D0707353

FALL
OF THE
DRAGONS

ALSO BY JAMES A. OWEN
Dawn of the Dragons
Time of the Dragons

JAMES A. OWEN

FALL
OF THE
DRAGONS

THE AGE OF DRAGONS · BOOK THREE

SAGA PRESS

LONDON SYDNEY **NEW YORK** TORONTO NEW DELHI

TO ALL THE BOYS WHO, LIKE
JOHN, JACK, AND CHARLES, REMAIN FOREVER
YOUNG NO MATTER HOW OLD THEY ARE.

SAGA PRESS
AN IMPRINT OF SIMON & SCHUSTER, INC.

1230 AVENUE OF THE AMERICAS, NEW YORK, NEW YORK 10020

This book is a work of fiction. Any references to historical events, real people, or real places
are used fictitiously. Other names, characters, places, and events are products of the author's
imagination, and any resemblance to actual events or places or persons, living or dead, is
entirely coincidental. • *The Dragon's Apprentice* copyright © 2010 by James A. Owen • *The
Dragons of Winter* copyright © 2012 by James A. Owen • *The First Dragon* copyright ©
2013 by James A. Owen • All titles were previously published individually. • Cover illustration copyright © 2016 by Levante Szabó • All rights reserved, including the right to
reproduce this book or portions thereof in any form whatsoever. For information address
Saga Press Subsidiary Rights Department, 1230 Avenue of the Americas, New York, NY
10020. • Saga Press and colophon are trademarks of Simon & Schuster, Inc. • For
information about special discounts for bulk purchases, please contact Simon & Schuster
Special Sales at 1-866-506-1949 or business@simonandschuster.com. • The Simon &
Schuster Speakers Bureau can bring authors to your live event. For more information or to
book an event, contact the Simon & Schuster Speakers Bureau at 1-866-248-3049 or visit
our website at www.simonspeakers.com. • The text for this book is set in Adobe Jenson
Pro. • Manufactured in the United States of America • First Saga Press paperback edition
March 2016 • 10 9 8 7 6 5 4 3 2 1 • Library of Congress Cataloging-in-Publication
Data • Owen, James A. • Fall of the dragons : The dragon's apprentice ; The dragons of winter ;
The first dragon / James A. Owen.—First Saga Press paperback edition. • p. cm.—(The age of
dragons ; 3). • Previously published as three separate stories. • Summary: To save the world,
Charles, the Grail Child Rose Dyson, and Edmund McGee must travel deep into the past to dis-
cover the identity of the mythical Architect of the Keep of Time. • ISBN 978-1-4814-2998-6
(paperback) • ISBN 978-1-4814-4145-2 (eBook) • [1. Fantasy. 2. Time travel—Fiction.]
I. Owen, James A. Dragon's apprentice. II. Owen, James A. Dragons of winter. III. Owen, James A.
First dragon. IV. Title. • PZ7.O97124Fal 2016 • [Fic]—dc23 • 2015018359

CONTENTS

THE DRAGON'S APPRENTICE

PROLOGUE

UNTIL IT HAS *been mapped, no thing truly exists. Not even time. To create maps is to be a Namer, and Naming makes things that are real more themselves, and things that are imaginary, real.*

But even as there are Namers, there are also Un-Namers in the world. And these seek to undo all that the Namers have mapped, in both time and space.

Safeguard the maps within this atlas from such Shadows. Give to it your Names. And believe.

This simple inscription, written on the first page of the Imaginarium Geographica, *bore no signature. It was possibly written by its maker, the Cartographer of Lost Places, but no Caretaker had ever asked, nor was the information ever volunteered. But someone had written it, and someday, someone would ask, and perhaps be answered.*

From the foredeck of the White Dragon, *the Far Traveler watched as the three new young Caretakers of the Geographica disappeared down the cobblestone streets to resume their lives. Not all that long before on that very spot, they had boarded another ship, the* Indigo Dragon, *as they fled from a terrible horde of creatures and their dark master, the Winter King. The days that passed between that moment and this, a scant few weeks, had changed the fates of two worlds and irrevocably altered their lives. He wondered if they knew how much. No matter—they would learn soon enough.*

"*They are the three, aren't they?*" said a voice from somewhere on the docks. "*The three Caretakers of the Prophecy. You would not have succeeded otherwise.*"

With a lively step that belied his girth, the Frenchman stepped from the fog and shadows enclosing the pier and onto the Dragon-ship.

"*Master Wells,*" he said with a smile and a bow.

The Far Traveler returned the bow, if not the smile. "*Master Verne. Well met.*"

The two men stood for a long moment, looking not at each other but at the city where the three young men had been swallowed by the winding streets.

"*It was a close call, Jules.*"

"*It was, Bert.*" Verne nodded. "*Too close. But they handled themselves well, especially that young Jack.*"

"*Everyone thinks that John is the fulcrum,*" said Bert, "*but he's not. He's just the most adept at fulfilling the duties of a Caretaker. Jack may yet prove to be his equal.*"

"*Of that I have no doubt,*" Verne said in agreement, "*but Charles may outshine them both. He has the potential—he just doesn't know it himself yet. Did you give them any inkling that this was only the first conflict of several to come with the Winter King?*"

"*Of course not!*" Bert shot back. "*We have disagreed on a number of things, Jules, but not that. They were unprepared enough as it was for the conflict with the Winter King. What would it do to them to know it isn't over?*"

"*Not much worse than being thrown in headfirst to what they've already come through,*" said Verne. "*They are, after all, the Caretakers of the Prophecy.*"

"Set aside your condescension, Jules," Bert said, irritated. "I know you don't believe in prophecies. Especially that one."

"I believe enough to help you, Bert. And them. And they show great promise. That's why we must keep their path as clear as we can, using all the allies we can recruit who will join our cause."

Bert raised an eyebrow and leaned against the railing. "You're still moving forward with the splinter group, then? These 'Mystorians,' as you call them?"

"Pshaw." Verne snorted. "Hardly a splinter group—Poe himself endorsed it. Hell's bells, Bert—he suggested it!"

"Yes, I know," Bert replied evenly, "but still not Caretakers, or even really apprentices." He took a breath. "They think I'm retiring, you know. They don't realize the process has just begun, and they won't comprehend it until it's all over."

"I understand," Verne said with sincere sympathy. "I know you want to tell them how quickly all of this is going to happen."

"Quickly for us, you mean," said Bert, "but not for them. To us, events will transpire over less than a year. But to them, it will seem to be decades. How do you explain to someone that all the years of service, and learning, and effort are all to prepare them for their truly important work, which may not begin until after they are dead?"

"That's as it must be, Bert," Verne said, gently chiding his colleague. "If Stellan had not been killed by the Winter King, it would not be necessary. But he was, and there it is. They had to be recruited now. He'll tell you that himself tonight back at Tamerlane House."

"Stellan . . . ," Bert said sorrowfully, shaking his head. "What were the odds of that happening?"

The Frenchman shrugged and smiled. "The same as everything, my friend. Zero, until it actually happens. Then it's a hundred percent."

"Is this going to work, Jules?"

"Yes," Verne answered firmly. "As long as the will persists to change events, everything is possible. Everything."

PART ONE

INDEPENDENCE DAY

CHAPTER ONE
THE GHOST OF MAGDALEN COLLEGE

—✳—

TWILIGHT HAD JUST fallen across the sky when the ghost pirate appeared at the base of Magdalen Tower. At first it seemed as if the ghost was on fire, but that was only a trick of the light. It was already quite dark along the cobblestone walk that crossed beneath the tower, so the light that emanated from the ghost filled the courtyard with an unearthly brilliance.

Eleven people were passing the tower in the moment that the apparition appeared. Three were professors who had seen many ghosts in Oxford, and so gave it no notice. Two more, also faculty at Magdalen, felt similarly about pirate costumes, and merely sniffed their annoyance as they passed, assuming as they did that it was some sort of student mischief. Four more were actual students, who reacted with surprise, awe, and no small amount of fear, and they scattered into corridors adjacent to the tower.

The last two people who witnessed the ghost's appearance were Caretakers of the *Imaginarium Geographica*, and a ghost pirate was at least as interesting as some of the other fantastic things they had seen, so they moved closer to have a better look.

John had arranged to meet his friend Charles at the base of

Magdalen Tower so that they might walk together to their friend
Jack's private rooms there at the college, and they met just as the
sun was setting. It was in that moment that the apparition had
appeared.

Even if they hadn't been Caretakers, a ghost would have been
nothing to cause them alarm—Oxford had long had a reputation
of being a haven to spectres and spirits of all kinds, and as long as
they didn't disrupt the business of the university, no one made a
fuss. Even in the midst of the Second World War, it was also good
for tourism.

"I didn't think I'd ever actually see this fellow," John whispered
to Charles. "I've heard about the Old Pirate for years but never
had the pleasure of seeing him in person, uh, so to speak."

"How many other ghosts have you met here?" asked Charles.

"Ah, none, I'm afraid," John admitted, "although I haven't
exactly sought them out, either."

"Well, why not?" Charles retorted as he approached the ghost,
hand outstretched. "They could prove to be really helpful to my
writing, you know. Worth asking, anyroad."

The ghost simply stood there, hunched over, staring into the
darkness as the Caretaker introduced himself. "Well met, old
fellow. My name is Charles."

Suddenly the ghost began to move, jerking about awkwardly,
as if it were a puppet in a penny nickelodeon. It seemed as if
speaking to it had engaged it in some way. Charles dropped his
hand. "Are you in distress?" he asked the ghost. "Why are you
here?"

The ghost stopped, then turned and focused its rheumy eyes
on Charles, who took full stock of it for the first time. The spectre

had presence and looked as if it stood in bright sunlight—but it was transparent, ethereal.

By appearance, it was certainly a pirate, no doubt, but an ancient one, many, many years old. His hair was long and straggly, and the clothes he wore, once fine, were tattered with age. His hands were shaking, and his head twitched nervously. But his eyes were piercing, intense—and, Charles thought with surprise, oddly familiar.

"Caretakers?" the ghost said with a trembling voice. "Be ye Caretakers, here, at Oxford?"

Charles and John exchanged surprised looks. This was no run-of-the-mill ghost. Not if he knew who they were. Then again, there had been stories of the Pirate Ghost appearing in this spot for two centuries, and no one had ever reported that he spoke at all, much less that he had mentioned anything about Caretakers.

"Who is asking?" said John, stepping forward. "Who are you looking for?"

"Jamie?" the ghost answered. "Jamie, is that you?"

John sighed. "The only one of us who ever quit," he said to Charles, "and he's the one everyone asks for in a crisis."

"No," the ghost said, shaking his head. "Ye be John, I think. Ron John Tollers, unless I miss my guess."

John stepped back in surprise at hearing a mishmash of his nicknames. "That—that's right," he said. "I'm he. Do I know you?"

The ghost spread its arms and smiled. "In another life, another time," he said, his voice weary, "I was your friend Hank Morgan."

"Good Lord," said John, glancing again at Charles, who was equally stunned. "We can't even walk across Oxford without stumbling into an adventure."

The old saying about absence making the heart grow fonder is over-rated, John had thought to himself as he prepared to go out earlier that afternoon. *Absence doesn't do anything except create longing, and an ache that cannot be remedied until the waiting is through.*

He and the other Caretakers of the *Imaginarium Geographica,* Jack and Charles, had been waiting for seven years for a chance to return to the Archipelago of Dreams. In earlier times, they had gone for longer periods without visiting, but there had been less urgency in those days—and maybe that was what stirred John's unease. That, or the fact that they'd been forbidden to return. *We never truly know we want something,* he thought, *until we've been told we can't have it.* Or perhaps it was the dark days of war covering the earth that made him long for the escape of the magical lands in the Archipelago.

Whatever it was, the price they'd had to pay for a victory in the future was steep. They'd jumped forward in time and defeated a terrible enemy, before returning to the time where they were meant to be. But to ensure that the victory remained certain, they had to stay away from the Archipelago, so as not to risk changing the outcome that had already happened.

They hadn't realized how hard it would be to wait through most of the new Great War that had swept the Summer Country.

The Darkness of the shadows was hardest to bear. In those days when the shadows of the Dragons swept over all the Earth,

John in particular struggled mightily against the impulse to act.

"We *are* acting," Charles and Jack would remind him, "and we have. By waiting. We know that this is a battle we have already won, John. We just need to do our duty—and do nothing. Nothing but wait."

Now, however, the waiting was almost over. The clock had caught up with the past, and the future was about to become the present again. And they could finally return and fully take up their mantle again as true Caretakers.

John had put on his jacket and looked at himself in the mirror. He was finally feeling the years of his life—and not just because of the Wars. He had now been a Caretaker for longer than he had not. It was one of the roles that defined him—and yet it was still one of the greatest secrets he kept from all but a few. *Until*, he thought with a smile, *the new calling of Jack's comes to fruition. If that works, well . . .*

Everything could change. Everything.

He had kissed his wife and children good-bye and stepped out the door.

It was less than an hour later that he and Charles began their conversation with the Pirate Ghost of Magdalen College.

"Hank!" John exclaimed. "What's happened to you? You look so . . . so . . ."

"Old?" Morgan replied with a cackle. "Two centuries of waiting will do that to a man."

"Waiting for what?" asked Charles.

"For you," the ghost replied simply. "I was waiting for you, Good Charlie, and Ron John, and Jack-Jack the Giant Killer. I was waiting for the three of you." He narrowed his eyes. "Where be Jack, anyroad?"

"He's finishing a discussion," said John. "We, ah, we weren't exactly expecting to see you, Hank."

"And why should ye?" Morgan retorted. "I've only been appearing in this same spot for two hundred years, give or take."

"No need to be snappish," said Charles, "but you never spoke to anyone before now."

"Because no one has ever spoken t' me!" said Morgan. "It only works if *you* speak first."

"What are you talking about?" John said, clearly puzzled. "You've lost me."

"No time, no time," said Morgan, waving his hands. Then, he laughed, wheezing. "Or just enough, I suppose. Yes—it was just enough.

"Listen to me," the ghost insisted with a new urgency in his voice. "You must build the bridge. Shakespeare's Bridge. You can't get back without it. But the bridge won't work without a trump."

He stopped and pulled one of the familiar silver watches from a broad pocket. He flipped it open and grimaced. "I've told them," he murmured to himself. "The loop should have closed."

Charles gripped John's shoulder, and looks of worry creased both men's faces. They were missing too many pieces of a far bigger picture here.

"Hank," John began, "perhaps if we—"

"You must build Shakespeare's Bridge," Morgan said again. "It's the only way! The only way for you to—"

He stopped and looked down at his watch, which had begun ticking. "Oh, thank God," he murmured as he adjusted the dials on the device. "You've finally managed to make a new—"

In midsentence, Hank Morgan vanished.

"Oh my stars," said John. "What just happened here, Charles? What did we just see?"

"Nothing we can sort out on our own," Charles replied as he looked around the courtyard. Morgan was indeed gone, and whatever his cryptic message had meant, it was apparently all they were getting. "Hank's supposed to be joining us at dinner later at Tamerlane House, anyway. We'll just take it up with him then. Maybe it's some sort of joke. To welcome us back?"

John shook his head. Whatever else the ghost was, it was no joke. The age, the hard years that weighed on their old friend, were real. And that meant the warning was too.

"Let's go," he said, spinning away on his heel. "Jack will be waiting for us."

"What is it?" Jack asked his friends as he ushered them into his rooms. "What's happened?"

He knew by their demeanors that something was amiss. John went straight to the cupboard to fetch glasses for a drink, while Charles wearily draped himself in one of the chairs. "I'm not sure how to begin," Charles said. "Let's just say we've been having a little chat with a ghost."

"Really?" said Jack, smirking, as John handed him a snifter of brandy. "Which one?"

"The Old Pirate," Charles replied. "You know, the one that appears at the base of the tower."

"Good Lord," said Jack after a moment. "You're serious, aren't you?"

"Quite," John said, sitting next to Charles, "but that's just the start of it."

Over the next several minutes, and a round of drinks, John and Charles related to Jack their experience with the ghostly Hank Morgan. When they had finished, he sat back and rubbed his forehead.

"Amazing," Jack said. "Two centuries is a long time to wait to deliver such a cryptic message."

"I got the impression that's all he could give us in the time he had," John noted, "relatively speaking, that is."

Charles rubbed his chin, deep in thought. "I think it's more than that," he mused. "He said it only works if we spoke to him first, remember? I think that ghost may not have actually been Hank, but some kind of avatar that could speak only when spoken to."

"A recorded message?" asked Jack. "And interactive, to boot? That's some trick."

"Exactly," said John. "Who else but Hank would have the skills to pull it off?"

"Manipulating space as well as time," Jack said, pacing the width of the room. "Not too many, I think. Alvin Ransom, probably. Rappaccini's daughter, maybe. Verne. Bert. Possibly Kipling. That's about it. There are others, associates of the Cartographer, who might have the skills, but they wouldn't have the need to send a message so indirectly. Not now."

"Associates?" Charles asked. "You mean apprentices, don't you?"

"Not necessarily," replied Jack. "Several of them were, but others ended up joining with Burton's Imperial Cartological Society."

"Ah," Charles said as he leaned back in his chair, crossing his legs. "I see."

The Imperial Cartological Society had operated as a sort of shadow organization to the Caretakers Emeritis. Comprised of rejected Caretakers, former Caretakers, and those men and women of history who might have been Caretakers in another time and place, the Society was dedicated to spreading knowledge of the Archipelago of Dreams and all its secrets—by any means possible.

It was only after the Society was subverted by the Shadow King that there was a split among its ranks, and the de facto leader, Sir Richard Burton, brokered a truce with the Caretakers.

The Society would not attempt to spread knowledge about the Archipelago without the involvement and approval of the Caretakers Emeritis. And in return the Caretakers, under Jack's supervision, agreed to start a formal educational program at Cambridge in order to begin creating a greater awareness of the Archipelago among those who proved worthy to know of it.

It was an imperfect alliance, and it was likely to go through a succession of growing pains. But a tentative peace was better than war—and they had all already had more than enough of war.

"I'll just say it, then," John said, rising to his feet. "Shouldn't we consider that this could be some sort of trick of Burton's? He's done it before."

Jack dismissed the question with a wave of his hands. "Not using Hank, no," he said. "And besides, he's sitting at the Caretakers' table, so to speak. There's nothing he can gain through deception that hasn't already been offered to him on a silver platter."

"We can just bring it up with Hank when we get to Tamerlane House," Charles said, stretching as he rose to stand with his friends. "After all, it can't be much of a crisis Hank was warning us about. Not if he had to go walking through two centuries just to deliver the message. Another day shouldn't matter that much."

"Speaking of walking," said Jack, "we should start heading for the Kilns. That's where Ransom is expecting to take us through, and besides, I want to check in with Warnie and see if Mrs. Morris has shredded Magwich yet."

"Mrs. Morris?" Charles asked. "I thought your cat was a he."

"Morris *was* a he," Jack replied, "right up until the point she had kittens. It's been Mrs. Morris ever since."

"You have kittens? Charles asked. "I hadn't seen any."

"Oh, we don't let them roam the house," said Jack. "We keep them in the storeroom with that stupid talking shrub."

"I really do appreciate you taking him on," Charles said apologetically. "He and Michal were getting on horribly, and I had enough trouble with her already after I explained about the map tattooed on my back. Apparently, wives like to be consulted about that sort of thing."

Jack shrugged. "Maybe I ought to put him at Cambridge," he mused, "make him the centerpiece of the new Imperial Cartological Society. Sort of a living cautionary tale about what

happens when an evil henchman turned green knight misman-
ages his chance at redemption."

"Does it really count as a secret society if everyone knows it
exists?" Charles asked.

"As I have begun to plan it," said Jack, "it is most definitely
not going to be a secret society. It's more like an invisible college.
Those who know about it don't talk, and those who don't know
don't care."

"I think that's half the reason the Caretakers Emeritis worked
out a truce with Burton and the others," said John. "The number
of people on the planet who would even give a flying fig about the
Society is going to be roughly the same as the number of people
who can be trusted to know about it."

"I still think we should have drawn straws," Jack complained.
"No one warned me that being the Caveo Secundus would mean
going to Cambridge."

"That was Burton's call, not to base it here," said John, "and
besides, once we get you into a proper appointment there, you'll
have a good shot at redeeming the whole University."

"It's strange how far apart we once were with Burton," said
Charles. "We got the jobs he wanted, and he went renegade
because he thought he could do it better. And now we have nearly
identical goals. A bit chilling, that."

"We've been very bad at the job, by my accounting," said John.
"After more than two and a half decades, the separation between
the Archipelago and our world is more pronounced than ever.
Sometimes I feel as if all we are doing is treading water."

"Holding the line," Jack echoed.

Charles let out a heavy sigh. "Our victories do seem to be

becoming hollower and hollower, don't they?" he mused. "Of course, it doesn't help that we've had to put down the Winter King—Shadow King—Mordred. . . ."

"Madoc," said Jack.

"Whatever his name is, three times," said Charles. "Hopefully now he's contented enough not to come back around looking to conquer or subvert or whatever it is that's the fashion for dictators these days."

"We've seen the last of him," said Jack. "And time will prove we've made the right choices all along."

"That's what worries me," Charles countered. "Whatever else we decide to do now, the possibility remains that everything we know—everything we have done—may be completely wrong."

The Caveo Principia inclined his head in acknowledgment. "It's possible," he said. "I just get the impression that we're still being trained, being tested. That we have not fully been given the mantles of Caretakers."

"Well," Jack said jovially, "if they haven't made up their minds about us after almost a quarter century, then either they're very indecisive, or they're very, very selective."

John shook his head. "I don't know which one of those would be worse."

"I'm sorry Hugo wasn't able to come," Jack's brother Warnie said with real regret when they arrived at the Kilns. "It's quite nice to have someone else around to chat with when you three are off on one of your, ah, jaunts. And besides," he added with less regret, "I have this nice bottle of Château Lafite I was hoping to share with him."

"You could save it for another time, or for our return," Jack suggested.

"That wouldn't do," Warnie replied. "I've already begun to let it breathe. To recork it or set it aside would be criminal. No, I suppose it's just going to be for myself and Magwich over there," he finished, tipping his chin at the shrub sulking in the corner.

"In case you hadn't noticed," Magwich grumbled, "I don't really have a mouth like I used to. I'm not exactly able to enjoy a fine wine anymore, thank you very much."

"Oh, I have no intention of wasting good wine," Warnie said, winking at the companions. "But I promised Jack I'd look after you while he was out—so I'm going to drink this wine myself, and then in an hour or so, I'm going to make sure you're good and watered."

"Eww," said Magwich. "I think I'd rather be back in the room with the cat."

"That can be arranged," said Warnie.

At that Magwich started up such a clamor of moaning and whining that the companions thought Warnie might just chuck the plant straightaway into the fire.

"I don't see why I can't come," Magwich sniffed. "I was a Caretaker's apprentice too, you know. And after that, I was the Green Knight. Is it my fault I'm a weak-willed traitor at heart?"

"Well, that's honest enough," Jack admitted.

"We're not taking him," said John flatly. "All he's ever done is cause trouble. Why take the risk?"

"Just as risky to leave him here," said Jack. "Maybe more so. At least here, one of us has always been around to keep an eye on him."

"Which Warnie is more than capable of doing," John pointed out, "especially if he needs any kindling."

"Murderers!" Magwich howled. "Cutthroats and murderers, the lot of you!"

"For heaven's sake," Charles said, exasperated. "All right, we'll take you with us, you sorry excuse for an overgrown radish! But you're going to ride in the burlap bag."

"You know, Warnie," John said as the others bundled up the still complaining Magwich, "you're more than welcome to come along. There are a number of people at Tamerlane who would enjoy your company."

Jack's brother held up his hands. "Thank you for the invitation, but the first time Hugo and I went into the Archipelago has more than sated my thirst for adventure. Although," he added with genuine regret, "I would not have minded a rematch with the centaur. That was an excellent game of chess."

"It's your right, as an honorary Caretaker," John said, "as it would be for any others who know about the *Geographica*. I'm looking forward to finally taking my boy Christopher over myself."

"And I Michal, now that we aren't using the boats," said Charles. "You know she hates the water."

"It is easier on all of you, isn't it?" Warnie asked. "Being allowed to share what you know with those closest to you, instead of keeping it all to yourselves."

"Much easier," Jack said, clapping his brother on the shoulder. "It halves the burdens and doubles the joys."

"And besides," added Charles, "if anyone slips up and mentions anything about the Archipelago, everyone just assumes we made it up anyway."

Suddenly there was a knock at the door.

"I'll get it," said John, "although if it's anyone who wants to give me a magical atlas, I'm going to flip a coin before I let him in."

He strode into the next room and opened the door, holding it firmly against the gust of wind that entered with the tall, familiar visitor in a trench coat.

"Alvin!" John exclaimed in delight. "Come in, come in! So good to see you, old fellow!"

Alvin Ransom shook his head, scattering raindrops everywhere. "Sorry about that, old friend," he said, accepting Jack's offer of a dry towel. "It's quite the night outside."

"The storm's just come up," said Charles, "but we'd have let you in anyway."

"Maybe you should stand guard at the door," Ransom suggested to Charles, "in case someone with two shadows tries to enter."

"Still smarting over that one, are we?" Charles asked with a barely suppressed grin. "If it helps, I was just having an exceptionally good day."

Ransom scowled, then grinned back at Charles and clapped him on the back. "It doesn't, but I'm not offended. I'm more embarrassed that I spent all that time trying to suss out the identity of the Chancellor, and you spend five minutes examining a few photos and nail it on the head."

"That's why we got the job," Jack said, grinning, "and you're still a messenger boy."

Ransom took a playful swing at his friend and pretended to

be insulted. "Fred sends his regards," he said to Charles. "He can't wait to see you tonight."

"Twice," Charles lamented. "Twice in seven years. That's far too little time to spend with an apprentice—or a friend, for that matter."

"Fred knows all the reasons you had to remain here," said Ransom, "and he understands."

"Alvin," John said, his voice tentative. "Have you spoken to Hank Morgan recently?"

"Henry?" Ransom replied. "Why, yes, just yesterday, in fact. He'll be at the dinner, if you're wondering."

"Glad to hear it," John said, with a quick glance at Charles and Jack. "It'll be good to see him again."

Ransom rubbed his hands together. "Well, I'm all warmed up. Are we ready to go?"

"Ready enough," Jack said, handing a pack to John. "We ought to take this along, don't you think?"

"You have the *Geographica* there?" Ransom asked, pointing to the pack. "You haven't left it in the back of your car again, I hope."

John rolled his eyes and sighed. "That was twenty years ago!" he exclaimed. "Who told you about that?"

Ransom chuckled. "It's one of James Barrie's favorite after-dinner stories," he said. "That's not the worst of it, though. Laura Glue has told it too."

"Uh-oh," said John. "To whom?"

"Charys. And the centaurs. And the Elves. And the Dwarves. And—"

"Enough already!" John yelled as the others convulsed with laughter. "Let's get going!"

Still grinning, Ransom removed a small case from his coat. In it were the trumps—the magical cards that allowed him and a few other associates of the Caretakers to traverse great distances as easily as walking across a room.

He removed the trump that held the drawing of Tamerlane House and held it out in front of him. Ransom concentrated on the card, and it began to grow.

The trump grew wider and wider, filling the anteroom. The smell of the sea swirled around them. In moments the passage was open, and they could see the towers and minarets of Tamerlane House.

Grimalkin was sitting at the front door, idly licking one of his two visible paws. "Hello there, Caretakers," he said lazily. "Welcome back."

CHAPTER TWO
ARIADNE'S THREAD

—✳—

ROSE WAS STARTLED but not surprised when the crescent moon appeared at one end of her attic room in Tamerlane House. What was surprising to her was that the moon wore a frock coat, fingerless gloves, and sensible shoes.

She was already awake, having been woken by the thunderstorm that had descended on the islands that evening. The wind was howling, and rattled the shutters, and the frequent flashes of lightning and rolling thunder made sleep all but impossible, so she had been reading Lord Dunsany when the strange visitor appeared. There was a flash of lightning that illuminated everything in the attic in high relief, as if it had been carved in white marble, visible only in that instant—and when it flashed again, the moon was there, sitting in the chair across from Rose's bed.

On reflection, she decided that if a moon were to come a-calling, that would be precisely how it would dress, so she shouldn't be surprised at all.

She changed her mind again when the moon spoke, addressing her by name.

"Hello, Rose."

"Hello," Rose answered. "Would you like a sandwich?"

She wasn't certain this was the sort of thing a girl who was barely into her teens should offer a visiting moon, but Bert and Geoffrey Chaucer had been instructing her in the rules of etiquette, and she didn't want to be rude.

The apparition paused for a moment, then bent forward in acquiescence.

Rose clambered from her bed and walked across the attic to the small icebox she kept in an alcove. She hadn't expected to have guests, but she spent a lot of time in the attic, and keeping a store of food and drink handy was easier than having to make her way downstairs to the kitchen.

For one thing, many of the rooms seemed to rearrange themselves at will, following no particular pattern or schedule, which frequently meant that she would take a customary route only to find she'd ended up on the wrong side of the house. She sometimes suspected she could hear the house snickering at her when it creaked and groaned under a stiff wind.

Tamerlane House, as its owner, Edgar Allan Poe, explained to her, was a house with a mind of its own. Thus, as a sentient structure, it tended to change and evolve, as do all living things. This also meant it could get grouchy, or play practical jokes—although, to be fair, the house never really messed around with any of its occupants except for Will Shakespeare, but then everyone there teased him, so that was all right.

Deftly Rose threw together a liverwurst and cream cheese sandwich and cut it in two; then she poured two glasses of milk from a chilled pitcher. She put the sandwich halves on plates, set one along with a glass of milk in front of her strange visitor, and climbed back onto her bed.

She blushed slightly when her visitor made no move to touch the sandwich or milk, and she realized that her offer had been accepted, as it was itself made, out of courtesy. She also noted, again with slight embarrassment, that the moon had no visible mouth.

"We thank you for your hospitality," the moon said, "but it is not necessary. We have come to speak to you regarding matters of the greatest importance."

"Who are you?" asked Rose.

"We are Mother Night," the apparition said, as if that explained everything. Rose took a bite of her sandwich and chewed as she considered this interesting happening.

For someone who had just appeared out of thin air, Mother Night gave no indication that her intentions were not good. Even in the event that she was some sort of enemy, the sword Caliburn was just under Rose's bed and could be drawn out in a trice.

There was a lot of comfort to be taken in being the wielder of the sword of Aeneas and King Arthur, Rose had often thought. Even if she hoped never to have the need to use it again.

Rose was at Tamerlane House in part because it was impossible to break into. For one thing, it was located on the centermost island in a group called the Nameless Isles, and as far as she knew, only a small number of people even knew they existed, and an even smaller number could actually reach them.

The great stones that stood on the smaller islands acted as a Ring of Power and protected the house from supernatural threats; and downstairs, in the Pygmalion Gallery, were some of the most significant men and women from history, who could be summoned by ringing a small silver bell.

True, most would have to be called forth from their portraits, which would take time—but Jules Verne, who had invited her here, was always close at hand. And Nathaniel Hawthorne, who was the de facto head of security—based on his ability to out-wrestle every other occupant—had not re-entered his portrait since she arrived, just in case.

There were enemies searching for her through time and space, so she had been required to spend all her time within the walls of Tamerlane House. But in just one more day, she'd have the chance to return to another place she considered home. It was possible that Verne's caution had lessened, and this visitor had slipped through the cracks. It was also possible that this Mother Night was not the type of creature who would be hindered by any pre-caution.

"Are you one of the Morgaine?" Rose asked.

"The Three Who Are One are an aspect of ourselves," answered Mother Night, "but they are not all that we are.

"Your education is about to begin," Mother Night went on, "and your true destiny will at last be revealed."

"I've had quite an education already," said Rose politely. "I've been to boarding school in Reading, and was privately tutored in Oxford, and have spent the last while as a student of the Caretakers Emeritis of the *Imaginarium Geographica*. So there's very little I haven't had the chance to learn before now."

"Arrogant words," Mother Night replied, but in a gentle tone of voice. "Knowledge is not the same as wisdom. And you are still far from wise."

Rose blushed and took a large bite of her sandwich, so that she'd have to chew for a while before responding. She swallowed, then took a sip of milk. Lightning flashed in one of the windows, and in her head Rose counted silently *one, one thousand, two, one thousand, three, one thousand* . . . until the answering rumble. Three miles away. The storm was coming closer.

"I apologize," Rose said at last. "I know there is still a lot I need to learn. But it's also very frustrating," she added. "It seems as if my entire life is about going where others want me to go, and doing what others want me to do, and never being able to decide for myself."

Mother Night shimmered slightly, and Rose got the impression that the moon was somehow pleased by what she'd said. "This is a wise thing, Rose," said Mother Night. "This is what separates childhood from maturity—the decision to act, and to take responsibility for those actions."

"If that's the difference," said Rose, "then some people never really grow up."

Again, Mother Night shimmered and bowed slightly. "Indeed. To be given a choice and still refuse to choose is to volunteer, whether one realizes it or not."

Rose's eyes narrowed, and she leaned back on her pillows. Had she just been tricked into volunteering for something?

Mother Night reached into her frock coat and pulled out a luminescent ball of string, which she handed to Rose.

"What is this?" asked Rose.

"Ariadne's Thread," Mother Night replied, as if that answered everything. "The skein of eternity has come undone. History itself has unraveled, and none remain who may yet reweave it. None," she said, her voice rising with emphasis, "save for you."

There was another bright flash of lightning, followed by an immediate crash of thunder. The storm was right above Tamerlane House now.

"You will be visited by two other aspects of myself," Mother Night went on, "at the points in your journey where you reach a crossroads. They will offer you counsel and answer any questions you choose to ask. But they will not compel you to action. That choice, as always, will be yours and yours alone."

Journey? Rose thought. Was Verne planning something he hadn't told her about? Or did Mother Night perhaps mean she'd be returning to Oxford at last? "Where will I meet them? The aspects of you?"

"You must seek out the Dragon," Mother Night said, ignoring her question. "Seek him out, and speak to him these words:

> *To turn, from time to time*
> *To things both real and not,*
> *Give hints of world within a world,*
> *And creatures long forgot.*
> *With limelight turn to these, regard*
> *In all thy wisdom stressed;*
> *To save both time and space above—*
> *Forever, ere moons crest.*

"When you have done this," she said, "you will be ready. Your true education may begin."

"My true education?" said Rose. "And . . . a Dragon? But . . . there aren't any more! Unless you mean Samaranth."

"No," said Mother Night. "There is another. He is an

apprentice, who has not yet chosen to become a Dragon. If he chooses not to be, all will be lost. You must help him to choose."

"What happens if he chooses not to? Become a Dragon, I mean?"

"The Shadows will be coming for you, child," Mother Night said. "They are coming for you now. Be ready."

"I'm not afraid of shadows," Rose said with self-assurance. "I defeated the Shadow King with the sword Caliburn, and I used it to free the shadows of the Dragons. My teachers have told me about what shadows can do, and I've learned to never be afraid of them."

"Afraid you may not be now," said Mother Night ominously, "but you will be, child. You will be.

"The shadows you have fought were only the servants, not the masters. The Shadows we are speaking of are those of primordial darkness—the Echthroi. They have labored long to keep this world in darkness, and have tried again and again to create a champion. Again and again they have failed. But there are those more powerful, who may yet be Un-Named and come to serve the Echthroi, and help them destroy the world. *You* are one of these, Rose."

Rose blanched. "Me? But all our enemies have tried to kill me, not convert me, or steal my shadow."

"And they were defeated," said Mother Night. "Now the attention of the Echthroi will turn to you. You will either be named, or Un-Named. You will become either the Imago or the Archimago. But you are our daughter, and it will be yours to choose."

"Mine?"

"You are the Moonchild," said Mother Night, "and this is your destiny, to use the greatest ability given to the Sons of Adam and the Daughters of Eve: to choose."

Rose lowered her head and closed her eyes. "What if I don't choose?" she asked softly. "What if I see a better path to take, or what if I simply don't want to choose? What then?"

There was no answer. Rose opened her eyes and looked around. The attic was empty.

A rumble sounded in the distance. The wind had died down, and the storm was passing. All that was left of the strange encounter was half a sandwich and a glass of milk, the glowing ball of string Mother Night had called Ariadne's Thread, and about a thousand questions. What journey was she supposed to be taking? To seek out a Dragon's apprentice and tell him a riddle? And what was this about Echthroi . . . or Echthros . . . She couldn't quite remember. Whatever else Mother Night had said that was confusing, that part was clear. The Echthroi, the true Shadows, would be coming for her. And perhaps already were.

"Are you going to eat that sandwich?" a broad smile said from atop one of the curio cabinets. "The storm woke me, and I smelled liverwurst."

"Grimalkin!" Rose said, happy to see a familiar face—or a part of one, at least. The Cheshire cat's smile filled out with whiskers, then nose and eyes, and ears, by the time he climbed down to the floor. He had attached himself to her uncle John, who was the Principal Caretaker of the *Geographica* but spent most of his time at Tamerlane House.

"Were you expecting a guest?" said Grimalkin, noting the extra glass of milk.

"Not really," said Rose, "but it's yours if you want it. Saucer?"

"Please."

She poured the milk for the cat and scratched its neck under the thick leather collar. The runes on it glowed faintly as she touched it.

The cat finished the sandwich and milk in pretty short order. "Anything else?" he asked, licking his lips.

"Not up here," Rose replied. "It'll be breakfast soon, anyway. Join us?"

"Perhaps later," said the cat, who had started to disappear again. "I was just looking for some ways to kill time while the storm was doing its blustery thing. I think I'll go downstairs and scratch on Byron's portrait."

With that Grimalkin vanished, although she could never really be sure he wasn't still lurking about somewhere. That was the only problem with a Cheshire cat—even when they weren't there, they might be.

Rose pulled on a sweater and some slacks, then brushed a few tangles out of her hair before heading downstairs. Almost as an afterthought, she tied the loose end of the thread to her bedpost and set the faintly luminescent ball on the floor. She wasn't certain what she was meant to do with it, but at least, she decided as she closed the trapdoor to the stairs, if she tied it to something, it wouldn't get lost.

"That was no ordinary storm," Bert proclaimed as the Feast Beasts cleared away the platters of food from the breakfast table. Ever since Rose had arrived as a resident, it had become traditional for several of the Caretakers Emeritis to take breakfast together in the southern dayroom. Bert still needed to eat on a routine schedule, and while Verne didn't, not eating still made him vaguely uncomfortable.

The rest of the Caretakers, who resided within their portraits in the Pygmalion Gallery, did not require food or drink at all—but they missed the memory of dining, and so were more than happy to accept Bert's invitation to have breakfast together.

Mark Twain was almost always there, as were Charles Dickens, James Barrie, and Alexandre Dumas. Jonathan Swift would occasionally join them, as would Rudyard Kipling, who, like Verne, was not a resident of the gallery but a tulpa—a younger, virtually immortal version of himself.

More unusually, Franz Schubert had often joined them as well, although he never spoke. Schubert virtually never joined in any of the activities at Tamerlane House unless they were a matter of official Caretaker business, for which his attendance was compulsory.

"I agree," Charles Dickens said, picking at his teeth with a pewter toothpick. "Something has changed."

"What do you mean by that?" Rose asked as she came down the stairs to join them.

"Ah, Rose, my dear!" Bert proclaimed, jumping to his feet. "When you didn't come down at six, we assumed you wanted to sleep in, especially with such an eventful day ahead. I'll summon the Feast Beasts back," he finished as he started to reach for a silver bell.

"No need," she replied as she took a crust of bread and sat down next to Twain. "I ate a snack rather late, so I'm not all that hungry. What did you mean when you said that something had changed?" she asked, looking through Twain's smoke at Dickens.

"It's the storm last night," Dickens answered, with a surreptitious glance at Bert. "Storms are omens of change, especially in the Archipelago. And after all the Time Storms that had battered the lands in recent years, we were keeping a close watch on this one."

"I thought the Time Storms had nearly stopped?"

"They had, young lady, indeed," said Twain. "That's part of the bother and the worry. Their absence meant that the energy was going elsewhere, not that it had disappeared altogether."

"Perhaps it was an Echthroi . . . or is it an Echthros? I can't remember." She looked at Bert. "Whatever it is that the primordial Shadows are called."

All the Caretakers sitting at the table, including the dead ones and the nearly immortal ones, had gone white.

"Where, pray tell, my dear Rose," Twain said, having regained his composure first, "did you hear those names?"

"I had a strange visitor in the night," Rose replied. "You'd be quite pleased, Bert. I was very hospitable, although I don't think she really liked the liverwurst and cream cheese sandwich I made for her."

"What did this visitor say to you, Rose?" asked Bert, still a bit shaken. "How did she come to mention the Echthroi?"

"She told me that history was broken, and that it would be up to me to fix it, otherwise the Echthroi would win, and the world would end," Rose said as she reached for the silver bell on the table. "Does anyone mind if I request something more to eat? It turns out I'm feeling hungrier than I thought."

The table was soon restocked with baked goods of all kinds and fresh fruit. The Caretakers waited patiently as Rose heaped a pile of crepes, strawberries, and whipped cream onto a plate—which she put on the floor for Grimalkin, who wandered in preening with his just-sharpened claws. For herself, she made a sandwich of lettuce, mayonnaise, and crunchy peanut butter.

"It's when I watch her eat," Dickens confided to Twain, "that I suspect Bert and Jules are teaching her all the wrong things."

"Never mind that," said Bert, more irritated at the pause in the discussion than the fact that he agreed with them about Rose's dining habits. "Tell us about your visitor, Rose."

As she ate, Rose recounted the discussion that had transpired in the attic, occasionally pausing to answer questions or clarify points she wanted to make. When she was done, she had some questions of her own.

"What is this about a Dragon's apprentice?" she asked. "I thought they were all gone. I would know—I freed most of them myself."

"All the Dragons in this world, save for Samaranth, were corrupted by the Shadow King," Bert said with a still tangible melancholy, "and any apprentices they might have had were lost long ago."

Rose waited patiently for Bert, or any of the others, to continue. Twain leaned over to Dickens and whispered something, which Dickens wrote on a piece of paper and passed to Grimalkin under the table. The Cheshire cat's eyes narrowed as it scanned the paper, and it seemed about to protest about being a mere messenger, but a sharp look from Twain silenced it, and the cat disappeared.

"It's possible," Twain said into the silence, "that there are still Dragons somewhere, somewhen, in the Summer Country. But as

Samaranth said, they would likely never return to the Archipelago, even if they exist."

"Mother Night said he wasn't a Dragon yet," Rose reiterated. "That he was an apprentice, who still had to choose."

"There have been rumors of such men and women," said Verne, who was looking cautiously at Bert as he spoke, "but none since the Histories have been recorded, and none since the creation of the *Geographica*."

"That we know of," said Twain.

"That we know of," Verne confirmed. "Although there's one possibility, which would make a strange sort of symmetry if it were true—"

"I'm more concerned about what this moon told Rose about the Shadows," Bert said, interrupting. "For her to have even spoken the *name* of the primordial Shadows . . ."

"Echthroi," another voice said. "Echthroi. Echthros."

It was Schubert.

Up to now he had been silent as he usually was, and so everyone had ignored him as they usually did. The Feast Beasts had dutifully placed trays and platters of food in front of him, but most of it remained untouched, save for a few cherry tomatoes, which he ate when no one else was looking.

"The Shadow. The Darkness. The Many-Angled Ones," Schubert said dully. "The Lloigor. The Nameless. The Unwritten. The Anti-Erl Kings. The Un-Makers. The Un-Namers. By all these names and more are they known. Against these, by any name, we fight. But they are always the same. . . ." He stood, looming over the table.

"They are the *Enemy*. And we must be strong, for they will not relent."

For the first time since Mother Night's visit, Rose felt genuinely frightened. For the Caretakers Emeritis to be taking this discussion so seriously was alarming, but for Schubert to be so actively involved sent a thrill of fear up her spine. Bert had once explained to her that he was more attuned to the supernatural than any of the rest of them, with the exception of Poe himself. And for Schubert to speak meant that there was something dangerous brewing.

"The Echthroi," Twain said gravely, "are why there must always be Caretakers, my dear Rose. They are who we protect the world against."

"But the Winter King—," she began.

"Was merely their agent on this planet," Twain interrupted, "and he had a mere fraction of their power."

"Why are they worse than anything else the Caretakers have faced?" Rose asked. "We've defeated shadows before."

"We've defeated their agents," Dickens corrected. "We have not yet faced the true Shadows. But," he added with a tense expression on his face, "it seems that time is finally upon us."

"Rose, dear girl," said Twain as he laid a reassuring hand over hers, "don't worry. This is what we do, we Caretakers. And we are going to use all the powers at our disposal to protect you."

That may be part of the problem, Rose thought. *If I am able to choose, and I don't because I know you'll try to protect me, will that be a mistake? Will we all pay a price, just because I'll be afraid to act on my own?*

"At any rate," Bert said as they all stood, "we should be discussing this with your three uncles when they arrive for the party. They'll feel terribly left out if we don't."

"Agreed," said Barrie. "I'm looking forward to their return as well."

"The storm has passed," said Dickens. "Take some comfort in that, Rose."

"What do we need to do now?" asked Rose.

"We have to prepare the banquet hall," Verne said as he swept past her into the foyer. "Today Time finally catches up with itself, and we want to make the Caretakers' return to the Archipelago a day they won't forget for *centuries*."

CHAPTER THREE
CHRONOS & KAIROS

CELEBRATIONS, LIKE MANY things, are happiest after a long separation, or a period of trials and tribulations—and the event at Tamerlane House came at the end of decades of fear, and conflict, and dark days. Several of the Caretakers Emeritis had come into the front reception hall to receive the new arrivals, and everyone was moving about in a swirl of hugs and handshakes, greetings and salutations.

"Rose!" Jack exclaimed as she hugged each of the companions in turn. "You've cut your hair!"

"It *has* been seven years, Jack," said Charles as he kissed the young woman on the top of her head. "I'm surprised we even recognize her."

"Seven years for you, you mean," Rose corrected as she hugged John a second time. "For me, just days."

"Hugo is sorry he couldn't come," said Jack. "Warnie, too. They've both missed you terribly. You should come to visit as soon as possible."

"Now, lads," Bert said, even though they were well into middle age, "we shouldn't go rushing to make plans so quickly. We've got time to do things now."

"We've waited a long time," Jack protested. "What's wrong with a short trip to Oxford?"

"We'll discuss it later, Jack," Bert said, trying to change the subject. "Let's just enjoy the celebration, shall we?"

"Fine," said Jack as he hugged her again. "But Rose will be coming to see us shortly, I think."

"I agree," said Charles.

Rose folded her arms, closed her eyes, and smiled. "That's what we're going to do, then."

Jack grinned at Charles. "That's it and done," he said. "There'll be no persuading her otherwise, not now."

"Well enough and good," Bert said, knowing he was beaten. "But we'll still be having a discussion before you leave."

"What's this?" a gruff voice said. "I smell Caretakers about."

"Hello, Burton," said John, reluctantly offering his hand. "It's, ah, good to see you again."

Behind the self-professed barbarian were his two colleagues, the former Caretakers Harry Houdini and Arthur Conan Doyle, who were arguing about something.

"Three is a good number," Burton had said when the Caretakers Emeritis had pressed him for the whereabouts of the other members of the Imperial Cartological Society. "Consider us the Society's version of your three Caretakers—emissaries to an unknown region."

"All secrets out, Sir Richard?" Twain had asked him. "All trust, in the open?"

"That's a journey, not a destination," Burton had replied. "We should just focus on the progress we're making, and not on what we expect of the future."

"Benevolent, malevolent, what does it matter?" Houdini was

saying, making frustrated gestures with his hands. "I just want to know how it was done."

"How what was done?" asked Jack.

"We made the mistake of showing Harry the Serendipity Box," said Twain, "and of course, he opened it straightaway."

"What happened?"

"It vanished," said Doyle. "Disappeared into thin air. He's been trying to suss out what happened. I keep telling him it was the faeries who took it."

"Oh, spare me," said Houdini. "They'd have returned it by now if they had."

A deep compulsion for finding things out was a trait shared by the Caretakers and members of the Society, and it had served them all well in various circumstances—but in none of them was the compulsion as deeply rooted as it was in Harry Houdini. He simply could not tolerate not knowing how a trick was done—even a trick involving time and space.

"All tricks involve time and space," Houdini huffed. "Any decent illusion is nothing but the manipulation of the viewer's perceptions. That's it, and that's all."

"What do you think, Bert?" John asked as they moved from the reception hall into the banquet room, where the rest of the Caretakers and their guests were waiting.

"I think," said Bert as he and Verne opened the great double doors, "that it gave him exactly what he needed. It's just going to take him a while to realize it."

Two of the special guests at Tamerlane House were among those the companions most wanted to see: Laura Glue, the Lost Girl who had grown up to become the leader of the flying Valkyries; and the badger Fred, who was Charles's apprentice Caretaker. Both completely ignored decorum and bounded across the table the minute they saw their friends.

"Hello there, Laura dear!" Jack exclaimed as the girl threw herself into his arms and hugged him tightly.

"That's Laura *Glue*," she chided gently. "I'm so happy to see you all!"

Fred was only slightly less reserved and couldn't stop himself from hugging Charles before he stepped back to offer a more dignified handshake.

"Good to see you, Scowler Charles," he said, still beaming. "I've kept my watch in good order."

"I have no doubt," Charles said, beaming. "And how are your father and grandfather?"

"Tummeler is well, but not fit to travel out of Paralon," replied Fred. "As for Uncas, he and Don Quixote are off on some secret mission for the Prime Caretaker, or else you know they wouldn't have missed you."

"I know it," Charles said as he led them to their seats. "You're a good fellow, Fred."

"Where's Archie?" John asked Rose as they sat at the table. "I would have expected he'd be here too."

"He usually is," Rose answered, "but he hates it when all the Caretakers are present for a big party, so he stays in my attic. He says the proportion of authors to scientists fills the room with the stench of arrogance."

"From which side?"

"He never really clarified that," said Rose, "but then again, I'm not sure it matters."

◆ ◆ ◆

The celebration was in full swing. All of the Caretakers Emeritis had come out of their portraits for the party—including, John noted, one who had gone renegade while still a Caretaker.

"So," he said to Bert, "you decided to let Lord Byron out, did you?"

"Yes," Bert said, sighing. "After the truce with the Society, we couldn't exactly treat him like a traitor any longer, so we took a vote. He managed to squeak through, so he's here. But on probation," he added. "Mary and Percy keep threatening to set him on fire again."

True to form, the contentious friends were already bickering when John, Rose, and Bert sat down across from them. "We haven't met," he said, offering his hand. "I'm John."

"George Gordon, Lord Byron," the Caretaker-on-probation said amiably. "A pleasure, I'm sure."

"Your attire is atrocious, George," sniffed Percy Shelley. "Also, you smell of smoke."

"Brilliant deduction, Watson," Byron shot back.

"Manners," said Doyle, who had taken a seat next to Bert. "At least I'm still in print. No need to show your temper."

Byron scowled at the Detective. "But," he continued, undeterred, "might it not be because one of my closest friends, someone with whom I have shared—"

"Mind the young ladies," said Houdini. Rose giggled, and to everyone's surprise, Byron reddened.

"—practically everything," he ad libbed, "tried to murder me by burning my portrait? Isn't that a good reason to be a bit testy?"

"There'll be no arguments here today," Verne said, holding up a glass. "Today we mourn old friends who are lost and celebrate the victory that was won at dearest cost. But above all, we're here to celebrate the new freedom we have as Caretakers. . . ."

Burton cleared his throat loudly at this, which got a scowl from Twain.

"The freedom," Verne went on, "to begin the process we have hoped for, been divided over, and thought might never be a reality— the reunification of the Archipelago and the Summer Country. Today is, as Jack named it, truly our Day of Independence."

To this, all the celebrants raised their glasses and let out a resounding cheer.

"Independence Day?" Charles whispered to John.

"Jack's way of tweaking our American counterparts," John answered. "I don't think he intended for it to stick. Did you know he was going to say all that?" he whispered to Jack.

"Not exactly," said Jack. "It's certainly a long-term goal for the New Society."

"Which you are in charge of at Cambridge," Charles whispered. "No pressure, Jack."

During dessert, which Rose had designed herself with the aid of the Feast Beasts and Alexandre Dumas, who was a surprisingly good cook, another guest dropped in, much to the relief of John, Jack, and Charles.

"So sorry I'm late!" Hank Morgan exclaimed as he strolled in and grabbed a sandwich from one of the trays. "It seems I've missed dinner, but the dessert looks exceptionally good."

"They're called beignets," Rose said proudly. "They're a sort of French doughnut, except for these, we've added a special touch—each one you eat will suddenly be filled with something you love. Something delicious. Alex and I made the beignets, and the Feast Beasts arranged the filling."

"Don't mind if I do," said Hank, taking one from the overflowing tray. He bit into it. "Mmm," he said with real admiration. "Hazelnut."

"Mine's chocolate cream," said Charles. "Well done, Rose!"

"Mine's plain," said Fred, "but I like 'em plain."

"Eww," said Byron. "Is this spinach?"

"You must have gotten a faulty one," Dumas said, winking at Mary. "Try another."

"This is . . . ," said Byron, making a face. "Is this wax?"

"A shame," said Dumas. "Ours are delicious."

"Jules," Morgan said, stepping to the door. "A word, if I may?"

"Of course," Verne said with a glance at Bert and Twain. "We'll be back shortly. Carry on with the party!"

When the dinner had concluded, the Caretakers and their guests retired to one of the great libraries of Tamerlane House to have a smoke, drink brandy, and generally catch up on the affairs of the two worlds. Fred, Rose, and Laura Glue decided to forgo the cigars, pipes, and brandy in favor of aged Vernor's Ginger Ale and some warm Mexican pastries.

The library was shaped like a star, with fireplaces at the center and at each point. This allowed for an expansive meeting space that at the same time offered the opportunity for smaller groups to congregate.

For the first time, John realized that one of the Caretakers had not been present, either to greet them at the door, or at the banquet. "Samuel," he said, pulling Twain aside, "Poe hasn't come down yet. I know he rarely does, but for today I thought . . . Is everything all right?"

"We're trying to discover that," Twain answered ominously. "At any rate, we'll discuss it with you when Jules returns."

"I don't remember being in this library before," said Jack as he scanned the walls. "Of course, the last time I was here, we were rather preoccupied."

"This is the Library of Lost Books," Twain said proudly. "I've assembled much of it myself."

"What kind of books are lost books?" asked Jack. "If they're lost, who would know about them at all?"

"Ah," said Twain, "so you understand the challenge I had. Originally this was a repository of our own lost or unfinished works. Charles finished *Edwin Drood*, and I wrote a sequel to *A Connecticut Yankee*, among others, but mostly it contains books that were mentioned only once, in some obscure text, and never again."

He pointed with his cane at a leather-bound book just above their heads. "That one, there? It's a defense of Christianity written by Origen, who wrote it as a rebuttal to an anti-Christian Platonist named Celsus."

"Ah," Jack said, looking at Origen's book. "A kindred spirit."

"Don't relate to him too closely," said Twain. "He also grossly misinterpreted a verse in the Gospel of Saint Matthew and castrated himself. It was a terrible way for him to learn about metaphor and allegory."

"I'll keep that in mind," said Jack.

✦　　✦　　✦

After an hour had passed, Verne came into the library still deep in discussion with Morgan.

"It's nice to see Hank in the flesh," Charles whispered to John, "and still younger than us."

"That's not so hard to do these days," John whispered back as Verne and Morgan approached them.

"Sorry I was late," Morgan said again. "It couldn't be avoided, I'm afraid. There's been a lot to do to get ready for your return."

"If we hadn't had obligations and family to return to," said John, "we might just as well have stayed to help you out with things here, then gone back to our proper time later."

"No," said Verne. "You couldn't have."

"Why not?" asked John.

As he spoke, Hawthorne and Fred came back into the library with trays of fruit that they set on the table.

"Because you are still alive, in what we have come to call your, ah, 'Prime Time,'" said Verne. He took an apple from one of the trays and began to munch on it as he explained further.

"You have an allotted span within which you are meant to achieve certain things," he said, sitting. "An allotted lifetime, if you will. You've already experienced how dangerous and difficult it is to go skipping around in time—and those occasions have been of brief duration. If you were gone for a more extended time, it would be even more so."

"The difficult part probably has to do with explaining one's whereabouts to the wife," said Hawthorne.

"Actually, I was thinking that's the dangerous part," said John. "But why couldn't we have stayed, especially if we could return to whenever we wanted, ah, whenever we wanted?"

"Because," said Verne, "you'd have started to burn more quickly through the years of your own Prime Time. And you can't afford to spare even one."

"If we can't, how is it that you can?"

"Easy," Verne replied as he began to devour the apple's core. "We're already dead. We have no more obligations to our natural span, and can therefore operate outside the bounds of Prime Time.

"Come with me," he went on as he grabbed a pear from the tray. "I want to show you something."

"For a professed dead man," Charles said as the companions followed the Prime Caretaker out of the library, "he certainly can put away the fruit."

"You'd be surprised," said Burton, "how much sweeter it tastes when you're living on borrowed time."

Verne led them all into the center of Tamerlane House, to a room that stood under the tallest of the minarets. In the center of the room stood a massive clock of stone, wood, and silver. It reached high into the room, standing some four stories taller than the ground floor, and it fell away below their feet into a vastly deep subbasement.

"How far down does it go?" John asked, leaning over the balustrade. "I can't see the bottom."

"We don't keep the lower floors lit, unless the clock needs maintenance," said Verne, "but it goes down some dozen stories. The house was built around it, in fact."

"Poe calls it the Intuitive Clock," said Bert, "although Jules added his own unique touch to it." He pointed at a plate that had been mounted on the clock at eye level. It read:

The Moving Finger writes; and, having writ,
Moves on: nor all thy Piety nor Wit,
Shall lure it back to cancel half a Line,
Nor all thy Tears wash out a Word of it.
—*Omar Khayyám*

"Ironic," said Charles. "I think."

The face of the clock was twenty feet across and bore two elaborate overlapping dials—the inner one of silver, and the outer one of gold. From somewhere inside the mechanism, they could hear a steady thrumming sound.

"The center dial represents Kairos—real time, of pure numbers with no measurement," Verne explained, "while the outer dial represents Chronos, which is ordinary wristwatch, alarm-clock time."

"One mechanical, one metaphysical," said Charles. "Fascinating."

"You all have similar mechanisms on your watches," said Bert, "the ones that have been activated as Anabasis Machines, at any rate."

"The Summer Country is on Chronos time," said Verne, "while the Archipelago is on Kairos time. Now at the moment, they should be in sync. But the longer you remained here, you'd see . . ." He stopped, puzzled. "Hank?" he asked. "What do you make of this?"

Morgan looked up at the clock, and his jaw fell open. He looked at his watch, then back at the clock, and shrugged. "I have no clue what this means, Jules. I've never seen this before."

"What is it?" asked John.

"The Kairos time should be behind Chronos time," said Verne, "but it's exactly the reverse. The Archipelago is moving faster." He looked at Hank. "That explains why you were late."

"Maybe so," said Hank. "But we should consult with Poe just the same."

"I agree," said Verne. He turned to the others. "I'm sorry, but we're going to have to cut our evening short," he said, suddenly somber.

As the group began to filter their way back to the main hall, John, Jack, and Charles pulled Verne, Twain, and Bert aside.

"There's something else we need to discuss with you," John said quietly. "We didn't want to discuss it openly in front of Burton, but it concerns Hank Morgan."

Briefly the companions explained John and Charles's encounter with the ghost pirate at Magdalen Tower. When they finished, Bert turned to Verne with a puzzled expression. "An anomaly?" he asked.

"It must be," Verne replied, looking just as baffled. "I did recently send Hank on a mission to the seventeenth century, but as you saw, he returned just as he left. There must be some other answer. And as far as I know, Shakespeare never built a bridge in his life—or after." He put a hand on John's shoulder. "You were right not to discuss it openly—or mention it to Hank. Anomalies are my responsibility. I'll look into it."

"We also have something we need to tell you," Twain said to the companions, "and in just as much secrecy, I'm afraid."

The three men listened as the older Caretakers told them about Rose's strange visitor.

"A Dragon's apprentice?" said John when Twain was done. "I didn't know there was such a thing."

"Never mind that," said Jack. "Why is this the first time we've heard about these . . . Echthroids?"

"Echthroi," Bert said, glancing at Verne, "and we have no good excuse, I'm afraid, Jack. We were waiting until you were ready, and—"

"If you'd waited any longer, we'd all be dead," said Charles, "but we know now. Do you think the Echthroi have anything to do with the ghost-Hank we saw?"

"I don't know," said Verne, "but we'll not get this figured out tonight. Come back tomorrow, and we'll have a proper council to discuss everything."

"Good enough," John said, yawning. "It's always easier to fight primordial evil after a few hours' sleep."

"Not for me, I'm afraid," said Jack. "I have several papers to grade and two lectures to prepare. But yes, I'll come back with John."

"Just the idea is going to be a weight off my shoulders," said Charles. "This whole matter of not being able to travel to the Archipelago has had my sense of obligation all in a twist. I kept worrying that there was going to be some crisis I wouldn't be able to help with—sort of like listening to a radio report about your brother's house burning down. You might be able to do something eventually, but there, in the moment that you're needed most, you can't really do anything. Terribly frustrating."

"I know," Bert said. "I know how hard it's been for all three of you. But that's all, erm, behind us now, so to speak. For now, let's get you home, hey?"

They rejoined the rest of the Caretakers and guests in the main hall, where final good-byes were said, hugs given, and hands shook, and at last the three companions were ready to return home.

"Remember," John said to Rose, "we want you to come back to Oxford as soon as you can arrange it. We've missed you terribly, and Warnie and Hugo would be terribly hurt if you couldn't spend time with them as well—although your uncle Hugo is going to be merciless about your hair."

Rose kissed him on the cheek, then Jack, then Charles. "I shall, I promise," she said. "That works both ways. If you find you have a free hour or two, you can always come here. This is home too."

"Indeed it is," said Charles, "and you have my word, dear girl—I'll be back here before you know it."

"All right, fellows," said Ransom. "Let's have a little walkabout." He pulled a small leather case out of his jacket and untied the binding. Removing the stack of trumps from the enclosure in the back of the case, he shuffled to the one he wanted and held it out in front of him, concentrating.

Nothing happened.

"Hmm," he said after a minute. "I must have had a bit too much to drink. I can't seem to focus."

Hank stepped forward and extended his hand. "I've just gotten back from a visit to the seventeenth century," he said with a half-concealed smile, "so I haven't yet had the chance to indulge in as much brandy as you. May I?"

Ransom scowled a bit but handed his colleague the card.

Hank held up the drawing of the cottage where Jack lived with his brother Warnie—who could even be seen through one of the windows, reading and smoking his pipe—and began to concentrate. Again, nothing happened.

"If this is all a trick," Houdini said at length, "the setup has been astonishing so far. I only hope the payoff is just as good."

"It isn't a trick," Ransom snapped testily. "The card just isn't working!"

"Something's wrong with the picture," said Rose, looking closely at the card in Ransom's hand. "With Uncle Warnie."

"Is he all right?" Jack asked, suddenly concerned. "What's happening? Is he in danger?"

"No," said Rose. "It's nothing like that. I'm looking at his pipe. The smoke isn't moving."

John arched an eyebrow as he and the others moved in to peer more closely at the card. Rose was correct—there was smoke coming from the pipe, but it was frozen. In fact, nothing in the picture was moving.

"How is that unusual?" asked Doyle, who had not seen the cards used very often. "It's just a drawing, isn't it?"

"The drawings change with the passage of time," Ransom explained. "It was Hank who first figured it out, after our escapade in 1936. They move along with us, and change as time advances. It isn't usually noticeable, except when we're using one. Then, the scene begins to move as we step through. But the card isn't even expanding, so I don't know what to think."

"So the one we used to get to the keep," said John, "the one that jumped us from 1936 to 1943. What is it like now?"

"It's blank, save for the frame of runes," Ransom said. "The last time I looked, where the Keep of Time had been drawn, there was only open, empty sky." He shuffled the cards again and pulled one out. "See? It's . . ." He paused, frowning.

"What's the matter?" asked Charles.

"Something's off with the trump," Ransom answered. "Here, look for yourself."

Charles took the card and whistled. Ransom was right. The card was not so much blank as overfull with static. A pulsating gray crackle swept back and forth over the surface of the card.

"Perhaps it looks like that because the keep is finally gone," offered Jack. "A temporal flux of some sort, like the Time Storms."

"No," Ransom replied. "I looked in on it just a few days ago, and it was fine. Water, sky, a few seagulls—but a normal trump, otherwise."

"It's not just that card," said John, pointing at the others on the table. Ransom spread them out and took a quick accounting. All the trumps that led to places in the Summer Country had the same problem as the one for the Kilns—they were frozen in time. But all the trumps that led to locations in the Archipelago were filled with gray static.

"That's really disturbing," Morgan said as he examined his own cards. "Mine are the same way. And I just used one earlier to get here from London."

"How did that work?" asked Verne.

Morgan shrugged. "It seemed to be fine, mostly. I didn't give it much thought at the time, but now that this is happening . . ." He frowned. "It was a bit difficult getting back. I thought I was just tired, but it took me more effort than usual, since I was also using my Anabasis Machine to travel through time. That's why I was late arriving here."

"So were we," said Ransom. "By several hours, in fact. I thought it was just a fluke, though. And the trump seemed to work fine— but now it won't work at all."

"Oh dear," said Bert. "That's going to present a problem."

"How so?" asked John.

"There is currently no other way to cross the Frontier," Bert said, hands spread apologetically. "If the trumps don't work, there's no way for you to go home."

CHAPTER FOUR
THE BRIDGE

—*✳*—

"THIS IS A fine how-do-you-do," said Jack. Traveling by trump was so convenient, and so easy, that it had never occurred to any of them what might transpire if the trumps suddenly stopped working properly.

"If only we still had a Dragonship," said Charles, "getting back would be a walk in the park."

Bert and Verne exchanged nervous glances. "Yes, if only," said Bert. "Don't worry, there has to be a reason this is happening. We'll get you home, never fear."

"How about one of the principles?" Jack suggested. "The Royal Animal Rescue Squad would be more than eager to come and bail us out with a ride to Oxford."

"The vehicles are also unable to cross the Frontier," said Bert. "The magic feathers that allowed them passage lost their power when the Dragons died."

"Samaranth has feathers," said John. "Perhaps we should ask him for a few?"

"You're forgetting the first thing he ever said to us," said Charles. "'Will you drink tea with me, or plunder and die?' Do you really want to go ask him if he's molted any feathers we could borrow? Especially after that last speech he gave about the race of men being on their own?"

"I agree," said Ransom. "There's our dignity to consider."

"I'm fine staying here, if it's all the same to you," said Magwich the shrub. "They really do treat me poorly in Oxford. Why, just watering time alone . . ."

"Oh, do shut up," said Charles, "or we'll give you to Grimalkin. And if you thought Mrs. Morris had large claws . . ."

"Sorry, sorry," said Magwich.

"All right," said Twain. "So far we've got a stack of malfunctioning playing cards and our dignity. What else do we have to work with?"

"Burton," said John, "the Society has ways of traveling around expeditiously. Can you do anything here?"

Burton's eyes grew wide—he'd been enjoying the predicament the Caretakers were in, but only as an observer. He didn't expect to be drawn in as a participant.

"In time, yes, but not in space, and not across the Frontier," he said in clipped tones. "That's why I stole the *Indigo Dragon*, remember?"

John could tell that Burton hated admitting he couldn't do something. "Fair enough," he said before anyone could probe any deeper. "It's seems our work is cut out for us, then."

As the other Caretakers Emeritis began to discuss a plan of action, Rose noticed that William Shakespeare had been present throughout the entire discussion.

He didn't often join in, and on the few occasions when he tried, he was either maligned by the others or just dismissed entirely. The most useful contribution Rose had ever heard him make was

to suggest that someone be flogged—but then that was usually all
he ever suggested.

"Lord," Shakespeare said under his breath as he quietly rose
and moved into the adjacent corridor, "what fools these immor-
tals be."

Rose caught him by the arm before he could disappear into
the bowels of Tamerlane House. "I heard you," she said plainly.
"You know what we need to do, don't you?"

Shakespeare looked uncomfortably flummoxed and tugged
at his collar. "I, er, I don't know what you're talking about, child,"
he said, guiding her over to a more remote corner of the hallway.
"After all, there's no one to flog."

Rose didn't reply to this but simply kept a steady gaze on the
increasingly uncomfortable Caretaker until he finally sighed and
shook his head.

"All right, I submit. You're more perceptive than I gave you
credit for."

"Everyone here in Tamerlane House is more perceptive than
anyone gives them credit for," said Rose. "You have an idea, don't
you? Why don't you tell them?"

"Do you know," he said with a mingling of resignation and
melancholy, "what they say about me? Out there, in the world?"

Rose was confused. "You're honored and adored," she finally
answered. "Your work is held up as the greatest of achievements—
greater than any produced before or since."

Shakespeare put his head in his hands. "That's exactly what
I mean. Do you know what kind of a burden it is to have such a
reputation? To be, as I am, revered? It is troublesome bad, and
more than any man should be expected to bear. And it was worse

when I was recruited to be a Caretaker. My fame had outstripped even my life, and always, those around me—even my elders and betters—looked to mine own words for counsel."

He sighed heavily and looked at Rose. "It is a great responsibility to make decisions, and more so to be trusted, and risk being wrong in the counsel given, the choices made. Much, much worse."

At last Rose understood. "But," she said gently, "if you could convince them it was all reputation and not reality, that you were not as well-suited to the task as they thought you to be, then no one would ever look to you for advice."

Shakespeare nodded once, then again. "It has been a difficult fiction to maintain, especially in those dark days when no one quite knew what path to take, save I—and I could not break my act, lest it give me away."

"Sometimes it's better to do the right thing than the comfortable thing," Rose said firmly. "Like right now. You know, and you won't help. How is that a good way to live?"

"It isn't," Shakespeare agreed, "but after so long, I don't know how the fellowship would countenance a newly confident Will."

"They'll accept you," Rose prompted, "if you'll just go tell them what to do."

For a moment his eyes brightened, as if his resolve had returned—but then he slumped back onto a couch in the corridor. "I—I can't," he admitted. "You just don't know how hard it is, being William Shakespeare."

Rose folded her arms and sat back. "Oh, you don't think so? Would you like to trade places with me?"

"What do you mean?"

"I mean, I'm the one they call the Grail Child, even though

I'm no longer really a child, and I'm supposed to be the descendant of more gods than even exist anymore. Odysseus was my
grandsire. Merlin was my uncle. And my entire childhood was
about being ready to give up my life to save my cousin Arthur.
Believe me, I understand what it is to live under the pressure of
high expectations."

Shakespeare rubbed his chin, appraising her. Then he smiled.
"I do believe you've cornered me, dear child," he said at last, still
smiling. "If you'll be so good as to accompany me, we should go
have a word with Jules."

Rose stood and offered him her arm. "My pleasure, Master
Shakespeare."

He groaned and took her arm. "But please," he said as they left
the room, "just call me Will."

"Pull the other one," Shelley said dismissively when Rose suggested to the assembled Caretakers that Will had a plan. "His
wick isn't lit. How is he going to be of any help? All he ever wants
to do is have people flogged."

Will reddened at this, but Rose shook her head. "He's brighter
than you think," she said firmly, "and if you'll just give him a
chance, maybe he'll surprise us all."

"I have not been myself," said Will, "not for a very long while.
But circumstances dictate that I need cast away the mask of the
fool, if we're to succeed."

"It was all a ruse, was it?" Twain said with a wan smile. "Well
played, Master Shakespeare."

"I knew it all along," said Byron. "I was just playing along to be
polite."

"Oh, do shut up, you nit," said Shelley. "All right, Master Wordsmith," he said to Will. "If you are indeed a closeted genius, what pray tell is your great plan to solve our dilemma?"

"We're going to build a bridge," Will declared firmly, and with as much courage as he could muster. "A bridge between the worlds."

John's mouth dropped open in a mix of amazement and shame, and he noted a similar expression on Charles's face. In the stress of the moment they'd forgotten the message from the ghostly Hank Morgan: *You must build the bridge. Shakespeare's Bridge. You can't get back without it.*

Charles began to say something about the ghost pirate, but Verne caught his eye and shook his head. The meaning was clear: not yet.

"If the trumps won't work, then why would a bridge?" Ransom was asking. "That's quite a conceptual leap."

"We don't even know *how* the trumps work," said Will, "just that they do. But I have another plan.

"It was the stones that gave me the initial idea," he explained, "after I'd read about them in your books, Bert."

"Mine?" Bert said in surprise. "What did my books have to do with your discovery?"

"The cavorite," Will answered. "The material in your stories that made space travel possible."

"It's also a major component in the watches," said Verne. "It's part of what allows them to function as time machines."

"That's what I'm driving at," said Will. "When you activate them, one doesn't simply view another time, one is transported to that time, whole and unharmed."

"Or whole and unclothed, in Morgan's case," Twain said with mock seriousness.

"Har har har," Morgan said drolly. "Only you would see traveling in time as an opportunity for a practical joke. But I think I see what Shakespeare's getting at. The Anabasis Machines do have an effect on the physical person, so it's as if there is an effect on space as well as time."

"Better," Will said, smiling. "I think it means space and time may be, in fact, the same thing."

"Pppthhbbbth." Burton blew a raspberry and folded his arms. "This is why we never tried to recruit him," he said dismissively. "He *is* a moron."

Will blushed slightly but refrained from responding to Burton's slur. Instead he continued. "We know there are cavorite mines where the material can be found in large quantities, which is where we've gotten it for use in various devices. But I've found another place where it resides, if in less abundance. It's laced throughout all the stones in the Ring of Power. And it's in the very foundations of the Nameless Isles."

That got the Caretakers' attention. There was a flurry of discussion, argument, and expressions ranging from intrigue to disbelief. It took several minutes before Verne was able to bring the room to order again.

"These are indeed astute observations, especially coming from . . . ah, one such as yourself, who is not trained in the sciences. But I fail to see the significance of your discovery."

"There's one other place where the cavorite is plentiful," Will went on, nonplussed by the resistance of his colleagues. "Avalon. The island that exists in two worlds at once."

"Half there, and half not," Grimalkin said, having suddenly appeared over Burton's shoulder. "Sounds implausible to me."

"Get away from me, cat," Burton exclaimed, swatting at Grimalkin with a fork as its midsection disappeared, leaving two thirds of a cat, which then walked away in opposite directions.

"What is it you're proposing, Will?" asked Verne, pulling them all back to the discussion at hand.

"Come with me," Will said, rising from the table. "I'll show you."

Shakespeare led them all out into the night air, to one of the large storage sheds at the back of the house. He walked inside and took a seat at a makeshift desk, amid the straw, and gardening tools, and odds and ends. Above the desk on a support beam were several drawings of a bridge, all drawn in Shakespeare's hand.

"I've done all my work out here," Will explained, "so no one would see. Nobody comes out here much anyway."

"Who helped you with these?" said Ransom, amazed. "No offense, but I didn't know you had engineering skills."

"None taken," Will said, hooking a thumb over his shoulder. "I did indeed have some help."

Standing at the rear of the shed was the giant Tin Man—formerly the Caretaker Roger Bacon, one of the great inventors of history. He moved forward and put a supportive hand on Will's shoulder.

"It appears," Verne said, putting his arm around Rose, "that you and Master Bacon have both been better judges of character than the rest of us."

Morgan and Ransom, who were both examining Will's drawings, looked at Verne and nodded. The bridge might work.

"All right," Verne said to a beaming Shakespeare. "Ask what you will of us, and then get to work. Time's a-wasting."

Will chose several of the burlier Caretakers—Hawthorne, Dumas, and Irving among them—to help him and the Tin Man build the bridge. Bert, Rose, Laura Glue, and Fred decided to go into the kitchen and find something else to eat, while the others returned to the meeting hall. Before they got there, Charles had already started an argument with Ransom about Chronos time and Kairos time.

"You're far too concerned about reconciling your own experiences with everyone else's," said Ransom. "You need to understand: There is no such thing as past or future, not to the individual. To the individual, there is only the Now."

"It's one great advantage to being a tulpa," said Verne. "We get to live in Kairos time, because we've already done our years in Chronos time."

"That stands to reason when we're talking about you, and Burton, and the other members of the Society," said Charles, "but where does that leave Bert? H. G. Wells is still a contemporary, still in our, uh, 'Prime Time.' Yet he seems to travel as freely between worlds and times as you do."

"Bert is a dimensional anomaly," Verne explained. "The one I originally recruited is the one you know, the one you have met, Charles. In the beginning of his apprenticeship, they were one and the same, until his first trip through time.

"We were equally inexperienced with the intricacies of time travel, and the problem arose when he took his trip into the future."

"The one he wrote about in *The Time Machine*, yes," said John.

"Exactly," said Verne, "but unlike his unnamed time traveler, Bert did not safely return to the point at which he left, or moments after. He overshot the mark and arrived two full years before he ever left, and at a point when he was barely an initiate as a Caretaker. Bert, our Bert, was older, more experienced, and brought with him a three-year-old daughter."

"Aven," Jack said, exhaling. "That was Aven."

Verne nodded. "We didn't know how to send him back to try to fix the anomaly, and we weren't even sure what had gone wrong to begin with. Even Poe himself was at a loss as to what to do. Finally we realized that Bert could not leave, but also that the younger version of himself could no longer be a Caretaker."

"How did he—the young one—take the news that he was being displaced?" asked John.

"To the Devil with that," said Charles. "How did he react when he met himself?"

"The other Wells—let's call him Herb—and Bert have never met," Verne replied. "To have another version of himself walking around—and to be fully aware of him—would have interfered too much with Herb's Prime Time. Too many variables would come into play. So Dickens and I conferred with Bert, and we agreed that he should continue in his role as the third Caretaker. As for Herb, I realized I would have to not only cease instructing him in the disciplines needed to become a Caretaker, but I would also have to convince him that many of the secrets I had shared were fictions. Only one man was meant to live the lifetime that was already being lived."

Charles cleared his throat and raised his hand for attention.

Jack slapped his forehead in resignation—he and John were comfortable mingling with the Caretakers Emeritis as equals, but Charles, for some reason, still felt like he was in grammar school among the greats.

"I don't mean to contradict you, Jules," Charles said, "but then how do you explain Chaz? I wasn't there myself during the Dyson affair, but he was essentially me from an alternate dimension. Yet he was able to come here to this one without changing my position with you at all." He paused and looked around nervously. "Or has he?"

Twain clapped him on the back and blew a puff of well-intentioned cigar smoke in his face. "Worry not, dear boy, worry not. For one thing, you were already far deeper into your course than young Wells was. Shades, you were already a full Caretaker! And for another, your friends didn't bring him back here—they dropped him off several centuries back. No fuss, no muss."

"Samuel's right," said Verne. "He fulfilled a purpose in this dimension, but in a different time. Think of the temporal plane as a great map." He pointed to a whorl of wood on the top of a table. "This is you, in this time. And this," he said, pointing at another pattern on the opposite side, "is where Chaz ended up living his life. One person, two temporal places. He never interfered with your Prime Time. But if we had kept Herb in the loop, so to speak, then both he and Bert would have been in one spot," he finished, tapping the first whorl. "Not good, temporally speaking."

"Also, Chaz wasn't precisely you, Charles," said John. "He was Charles-like, but he had lived in a different world there in the Winterland. He might have started taking on more of your attributes, but he was not you, and his thinking had become different enough that he certainly could not have taken your place."

"Bert and Herb also diverged in this same way," Verne said, vigorously nodding his approval. "You've no doubt noticed that Herb's viewpoints and my own were often at odds when it came to writing."

"And science, and politics, and social development," intoned John. "You were at opposite ends of the spectrum on just about everything, Jules."

"And so it is with Bert, also," Verne agreed, "but with the difference that he and I are colleagues, whereas to Herb, I was a potential mentor who abandoned him."

"Why abandon him if he was going to end up going into the future in two years anyway?" asked Jack. "What was the need?"

"That's just it," Dickens put in, as he went to refill his pipe. "He never went."

Verne coughed. "Yes. We made certain that his studies never reached the point that he really believed in time travel, not really, and we made equally certain that he would never lay eyes on the device, much less use it."

"How much did he know?" asked John.

"Enough to know that I was no longer being truthful," Verne said, casting a sorrowful glance at Dickens, who nodded. "That single rift widened into a chasm, and in only a few years, he was no longer the man who was once so suitable as an apprentice Caretaker. The imagination, and integrity, and ingenuity were still there, but the spark of belief was gone."

"But he still wrote *The Time Machine*, didn't he?" John asked. "Or was that our Bert?"

"They both did," said Twain, "only Bert's will never be published. Of all of us, only he has written the full and accurate version of his adventures into the Histories. He feels no need to express himself outside of our quorum because in a way, he's already out in the world doing it.

"Granted, he reads his counterpart's work—and, I daresay, improves upon it, especially in his nonfiction—but the paths of Bert the Caretaker and H. G. Wells the respected author diverged a long time ago."

Jack scratched his head and squinted at the others. "But without being involved in the Archipelago," he said wonderingly, "how was he able to create all those extraordinary stories?"

"Because he's a brilliant writer," said Dickens, who had just come back into the discussion. "A great many of us have been inspired by our adventures in the Archipelago and incorporated some of those tales into our stories. But not everything is borrowed—we are, after all, still writers of great ability."

This last comment brought up a round of grunted assent and table thumping, which, Jack figured, was probably why Dickens said it.

"Conversely," Dickens continued, "there have been many talented men and women who had the imagination to be Caretakers, and who believed in the Platonic idea of the Archipelago, even if subconsciously, but yet never had the chance to become Caretakers themselves."

There was more grunting and "hear, hear's" and table thumping, and several of the Caretakers recited names.

"Chesterton," said Barrie, "and he's still living, I should note."

"Charlotte Brontë," said Dumas. "And Jane Austen."

"Longfellow," said Barrie, "and John Ruskin."

"George Gordon," said Twain.

"I'm *right here*," Byron said, irritated.

"So you are," Twain said, winking at Jack.

"We could name a hundred, or a thousand like them," said Dickens, "all brilliant, and all completely ignorant of the affairs of the Archipelago of Dreams. Yet still, they created great works. As have those here. After all," he concluded, looking at Jack, "you don't base all of your own writing off of your experiences as a Caretaker, do you?"

"All of it?" Jack asked, fingering his collar. "Well, I mean . . . that is, of course not!"

"Right," said John.

"Uh-huh," said Charles.

"What?" said Jack.

"What are we discussing?" Bert said as he entered the room, pocketing a now empty vanilla bottle. "Sounds lively."

"Plagiarism," John replied, grinning.

"Swipes," said Charles.

"You can't plagiarize from history!" Jack exclaimed, giving both of his friends the stink-eye. "*Homages*."

"Ah," Bert said, as if he completely understood. "Shakespeare and Kit Marlowe been at it again, have they?"

"Then our Bert, the one who's been in the kitchen sipping the cooking vanilla," said Jack, "shouldn't exist at all. If Jules stopped him from going to the future, then the Bert who returned shouldn't have existed to begin with!"

Twain thumped the younger Caretaker on the arm with his cane. "Boy," he said with equal parts exasperation and mirth, "just what part of the word 'anomaly' don't you understand?"

"They're telling you I'm an anomaly, eh?" asked Bert. "Well, in this crowd, I'd have to be."

"How's that?" asked John.

"Simple," said Verne. "He's the only time traveler who is still among the living."

The construction of Shakespeare's Bridge took more than three days, but before the rays of the morning sun broke over the Nameless Isles a fourth time, it was complete.

The bridge was made of cavorite-laced stone, and arched shallowly from a bend in the path behind the house to a spot in the sand about fifteen feet out. It was a fairly ordinary looking bridge, except for the two stones at the apogee of the arch.

"That's what should allow it to function," Will explained. "The capstones, into which we'll be placing these," he said, showing the others two small golden orbs. "They should allow the bridge to span the two worlds, and if we've designed it right, it should take you to somewhere in Oxford, if not directly home."

"What are they made of?" Jules asked, examining one of the orbs. "They look like . . ."

Will nodded. "We believed that the life force of the Dragons was not all that allowed them to cross," he said somberly.

"Their eyes," said Jack. "The golden eyes of the Dragons."

"Ordo Maas built them to cross over," Will said, "before they were living ships. I think we can still use the eyes and this bridge to breach the Frontier."

With no ceremony, Will stepped onto the bridge and placed one orb in each capstone. Nothing happened.

"Will?" Ransom asked. "Are you supposed to throw a switch or something?"

"I don't understand," Will murmured, more to himself than the others, as he examined the bridge. "It should have worked right away."

Verne looked at Charles and pursed his lips. "Now," he said softly. "Now is the time to share what you know."

Charles looked nervously from Verne to John, and then at Morgan. "I ah, er," he started, tugging at his collar. "That is, John and I, we know how to make the bridge work."

"How do you know that?" asked Will, surprised.

"We know," said Charles, "because Hank told us."

With all the Caretakers and their guests gathered about them, John and Charles related the details of their strange experience at Magdalen Tower.

"Interesting," Hank said when they were done, "but I'm afraid it wasn't me. I've never actually been a pirate, much less a ghost pirate."

"The timing is right, though," said Verne. "You were just there, two centuries back."

"The problem is with the trumps, not the Anabasis Machines," Morgan protested, "and I made it back just fine. Although . . ." He paused, finger aside his nose. "I have been working on a new device. Remember, Alvin?"

"Yes," said Ransom. "It's a modified version of the Lanterna Magica, but without the limitations of the slides—"

"Because we'd be using trumps," Morgan finished, snapping his fingers. "I'll go fetch it and we'll give it a try."

"So," Burton rumbled as Hank ran back into Tamerlane House, "you are keeping secrets, Caretaker?"

"Not just from you," Verne answered. "I didn't want Charles and John to tell what they knew. Not until now."

"Why?" asked Dickens. "Why not tell *us*?"

"Why not?" asked Hawthorne. "We might have believed in Shakespeare *more* if we'd heard Charles and John's story first."

"Maybe *you* would have," Verne said, looking over to where Will was adjusting stones on the bridge, "but he might not have believed in *himself*. It needed to be his choice to offer—not just because of a ghostly warning from an ally who is decidedly unghostlike."

"Whether or not he's an idiot has yet to be proven," said Burton. "The bridge doesn't work."

"Not yet," Morgan said as he hurried back to the group, "but this might do the trick."

He was carrying a strange contraption that resembled an electrified diorama box. "It's meant to be portable, usable anywhere," he explained as he set it up at the foot of the bridge, "and it operates using a trump."

He took the front off the box, revealing lenses and gears, and a slot where a card could be inserted. Carefully, he and Ransom removed one of the stones in the center of the bridge and placed the box inside the shallow hole. Morgan ran leads to both capstones, then turned to face the Caretakers.

"It's already functional," he said, nodding at Will. "You were right about the Dragon's eyes. But," he went on, "you gave it nothing to connect to on the other side." He leaned over and swiftly inserted a trump into the slot.

Instantly, half of the bridge vanished.

"Gentlebeings," said Morgan, "I give you Shakespeare's Bridge."

Will turned to the companions, beaming. "I think," he said, bowing, "you have a short walk to take, and you'll be home, safe and sound."

"I'm impressed," Ransom said, giving the functional bridge a once-over. He checked the time, then shook his watch, tapping it on his hand. "Dratted thing. I'm going to go in and check it against the Intuitive Clock. John, Jack, Charles," he called out as he left. "See you soon?"

"Of course," said Jack, who was hugging Rose one last time. "We'll get things caught up at home, then we'll be back."

"I'm going to have to explain we weren't out at the Bird and Baby," said John. "Again."

"Don't work too hard," said Fred, waving.

"I can't promise," Charles called back over his shoulder as he waved good-bye. "After all, some of us have less time than others—and we need to be making hay while the sun shines."

"Where in heaven's name did you get that expression?" John said in mock disgust. "You've been fraternizing with the American scholars again, haven't you?"

The three companions laughed as they stepped onto the bridge—and disappeared.

"Well done, Will," said Verne. "You've just changed the game."

Ransom was crossing through the dining hall when Grimalkin appeared. "So," said the cat. "Does it work?"

"Well enough to get them home," Ransom answered without looking down at the cat, which probably wasn't there anyway. "Although I'm sure I can figure out what's wrong with the trumps, given enough time."

"The trumps?" asked Grimalkin's voice. "Like the one you just used?"

"Yes," Ransom said. "I—" He froze midstride. "It still shouldn't have worked," he murmured. "Not if it was a spatial problem . . ."

He looked down at his watch, and his eyes widened in horror. Quickly, he spun about and ran back toward the other end of the house.

"It's quite a relief, actually," Morgan was saying as he congratulated Will. "Your bridge will make traveling back and forth a lot easier."

The other Caretakers Emeritis voiced their agreement—this was a paradigm shift of a rare kind.

"Of course," said Burton, "you've also rendered your safe house functionally unsafe. As of now, all roads lead to Rome, as it were."

Suddenly a voice rife with terror rang out as Ransom burst out of Tamerlane House, waving his watch. "No!" he shouted. "Don't cross over! Don't cross the bridge!"

"You're a moment too late, I'm afraid," said Bert. "They've already gone through."

"It's a discontinuity!" Ransom exclaimed, panting. "A rift! A rift in time, between this world and the Summer Country! We've got to get them back!"

Without warning a terrible earthquake shook the island,

throwing them all to the ground. A howling noise like a hurricane filled the air, and for a moment it seemed as if Tamerlane House was going to be shaken to pieces.

More ominously, the other half of the bridge had reappeared—and it brought something else with it.

"We aren't in Kansas anymore," said Twain, "or even in the Archipelago."

Through the bridge, they could see the ghost image of England, almost real enough to touch. Behind them, they could still see the Nameless Isles, but beyond that, gray mists.

"Oh my stars and garters," said Bert. "I think we've been ripped free of the Archipelago altogether."

"And what of the Caretakers?" asked Twain. "Where did they go?"

"Not where, when," said Ransom. "And there's only one way to find out. We've got to follow them across."

PART TWO

THE DISCONTINUITY

CHAPTER FIVE
THE PIRATE

THE MAN CALLED Elijah McGee dipped his quill into the watery ink and continued to draw on the broad parchment on the desk before him. The map, which was the seventh he had created for the man who was not quite a friend, and yet was more than an acquaintance, was almost completed. It was the most unusual of the maps he had made, and the most complex. But it was correct in a way he could not explain—as if it had existed in the parchment already, and was only being pulled forth by his penstrokes, not drawn upon it by his hand.

Mapmaking was not his original calling; Elijah McGee was a silversmith of great renown in the Colonies, and particularly there in Charles Town. None had a greater reputation save for one or two in Boston. But for the finest detail work, every man in every trade knew to seek out Elijah McGee.

Even if such a man was a pirate.

The young man who had first come to him was barely thirty years old, if that, but his face bore the lines of a longer life, as if the years he lived had worn down his spirit before they showed on his flesh.

He had approached Elijah with a strange watch, which was

made of a metal he had never seen before. It had been damaged in some way, or so the man had claimed. At the first meeting, he was strangely reluctant to describe to Elijah all the supposed workings of the device, but during subsequent encounters he shared more and more extraordinary tales of what it was capable of, and the adventures he had had through its use.

He had taken it to other silversmiths, some in London across the ocean, and some in the Colonies, but none could help him. One of them in Boston had agreed to allow him to try to repair it himself—but the young man had fired up the smelter when his master was at Sunday services, and had a terrible accident: He had tripped and burned his hand in molten silver. A surgeon later restored much of its usefulness, but the hand would never be the same.

Without the watch, he explained to Elijah, he could not communicate with his colleagues, and worse, he would be consigned to remain here in this *time*, rather than return to his own.

He had said "time" as if it were a place, Elijah remembered thinking. As if it were something to be traveled to. And he spoke of it reluctantly, as if a great confidence were being breached.

More was the pity then, Elijah mused, that he was unable to determine the reason for the device's malfunctioning. It operated as a watch, and nothing more, and that would have to be good enough.

He had always taken the story of the watch as he had taken the other tales—with a grain of salt. The stories were simply too outlandish to believe: accounts of a group of men and women called Caretakers, and an extraordinary place called the Archipelago, and of a singular personage the man had called the Cartographer, from whom the man had begun learning the art of mapmaking.

If even a few of the stories were true, it would be extraordinary enough, but they were generally too impossible to believe. Still, he seemed a decent enough sort, and he paid in gold (albeit coins of ancient origin), so Elijah had come to look forward to his visits.

When it was evident Elijah could not fix the watch, the young man disappeared for several months, then reappeared. He had become a pirate, which was not all that disreputable a profession—and quite a successful one at that. And he had a curious request: that Elijah draw for him a *map*.

With his ruined hand, he could no longer do it himself—but he could teach Elijah, and Elijah, with his skilled fingers, could create it. And Elijah agreed, in part out of sympathy, and in part because one does not argue with pirates.

That request was the first of several to come over the years, and in time, Elijah developed a reputation among the other pirates. Before he realized it, he had entered a new, secret profession. And it was all begun by the strange young man with the watch who had become a pirate.

I was a silversmith, Elijah thought, *before I became a mapmaker to pirates—so who am I to criticize a craftsman such as my young friend in his choice of careers?*

The visits from the young pirate became more sporadic, and Elijah wondered if some mischief had befallen the man. And then one day he returned, with the strangest request of all: He asked that Elijah try to create a map that would guide him not to a specific place . . .

. . . but to a specific *time*.

The years had taken their toll; both Elijah and his pirate friend had aged and weathered. But as Elijah was about to protest that such a thing could not be done, he noticed the fellow fingering the silver watch—and for some reason, he heard himself agreeing to try.

It did not come easily. Many conversations were had about the nature of maps, and time, and the paths that men take in their lives. And Elijah realized that it might be possible that his whole purpose in life was to create this single drawing. It was, he thought with astonishment, going to *work*.

And besides, he thought as he dipped the quill again to finish the drawing, even a failure would bring him gratitude from someone who had become a very influential man. If one was to find oneself an ally and friend to a pirate, he could do worse than to have that pirate be the most successful, ambitious, and noble of them all. So if Captain Henry Morgan wanted a map of time, Elijah McGee would oblige him. After all, isn't that what friends are for?

It was decided that Verne, Bert, Ransom, and Morgan would cross the bridge to see what had happened to the companions. Twain and Dickens stayed behind to alert Poe, and to console an inconsolable Shakespeare.

"A bit risky, isn't it, Caretaker?" Burton said to Verne. "Crossing over with so many?"

"It's my responsibility, mine and Bert's," said Verne, "and if we get stuck ourselves, we'll need Ransom and Morgan to find a way back."

"Fair enough," Burton replied, sweeping his arm in a grand gesture. "Be my guest."

Bert stepped across first, then the others.

They were in the garden just outside the Kilns, and it was in full bloom. "Spring, not autumn," Bert said bleakly. "This bodes ill for us all."

Verne was looking at his watch and shaking his head in disbelief. "This can't be right," he murmured to himself. "It's not possible."

"It's all too possible, Jules," Ransom said grimly. "And all too real."

They moved around to the entrance that led to the large drawing room, where they hoped to find the three Caretakers. John appeared at the door, nearly trampling over Bert in the process.

He was dressed differently than he had been just minutes before in Tamerlane House, and he held a drink in his hand. After a few seconds of stunned disbelief, he set the drink aside and embraced his mentor.

"Knew you'd come," John said, his voice a mix of joy and barely restrained sorrow. "I knew you'd find a way!"

Behind him they could see Jack, his brother Warnie, and Hugo Dyson. All were dressed very formally and were drinking strong liquor.

There was some confusion as the new arrivals entered and introductions were made. Warnie and Hugo had never met Verne or Bert, and Ransom and Morgan only briefly.

"We're so glad to see you're all right," said Bert. "When the earthquake happened, we worried something had gone terribly wrong."

"Earthquake?" Jack asked, looking at John, who shrugged. "Nothing like that happened. The bridge worked like a charm, but then it vanished. We've been terribly worried all this time about *you*. And when we didn't hear from anyone—"

"All what time?" said Bert. "You just left, not five minutes ago!"

"Bert," Jack said slowly, his voice trembling, "we came home two years ago. We've been trying to reach you the entire time."

Verne closed his eyes as he suddenly realized: They were having a wake. "Then Charles . . . ," he began.

"You've come too late," said Jack. "Charles is dead."

It took a few minutes to let the terrible news sink in before the Caretakers could even speak. Charles was dead—which meant that it was no longer 1943, but 1945. Somehow, the creation of the bridge between worlds had shifted Tamerlane House forward in time two full years.

"We have to speak to Poe," Bert said when he had regained his composure. "He may be able to help."

"What about Poe's portraitist, Basil?" John said, suddenly animated. "He was working on one of Charles. Can he still—"

"He never finished it," Bert interrupted. "Charles asked him not to."

"Oh," said John, suddenly crushed. "But he still has it, doesn't he? It can still be completed, correct?"

"Yes," Bert said, casting a hesitant look at Verne. "But . . ."

"There's something you need to know," Verne said, "but it may be best discussed when we get back to Poe's house. Please, John—trust us on this. Charles has not been abandoned."

"All right," said John, deflated. "I do trust you, Bert."

"We don't even know if we *can* get back," said Ransom, who seemed to have taken the news of Charles's death worse than any of them. "Do we?"

"We do," said a voice from the door. It was Mark Twain. "We've crossed back and forth several times," he said as he entered the Kilns with Burton close behind. "Tamerlane House, in fact, all of the Nameless Isles, are now connected to Oxford."

It was true. From the garden, all that could be seen was half of a stone bridge, leading to nowhere. But looked at straight on, one could see the ghost images of the other Caretakers and Tamerlane House just beyond.

"Whatever it was that caused this particular problem seems to have ended when the Nameless Isles were wrenched away from the Archipelago," said Twain. "Tamerlane time and Oxford time are the same, now, so it's safe to cross."

"Maybe," said Verne, "but we still have no idea what's caused the discontinuity to begin with."

"That matters less to me," Jack said, wiping tears from his eyes, "than it would have just a week ago, when Charles was still alive."

Warnie and Hugo stayed behind while John and Jack returned across the bridge with the others to tell the bad news about Charles to the rest at Tamerlane House. One among them took the news worse than the rest. The sorrowful howling echoed throughout the isle.

It was Fred. "Awooo . . . ," he howled again, eyes filled with tears. "I—I should have crossed over with him!" the little mammal said, sobbing. "I'm his apprentice! I should have been there! He didn't have to die alone!"

John and Jack both knelt and grasped the small badger by the shoulders. "He didn't, he didn't, Fred," Jack said soothingly. "There were many people with him, all of whom loved and admired him. He wasn't alone."

"Take heart, little apprentice," said Burton in an almost sincere effort to seem supportive. "You'd have been broasted by the fellows at Magdalen the minute they caught sight of you. So really, you saved him a bit of grief already by not having to mourn you."

Strangely enough, Burton's poor attempt at a joke was more buoying to Fred than anything else anyone said, and after a few moments, he regained his composure.

"Does this mean I'm to take his place?" Fred asked Bert. "Not that I'm in a hurry to, or in any way as capable as Master Charles," he added quickly, glancing at John and Jack. "I'm just thinking that in a crisis I don't want the Caretakers to be left shorthanded."

It occurred to John that at that particular moment, between the Caretakers, past and present; the members of the Imperial Cartological Society; and the Messengers, Morgan and Ransom, they were anything but shorthanded when it came to bootstrap Caretaking. But he kept this to himself—Fred didn't need to hear something that made him think he wasn't essential.

Once more the Caretakers Emeritis gathered in the meeting hall, where, for most of them, they had dined just hours before. But for John and Jack, it had been two years.

"The war is all but won," said John. "There's a new American president, and the Germans surrendered only a week ago. It was terrible—especially the waiting, knowing it would have to eventually end. But we stuck it out, and I think Charles held on just long enough to know that we'd done what was needed. And then he let himself go."

"When we didn't hear from you," Jack said, "we feared the worst, especially as the war continued. But then suddenly things turned around—and we realized that our defeat of the Shadow King was finally being reflected in events in our world."

"We're very happy to see you," John said, "even as sad as we are to have lost . . . to have . . ." He stopped, groping for words, and wiped at his eyes. "Well, yes. I wish Charles were here. But tell us: What happened? Obviously the bridge works."

"Works now, you mean," said Shakespeare miserably. All of Rose's consoling words could not bring back his earlier confidence. From his point of view, he'd done worse than fail. He'd failed because he was too confident he'd succeeded.

"The best we have been able to figure," said Morgan, "is that Will's principle was sound, but he missed a few things in the execution."

"Indeed," said Ransom, who was still a bit ashen. "The orbs allowed the Dragonships to pass between worlds, but they were also moving. At some point, they would cross. The bridge didn't move—it was forming a fixed point in both worlds. And because of the discontinuity I discovered, we think that the Nameless Isles were pulled out of Kairos time and into Chronos time, and we lost two years in the process."

"But how is that possible?" asked Jack. "I thought time moved more slowly in the Archipelago."

"It did," said Verne, "but now it appears to be speeding up. We think that's why you couldn't use the trump—the time differential was too great. The cavorite in the bridge let it function enough for you to cross over, but we lost two years in the transition when the chronal stresses became too great, and now we've been completely cut off."

"Tamerlane House is now connected to Oxford," said Ransom,

his voice shaky. "But that is nothing compared to what we fear is going on back in the Archipelago."

Before he could elaborate, Ransom's eyes widened, then rolled back in his head as he collapsed to the floor, unconscious.

"What's wrong with him?" Jack asked as they got Ransom to bed in one of the spare rooms. "He looks deathly ill."

"He may be," said Bert. "He's gone past his Prime Time in Chronos time now. We've never seen that happen before."

"His Prime Time?" asked John. "Then he was meant to . . ." He paused. "Like Charles," he said suddenly. "He's *exactly* like Charles."

"An aspect," said Verne. "Not so much a direct analogue of Charles, as your fellow Chaz was. But an aspect is enough. Think of him as a Charles from another dimension—somewhat like your H. G. Wells, Herb, is to our Bert."

"However you choose to think of him," said Bert, "Alvin Ransom is dying."

"It's time to call a full council of Caretakers," said Twain, "and you, as well," he added, waving at Burton. "We need all our friends now, and our old enemies, too."

The group waited to start the council until the elder members of the Caretakers Emeritis had joined them. Some, like Chaucer, had been at dinner the night before. Others, like Malory and Tycho Brahe, had been busy with other matters. But the one they were all waiting for was Edgar Allan Poe.

He was the master of Tamerlane House, and more of an anomaly than Bert was. John was the Principal Caretaker of the *Imaginarium Geographica*; Verne was something called the Prime

Caretaker; but Poe stood above them all as an enigmatic adept in matters involving time and space. His abilities and counsel were oracular in nature—he was not always present, not always involved, and did not often offer advice unless Verne specifically requested that he do so. But when he did choose to involve himself in matters at hand, it was both a relief and an added fear. For despite all the good he could do, he only got involved when the situation was most dire.

The rest of the caretakers had been seated for several minutes when Poe finally took his place at the head of the long table. "This note," he said to Twain, "about Rose's visitor. Perhaps we should start there."

Rose recounted the details of her visit from Mother Night. Following that, Verne, aided by Morgan and Bert, elaborated on the happenings after the celebration, when they discovered that the trumps weren't working. When they got to the part about the bridge, Shakespeare bravely took the stage himself to explain.

"Interesting," Poe said when he had finished. "You demonstrate the same sort of genius that Arthur Pym had."

"Thank you," said Will.

"You also made the same mistakes," added Poe.

"Oh," said Will.

"Do you think the events are related?" Verne asked. "Could the discontinuity be the fault of the Shadows?"

Poe pondered this. "The Echthroi," he said at last, "exploit weaknesses, but I don't think they are the cause of this. I think we are."

"How so?" asked Twain.

"Independence Day marked another event," said Poe. "The

final destruction of the Keep of Time. I think this is what Mother Night was referring to when she said the threads of history had come undone. I think that caused the discontinuity."

"Great," said Burton. "You fools have broken history."

"I hate to admit it, but he's right," said Jack. "We have. And we've just assumed that it would take care of itself, but it hasn't."

"So how do we fix it?" asked John. "It isn't like the *Geographica*, where we can just replace the tower with a book of maps."

"Maybe we can, at that," said Verne. "Time *is* mappable, you know. It's difficult in the extreme, but not impossible."

"Only one among our number has ever had the facility to map time," said Chaucer, "and I know it pains you, Bert, to hear him referred to thusly, but it was our renegade, John Dee."

"Cambridge man," Fred said, before spitting over his left shoulder and winking twice.

"Hey now," said Jack. "Enough of that. Or have you forgotten I'm a Cambridge man too? Or about to be one, anyway."

"Big diff'rence between being drafted an' enlisting," said Fred. "We know your heart will stay pure, Scowler Jack."

"Actually, that's exactly what we were using Morgan, Ransom, and the other adepts to do," said Verne. "We had begun by mapping the Keep of Time itself. The Messengers were our primary exploration force, venturing through each doorway and then reporting on what they found there."

"Ransom was one of the latecomers," Twain added, "though he certainly made up for his relative inexperience with a marked ability to report on unorthodox environs."

"With their experiences in time travel," John said looking at Burton, Houdini, and Doyle, "it had to be helpful to draw on the

Society's collective knowledge. Was that part of the reason you agreed to the truce?"

"It was a bit of a Hail Mary pass on their part," Verne said with a barely concealed smirk. "There was practically nothing left of the original Imperial Cartological Society after the split in the ranks, and other than Burton's core group, all of the members were either missing, dead, or permanently indisposed."

"Permanently indisposed?" asked John.

"Kit Marlowe was stranded on a fictional island, which is entirely different from being stranded on an imaginary one," Chaucer said, his face an impassive mask of memory. "De Bergerac is on a comet, I believe. Or the moon. I forget. Anyway, he's no longer of this physical world. Defoe you know about, and also Coleridge, who still sits in despair on that island past the Edge of the World.

"Wilhelm Grimm was killed by the Shadow King," he continued, "and Byron is on probation, so he will remain out of circulation as either a Caretaker or a member of the Society."

"We can still make that a more permanent state," Percy Shelley grumbled.

"Christina Rossetti is in Fairy Land," Dickens said, consulting a notebook, "and Milton was last said to be in the Underworld somewhere."

"Which underworld?" asked John.

"Does it matter?" said Dickens.

"So," Chaucer concluded, taking a tally on his fingers, "that's six we know of then. Burton, Houdini, Conan Doyle, Byron, and Magwich here—and Dumas *fils* and William Blake unaccounted for."

"Does Magwich really count?" said Jack.

"I heard that," came a whining voice from the next room. "Just because I'm a tree doesn't mean I can't hear you. Trees have feelings too, you know."

"Here," John said as he handed his jacket to Fred. "Cover up the shrub, will you?"

"My pleasure," said Fred as he covered up the vehemently protesting plant. "Time for a nap, Maggot."

"Blake was never one of us," Burton said. "We had . . . diverging opinions about the direction of the Society. One day he simply left. I've not seen him since."

"We can discuss Blake another time," Verne said with a mysterious expression on his face. "For now, the one I'm concerned about, who may be the most significant player on the other side, is still unaccounted for."

"Who was that?" said Dickens, consulting his notes. "I don't—"

"Dee," Poe said. "Dr. John Dee. The renegade."

All eyes turned to Burton, who scowled.

"No one really knows what happened to him," Burton said. "He was the originator of the Society, but he operated more as a mythic archetype than a colleague. I've never met him myself—not face-to-face."

"We'll take your word on that," said Twain, "for now."

"If it's just one man," said Jack, "then why would he be of any concern? Can't we just put him in the 'missing' column next to Blake and young Dumas and focus on other matters that are in the here and now?"

"Not like Blake," Verne said brusquely, "and perhaps not

missing. Just because we can't find him doesn't mean he hasn't already found us."

"And he's not likely alone, either," added Burton. "There were always other recruits to the ICS, but Dee was never forthcoming about who they were, or in what numbers he'd recruited them."

"So what *do* we know?" John said, exasperated.

"Only this," said Verne. "Our enemy is more skilled than any here in mapping time, and he may already know everything he needs to know about *us*—while we know almost *nothing* about him."

"I'd like to ask something," said Rose. The Caretakers fell silent, in deference to Poe, who immediately turned to her. "The keep has fallen—that was going to happen regardless. But how does that affect your ability to move through time?"

"That's a good question," said Bert, "which I can't begin to answer."

"I was just thinking," Rose continued, "that if I'm supposed to restore the threads of history, then maybe I'm meant to go back in time and fix the keep before it can be damaged?"

"That's a tall order," said Verne. "Too much of that can just make things worse. And besides, we don't even know if we still *can* travel in time."

"We can certainly find out," Morgan said as he whipped out his watch and twirled one of the dials. "We *are* a part of the Summer Country now, right? So why not have a look? Back in just a bit," he added with a wink. "Don't let the badger steal my chair."

"I would never . . . !" Fred huffed before Laura Glue elbowed him in the ribs. "Uh, I mean, not again, anyway."

Morgan disappeared. There was a soft popping sound as the displaced air rushed in to fill the Messenger-shaped void where he had been standing.

A few moments later, the air pressure of the room increased ever so slightly as he reappeared—but it was not the Hank Morgan who had just left. Or rather, it was, but he was not in the same state. This Hank Morgan was old—impossibly, inconceivably old—and he was dressed as a pirate, exactly like the apparition Charles and John had seen at Magdalen Tower.

"Zero point!" Hank said as his eyes rolled back in his head.

John, Jack, and Twain rushed forward to grasp hold of the old man as he collapsed in front of them. He was sobbing, not from pain, but from relief.

"Oh mercy," he cried. "I'm back! I'm finally back!"

"You weren't gone but thirty seconds!" Jack said as they lowered the fragile Messenger into a chair.

"Fifteen," Fred said as he offered some silver to boost Morgan's strength. "Twenty, tops."

Morgan's eyes widened in alarm, and he pushed aside the silver and mug of ale proffered by the badger. "Twenty seconds?" he wheezed. "I've been leaping through time trying to return here for over two hundred years!"

"I was going to say he looked pretty decrepit," Houdini said to Doyle behind his hand, "but for two hundred and forty-odd years old, he actually looks pretty champion."

"At least we know when he was," Verne said, "or at least, when he was *last*."

"Tried to send you a message, yes I did," said Morgan.

"We got it," John said, leaning close. "Charles and I—we got your message. How did you do it?"

Morgan closed his eyes. "Chronal stereopticon," he murmured weakly. "Like I made for Shakespeare's Bridge, only better. Projected a message through time, to tell you how to make it work."

"But why did you project it at Magdalen Tower?" John asked. "Why not the Kilns, or our offices?"

Morgan cackled. "Weren't built yet," he said, "not in the seventeenth century. But the tower was. Had to make a trump of what was there then, to reach you here now."

"I wonder how his watch malfunctioned," said John. "Will ours do the same?"

"Yes!" Morgan said as he staggered to his feet and clutched at John's lapels. "But it wasn't a malfunction! There are no zero points! Don't you understand? There was nothing for the Anabasis Machine to cling on to. Nothing to show where, or when, I was. I have spent three lifetimes leaping blindly from instant to instant trying to find my way back to now."

"No zero points?" asked Jack. "What does he mean?"

"A zero point is created by events of great significance," said Bert. "The watches are attuned to all of them through history. He should have been able to leap straight back. And for some reason, he didn't."

"But here you are at last, my dear young lad," Twain said gently, taking Morgan's hands in his own, "and here you'll stay. The watch finally brought you home."

Jack found it a bit disconcerting to hear Twain refer to the more elderly-appearing Morgan as young, but not as disconcerting as he would have when he himself was younger. Still, neither the gesture nor Twain's soothing words seemed to help—Morgan was still frantic.

"That's just it!" he said as he loosed Twain's hands and rummaged around in his pocket. "The watch still doesn't work!"

This, at last, seemed to get Poe's attention, and he leaned farther over the table. "That isn't possible," he said softly. "The cavorite in the watches never loses its energy. They will function indefinitely."

"To keep time, yes," Morgan shot back, clearly incensed by the fact that no one was really paying attention to his protestations, "but not to traverse time. It took me out, then stopped functioning as it's supposed to." He pulled out a rumpled parchment from his pocket and flattened it out on the table. "This is the only reason I'm here now."

It was a map. Slightly charred around the edges, and shot through with a few holes, but a map nonetheless.

The drawing on the parchment was almost holographic in nature and gave the impression of being a palimpsest, as if several drawings had been created, then erased, leaving a faint impression of what had been drawn before under what was now there.

The locus for Tamerlane House and the Nameless Isles was clearly visible in the center, and other markings indicated the placement within the Archipelago of Dreams, but there were additional lines that were almost mathematical in nature, and calculations that involved symbols, pictograms, and runes, all wedded to the location of the islands. It was at once simple and complex, and unlike any map any of the Caretakers had ever seen—the images drawn upon it almost . . . *moved.*

"Is that one of the trumps?" asked John. "It looks too large."

"It *is* too large," countered Jack. "It's one of Merlin's spares, isn't it, Bert? One of the extra sheets he pulled out of the *Geographica.*"

Bert moved around the table and peered more closely at the sheet, then at Morgan's harried expression, before turning to the others and nodding. "It is. I didn't know Hank had it, but I'm glad he did."

"He needed a new map, because the old one, the one that catalogued all the zero points, is gone."

"What map?" asked John.

"The keep," said Bert. "The Keep of Time was how we mapped zero points."

"Take this," Hank said to Twain, pressing the parchment into his hand. "Take what I've done and learn from it. You can still find a way. I know you can, Samuel."

"We will, we will," Twain assured him as he leaned him back in a soft chair. "You've done a marvelous job for us, Hank. We're very grateful."

Morgan didn't respond, but instead closed his eyes and took a deep breath. A moment later his watch fell out of his hand and to the floor.

"Ah, me," Twain said heavily. "Good-bye, my noble friend. Sail well into that good night."

The others stared at one another in disbelief. Hank Morgan was dead.

CHAPTER SIX
STRANGE DEVICES

- ✳ -

MORGAN'S BODY WAS put into his room to lie in state until the Caretakers could get a better grasp on the escalating crisis. In just one day a Caretaker and a Messenger had died, and another Messenger lay on the edge of death. They returned to the meeting hall, frustrated, saddened, and subdued—most of them, anyway.

"I'm thinking we chose a terrible time to ally ourselves with this lot," Burton said to his two colleagues. "The Caretakers are dropping like flies."

With a sudden explosion of energy that none of them had expected, Mark Twain burst out of his chair and struck Burton full in the jaw with a brutal right cross. Burton flew backward and fell flat on his back, cracking his head against a cabinet.

"What the hell . . . ?" Burton sputtered as Doyle and Houdini helped him to his feet. "I should kill you for that!" he spat at Twain as he glowered, held back only by Doyle's good sense and strong arms.

"Better men have tried," Twain answered as he straightened his cuffs and sat down, "and anyway, I'm already dead, so you'd be trying to harvest when the cows already ate the cabbage. You can be angry at me if you like, but we will have respect in this house, especially for our own fallen."

Burton didn't reply, but relaxed his stance and shrugged off Doyle's grasp. "It's a strange business," he murmured gruffly, "when dead men such as we must mourn another dead man."

"Does he have to stay that way?" Jack asked with a burst of excited insight. "This *is* Tamerlane House! Can't you bring him back with one of the portraits?" He started for the stairs to the upper rooms. "Where's Basil? We need to fetch him, quickly!"

Several of the other Caretakers reached out to Jack to stop him, offering gestures of comfort for the words they knew he was about to hear.

"It's not possible, young Jack," Chaucer said as they moved him back to the table and his seat. "Not for one such as Henry Morgan. I'm sorry."

"How about you?" Jack said to Verne. "And you?" he said to Burton. "Can you make him a tulpa?"

"It doesn't work that way," Burton said dismissively. "For one, it's the same problem—it wouldn't work for Morgan. And anyway, our methods take longer—at least a year would be necessary."

Bert took his protégé by the arms and looked into his eyes. "Jack," he said, "the reason that we cannot create a portrait for Hank Morgan is because he is a Fiction."

Jack blinked and narrowed his eyes. "You mean, as in Samuel's book? But all of us have fictionalized things we have seen and people we've met."

"I don't mean to say he is a fictional *character*," Bert said with emphasis, "but that he is unique—what we refer to as Fictions. Unique works in creation."

Verne stepped in to elaborate. "You know that there are ana-
logues of us all in other times, other worlds, other dimensions.
You've even met some of them."

"Like Chaz," Jack said.

"Precisely," said Verne, "but Hank was not like that. He was
unique in all the worlds. There was one of him, and one only.
There have been others like him, but very, very few."

"Herman Melville," said Chaucer. "Prime Caretaker material,
just prime. A brilliant creator, with marvelous insights."

"We considered him before Jules," said Dickens. "No offense,
Jules."

"None taken," said Verne.

"He would have been a Caretaker," Dickens continued, "but
there were . . . ah, complications. And we moved on."

"Complications?" asked John.

"Crazy as a bedbug," said Hawthorne.

"Nathaniel!" Dickens exclaimed. "Bad form."

Hawthorne sighed. "His creative genius was coupled with
madness," he explained to the others. "We could never be certain
which of the traits would become dominant, and we couldn't take
the risk that the insanity would prevail."

"We still wanted him," Twain interjected, glancing sternly at
Hawthorne, "if only to have him as an apprentice to our group.
That was when we discovered he was, in fact, a Fiction. Unique."

"We tried to get him ourselves, for the Society," said Burton,
"but we noted the Caretakers' apparent disinterest and withdrew.
If we had only known . . ."

"It would have done you little good, Richard," Twain said in as
stern a voice as they had ever heard. "He would not have become

a tulpa, and as we discovered, painting a portrait does not work on Fictions. It drove Basil nearly insane, mixing and remixing the resins to try to fix what he saw as his own mistake. But it had nothing to do with the resins, or the quality of the painting. It was because Melville could not be duplicated. And Hank Morgan was unique in exactly the same way."

"Despite Morgan's rashness in testing the theory," said Poe, "Rose's suggestion still has merit. There may be a point in time where something may be fixed. And as he demonstrated, zero points may still be created—and mapped."

"We can't stop the fall of the keep," said John. "That risks sacrificing our victory over the Winter King."

"I wasn't even thinking that far back," said Rose. "What if we just went back far enough to avoid the discontinuity?"

"To keep Tamerlane House from being separated from the Archipelago?" asked Chaucer.

"No," Rose said. "I was thinking that we'd start by saving Charles and Mr. Morgan."

"You're a sweet girl," said Bert. "Your heart is in the right place. But before we could even try, we'd have to find a way to do it. And we already discovered that the watches will not work."

"Let's try the repository then," Verne said, rising, "before anyone else tries something rash."

The repository was by far the largest room the companions had seen within Tamerlane House, with the sole exception of the Trophy Hall that Poe kept in the basement. It contained, among other things, a stuffed tyrannosaurus rex, a giant American penny, and both halves of the Titanic—from which, Poe had claimed, they had gotten all the dinnerware used at Tamerlane House. John kept meaning to turn one of the plates over to check for the maker's insignia, but always forgot until after the tables had been cleared.

All the various time travel devices used by Verne and Bert were stored in the repository, Poe explained, including the ones that had never quite worked as they were meant to. There was one that resembled a blue police box from London—"Stolen by a doctor with delusions of grandeur," said Poe—one that was simply a large, transparent sphere—"Created by a scientist with green skin and too much ego," said Verne—and one that was rather ordinary by comparison.

"This one looks like an automobile," John said admiringly, "with wings."

"The doors open that way for a reason," Verne explained, "we just never figured out what it was. The inventor of this particular model tried integrating his designs into a car, an airplane, and even a steam engine train. He was running a crackpot laboratory in the Arizona desert, and he never realized that it was not his inventions themselves, but his proximity to some sort of temporal fluctuation in the local topography, that allowed them to work."

"What happened to him?" asked Jack.

"He'd get the machines up to one hundred and six miles per hour," said Bert, "and then he'd run out of fuel and promptly get arrested by whatever constabulary had been chasing him. The sad part was that Jules figured out if he'd just gone two miles an hour faster, he'd likely have been successful in his attempt."

"And this one?" asked John. "It looks like a treadmill."

"The Cosmic Treadmill, if you please," sniffed da Vinci. "It may have never operated as I planned it to, but the theory behind it is sound."

"Only if you can find someone who is capable of running one hundred eight miles per hour," said Bert.

"It's hardly my fault that human potential has not yet risen to match my invention," da Vinci replied. "At any rate, I'm not going to stand around here just to be insulted. I'm going back to my portrait."

He stormed off in a huff, and Bert flipped open a book to make a note. "Insult the treadmill, da Vinci leaves the room," he murmured, clicking his tongue as he finished and snapped the book shut. "Good to remember. He's going to drive me up a wall someday."

John and Jack moved away from the mobile devices toward one far more elaborate. It resembled a theater balcony, with a low banister across the front and a wide, red velvet seat in the center. In front of the seat was an instrument panel filled with switches and dials, and behind was a large metallic disk.

"This is the one you traveled in, isn't it, Bert?" John asked, circling the machine with unabashed admiration. "It looks brilliant."

Bert folded his hands behind his back and blushed. "Well, yes. Thank you, John. It's the only machine here created entirely from my own design."

"After all the grief you fellows gave Arthur and me," Houdini complained, "it's a bit insulting to find you sharing Archipelago secrets in your books."

"Technically speaking, the machine and my accounting of the journey were not of the Archipelago," said Bert. "The trip was done entirely in London."

"Also, it wasn't so much that you broke the rules," Verne chided, "but that you were so noisy about doing so."

"The man has a point," Burton agreed, glaring at Houdini and Doyle. "Now will you please be quiet?"

"You have a lot of machines here," said John. "Will any of them work better than the watches do?"

"That's a difficult question to answer," said Bert.

"Here's the main problem we have encountered," said Verne. "While it's true that we have discovered many ways to travel through time, each way works only once for each traveler. Once, and never again."

"The main reason we turned almost entirely to the watches—the Anabasis Machines," said Bert, "is because they *could* be used over and over again. What they didn't have is range—to be able to go more than a millennium required either a Lanterna Magica, which was limited in use too, or one of these devices."

Chewing on his lip, John turned to Bert as another piece fell into place. "So your first journey out, when you traveled eight hundred thousand years in the future . . . ," he began.

Bert took a deep breath, then nodded. The sorrow was undisguised, and it occurred to John that perhaps the old man wanted them to realize the depth of his feeling on the matter.

"Once, and never again," Bert said, echoing Verne. "I took one of our earliest devices, a contraption designed by Leonardo da Vinci and assembled by Nemo, Bacon, and the animals, and a few minutes into the trip, I made a terrible miscalculation. I tried to correct it, but the knob broke off in my hand. By the time I was able to replace it, I had traveled more than eight thousand centuries."

"With such an accident," said Verne, "there was no way to track or follow him. He was utterly on his own."

"As you found out, I discovered I could be happy there," said Bert, "but I also thought I could leave again and return at will— that the accident was only that. Not that I couldn't go back."

"So when you returned here . . . ," Jack began.

"We didn't know," Bert said with painful bluntness. "We were monkeys playing with . . . well, with a time machine. I believed that I could easily move back and forth as I liked, and so when Aven was only a few years old, I offered to take her on a short trip to the Archipelago, to visit, only to discover I'd abandoned her mother in the far future. I can only imagine," he said tearfully, "how lonely she must have gotten."

"Well, from a certain point of view," offered John, "she hardly knows you've left. That is one of the advantages to traveling in time, isn't it? That you can go back almost to the moment that you left, with no one the wiser?

"After all," he added conclusively, "isn't that what you did with us when you returned us to the Inn of the Flying Dragon shortly after we'd left?"

"Not quite," said Verne. "Always moving forward, remember? You still aged the days you were in the future—you didn't shed those years when you came back."

Jack nodded in understanding. True, Bert and Aven could possibly return to almost the same point they'd left, if a means for returning could be finely tuned enough to do so. But they would be the age they were now—an elderly Herbert George Wells instead of a young adventurer, and a pirate queen named Aven, a mature, fully grown woman, rather than a child bubbling with laughter on her father's lap as they vanished into time.

Like Morgan, they could go back, but they would not be the same two people who had left. It was possible that Weena, Aven's mother, would not miss them at all, but it would become immediately apparent to all three of them that something had been lost—three lifetimes together, never to be recaptured.

"Why do you think he gave up being a full-time Caretaker?" Verne murmured. "Stellan was killed, true, but Bert had become semiretired already—although he never took it to the extent that Jamie did in refusing to be involved at all."

"So all those occasions, all these years," John said, "all the moments when you were unavailable to us as a mentor . . ."

Bert choked back a sob and gave one short, sharp nod of his head.

Verne put a steadying hand on his friend's shoulder. "Yes," he said gently. "He was here, in the repository, trying device after device in hopes he might finally be able to return to Weena."

"The most ironic thing about mourning her?" Bert said as he wiped a sleeve across his eyes. "She won't even be born for more centuries than I can count."

"Can you leave her a message somehow?" John asked. "Like Hugo did when he went back to Arthur's time, with the message he wrote in the Booke of Dayes?"

Bert shook his head. "I was there, remember, lad? In that much time, cultures fade and vanish. To be sure, it's not geologic time, or even Deep Time—but eight thousand centuries is too long to expect anything familiar to persist. No Caretakers, no Archipelago to speak of—at least in the form we know it today, or

whatever day this is. The libraries were gone, the buildings, the—"
He stopped and stared curiously into space.

"No, wait," he continued after a moment. "There *was* one arti-
fact that did survive, although I seldom spoke to her myself. She
was a frosty one."

"The Sphinx!" Fred exclaimed. "That's who you mean, isn't it?
My father and Quixote told me about her."

"Yes," said Bert, "but other than her, I saw almost nothing—
nothing—in the future that had survived from our time, or any
other. Nothing that she would be able to recognize, at any rate."

"Hmm," said John. "I wonder why they only work once? There
has to be a physical principle at the heart of the dilemma somewhere."

"There's a rule of conservation of energy of travel in time," said
Poe, who hadn't spoken since they'd entered the repository. "A
journey into the past must be balanced by one into the future."

"This is one of the reasons we know as much as we thought we
did about the near future," Verne put in. "All the voyaging Hank
and Alvin were doing into the near past had to be counterbalanced with similar trips into the near future."

"What we didn't understand at the time," said Bert, "is that in
time, distance equals energy. Thus, a trip into the deeper past had
to be counterbalanced by one into the far-flung future."

"What happened when you didn't balance the energies?" asked
Jack.

"It wasn't an academic question," said Verne. "The energies did
just fine at balancing themselves—sometimes in a catastrophic
fashion."

"We lost Pym that way," Bert said with a reproachful glance at

Poe, who remained impassive. "Arthur took an ordinary trip out into what should have been the fourth century. Instead, as far as we have been able to determine, he was ripped from his planned pathway and flung into Deep Time. To where—ah, when, we have no idea."

"Hank didn't have to come back, but he did anyway," Jack said in awe. "He spent two centuries trying to get back just to tell us what he'd learned."

"Small acts of conscience are what make the world, and eternity," said Poe. "Those little choices, those moments, when everything diverges. Those are what we are trying to preserve."

"We didn't change the past, we changed our own future," said Jack. "You said that it was necessary that we do so, and jump forward, because according to a 'possible' future history, we already had."

Poe inclined his head. "That is so."

"But," Jack went on, not giving ground, "it seems to me all we've done for decades now is meddle in time trying to make up for mistakes we'd already made! Instead of trying to patch up the mistakes, and fight the Winter King over and over again—"

"He's dead now," Fred offered. "The bad part, anyway."

"I know that, Fred," said Jack. "But that's my point. No disrespect to our own dead friend, but if all this grief and suffering is because of the accident that destroyed the Keep of Time, why *don't* we go back and try to stop ourselves from doing it? Or better yet, find a way to go and defeat the Winter King in the first place, so that all the rest never needed to have happened at all?"

"It didn't have to happen, although it did," said Poe. "Master Wells, do you have the book?"

Bert's eyes widened in surprise, and he looked not at Poe, but at Verne. He paused a moment, as if considering a response; then, without answering, he stepped out of the room, only to return a moment later carrying one of the Histories.

Bert handed the book to Verne, who skimmed through the pages to the one he expected Poe was seeking. He tapped the page and handed it to Jack.

"This was, at one point in time, another future history," Poe said, looking Jack directly in the eye. "It was what we call a 'might-have-been.' That's a history that has not happened, but is likely to. In some cases, a might-have-been can even be viewed, as this one once was, by Masters Wells, Verne, and Sigurdsson. They recorded what they witnessed here and shared it with only one of their successors."

"Charles," Jack murmured as he scanned the page. "Charles knew about this?"

Poe didn't reply. Jack continued reading, and suddenly the blood drained from his face. "Dear god in heaven," he breathed. "I—I never realized . . ."

"What is it?" asked John, a look of concern etched on his face. "What does it say?"

Jack looked up, his face still ashen. "The destruction of the keep wasn't supposed to happen," he said slowly, as if he could not quite accept the words he was speaking. "In fact, according to this, we weren't supposed to reach the keep at all."

"Then what did happen?"

"You were the three Caretakers of prophecy," said Verne, "who were meant to defeat the Winter King. And you did, during your *first* encounter."

"We did?" John said, astonished. "What went wrong?"

"Indeed," said Bert, "but nothing went wrong, practically speaking. What happened is that something went *right*."

"Our first meeting," Jack said to John, pointing with a shaking finger at the pages, "when the *Black Dragon* overtook the *Indigo Dragon*. The Winter King offered me a choice, remember? To join him?"

"And you declined," John said, meeting his friend's eyes, "as you knew you must."

"But that's just it," said Jack. "I almost didn't decline. I nearly chose to go with him! And according to this book, that's exactly what I did!"

John looked at Bert and Verne, who didn't reply. Their silence was confirmation enough.

"A man's greatest enemy is himself," Twain said as he lit his pipe, "and that day, in that might-have-been, Jack was defeated, and he sided with Mordred. You—and he—never went to the keep, but back toward Paralon, where Nemo was already prepared to engage in a battle. The *Black Dragon* attacked, and this time, was defeated. The *Imaginarium Geographica* was recovered, and Mordred was bound, and imprisoned in the keep along with his brother, and," he added, eyes glittering, "you."

Twain was pointing his pipe at Jack, who lowered the book to the table and gently closed it. "After that, Artus still became king. Nemo never died. E.R. Eddison becomes the new third Caretaker. . . ."

"The Great War ended a year later," said Poe, "and this new conflict, which some call the Second Great War, never began— but not because Mordred's shadow, as the Chancellor, wasn't there.

It never started because the Archipelago was in harmony with the Summer Country. The entire world moved forward into an idealized society, much like the kind Master Wells espouses in his writings. And all because, in that moment, you succumbed to Mordred."

"I—I wish I didn't know about this," Jack said wearily. "It's too great a burden to bear. That all the grief of two worlds is my fault . . ."

"You misunderstand," Verne said gently. "We don't tell you this so you'll be burdened. We're telling you so you'll understand how great, how important it is to be able to choose."

"And was my choice good or bad?" Jack asked. "I'm not sure I know."

"Yes, you do," answered Bert. "You always have, Jack. You chose according to the dictates of your heart. And you chose wisely and well. It was in that choice that you set the course of the future, and we have rallied all the powers at our disposal to see that it was not a choice made in vain."

"My heart was tempted," said Jack. "I really was considering his offer. I didn't really know John or Charles. I didn't know you. And . . ." He paused. "I was probably just trying to impress Aven, if you want to know the whole truth. It wasn't an epic choice of good versus evil. It was just a choice. I'm going to have to grapple with that, Bert."

"We all do," Verne put in, "every day. We all grapple with the two sides of ourselves—but it's not what you consider that matters, Jack. It's what you do. And when it did matter, you chose not to betray the trust of your friends."

"Small moments of conscience," Poe repeated. "Those are

worth the world, and more. So to answer your question, yes—there are zero points in time wherein we could have changed a might-have-been to an is. But in doing so, we would have lost you, and lost the man you have become. We would have Un-Named your choice. And that is the one thing we could not countenance."

"I'm glad I never knew," said Jack. "It would have been harder, not easier, to choose."

"The future Histories are guides," said Verne, "not instruction manuals. But they should never replace free agency. That's why we didn't tell you what we knew before—we needed you to choose, freely and unafraid."

"I don't see how we can risk trying any of these machines," said John. "If they only work once for each of us, then there's no point in risking another accident. We'd just be losing someone every time we tried to find a zero point that can be changed. We simply don't know enough about what's happened."

"We need someone who knows a lot more about time travel," said Jack, "and if that isn't any of you, then I'm out of options. We'd be better off sending Hugo again."

"That would at least be interesting," a voice said from the ceiling, "considering the mess he made the last time."

"Cats should be eaten, not heard," Burton said, irritated. "What are you doing down here, anyway?"

"He's a Cheshire cat," said Bert. "He goes pretty much wherever he wants to go."

"Uh-huh," said Burton. "Poe doesn't strike me as an animal lover."

"You'd be surprised," Bert replied. "He keeps an orangutan

in the larder—mostly to guard the pistachio nuts. But the cat belongs to John—or more properly, John belongs to it."

"It sort of adopted me," John said as Grimalkin's torso disappeared, leaving a head and tail floating in midair. "It used to be Jacob's cat, I think."

"And Edmund Spenser's before that," added Bert, "and . . ." He stopped and scratched his head. "Who had him before that?"

"Dante, I think," said Verne, "but I think Roger Bacon had him first."

"He's sort of the animal familiar for Tamerlane House," Bert said. "It's hard to remember a time when he wasn't there."

"He wasn't there five minutes ago," said Jack. "And then suddenly, he was."

"That's a Cheshire cat for you," said Bert.

"Grimalkin," John said as a tail appeared above his head. "What *are* you doing down here?"

"Offering advice," the Cheshire cat said as its head appeared, sans body. "There is an expert in time who is here and not in the Archipelago."

"I hadn't actually considered him," Verne said thoughtfully, "but if all the Nameless Isles are here, the chances are good he is too."

"What are you suggesting, cat?" asked Twain.

"You already know what to do," Grimalkin said. "You need to seek the counsel of the Watchmaker."

CHAPTER SEVEN
THE WATCHMAKER

—✳—

HAVING MADE THIS pronouncement, the Cheshire cat promptly began ignoring everyone in the room. Verne stroked his beard in thought, considering the idea. John and Jack had no idea what to think. Houdini was intrigued, as were Doyle and Burton. Having been separated from the Caretaker culture for so long, they knew very little if anything about the being who made the watches.

"If that's such a wise course of action to take," Burton said to the cat, "perhaps you would like to go along and make introductions."

"For one thing, I'm not allowed there," Grimalkin said as he licked one of his paws in apparent disinterest. "He is a Maker, one of only seven in all of creation, and as such, creatures like myself are not welcomed. Also, there are dogs."

"What do you mean creatures like yourself?" asked John. "You're a cat."

"So you understand," Grimalkin replied. His lines were beginning to fade, and his tail had already disappeared. "Cats and Makers should not mix, especially this cat, and this Maker. It was bad enough when we saw each other socially, but this is business, so it's best for all that I stay behind."

"I'll go," said Verne. "He knows me well enough, and Bert will be needed to explain what's happened. John and Jack as well."

"I insist—," Burton began.

"No," Verne said, cutting him off. "Principal Caretakers only." His expression said that he would countenance no argument on this point, and Burton withdrew.

"What about me?" asked Fred. "Shouldn't I go along as well?"

"In other circumstances, yes," Verne said, patting the badger supportively, "but not here. The Cheshire cat is correct—the Watchmaker does not socialize well with your kind."

"With animals, you mean?" said Fred, chagrined.

"No," Verne answered. "With intelligent animals."

"Mmm," Fred mused. "That's a little better, I guess."

"I thought we were cut off from the Archipelago," said Jack. "How are we to get to him?"

"He's not in the Archipelago," Verne said with a sly grin. "In fact, he's much closer than you realize."

Within an hour the tides were low enough that the companions were able to cross to the small island in the northeastern corner of the Nameless Isles, where Verne said the Watchmaker could most likely be found. "He's often here, working," the Frenchman explained as they waded through the shallow water. "He isn't confined, as Merlin was."

"Is he like the Cartographer, then?" John asked.

"In some ways yes, in others, no," Verne replied. "We don't know much about him, to be honest. We know he's old, very, very old, but doesn't look it. He's a friend of Samaranth but seldom speaks of him and how they met. And once, when I came to see him with no advance notice, I saw him—only it was not him. He appeared to be a twelve-foot-tall mantis. I blinked, and an instant later he was just a man again."

"Did you ask him about that?" asked Jack.

Verne laughed under his breath. "I did. He apologized for being dressed too formally and said he had not yet had time to change after another meeting."

"Intriguing," said John. "So he isn't human, then?"

"Oh, he's human," said Bert, "or at least, he started as one. Whatever else he became, who can say?"

The companions traversed the next hollow, where Verne signaled for them to stop. Up above them were three massive dogs standing guard at the crest of the hill.

One was the size of a normal, large dog. The next was the size of a small pony. And the third was the size of an ox. All three had massive round eyes the size of dinner plates—and those eyes were fixed intently on these possible trespassers.

"Ho, Fios," Verne said as he raised a hand in greeting.

"Well met, Master Verne," the smallest of the dogs replied. "Is your hunting good?"

"It is," Verne replied. "Ho, Luaths."

"Well met, Master Verne," the second dog said, sniffing. "One of your friends—he smells of cat."

John frowned. "Uh, sorry about that."

Verne looked slightly alarmed but continued to smile. "Ho, Tron," he said to the largest dog. "May we pass?"

"Well met, Master Verne," the dog replied, stepping aside to make an opening between himself and the other dogs. "You may pass."

The four companions walked between the huge animals and down the other side of the hill, where there was a small structure made of stone and marble. It resembled a crypt, or an elaborate barrow, and it had a broad door that opened onto steps that led to a shallow chamber.

"That was a bit chilling," Jack said as he and Bert removed four torches from a niche in the wall. "I suppose if you're being guarded by fellows like that you don't need fancy locks or a riddle in code."

"Exactly," Verne said as he lit the torches. "The dogs, whose names mean Knowledge, Swiftness, and Heaviness, incidentally, are good judges of character. They go by scent alone—anyone who doesn't pass is ripped to pieces."

"So the cat thing . . . ," John began.

"Oh, I'm sure it would have been nothing," said Verne as he stepped down into the darkness, "although for a moment there, I did think it was a shame we hadn't had Basil start a portrait for you yet."

Inside the chamber a great stone tablet was set into the earth and ringed about with smaller stones, all covered with runes.

Jack touched some of the stones, which were worn smooth with age. He looked questioningly at John, who shook his head. "They're beyond my skill," he said. "They may be some sort of proto-Aramaic, or Akkadian. The forms are vaguely familiar, but I can't suss out the structure."

"Not Akkadian," said Verne. "Think older."

"Cuneiform? Sanskrit?"

"Older," said Verne. "Poe thinks they may be prehuman."

"What can possibly be prehuman?" said Jack. "Except . . ."

"Angelic," said Bert. "There's no way to know for sure, but that's our belief. We haven't dared ask the Watchmaker."

"For fear he won't tell you?" asked John.

"No," said Verne. "For fear he *might*."

Bert placed his watch into an indentation in one of the stones. Suddenly the great stone slab began to slide back into the hill, revealing a narrow set of steps that dropped away into the darkness.

Bert nodded in satisfaction as he pocketed the watch and lit up the torch he was carrying. "It's always a comfort to do that," he said, grinning. "It's like a ritual of acceptance, to ask for entry and be approved."

"I'm all for security," said Jack, "but really, after the dogs, this might be overkill."

"Oh, we only just put the dogs here seven years ago," said Bert as he stepped down onto the stone stairway. "Verne thought it was time to start considering some extra security, just in case."

"How long had he gone without the extra security?" John asked as he followed Bert.

Bert shrugged. "How old are the runes? Those were the first safeguards set up. I really can't tell you when."

John looked back at Jack, and they traded an expression of wonderment. The runes were deep, and carved in granite. To have been worn smooth by the wind and rain would take hundreds, if not thousands, of years. Their suspicion that the runes were Angelic in nature might not be so wild an idea after all.

Wordlessly they followed their mentor into the earth as the tablet slid closed above them.

✦   ✦   ✦

The passageway was neither steep nor narrow, and the torches they carried provided more than enough light for the companions to clearly see the steps above and below. The descent to the Watchmaker's cavern did not take long—less than twenty minutes passed from the time they entered until they reached a place that was well-lit enough for them to extinguish their torches.

The enormous room looked to John as if someone had filtered a cave from one of Jacob Grimm's stories through a London clockmaker's shop, and then sprinkled in some Greek myths for good measure.

There were mirrors of all shapes and sizes spread throughout the space, mingled with crystal formations and stalagmites. Each one reflected not just the observers, but also some additional form—some were human; some, like the giant mantis Verne had mentioned, were not. They appeared as ghost images laid over the real reflection.

John found himself in front of a tall mirror that showed a rough-looking woman, dressed in skins and carrying a Bronze Age hammer. For a moment John thought she was real enough to touch, and he reached out with his hand.

"I wouldn't if I were you," Bert murmured, grabbing his hand, "unless you fancy living out your years in a form very different than you'd imagined."

Verne moved around the others and walked to the Watchmaker, who had been too absorbed in his work to notice he had company.

Predictably, he was sitting at a broad workbench amidst a scattering of tools, wires, cogs, and other sundry items that had no apparent purpose. Some of the objects were made of gleaming metal, while others were obviously stone. At the moment he seemed to be trying to coax a miniature sun into a porcelain clock.

The Watchmaker himself was shorter than the companions, but not noticeably older. He had a prominent nose that curved up and into his brow, and small, close-set eyes. His hair was black and slicked back over his head out of the way of his face, so as not to obscure his vision as he worked.

He was dressed simply in a tunic and breeches, and he wore a thick leather apron covered with pockets that were all laden with tools. On the companions' approach, he stood and greeted each of them, shaking their hands and repeating John's and Jack's names.

"I've met so many people over the centuries, you see," he said in explanation, "that I find repeating the names helps me to recall them. Of course, the fact that you are Caretakers who bear examples of my handiwork will help to narrow it down a bit," he added, winking conspiratorially.

On his prompting, both John and Jack pulled out their watches for him to examine. "Nice, very nice," the Watchmaker proclaimed on seeing Jack's, which was all silver, with a silver bas-relief dragon on the cover. "Egyptian. Or maybe Chinese. I forget. I can never keep track of these young cultures and the things they do—but I know when they've done something worth incorporating into my own work."

He moved on to John's watch. "Ah, the classic," he murmured approvingly. "Silver case, silver chain, glazed ceramic disk with the Red Dragon on it." He turned the case over and noted the engraving: caveo principia.

The Watchmaker looked up at John appraisingly. "You're the Principal Caretaker, then?" He looked at Verne. "Well, Frenchman? Is he worthy?"

Verne nodded. "Eminently so."

"Good enough," said the Watchmaker as he handed the watch back to John. "Not that my opinion should matter, overmuch. You have a harder row to hoe than I."

"For a Watchmaker, you don't seem to have many actual, uh, watches hanging around," Jack said to their host. "No offense."

"Why would I want to surround myself with watches?" said the old man matter-of-factly. "I spend a great deal of time making them, but they aren't an all-encompassing obsession."

"How many have you made?" asked John.

"Several hundred for the Caretakers, of course," the Watchmaker replied, "and perhaps fewer for others."

"You make watches for people other than Caretakers?" John replied before Verne could caution him not to ask. "Isn't that dangerous?"

The Watchmaker fixed John with a gaze that was so intense it was almost a physical blow, and his smile belied the gravity of his words. "I am not the judge of all the Earth," he said, unblinking, "nor do I wish to be."

"These are very interesting mirrors," Jack said, trying to steer the conversation in a less tense direction. He was peering at an oblong one that reflected some sort of multi-tentacled creature. "They don't actually reflect very well."

"They reflect well enough for me," said the Watchmaker, "as they should, since they are my mirrors. What good would my mirrors do to me if they reflected someone else better than I?"

"I guess you have a point," Jack admitted. "Is that a winged centaur?" He pointed to a large rectangular mirror above a work-table.

"It is," replied the Watchmaker, "when that's what I want to be."

John threw a surreptitious glance at Jack, who widened his eyes in response. Whatever this Watchmaker was, he was not a kind of creature they had met before. It was no wonder he was friends with Samaranth—they were similar in both mystery and temperament.

"You all have watches," said the Watchmaker, "so I expect you have come for some other reason."

"We've come," Verne began, "because they don't seem to be working properly. In fact, one of the Messengers has died because he could not return to us in, ah, time."

"Not working?" the Watchmaker exclaimed. "Improbable. Let me take a look."

Verne handed over his watch, and the Maker looked at it for barely a moment before he handed it back. "The watch is fine," he proclaimed. "Something else must be broken."

"History," said Bert. "History has come undone."

"History?" the Watchmaker repeated. "History is a self-defining term. By necessity, it is an accounting of the past—and that past is not real, not solid. At least, not as much as we'd like to believe.

"The present is real. The future is malleable. And the past is both, because although all stories are *true*, some of them never *happened*.

"Events and accountings may become undisputed components of history not merely because of the truth they hold, but because of their perpetuity: The stories we believe are the stories we know."

"He talks just like Merlin used to," Jack said to John. "I never thought I'd miss it so."

"Merlin?" the Watchmaker asked. "I know that name, don't I?"

"The Cartographer of Lost Places," said Verne.

"Oh yes," said the Watchmaker. "I remember him now. The young stallion with fire in his belly."

"Young?" Jack exclaimed. "Merlin is one of the oldest people I ever met."

"Youth is a relative term," the Watchmaker replied. "I prefer to think of it as a state of mind."

"I know a lot of youthful students who might argue that point," said Jack.

"I've no doubt you do," the Watchmaker replied. "That's what gives my point of view credibility. Everyone argues against it at first, but eventually they all come around. So," he said to Verne, "how is young Merlin?"

"Gone," Verne said simply. "Freed from Solitude, just before the Keep of Time fell."

"Ah," the Watchmaker said, leaning back in his chair. "I suspected that might be why you've come. Sit, and tell me what's been occurring."

As quickly as they were able, the four Caretakers related all the events that had happened, including the mystery of the discontinuity.

"It's not a mystery," the Watchmaker said when they had finished. "Without the Keep of Time, there is nothing to connect Chronos and Kairos, and Kairos itself is loosed.

"Chronos time is merely a record of the passage of objects

through physical space," he explained, "but Kairos time is what gives those events meaning. This is why your watches cannot find any zero points. The meaning has been lost. The connection is gone."

"Is that why there were doors in the keep?" asked Jack. "To connect to zero points in time?"

"The doors merely acted as focal points for the energies within the keep," the Watchmaker said. "Once attuned to a specific time, they would continue to work, as you noted with the false tower the Barbarian—Burton—built for the Shadow King."

"And the door that Hugo Dyson stepped through in Oxford," added John. "That makes sense to me."

The Watchmaker nodded approvingly. "The Barbarian's design was faulty to begin with—the doors opened to the same energies, and had you not dispatched it, it would have no doubt eventually fallen on its own accord. But it was in his original premise that he made his most grievous error. The doors were not the aspect of the keep that made it function—that was something integral to the keep itself. Something about the construction design, and the stones used, and perhaps even the runes carved into the stones. The doors focused the energies to allow passage, but the Keep of Time served a larger function: It anchored Chronos and Kairos. And now that the anchor has been lost, time is flowing freely in the Archipelago, and there is no way to harness it again."

"How can we repair it?" John asked. "We've gone back in time before and managed to not do so badly. We believe we can do so again—we just don't know where to start, or how to get there without the watches."

"So, you need the watches to fix time, but you cannot use the watches until you already have."

"A paradox?" asked Jack.

"A pickle," said the Watchmaker.

"I wish we were able to consult Samaranth on this," John said miserably. "I think he'd have an idea or three as to what to do."

"I spoke with him before the fall of the keep," the Watchmaker said. "He anticipated that this might happen—but he is also reluctant to participate in the matter."

"You've spoken to Samaranth?" John exclaimed. "Did he say anything else?"

"All that he would volunteer was to say that as he has already given you the means to solve this problem, he is not obligated to do anything further. A Son of Adam put these events into motion, and only a Son of Adam should put them right."

"He isn't going to help us, then," said John.

The only response the Watchmaker gave was a steady, almost sorrowful gaze, and silence.

Jack's shoulders slumped. "What are we to do now?"

"Find a way to create zero points," the Watchmaker said. "Find a way to give meaning to Chronos again. And then you will be able to use the watches."

"We *have* traveled through time without the watches before," said John, "when we used a trump from the future, remember?"

"Except that didn't really work out so well the last time," said Bert. "Needed a bit of a push to get through. And you lost seven years of Chronos time. We can't risk another loss like Hank—not when the trumps aren't working properly anyway."

"We never discovered who your mysterious benefactor was

either," said Verne. "The old man in the white room."

"People have a way of becoming their own benefactors," said the Watchmaker. "That may be the case here."

"Not the future," Jack said, thinking about the trumps. "That won't help. We need to go into the past."

"The Histories?" asked John. "Can we use those?"

"They're just books," said Bert, thinking. "No spatial or temporal properties to them."

"But," said Jack, snapping his fingers, "we do have something with those properties. Remember the map that Hank brought with him? He said it was what brought him to Tamerlane House. He used a map to go through space and time. And he made it using one of the spare pages from the *Geographica*."

"I'd almost forgotten!" Bert exclaimed. "I have the rest of those extra pages, back at Tamerlane House."

"If we can use those to create zero points," said Jack, "then we'll have something to attune the watches to. We can create a sort of chronal *Geographica*."

"A sort of Archipelago of Lost Years," the Watchmaker said as a thoughtful expression flashed across his face. "It could be done in such a way. Yes, exactly so. In fact, one of your own tried such a thing many years ago. He even came to be called by a name that reflected this: the Chronographer of Lost Times."

"He went renegade," Verne said with a careful look at Bert. "We haven't seen him since, and have no idea how to find him."

"Ah, that's right," the Watchmaker said. "I did hear about that. There's no way to contact him, then?"

Verne shook his head. "Not that we know of."

The Watchmaker spread his hands and tipped his head. "It

seems simple then," he said. "You need to find *another* Cartographer. Another Cartographer of Lost Places. You have apprentice Caretakers," he added, gesturing at John and Jack. "Surely there were also apprentice Cartographers?"

Bert sighed heavily and traded resigned glances with Verne. "There were, in fact, a number of individuals who trained with Merlin, but replacing him isn't going to be anywhere near that easy," he said wearily. "To do what the Cartographer did, to attain his skill and intuition, would take generations. Centuries, perhaps. And no one I know who studied with him possesses either. Not to the degree we would need."

Verne pursed his lips and nodded tersely at John and Jack in answer to their unspoken question. There had been one apprentice and one only who might have taken the Cartographer's place: Hank Morgan. But he had been drawn away by his escapades through time with Verne. Ironically, his experiences with time travel would have made him an even more ideal choice to do what the Watchmaker said was necessary. And now, just when they discovered he might be the one man they needed most, it was too late.

"Remember what Samaranth said," the Watchmaker reminded them. "You have the tools you need to fix this. All you need to do is believe that you can, and then do it." He turned back to his workbench. The audience with the Caretakers was over.

"Thank you for all you've told us," Verne said, bowing. "Hopefully, much good will come of it."

"All good things happen in time," the Watchmaker said. "Trust in that wisdom, as I have."

"A chronal *Geographica*?" John murmured to Jack. "Do you really think we can create one?"

"Someone already has," the Watchmaker cautioned without pausing in his work or glancing up. "The watches still work, so time is flowing. Someone's found a way to begin mapping time, and unless you discover who is doing so and why, your race may already be lost."

It occurred to John that the Watchmaker's last remark may have referred to the human race, and not the ensuing conflict to somehow fix the flow of time in the Archipelago, but by the time he had the presence of mind to ask, the old Maker was already engrossed in his work, and Verne was closing the door, a finger to his lips.

CHAPTER EIGHT
THE BLACK DRAGON

—✳—

THE MARCH BACK to Tamerlane House was largely silent, as each of the Caretakers pondered what they had learned from the Watchmaker. The visit had birthed almost as many questions as it answered, but still, it seemed there was no way out of their dilemma. If there was no way to traverse time, then there would be no way to fix it. And worse, it seemed that far from reuniting the two worlds, they had lost the Archipelago of Dreams completely.

"We move into the future one second at a time," John murmured to no one in particular. "It seems it would be an easy enough thing to move a few days into the past."

"I know what you wished to ask him, John," said Verne as they began their crossing to the central island. "It would not have aided you to know."

"Sometimes information is a comfort," John countered. "I'd like to have known if it was possible."

"To make Charles's death into a zero point?" Verne answered. "I don't know that he could answer that. Or would."

"It would have been a start," said John glumly. "Can you tell me," he went on, suddenly switching direction, "why Charles chose not to have Basil finish his portrait?"

Bert inhaled deeply. "He didn't want to have the limitations that the others did," he said consolingly. "After what happened to Stellan, Charles saw that as more of a living death than a chance to carry on as a Caretaker. I disagreed with him, but it was his own choice."

"I only wish," John said to Verne, "that he had chosen your path. That you had been able to be with him before his death and create a tulpa. I keep feeling that if he were only with us, he'd know exactly what must be done—and it would be a plan too outrageous for any of the rest of us to think of."

Jack quickened his pace and put his arm around his friend, whispering words of comfort to him as they walked.

Bert started to approach them both to say something, but Verne held him back, shaking his head sternly. "Not yet," he said softly. "We can't say yet. Later, when it's sure, we'll tell them. But not now."

Bert stared at his mentor, struggling to form a response, but finally nodded in agreement and turned away.

"We have to return to the Archipelago," John declared firmly. "That's the only way to discover what's caused all this."

The report of the meeting with the Watchmaker had not gone over well at Tamerlane House. The Caretakers split into factions, all arguing over what they thought should be done, and why everyone else's plans were impossible. Fred, Laura Glue, and Rose did their best to mediate, while it was all Burton and his colleagues could do not to make things worse by venturing any opinion at all. Only John's pronouncement ended the arguments. The room went silent so they could hear what he had to say.

"We have to recreate a map of the zero points in Chronos time," he said calmly, "but time travel here is impossible at the moment. So we must go to the source of the problem. This all began when the keep fell. We caused that to happen. Samaranth said we have the means to repair what is broken, and I don't think that can be done here, in this world.

"There's another reason to restore the zero points. I don't think Rose being visited by the Morgaine—or one of them, anyway— was a coincidence. I think she was giving us a warning. 'The threads of history are undone,'" he quoted. "That's exactly what has happened.

"And Mother Night said to seek out the apprentice of the Dragon," he reminded them. "Samaranth is the last Dragon. Where else should we seek his apprentice if not in the Archipelago?"

"Well reasoned, young John," said Twain.

"But how will you cross?" asked Chaucer. "The Nameless Isles are connected to the Summer Country now."

"We might try modifying the bridge," Dumas suggested. "It did shift us forward in time."

"But at what cost?" asked Twain. "What happens to Tamerlane House if the bridge is severed, or reset?"

"He's right," said Verne. "We can't risk that. It's the only stability we have."

"Where did the orbs come from?" John asked Will Shakespeare. "The Dragon's eyes you used in the bridge?"

"The *Indigo Dragon*," Will answered. "In the south boathouse."

"Could we use another Dragonship?" asked Fred. "I'd be willing to risk it."

"There aren't any more. When the Shadow King corrupted all the Dragon shadows, we also lost the use of the Dragonships," lamented Jack. "As living ships, anyway."

"And when we were ripped out of the Archipelago," said John, "you left all the other Dragonships there, so we don't even have any extra eyes to experiment with."

"Ah," said Verne, rising. "But we just might have an extra Dragonship."

"What?" John exclaimed. "Even with the golden eyes, they're still just ships, and may not be able to cross."

"Not all of them," Bert said with an unusual twinkling in his eyes. "There's one left that is still a true Dragonship."

"I'm sure the Shadow King made particularly certain to get the Dragons who became our ships," said Jack, "just to keep us from being able to voyage back and forth across the Frontier."

"A plan that worked, for the most part," said Bert, "but recall, he was going by the History of Dragons in the Last Book, using their true names to seize their shadows. That's where he missed one—a Dragon who was never named, because he was never known. A cipher, a mystery . . ."

"An enigma, a conundrum, yes, yes, yes," Houdini said in exasperation. "How is that possible? Whose Dragonship did he overlook?"

Bert smiled. "His *own*."

The south boathouse was large enough to hold several ships within two enclosures. One contained the *Indigo Dragon* and several smaller boats. The second enclosure, which was double-locked and safeguarded with runes, spells, and the seal of both the house of Arthur and the Caretakers, housed the *Black Dragon.*

During the companions' first encounter with the Winter King, he attacked them and the much smaller *Indigo Dragon* with this dark, foreboding warship. It was only in the heat of battle, when the *Black Dragon* shifted course of its own accord, that they had realized it was a Dragonship in more than name alone. It was a true Dragonship—one that had melded the heart and living soul of a flesh-and-blood Dragon with the hull of a ship.

Ordo Maas, the great shipbuilder of ancient days gone by, knew of it, but not who built it. The Winter King claimed to have done so, but only Ordo Maas and the Dragons themselves ever knew the secrets of passage between the worlds—or so they had believed.

The ship was sleek and undamaged, and the chest of the great Dragon on its prow heaved with restrained energy and life.

When it was first captured, Ordo Maas had taken possession of it, but because of its mysterious origins, he relinquished it to the Caretakers' stewardship. It had been locked in the boathouse ever since.

"We can only assume that the Shadow King thought we had destroyed his ship, Dragon and all," said Bert, "or else why wouldn't he have sought her out?"

"It makes sense," said Burton. "Destroy what you do not use. It's standard tactics. It's what I would have done."

"Lucky that it wasn't you, then," said John, "or we'd be out a resource now."

"Even a stopped Caretaker is right twice a day," said Burton. "If he wins the coin tosses."

"Can it be controlled, is what I want to know," asked Jack. "Not to sound too prejudiced against Dragons, but I was scared enough of the ones I knew of, and even more of the ones who actively liked me. I'm not sure I want to trust my life to one who has tried to actually kill me."

"I think it can," said Bert. "The Winter King was its master, but I don't think it was a willing servant. Not completely."

"All right," Jack said. "I think we have the means. Now we just need to decide on a plan of action."

The Caretakers reconvened in the great meeting hall to call for a consensus. The vote was unanimous, even including Byron and the Society members. Only Magwich and Grimalkin weren't permitted a vote, and likely wouldn't have voted if they had been. Or at least not quietly, in Magwich's case.

"It's decided then," Chaucer said, thumping on the table for order. "We must discover what has happened in the Archipelago. The Dragon Samaranth must be sought, so his apprentice may be named. And somehow the zero points must be mapped so that time itself can be repaired."

He turned to John. "Caveo Principia," he said with respect and reverence, "this is under your purview."

"We'll sort it out," John said, glancing quickly at Jack, who winked in agreement. "We may not be the young Turks we once were, but we're still the Caretakers. It shouldn't be anyone else's responsibility."

"And risk," Jack added. "The two of us—"

"Ahem-hem," Fred interrupted, clearing his throat. "That would be three of us."

"My apologies, Caretaker," said Jack. "Three of us."

"As you wish," said Chaucer, to a round of table thumping by the others.

"Hold on," Burton said suddenly. "I see three—make that two and a half—Caretakers planning to go, but no representatives of the Imperial Cartological Society?"

"Pardon me?" said Jack, who was slightly offended. "I can represent both."

"I'll keep my pardons for myself," Burton replied. "You may represent the ICS to the outside world, but in matters of the Archipelago, we all know what the reality is. I'm going along as well."

"The Caretakers and Sir Richard—," Chaucer began.

"Three and three," Burton interrupted, gesturing to Houdini and Doyle. "They come with me. More witnesses, better reportage."

"He has a point there, Geoff," Twain said, tapping out his pipe. "And Richard is the most experienced among us for reporting on odd cultures and unusual scenarios."

"It will be dangerous . . . ," Dickens began.

"If anyone else has the scars to match mine," said Burton, stroking his cheek, "I'll listen to their arguments. But I think I'm beyond contestation in this."

"I have some bad scorch marks," said Byron, raising his hand.

"Oh, do shut up," Shakespeare said, "or I'll ask the faeries to give you the head of a donkey."

"Can he do that?" a horrified Byron whispered to Twain.

"Probably," Twain said, winking at Shakespeare, who returned a halfhearted smile. Will was still stuck in a mood that was half

elation and half misery. The first, because his bridge had worked—
and the second, because the rest of the Caretakers, with a few
exceptions, still wondered if his cleverness was just another mask
he wore to conceal the idiot underneath.

"Burton does address a valid point," said Chaucer. "This could
be dangerous in the extreme. We should send someone else to
help safeguard the Caretakers."

"Whom did you have in mind, Geoff?" asked Twain. "Hawthorne, maybe?"

Nathaniel Hawthorne was, among the Caretakers Emeritis,
the most able-bodied and skilled scrapper. He was precisely the
sort of man one would want to have in a fight. There was only one
problem.

"He can't," said Chaucer. "This is a matter of time, and we have
no way of knowing how that would affect a Caretaker who has
already passed and is now a resident of Tamerlane House and the
Pygmalion Gallery. We can't risk a loss like . . ."

His voice trailed off, but everyone at the table knew he was
thinking of John's old professor Stellan Sigurdsson. He had traveled with Rose, Quixote, and Archie beyond the Edge of the
World, but he'd exceeded the one-week time limit imposed on all
Caretakers who resided inside the portraits. One week away from
Tamerlane, and no more. And to take such a risk so close on the
heels of the loss of Charles would be too much to countenance.

"Burton, Harry, and Sir Arthur are tulpas," Chaucer said,
hardly masking the distaste in his voice, "and so are not at risk
with another time displacement. John, Jack, and Fred are still
living in their Prime Times, and so are also at less of a risk. So
there's only one other among us we can send."

"Of course!" Bert exclaimed. "Roger!"

"You do know he hates that name, right?" Twain said bluntly. "He prefers to be called the Tin Man now."

John and Jack looked at each other in surprise. They hadn't considered him as an option. Roger Bacon, one of the great Caretakers of antiquity, had never died—he had manufactured for himself the massive mechanical body that kept his brain, his soul, and his intellect intact. All within a form that could shatter boulders and wade through doors as if they were tissue.

"I'll go fetch him," said Hawthorne, rising from his seat. "I think he's still in the workshed he shares with Shakespeare."

"I'm going too," said someone from the back of the room.

Jack started to shake his head in protest. It was Laura Glue who had spoken, and she was already glaring at him defiantly.

"Laura Glue, you can't think—," John began.

"You really expect to go?" said Dickens. "It could be very dangerous, child."

"Of course I'm going!" Laura Glue exclaimed indignantly. "I was *born* in the Archipelago, and I've spent my entire life there, remember? Can anyone else here say the same?"

"Ahem-hem." Fred cleared his throat.

"Except for Fred," she added, winking at him.

Burton chuckled. "She has a point, I think."

"That's where home is for me," she continued, walking the perimeter of the table so that she could look at each Caretaker. "You may think it's safer to be here in Tamerlane House, but I'll remind you, I am the head of the Valkyries. I can take care of myself. And no one here is going to stop me."

Bert and Verne both looked askance at Jack, who shrugged his shoulders and raised his hands. "Don't look at me," he said sheepishly. "I couldn't win an argument with her when she was eight."

"I want to go too," Rose suddenly said, realizing that her request sounded more like an afterthought once they'd given in to Laura Glue. "I think I could be helpful to you, Uncle John. And Mother Night did say that I was the only one who could reweave the threads that had come loose from history. Isn't that just what the Watchmaker said we needed to do? To find those special points in time, to make them significant again? For that reason alone, I don't think you can do this without me."

As if her argument had been decisive enough to end the discussion, she folded her arms, closed her eyes, and smiled.

"She must," Poe's quiet voice spoke from somewhere above them. "Rose must go."

"I disagree," said John. "We've already lost Charles and Morgan—and that's without the threat of these Shadows, these Echthroi, that Mother Night said were coming for Rose. I think she'll be much safer here in Tamerlane House."

"Not anymore," said Burton. "The door has been opened for good, by way of Shakespeare's Bridge." He looked up into the shadows. "The islands are still Nameless, but they're no longer lost, are they?"

Poe didn't answer, but simply stood there, watching.

"This is going to be dangerous, Bert," John reiterated, folding his arms. "She should stay behind, with the rest of the Caretakers."

"I don't think anywhere is going to be safe," Rose said mildly. "Is it, Bert?"

The Far Traveler shook his head. "The girl is right, John," he said with obvious resignation. John realized in that moment that

Bert didn't want her to accompany them any more than they did. But for some reason, she was meant to go. He looked at Rose and realized that she had not offered just to have a chance at an adventure. She really believed she was meant to do this. And he had no good argument why she shouldn't go.

"She may not be safe anywhere," said Poe, "least of all with you, in the Archipelago. But the fact remains that this may be what she is meant to do—even if it costs her everything else."

John stepped into the center of the foyer underneath the railings where Poe stood. He looked up at the shadowed face of the great Caretaker. "Tell us why," he said, not bothering to keep the anger out of his voice. "We have done many, many things on faith, Edgar. Sometimes things work out, but sometimes they don't. And we have never defied you or the Caretakers Emeritis.

"I don't believe you're all-knowing," John continued, his voice still sharp with fury. " I think you're making this up as you go along, the same as the rest of us. So I think we deserve to know why we should have to do as you say."

Burton chuckled under his breath. "So, the little scholar has some dung up his neck after all."

"That was, ah, brave," Houdini whispered to Doyle. "I don't think anyone, even Chaucer, calls him Edgar."

"You don't," said Poe simply. "You have always had your free agency to choose—as does Rose.

"There are threads that are lost, and must be found again," he continued, echoing Rose and Mother Night's words. "She is the only one who can find them."

"What else haven't you told us?" asked John. "What else is happening here?"

"The Darkness is coming," Poe said somberly. "Perhaps not now, this instant, but soon. Some of its agents already work against us. Some of them have been here, in this house. But make no mistake—the Darkness *will* come. And all of our work over the centuries has been to find the one light that will be able to stand against our enemy."

"Echthroi," Schubert said from the far side of the stairway. "Our enemy."

"And you believe that Rose is that light?" John demanded. "Do you?"

Again Poe was silent. And John realized why. He didn't need to answer a question John had known the answer to all along. Rose *was* the light. She was the one they had protected, who had come out of history to save them once before—as she might do again.

"All right, so the Grail Child has to go," Burton said, "but with the addition of the mechanical man and the birdy-girl, you've got two more representatives of the Caretakers. I demand equal representation for the ICS."

"As the Valkyrie noted," said Poe, "she is simply returning home. She represents only herself."

"Fine," Burton acceded, "but you're still up one with the Tin Man."

"I had already planned on sending someone else along with you," Poe said as a door to his right opened slowly. "I trust you'll approve."

From behind Poe, a tall, muscular, dark-skinned man stepped onto the landing and descended the stairs. He was dressed in the manner of an Arab, with a linen robe and head wrapping and broad leather belts. He was barefoot, and his skin was so black it was almost purple-hued in the light of the meeting hall.

He moved through the Caretakers and went straight to Burton—who, to the shock and amazement of everyone there, embraced the tall man.

"The End of Time," Burton exclaimed. "I did not know you were still alive, but I'm not surprised!"

"Master Burton," the man said in a deep baritone voice that was flecked with a French accent. "It gladdens me to see you again."

"What are you doing here?" said Burton as he clapped the man on the shoulders. "When did you get here?"

"I have been here, in these islands, for a very long time," he replied. "I have been waiting for you, in fact."

Burton wheeled around and pointed at Poe. "What kind of game are you playing, Poe? You had my friend here, with you, all this time?"

Poe didn't answer.

"The End of Time?" Jack said. "I'm sorry, but I don't understand the reference."

"It isn't a reference, it's his name," said Burton, still eyeing Poe above. "He was my guide across Somaliland in the 1850s. I would not have survived if not for him. We called him Theo for short, and . . .

"Wait a minute," he exclaimed suddenly. Burton looked over the man he called the End of Time from head to toe, then took a step back. "How is it that you're here now? That was nearly a century ago."

"He's one of the Messengers," Verne said, trying without success to conceal the smugness he felt at disorienting Burton so. "An adept, like Ransom and Morgan. Or didn't you know that?"

"I . . . did not," Burton said frankly. Doyle and Houdini looked at each other in surprise. This was a rare admission for Sir Richard, to not have known something about his own man.

At that moment Hawthorne reappeared with the Tin Man, who agreed to go. "And I'm taking Archie," said Rose, as if defying Burton to argue with her—but he was too stunned by the appearance of the End of Time to care.

"Then we have our fellowship," Chaucer declared. "Luck be with you all."

The travelers left Tamerlane House to go prepare the *Black Dragon*, just as another argument broke out among the Caretakers Emeritis. "We've already shared so much," Bert was saying, pleading with the others. "Why couldn't we have told them this, too? Why not put all the cards on the table, so they can be fully informed about their choices?"

"It isn't a matter of being fully informed, Bert," said Twain, "but about how much they can bear."

"It would have only added to their burdens," Verne said wearily, "to reveal that according to the future Histories, today, Jack's 'Independence Day,' also marks the first day in the War of the Caretakers."

PART THREE

THE SHADOWED WORLD

CHAPTER NINE
THE WASTE LAND

—✳—

IN A WORLD where the power of a nation was determined by the power of its naval forces, a skilled mapmaker was as valuable as the most ruthless of privateers. The ability to see what others could not see, and know what they could not know, was embodied in the accuracy of the maps made for the various principalities, and the brotherhood of mapmakers skilled enough to have come to the notice of the kings and admirals was small and select. But even among these there was a hierarchy, and the best, most elite of their number was a man who had never drawn a map for a king or country.

In mapmaking circles, no one was better than Eliot McGee, and he only made maps for pirates.

It was the family trade, begun by his father Elijah, who was recruited by the pirate governor, Henry Morgan, to make maps to his own hidden treasures. In time, word of both Elijah's skill and his ability to keep tightly bound the most fragile of secrets brought all the pirates of the age to the McGees' door.

Eliot's childhood, once meant for his apprenticeship as a silversmith, became an endless game of art and imagination, of hidden lands and lost treasures, as his father taught him the art of mapmaking.

Once, during one of Morgan's late-night meetings with Elijah, Eliot thought he overheard something about a Cartographer, and Caretakers of a place called the Archipelago of Dreams. He had assumed it was just another discussion about the Caribbean. Almost all the maps that Elijah made were for islands in that part of the world—in part because that was where all the pirates were.

Then, when he was old enough to have passed from apprenticeship to mastery, he met another man who spoke of the same things, in the same way. They spent many long nights talking of imaginary lands, and in the process became the best of friends. And in due time, his friend introduced Eliot to his own master—a man who referred to himself as a Caretaker. And this Caretaker had also taken on another apprentice, who was destined to have a great impact on the life and career of Eliot McGee.

And thus did Eliot McGee, Charles Johnson, and Daniel Defoe become apprentice Caretakers to Cyrano de Bergerac.

Burton argued with Jack about which of them was to captain the *Black Dragon*, until Fred pointed out that John was actually the Caveo Principia, and he should choose. John, for his part, didn't want to embarrass Fred by ignoring his obvious show of loyalty, but he also didn't want to overrule Burton in so blatant a manner. So, he asked one of the others to flip a coin, and Burton was to call it.

It turned out the only one of them who actually had a coin was Houdini. "All right," he said, readying a quarter on his thumb and finger, "I'll flip it. But how do you know I won't cheat? I can make the quarter do anything I want, as you probably know."

"If you do it fairly," John said, "I'll tell you the secret of how the Serendipity Box works—uh, worked."

Houdini's face lit up. "Deal!" He flipped the coin expertly into the air. "Call it, Richard."

"Tails," said Burton.

Houdini caught the spinning coin and slapped it on his wrist.

"It's heads," Fred said as Houdini showed him the coin. "Scowler John chooses."

Burton started to protest, until John interrupted him. "Burton should captain the ship," he said. "Any objections?"

"Not really," said Jack.

"I don't understand," said Burton. "Why put us through this little game if you were going to let me do it anyway?"

"Because," said John, "I wasn't going to 'let' you do anything. I was going to choose you, because you've had more experience, and more recent experience, than any of us. And I made us flip the coin to point out who's in charge here."

Burton's eyes narrowed, then he grinned and moved to the foredeck to loosen the moorings, while instructing the Tin Man to loosen those in the aft.

"How did you know you'd win the toss?" asked Doyle. "Not much of a way to establish yourself as leader if you'd lost."

"Oh, Harry made sure I won, didn't you, Harry?" John said with a wink at the magician.

"Well, er . . . that is," Harry stammered, glancing over his shoulder to make sure Burton wasn't in earshot. "You did win, and that's what counts. So," he added, rubbing his hands together in anticipation of an earned reward, "how does the Serendipity Box work?"

John clapped him on the back and leaned close. "Magic," he whispered before striding to the cabin with Jack and Fred. "It's *magic*."

"That was dirty pool," Houdini fumed as Doyle laughed. "Completely dirty pool."

The *Black Dragon* seemed almost grateful to be free of the boathouse, giving Burton only a little bit of resistance as he steered her out to sea. The water that had come with the Nameless Isles extended only a few miles from the shoreline, where it vanished under the gray mists that now surrounded the islands.

"If this works," John said to the others, "we should know right away. And if it doesn't, we'll just take a little jaunt around the islands."

"It will work," said Rose. "I can feel it."

As if she had predicted it, in short order the Frontier loomed up before them, replacing the gray haze with a stark blackness and Jack was suddenly glad and relieved that Burton was in command of the ship instead of him.

The barrier between worlds usually manifested itself as a line of thunderheads, electric storm clouds roiling with wind and rain and crackling with lightning. The Dragonships were designed by Ordo Maas to withstand the crossing, but most ordinary ships—those that would dare approach such a fearsome storm—would be driven back. Even the occasional few that made it past the Frontier were usually battered into uselessness and had to be abandoned soon after.

The ruins of Atlantis, the drowned lands past Avalon, were littered with the wrecks of vessels that had crossed the Frontier but were unable to continue.

The mermaids usually took care of whoever survived of the crews that sailed them. Mer-people were not ones to waste food, whatever its source.

This time the situation was different. The storm clouds reached to—past?—the surface of the torrential seas and formed a distinct, almost solid wall of darkness. Even Burton, who was usually in complete control of his reactions, was showing trepidation, if not fear. He was a cunning and bold captain—but the *Black Dragon* had not been built by Ordo Maas. There was proof in the Histories that it had gained passage through the old Frontier more than once, but there was no way of telling how it would fare against the nightmare that lay ahead.

Archimedes, Rose, and Laura Glue were already strapped to mainbeams inside the cabin, and John and Jack were considering joining them. There was little else they could do on deck that Houdini and Doyle were not already doing—and the two tulpas were both younger and more physically fit than they. Even Theo was more actively involved, as he seemed to be helping Burton choose a path to take through the blackness ahead.

It was all Jack could do to resist offering unsolicited advice, which Burton would probably throw back in his face anyway. He had a terrible urge to grab the ties to the sail and leap on top of the cabin, steering the ship into the storm like a bullrider.

A spar broke on one side of the deck and spun crazily across the planks before spinning off into the night.

"I had the thought that this might have been better if we'd converted the old girl to an airship," John shouted to Jack over the roar of the wind. "Fly over the clouds, you know? But I'm reconsidering."

The hull shuddered and groaned with the strain as the sails whipped about in the wind, tearing, pulling.... And then, without warning, the center mast snapped and fell directly toward Burton.

In a trice, before any of the others could react, the Tin Man leaped in between the massive wooden beam and the wheel and caught it before Burton could be crushed.

With an immense effort, the Tin Man slowly pushed the mast back into position and over, snapping it off completely.

"What have you done?" Burton screamed over his shoulder. "You fool! You've killed us all!"

But Jack realized that the Tin Man had in fact done just the opposite—the main mast, which was taller than the others, was catching more wind in its sails and making it harder to maneuver the ship. Broken, it was even more of a danger to them. But gone completely, there was more leverage for the rudder, and more control for Burton.

"I should have let you drive," John said, seeing the familiar look on his colleague's face. "Sorry, Jack."

The darkness of the storm seemed to be reaching for the ship itself, as if the very storm had will, and intent.

"It is an Echthros," Theo said, his voice strangely clear in the din. "It is trying to prevent us from passing through."

"You mean the Echthroi," Jack called back. "Our enemies."

Theo shook his head. "Not many. Only one."

"Oh, for cat's sake," John complained, looking at the breadth and intensity of the storm surrounding them. "If this is just a single one of our enemies, we're going to be in a lot of trouble."

"Hold on," said John, lowering his head. "We're about to go into the worst of it now."

With a barbaric yawp, Burton spun the wheel and steered the *Black Dragon* into the heart of the darkness.

The ship crossed the Frontier.

There was a great deal of damage, but no cracks in the hull. And none of the companions had been injured or swept overboard. The Frontier disappeared behind them as quickly as it had arisen, and the dark storm clouds gave way to gray fog and endless open seas.

"I can't believe we've come through alive," John said, brushing off his jacket and checking his pack to make sure the *Imaginarium Geographica* was safe. "Well done, Sir Richard."

Burton acknowledged the compliment with a shrug and continued to examine the boat to better appraise the extent of the damage, but everyone who'd been on deck knew what had happened, and who was deserving of the credit. The Tin Man was the only reason the secondary masts were intact, and after saving Burton's life he had ridden out the passage holding fast to the rudder, which was nearly ripped free from its bracings.

Houdini seemed unperturbed, as did Doyle. Both men were in remarkable shape, particularly Houdini. It probably didn't hurt, John thought, that they were both tulpas—they had already gone through death itself. So what was a little hurricane to them?

Fred was the only member of their company who seemed distressed, and John knew that was probably just because he was wet. Badger fur did not take well to water and smelled horribly even in damp weather, never mind after being drenched in a thunderstorm at sea.

Fred noticed John looking at him and gave a cheerful salute to show he was all right—but conscientiously kept to the far side of the deck, downwind, just to be safe.

"Theo," Jack said, putting his hand on the tall man's shoulder and speaking quietly, so the others would not overhear. "The Echthros—is it gone?"

The End of Time didn't answer immediately, but stood on the deck, looking into the wind. He turned and looked back at the imposing blackness of the Frontier, then back at Jack. "I cannot tell," he replied at length. "It may still be with us, or waiting somewhere nearby."

Jack folded his arms and bowed his head. "Is there any possibility that the Frontier kept it out of the Archipelago? That it didn't cross over with us?"

Theo looked at Jack, then, oddly, at Burton, who was still at the wheel, shouting curses and orders in equal measure. "All of this is being caused by the Echthroi," he said finally. "If one of our enemy chose to follow us through the barrier, there is nothing to prevent it from doing so. It could be with us even now, just biding its time, waiting."

"Waiting for what?"

"To do whatever it has been sent to do," Theo replied, "to prevent us from reaching our goals."

"I see," said Jack, looking up. "And if that's the case, is there any way to stop it?"

Theo never answered, instead moving to help the Tin Man clear debris off the decks. After a moment, pondering, Jack went to help.

✦   ✦   ✦

After the ship was secured, and food and drink had been passed around, John and Burton huddled close over the *Geographica* to determine where in the Archipelago they were. "I can't quite figure it out," said John. "We didn't start at a normal place, and I haven't seen any landmarks yet."

"Technically, we sailed from Oxford," said Jack, "so we ought to be close to Avalon."

"If we're lost," Houdini suggested, "then perhaps we ought to just ask that fellow over there for directions."

The surprised companions looked in the direction Houdini was pointing. There, on a protrusion of rock, stood a man. He was nattily dressed in a waistcoat and tails, with a boutonniere, and spats on his shoes. He was slightly stout at the middle, and his reddish brown hair was beginning to thin.

To one side, on a smaller protrusion of rock, was a table set for tea; on the opposite side, a large steamer trunk rested on another rock just above the waterline.

The man waited, arms folded behind him, as they approached, then lifted a hand in greeting as the *Black Dragon* bumped up against the rocks.

"Greetings, travelers," he called out with restrained cheer. "From whence do you travel, and to what destination?" If he was in any way taken aback by the strange assortment of characters aboard the ship, it didn't show.

John stood at the railing and quietly gestured for the others to hang back until he could better assess who and what they were dealing with.

"I'm the Caretaker Principia of the *Imaginarium Geographica*," he announced to the man. "Whom do I have the pleasure of addressing?"

"Oh my stars and garters!" the man exclaimed. "I never believed I would be so lucky as to see you myself! All of us have imagined that we might be the one, but after so many generations, a hope unrealized becomes a dream and only a dream."

The man bowed deeply. "I am George Chanticleer, descended of the Chanticleers of Dorimare, and it is my honor to be of service to the Caretakers."

"I've read of a Chanticleer of Dorimare," said Jack. "Nathaniel, wasn't it?"

George bowed again. "My eldest forebear. You honor me by invoking his name."

"Eldest forebear?" Jack asked, a puzzled expression on his face. "Begging your pardon, but you and I seem of an age, and from what I knew of Nathaniel, he wasn't much older than I am. So at most, he'd be your father, wouldn't he?"

George stuck his finger in his ear and wiggled it about, as if Jack's words had gotten stuck there and not quite penetrated to his brain. "Father? Well, I suppose after a manner of speaking, that's true. To be precise, however, he would be my great-great-great-great . . ."

"Uh-oh," said Fred. "A genealogist."

". . . great-great-great-great . . . ," George continued, counting off the "greats" on his fingers as he went. ". . . great-great-great, uh . . ." He paused. "Maybe if I named them instead. I'm the son of Diggory the fifth, who was the son of Orson the ninth—"

"I'm starting to get the picture," John said interrupting him. "How long have you and your family been waiting for us here?"

"From the Day of Sorrows to this," replied George, his eyes welling up with tears, "it has been two thousand sixty-three years and a number of days. If you desire it, I can calculate the days."

"What deception is this?" Burton fumed as he grabbed John roughly by the shoulder. "Are you trying to deceive us, Caretaker?"

"You're seeing everything I am, Sir Richard," John shot back. "You're experiencing this in exactly the same way I am, so do all of us a favor and shut up!"

Theo stepped between the men and put his hand on Burton's shoulder. "Chanticleer speaks the truth," he said, his voice soft but clear in its conviction. "Twenty centuries have come and gone since any of you were last in this place."

Burton started to retort, then thought better of it and nodded. "All right," he said, turning to look at John. His temper had been cooled by the dark-skinned guide.

"I'm guessing that's why *he* needed to come along," Houdini whispered to Jack. "No one else I've ever seen has had that effect on Burton. No one."

"What happened, George?" John asked.

"There was a ferocious storm on the Day of Sorrows," said George, "and Avalon was caught up in it in a terrible way. The ocean heaved, and the black clouds descended from the sky and ripped the island into pieces. What you see," he finished, gesturing around him sadly, "is all that remains."

Instinctively, John and Jack both looked at Rose. Avalon was where she had been born and raised by her mother Gwynhfar and grandfather Odysseus. Once before they had come here, and they had not realized how strongly she identified with it as her home.

On that voyage, they had found the island to be much as they had known it—a ruined echo of what it once had been. But Rose had only ever known it as a pristine, gleaming jewel that could have been lifted out of mythic Greece, and in fact, all but was.

To see it in its dilapidated state had been a shock then—so how much worse would it be to find it utterly destroyed?

Rose saw their looks of concern and took them both by the hand. "It's all right," she assured them. "I had prepared myself to see . . . well, something worse than before. I knew it was not going to look like I remember it."

"It must have happened when the last of the tower fell," said John. "After the rift started to widen, Avalon couldn't stand the strain of the difference in time flows, and it was destroyed."

"That could have happened to Tamerlane House, too, then," Jack said with a shudder. "I think I need to sit down."

"I wonder what made the difference," Burton wondered aloud. "Your reasoning is sound, young Caretaker," he said to John, "but your conclusion isn't. The same thing absolutely should have happened to the Nameless Isles. Absolutely. So why didn't it?"

"Shakespeare's Bridge and the golden eyes of the Dragon," said Jack. "I think that made all the difference. John and I lost two years, but Tamerlane House was spared the fate of the rest of the Archipelago."

"So," John murmured to Rose, "the *Indigo Dragon* saved us yet again."

"So what now?" Burton asked. "What are we supposed to do?"

"Go on to Paralon," said George. "You're expected. Or at least, you were, long ago." He straightened. "No matter. You've come at last. In the end, nothing else will be important. Do you know how to get there?"

"Finding our way from Avalon, uh, rock, to Paralon shouldn't be a problem," said Jack. "We've done that voyage a hundred times. It would be pretty hard for us to lose our way and end up at the wrong island."

"It's harder than you think," said George, "being as Paralon is the only island left."

"What?" Jack, John, and Fred said in unison.

"What are you talking about?" asked John. "What do you mean it's the only island?"

"That's all I know, all I can tell you," George said in apology. "The rest you will discover on Paralon."

"How can all the islands just disappear?" said Burton. "There's no sense to it. There must be an explanation."

"They were left on their own," George replied softly, his face reddening. "Not to put too fine a point on it, no one was here to, ah . . . take care of them."

John and Jack exchanged a rueful look. This was one of their worst fears—that in the time of greatest need, they would not measure up to the task. Or apparently, be there at all.

"You've done your duty," John said with a wave. "Do you wish to come with us?"

"Thank you no," said George. "I'm going to write this up—so exciting! And then, I think I'll have tea, and watch the sun set. Now that you've come, there won't be any need for a Chanticleer to wait. And there's no greater honor I can think of . . .

". . . than to have been the last, very last, Green Knight in the Archipelago."

John was able to give Burton an exact heading to take them to Paralon, and he and the Tin Man put the remaining sails to use to gather as much speed as possible. He even suspected that the ship itself was adding to their momentum, as if it had understood the urgency of their mission and had chosen to help them, rather than hinder them.

"I have to say," Jack remarked to John and Theo, "that I'm starting to gain a new respect for the Winter King. If he did build the *Black Dragon*, he did a bang-up job. I don't know how he persuaded the Dragon to go along, but it's an impressive combination."

"It is at that," John agreed as Rose, carrying Archie, came to stand with him at the railing. "She'll have us in Paralon in no time at all. So to speak."

Only Fred noticed that Laura Glue had withdrawn from the others to stand alone at the aft of the ship. He made his way back to where she was watching the wake in the water and sidled up next to her.

"A muffin for your thoughts," he offered meekly.

"Isn't the expression 'a penny for your thoughts'?" she said without turning or looking away from the water.

"Maybe for human beans," Fred replied, "but badgers seldom have pennies. However, we almost always have a muffin or two." As proof, he rooted around in his pocket and produced a small chocolate-banana muffin.

Laura Glue dipped her head and laughed, then turned to look down at the grinning mammal. "What did you bring that for?"

"First rule of being a Caretaker," he said nonchalantly. "Never go anywhere unarmed if you can help it."

"Wouldn't a dagger, or a slingshot, or something like that be more handy?"

"Maybe," Fred admitted, "but if you find yourself feeling peckish, you can't nibble on a slingshot."

"True enough," she said as she turned to look at the water again.

"Why are you looking at where we've been?" Fred asked. "Home is in the other direction."

"Is it still going to be home when we get there?" she asked somberly. "After so many years, will we recognize anything?"

"One thing I've learned," Fred said with as much authority as he could muster, "is that you must trust in the Caretakers. Not me, I mean—but Scowler John and Scowler Jack. They will do everything they need to do until things are set aright. I didn't doubt them before, and I don't doubt them now."

Impulsively, Laura Glue leaned over and hugged her furry companion. "Thank you, Fred," she said. "That helps. A lot."

Yes, Jack thought from the port side of the cabin, where he'd inadvertently been listening in on their conversation, *thank you. I only hope that we can live up to your expectations. And our own.*

CHAPTER TEN
FALLEN IDOLS

·—✳—·

AFTER AN UNEVENTFUL night of sailing through the gray, starless gloom, the *Black Dragon* glided through the shallows and onto the beach at Paralon—or what was a pale, nightmare reflection of the Paralon they all remembered.

The island had changed.

The docks and the bustling business quarter were gone as if they had never been. Most of the buildings that lined the paved streets were gone. In fact, the only thing that resembled the old Paralon was the citadel that was carved into the mountain ahead. Everything else was gone.

"I was here just yesterday," Laura Glue said dully. "How can it have changed so completely, so quickly? How is that possible?"

"Two millennia makes a difference," said Jack. "Everything changes in that much time."

"I don't care about the island!" she said angrily. "I care about all my friends. What's become of them?"

Fred swallowed hard and hugged her tightly. She was right— his father, Uncas, and grandfather, Tummeler, had been here on Paralon. If what they saw around them was true, then Fred would have lost his family just as Laura Glue had lost all her friends. It was a prospect that became even more chilling the longer the companions thought about it, as the understanding of the magnitude of their predicament became ever more manifest.

Everyone was gone. Everyone they had ever known in the Archipelago.

"Surely there might still be someone left?" Jack stated as bravely as he could manage. "Samaranth, almost certainly, and perhaps Ordo Maas. Didn't they call him the Ancient of Days? Surely two thousand years would be nothing to him."

"It's not just the passage of time that worries me," said John, "it's that the worlds have been severed. The Summer Country, our world, is the living twin to the Archipelago."

"A Siamese twin," Burton said. "And what happens if the blood flow from one is disconnected from the other?"

John didn't reply, but merely frowned and turned away. Jack knew what his friend was thinking. John's son Christopher was still in the RAF, and the war, while winding down, was not yet won. What if, because of this crisis in the Archipelago, the war would not end? What then?

"Look!" Archimedes called out. "Over here!"

He'd been flying above the companions, looping in wider and wider circles, searching for someone or something they might recognize—and it appeared he'd found both.

It was an immense statue, half broken, as if it from the impact of something equally large. Still, the form was unmistakable: It was a centaur.

"Charys?" Jack asked Fred, who had scampered over to read the inscription at the base.

"Same vineyard, different vintage," Fred replied. "This is a statue of his great-grandson, Kobol, who was killed while defending Paralon in the Second Great War of the Races." He turned to Jack. "I don't remember there being a First Great War of the Races."

"You can miss a lot of wars in two millennia, little Caretaker," said Burton.

Fred's whiskers twitched. "He was my teacher, you know. Charys."

"Do you suppose this is the Winterland?" John suggested to Jack. "Could we have crossed back into that place?"

"I doubt it," Jack answered. "For one thing, the Winterland was back in our world, not here. And for another, that entire scenario was caused by a specific bit of chronal sabotage."

"What was that?" asked Burton.

"You," John said pointedly.

"Oh yes," Burton said. "The Dyson incident. Verne told me about your end of that tale. I have to admit, I was rather impressed by the accounting of Bert."

"How so?"

"The fact that he was willing to sell out his colleagues to Mordred to save his own skin," said Burton. "It sounds like something I would do."

"Yes," John said drolly. "It does. And it was barbaric. I'd rather you not bring it up again."

"Not to defend Burton," said Jack, "but Jules *does* keep his own skull on his desk. If anyone has reason to be tweaked by the whole thing, I'd guess it was him."

"It may have seemed like a disaster to you," said Burton, "but this 'Winterland' you experienced managed to do one thing right that not a thousand years of Caretakers have succeeded in doing."

"What was that, Burton?"

"Unite the worlds," Burton replied. "In the Winterland, the Archipelago and the Summer Country were one again."

"Under the tyrant's rule, you mean."

Burton shrugged. "I didn't say it was perfect. But just so you know—it is possible."

"That's almost reassuring," said Rose. "If you ever try to do it again, I hope you choose a better ruler."

"Your own father ruled the Winterland," said Burton, "did he not?"

"No," said Rose. "*Mordred* ruled the Winterland. My father is Madoc."

"From the position of the city gates," Laura Glue said, shading her eyes to peer into the distance, "I'd say that we're standing where the royal docks used to be."

"Either they don't use boats very often anymore," said Jack, "or they haven't needed to in a very, very long time."

"Archimedes," John called out to the bird, "go do another aerial reconnaissance and see if there's anyone else about."

In only a few minutes, Archimedes swooped low over the companions and gave his report. Farther up the beach, he had found someone, the first living being they'd seen since Avalon—a single man, sitting close to a cold fire.

They approached him cautiously, but he barely gave any notice that he knew they were there until they were directly opposite the fire. The robes he wore were of a fine, rich material; ebony-hued, sleeker than silk. They dropped over one shoulder and wrapped around his midsection before falling almost to his shoeless feet.

"He has the features of an elf," John whispered to Jack. "But . . ."

"I know," Jack answered. "I've never seen an elf who actually looked . . . *old*."

The man stood and looked at the companions oddly, as if he knew there should be some sort of decorum involved when greeting newcomers and simply couldn't remember what it was.

He moved his mouth in fits and starts, clearly wanting to speak—but he said nothing. His eyes were not quite vacant, but both John and Jack had seen the expression he wore all too often.

Shell shock. Battle fatigue. A war, perhaps many wars, had taken their toll, and destroyed whatever there had been in him that had made him walk tall and strong and confidently in another life that was long past.

Strangely, it was Houdini who first decided to approach this strange, emaciated figure. "Hello," he said tentatively. "My name is Ehrich."

Doyle reacted visibly to this—Houdini hated being called by his real name and rarely used it.

The man tilted his head, examining the magician as if assessing his intent. Then, without warning, he stepped forward and collapsed into Houdini's arms, sobbing.

"Are you really here?" he asked between long, choking gasps. "Are you real, or fantasy?"

"I sometimes wonder that myself," Houdini murmured as he held the man closer. "I'm here. We've come to help."

"You're too late!" the man said, still crying. "You're just too late."

The others moved closer, and John and Laura Glue brought out some of the stores of food and water that had survived the passage of the Frontier. Burton, Doyle, and Theo gathered together more driftwood to add to the fire.

"This was all within reach," Burton grumbled as they added more sticks to the pile. "Why didn't he build it up? Why was he just sitting here, shivering and suffering?"

"I don't think he could build the fire," John said quietly, glancing over at the emaciated man. "I don't think he had the strength—or the will."

"If I have the will, I'll find the strength," Burton answered, scoffing.

After half an hour, the man seemed to have gotten enough of his strength back to converse with the companions.

"How do you come here?" he asked Houdini.

"In a ship," the Magician replied. "The *Black Dragon*."

"You have a Dragonship?" the man said. There was more interest in that single question than anything else he'd said to them.

"We do," said Jack, pointing down the beach to the faintly visible silhouette of the *Black Dragon* and the Tin Man. "We've only just arrived in it, though it's seen better days, I'm afraid."

"I have a Dragonship too," the man replied, weakly lifting his arm to point in the other direction. "It's there, on the sand. I hope to see it sail again someday, but sometimes . . ." He paused, and his eyes welled up with tears. "Sometimes I have had to use the wood for my fire, when there is no skrika, and the rain is coldest."

John cupped his eyes with his hands and peered in the direction the man was pointing. He'd seen a shape in the distance but thought it was simply an outcropping of rock; now he could make out the contours of a ship.

"Archimedes," he began.

"Wait," said Laura Glue. "I'll go take a look. I've been needing to stretch my wings."

"All right," John said, "but not alone. No," he added as she started to protest, "it's not because you're young, or because you're a girl. We don't know anything about this place. This is not the Paralon you know. None of us are going anywhere alone."

"I'll go with her," offered Doyle. "Won't be but a few minutes."

The bird, the Valkyrie, and the Detective disappeared into the mists along the beach, and were gone for only a short while before they returned. Doyle was nonplussed by their find, but Archie was excited and Laura Glue was visibly upset—enough so that she walked back alongside Doyle instead of flying.

"Laura Glue?" Rose asked, taking her friend's hands. "What was it? Is it really a Dragonship?"

Laura Glue wore the stunned expression of someone who had seen an impossible thing—and perhaps she had.

"It *is* a Dragonship," she said, incredulous. "It's the *Blue Dragon!*"

The companions all ran down the beach together to take a closer look at the legendary ship. It was the most elusive of the Dragonships, and the most powerful, because it belonged to one of the Elder Races in the Archipelago: the Elves.

It had been John's experience that when one spoke of Elves, people tended to think about sprites, and gossamer-winged fairies, and gentle, folklore magic. These were not those kind of Elves.

Bert had explained to him early in his apprenticeship about the Elves—that they had not come to maturity during the time of the Archipelago, as had many of the other races, but had in fact come from a far older culture, from when there was no separation between the Summer Country and the Archipelago.

Their land was contemporary with Atlantis and Mu. Some heard it was called Númenor; some Ys; others still Melniboné. But whatever it had been called was lost to all but the Elven race itself, and they had had enough of dealings with men.

When the Frontier was erected, Arthur himself went as an emissary to the Elf King, Eledir, who reestablished trade with the rest of the Archipelago, and by extension, the rest of the world. As a gift of good faith, Arthur allowed Ordo Maas to build the Blue Dragon, which he presented to the Elf King. In subsequent years the Elven craftsmen improved on the old shipmaster's design, turning an already formidable craft into a truly impressive instrument of war.

A remarkable history, John thought, that comes to its conclusion here, half-buried in the dust of Paralon.

Several dozen feet above their heads, the masthead of the great Dragon stretched high into the dusky air. Reaching away behind it were the spars and boards that had once formed a tight hull, now spread wide with age and disuse. The sides of the ship looked like a moth-eaten blanket, shot through with holes. The frame spread out on both sides like a skeleton, ribs pulling away from the spine—proof, stark and cold, that the living heart that it had once housed was long dead. Even the golden eyes of the Dragon were gray and cold—or at least one of them was, John noted. The other had been pried out of its socket, leaving a gaping hole in the noble face.

"Were you a sailor aboard the ship?" Rose asked gently, "or its captain, perhaps?"

"Not captain," the man said. "My ship. I built her. I and the Ancient of Days."

"Eledir?" John gasped. "Are you Eledir?"

The fragile face changed into a mask of hope. "Do you know me? You know my name?"

"Yes, yes I do!" John exclaimed. He wasn't certain what to think about this incredible and disturbing new discovery, but for the moment, he was happy enough just to find someone—anyone— he knew.

"Oh, thank you," Eledir said. "Do you have any skrika?"

John's face fell. He looked at Jack, who was similarly confused. Only Houdini and Theo seemed to understand what had happened.

This was indeed Eledir, the great Elf King of legend, who had fought beside Arthur in his youth, and with John and Jack in his golden years. But time, and whatever dreadful events had befallen the Archipelago, had taken their toll. His mind was gone—and with it the noble, majestic warrior who had led the Elven race for millennia.

"There must be a way to aid him," John said as he led the companions a few feet away to confer. "Fred? Is there anything in the Little Whatsit that might help?"

The little badger looked through page after page of ailments and maladies and remedies, only to come up regrettably short. "I'm sorry, Scowler John," he said sadly. "There's nothing here that really addresses this sort of thing. The only references that even come close say to consult the Elves—and he's the only one we know of here."

There was nothing the companions could do except leave

the Elf King where they had found him, next to his fire. Doyle, Houdini, and Theo gathered up more wood for him, and Laura Glue and Fred gave him more rations of food and water. After a moment, Fred even went back and placed a packet of his beloved Leprechaun crackers in Eledir's hand.

"Tell the Tin Man," John instructed Archimedes, "that we're going to go into the city, but we're leaving Ele—we're leaving this fellow here. He doesn't need to do anything, just watch from a distance, but I'll just feel better if we're not leaving him completely alone."

"I don't think it matters, little Caretaker," Burton said as he shouldered his pack. "He's not in there."

"It matters to me," said John, turning away, his fists clenched in helplessness. "It matters."

CHAPTER ELEVEN
THE LITTLE PRINCE

SILENCE RULED IN the streets of the city on Paralon. The broad, stone-lined thoroughfares were still there, but empty save for weeds and dust. The canals had gone dry, and most of the lower structures were too crumbled and broken down to even safely explore. The only structure that bore a resemblance to what had stood there before was the great citadel—the seat of the Silver Throne.

"I'll say this for him," John said, whistling in admiration. "Artigel built things to last."

Laura Glue was taking the destruction in stride. After the discovery of Eledir and the *Blue Dragon*, everything else seemed to be revealing itself in a natural, terrible progression. Still, John noted that she remained aloft on her wings as much as possible, and she spoke only to Archimedes. She might be feeling the impact of all this more than she was revealing.

As for Fred, he was putting up a brave front. John could tell by the nervous twitching of his whiskers that the badger was highly agitated—but he kept his composure, mostly by stroking his watch.

Ah, Charles, John thought. *You chose better than you knew, when you picked this little fellow to be your apprentice. He knows instinctively that bravery is not the absence of fear, but the willingness to act in spite of it.*

There were high walls erected in concentric circles all around the main towers of the citadel. They were massively solid but seemed also to have been hastily constructed, with some of them built over, on top of, and through the surrounding structures. The patchwork construction of some of them attested to the fact that they were built while Paralon was under siege—they were made of the materials that were readily at hand. That meant roads, castles, hovels—whatever could be broken down and used again to reinforce the battlements.

"Those wars George mentioned," Jack said, drawing his finger through the dust on a rampart. "I think I believe him now."

"They were trying to protect something," said Burton. "These are battlements, and well-built ones."

"Something, or someone?" asked John. "And the more important question: Were they successful?"

"I don't think the citadel would still be standing if they weren't," offered Doyle.

"I can't believe we haven't found anyone else here," said Laura Glue. "There were thousands of people living on Paralon."

"There is probably no one left around except for the animals," Burton said as he pushed aside a fallen pillar. "They're usually what remain when the people have gone."

"Talking, or the other kind?" asked Houdini. "I wouldn't really mind meeting more animals that can talk."

"What does it matter?" answered Burton. "If they talk, they're just servants and chattel. If they don't, they're dinner tonight and food storage for tomorrow."

"Ahem-hem," Fred interrupted as politely as he could manage. "I know some animals who would say exactly the same things about *you*."

"That matters less to me," said Burton. "I don't believe in making friends with something I ought to be eating."

"Don't take that personally, Fred," said Jack. "He's eaten a lot of his friends, too."

"If there is anyone still left here," Fred went on, undeterred by Burton's disdain, "it's sure t' be the animals, precisely *because* we're a servant class race."

"So you admit you're inferior?" asked Burton.

"I said nothing of the kind," Fred retorted. "We do it because it's a calling humans can only aspire to."

"Hah!" Burton barked. "How do you figure that?"

"Animal logic," answered Fred. "We figure we're here in this life to help others, to be happy, and to try not to eat our neighbors. And not necessarily in that order," he added.

"Those are three qualities that Burton will never understand," said John, "including the part about eating his neighbors."

"Only when it was necessary," said Burton.

The last of the great walls was the stoutest, and tallest, and least damaged.

"I don't even think it's just a wall," Jack said, shading his eyes to look skyward. "It looks like they were trying to enclose the palace completely and never finished the job."

The massive doors resembled those that guarded the ancient library known as the Great Whatsit, or those of Samaranth's own cavern. There were Elven runes carved throughout the metalwork and stone.

"That may have been why Eledir was here," Jack suggested. "He closed them in and sealed the door."

"Possibly," said John, "but someone was expecting us to open them again." He pointed to the locks. "See here? *Alpha*, the mark of the House of Arthur. And here," he indicated the other side. "*Pi*. The Caretaker's mark. We were meant to come here together, Rose, to find this place."

John and Rose each placed their hands over their respective marks, and there was a faint glow and warmth as the magic engaged. But the doors did not open.

"Come here, Burton, Theo," said Jack. "Let's give it a push."

"Rusted shut," Jack declared after a minute of straining at the doors. He wiped his hands on his trousers and looked at the Magician. "I don't suppose you can do anything about this?"

"Me?" said Houdini. "Locks aren't a problem. Rusted twenty-foot-high doors . . . that's a different kettle of fish."

"Archimedes . . . ," John began.

"I know, I know," the bird grumbled. "You want me to go fetch Bacon. Your wish is my command, O master."

Archie wheeled around and flew toward the beach, grumbling as he went. "Servant class my feathered rear," he muttered. "I'm a teacher."

"Sorry to burst your bubble," Jack called out, "but in my experience, that's about the same thing."

"We're not going to wait," Laura Glue declared suddenly, as she caught up Rose under the arms and soared up the face of the wall.

"Laura Glue!" John shouted. "Oh, for cat's sake," he grumbled. "There's not much we can do, I suppose, if she won't listen to us."

"And why should she, Caretaker?" asked Burton. "In her world she's a trusted soldier. But you still see a frightened child. Is it her obedience or your vision that is too small?"

Archie arrived with the Tin Man in tow, and once more they put their shoulders to the doors. But again, even with the Tin Man's amazing strength, they could not move the doors an inch.

"Now what?" Jack panted. "We can't exactly have Laura Glue fly all of us over the top, can we?"

"You don't need to," Rose said as the mighty doors swung open—*toward* the companions. "All the pushing in the world won't do you any good if you're pushing in the wrong direction."

All the men looked around sheepishly at one another as the young women and the animals laughed and trooped inside. "Did you even try pulling on them?" John asked.

"Didn't even occur to me," said Jack. "If it was up to us, we'd have ended up sitting on the beach with Eledir."

"I was going to mention the huge silver rings on the outside," said Houdini.

"Oh, shut up," said Burton.

Inside the great wall, which they could now see was really a half dome, stood the palace of Paralon. Its defenders had been trying to erect a great protective shell around it, to better preserve whatever it was that remained inside. But of everything the companions had witnessed, the castle was the one thing that resembled their memories, and Laura Glue teared up at the sight of it.

"Now we're getting somewhere," said Fred, thumping a fist into his paw. "As long as there sits a descendant of Arthur on the Silver Throne, then the Archipelago is not alone."

John looked askance at Jack, who remained placid. After all these years, any mention of the Silver Throne pushed Jack into an emotional reserve of coolness. The last King they knew, Stephen, was the son of Jack's first great love—and he had never truly gotten over that feeling.

"Let's go see what there is to see," Jack said brusquely, pushing ahead of the others. He strode through the familiar corridors as quickly as he could until he finally reached the great hall where the Silver Throne of Arthur had stood.

Jack pulled open the doors—pulled, not pushed, John noted with amusement—and entered the hall.

Immediately he was surrounded by dozens of animals bearing a strange assortment of weapons. They were all chittering and howling and creating a terrible racket. Some were foxes, and others were smaller creatures he couldn't identify in all the melee.

They were pointing crude spears and long knives at Jack and the others who had come up quickly behind him—but some among the animals had weapons that resembled those of Nemo's time. That meant they were deadly, if not accurate.

"Stop!" Fred shouted, throwing himself in front of the companions. "We mean you no harm!"

At the appearance of another animal, all the rest stopped and grew silent. They seemed slightly confused, as if they'd been ready to go to war, and the appearance of this little badger had changed their minds.

"Who be you?" one of the foxes asked. "Be you friend, or be you foe?"

"I be . . . I mean, I am Fred, son of Uncas, son of Tummeler," said the little Caretaker, "and we mean you no harm."

"Caretaker?" the fox exclaimed. "Are the rest of you also Caretakers?"

"Some of us," said Jack. "I'm Jack, and this is John."

At this, all the animals, which they now saw were foxes and hedgehogs, dropped their weapons and sank to their knees. "Scowler John and Scowler Jack," the fox said reverently, "I am Myrret, and I am your humble servant. We have cared for him the best we could until you could arrive."

"Him?" asked Jack. "Him who?"

"The prince," Myrret replied with some surprise. "The last prince of the Silver Throne."

The animals led the companions through the great hall, and for the first time, they could see how it had been transformed. Far from being a place of government, it had been made over to resemble a giant nursery. There was a theater to one side, with half-completed sets from what appeared to be a Brothers Grimm story. There were books scattered everywhere, and stained-glass friezes that depicted a plethora of fables and fairy tales. There was even a miniature planet, large enough to climb on, that hovered above a silver base. It was every child's dream—or would have been, had it not been locked inside a fortress.

"Where is he?" John asked Myrret. "Is he here?"

In reply, the fox pointed to the fore of the room, to the Silver Throne itself.

There, peeking from behind the timeworn throne, was a child. A boy, dark-haired, bright-eyed, and all of six years old, if that, thought Jack—although the curious expression on his face and the absence of fear made him appear to be older.

He hesitated—these strangers were the first people he might have seen in a long time, if ever. Rose read his fear and approached the throne slowly.

"Hello," she said softly. "I'm your cousin Rose. Who are you?"

"I am the son of Radamand, who was the son of Homer, who was the son of Karal," he said, "who was the son of . . ." He paused and scratched his head. "I forget who else. But I am the last king of the Silver Throne."

Burton laughed, a short, sharp bark. "Hah! King? You're barely old enough to dress yourself."

"Richard, shut up," Jack hissed.

"You are a prince, and may be king someday," said Rose. "When you are older."

"I read about the king in the stories," said the boy. "The king of rocks. You know—Old King Coal was a merry old soul."

"You can read?" asked Rose.

"The animals tell me stories," he said. "They've also taught me how to read, so that if they are busy, I can read them myself," he said with no small pride.

"C-O-L-E, not C-O-A-L," Fred corrected, trying to be helpful.

"The animals call me Coal," the boy said. "I never got a real name. When I was born, there was no one left to name me. So I decided I came from a story instead."

No one left? John thought. Had they come too late? Just in time to witness the end of the Silver Throne?

"Knew you'd come," said Coal. "The stories all said you would. And now we can listen to the last story together!"

"What is the last story?" asked Rose. "Is it a book?"

"No," Myrret answered. "It's in the Whatsit."

"The Great Whatsit!" Jack exclaimed. "It still exists?"

"Not the Great Whatsit," Myrret corrected, "just the Whatsit. The Great Whatsit was destroyed by the Trolls in the Second War of the Races, and the last of the crows and the hedgehogs moved what they could save here, to the new Whatsit that a badger built underneath the palace."

"Badger?" said Fred, perking up. "What badger?"

"Charles Montgolfier something something," said Myrret. "I could look it up if you like."

"No need," Fred said as Jack squeezed his shoulder. "Attaboy, Pop."

"The prince's own ancestress left the last story for you," said a small hedgehog, "and she has guarded it herself all these centuries."

"She's still alive?" asked Rose.

"She sleeps forever in the crystal," the hedgehog said reverently, "never to be awakened. Come with me, and I'll take you to her."

CHAPTER TWELVE
THE REGENCY

MYRRET AND THE other animals led the companions and the little prince to a spiral flight of stairs that was secreted behind the throne itself. It dropped away almost straight down, farther than the light from the torches showed. One by one they climbed down into the stairway, first the animals, then the Caretakers, with Burton and his colleagues bringing up the rear. The Tin Man stayed behind to make sure they weren't followed.

Shadows danced along the walls of the tunnels as the companions passed down into the new Whatsit. Jack occasionally looked back at Theo, who had taken up the rearmost position, and who was pausing every now and again to peer back into the darkness behind them. Each time, Theo would return Jack's unspoken question with a short shake of the head. No enemy was following them—not that they knew of. Or could see.

The stairway ended in a tall cavern filled with crystalline structures. All along the walls were tubes full of crystal shards, some of different colors, and they seemed to be organized by size.

"We started keeping all our records on the crystals," Myrret explained, "when the parchment and books became too unwieldy. Far more expedient this way, don't you think?" The fox was twisting his paws together, and it was obvious he was seeking some sign of approval from his esteemed guests.

"It's remarkable," said John. "Very good work, Myrret."

The fox beamed and scampered across the room to fetch one of the librarians. He returned with a ferret who was dressed in several weathered robes, all of which had been meant for larger animals.

"Glory be," the little tatterdemalion whispered as he pulled up his trousers. "The Caretakers! I never thought I would live to see them myself!"

The ferret was thrilled to be able to show them the pride and joy of the Whatsit—what they called the Last Story.

"Good heavens," Jack said, whistling. "It's a projector."

There on a pedestal in the center of the room, facing a tall structure of giant crystals, stood a very familiar-looking device. It was a reel-to-reel film projector, much like they had in the cinemas back at Oxford, but with a double set of lenses.

"It's definitely Hank's design," John said admiringly. "I think this is what he intended his chronal stereopticon to eventually become."

"Is it like the Lanterna Magica?" asked Jack, as his face lit up with the possibility. "Can we use it to leave the Archipelago?"

Myrret shook his furred head. "The ancestors had access to neither the Prime Caretaker nor the Tin Man, and the great Captain Nemo was long dead. Without their knowledge, we had no way to build such a device. All we could do was use what we had to keep a memory alive. And keep it we have, for many, many centuries."

"I've tried to turn it on," said Coal, "but it never would work.

Not for me, even though I can work other things by touching them."

"The seal bears the Caretaker's mark, not the king's mark," Jack explained to Coal. "That's why you were never able to turn it on."

"Archie," John began.

"I'm way ahead of you," the bird replied. "I'll go get him."

With some difficulty, the Tin Man made his way down the stairs to the Whatsit, where he examined the device briefly, then shook his head. Whatever he might have been able to contribute to its construction was not possible now. It would do what it would do.

"We've replaced all the parts many times to keep it in order," Myrret said proudly, "but it is the selfsame generator that the great Hank Morgan built in the time of Arthur, lo these many centuries ago."

"How would you know about that?" asked Houdini. "That was in another world, wasn't it?"

The small animal brandished a familiar-looking if ageworn book. "The Little Whatsit," he said proudly. "The Histories are complete, at least in regard to the important things. And there was none more important than the story of the Great King and the Silver Throne."

"It isn't the same machine, you know," Burton said as he peered at the projector. "If you've replaced all the components, then the original doesn't exist anymore. It would be like taking your grandfather's ax and replacing the handle, then replacing the blade, then replacing the handle again, and then still insisting that it was your grandfather's ax."

The little animal was crestfallen. "I meant no offense, great Lord," he said meekly.

"Never mind him," said Jack, frowning at Burton. "He's only a barbarian."

Myrret opened a velvet-lined box and removed a large reel, which he carefully placed on the empty arm, then threaded into the projector. "Legend says the ancestor made this for her own son, who was king," he explained, "but that was many years ago. I don't think she expected it to be so long before you returned."

"Neither did we," said John.

"Great Caretakers," the ferret said, "would you do us the honor of turning on the device?"

"Be my guest," John said to Jack.

"How about our third?" Jack replied, smiling at Fred. "Will you?"

Fred swallowed hard and reached his paw up to the seal, which melted away at his touch. There was an awed hush among the other animals—to see one of their own as a Caretaker would create a new legend in the Archipelago. Or whatever was left of it.

The projector sputtered to life, and a broad rectangle of light appeared on the glassine wall of the crystal across the chamber. A logo appeared, bearing the insignia of Mr. Tummeler's production company, followed by an ad for the twenty-eighth expanded edition of the *Imaginarium Geographica*.

"Good old granddad," Fred said, wiping a tear from his furry cheek. "Never missed a trick."

"Now I'm getting hungry for blueberry muffins," said John.

"Same here," said Jack.

"What in Hades does that mean?" asked Burton.

"Never mind," Jack said, winking at Fred. "Inside joke."

A moment later a fox appeared on the wall and introduced himself as Reynard. He bowed, then stepped offscreen.

"Reynard, of course!" John said to Jack. "Just like back at Sanctuary."

"Yes," said Jack warily, "but didn't Verne set that up?"

"For all we know, he set this up too."

"Hush," Jack replied. "Someone's coming into view."

The image on the crystalline wall was of a woman, mature but not yet elderly, who was dressed in simple clothes, save for the elegant silk robe draped across her shoulders. Her hair was auburn shot through with silver, and it seemed to Jack for a moment that he recognized her.

"Hello, my young firebrand," the image said as she appeared to look fondly at Jack. "I'm not surprised to see you, although I wish it had been far, far sooner."

Jack and the others gasped—he had recognized her after all. It was Aven.

"Did she record this for me, then?" Jack whispered to Myrret. "I thought she meant this for Stephen."

"I did," the image replied, to the consternation and surprise of everyone in the chamber, "but I do not believe it is a coincidence that you should be the one to open the seal, dear Jack. You saved me once," she added with a wry smile. "Perhaps it is now written in your destiny to save us all."

"How is this possible?" Jack exclaimed, hardly daring to move closer. "Is it really you?"

The image of Aven laughed. "It is, Jack. It is the Aven you knew. But I'm not here—or 'there,' I suppose—in the flesh. I am just an image, but still, I have been waiting for a very long time, and I'm very glad to see you again."

"Actually, I opened it," Fred said, meekly raising his paw.

"Ah," said Aven. "So you've become a Caretaker too, Fred. Your family would be very proud of you."

John realized that just like the ghost of Hank Morgan, she couldn't see or hear the viewers until they had engaged the projection first. "I'm here as well," John said. "Hello, Aven."

"John," she said. "You haven't lost the *Geographica* again, have you?"

"Not so far," said John. "But I seem to have misplaced the Archipelago."

"Yes," she said, head bowed. "I imagine it would seem that way."

"What happened, Aven?" asked Jack.

"When it seemed that the Caretakers abandoned the Archipelago," she began, "we had no way of knowing what had happened to you—only that you didn't return, and there was no way to contact you.

"The Frontier had become impassable, as if the storm clouds had been replaced by stone walls," Aven went on, "and nothing we built could breach it. Stephen and the animals built machine after machine, but nothing worked. After almost a decade of trying, he abandoned his efforts and turned his attention to guiding the future of the Archipelago."

She paused, and bowed her head. "It did not go well."

"In the twenty-second year of the new republic, several of the races rebelled, and there was a violent split in the Senate. Several lands withdrew their support, and war was declared."

"War?" John sputtered. "There was a war in the Archipelago?"

Aven nodded. "Four wars, to be exact. The severing of the bonds between the races was all it took to divide the republic, and all the lands took to looking after their own interests.

"It was after the battle with the Shadow King that I stepped down as queen, and Stephen took over the affairs of the Archipelago," she continued. "I had lost my husband, but he left me with one final gift. I was with child."

"You and Artus had a child?" John exclaimed.

"Yes," said Aven. "I named him Charles. It was Tummeler's suggestion."

"Of course it was," Jack said, noting that Fred was practically beaming at the mention of his grandfather. "And what of Stephen?"

At the mention of her elder son, Aven's countenance darkened. "He went on a quest," she said after a pause. "The last great quest of the Archipelago. It remains to be seen whether or not his sacrifice will have been worth all we lost.

"There was one final message from him, before he . . . ," she said, her voice breaking. "He said that the sacrifices he made were not just for the Archipelago, or the Summer Country, but for the love he had for one girl, which he never got to share."

Laura Glue's face reddened. "I knew," she said.

Aven looked at her with gentle eyes. "He did love you, you know, even if you didn't feel it as strongly as he did. He spoke of you often, and regretted not having gone with you to Tamerlane House."

The Valkyrie's eyes began to well with tears, and Fred reached over to take her hand in support.

"So Arthur's own line did continue," said John. "That means the child had the same lineage as Rose."

"It became stranger than that," said Aven, "when Charles married Tiger Lily. It turned out to be a very successful union despite the matter of Lily's parentage."

Burton cleared his throat. "I'm right here, in the room," he said a bit brusquely, "but I forgive the slight breach of etiquette, as you have given me news of my daughter." He bowed slightly—not deeply enough to be subservient, but just enough that the gesture was sincere.

"Burton?" Aven asked, startled.

"Yes," said Jack, in a tone that was almost embarrassed. "You remember, Aven—the Caretakers Emeritis brokered a truce with the Imperial Cartological Society. We're all operating cooperatively now. And the ICS is being developed as an official organization at Cambridge by, uh"—he swallowed hard—"me."

"So he's your ally now," Aven said, her voice subdued. "Not enough time has passed, it seems, for that not to be a surprise. And you, Jack," she finished, looking up again and meeting his eyes, "you've become a true pirate at last."

Jack winced slightly. He couldn't tell if she was teasing or not.

The projection laughed. "Of course I'm teasing you, Jack. I know full well that appearances are fleeting, and you did what was necessary."

"What happened to the Archipelago, Aven?" asked Jack. "Where *did* all the lands go?"

"Samaranth took them," Aven said simply. "He took them all, to a place that cannot be reached in space or time."

"Where is that?" asked Burton. "Nether Land?"

"Farther still," Aven replied. "He took them beyond the great wall."

"Why would he do such a thing?" John asked. "How is that even possible?"

"The Shadows came to claim them," Aven said with deep sorrow. "The true Shadows, the Darkness that cannot be broken. Our great enemy."

"The Echthroi," said Theo.

"Yes," said Aven. "The Echthroi. That is the name of the Shadows. They have another name for those shadows they claim from the living: Lloigor. When a good creature, a servant of the Light, is turned, its shadow disappears—but not completely. It becomes a servant of the Echthroi. A Lloigor."

Jack exhaled hard and looked away. "Then that's what was happening to me when I started to follow Mordred's path," he said somberly. "My shadow was becoming a Lloigor."

Aven nodded. "But you chose to take it back, Jack. You chose to return to the Light. As long as there is life, there is always a choice. No matter what else has gone before, no matter how terrible the crimes or how strong the temptation, one may still choose to turn away from the pit of darkness, away from the lure of shadow. This is how the Echthroi are defeated."

"And what about after life?" Burton asked abruptly. "What about those living a second go-round?"

"Life," Aven said evenly, "is intelligence, and the ability to choose. Death is rejecting all choices."

"I don't think that quite answered the question," he murmured under his breath.

"I think it did," said Theo.

"If my shadow was becoming a Lloigor," said Jack, "what happened to Mordred's shadow?"

"He was to become their greatest champion," said Aven. "A Lloigor who goes willingly is nearly unstoppable. That's why it was able to return so often, first as the King of Crickets, and then as the Shadow King."

"If such a creature is so powerful," said Jack, "then how was it Rose was able to defeat it with Caliburn?"

"Because Madoc chose," said Aven. "He chose to turn his back on the Echthroi and what they represented. And in that hour the Shadow King lost much of his power, and the Echthroi lost their great champion."

"But it isn't always those who choose the darkness, as I nearly did, who become servants of the shadows," said Jack. "What about those peoples of the Archipelago who were made into Shadow-Born by Pandora's Box?"

"Or the Dragons themselves, who were touched by the Spear of Destiny?" added John. "None of them were willing, but they became servants of the Echthroi nonetheless."

"Their minds were clouded," said Aven. "Samaranth told me that the Echthroi could compel obedience through magic, or lies, or betrayal. But that is only a last resort—they prefer to convert, not compel. And sometimes they appeal to the darkness in all men's souls, and can confuse good men into service. Surely you can understand this?"

"Yes," Burton answered, as if she'd been speaking to him. "Yes, I can."

"A century after the Day of Sorrow," she continued, "we discovered that lands along the western edge were vanishing—being covered in Shadow. At first we feared that the Winter King had in some way returned. But we knew his Shadow had been destroyed, as much by his own choice to aid you when he repaired the sword, as by the sword itself. There have been other agents throughout history, others who served the Echthroi, but Samaranth came to us here and said that it was far worse. The Shadow covering the lands was the Echthroi *themselves.*

"That was when Samaranth opened up his own archives to us and shared all the knowledge he could. And I realized that I would never be seeing him again."

"What did he do?" asked Jack. "Is that when he left?"

Aven nodded. "It was. He invoked the Old Magic, and as the first Caretaker of the Archipelago of Dreams, he took up all the lands and bore them away so they would not fall victim to the Echthroi."

"It seems that I've outlived my usefulness," John said ruefully, looking at the atlas in Fred's pack. "If there's no Archipelago of Dreams, then of what importance is the *Imaginarium Geographica,* or a Caretaker who can translate it?"

"Of great importance, John," Aven answered with a tone of reproach. "The greatest. Without the *Geographica,* it will be impossible to put them all back."

"What?" asked Jack. "The islands of the Archipelago? They can still be restored?"

"Yes," Aven said. "But not until you repair what was broken, and connect our worlds once more. Until then, only shadows remain."

"If all that remains of the Archipelago is shadows," Jack asked, "then will the images in the *Geographica* vanish?"

John understood the concern behind his friend's question. During their first conflict with the Winter King, they discovered that whenever a land was conquered, the corresponding map faded and vanished. The longer the Winter King was loosed in the world, the more likely he was to have control of all of the lands. Only restoring the shadows to the people of the lands brought the drawings back.

"Never fear, Jack," Aven answered. "The lands have not been taken by force, not even those of our enemies. They went willingly and unafraid, because they knew that taking them from these waters was Samaranth's responsibility, and his stewardship, as it has always been."

"What if Rose called him?" asked Jack. "Samaranth *would* come, wouldn't he?"

At once her expression grew dark and stern. "That you must never do," she cautioned. "You must never summon the Dragons again." This last she directed at Rose. "Even if Samaranth is the only one left, should he be summoned by one of noble intent, he would come and restore the Archipelago. And until time is properly restored, that cannot happen. Must not happen."

Jack was taken aback by the tone and fervor with which Aven spoke. Nothing else she had said had carried this degree of firmness. "We'll listen, Aven, and the Summoning will not be spoken. But why is it so important? Wouldn't Samaranth be a help to us?"

"It's too late for Samaranth to help you, even if he chose to," said Aven. "But there is still time to seek out his heir."

Rose looked sharply at John. Samaranth's heir? Could she mean the Dragon's apprentice?

"The two worlds were once one," the projection continued, "connected. And even when the connections were severed, and the worlds separated by the Frontier, there remained resonances . . .

reflections. What happens in the one is mirrored in the other. What happens in one can impact the other. And with the flow of time set loose here in the Archipelago, the effects were mirrored a thousandfold."

"There's a lot you need to know about what's happened," John began, but Aven cut him off.

"The film isn't an endless loop," she chided, "nor is it infinitely expandable. It was shot using Verne's processes, so that a time loop could be instilled within the frames—but once it has been exposed to the projector light, the frames are set. This film can never again be replayed as it is being played now. When our time has run out, you'll have a recorded copy of this discussion, but nothing more. I'll be gone, forever."

Suddenly the images on the wall began to flicker, and chemical burns began to strobe along the edges of the frames.

"Wait!" Jack shouted. "We aren't done yet! Wait!"

"We don't know what to do!" John exclaimed. "There's no way to repair the Archipelago!"

"But there is," Aven said, her voice strained and growing weaker. "I would not have charged you with such a task without giving you the means to carry it out."

Without any further warning, the projection went blank, then the end of the strip started flapping noisily through the reel until Jack reached over and shut it off.

"That wasn't really a very good story," said Coal. "Do we have any more?"

"She couldn't tell us," Jack lamented. "She said she left us the means, but we don't know what that is!"

"I know, Master Caretaker," said Myrret. "It is one of the

greatest stories we have after the Day of Sorrows. The great quest of King Stephen. It cost him his life, but he was successful. And it will perhaps give you the opportunity you seek."

He motioned to the other foxes, who guided the companions into a second chamber in the Whatsit. This one was broader, and covered in sand and stone rather than crystal. But something stunningly familiar sat in the center of the chamber.

It was a door. One of the doors from the Keep of Time.

PART FOUR

THE FAMILY TRADE

CHAPTER THIRTEEN
THE PASSAGE

—◈—

CURSING UNDER HIS breath, Ernest McGee swept his arm across the table, scattering parchments and spilling ink. His family trade was mapmaking, and as far as Ernest could tell, it had brought both wealth and fame, and grief and misery in equal amounts.

His father's best friend, Captain Charles Johnson, had disappeared years earlier, and the subsequent deception that was put forth was an insult and a travesty.

True, the *History* was published, and it bore Johnson's name, but for Ernest's father, Eliot, to deny all knowledge of the man was not right.

It didn't bother Ernest that his father's collaborator claimed credit for work that was not his—it bothered him that they had created the fiction that Johnson never existed at all.

It had taken Ernest most of his adult life to properly assemble the two books that his father had worked so hard to complete: One described the wealth of the world, hidden in strange and curious places by terrible men who no longer sailed the oceans; and the other described entire worlds that might or might not even exist.

He might not have inherited the desire, or even the skill—but he was loath to deny the family a legacy. He only hoped that it would end with him, that perhaps his own son might choose to return to silversmithing, rather than follow the family heritage of making maps for pirates and madmen.

Even as he wished it, he knew it wasn't to be. Some things in life run too deep.

Some things are just in the blood.

Picking up the quill and a fresh parchment, he dipped the point into the ink and started to draw again.

"Oh my stars and garters," Fred whispered. "Is that what I think it is?"

"It's a door from the keep, you idiot," Burton said gruffly.

Rose laid a comforting hand on the badger's arm before he could draw a sword and defend his honor by having the stuffing beaten out of him by Burton. "He knows what it is," she said placidly, "because he's seen it before. We all have. That's the door we dropped over the waterfall.

"That's the door we gave to my father—to Madoc."

"So we may have a way out after all," said Burton. "Excellent."

"Is this what we want to do?" John asked the others. "We might be saving ourselves, but would we be giving up on the Archipelago?"

"Pardon my saying so," said Fred, "but what would we be giving up? Other than Paralon, there's nothing here. And the queen said that Stephen gave his life to give us this opening, so we could fix things. What else do you need to know?"

John scratched the badger on the head. "You may be the wisest of us all, Fred. We'll go through the door."

"Myrret," Jack said suddenly, "may I take the reel from the projector with me? Please?"

The little animal sniffed loudly and nodded its assent through a curtain of tears. "It was f'r you that we preserved it all these years, so it's well and just that you should have it. Besides, it can't be used again, so there's no point, is there? No point in us keeping our stewardship any longer."

"There's always a point, little fellow," Jack said, "and stewardships kept are among the noblest of causes."

"All we have to do now," said Myrret, "is say good-bye to her."

Jack's brow furrowed. "What do you mean?"

"The queen," Myrret said, confused. "We promised that when you came, we would wake her. She sleeps in crystal, here in the Whatsit."

"I thought you were talking about the projection," said John. "A metaphor."

"Take us to her, Myrret," Jack said. "Take us to her now."

In another chamber adjacent to the projection room lay a deep cradle of crystal and silk, and in it, covered by a sheath of the clear stone, lay Aven.

"She's still here," Jack breathed. "She's alive."

Aven was ancient, impossibly old. Her face and hands were pale, and her hair, which was draped behind her as if it were floating, was pure, colorless white.

"I'll wake her now," said Myrret. He touched a contact at the base of the cradle, and the crystal sheath slid back. Exposed to the open air, Aven suddenly took a deep breath, then another, and another. Then, slowly, she opened her eyes.

"Ah, my young corsair," she said when she saw Jack. "You came back. You came back to me."

"Of course," Jack said, his voice choked with emotion. "Of course I did."

He leaned in close as his ancient friend slowly closed her eyes, then opened them again. They still sparkled, but the light in them was fading.

"We should ask her to answer more of our questions," Burton began, but Theo pulled him back, and both Houdini and Doyle stepped in front of him. The purpose of waking Aven was not to ask questions. It was to allow her, finally, to rest.

"You saw the message?" she asked weakly. "You understood?"

"We did," said Jack. "We'll use the door, never fear. We'll right this, Ave. And we'll look after the prince."

Her expression darkened. "What prince?"

"Coal," he said. "The little prince. Your heir."

"He mustn't leave," she said. "It isn't safe." She drew a shallow breath. "Look after Charles, will you, Jack? Take care of him. He needs you. He can help you."

"Of course," Jack said, looking over at John. She was obviously fading—her son was long gone.

"Ah, Artus . . . ," Aven breathed. "You don't need to wait for me any longer. . . ." As the companions watched, the strength left her arms, and her eyes fluttered closed. Slowly she took a breath, her chest rising faintly with the effort. Then another. Then, nothing. She was gone.

Jack squeezed his eyes shut as the tears flowed down his cheeks, and he murmured a quiet prayer as he placed Aven's hands on her chest and stepped back from the cradle.

+ + +

"It's decided," John said flatly. "We can't take the boy with us."

The companions had retreated to the projection room to decide what to do. They had already planned to go through the door—but there was some dissent about whether all of them should go.

"That isn't your decision to make, Caretaker," Burton said with obvious anger. "Not alone."

"I have to say that I agree with him," said Doyle, "and not just because we're both members of the Society."

"I agree with them," said Houdini. "After all we've been told, how can we consider leaving him here? There's nothing left, John. The Archipelago is a wasteland. There's no future for him here."

"That's part of the problem," said John. "It's *all* future here. We've already had too much experience with dropping people in the past, where they didn't belong. What kind of chaos will we cause if we bring back someone from the future?"

"That's not quite it," said Jack. "Remember what Ransom said? This isn't the future, not to us. It's our present. It's also," he added, jerking a thumb over his shoulder at where the boy was chatting with Fred and Laura Glue, "his present. It all moves forward."

"You're wiser than I gave you credit for," Burton said to Jack. "You're outvoted, Caretaker."

"I didn't say I was siding with you," said Jack. "I have reservations of my own. And Aven herself said he shouldn't leave."

"She's been sleeping in a crystal for two thousand years," said Burton. "She didn't know what she was saying."

"I still say we vote," said John.

"And of course the rodent will be voting with you," said Burton.

"Fred," Jack said pointedly, "qualified to be something you flunked, Burton. So try to have a little respect, if only for the office he holds."

"I have some respect for the badger," Burton shot back. "It's the office I think is weak."

The End of Time looked at Burton. "The child must stay," he said impassively. "He must."

Burton's jaw dropped open in amazement. Of all of them, the End of Time was the one man he had expected to back him in his arguments.

"Why?"

Theo refused to answer, and merely stared at Burton, who dropped his eyes.

"All right," Burton finally agreed, still reluctant. "The boy stays here, God curse you all."

It took some intense discussions and the direct involvement of both Fred and Archimedes to convince Myrret and the other animals that it would be best for Coal to remain on Paralon. By that point, even John was wavering—but Jack took both Aven's request and Theo's warning very seriously and persuaded the others that it really was for the best.

As Myrret distracted Coal up in the Great Hall, the companions began to examine the door. It was framed in stone, and despite all its travels, looked none the worse for wear.

"I'll give this to the Dragons," said Burton. "They could build a door."

Jack reached out and touched the door. It swung open slightly and vibrated. Peering through the crack, he could see some kind of street, and the sounds of horses and street vendors wafted through, along with an assortment of odors. There was no question—the door still worked.

Suddenly a stone fell from the arch and landed with a dull thump in the sand. "Uh-oh," said Houdini. "That's not a good sign."

"It's thousands of years old," said Fred, "and it's no longer being supported by the energies of the keep."

"We'd better go through quickly," said John. "It may not last for another trip."

But before the companions could open the door farther, an earth-rattling tremor threw them to the floor.

"What the hell?" said Burton. "Is it another discontinuity?"

"No," Theo said, looking up the stairwell. "That was something else. Something living."

There was another tremor, and then a deep, malevolent voice rang through the entire palace. "Little things," the reverberating voice said, "why have you come here?"

Rose's eyes widened in recognition. She had heard that voice before, not all that long ago. "It's the star!" she exclaimed. "The star, Rao, from one of the islands past the Edge of the World!"

"It is a dark star," the ferret said. "It is a creature of Shadow now."

"A Lloigor," said Theo, "with the power of a living star. We must go. We must go now."

Somewhere up above the palace, the star called Rao roared, and the earth shook. Two more stones fell from the frame around the door.

"It's not going to hold!" Fred cried as he pushed open the door. "The frame is breaking up!"

A huge figure lumbered around behind the door and grasped the stones, and Fred pushed it open all the way.

The Tin Man braced himself around the crumbling archway and held the stones together as, one by one, the companions passed through the vortex of energies that was the doorway into time.

Rao continued to rage, and now the roaring was closer—the star had entered the palace itself.

"Good-bye, Great Caretakers," the ferret said sadly. "Remember us."

"Ah, me," said John, closing his eyes. "How can I leave them like this?"

Suddenly a cry rang out—a plea. It was a child's voice, calling to them from the far chamber, and he was begging not to be left behind.

Coal.

"We can't!" John shouted, steeling his resolve. "I'm sorry, we can't!"

"We understand," Myrret called out as he barred Coal from entering the chamber. "Go! Go!"

"How stony is your heart, Caretaker?" Burton argued from the world beyond the door. "You'll leave him here, to face this, alone?"

John looked back and forth between Burton and the terrified boy, then dropped his head in resignation. Jack knew the expression on his old friend's face. He was thinking about his own son, Christopher, who was in the Royal Air Force back in England. One young man against a war was too much for a father to carry—and it was too much here, in the face of the dark star, the Lloigor Rao. "All right!" John said to Burton. "Go! Grab him! We'll keep the door open!"

Burton dashed back through the door and took the terrified boy from the fox just as a dark, living mist began to descend the staircase. "Little things," the booming voice called out, "come to me. Come to Rao."

"Scowler John," Fred said, trying to keep the pleading out of his own voice, "what would Charles do?"

"All for one and one for all, then," John said under his breath. "Myrret!" He shouted. "Come on through! Bring everyone!"

Burton, carrying the little prince, passed through the door just before a rush of animals nearly bowled him off his feet. A dozen foxes, as many hedgehogs, and the ferret raced though between John's legs.

The outer chamber of the Whatsit was full of the black mist now, and the entire palace seemed to be falling to pieces. The rumbling was constant now, and the angry voice of Rao filled the room.

"What about Aven?" Jack shouted over the rumbling. "And Eledir?"

"Aven's already gone," John shouted back, "and Eledir's too far away to help. We're done here, Jack."

John was the last to pass through, and for a brief instant he considered suggesting that the Tin Man try to step around and through the door—but the great behemoth saw the thought pass fleetingly over John's face, and shook its head no.

There was no time left. The Tin Man was here, now, for this purpose—to ensure that the last efforts of Aven and Stephen had not been in vain.

"Little things," Rao boomed, "I see you!"

A great tendril of darkness shot out from the formless Lloigor, past John and through the open door, where it wrapped itself around Rose and began pulling her back.

"No!" John shouted, clutching at the darkness. "Burton! Jack! Hold on to her!"

The men grabbed Rose by the arms, and she screamed. For a moment it seemed as if Rao was going to pull her apart—then suddenly the tendril loosed and pulled away. It had gotten what it wanted.

"My shadow!" Rose exclaimed in horrified wonder. "It's taking my shadow!"

"Close the door!" John yelled up at the Tin Man. "Do it now, before it's too late!"

Something shoved John hard in the chest, and he fell backward through the door. The tendril had released Rose's shadow, which followed him through the door, writhing on the ground at his feet as Rao rose up to confront the Tin Man.

The companions despaired. The machine man was powerful and had a great will—but he would not last long against the power of the dark star.

As the door closed behind him, John heard the voice of the Tin Man speaking to him through the din. "Fix this," it said, in the softly accented continental English of Roger Bacon. "Fix this, Caveo Principia."

Then the door slammed shut and exploded with a violent burst of light and splinters and the shards of time.

CHAPTER FOURTEEN
CRAVEN STREET

—✳—

THE COMPANIONS FOUND themselves standing in an alley off a busy street in London. It was dark, and narrow, and smelly, but it was concealed enough that they weren't going to immediately attract too much attention for the fact that they were accompanied by dozens of animals that walked on their hind legs, were dressed in human clothes, and spoke in accented English.

It took several minutes for the companions to gather their wits about them after the narrow escape from the dark star Rao. John's last act of compassion had brought them not only the little prince, but also an entourage. It also cost them precious seconds during which they'd nearly lost Rose to the Lloigor.

"She'd never have been at risk if you'd just allowed the boy to come with us from the start," Burton said to John, glowering. "You are a stupid man, Caretaker."

"It's all right," said Rose soothingly, her voice still a bit shaky from the fear and the adrenaline. "Because of the Tin Man, we all came through fine, with no harm done. That's all that matters."

"Not completely," Jack said, pointing at the ground. "Something's come loose, Rose."

He was right. Her shadow lay on the ground at their feet, completely disconnected from her—and pointing *toward* the light from the street.

Rose's eyes widened, and she leaned down to touch it, but it darted away and up a nearby wall.

"What does this mean?" she asked the Caretakers. "How can my shadow move on its own?"

"People have lost their shadows before," said John, "but usually they have to be given up willingly, or in the cases of the Shadow-Born, taken. But this is an entirely new dilemma."

"Does that make her a Shadow-Born, then?" asked Fred. "That would be terrible for you, Rose."

"She didn't lose her shadow," said Jack. "It's right up there. It just isn't attached to her anymore."

"To give up a shadow means choosing a dark path," said Burton. "Be wary, girl."

"I don't want to give it up!" Rose exclaimed, almost petulantly. "I haven't chosen a dark path! I'm the Grail Child."

"Well, it doesn't appear to be leaving you," John remarked, noting that the shadow was now dancing among the shadows cast by the other companions. "I don't think you have to worry about becoming a Shadow-Born, Rose."

"Not permanently, anyway," Jack said with a grin. "But if you wanted, you could get up to all sorts of mischief now, and just blame it on your shadow."

Rose's eyes widened. "Really?"

"Shame on you!" Archie squawked. "You of all people should know better than to joke about that, Caretaker."

"He isn't too bright either," said Burton.

"I'm sorry," Jack said, chagrined. "Forgive me, Rose. We'll figure out how to reattach it somehow."

"There's nothing to forgive," Rose answered. "We have bigger things to worry about."

"First things first," said John. "We've definitely returned to the Summer Country—but when?"

Burton checked his watch. "Hmm," he mused. "1768. That's not too shabby. And at least we're in the right hemisphere."

"1768?" Houdini repeated. "Are you certain?"

Burton simply scowled in response.

"Drat," said Houdini. "I've missed him by more than a dozen years."

"Missed who?" asked Doyle.

"Katterfelto," the magician replied. "The Prince of Puff, one of the great performers of the age. He doesn't arrive in London until 1782, blast it." He paused and rubbed at his chin in thought. "Then again," he said, his countenance brightening, "there was an influenza epidemic that year too, so I suppose it's not all bad."

"Not all bad!" John exclaimed. "We're in the eighteenth century! And worse, the entire Archipelago is all but destroyed! Are you out of your bloody minds?"

"Calm down, little Caretaker," said Burton. "They've traveled in time more often than you have and adjust more quickly to the novelty of it."

"If we're home," said Rose, "shouldn't there be someone who can help us? Another Caretaker, maybe?"

"Who is the Caretaker in this time?" Jack asked. "I can't recall offhand."

John removed the *Imaginarium Geographica* from Fred's pack and unwrapped it. He turned to the endpapers, where all the Caretakers had inscribed their names, and ran his finger down the list. "It was after the point when they chose to enlist three Caretakers at a time," he said as he read the names, "so it's possible we could meet up with more than one."

He frowned. "Goethe, from what I can tell. But he may still be too young to have been recruited, and he'll be in Germany, not London. And Swift, although he would be at Tamerlane House by this point, having died already."

"William Blake?" Jack suggested, peering over John's shoulder. "I know he later went renegade with some of the others, but he was a Caretaker around this time."

"Not yet," Burton said, ignoring the remark about renegade Caretakers. "He's only about ten years old here. He won't be approached by the Caretakers for another decade, and he won't start painting the portraits for years after that, so Swift is right out too."

"Then who?" asked Jack.

"I can't tell," said John. "There's a gap here. No one is minding the store, so to speak, until Blake comes of age, and then Schubert after him."

At this Houdini, Doyle, and Burton exchanged surreptitious glances, but said nothing.

"Then we're on our own," Burton said as he snapped shut his watch. "Brilliant, young Caretaker."

"You have one of the watches?" Fred exclaimed, as his face wrinkled up in an expression that was a mix of both shock and distaste. "Aren't they s'pposed t' vanish when you become a traitor?"

Jack tried to hush the little badger, but Burton brushed off the implied insult. "It depends on what you've become a traitor to," he said, fingering the watch. "I've always remained true to my own code, and I'm guessing the watch would recognize that—if," he added with a dark smile, "it was one of your cheap Caretaker watches."

"It's not?" Jack said in surprise.

"Of course not," said Burton. "I gave that one back to Dickens ages ago. I got mine from Blake—and it doesn't have any image of a false god on the cover to slow it down."

"Samaranth isn't a god," Jack countered, "and you're still as misguided as ever, Burton. You scorn the wrong things, you're slow to learn, and you see yourself as infallible, even in the face of evidence that proves you aren't."

"You know what they call a person like that?" said Burton. "Caveo Principia."

"I'm nothing like you, Burton," John shot back. "Nothing."

"I'd be disappointed if you were," said Burton.

"Pardon me, gentlemen," Houdini interrupted, "but is this really the best time? People are starting to stare."

"We're just having an argument," Jack retorted. "Why would that be anyone else's business?"

"I'm not saying it is," Houdini said mildly, "but if none of us being dressed like the locals doesn't eventually get someone's attention, the two dozen talking animals and girl with wings will."

"You're right," said John, slapping his forehead. "Of course you're right. We've got to find someplace where we can regroup and get our bearings. It won't do the timeline any good if we end up in jail in eighteenth-century London."

"Speak for yourselves," said Houdini. "At worst, I'll start an entirely new career by escaping."

"What do you want to do, John?" Jack asked.

John pointed to a sign that was attached to the wall above their heads. "The door from the Keep of Time brought us here," he said, drawing a deep breath. "Let's have a look around and see why the Dragons thought this was an important time and place to visit."

The Caretakers explained to the animals of Paralon that they would have to remain in the back of the alley while the humans found a place for them to stay. The animals, being well-educated and mostly librarians at that, readily agreed.

"We lived in secret on Paralon for all these years," Myrret said with understanding. "We can certainly manage to stay hidden in an alley for a few hours."

"Maybe," Jack said, looking around nervously, "but there you were locked in, and almost everyone else was gone."

"Point," said Myrret.

"I can help with this," Houdini said, stepping forward. He licked his thumbs and peered up at the walls that framed the alleyway. Reaching up, he touched his thumbs to points just above his head on both walls, and then repeated the motions on several points farther down. All the while, he was murmuring words in some strange tongue.

"There," he said, straightening his vest. "As long as they stay behind this spot, no one on the street will be inclined to look inside the alley."

Doyle and Jack tested Houdini's claim by stepping out into

the street and turning around. The illusionist was correct—from without, none of the animals or companions were visible.

"That's not an illusion," Burton murmured to Houdini. "That's something real—someone else's magic. And knowledge like that comes with a price."

"I paid it," said Houdini primly. "It's *my* magic."

"That's them taken care of," said John. "What of the rest of us?"

Houdini excused himself for a moment, then disappeared around one of the corners before John could protest. He reappeared only a minute later carrying period clothes for all the men, the two young women, and the little prince.

"We'll be able to move more freely if we look the part," he explained. "Everyone, strip."

The men hung a sheet in the alley so the girls would have a place to change in semiprivacy, while they dressed on the outside.

"Where did you get these, Harry?" John asked as he pulled on a pair of breeches. "More magic?"

"Mmm, probably best not to ask," said Doyle. "Harry has a bit of a 'don't ask, don't tell' policy when it comes to this sort of thing."

"Wonderful," Jack grumbled. "Stolen. What happens if we end up in jail?"

"As I mentioned, I'd be fine," said Houdini as he pulled on a nicely appointed topcoat, "but the rest of you would probably be hard-pressed to find a way out."

"You wouldn't leave us there?" Laura Glue exclaimed from behind the sheet.

"Of course not!" Houdini called back. "I'm sure I'd break you all out—eventually." He smirked at the Caretakers.

"Rose? Laura Glue?" John called out as he and Burton helped

the prince with his shirt. "Are you ready yet, or do you need a few more minutes?"

"They're both dressed," said Fred.

"How did you know?" Laura Glue asked as she pulled back the sheet. "Were you peeking, Fred?"

"Not intentionally," Fred answered, "but you did hang the sheet kind of high, and I'm pretty short."

"So you watched us dress?" Rose asked. "Fred. For shame."

The badger rolled his eyes and made gestures with his hands that said he was embarrassed, but the broad smile on his badger face said otherwise.

"Fred, you scamp," said John. "If you were my son I'd take a switch to you."

"Oh, leave him alone," said Burton. "That's the first thing he's done since I met him that's made me not want to eat him."

"Uh, thanks," said Fred. "I think."

The clothing Houdini had gotten for the young women was innocuous enough and fit them well, but not even the hooded cloak he gave to Rose could cover the fact that she was shadowless. Occasionally her shadow came close enough to look normal, but then it would swing around in the wrong direction, or jump underneath a crate or passing carriage.

"I know it's making you crazy," Jack told her. "Best if you try to ignore it for now. It probably won't go too far, and most people won't notice that it's not playing by Hoyle."

"All right," Rose said, not entirely convinced. "I just hope it doesn't cause any trouble."

"It won't," Jack assured her. "It's still you, Rose. It's only your shadow—it can't do anything real, or harmful, while it's still yours. It's only when you give it up that it starts to stir things up on its own."

"So it's your shadow that makes people do terrible things?" she asked.

"It's more like your conscience," Jack replied. "There's no shadow if there's no light. As long as you are the light, you'll have a shadow. That's why giving it up willingly, as your father, Mordred, did, or"—he swallowed hard—"as I myself once did, is so terrible. You aren't giving up your shadow—you're giving up your light. Do you understand?"

"I think so," she answered, still pensive.

"Good," Jack said as he stepped over to the other Caretakers. "Don't worry, Rose. It's usually the grown-ups who make all the stupid choices, not children. So you ought to be just fine."

Rose didn't respond to his last remark, but instead looked down at her shadow, which was floating underneath her, almost touching her.

Almost.

Archimedes became a one-bird reconnaissance squad, being the only one of the group who could observe and report on where they were without drawing any undue attention.

"I was here once, you know," he said as he landed next to Rose to give his report. "The air was cleaner, but because of the horses, the streets were filled with more—"

"And that's enough of that," said John, clearing his throat. "Decorum, Archie."

"What?" said the bird. "Rose was raised by an old fisherman, and the Valkyrie didn't bathe until she was twelve."

"I'm not worried about them—I'm talking about the boy," said John.

"What boy?"

"Oh no," John said, looking around. "I thought you were watching him, Burton."

"He was here just a moment ago," Burton snapped. "He can't be far."

They started out into the street, when a tall, finely dressed man with an imposing manner and a cane stepped into their path. His dress and markings said that he was the local magistrate—and his cane and tilt of his head said that he was blind.

"If it's a young lad you're looking for," the magistrate said, "you might follow the laughter and the running children." He lifted his walking stick and pointed to the far end of the street, where several boys were indeed streaming past, whooping and hollering.

"You could tell that just by listening?" Houdini asked, honestly curious.

"These old ears still hear very well," the magistrate replied. "I can distinguish among all the children in London, in point of fact."

"Can you now?" John said. He smiled and glanced at Jack, who seemed to be having the same thought. This was a preposterous claim on the magistrate's part, but a harmless one. No point in antagonizing the old fellow.

"I can hear well enough to catch that thought," he said to John, much to the Caretaker's surprise and chagrin, "and to know you are a stranger to London."

"Not a stranger, exactly," John stammered, "but yes, I'm not from around here."

"Hmm," the magistrate sniffed. "Oxford. And . . . a little Yorkshire."

"Impressive," said Jack.

"Hah," replied the magistrate. "You're perceptive, for an Irish."

At this Fred let out a short, sharp laugh—and was immediately silenced by a look from Burton. Rose put her finger to her lips and quietly shook her head, just for good measure.

At the sound of the badger's laugh, the blind magistrate stopped and lifted his head. "What was that?" he asked, turning his head from side to side. "There are no dogs on Craven Street."

Craven Street, John thought. *I thought some of these buildings looked familiar.* "The boy found it over near Trafalgar Square," he said quickly, gesturing apologetically to Fred. "He chased it here, and then we lost him."

"I see," the magistrate said, not sounding wholly convinced. "In any regard, follow the children, and you should find your boy."

"Thank you," said John, as he and the others turned to head down the street. "Good day to you."

"And to you," the magistrate replied.

"That was close," Jack said when they were a safe distance away. "We're going to have to wrap Fred in a scarf or something."

"Why is it always a dog?" Fred complained. "I never have this problem in the Archipelago."

"Just try to keep your head down and don't talk," Jack advised. "It'll be fine."

"He should have stayed with the other animals," said Burton. "We're taking an unnecessary risk bringing him along."

"He's a Caretaker," Jack responded, half-ashamed that he did, in fact, agree with Burton. "He goes with us."

"There," said Doyle, pointing. "The boys are all congregating there."

At the end of the street that ran perpendicular to Craven Street was an open plaza. It was not quite a park, and not quite a broad intersection. There were trees and grass, and a bustling market at which vendors sold geese, and vegetables, and even hot cakes.

In the center, near the trees, a dozen or so boys were flying kites and cheering.

The kites were made in several different styles and were painted in a rainbow of colors. Some of the tails were too long and kept getting caught up in the trees, but others were flying free and high above the rooftops.

One of the boys in particular was having a lot of difficulty getting his kite out of an elm. He pulled at the string as if he'd never held a kite before—which, in point of fact, he hadn't.

"There he is," Jack said, exhaling in relief. "That was a bit of a scare. Let's go get him."

But at that exact moment, a constable appeared on the far side of the park, and he shouted at the boys with the kites.

"Oi! You lot!" he called out harshly. "No kites here! Stop where you are, in the name of the magistrate!"

John thought it was strangely funny that the magistrate knew all about the boys and their kites and didn't seem to care less. But this constable was certainly stirring things up. The boys were scattering in all directions—but several were coming straight toward the companions, with the constable in hot pursuit.

"Quick!" John yelled. "Grab Coal!"

Burton dodged between the fleeing boys and caught the little prince, who was clutching a green kite for all he was worth. "I have him!"

Two more boys plowed into Fred, knocking him sprawling. Rose and Laura Glue immediately jumped in to pull him up.

The constable stopped. "Is this your boy?" he asked Burton sharply. "You ought to know better, my lords."

Jack suddenly forgave Houdini for stealing the clothes. His good taste might have just saved them from a lot of trouble.

"I'll mind the boy's business," Burton said haughtily, "and I'll expect you to mind yours."

The constable flushed, then tipped his hat and ran on after another of the boys.

"Good enough," Jack said. "No harm done."

"Uh-oh," said Fred, who was frantically searching around in his pack. "We've got a problem."

"What's that?" asked John, kneeling. "Are you all right, Fred?"

"I'm fine, but it's gone!" Fred exclaimed, his whiskers atremble with anxiety. "I think one of those boys took it!"

John had a sudden sinking feeling. "Took what, Fred?"

"The *Imaginarium Geographica*!" the little badger cried. "It's gone!"

Magistrate Hawkins made his way down to the other end of Craven Street and found a familiar door. He knocked twice, then again, until a voice from the inside yelled out, "Come in!"

He entered and closed the door behind him, sniffing at the air inside the house as he did so. "Sulfur," he said, more of a statement than a question. "Calling up an evil spirit, or constructing some kind of infernal device?"

"What's the difference?" the occupant replied, his voice cheerful. "Either way, I'm likely to learn something new. What can I do for you, Magistrate?"

"I just thought you ought to know," the magistrate said as he settled into a chair with the familiarity of a frequent guest, "that some very unusual people have just come to Craven Street."

"I know many unusual people," came the reply, "including several on Craven Street. So you are bringing this to my attention, why?"

"Several of them are men who speak with strange accents," the magistrate replied, "and there are two young women, who speak the same. But what makes them really intriguing is the talking dog."

"A talking dog?" came the reply. "Do tell, Magistrate. Do tell."

CHAPTER FIFTEEN
THE RELUCTANT MAPMAKER

— ✳ —

"WHICH BOY WAS it?" Jack asked. "Could you tell?"

"I think it was the taller one," Fred replied. "He had copper-colored hair and a brown vest."

"Almost all of them wore brown vests, you idiot," said Burton.

"Oh," said Fred, crestfallen. "Then I'm not sure."

"I remember him," said Laura Glue. "I'll get the book back, never fear." With that, she turned and took off at a dead run in the direction the constable had gone.

"This is getting out of control," John said miserably. "Archie, follow her and try to keep track of where we are. We'll stay on Craven Street until we hear from you."

"Not a problem," Archimedes said as he launched into the air after the Valkyrie.

"Hey," Jack said, looking around. "Where did Houdini and Doyle go?"

"I'm not their nursemaid," said Burton. "I was watching the boy. Besides, they're grown men. They can look after themselves."

"That's exactly what worries me," said John. "We're about one public disaster away from destroying the entire timeline."

♦   ♦   ♦

There were many reasons why Laura Glue had become the captain of the Valkyries at such a young age. For one, she was raised among the Lost Boys, and thus was a world-class authority at hide-and-seek. She was also the best flyer of her generation and could maneuver herself in ways that other flyers couldn't even fathom doing. But above all, she was captain because she never lost her quarry once she started tracking it. And a thieving boy in eighteenth-century London was not going to be any challenge at all—or was he?

She found him in short order, running about two blocks ahead of her, but when he realized he was being followed, he disappeared.

Twice more she found him, and twice more he lost her—until finally she took to the air and tracked him from above, finally dropping down and cornering him in an alley. It didn't hurt that she had Archie flying above to help her narrow down his possible paths.

"How did you find me?" he gasped, less startled by a flying girl than by the fact that he couldn't lose her. "No man is able to track me when I don't want to be tracked!"

"In case you hadn't noticed," Laura Glue said primly, "I am no man. And I've played hide-and-seek with boys a lot smarter and more skillful than you, so no matter where you went, I'd have found you eventually."

"But it took you no time at all!" he exclaimed. "How is that possible?"

"I have a secret weapon," she said, holding out her arm. There was a flapping of wings, and to the boy's utter astonishment an immense owl landed on her arm and fixed him with an intense glare. If he hadn't known better, he'd have thought the bird was preening at having tracked him so easily.

Laura Glue held out her other hand. "The book, if you please," she said sternly, "or you'll find out what else Archimedes is able to do."

He reluctantly handed over the atlas as Rose, Fred, and the men came running up behind her, having followed Archimedes.

"Bloody hell, girl," Burton huffed as the men caught up to the Valkyrie and her quarry. "You can run, can't you?"

"It helps that she's a tenth of your age, Sir Richard," said John, who was breathing hard himself. "I thought your type didn't get tired."

"We're hardy, healthy, and younger than you," Burton countered, "but we can still get winded."

"You wouldn't be," said Jack, "if you kept yourself in the same kind of shape as your colleagues."

"What are you doing stealing from people anyway?" Laura Glue asked the boy. "It's not polite to steal."

"I didn't damage it at all," said the boy. "I only wanted to look at the maps."

"Argh," John growled. This whole escapade was coming apart at the seams. "How did you know there were maps?"

"When I knocked over the little fellow, it spilled out of his pack, and I saw what it was. I only wanted a look."

"He's damaged it, Scowler Jack," said Fred. "Look, some of the pages have come loose."

"Come loose?" John said. "That's impossible."

Fred handed him several maps, all drawn on thick parchment. They bore a superficial resemblance to those in the *Geographica*, but on touch, John could tell they were different.

"These aren't from the *Geographica*," he said in astonishment. "These are entirely new maps. I've never seen them before in my life!"

"Where did you get these, boy?" Burton exclaimed as he grabbed the youth by the lapels and lifted him off the ground. "Tell us, and tell us truthfully, or I'll cut your tongue from your head."

"I didn't steal them!" the boy exclaimed. "I didn't! I swear by King George I didn't! I just stuck them in the book when you started chasing me!"

"Oh for heaven's sake," said Jack as he pushed Burton aside and smoothed out the boy's collar. "There are better ways to persuade people, Burton."

He held up one of the maps with one hand and grasped the boy's shoulder with the other. He didn't approve of Burton's manner, but he knew a street-sharp boy when he saw one, and he didn't want to go through another chase-and-evade if he could help it.

"These maps you had," Jack said. "We just want to know where you got them." The boy didn't answer, just stared sullenly at Jack and the others.

"If you won't report me to the magistrate," he said finally, "I won't tell anyone about your talking dog."

"I'm not a dog, I'm a badger!" Fred retorted.

"Right," said the boy. "Pull the other one."

"Really," Jack went on. "We're not going to report you for stealing the maps. And no one will believe you about the badger, anyway."

"My master would, and for the last time I *didn't* steal the maps!" the boy retorted. "I *made* them."

✦   ✦   ✦

"What's your name, boy?" asked John.

"Edmund," he replied. "Edmund McGee."

"Who taught you how to make maps like these?"

"My father, but he hates making maps," Edmund explained, "even though that's what our family has done for three generations. When we lived on St. Lucia, in the Caribbee Sea, I was never allowed to touch his maps. I only made these because I'm apprenticed to someone here in London, who teaches me other things in exchange for the maps I make for him."

"But these maps," John said, "don't depict any lands I know, and I know all of them. Where did these come from?"

"I made them up," said Edmund, as if it were the most obvious fact in the world. "In the Old Way."

"Hah," said John. "I haven't heard that in a while."

"What does it mean, the 'Old Way'?" asked Fred.

"It's something the old explorers used to do many ages ago," John explained, kneeling to draw in the dust with his finger. "They'd start out on an expedition with only a vague notion of where they were going. They might have been spurred by some fragment of a myth, or a legend passed village to village, about some enchanted land just beyond the bounds they knew."

He traced a jagged outline of an island in the dust, then added a rough compass, and almost as an afterthought, a sea monster. "You see, they'd make the maps first—then sail out to prove that they existed. And more often than you'd believe, they found something at the end of their journey. Sometimes it was an island in the Archipelago, and sometimes it was Greenland, or Australia."

"So did wishing make it so?" asked Fred.

"Not wishing," John replied. "Believing. They believed, and they found what they were looking for."

"Namers," Rose said suddenly. "Like Mother Night and Mr. Poe mentioned. They were Namers, and they found the places they named."

"That's a remarkable insight," said Jack. "I suspect you're very close to the mark."

"Here," John said as he leaned over again. "Let's see if we can't make this one happen." He wrote "Fred's Isle" under the drawing and stood up. "Perhaps we'll run across it one day."

"Don't forget this," Edmund said as he crouched and added a notation in the dust. "You don't want anyone going there unawares."

John whistled. The boy had added the words *Hic sunt Dracones*—"Here Be Dragons."

Edmund shrugged. "I know that Dragons aren't real," he said matter-of-factly, "but it's bad form not to give people the warning."

"What does your master teach you in exchange for these imaginary maps you make?" asked Jack.

"Lots of things," Edmund said brightly. "Chemistry, and geology, and philosophy. He also invents things like kites, and, well, a lot of other things."

"He sounds like quite a fellow," said John.

"You probably know him," Edmund said, shoulders slumping as he realized he might be getting into trouble after all. "He wears a pocket watch just as you all do."

The Caretakers and Burton all glanced at one another. This might be exactly the stroke of good luck they needed. A watch meant a Caretaker—or did it?

"He can't be," John whispered to the others, "or we'd already know who it is."

"Maybe he's an apprentice we don't have a record of," offered Jack.

"Don't look at me," said Burton. "I haven't a clue who the boy is talking about."

"We'd like to meet your master," John said to Edmund. "Right now."

"He's a scientist, except for when he's a publisher," Edmund said as he led them back toward Craven Street. "Or a historian. Actually, I suppose he's a lot of different things rolled into one."

"And he makes kites," said Jack.

"That too," said Edmund. "Most of the children just call him the Doctor."

He marched the companions to a broad, well-appointed house that was several stories tall. It was in the nicer part of Craven Street, more sparsely populated than where they'd just come from.

"Privacy is good," Jack murmured.

"Doctor Franklin?" Edmund called out at the door. "May I come in?"

"Enter freely, and unafraid," came the response from somewhere in the bowels of the building. "Unless you owe me money—then I hope you'll pardon me while I locate my pistols."

"He's just joking," said Edmund, waving the others inside. "I think."

The companions followed the boy down a narrow corridor and past a staircase to a large room in the back, which was sunlit through an expanse of windows that ran almost floor to ceiling on the north wall. Every other wall was covered edge to edge with art, and newspapers, and maps, and all manner of bric-a-brac.

The room resembled an Aladdin's cave, if the genie had been some combination of Copernicus, Aristotle, Newton, and Hadrian. An immense round table sat in the center of the room. It was claw-footed and was covered with all manner of books and pamphlets in every conceivable language. On one side of the table and spilling onto the floor were small models in clay and metal, the use for which the companions couldn't even begin to guess.

Across the floor and piled on numerous bookshelves were volumes on the sciences, the supernatural, diplomacy, agriculture, history, and several other topics that John thought might get their owner either arrested or burned at the stake were the public aware of them.

Another worktable on the east wall was laden with more papers and scrolls, and several scientific instruments, only a few of which were readily identifiable. But of all the extraordinary paraphernalia that filled the room, those that were most intriguing were the expansive maps tacked along the west wall down to the floor. They were covered with notations that were more metaphysical in appearance than cartological, and seemed to include several hand-drawn corrections. Many were of European regions, based on the topography, but several others were completely unfamiliar to John, the Principal Caretaker of the greatest atlas in the world.

That alone, if for no other reason, made the stout occupant of the room compelling to John—and there were many other reasons to find him compelling. He wore a black skullcap that seemed barely able to contain the explosion of hair that sprouted underneath. He had on a silk dressing gown that was embroidered with numerical symbols and equations, as if he were an alchemist who was unwilling to walk the length of the room without his formulas at his side. The house was old and crumbling at the seams, but this room alone justified its existence—and the owner himself seemed as if he could justify anything by sheer charisma alone. His bearing was one of gravity and sage wisdom; but his face, dusty with plaster and drying powder, bore the liveliness and delighted curiosity of a child.

It's no wonder, John thought as he moved forward and offered his hand in greeting, *that the local children are drawn to this man. I've only just seen him, and already I find myself hoping to talk to him about anything and everything.*

"Greetings, gentle sentients," he said, rising from his chair. "I'm Benjamin Franklin."

One by one, the companions introduced themselves to the Doctor, leaving out the fact that they already knew exactly who he was and what role he'd played in history. John and Jack introduced themselves as Caretakers, although they didn't say what for, and Burton said he was a traveling historian, and Theo his aide-de-camp.

Oddly enough, of all of them, Burton seemed the most impressed on meeting the Doctor, although Franklin paused and blanched when he shook Theo's hand.

He greeted the young women more formally, and looked with rapt interest at Archimedes.

"And you, my fine young fellow," Doctor Franklin said, scratching Fred's head. "You must be the third Caretaker, eh?"

"He's a talking badger," said Edmund, "but I promised not to tell the magistrate."

"You weren't supposed to tell *anyone*," John reminded him, rubbing his temples. "You're a bit of a trial, Edmund."

"I don't mind," said Franklin. "I'm rather fond of talking animals."

"How many do you know?" asked Fred.

"You're the first one," Franklin admitted, "but I'm a good judge of character."

While Edmund showed Burton, Rose, Theo, and Laura Glue around Franklin's study, Jack and John withdrew to a corner to converse privately.

"What do you think?" asked Jack.

John's voice dropped to a conspiratorial whisper. "I'm as impressed as you are, Jack. That's not my concern."

"It's Fred, isn't it?" asked Jack. "Franklin didn't so much as blink that a talking badger showed up in his parlor."

"If that was all it was, I'd be more relieved. What worries me is what he said to Fred about being the third Caretaker. We introduced ourselves as Caretakers—but we never said anything about whether the others may or may not be. So why assume there would be a third at all? And why go right to Fred?"

Jack pursed his lips and frowned. "Those are really good questions."

"Here's something else," John said, handing Jack one of Edmund's maps. "I recognize these."

Jack reacted with surprise. "You've seen them before?"

"Not these exact maps, but this kind of parchment, and the

hand in which the map was drawn," John whispered. "It matches the map that Hank Morgan had made to return to Tamerlane House."

"Remarkable," said Jack. "We need to meet Edmund's father, I think."

"Why so reserved?" Franklin said, interrupting. "So many wonderful things to see here, and you're whispering in a corner."

"Forgive our rudeness," said John. "We didn't mean any—"

"Nonsense," Franklin said, waving his hands. "I've been talking to Burton, and he's told me you have no place to stay. Is that correct?"

"It is," said John. "We've only just arrived in London."

"As it turns out," said Franklin, "I have an entire upper floor that is completely unoccupied. I never use it—I prefer to stay down here, working. If you would consider staying as my guests, I'd be happy to have you."

It didn't take any discussion to decide to accept. "We will," said John. "Thank you, Doctor Franklin."

"Pish-tosh," he replied. "It's my pleasure."

"There's one other thing," said Fred. "How would you like to meet a few more talking animals?"

"Do tell?" said Franklin. "Another badger?"

"Not quite," Fred replied, "but the hedgehogs are pleasant enough."

Franklin laughed. "Really?" he said. "Bring them on, Caretaker Fred."

It took another two hours to move all the animals that had been at Paralon from the alley over to Franklin's house without being seen. But once they were there, John realized that they had found in Benjamin Franklin the ideal host. He was fascinated enough by the creatures to be preoccupied with them for days; and he was an unusual enough character that they believed him when he agreed to keep their confidences.

It was growing dark by the time Jack and John could persuade Edmund to take them to his father's house. As reluctant as he was to take them there, he insisted his father would be even more reluctant to discuss the family trade.

The house of Ernest McGee was at the far end of Craven Street, closer to the tumbledown homes of the ne'er-do-wells and rabble of London. It was probably significant in some way, Jack thought, that there was very little difference between the children at the poorer end of the street and those from the more well-heeled households.

Edmund seemed to be walking slower and slower the closer they got to their destination, and John realized he really was dreading this visit.

They were greeted at the door by the McGees' servant girl, a slim, clean-faced young woman named Lauren, who was not much older than Rose or Laura Glue. It was obvious she was responsible for maintaining the entire household. Ernest greeted them in the drawing room, flashing a brief smile when he saw his son, which was replaced with a scowl when Edmund explained why they wanted to speak with him. It didn't take very long at all for the discussion to turn rancorous and short.

"I don't have the skill my father had, and not even he could keep up with old Elijah," Ernest spat, making no effort to conceal the bitterness in his voice. "What does it matter, anyway? The age of piracy is over. Not even the privateers are called upon any longer, so of what use is a mapmaker to pirates?"

"There are other uses for a mapmaker," Jack said softly, "than to work as an errand boy for pirates."

Ernest wheeled about in a fury, ready to unleash venom in response to the insult—but when he saw Jack's face, he understood. It was not an insult. It was a respectful call to action.

Ernest set his jaw and considered whether to say anything, then turned away. He used a bell to summon Lauren, and when she appeared he murmured a few words to her, then dismissed her. She returned a few minutes later with a tray of tea and cakes. Ernest McGee might not have liked the reason his guests were there, but he was still going to treat them as guests.

"It's been more than two decades since my father died," he said at last when they'd drunk the tea and eaten the cakes, "and almost ten years since I compiled that cursed atlas." He gestured at the workbench near the corner. "The *Pyratlas*, they called it. It was to be a complete assemblage of three generations of McGee family maps, bearing all the secrets of the pirates."

"And yet you forbade your own son from following in your footsteps," said John. "Why is that?"

"I forbade it," Ernest continued, drawing resolve from well-worn arguments, "because mapmaking has already consumed too many decades of my life, and I'll not see it destroy his."

"It didn't destroy your father, or his," Jack replied. "They were the best in the world, according to Edmund."

Ernest responded to the compliment with a half smile, appreciating the effort, even if Jack was exaggerating the truth. "We were silversmiths," he said, shaking his head as if he were recalling another life, or a half-remembered dream. "My grandfather was one of the most renowned in the world in his trade, before he became a mapmaker to pirates. He passed along the craft of silverwork to my father out of a sense of tradition more than anything else, which ended up being arbitrary anyway. My father was the one who fully embraced the family calling, as he referred to it, and we have been nothing but mapmakers ever since. At times I've thought we ought to just throw in entirely and become pirates. It would not have changed our lives overmuch had we done so."

"Forgive my noticing," Jack said, looking around at the well-appointed room, which would have been more in place in a house at the other end of the street, "but being mapmakers to pirates seems to have benefited you rather handsomely."

"You think I'm ungrateful, don't you?" Ernest retorted. "Well, perhaps I am. There has always been enough—more than enough—money for my family to do as we pleased. But I think that would have also been the case had we remained silversmiths. . . ." His voice trailed off as he stood at the window, staring out into the street.

"If only Elijah had never started," Ernest said at last, "if only that pirate, Morgan, had never taught him the craft, our lives might have been very different."

"Morgan?" John and Jack exclaimed together.

"Which Morgan?" asked Jack.

Ernest turned to them in surprise. "I thought you would have known," he said. "The pirate governor, Henry Morgan, was the man who first recruited Elijah to be a mapmaker, and he taught him how to do it besides. Everything that's happened to my family started with him."

CHAPTER SIXTEEN
THE PIRATE'S BIOGRAPHER

THE BEST THING about being a magician, Houdini had decided long ago, was that people believed that magicians could do *anything*. Which, in point of fact, was not too far removed from the truth where he was concerned. No cell could hold him, no locks could bind him. He could not be drowned, or burned, or sliced in two.

He could make anything disappear, given proper preparation, from a mouse to a freight train. And he could dazzle a crowd with nothing but a handful of ordinary household items and his rolled-up shirtsleeves.

He was a showman, no doubt. And his life was the stage. But when he met and befriended Arthur Conan Doyle, another aspect took hold and soon became the force that motivated everything he did.

Sir Arthur believed in an ethereal world of spirit, where magic was commonplace and the dead communicated with the living. Harry believed that magic was the result of skill and hard labor, and that the world of spirit was the realm of tricksters and charlatans. And he never believed in the ability to communicate with the dead until he became dead himself.

Harry had often promised his wife that if there was some means of communicating with her from the great beyond, he would. What she didn't expect was for him to actually turn up at her door, flowers in hand, still young and in his prime, in the company of his dead friend, the writer of detective stories, Sir Arthur Conan Doyle.

She declared him a fake and a fraud and threw him out. For years after, she still dutifully held a séance on his birthday, in the belief that the real Harry would somehow contact her.

Since then, he had thrown himself into his new calling: going about the business of the world, trying to save all of history, partnered with his friend who had embraced this new life to become that which he admired most—a Detective. But as for Harry, dead or alive, he remained what he always had been, a showman.

"What do you think, Arthur?" Houdini asked as they passed Trafalgar Square. "Is this a rational plan of action, or sheer madness?"

"All the best plans are always slightly mad," Doyle replied, "but I think the only way the Caretakers are going to sort this out is if we give them a hand."

Houdini chuckled. "They always underestimated us as Caretakers, and Burton wasn't much better," he said, nicking a couple of apricots from a nearby stand, then paying the vendor with a penny from his own till. "They're good about practical matters, but they just don't have any sense of style. Except maybe for the badger. He shows promise."

"Rose, too," Doyle said, taking one of the apricots, "as long as she is allowed to have her own head about things. She's growing up faster than any of them realize."

"If we don't figure out how to reattach her shadow soon, she may grow up faster than anyone is ready for," Houdini replied.

"Don't I know it," said Doyle.

"Over here, this way," Houdini said, pointing. "There's a street where there are horses and carriages, and it's smoky and noisy. That means blacksmith shops."

"It's as I've always said, Harry," Doyle mused. "These Caretakers lack focus. Always, they lack focus. Oh, a few of them have vision—but they're never going to be able to see anything through while they're stuck in that gallery, or arguing all the time."

"I completely agree," Houdini answered as he finished the apricot. He dropped the pit into the tin cup of a match girl and waved his hand over the cup. A shoot of green sprouted up from the pit, and in a few moments it was a miniature tree, full of leaves and bearing fruit of its own.

"They're so preoccupied with having come through the doorway," he continued, "that they've completely forgotten the most important thing . . .

". . . who it was who came through the door *last*."

The visit with Ernest McGee ended cordially enough, with John and Jack thanking him graciously for his time and trouble, and Ernest agreeing, somewhat reluctantly, to meet with them again. The revelation that Hank Morgan had been Elijah McGee's teacher was too significant not to share with the others—but they did not yet know enough about this family of mapmakers to speak of it openly in front of them.

Lauren saw them to the door, pausing a moment longer than

was needed to say good-bye to Edmund, who was returning with them to Franklin's house.

"I still have some work to do," he explained. "I was supposed to finish earlier, but it was too good a day to waste being indoors, and not flying kites."

At Franklin's door, they found Theo waiting for them outside. He asked to speak with Jack privately, and so John and Edmund went inside, leaving the others to talk.

"I have felt our enemy," Theo said quietly. "The Echthros followed us through the door. It's here, with us, now."

Jack looked around, his hackles rising with panic. "Here? On Craven Street?"

Theo nodded. "I have felt its presence at the edges of my mind since we arrived, but I have only just decided that it was a certainty."

"Is it going to attack us like it did the ship?" Jack asked, scanning the sky above, which was sparsely dotted with clouds. "Or will it attack us more directly?"

"The Echthroi corrupt and subvert," he replied. "This one's goal was to stop us, and at the Frontier that meant stopping the ship. At Paralon it tried to summon its allies. Here I do not yet know what it intends—but we must be alert."

"Could it be the star?" Jack suggested. "Rao? The animals said it had become a Lloigor."

"No," Theo said. "Not the Lloigor from the Archipelago. The Echthros—the same that has followed us all along."

"Should we discuss it with the others?" asked Jack. "Warn them?"

"No, not yet," Theo replied. "The Echthros can take any shape, appear to be anyone. It may have already done so."

"Great," Jack groaned. "So how do I know *you* aren't the Echthroi—Echthros?"

"If I were, you would already be dead."

"If we do discover our enemy, what then?"

"I have a way to control it," Theo replied, "so that we may escape."

"Escape to where? We've been in the Archipelago, and we've gone back in time. Where else can we go?"

The End of Time pondered this. "You are right," he admitted. "We can't hide. So we must be successful, or perish."

The night passed uneventfully, which was a blessing to the companions, who had had more than enough of commotion and chaos in the last few days. Better than just settling in, the animals had proved to be amazingly compatible with Doctor Franklin and had, in a single evening, reorganized his entire library.

"I can't find a single thing!" Franklin said, beaming. "It's glorious."

He was a gracious host and had asked Edmund for the loan of the McGee's maid to help prepare breakfast. The flapjacks went over extremely well with everyone, as did the fresh bread and fruit, but there was a minor diplomatic incident when Lauren lifted the cover on a platter of sliced ham.

The foxes were all for it, but the hedgehogs threw a fit and threatened to have a public protest. It didn't help matters when the ferret started quoting a book on cross-species ethics that had been written by Fred's grandfather.

Eventually everything settled back to a dull roar, and the animals went back to work while the others set about planning their day.

"I'm concerned," John began. "We haven't heard anything from Houdini and Doyle. Perhaps we should have Laura Glue out looking for them."

"Oh please," said Burton. "You're worried about them, but not the effect that might be caused by a flying girl being spotted in London?"

"What else can we do?" asked John.

"Wait," Burton said firmly. "Simply wait. They'll find their way to us."

Jack's eyes narrowed. That was too pat an answer, too assured. "Sir Richard," he said casually, "is there something you're planning that we should know about? After all, they are *your* acolytes."

"I'm here as your ally, Caretaker," Burton replied. "Don't question my motives or take me for a fool."

"All right, enough," John said, standing. "We don't need to be arguing. Houdini and Doyle will just have to look after themselves."

Theo had basically taken up the post of watchman at Franklin's house, which was serving as their de facto headquarters on Craven Street, and Laura Glue was helping him. Fred had been conversing with Franklin on a number of topics and chose to stay. So John, Jack, Burton, Rose, and Archie followed Edmund and Lauren back to Ernest McGee's.

The Caretakers' second reception at the house of Ernest McGee was much warmer than the first. He had been poring over his father's journals and seemed to have found something that changed his outlook on the strange visitors his son had brought to his house. Ernest set Edmund and Lauren to doing other tasks in the house while he opened one diary for his guests.

"Here," he said, showing them a particular passage he'd underlined, "in one of his diaries, from when he was very young. He had been working closely with his two best friends on their *History*, and on the Pyratlas, and he mentions that they were doing it in hopes to become apprentices to someone called a Caretaker."

John and Jack didn't respond to this, but Burton let out a short, sharp bark of a laugh. Rose scowled at him, and Archie simply looked on.

"That's, ah, very interesting," said John. "Why are you showing this to us?"

"Because," Ernest said as he led them upstairs, "I remember once, when I was very young, sneaking into my father's study and seeing the Caretaker. He was a Frenchman with a high-born manner and a very prominent nose. I remember little of what they discussed, but I will never forget," he added as he opened the door to a large room, "that he wore a silver pocket watch, with the picture of a dragon on the case."

"Centuries," John whispered as they followed McGee into the room. "We spend *centuries* trying to keep the secrets of the Archipelago, and when we drop, unannounced, into eighteenth-century London, everyone we meet seems to know about the Caretakers."

"A validation of my arguments," Burton said with a wry smile, "and a preview of your life to come, eh, Jack?"

"I don't even want to think about it," said Jack.

"Excuse me," said a voice from somewhere in the back of the cluttered workshop, "but if you're burglars, as I suspect you must be, then I'd ask that you take me along with you. It's dreadfully boring being in here all the time, and I'd do just about anything for a change of scenery."

"I'm sorry," Ernest said as he cleared away some of the debris that blocked the space between the shelves. "I didn't mean to leave you here so long, Charles."

"I know that voice!" Rose exclaimed. "Archie, don't you? Do you remember?"

Ernest pulled aside a tarpaulin and uncovered a large oil portrait inside an elaborate oval frame.

It was Captain Charles Johnson.

"Hello," Rose said. "It's nice to see you again, Captain Johnson."

"How is it that you know me?" Johnson said, the suspicion in his voice quite clear. "To the best of my recollection, we haven't met."

"We have," said Rose, "or rather, we will. In your future. You may not remember, but I do."

"Ah, the future," said Johnson. "That would explain it. You aren't old enough to have met me in the past, when I was still among the living. Not that I'd remember you anyway, young lady. I was quite the rake, you know. I do like your bird, though."

"Pardon me for saying this," offered Archimedes, "You may not be among the living, but you aren't exactly dead, either."

"I might as well be," Johnson retorted. "I'm stuck in this stupid painting, and even my best friend's son manages to forget I'm here."

"I did say I was sorry," said Ernest.

"What are you doing in here?" asked John.

"I'm a spy, don't you know," said Johnson. "I'm spying on the family McGee for Daniel Defoe."

"Pardon my asking," Jack said, looking at Ernest then back at the portrait, "but isn't part of the point of being a spy that you try to keep it a secret from the people you're spying *on?*"

"Yes," said Johnson, "except that I really, really hate Daniel Defoe."

"That would do it," said Burton.

"The last thing I remember before waking up in this portrait," said Johnson, "was one of my best friends, Daniel Defoe, pointing to something interesting over the side of a ship. One good shove later and I'm condemned to a glorious second life in oil paint."

"He murdered you?" asked John. "Not really a very good best friend."

"Don't I know that," Johnson said glumly. "Anyroad, he told me that if I spied on the McGees for him and tried to discover where the treasures were hidden by watching the maps they made, then he'd make sure I got credit for my book."

"You're speaking of *A General History of the Robberies and Murders of the Most Notorious Pyrates*, aren't you?" said Jack. "Well, I've got some good news and some bad news for you."

"I don't care what the bad news is as long as my name's on it," retorted Johnson. "It's practically the only thing that proves I ever existed."

"Uh-oh," said John.

"Never mind that," Rose said, steering them to another topic. "Can you tell us anything about Henry Morgan?"

"Ah, Morgan," said Johnson. "A gentleman and a pirate, in that order. He was the one who taught Elijah McGee how to make maps, and started this whole family down the pirate road. He never made much noise about his own skills, although he certainly could teach. It's funny." He paused, thinking. "He's the one who pressed Elijah to teach Eliot, and young Ernest here. He said it would take generations for them to be 'good enough,' although I never got to ask him what they needed to be good enough *for*."

"Why not?" asked Rose.

"Because," said Johnson, "after old Elijah gave him the last map he requested, Morgan up and vanished."

"You mean he died?" Burton asked.

"No," said Johnson. "I mean he disappeared, right in front of Elijah. All he left behind were the treasure maps and a note I stuck in my other book, *The Maps of Elijah McGee*. He said that the note was to be given to anyone who came looking for him who wore a silver pocket watch."

"Do you still have the note?" John said excitedly. "Is it still in your book?"

"I haven't the faintest idea," replied Johnson. "I'm afraid I lost it. I haven't seen it, page or cover, in over fifty years."

It took the Magician and the Detective the better part of a day and a night to deduce the answer they were seeking. They bribed, cajoled, and otherwise sweet-talked half of lower London into giving them clues, and finally they found the shop they were looking for—although it was not the one they had expected to find.

A young man, not quite a master, but obviously not merely an apprentice, was sitting in the open door. He was working over a piece of leather on a stool that seemed designed for the purpose. His tongue stuck out from his mouth as he concentrated on the leather.

"Pardon me," Doyle said to the man, "but we're looking for your master."

"He isn't here," the man said without looking up. "Come back tomorrow. It'll be done then."

"What will be done then?" asked Houdini.

"Whatever book it was you ordered," said the man. "It'll be done tomorrow, I swear."

"We're not looking for a book," said Doyle, "just your master. Is he"—he leaned back and looked over the shop—"is he really a bookbinder?"

"My master?" the young man asked, surprised. "Of course he is—the only one-armed bookbinder in London, as a matter of fact."

"A one-armed bookbinder," Houdini said, scowling at Doyle. "Who would have thought?"

"It's not my fault," said Doyle. "The last I knew of him, he was a blacksmith."

"I wouldn't know about that," the man said as he resumed his work, "but if you want to see him, he's in the back room."

Houdini and Doyle walked through the small but clean shop, which was filled with decoratively bound books, sheaves of paper and parchment, and new leather, waiting to be tooled. Toward the rear, with his back to the door, a large, stout man was working with a brush and paint on a large illuminated manuscript.

"He's a good boy, is Roger," the man said without turning around. "Mark me—in a few years Roger Pryce will be known as the greatest bookbinder in Europe."

He turned around on his stool, and Houdini couldn't help but gasp as he saw the arm that ended in a bright, curved hook.

"What can I do for you?" Madoc asked.

Doyle swallowed hard and looked at his friend, who took another step forward.

"Not to put too fine a point on it," said Houdini, "but we've come seeking a Dragon."

"More specifically," Doyle added, "a Dragon's apprentice. And we were hoping you might be able to tell us where we might find him."

Madoc's self-control was such that he didn't immediately react to their question. Instead he silently regarded them for a moment, then turned and strode to the door. He said something to his apprentice, who rose and left. He closed the door, then lifted the heavy crossbar that was leaning next to the frame and dropped it into the brackets.

"Uh, begging your pardon," Doyle asked, tugging at his collar, "but are you hoping to keep someone out, or keep someone in?"

Madoc ignored the question and walked to the cupboard in the corner, where he retrieved a small stoppered bottle. He pondered the bottle for a few minutes, turning it over and over in his hand before finally opening it and shaking a few drops of the liquid inside it onto his other arm, just above his scars.

"I was never much for scented oils," he said slowly, "but my brother favored them in our youth, and he once concocted a mix that was mostly cinnamon. I could always tell when he had been in a room by the lingering scent it left behind."

He turned and looked at them. "It smells of Greece to me, and of happier days."

Houdini and Doyle said nothing. Both were experienced enough showmen to know when someone was speaking in preamble. They waited, and Madoc continued to speak.

"The Dragon's apprentice," he said, voicing the words as if he were rolling them around in his mouth, tasting them. "That's something I never expected to hear spoken of again, not in this lifetime or any other. Especially now that the Dragons are all gone."

"We were told that Samaranth took on an apprentice once, long ago," said Doyle, "and as you are the only person we know in London who was there at the time, we were hoping you might be able to tell us who the apprentice is."

Madoc puffed on the pipe for a while, appraising them.

"Your watches give you away as Caretakers or their ilk," he said finally, "so I'm guessing that they are whom you represent."

"They are," Houdini said with a straight face, only slightly hesitant about the white lie. "*Did* Samaranth have an apprentice?"

"He did," Madoc confirmed. "He had exactly *one* apprentice . . . me."

PART FIVE

THE DRAGON'S
APPRENTICE

CHAPTER SEVENTEEN
NAMERS AND UN-NAMERS

.—✳—.

THE BARD WIPED his brow and set his quill aside. It was done—
or at least, as done as it was likely to be. Tycho Brahe had been
of more help than he'd anticipated, but then, he was the only
one among the Caretakers Emeritis who had been personally
acquainted with Dee while they were still living, and before they
had become Caretakers.

The fact that Brahe was looked down upon by some of the
other Caretakers made his contributions especially sweet.
Hierarchies were troublesome, especially among equals. And if
they were not truly equal, being dead, then what was the use in
trying to be accepted at all?

He shook his head to ward off the thought. That was past,
when his facade was up. Now all the ruses had fled him, and he
was being looked to for a glimmer of hope—even by those who
had mocked him for a simpleton.

But, he reminded himself, that was yesterday. Today the name
of Will Shakespeare might mean something different.

At least, he hoped it would.

"All right," he called out to the others. "I think I've gotten it.
Let's see what we may see."

◆   ◆   ◆

Several of the other Caretakers who had chosen to remain out of their portraits for the vigil clustered around the Bard to view his handiwork. "I've adapted the trump so that we might be able to see what's happening in the Archipelago," Will explained. "I used some of Tycho's calculations and a few of Jules's notes from the Watchmaker to give us a clearer image."

"Will we be able to use it to go through?" Kipling asked. "If so, I'd like to mount a rescue for our friends."

Shakespeare shook his head. "I don't think so. The time differential is too great—that's why we can't see anything through the trump. The passage of night and day is creating a strobing effect that renders the card gray to us. Our side of the card simply can't keep up.

"What I hope I've managed to do is to convert the card to resemble a one-way mirror," Will continued, noting the new symbols he'd etched onto the card. "Instead of a portal that must take both sides into account, it will simply function as a window we can look through."

"Will you be able to convert it back?" Chaucer said with concern in his voice. "These cards are willing scarce."

Will shrugged. "Who's to say? But we can't use it now, so there's no harm in trying."

"Go ahead," said Chaucer, nodding approval to open the card. "Let us see what we can."

Tycho Brahe swallowed hard and gave Shakespeare a thumbs-up. Will rolled his eyes and inhaled deeply, then activated the trump.

The card shuddered slightly; then, to everyone's surprise, the image came into focus.

"Paralon," Verne said. "Well done, Will."

Shakespeare blushed at the compliment but kept his focus on the card. "It seems to be fuzzy at the edges," he said, puzzled. "The structures on the island don't seem quite right."

Verne's shoulders fell as he realized what they were seeing. "The picture's fine," he said tersely. "It's the island itself that is fading."

He was right. The castle, which lay in fractured pieces, the great statues, even the island itself were being eaten away by the passage of time. The edges were indistinct because they were crumbling into dust.

"It's speeding up," Will said. "I'll try to expand it so we can see better."

He touched two of the symbols at diagonal points of the card, and it trembled, then expanded to the size of a large atlas. The detail made the process of decay even more difficult to witness— the principal isle, the seat of the Silver Throne, was falling apart as they watched.

"Look, there!" Chaucer said, pointing to the rear of the island. "What is that shape?"

A dark, shapeless mass was beginning to cover what remained of Paralon. In seconds—centuries in the Archipelago—it had overwhelmed the island and begun spreading across the ocean itself.

Suddenly the card went black. Shakespeare tapped it once, then again. "What's happened?" asked Brahe. "What's wrong? Is it broken?"

"No," Verne said heavily. "I think something just covered the sun."

"The Lloigor," said a voice from up above. Poe was watching

from somewhere in the upper hallways. "The enemy has taken over the Archipelago of Dreams."

"I can't believe he lost it," Jack said as they returned to Franklin's house. "A message from Morgan! It could be invaluable!"

"It could be nothing," Burton said dismissively. "For all we know, it could just be his last will and testament."

"Or instructions on how to make another map, like the one he used to return to Tamerlane House. That could be really useful."

"Because the other one worked so well," Burton sneered. "Thanks, but no. I'd prefer to get back while I'm still in my first century."

"Says the tulpa," Jack retorted. "You'd probably do fine, as would your fellows. It's those of us who are still in our Prime Time that I worry about."

A small figure appeared in the doorway and tugged hesitantly on John's coat. "Master John?" he said quietly. "Master Jack? Do you need any help?"

"Oh, Coal," John said, barely glancing up. "No, we're fine, thanks. Why don't you go play with Myrret?"

"He's busy," Coal answered, "and he didn't need any help either."

"Well, I'm sure there's plenty to read, isn't there, Coal?"

"I suppose so."

"I'm sorry, Coal," Jack said, hustling the boy out of the room. "We have some important grown-up business to conduct."

"So you still think he shouldn't have come?" Burton asked. "Or do you just tend to dismiss children out of hand?"

"There'll be time to deal with Coal later," said John. "For now, we need to speak with Franklin."

✦   ✦   ✦

"A book by Captain Charles Johnson?" Franklin said in bemusement. "He didn't really exist, you know. He was an invention of Edmund's grandfather, Eliot, and his writer friend Crusoe."

"Defoe," Jack corrected. "Have you ever seen such a book? We thought that if anyone would know the whereabouts of such an esoteric book of maps, it would be you."

"You flatter me," said Franklin. "I have one of the finest libraries in London and the best collection of books of maps. You're welcome to avail yourself of it, if it will help."

"Thank you, Doctor," John said. He turned to Rose. "When Edmund gets back from doing his chores at his father's house, will you tell him I'd like to see him? He may be able to help us."

"Can't I help you look for the book?" Rose replied. "I might be able to see something you'd miss."

"We're scholars," said John. "Books are our business. We'll have a better idea of what we're looking for, Rose. But thank you for the offer." He glanced at the door. "Edmund?"

"Of course." Rose nodded. "I'll watch for him outside."

"While you're chasing paper," said Burton, "I'm going to go look for Theo. I haven't seen him today."

"Fine," Jack said as he and John entered the library. "We'll let you know if we discover anything."

John thumbed through a stack of books on Franklin's desk, then handed several to Jack. "Has it ever occurred to you," he said, pondering, "that our presence here, at this particular time, and the disaster in the Archipelago, might be part of the impetus for the Revolutionary War? You know, the way the Winter King spurred the Great War?"

"I can't tell if you think we should get credit or blame if we were responsible," Jack said as he emerged from underneath the desk and took the musty books. "It might have been nice to retain control of the Colonies for a while longer, but then again, without the Americans we wouldn't be winning World War Two either."

"Just think it through," John continued. "Events in the Archipelago mirror those in this world and vice versa. Do you think something is about to happen there that results in the conflict here, or is it the crisis in time that's somehow reverberating backward?"

"If it's going backward, then I'm worried it might reverberate forward, too," said Jack. "Like the ripples in a pond. Anyroad, I don't think the Revolutionary War has as much to do with us as it does a bunch of plantation owners getting their knickers in a twist."

"Probably," said John. "But it can't be coincidence that we're here, with other Caretakers, and in the same basic era that Morgan had jumped to."

"Not coincidence," Jack stated flatly. "We're here because that's where the door opened."

"Yes," John agreed, "but the builders of the keep chose to place the door here for a reason, and I think it's because our coming here has made it one of Verne's zero points."

Jack stopped, mouth agape. "That's a really good argument," he finally said. "I can't believe I hadn't thought of that."

"Funny," said John. "That's just what Charles would—" He swallowed hard. "Sorry. I didn't think."

"I miss him too."

John looked down at the sheaf of maps in his hand, then shoved them back into a drawer. "I think we're done. If the book is here, I can't find it. I'm awful at espionage anyway. We should have asked Fred to do this."

"He wouldn't have fared any better," Jack replied. "And is it really espionage when you have permission?"

"I don't think we really know what we're looking for anyway," said John as he opened the door. "And I don't think we should underestimate Fred."

"Point taken," said Jack. "Shall we go find some dinner?"

"Sounds good to me," said John as the door closed behind them. "Lay on, Macduff."

Rose went to wait for Edmund, but she couldn't shake the feeling that that was all she was able to do—wait. She hadn't slept well, having nightmares about the dark thing on Paralon, and she felt that she was of little help with the Caretakers' efforts here in London. So far, the most important thing she had done was not make things worse—which wasn't really helping at all.

Then again, she thought as she absentmindedly played foot tag with her shadow, *the Caretakers never really ask for my help, or my opinion. Not really. To them I still seem to be a child.*

Without Rose, the Shadow King would not have been defeated. Without Rose, Arthur would not have been saved. When there was a crisis, and she was the solution, they listened, because they had no choice—and that felt really good to her. To be the hero who saved the day. Perhaps it was selfish, but in a small way, she understood that was why she was frustrated—she wanted them to listen to her, to help, so that she could save them all again. *Maybe,* she thought, *that's why heroes do the things they do, anyway.*

She had been out on the street for only a little while when she saw Edmund coming across the cobblestones. She started to raise her hand in greeting when he suddenly turned left into an alley at the end of the block.

She started walking in that direction when she saw Lauren, who had been following Edmund from some distance behind him. Rose crossed the street behind a wagon, so as not to be seen, and then moved to the opposite corner where the alley was in full view.

Edmund was at the far end of the alley . . .

. . . with Laura Glue.

They were simply talking, nothing more. But it was obvious by the efforts they'd made to meet in private that they wanted to keep their meeting a secret. They were partially successful.

Closer to the street, Lauren was also watching, and it was obvious that she was feeling heartache over Edmund's interest in Laura Glue. Rose decided she should speak to the girl, but she didn't want the others to know they'd been seen. She moved farther down the street before crossing, so that she could approach Lauren quietly.

At that moment several horsemen rode by, stirring up dirt and muck, and when they had passed, Lauren was nowhere to be seen. The girl had vanished.

"Lose someone, dearie?" a voice croaked from behind her. "Or something?"

It was an old beggar woman. She smiled at Rose with a faintly frightening snaggletoothed grin.

"Hello, Moonchild," the old woman said. "You have come to another crossroads, I think—else I would not have been drawn to you here."

Rose looked the woman up and down and only barely concealed the expression of distaste that was rising on her face. The woman was a beggar, or possible an escapee from a sanitarium, or both. She was humpbacked and seemed to be missing several teeth. She smelled awful, and her clothing was an assorted mishmash of rags, discarded blouses, and skirts, which she had layered with no particular finesse, and a collection of belts and necklaces that would have outfitted the entire British navy. She wore boots and carried a tattered umbrella.

"Been having bad dreams, have we, dearie?" the old woman asked. "Would you like to tell Auntie Dawn about them? You might feel better if you do."

"Did Mother Night send you?" Rose asked, looking around warily. Her shadow was nowhere to be seen, and she wished she had thought to bring Archimedes with her.

She needn't have worried—no one else on the street seemed to take any notice of her and the old woman at all. "I'm here for you and you alone, dearie," she said, almost as if she were confirming what Rose had been wondering. "No one else will give us a come hither or go thither. I've come to speak to you about your gift."

Suddenly Rose was overcome with feelings of shame and guilt. She had left the glowing ball of string in her room at Tamerlane House. With everything else that had happened after Mother Night's visitation, she had completely forgotten about it.

"No, dearie," Auntie Dawn replied, answering her thoughts, "you didn't forget it."

On impulse, Rose stuck her hand in her pocket and pulled out Ariadne's Thread.

"We gave it to you," Auntie Dawn said, "and you accepted it.

That can't be taken back, and it can't be left behind. It's yours now."

The way she said it was meant to be reassuring, Rose thought, but then why was the strange woman's face so sad when she said it?

"If I'm at a crossroads," Rose said, "what direction am I supposed to take?"

"You're about to discover the reason you are here," said Auntie Dawn. "To move forward, you must look behind. To gain something, you must sacrifice it. Nothing worth having comes without a price. And you needn't have nightmares, not if you don't want to."

Her head spun. What did all this mean? "I have nightmares," she said, addressing the last point honestly, "because the dark thing terrifies me."

"The only reason it's in your nightmares," Auntie Dawn said with a wink, "is because *it* is more terrified of *you*. Remember that, Rose. You have more power than you believe. You simply have to make the decision to act—and then see what follows."

"Rose?" said Laura Glue, hastily dropping Edmund's hand from her own. "Who are you talking to?"

"Who?" Rose answered. "I'm just . . ." She turned, but no one was there. Auntie Dawn had vanished. "No one, I guess. You're needed back at the Doctor's," she said to Edmund.

"We're heading over there now," he said. "We'll walk with you."

When the trio arrived at the house, they found there were other guests who had just come in the door—Harry Houdini and Arthur Conan Doyle. The two men were alternately greeting and being grilled by the rest of the companions.

"How did you know we were at Franklin's?" asked Jack. "We had no way to communicate with you after you went on your little stroll."

"It wasn't hard to deduce," Doyle said with the pride of a Detective who'd detected well. "You couldn't go far with all the animals in tow, which limited you to Craven Street or the surrounding neighborhoods. On Craven Street, there are two notorious residents—one an eminent scientist and philosopher, and the other a reclusive mapmaker. The odds were you'd be at one of those two homes, and Doctor Franklin is the one who's better positioned to help you as a resource of knowledge and connections, while still being in close proximity to the mapmaker's house."

"Good Lord!" John exclaimed. "That's brilliant!"

"Elementary, my dear Caretaker," said Doyle with a slight bow.

"Oh for heaven's sake," Houdini said. "We came back here because this is where we started, and then we just followed the trail of Leprechaun cracker crumbs between the two houses. The blind magistrate told us who lived in them."

"Ulp. Sorry about the mess," Fred said, pocketing the bag of crackers he was munching from.

"The magistrate would be Sir John," Franklin said. "Very little of what happens on Craven Street escapes his ears."

Houdini leaned close to Jack. "Should we be talking in front of him? Oath of secrecy and all that?"

"For one thing, to hear you asking about the Caretaker's oath of secrecy is the funniest thing I've heard all day," said Jack, "and for another, there are two dozen talking animals in his library right now, arranging his books according to smell. So we're a bit past worrying about whether he can keep a secret."

"I can," Franklin assured them. "Make yourselves at home," he told the two newcomers as he disappeared into his study. "Everyone else has."

John poked a finger into Doyle's chest. "Where did you go?" he demanded. "We were very concerned."

"That's good to hear," said Doyle.

"He means, we were worried about the kind of trouble you might cause," said Jack.

"Oh," said Houdini. "Honestly, I can't say I blame you. But we didn't get into any trouble—we may have just saved the day, so to speak. You need to come with us. There's someone you need to meet."

"Can I come?" Coal said, running into the room. "Please?"

John started to answer, but Burton walked through the door and interrupted him. "Yes," he replied, looking at John. "You can come. Where are these two idiots taking us, anyway?"

"You'll see," Houdini said, scowling. "We've been working to all our good, Sir Richard. What have you been doing?"

"Looking for the End of Time," he said, "but I haven't found him yet. So we may as well go for a walk." He put his hand on Coal's shoulder.

"The others, too," said Doyle. "Laura Glue, and Rose, and Archie, and Fred. We should all go. Except the animals," he added. "We are going to be walking a fair distance and don't want to attract too much attention."

"Can Edmund go too?" Laura Glue asked, blushing slightly.

"Edmund?" asked Doyle, looking at the young man who was standing between Rose and the Valkyrie. "Have we picked up a stray?"

"He's the mapmaker's son," Jack said, "and a better than fair mapmaker himself. We'll tell you about it on the way."

"Where are we going, anyway?" said John warily. "Who are you taking us to meet?"

"The person we came here to find in the first place," Houdini said as the group marched out the door. "We're taking you to meet the Dragon's apprentice."

CHAPTER EIGHTEEN
THE HEIR

-—✸-—

THE MEETING AT the bookbinder's shop was full of old history. Almost everyone in the room had been connected to Madoc in one way or another, for good and for ill. Of them all, only Edmund and Coal saw nothing but a one-armed bookbinder, who was large and still in the prime of his life, and who simply wished to be left alone to do his work.

To Fred and Laura Glue, he was the man out of legend, the mythical Winter King, whose Shadow had returned again and again to wreak havoc on their world.

To Burton, Houdini, and Doyle, he was the martyred brother of Merlin, the betrayer, who prevented Madoc from becoming the ruler of two worlds, united in peace.

The last time John and Jack had seen him, he was plummeting over the edge of a waterfall, having tried his level best to kill them.

And the last time Rose and Archie had met him, which was the first time she had ever seen her father in the flesh, he helped them repair the sword of Aeneas, so they could defeat his own Shadow-self and save the Archipelago and the Summer Country from a devastating war.

The Caretakers and their motley entourage filled the small

shop, where they sat with Madoc, who kept his distance from all of them except for one.

"Rose," he said quietly, extending his good arm. "Come to me."

She walked to her father and wrapped her arms around him. He embraced her, then stood back, indicating that she should sit on the stool next to him.

He looked her up and down, appraising her, and then his eyes narrowed and his expression grew dark. "Rose," he said slowly. "Where is your shadow?"

Rose blushed furiously, embarrassed. "It—it's outside, under a bench, I think. It should be coming in soon."

He leaned back, looking from her to the Caretakers. "So. You didn't give it up, then? It's still yours?"

"Oh no!" Rose exclaimed. "I mean, yes. It's still mine. There was an accident, and it came loose. But it's still mine."

Madoc nodded, and his expression softened. "I was not chastising you, daughter," he said. "It's not my place, not after all that I have done. But I was just . . . I was . . ."

"I understand," Rose said, laying her hand on his.

Madoc looked up at the others. "I agreed to this meeting in order to see my daughter again," he said brusquely. "She kept her word to me, and because of her, I have a new life. But I don't see any reason why I should speak to the rest of you."

Burton's face colored, and he turned away, chagrined.

"We are here because we were told to seek your help, Madoc." Jack spoke the last word with deliberate emphasis. He had once been swayed by this man's magnetism, and the promises he offered for power and influence in the world. He was wary about speaking with him again, however good the reason.

Madoc turned his eyes to Jack, and they glittered as he spoke. "Yes, Jack, so I'm told. You need the help of a Dragon. But as I told your two associates, there simply aren't any left."

"No Dragons, perhaps," said John, "but you were Samaranth's apprentice, were you not?"

Madoc bowed his head. "I was. A poor one, I'm afraid."

"Are all the Dragons really gone?" Rose asked. "We have come back in time, after all."

Madoc rubbed his chin and thought a moment. "It seems I have seen some, now and again. But not for some time."

"They would have been captured and taken back through the same door we used," said Jack, "so if there was a Dragon here, it would have been taken by the Shadow King."

"How long have you been here?" Rose asked her father.

"Nearly two years," he answered, "although if you used the same door, you should have followed right on my heels."

"There is a discontinuity," said John. "A rift in time. That's why we've come here, Madoc."

The bookbinder sighed. "All right," he said, looking at Rose. "Tell me what's happened."

Between Rose's accounting of her visit from Mother Night, and the others' mishmash retelling of the events since the party at Tamerlane House, it was almost two hours before Madoc spoke again.

"I don't know enough about cartography to help you with mapping time," he said when they had finished. "That became my dear brother's specialty. But I know why you were told to seek out a Dragon to solve your riddle.

"Samaranth told me there were certain things that could only be known as a Dragon," he continued, "things that I could not know as a man. He promised me that if I ever chose to . . . If I ever became a Dragon, then I would understand.

"It was the Dragons, did you know?" he said to no one in particular. "The Dragons who made the doors for the Keep of Time. So I'd imagine that only a Dragon would be able to tell you how to harness those energies again. If," he added, "it can be done at all."

"If that's true, then why didn't Samaranth just tell us himself, or leave us instructions?" asked John. "Why force us to go searching for you?"

"Either his idea of a joke, or my final lesson as his apprentice," Madoc said darkly, "and as I told you, I was a very poor student."

"Or because he simply chose not to," Jack said, "given what the Watchmaker said."

Madoc shrugged. "He moves in mysterious ways. But you probably know that better than I."

"You said you had seen other Dragons," Doyle said hopefully. "Maybe it's one of them we're meant to find. What kind did you see?"

"Dragonships, mostly," said Madoc, "but none I knew too well. The last one I saw had the look of a sea serpent. A long neck, which rose high into the air. Sleek. It moved through the harbor and disappeared. But I have no doubt it was a Dragonship."

"Which one?" John asked. "What color was it?"

"Color?" said Madoc. "If I had to call it anything, I'd say it was green."

"The *Green Dragon* then?" asked Rose.

"No," John said, shaking his head. "The *Green Dragon* is mostly blue. If the one Madoc saw was green, then it was quite possibly the *Violet Dragon*."

"Dragonships, maybe," said John, "but no other Dragons, then."

Madoc got up from his stool and moved to the window. He could see the Thames from there, and smell the tang of moisture in the air when the wind blew east.

"There were Dragons younger than Samaranth who had taken apprentices," he said at length, not turning from the window, "but they had taken no new apprentices in almost five thousand years. I think the last was during the Bronze Age, well before my time. Even so, I was not taken in as a student by Samaranth until I was quite old myself, chronologically speaking."

Archimedes nodded and squawked in agreement. "It was right around the time of the tournament, I believe."

"It was," Madoc acknowledged, returning the nod. "But you weren't there. How did you know?"

The bird shrugged. "I read things. I keep up."

"Hah!" Madoc laughed. "Of course you would. Anyway, it was after I left in a fury. I felt angry, betrayed. And Samaranth saw this, and decided to do something about it. So he approached me and made the proverbial offer you can't refuse."

"What does that mean?" asked Doyle.

"It's an old expression, coined by people conquered by Attila the Hun," explained Archimedes. "Basically, every time he approached a new country, he did it in the spirit of friendship, cooperation, and civilized, mutual progress."

"Really?" said Doyle. "How did that go over?"

"If his overtures were rejected, he'd basically order his armies to behead everyone until they changed their minds. It got a lot easier to offer his friendship to countries after he had a few of those under his belt."

"An offer they can't refuse," Doyle repeated. "So Samaranth threatened to behead you?"

"Not in so many words," Madoc replied, "but he made it clear that he thought I needed his guidance, and that were I to decline, the consequences would be drastic."

"We've had some experience with that ourselves," said Houdini.

"And the riddle?" asked Rose. "It doesn't mean anything to you?"

"It means one thing to a man," Madoc said, echoing his earlier remarks, "and another to a Dragon. To give you the answers you're seeking, I would have to . . ."

"Ascend?" said Jack.

"Call it what you like," said Madoc, "but I refuse to do it. Not for any reason. I am finally a whole man again—I will not give that up to become a Dragon."

"You were willing to sacrifice yourself once for a great cause," Rose said. "I know. I was there."

"I could never be that selfless," Madoc said, his voice subdued. "Not . . . again, at any rate.

"Once in my life, all that I sought was entry back into the Summer Country. But I chose poorly, in so many things, and eventually the reasons I wanted that so badly were forgotten. Only the idea of the prize remained. And then, when I lost it, and everything else, I started to remember. Then, miraculously, I was given a second chance—and I took it. And now, now that I truly understand what I have, I'm hard-pressed to ever give it up again."

Burton stepped forward. "I understand. Everything I have

done, everything I have sacrificed," he said, spreading his hands in supplication, "has been in your service, Lord Madoc."

Madoc looked at Burton, blinking impassively, then belched loudly enough to rattle the tools on the wall. "You chose your deity poorly then," he finally said, drawing out the words for emphasis. "I'm merely a bookbinder here, and a one-armed one at that. I'm no one to be worshipped."

"You were, once," Burton said, unwilling to drop his arguments, "and you could be again. I know. We are very much alike, you and I."

"We," said Madoc, "have very little in common."

"More than you think," Burton replied, as he pulled open the curtain. Through the rear window they could see into the courtyard, where Coal and Laura Glue were watching Edmund draw in the dirt with a stick. "That one, there," Burton said, indicating Coal. "That's our common link, Lor—Madoc. He is your nephew many generations removed, the heir to the Silver Throne, and my own descendant."

Madoc started, then peered more closely at the pastoral scene outside before turning around. He shook his head. "I've not had too much luck coming to the defense of my nephews," he said, holding up his hook. "I can count on one hand the number of times that choice turned out to be terribly wrong.

"Take it from one who knows," Madoc went on. "Your life will be what you make of it, and you draw to yourself that which you truly believe in. I've stopped searching for things that only cause me grief and pain. You ought to do the same."

"Twice I've been drawn to *you*," Rose said. "You helped us before. Will you please, please consider it again?"

He looked at his daughter's eyes—they were innocent, trusting. Hopeful. Then a movement at her feet distracted him. It was her shadow, shimmering, writhing, moving from darkness to darkness inside the shop. He could barely suppress the shudder that came over him, and the memories that came with it.

"It—It's too big, my dove," he said. Rose almost smiled—he'd never used an endearment with her before. "This is my final word. I have finally found a life that I . . . love. A work that gives me pleasure. And a peace I have never known. I have paid my debts, and more. So I want nothing more to do with the Archipelago, or the Caretakers, or any of it. I wash my hands of the whole thing."

With that, Madoc stood and walked out of the bindery. He did not look back.

Franklin's library was a treasure-house of knowledge, and even more crammed with books, maps, papers, and scrolls than his office downstairs had been. The windows were shuttered, so that the sunlight didn't fade the bindings on the books or the ink on the maps, and every other wall was covered with shelves that were full to spilling over with more books. The room had become much more organized since Myrret and the other animals had arrived—but the effect they had was to make the library more like the only other one they had ever known.

It was possibly the only place Coal could have been in all of London that felt like the Warren where he was raised back in the palace at Paralon. After the little escapade with the kite, John had given Myrret strict instructions to keep an eye on him—which, since the fox could not really leave Franklin's house, meant the little prince could not either. So to him, the jaunt to visit the mysterious bookbinder had been all too short.

"That was either a brilliant command performance," Houdini said as he slumped into a chaise in the library, "or we've just been dismissed as completely irrelevant."

"The latter, I'm afraid," said Doyle. "He's not going to be any help to us whatsoever."

Burton hadn't spoken for the entire walk back to Craven Street. Back at Franklin's house, he simply sat in a corner of the library, glowering.

"Would you like to read me a story now?" Coal asked, not really directing the question at anyone. "I've been very good, and I waited to ask."

"We've been giving you short shrift, haven't we, lad?" Houdini said as he knelt and tousled the boy's hair. "That's the way it is with grown-ups sometimes. We become too focused on the things that are urgent, so we forget the things that are truly important."

"We'll have time for that later, Coal," said Jack.

"I'm not surprised that he wouldn't help us," John said as he sat next to Burton. "All things considered, we're part of the reason he's had such a struggle all these years. We did play our part, however well-intentioned our motives were."

"He didn't seem too impressed by any of us, don't you agree, Burton?" asked Jack.

"He is," Burton said, then paused as his expression darkened, ". . . not the man I was expecting."

"This will sort itself out, Burton," John said as he laid a supportive hand on the other man's shoulder. "It will."

Burton glared at him and roughly pushed off John's hand. "When I need comfort from the likes of you, little Caretaker," he growled, "I'll ask. But don't count on that ever happening."

"So," said Houdini, diplomatically trying to change the subject, "Hank Morgan really trained Edmund's great-grandfather in mapmaking?"

"Nice to see you've been paying attention," said Doyle.

"I've been paying attention!" Houdini snapped. "I'm a marvel at paying attention."

"Except," put in Doyle, "when you're preoccupied by a trick you can't figure out."

"I haven't been preoccupied!" the Magician retorted. "Not entirely, anyway. It is possible to think of two things at once, you know."

"So your pretending to pay attention is just an illusion."

"I'm a magician, not an illusionist," said Houdini. "There's a difference. But then, you knew that."

Coal looked bewildered. "What is the difference?"

"An illusionist shows people what they want to see," Houdini said, smiling down at the boy, "and convinces them it's real, even if they know how the trick is done. A magician does things that are real, and seem to be miraculous. The second is far, far more work, by the way."

"I disagree with your assessment of illusionists," said Doyle.

"Was my life on Paralon an illusion, or magic?" asked Coal.

Houdini paused, not certain how to answer. Doyle stepped in and took the boy by the shoulder. "Let's just say that your life was an illusion until now, and everything that comes after will be magic, if you want it to be."

"That is such a load of horse manure," said Burton. "Why not tell the boy the truth? That everything worth having in life comes at a price. All that's left for you to decide is whether or not you're willing to pay it."

"It's always worth it," said Jack.

"Really?" asked Burton. "Do you think your friend Charles would agree?"

Jack didn't answer, but simply turned and strode from the room. After a silent moment, John followed him.

"I don't even know why the Caretakers Emeritis permitted him to come," Jack said in frustration as they climbed the stairs to the sleeping room and opened the door. "Houdini is not a bad sort—a bit irritating at times—and as far as I'm concerned, Doyle should have been a Caretaker all along. But I don't know why we need Burton at all."

"He is a Namer," said a voice from the corner of the room. In a smooth, fluid motion, Theo stood up from where he'd been reading and placed the book facedown on one of the beds.

"What were you doing on the floor?" John asked. "We've got plenty of beds."

"I find I am more comfortable on the floor," Theo replied. "It is how I have slept more nights than not."

"Look, Theo," Jack began.

"He is a Namer," Theo repeated. "Burton is fond of declaring himself to be a Barbarian, but he is a most educated man. His temper and impatience have caused him grief in his life, and closed doors that might otherwise have been opened. But he may yet become a champion of the Light, if we allow him to be."

"Allow?" said Jack. "I don't think anyone can stop him if he sets his mind to something."

"He can stop himself," said Theo. "The darker side of his own nature, which all of us share—as you know well, Jack."

"Yes," Jack harrumphed. "I do. But Burton's a different case."

"Not so different from you or me," Theo replied. "Not so different from Madoc."

"Are you saying that he is the way he is because someone wronged him?" asked John. "How do we fix that?"

"Do exactly as you are doing," said Theo. "Help him. Shape him. But do not disregard him. His choice is yet to be made, and you can still tip the balance."

The other men left the library soon after, arguing about magic boxes and reluctant Dragons, so none of them really noticed that they were leaving the little prince all alone. Again.

The door opened. And closed. Someone had entered the room.

Coal looked up, and his face broke into a wide grin when he saw the visitor. Someone familiar. Someone comfortable. Someone safe.

"It's a shame," the visitor said, "that you're left here alone while everyone else has all the fun."

"I don't mind," Coal answered. "I like to read. And they have many important things to do."

"I don't mind either," his visitor said. "It gives us more time together, and we've had some good fun, you and I, haven't we?"

The boy nodded, smiling happily. Then he stopped and frowned, curious.

"Why is it," he asked, "that you have no shadow?"

"Sometimes I do, and sometimes I don't," his visitor said. "I shall have one here if you like."

"No," the boy said, thinking of the dark thing on Paralon. He shivered. "I like you just as you are," he said, "and I'm glad we found this house."

Edmund had an errand to run for Doctor Franklin, and so he didn't go back with the Caretakers, but detoured to an outdoor market. Laura Glue, to everyone's surprise except for Rose, chose to go with him.

The men were mostly preoccupied with discussing the ramifications of Madoc's refusal, and so Rose and Archimedes continued down Craven Street past Franklin's house to the house of Ernest McGee.

"I'm sorry," Lauren said as she opened the door, "but Master McGee isn't in right now."

"I didn't come to see him," Rose answered. "I came to see you."

"Me?" the maid answered in surprise. "But why?"

"You love him, don't you?" Rose asked as the girl ushered her and Archie into the house. "Edmund."

Lauren snapped her head around, startled by the frankness of the question. At first she blushed furiously and twisted her apron in her hands, but then Rose's open and honest expression told her that there was no ulterior motive for the question. She really wanted to know.

"I—I do," Lauren answered, nodding. "I always have, I think. My mother and father served Master Elijah, and so as young children, it was natural that his grandson and I played together. But Master Ernest didn't approve. As he saw it, I was just being brought up as the next generation of Bonneville servants to the house of McGee."

"I see," said Rose. "And he wasn't happy about the prospect of his son courting a servant girl?"

Again, the blush rose in Lauren's cheeks. "Oh no! Nothing like that!" she exclaimed. "I mean, we never courted. Edmund doesn't . . ." She paused and looked around for anyone who might be eavesdropping, but the only other one in the room was Archie, who was busy plucking at a pinfeather in the far corner. "He—he doesn't know, mistress. At least, I don't think he does. How I feel about him, I mean. There was never a courtship to it."

"That's really quite a shame," a pleasant, cultured voice said from behind them, "for I do so look forward to meeting new generations of McGees."

Rose turned around and gasped.

Daniel Defoe stood in the doorway of the mapmaker's house, eating an apple.

"Well met," he said with a practiced air of indifference. "I'm guessing you are from the Archipelago," he said to Rose, "as I haven't seen any other mechanical owls in this part of the world—or anywhere else, for that matter."

He dropped the half-eaten apple on the floor, then locked the door behind him. "Let's have a little talk, shall we, ladies?"

CHAPTER NINETEEN
THE MAPS OF ELIJAH MCGEE

— ✳ —

"ACTUALLY, I'M FROM *this* world, you twit," Archie huffed. "You must be one of the stupider Caretakers."

"Archimedes!" Rose sputtered, grabbing at the bird. "Mind your tongue."

The bird looked at her strangely for a moment, then went silent when he realized what she was thinking. Defoe had been the great betrayer in the war against the Shadow King. He had not only turned his back on the Caretakers, but had tried to use the Spear of Destiny to become the King of the World himself. And while those events were yet to occur, this was still the same man. Still a traitor, who had murdered one of his best friends. And still someone who could be very dangerous, if they gave him any information he might use.

"You're wiser than the bird is," said Defoe, "although wisdom doesn't help much when you're caught in a mire."

"It does if you're wise enough to avoid it in the first place," said Rose.

Defoe smiled, and it seemed warm, but there was a calculating darkness behind it. "As I said, wise. But in the mire is in the mire . . . So what, pray tell, are denizens of the Archipelago doing in London? Especially at the home of Ernest McGee?"

Rose held her tongue, as did Archie, and surprisingly, Lauren.

"I see," said Defoe. "I don't intend to cause you any harm, you know. I shan't bite."

"Maybe not now," Rose felt herself saying, "but someday you will."

"So," said Defoe, "you distrust me not for who I am, or what I've done, but because of what I have yet to do? That's a pretty judgmental attitude from a girl . . .

". . . without a *shadow*."

His voice dropped to a near whisper with the last words, but they all heard it clearly. He had seen, and he knew what it meant to be without a shadow.

For her part, Lauren reacted with mild surprise to this. She probably had noticed Rose's elusive shadow, but that was the sort of thing servants weren't supposed to notice—or if they did, they weren't supposed to mention it.

"It's not what you're thinking," Rose said, stumbling for the words. "I haven't given it up, I've just . . . misplaced it."

"I haven't made any judgment about you at all," Defoe said, "except maybe that you aren't where you're supposed to be—but now I think maybe you're exactly where you're supposed to be."

"What do you mean?" asked Rose, drawing back protectively in front of Lauren.

"Nothing happens by coincidence," Defoe said. "If you'll come upstairs with me, I think I can explain it to you more clearly. Of course," he added, gesturing at the door, "if you decide otherwise, you are of course free to leave."

"Great," said Archie. "We're leaving."

"No," said Rose. "I think I'd like to hear him out."

"You don't—," Archie began.

"Don't tell me I don't understand!" Rose said, her temper flaring. "This is my choice, Archimedes."

"All right, then," said Defoe. "Let's all go upstairs, if you please."

The door to the upper room swung open with a loud squeal as the two young women and the owl entered, followed by Defoe.

"It's about time someone came back up here," Captain Johnson said primly. "I've gotten very bored, you know."

"Well then," said Defoe, "we'll have to see if we can't liven things up a bit."

"Oh, shades," said Johnson.

"Remember what Captain Johnson warned," Archimedes whispered. "We can't trust him. We shouldn't trust him."

"Wait, Archie," Rose said. "I really do want to hear what he has to say. I don't think he intends to harm us."

"Clever girl," Defoe said, "and you're quite right. In fact, it's just the opposite. I want to ask for your help."

"He's lying," said the captain. "Don't listen to him!"

Before Rose could respond, a patch of darkness darted through the great round window at the end of the room and covered the portrait. The effect was the same as if a wool blanket had been cast over it—Captain Johnson's speech was almost completely muffled, and he could no longer see the others in the room.

"A good use of your shadow, my dear," said Defoe. "I wish I'd thought of that."

"But," Lauren said, feeling brave enough to venture an opinion, "you still have *your* shadow."

"Indeed I do," Defoe said, looking down. "That alone should tell you something about my intentions."

Rose looked questioningly at Archie. This was unexpected. If Defoe was truly the evil man they expected, then why would he still have his shadow?

"All right," Rose said tentatively, "we can talk to you, if you like. What is it you wanted me to help you with?"

Defoe smiled. "I was hoping you'd ask that."

"This is a mistake," said Archie. "We should leave, Rose."

"Lauren?" Rose asked. "What do you think?"

Lauren blinked. She'd very seldom been asked her opinion— and never as a peer. "I . . . I think I could stay, just for a little while."

"Excellent," Defoe said, rubbing his hands together. "So we've just the one dissenter—but we can find someplace to put you out of the way, I think. Come here, bird."

Archimedes snapped out his wings and flew into the Caretaker's face, then wheeled about and flew to the far side of the room. In an explosion of feathers and metal, the great owl burst through the round window at the end of the room and out into the street.

"Well played, bird," Defoe murmured. He turned to the young women. "He might have been useful, but it's you and your shadow that I think I needed," he said. "Now the clock is ticking. And our time . . .

". . . is quickly running out."

Benjamin Franklin sat watching in fascination as Fred simultaneously recited stanzas from the *Iliad* and ate Leprechaun crackers.

"What?" Fred asked, his mouth full of crackers. "Did I do something wrong?"

"Oh no," Franklin said quickly. "I was just wondering how it's done. The talking, that is."

Fred frowned. "I'm not sure what you mean," he said warily. "This is because I'm a badger, isn't it?"

Franklin smiled disarmingly and held up his hands. "I mean you no disrespect, young Caretaker," he said jovially. "But you must understand, in my extensive experience, animals do not converse with humans. In any language. So having this particular group of houseguests has been quite an education."

"Maybe the animals you know didn't have much to say," said Fred. "Or they got a glimpse of your head wear and decided to keep their mouths closed." He tipped his head and indicated the raccoon fur cap hanging on the coatrack in the corner.

Franklin blew out a puff of air and chuckled. "I can't say I blame them. If it helps, that was a gift, not something I acquired myself."

"It really doesn't," said Fred, "but I appreciate the gesture."

"Who taught you how to speak, ah, English?"

Fred puffed out his chest slightly. "My father, Charles Mongolfier Hargreaves-Heald," he said proudly, "otherwise known as Uncas, squire to Don Quixote."

"You don't say?" Franklin replied. "Interesting. You know, I really hadn't expected to find you to be such a fascinating conversationalist. But it's the way you say things that's so intriguing."

"Well, there are some allowances made for the differences in our mouths," said Fred. "An animal's jaw is so much more adaptable to long vowel sounds, for example. But that's for spoken language. It's a lot easier than learning to read and write was, I can tell you that. So many of the words you use aren't spelled the way they ought to be."

"How do you mean?"

"For example," Fred started, warming up to his topic, "several letters in your alphabet are completely redundant. C, and *q*, and *w*, *a*, *x*, and *y* . . . a couple more, besides. You really don't need them, not if you want a word to look like it sounds."

"That's fascinating!" Franklin exclaimed. "To be frank, my friend Noah Webster and I have discussed something very similar."

"Then you get where I'm coming from," said Fred. "Also, if you made up a few combined consonants, like the 'ch' in 'chew,' you'd save a lot of time and trouble. It's not that the words are bad—just the rules about how they're spelled."

"Impressive," Franklin said in all seriousness. "Despite your short stature, may I compliment you on your thinking?"

"Thanks," answered Fred. "Despite your immense girth, may I compliment you on your civility?"

"Uh, ah," Franklin stammered. "Thank you."

Edmund and Laura Glue arrived with a box full of vegetables for the next evening's meal, and something else—Ernest McGee.

He stood hesitantly in the doorway, looking around at the interior of Franklin's house as if he was about to be pinched for some petty crime.

"It's all right, Father," Edmund said soothingly. "I'm his apprentice, remember? I'm allowed to have guests."

"I've never been here before," said Ernest. "I wanted to speak to the Doctor, and . . ." He paused. "Thank him."

Edmund beamed. "We can arrange that," he said. "Laura Glue? Would you see if the Doctor is about?"

While the Valkyrie went to look for Franklin, Edmund took

his father into the study, where a spirited discussion was taking place.

"I can't help thinking that the key we're missing is in Morgan's message," John was saying. "If only Captain Johnson hadn't lost his book . . ."

Edmund perked up at this. "Which book?"

Jack waved his hand dismissively. "It's not important now. He lost it decades before you were even born."

"You mean *The Maps of Elijah McGee?*" Edmund asked. "That book?"

John's jaw fell open. "How did you know?"

Edmund shrugged. "There were only ever three books that he worked on with my grandfather and Mr. Defoe," he replied. "The *History*, the *Pyratlas*, and the last one."

"Which does us no good if we don't know where it is."

"But we do," said Edmund. "*I* have it."

Every man in the room suddenly took on the same shocked expression. "You do?" exclaimed his father. "Since when?"

"Since I was a boy, and started making the maps," said Edmund. "When you made your, um, opinion clear, I started hiding them— and that book, the one Captain Johnson started compiling, was the best of our family's work. So I kept it, and have been adding to it ever since."

"Ah, me," his father said sadly. "I have done you a disservice, my boy. But we'll say our piece later—for now, let's see the book, hey?"

As Edmund went up to his attic workroom to fetch the book, Ernest took a seat among the Caretakers.

"He's a talented boy, you know," said John. "But then, it does run in the family."

"The talent, or curse, depending on which of us you ask and when, skipped a generation or two, I think," said Ernest. "Oh, I have the facility for it, as had my father. But neither of us has the innate skill that Elijah had. My son Edmund has it too. I'm more of a compiler, after the manner of my father," he continued. "We were always more interested in collecting them than we were in making them."

"It was good of you to let him apprentice to Franklin," said Jack.

"I didn't approve," said Ernest. "I'm still not sure I do. But I'm not a fool, either," he added as his son came downstairs to the study carrying a large book. "McGee maps are McGee maps, after all, and I'm loath to let the family legacy end just because I don't like it."

Edmund set *The Maps of Elijah McGee* in the center of the table and spread it open. It was not even a book yet, per se, but more a collection of notes written by Johnson, and maps, drawn on the same thick paper that Edmund had been carrying when they first met him.

"Do you know what these are?" Jack exclaimed excitedly. "These are maps to some of the places that Verne mentioned! To the places where imaginary lands never separated from the Summer Country!"

"You mean, like the Soft Places?" asked Fred. "Like the Inn of the Flying Dragon?"

"Not quite," Jack replied as he riffled through the pages. "More like places that found their own niches in our world and never pulled away when the Frontier was created."

"Pardon my asking, but did that badger just *speak?*" Ernest asked.

"Oh, that's just Fred," said Edmund. "Wait'll you go upstairs to meet the new librarians."

"Aha!" Jack exclaimed. "It's here!"

As Johnson had said, there was indeed a note from Morgan, tucked away in the pages of his book.

> To whoever finds this note:
>
> It was no accident. It was no malfunction. But for whatever reason, my watch will not work. I was kept here, in this time, through no will of my own. Someone is playing a deeper game and has learned how to manipulate time—someone better than the Messengers. Better than Verne. Possibly even better than Poe. Somehow I must reach you in the future—but the key to the past is hidden here, in the pages of this book. Find it. Use it. As for me, my friend Elijah and I are going to try to create a chronal map, which I hope to use to return to Tamerlane House. If it works, then we'll have a good laugh over this. If not, I hope you'll fare better than I. If Houdini is the one who finds this note, then I can only pray it remains intact.
>
> God be with you,
>
> Captain Henry Morgan, Lt. Governor, Jamaica

"Oh, now that's just a low blow," said Houdini.

"Intriguing," John said. "He believes that someone kept him here—someone better at time travel than he was."

"It's logical," said Doyle. "He was the one most likely to take the Cartographer's place, and according to the Watchmaker, that's what we needed."

"Whoever did this to him never expected that he might train someone else," said John, "or that he would stumble across a family like the McGees."

"I don't think it was accidental," said Houdini. "Not with what I've seen. Morgan chose Elijah McGee. Carefully, and with intent."

"I actually wish he were still here," said Jack. "I think it would be comforting, somehow, just to have him around."

"It's too bad he's dead, then," spat Burton. "The dead are useless, unless they're Caretakers, or we've run out of supplies."

"Do you remember reading anything about the McGees in the Histories?" John asked Jack. "Anything at all?"

"I can't recall," Jack said, thinking. "Those were more Charles's passion, not mine. Why do you ask?"

"I can't remember anything much about them either," said John, "nor can I remember any mention of them in anything having to do with the Cartographer. But just look at these, Jack! Can you imagine a family of this talent not coming to the attention of the Caretakers? Or the Cartographer?"

Burton clucked his tongue. "Maybe they just *did*."

"What's that supposed to mean?" asked John.

"I've had more experience in time than you have, young Caretaker. Just because something you think is important hasn't happened in the past doesn't mean it will not still happen in your own future. Even if that future takes you to the past."

"Every time he talks about this sort of thing, my head aches," said Jack.

"No, he's right," said John. "Time moves in both directions, isn't that what you said?"

"At the Eagle and Child, yes," Burton said with grudging admiration. "Maybe you aren't a waste of time, after all. And yes," he added, smirking at Jack, "the pun was intended."

"Oh, I got it," said Jack. "I just didn't think it was funny."

"What I'm thinking," John said, "is that the McGee family may in fact be Fictions, like Hank and Melville. That would explain why we haven't seen anything of them in the Histories before."

"When they met past the waterfall at the Edge of the World," he continued, "Captain Johnson told Rose that he and Defoe were training as possible apprentices to Cyrano de Bergerac, and that de Bergerac had his eye on Eliot as a possible apprentice to Merlin."

"The Caretakers don't document apprenticeships unless they become full Caretakers," said Jack, "no offense, Burton. And I don't think anyone but Verne knew of actual apprentices to the Cartographer."

"He never said that Eliot was a formal apprentice," said John, "just that de Bergerac thought he had a good hand for mapmaking."

"That's a good eye for talent," said Jack. "De Bergerac was one of the Cartographer's apprentices himself, remember?"

"There's another possibility," Doyle said. He paced the floor pensively, rubbing his chin in thought. "We've gone about this backward," he said slowly, "assuming that the McGees didn't come to the attention of the Caretakers, or were somehow overlooked. But what if they weren't?"

"What do you mean?" Jack asked.

"There are two possibilities," said Doyle. "One, that they were never meant to be mapmakers until Morgan came here to teach them, and so the Caretakers never knew about them in our time."

"Mmm, no," said Jack. "De Bergerac knew of them, remember? And he was also a skilled cartographer. He might have started training them even without Morgan."

"A possible paradox, then," said Doyle. "But it's the second possibility that's more troubling—that the current Caretaker *does* know about them and is trying to suppress them. Maybe even destroy them."

"Except there doesn't seem to be a Caretaker here now," said Jack. "There's a gap, unless it's Franklin—but surely he'd have mentioned it."

"There's no gap," Burton said with an almost regretful sigh. "Perhaps Verne wasn't brave enough to tell you the truth of it. Having three Caretakers at once was a safeguard, and kept the flames of prophecy fanned—but you three were the latecoming exception to the norm. There were not always three Caretakers available, not all at once. Sometimes there were two, and more rarely, one.

"There is a current Caretaker, but he's a tulpa, one of the first John Dee created after himself, and that fact extended his tenure for a very long time—well before making tulpas fell out of favor with the Caretakers Emeritis. It was before Blake began creating portraits, and well before Poe began traveling to the past, so the records of his tenure could be manipulated. So," he said again, "there's no gap. You just haven't figured it out yet, because the fact that he *was* a tulpa was kept a secret from all the rest later."

"He's correct," John said as he examined the list in the *Geographica.* "Swift was the last Caretaker in this era until he was

replaced by Blake, and Goethe is the current living Caretaker—
but he isn't one, not yet. That leaves only one name on our list."

"Oh fewmets," Jack said under his breath. "Really?"

"I'm afraid so," said John. "The Caretaker can only be Daniel
Defoe."

No one at the Doctor's house noticed when the End of Time
slipped silently out the door, just as no one had noticed the
Shadow leaving earlier.

The Shadow moved quickly and was difficult to track. But
the End of Time had tracked beasts in impossible terrains, and
London was no challenge. The End of Time leaped over the
chimney tops of the houses that ran perpendicular to Craven
Street as he followed it, until finally it was cornered and could
flee no more.

"You are not meant to be here, in this time, and in this place,"
Theo said calmly.

"I'm impressed," the Echthros said just as calmly. "There are
very few among your kind who are able to sense my presence, let
alone track me—especially when I don't want to be tracked."

"But track you I have," Theo said quietly as he removed a small
parchment from his pocket, "and now I will do what I must, and
bind you, and cast you out."

The Echthros laughed, a chilling sound that reverberated off
the walls in the narrow alley. "Go ahead and try," it said. "In fact,
I insist that you do."

A flickering of fear danced across Theo's usually placid features, but he unfolded the paper and then began to read. His eyes
grew milky and a faint shimmering appeared around him as he

softly, carefully recited the ancient words of power. When he had finished, he looked up at his enemy.

"All done?" the Echthros responded, seemingly bored. "Is that all you've got? Or did you have something else you'd like to try?"

Theo's eyes grew wide with alarm. The creature should have been bound. This was one of the oldest of the Old Magics, and it had never, never failed.

"That's the thing about the Old Magic," the Echthros said as it moved closer to the End of Time. "It is reliable. It operates according to rules and laws, and those may be bent, but never broken. Especially when it comes to things like Bindings."

"I don't understand," Theo said, bewildered. "I spoke your name—your true name. You should be bound."

"I am bound," the Echthros replied, as it began to shimmer and change, growing larger and darker and less distinct. "I was already bound, and cannot be bound again by the same curse until the first is broken. So you see," it concluded, now huge and towering over the man, "I am bound, but you are not my master!"

With a shrieking sound that shattered windows and a rending of flesh with massive claws, the Echthros fell upon the End of Time. There was no screaming, just dying, which irritated the creature somewhat. But for the moment, its secret was safe.

Changing back to its original shape, the Echthros walked away from the still steaming body and made its way back into the crowd, where no one saw it pass, nor would have stopped it if they had.

CHAPTER TWENTY
THE FALSE CARETAKER

--- ✳ ---

IT TOOK A while for Laura Glue to track down Doctor Franklin, but the second time she looked there, she finally found him on the upper floor, discoursing with Myrret about Arthurian history. He was reluctant to leave, until she told him who his visitor was.

"The fox has some very unusual takes on history," Franklin said as they descended the stairs, "but I think he's got his dates confused. He seems to be off by a millennium or two."

"Foxes make great librarians," said Laura Glue, "but they're not so good at math."

"Mr. McGee," said Franklin, offering his hand.

"Doctor Franklin," said Ernest, taking it. "I'm pleased to finally meet you."

"What's all this?" Franklin asked as he looked over the spread of papers on the table.

Briefly Edmund explained about the book and what he'd been doing with it.

"How fascinating!" Franklin exclaimed. "You know, Edmund, I've got some similar writings and drawings in an old book of mine I keep in my desk. You might call it my own apprenticeship. I'll have to show it to you sometime. I think you'll find it very enlightening."

"I'd love to see it," Edmund said, as a look of interest flashed among the Caretakers. A book like this one? One that Franklin had not yet shown to Edmund? And more importantly, that he referred to as his own apprenticeship?

At that moment John noticed that a shadow had followed Laura Glue and the Doctor down from the rooms upstairs. The boy Coal was holding a kite. He suddenly had an idea.

"Doctor Franklin," John said amicably, "I'd promised Coal that we'd go out flying kites, but I forgot that we were meeting with Ernest. You wouldn't have some free time, would you?"

"Actually, I do," said Franklin. "I was thinking of going over to Trafalgar Square myself to try out a new kite design. I'm sure the young man wouldn't mind helping me, would you?" He looked down at the boy, who nodded enthusiastically.

Jack started to protest that it wouldn't be necessary, that they could look after the boy well enough, but John's tap on his hand stopped him. John nodded almost imperceptibly, then to Franklin he said, "That will be fine. Thank you, Doctor Franklin."

"What was that all about?" Jack asked as the Doctor left with the little prince, two kites in hand. "With all our suspicions, are you sure it's safe to leave the boy alone with him?"

"What's he going to do, really?" asked John. "Benjamin Franklin isn't exactly going to harm a child in broad daylight. Besides, it's to follow up on our suspicions that I agreed."

"I hadn't realized you expected me," Ernest said, confused. "We had a meeting?"

"We're having it now," John said as he headed up the stairs.

"Harry can pick any lock, and we've got a good hour before they're back to look around unmolested. And I want to see that book."

The others laughed and trotted to catch up to the Principal Caretaker. "When you wrote about the little burglar in your book," Jack said, "I didn't realize you were writing from experience."

"Not experience," said John as they entered Franklin's private study. "Just unfulfilled ambitions."

"Do you like the kite, Coal?" Doctor Franklin asked as he led the boy into ever more crowded streets. "I made it just for you."

The boy nodded happily, clutching the brightly colored kite to his chest as the tail trailed along behind them. "It's very nice, thank you."

"What a polite young man," Franklin said, mussing the boy's hair. "I'm very glad we've gotten to be friends. We'll have some good fun, you and I, won't we? I was meaning to ask," he added, "where is it you come from, Coal?"

"I—I'm not supposed to speak of it," Coal stammered, looking suddenly very worried. Laura Glue and the Caretakers had given him very strict instructions not to talk about where he was from with strangers—but Doctor Franklin was not really a stranger, was he? After all, they had let him go to fly kites with the Doctor, and they had been staying at his house. If he could not be trusted, then who could?

"Perhaps you could tell me about it as a story," Franklin suggested. "You like stories, don't you, Coal? Like the ones in my library?"

"Oh yes!" the boy responded. "I love to read."

"Well, then," Franklin said as they located a suitable place from which to launch the kite. "Why don't I tell you a story about myself, and then you can tell me stories about yourself. Is it a bargain?"

Coal murmured in agreement as he untangled the kite's tail from his legs. "It is. A bargain."

"Excellent!" said Franklin as they tossed the kite into the wind. "I'll start. I came here from a land far, far away, called America. Where did you come from?"

"Once upon a time," Coal began, oblivious to the intense scrutiny being fixed on him by the Doctor, "I came here from a land far, far away. It was called Paralon."

The Caretakers were so intent on getting a look at Franklin's mysterious book that they didn't notice Edmund and Laura Glue slip away and out the back door. They ran through a maze of alleys and ended up at an old barn that was mostly used to store grain. It was spacious, and best of all, private.

"They were going to go look at the Doctor's book," Laura Glue said as they climbed up to sit on a high crossbeam. "Didn't you want to see his secret maps?"

"I draw maps all the time," said Edmund, "and when I'm not drawing them, I'm reading about them. I spend most of my life buried in maps. And I do love them—but I want to do other things too, and spend time with . . ." He blushed. "Well, do other things. Otherwise, I'd be no better off than if I was an old hermit, stuck in a tower, doing nothing but drawing maps. And what kind of a way to live is that?"

Smoothly, he leaned in to kiss her, and she shied away. "You don't kiss boys where you come from?"

"It's never really come up," Laura Glue said matter-of-factly. "There were always kissing games when we were children—girls chasing the boys, and all that—but the point of it was that the girls chased the boys, who didn't want to be kissed."

"Didn't they?" asked Edmund with a lopsided grin. "Weren't the boys faster than you were?"

"Mostly," Laura Glue admitted, "except for maybe Abby Tornado. She could outrun everyone."

"Mmm-hmm. But somehow you always managed to catch them, didn't you?"

Laura Glue's brow furrowed, then her eyes widened. "I never really thought of that. I suppose they must have wanted to be caught."

"That's my point," Edmund said as he moved closer. "Boys liked kissing as much as the girls did. They were just too young to admit it."

Laura Glue sighed. "We shouldn't, you know. Not because I don't want to, but . . ." She hesitated. "I may be going away soon. To a place a long . . . a long ways away. A place it would be impossible to visit."

"All the more reason to spend as much time with you as I possibly can," said Edmund. "Besides, sometimes things don't go as we plan them to. I wouldn't mind if you had to stay here."

"I wouldn't either."

She unhooked the harness that held her wings and let them drop to the barn floor below, then moved closer to Edmund until their knees touched.

"Aren't you afraid you'll fall?" asked Edmund, peering down at the wings.

"I'm sure if I do, you'll do your best to hold on to me," Laura Glue said, her voice barely a whisper.

"And if I fall?"

"Then I'll catch you," she said, and then she leaned in and kissed him. Neither of them ran away.

It took Harry only a few seconds to open the lock on Franklin's desk, which was disappointing to Fred, who was ready to jimmy it with an awl.

"It doesn't hurt to have a backup plan," said the badger.

"He's quite a smart fellow for a badger, isn't he?" asked Ernest.

"You don't know the half of it," said Jack as Houdini handed him the book.

"That book," Fred said wonderingly. "It's almost like the Little Whatsit. Almost exactly like it, 'cept maybe a little older."

"Yes," said John. "Strange. It's very like the Little Whatsit."

"Not the Little Whatsit," said Jack. "One of the Histories. Just look at it!"

Jack held it up and pointed to the cover. He was right—it was identical to one of the Caretakers' Histories.

"I'm right, aren't I?" asked Jack.

"I'm afraid you are," John said, gritting his teeth in frustration. "It's the only explanation that fits. He *is* an apprentice of Daniel Defoe."

Just then there was a knock at the front door. Fred peered out the window. "It's that blind magistrate," he said.

"Uh-oh," said John. "I'd better go see what he wants."

◆　◆　◆

If the body of the End of Time had lain in any other district in that part of London, it might have been discovered sooner. As it was, his body had already gone cold and rigid when the match girl found him. She told the potato vendor at the corner, who told one of the newly commissioned police force, who, in an effort to demonstrate his worth to his employer, told the magistrate. And it was he who realized who the victim was, and who needed to be told about the murder.

It was a good day for flying kites. Warm and overcast, the cloud-filtered sunlight cast no shadows. And so the boy was unafraid when he was led away from the park by his friend who had no shadow at all.

On days such as this, the trees ate many kites—and so no one questioned, or even noticed, when two kites were left unattended, to flutter in the breeze.

Under the circumstance, Jack felt compelled to tell his companions about the private discussions he had been having with Theo since the crossing of the Frontier.

"He wanted to wait to say anything," Jack explained, "until he'd gotten a better handle on what our enemy might be planning. I trusted him entirely."

"As you should have!" Burton roared. "I'll not have you talking about him like he was some laggardly half-wit. It would have taken someone—something—truly inhuman to have killed him like this."

Burton's words were brash and full of anger, but more than one of the companions noticed that as he paced back and forth his hands were trembling.

"You said Theo told you the Echthros had followed us through the door," said Doyle. "Do you think it's possible . . . I mean, the boy—"

"No!" Burton roared. He grabbed Doyle and threw him roughly to the floor.

"It's worth considering," said Houdini as he helped his companion back to his feet. "If you were not so upset, you'd see that, Richard. And the End of Time would say the same if he were here."

Burton stared at them, breathing hard, his eyes crazy with rage. But then the mood passed as he slowly realized the wisdom of Houdini's words. It was true—if it had been Theo speaking, he'd have at least considered the possibility. The boy, Coal, might be the very Echthros they were fighting against.

"Theo said that he had a way to control it," said Jack, "and I think I know what that way is." He reached into his pocket and pulled out a bloodstained piece of paper. "The magistrate said that Theo had this in his hand. They had to pry his fingers open to get it loose. It's a Binding. An Old Magic Binding."

Burton stared. "Why would the End of Time have such a thing?"

"Never mind why," said John. "How would he be able to speak it and make it work? I didn't think it was possible for just anyone to speak a Binding."

"It must have been possible," Jack replied, "or else he wouldn't have meant to try it. Poe did send him with us, after all. And as one of Verne's Messengers, he certainly would have known what it was."

"Not that it did him a lot of good," said Doyle. "Either it didn't work, or he didn't have time to speak it. Which means that the Echthros either caught him unawares . . ."

"Impossible," said Burton.

"Or," Doyle went on, "it appeared to him as someone he trusted and would not think to question."

"It may not be the boy," said John. "There's another possibility, remember?"

"That's almost as bad," said Burton. "If it is Defoe, then it's my fault the End of Time is dead, because I'm the one who recruited him to the Society."

"There's one way to find out," Doyle said, taking the paper from Jack. "We can bind him ourselves, and we'll ask."

"We can't," said John. "If we interfere with Defoe too much here, we'll risk derailing everything we've already accomplished back in 1945."

"And what do we do about Coal?" said John. "It's an unanswered question. What if he is our enemy?"

"Maybe *he's* the Fiction," Jack suggested. "He's certainly unique, given where he came from. He might not be an Echthros—he might just be a cypher. Something that shouldn't exist, but does."

None of them saw the shadowy figure that had been listening outside the cracked door, and none of them saw it leave. But it had heard everything it had to hear to know what it needed to do next.

PART SIX

"ALL OF ETERNITY
IN A SPECK OF DUST"

CHAPTER TWENTY-ONE
THE SUMMER KING

THE BOOKBINDER SAT in darkness, watching the dying light of the embers in his fireplace as he removed the hook from the stump of his arm. He rubbed at it gently, as if it was still raw, even though it had healed over long before.

Twice in his exceedingly long life he had been an apprentice—once to his brother, whom he had believed to be wiser than he, and once to a Dragon, who actually was. The first time, he was betrayed—and the second, he was the betrayer. Samaranth had never been anything but patient with him, showing faith and fortitude as he tried to teach the young man called Madoc how to make his way in the world.

But somehow he changed. The betrayals of his brother, and his nephew, Arthur, and especially the woman he loved, Gwynhfar, had taken their toll, and Madoc became Mordred, and all he knew was anger, and hatred.

But through all the years from that time to this, one thing still haunted him: Arthur's belief that Madoc was still Madoc, and that he was a good man.

The Dragon, Samaranth, had believed in him too. As had Gwynhfar. And in the end, it was he who had walked away from them, determined never to look back.

It was he who had killed Arthur once, and then again, for the final time. And he who cast aside the mother of his child, and rejected all that Samaranth had offered to him.

You are strong enough to bear this, Arthur had said to him once. But that was before Mordred had become the Winter King—before he surrendered his Shadow, and made his choice about what kind of man he would be.

He never expected a second chance to live his life, free and unfettered by the choices of the past; but it seemed the past had come calling for him, and once more he had to make a choice. All that remained for him was to decide who would do the choosing. . . .

Madoc, or Mordred?

None of the humans in Doctor Franklin's house had ears sharp enough to hear it, especially while they were having a vigorous discussion. But the badger's ears were sharp, and he would have heard the sound right away, even if the mechanical owl hadn't been calling him by name.

At Fred's urging, the companions raced to the front door, where they found a bruised and battered Archimedes, dragging one wing behind him.

"I had to bust through a window to get here," the bird exclaimed, seeming nearly exhausted, "and methinks I have a screw loose. No jokes, please."

"What's happened, Archie?" John asked as he picked up the injured bird. "Fred, go find some tools."

"Trouble, right here on Craven Street," Archie replied as Fred ran to the shop. "Daniel Defoe—he's here, in London!"

"We know that, Archie," said Jack. "We just figured it out ourselves."

"No!" the bird exclaimed, growing more frantic by the second. "You don't understand! He's got Rose at the McGees' house!"

"Defoe is at my house?" Ernest said, frowning. "I have to get back there."

"We're all going," said John. "I think a lot of our questions are about to be answered."

His wing repaired, Archie flew ahead to keep an eye on the McGee house while the companions ran along below him. At the corner, they nearly collided with Edmund and Laura Glue.

"What's happened?" Laura Glue asked when she saw the alarm etched on all their faces.

"No time to explain," John said without slowing. "Come with us!"

Edmund and Laura Glue fell into step behind the Caretakers. "We've got to leave him be," John was saying in a tone that said he'd brook no resistance. "I'm pulling rank here, Jack. I mean it. Don't touch Defoe."

"I'll do my best," Jack replied, "but if he's hurt Rose, no promises."

"Are you up for a fight?" Doyle asked. "He was our ally once, you know."

"That was then, this is now," Houdini responded with a distracted expression. "We'll do what we have to do."

"Good enough," said Doyle, peering down the darkening street. "And if we find that—" He stopped and looked at his companion, frowning. "I don't bloody believe it. You're thinking about that cursed box again, aren't you?"

Houdini started to protest, then sighed in resignation. "I can't help it, Arthur," he said, shrugging. "It eats at me. There was no displacement of air, and no evidence of kinetic energy expended. . . ."

Doyle closed his eyes and thumped his forehead with his fist. "The. Box. Is. GONE," he said through clenched teeth. "Will you just drop it already?"

"Shut up, you idiots," said Burton. "Look—there he is."

The companions turned the corner just as Defoe was exiting the house, carrying something with a sheet draped over it. He started when he saw them, then took a menacing stance. They stopped on the other side of the street, unsure of what to do, while Archimedes circled overhead. It was a standoff.

"You have your business and I have mine," Defoe said, just loud enough for them to hear. "I don't know what denizens of the Archipelago are doing in London, but this need not go in a bad direction for any of us."

"He thinks we're from the Archipelago," Jack whispered. "He doesn't have any idea who we are!"

"We're running around with a badger and a mechanical owl," said Houdini. "It's not a bad guess."

Burton took a step forward. "I know you, Caretaker," he called out. "We can discuss this amicably."

Defoe's eyes narrowed. "You know *nothing* about me."

"In point of fact," Burton said, eyes glittering, "I know you died in 1731, and I know that you're only here now through the good graces of John Dee."

That took the stuffing out of him. Defoe suddenly looked more confused than menacing.

"My name is Burton," he continued, "and I can give you access to the treasures you seek."

"Is he insane?" asked Jack. "We can't barter with Daniel Defoe!"

"All right. Perhaps we can do some business, Burton," Defoe said. "Let us talk of this further."

"Excellent," Burton replied. "But first, where is the girl?"

Defoe paused. "She's upstairs. She has her own role to play tonight—which is more than you ever allowed her to do."

"You dung heap!" Ernest shouted as he suddenly flew across the street. "You'll pay for what you've done to my family!"

"Drat!" John exclaimed. "Grab him! Quick!"

Before Ernest could reach Defoe, Doyle and Houdini caught him by the arms and held him fast. "You don't know!" Ernest bellowed. "You don't know what he's done!"

"I'm a Caretaker," Defoe exclaimed, his temper rising, "and I'll do as I please, boy!"

"You're evil, is what you are!" said Fred. "Even if you still have your shadow!"

"Hah!" Defoe said, smirking. "Maybe. But it isn't *my* shadow."

"Defoe, listen to me," John began, trying to contain the situation. "We've no wish to hurt you."

"I'm immortal!" Defoe proclaimed. "What can you possibly do that can hurt me?"

Fred's well-aimed muffin struck Defoe squarely between the eyes. He was unconscious before he hit the street. The parcel fell out of his hands, and the sheet dropped away from the portrait of Charles Johnson.

"Sorry," Fred said to John. "He was giving me a headache with all that hot air."

"Help me!" Johnson called out. "I'm being abducted! And oppressed!"

"And now the other shoe drops," said Burton, pointing away. "Look, John!"

Behind them, coming around the opposite corner past the park, Franklin and Coal were running toward Defoe. They hadn't yet seen the Caretakers, but Franklin had a firm grip on the boy, who was obviously terrified.

"Not on my watch," Jack murmured. "Doyle? Harry?" The men nodded, and as one they took off at a run, tackling Franklin as he rounded the corner. He fell roughly to the ground under the three men's assault, and the boy went sprawling into the grass.

By the time the others ran over, Jack had Franklin pinned to the ground.

"We know who you are, and we know what you are!" Jack said, his voice shrill with anger. "We're done being played by you!"

"Played?" Franklin exclaimed with genuine surprise. In an instant, his face turned stern. "You have completely misunderstood me, Jack," he said in a clear, direct tone they had never heard from him before. "Coal and I were flying kites in the square, and something led him away. I was more than an hour finding him again."

"What have we misunderstood?" said John. "We found the History, Doctor. We know you're an apprentice Caretaker to Daniel Defoe."

"Oh, do you now?" Franklin said, eyes flashing. "And what, pray tell, is your proof of this? The fact that I knew about the Caretakers before you arrived? The fact that walking, talking beasts are no surprise to me? Or the fact that the heir to the

Cartographer's mantle has been training as an apprentice in my own house?"

Jack looked up in shock and surprise. Franklin had just named all the things they meant to accuse him of, and he really wasn't sure what to say next.

"Proclaim your own sins publicly," said Franklin, "and you take away the naming as a weapon in your foe's arsenal. Even if what you name aren't really sins."

"Something is amiss here," said John. "Pull him up."

Jack and Doyle pulled Franklin to his feet but kept a solid grip on him. "All right," John said. "We're listening."

"Not everyone who looks out for the welfare of this world has to travel to imaginary lands to do it," said Franklin, "or to the ends of time. Some of us like to remain involved in the affairs of this world, and help others where we can.

"I am not a Caretaker," the Doctor went on, his voice low, "I am a Mystorian, and I have only one other thing to say: Verne is with you."

"Verne!" John exclaimed. "What does he have to do with this?"

"When you're losing the game, sometimes you have to change the rules," said Franklin. "This is the Great Game, and there are new pieces on the board—Verne's Mystorians. The Caretakers cannot do all that is needed on their own, not even with the help of your enemies. So Verne has recruited more friends. It is the only way to defeat the Echthroi."

"I still cannot believe—," John began.

"John, the boy!" shouted Burton. "We've been focused on the wrong opponent!"

Defoe had retrieved the portrait of Charles Johnson and was

holding it under one arm. The other was casually draped around the shoulders of the little prince.

"Don't hurt him, Defoe!" John shouted.

"Hurt him?" Defoe said mockingly. "I won't hurt him." He looked down at Coal. "We're friends, aren't we?"

The boy smiled hesitantly, then nodded.

"Coal," Jack said slowly, beckoning to the boy, "come here."

"You aren't my friends," the boy said softly. "You won't read to me, or play with me. But he gave me a present. No one's ever given me a present before."

"I don't think you'll be able to track him," said Defoe, "but you're more than welcome to try."

The Caretakers gasped as they realized what Coal was playing with, what gift Defoe had given him.

It was Defoe's watch. His Caretaker's watch.

An Anabasis Machine.

"They don't work, you know," John said, his voice steady. "There's something wrong with them."

"You mean they don't work properly," Defoe shot back. "That's why I've been stuck here in London for so long. But they're working now—at least as long as you don't care where—or when—you end up."

"Oh no," John breathed. "He wouldn't."

"You trust me, don't you?" asked Defoe.

The boy looked up at him, face open and hopeful, and nodded.

"Then," Defoe said, "turn the dial at the top of the watch just as I showed you . . .

". . . and make a *wish*."

"Coal, no!" Jack shouted. "Don't touch it!"

But it was already too late. The little prince spun the dial at the top of the watch . . .

. . . and *disappeared.*

"Defoe!" Burton roared. "I'll have your head on a stick for this!"

Suddenly an explosion rocked Craven Street, and all the companions were thrown to the ground. The force of the blast made their vision blur and their ears ring, and when they had regained their senses, Defoe and the portrait were gone. Worse, the house of Ernest McGee was in flames.

"Oh dear God," John exclaimed. "Rose is in there!"

"It's on fire!" Edmund yelled. "They've set my father's house on fire!"

"All our maps!" Ernest cried. "All of our family's work! It's burning!"

The companions had a choice: pursue Defoe and the portrait of Captain Johnson, or go rescue Rose and try to salvage what they could of the McGee legacy.

"The boy is already gone," John said to Burton. "There's no point in pursuing Defoe, not now. Rose comes first. It's not even a question."

Burton looked in one direction, then the other, wrestling with the choice before him, and finally, cursing, turned toward the fire. "Promise me, Caretaker," he hissed, "when this is all done, we'll have a reckoning with Defoe."

"I swear it," John said over his shoulder. "We will."

The flames had not yet reached the stairway, which was where John found Rose. She was already unconscious, but still breathing. Burton and Doyle ran past to look for the *Pyratlas* and the rest of the maps, but the heat was too intense. The fire had started in the library, and all the aged paper made for excellent tinder.

"Please!" Edmund pleaded. "Please, Jack! All the maps are there! Everything my family has created! We can't just let them burn!"

"There's nothing we can do, Edmund," said Jack as he held tightly to the panicked young mapmaker. "It's too late. I'm so sorry."

"Son, oh my son," Ernest gasped. "It's all right. They're only maps."

Edmund leaped up and embraced his father. "But it's your life's work!" he sobbed. "Yours, and Grandfather's, and Papa Elijah's!"

"Shh, now," Ernest said, stroking the boy's hair. "Never mind the maps. We'll make more. We are McGees, are we not?"

Suddenly a bolt of furry lightning zoomed past them and into the conflagration. "What was that?" Doyle shouted.

"That was the stupid badger!" replied Burton as they backed down the stairs, coughing. "Caretakers," he muttered. "They're all the same."

They got Rose to a clean spot on the grass where they could give her air, and she started to cough.

"She'll be all right!" said John, thrilled and relieved at once. "She's going to be all right."

"Hey—where did Franklin go?" Jack exclaimed, looking around for the Doctor. "John, he's disappeared."

"Curse it," John muttered under his breath. He hadn't been able to ask what the Doctor had meant by his cryptic remarks about Verne and being a Mystorian. And he was still not convinced that Franklin was not in league with Defoe, or worse, the Echthroi.

"Fred's in there!" Burton shouted. "He went in for the maps."

"I'll get him," said Laura Glue, her face set with determination. She pulled a cord on her blouse, and in an instant her wings popped out from the pack she wore on her back. In another moment she was airborne and winging her way toward the upper stories of the house.

"Good Lord!" John exclaimed. "When did she do that to her wings?"

"I did it," said Houdini, "when I was tinkering around in Franklin's workshop. It's nothing, really—just a simple matter of miniaturizing the mechanism."

"No doubt, you're a genius," John said. "I just hope the wings are flameproof."

Archimedes hovered at the edge of the flames and smoke and shouted instructions to Laura Glue as she darted close to the conflagration, searching for a way in.

At last she found her opening and dove inside. She emerged a minute later, wings trailing smoke, with the little badger draped over her slim arms. He was holding on to a stack of papers for dear life.

The flames took a terrible toll on her wings, nearly crippling their maneuvering ability, and she corkscrewed crazily against the firelight before plummeting toward the cobblestones below. But just before she hit them, a bulky figure threw itself across the street and under her and Fred, absorbing the brunt of the fall.

John, Houdini, and Burton rushed over to where Arthur Conan Doyle was staggering to his feet. "Never mind me," he wheezed, waving them off. "Just knocked the wind out of me. Look to the girl and the badger!"

Fred was in worse shape than the Valkyrie, but he was alive, and he had salvaged a large stack of maps.

"You were amazing, Fred!" said Jack. "I can't believe you got them all!"

"Not all," he said in a small voice. "I gots all I could, Scowler Jack." He was curled up in a ball, and the edges of his fur had been badly singed. His clothes and cap were blackened from the smoke and fire, but the maps were in near-perfect condition.

"I wouldn't have been burned at all," he whimpered, "'cept that my stupid scarf got caught on a windowpane when Laura Glue was helping me make my great escape."

"Any escape you walk away from is a good escape," Houdini said with real admiration, "but when it's by the skin of your teeth, it's truly a great escape—and everyone around you knows it."

Ernest and Edmund were examining the maps Fred had managed to salvage, and as they set aside each one the old mapmaker's eyes shone brighter and his smile grew wide.

"Bless your badger's heart," Ernest exclaimed as he laid down the last map. "You saved them all."

"All?" Fred said in surprise. "I only managed to get a dozen or so."

"Fourteen, to be exact," said Ernest, "but the *right* fourteen. The most important ones in the lot. The ones I could not have recreated, because all those who gave me their secrets are dead."

"The legacy of the McGee family will live on then," said Houdini.

"Of that," Ernest said as he hugged his son again, "I have no doubt."

Rose was sitting up now and seemed to be in shock. Her eyes were wide and her breath was coming in short gasps—and despite the bright light of the flames, her shadow was nowhere to be seen.

Suddenly a scream rent the night air, sounding clear and shrill even over the roaring of the flames.

"Dear God in heaven," Ernest wheezed. "Someone's still inside!"

"There! Look!" Laura Glue exclaimed. The others looked in the direction she was pointing and saw a face in the upper attic window. It was Lauren.

Edmund looked at Laura Glue and Rose with a mix of shame and fear; then his expression changed to one of resolve. He leaped to his feet and bolted for the building's facade—but the heat was too great to even approach.

Laura Glue jumped into the air, wings straining, but after a few staggered bursts upward, she fell back to the cobblestones. The effort to save Fred had taken its toll.

"Can you fix my wings?" she yelled at Houdini. "Make them work again?"

The magician shook his head and looked at the fire. "Not quickly enough!"

Lauren screamed again, then went silent as the flames and smoke covered the windows and rose past the rooftops.

"She's gone," Ernest said, sobbing into his son's shoulder. "Oh, Edmund, we've lost her!"

Suddenly a huge, muscular figure burst out of the adjacent alley, running full-out. Without a pause or look backward, he leaped over the threshold of the ground floor and disappeared into Ernest's house.

The companions looked at one another in amazement, as if they couldn't believe what they had just seen.

"Bloody hell," whispered Burton.

"That's the way to do it!" Archie exclaimed, whooping and screeching as he launched himself into the air. "Go, boy! Go!"

"Oh, Father . . . ," Rose began.

Then, as quickly as he had entered the burning house, Madoc crashed through one of the upper windows carrying a limp figure wrapped in a sodden blanket. He plummeted to the earth with a sickening crunch, then rolled free of the unconscious girl. "Quickly!" he gasped, his face drawn tight with pain. "Get her to fresh air! Hurry! She may still live!"

Houdini, John, Jack, and Fred tended to Lauren, while the others moved Madoc to a cool spot on the grass. He was badly burned—all of his hair and beard were gone, and one eye was blistered shut. He was covered with burns—too many to survive for long.

"Why did you come?" Rose asked him, sobbing. "How did you know where we were?"

"He said . . . my daughter needed me." Madoc coughed. "How could I not come?"

"Who said that?" asked Jack. "Who told you, Madoc?"

In answer, Madoc lifted his hand and pointed . . .

. . . at Benjamin Franklin.

CHAPTER TWENTY-TWO
THE CHOICE

—❋—

"YOU KNEW THERE was going to be a fire," John said, rising to his feet with fists clenched. "How?"

"I didn't know for certain," Franklin answered. "Let's just say it was a very strong might-have-been that ended up happening after all."

Burton growled and stood next to John. "All I want to know," he said, his voice low, "is whether you're in league with Defoe."

"Had I been formally apprenticed as a Caretaker, Defoe would have known about me, and I wouldn't have been able to help you," Franklin answered. "I was here in London for a different purpose. Hank Morgan started the process with Elijah, but someone had to be here a century later to build it up in young Edmund. That job fell to me. And I believe he's now ready for what you need him to become."

"The girl," Madoc rasped. "Is she all right?"

"Why did you go in there?" Rose asked him, sobbing.

"Thought . . . she was you," said Madoc. "Wasn't going to leave you in there alone."

"Rose is fine, Madoc," said John. "I got her out in time. But Lauren . . ." His voice trailed off.

"I didn't know she was still in there!" Rose exclaimed, her voice breaking. "Defoe told me she was leaving with him!"

"What?" John said. "Weren't you his prisoner, Rose?"

"That's not exactly what was happening," Archie said as he landed in the grass nearby. "It was more of a conversion than a kidnapping. He's a smooth talker, he is. And Rose is still very young."

"A conversion?" Fred asked, confused. "You shouldn't ought to have talked to him, Rose." He shook his head sadly. "He in't t' be trusted."

"Nor was I, once, too," Burton said quietly. "Yet here I am, your ally. Let her speak."

"I—I'm so sorry," Rose stammered. "I didn't understand. . . ."

"It's all right," said Madoc, taking his daughter's hand in his own. "I think I finally do."

Laura Glue reached out instinctively and took Edmund's hand in hers. They intertwined fingers and silently wept.

"John," Houdini said, his voice breaking with anguish, "I don't think the girl is going to make it. There's just too much damage."

"No!" roared Madoc as he lurched to his feet. He threw himself to the ground next to Lauren and clutched her hands. "No," he said again. "I won't allow it. Not while I can still prevent it."

"Madoc!" John exclaimed as he and the others tried to pull him back. "Don't make yourself worse. You've done all you can."

"Not yet," Madoc rasped. "Ask . . . my daughter. She knows. She knows there is still a way."

They looked at Rose, but she didn't answer. She was staring at her father.

"I don't think I can," she said finally, her voice dulled with remorse. "My shadow is gone, father. I've lost it. It isn't that I'm not willing—but I don't think I'm worthy. Not any longer. Not after this."

"Oh, my girl," Madoc said, touching her face. "I wasn't . . . wasn't suggesting that you offer yourself. You paid my price, a long time ago. Now . . ." He coughed, spitting smoke and blood. "It's my turn to pay yours."

With John's help, he sat up and moved close to Lauren. Madoc bent his head over the dying girl and whispered, so softly that it could barely be heard.

"Mine for hers," he said with faint breaths. "My life for hers . . . I offer this freely. . . . It is my will. . . . Mine for hers."

In that moment, a blinding light erupted from the injured girl. It enveloped all the companions, and when again they could see, the girl was gone. In her place, sitting on the grass, with Madoc's head on her lap, was a regal woman, dressed in a fine Elizabethan gown. Her skin was porcelain, and her eyes gentle. She could have been fifteen, or five hundred—either would have looked the same.

"Hello, Rose," she said with a voice of crystal. "I am Lady Twilight."

"The Starchild has been lost, but the Moonchild still remains," said Lady Twilight. "The new thread remains unbroken. And thus the tapestry may yet be woven once again."

"But I've failed!" said Rose. "All the choices I've made have been wrong."

"You have made the choices you made," came the reply, "and those choices have brought you here. Every choice, every decision, shapes you into who you will become."

"And my choices have ended an innocent life," said Rose bitterly, "and maybe my father's as well."

"The girl you called Lauren is a part of us now," Lady Twilight said. "It was her purpose to be here, now, so that you could be tested—but she lived a worthy life, and her heart was pure. And now she—I—am serving the Light as I was meant to, as the Three Who Are One."

"Like Gwynhfar," Jack murmured to John. "When she died, she became one of the Morgaine too."

"If I was being tested," said Rose, "then I failed."

"Perhaps not," said Lady Twilight, "but then, you were not the only one being tested.

"Now only one choice remains. Tell them."

This last she said to Madoc.

"Tell them," she repeated, her musical voice stern.

Madoc closed his eyes. "It was Rose. You started the fire, didn't you, daughter?"

Rose didn't answer, but simply closed her eyes.

"That's why Franklin went to find him," said Jack. "Somehow, he knew."

"This is exactly how it happened before!" Fred said bluntly. "She's being accused of something she didn't do, just as her father was! And all of history condemned him for it. This isn't right!"

"Hush, Fred," said John. "That isn't what's happening here, is it, Rose?"

"No," she answered, her voice shallow with anguish. "I didn't know Lauren was still—I—I only wanted to destroy the maps."

"Destroy them?" John said, incredulous. "But why, Rose?"

"Mother Night told me it was up to me to set things right, to find the Dragon's apprentice," said Rose, "but when I failed to convince Father to become a Dragon, everyone stopped paying any attention to me at all. Then another of the Morgaine reminded me that I still had Ariadne's Thread and told me I needed to act. And that was when I met Defoe."

"But Rose," Jack exclaimed, "you know what Defoe is! You know what he's done! How could you listen to him?"

"He hasn't done it yet," said Rose, "and the one I met here is still a Caretaker. He had to have been good, once."

"But he became evil," said Fred.

"So did my father, once," said Rose, "and then he changed again, when we gave him a second chance."

Jack sighed heavily and looked at John. They'd made a terrible choice themselves, and they were partly to blame for the events happening right now. They were both expecting Rose to act like an adult who had saved the world, while at the same time treating her like the child she still seemed to be. Defoe had taken advantage of that—and Rose was suffering for it.

"Everyone was sure that the McGees' maps were going to save us all," Rose went on, "and so when Defoe told me I needed to burn them, I thought you'd have no choice but to turn back to me to save us all. You'd have to listen to me again."

"Ah, me," said John. "I'm so sorry, Rose. We didn't see—didn't realize."

At this Madoc started weeping, and Lady Twilight pulled him closer.

"Now, Rose," she said. "Only you can make him believe. Only you can ask this last choice of him."

Madoc turned his head away. "No," he said. "I'm not worthy of it. Not any longer. And not for a long time."

"Not true," Lady Twilight said gently. "You earned your redemption when you chose to pay the price for your daughter's mistake with your own life. Your offer was true, and real, and you *are* worthy, Madoc."

Madoc turned his head to look at his daughter. "Rose," he said, his voice soft, "look at me."

Rose blinked and opened her eyes, looking at her father. She was afraid of what she would see there, in his eyes—but found nothing but love, and trust, and hope, and acceptance.

He believed in her, as she would always believe in him. And in that moment, she made her decision.

"If you can do it, I want you to become a Dragon, Father," she said, weeping again—but this time the tears were full of hope. "I believe in you—but I still feel as if I've cost you your life."

"You made the mistakes you needed to make to learn," said Madoc, "and growing up isn't just about making decisions—it's about taking responsibility for what happens after. I was just here to help you through it—because after all, isn't that what a father is for?"

Sobbing, Rose clutched her father and hugged him tightly.

"That's the most wonderful thing I've ever heard," said Fred, "considering th' source."

Madoc reached up and stroked his daughter's hair. "If," he said slowly, his voice strained and weak, "if I do this thing, will you make the badger stop talking?"

Fresh tears burst forth from Rose's eyes. She nodded. "I will, I promise."

"Wisdom runs in the blood," said Archimedes.

"Hey, now," said Fred.

"Rose," Jack said, touching her shoulder. "Look."

There, mingled with the shadows cast by the fire, was Rose's own elusive shadow. Still unattached, but not lost.

"You're still making choices, my daughter," said Madoc. "Make them good ones. Remember me. And do not despair—because this is why I was sent here through the door, to be here, for this moment, now." He looked his daughter in the eyes, strong and unafraid. "I can choose too. I can ascend. I can choose to become a Dragon."

The moment those words were spoken, there was a terrible shrieking sound that seemed to be everywhere and nowhere all at once. It pierced everyone who heard it to the core, as if it was trying to shatter their souls with its pain and anguish. As it sounded, a shadow passed across the setting sun, then vanished. The shrill cry faded into nothingness, and in seconds, it was as if it had never happened.

"The Echthroi," said Fred. "The enemy have lost one they hoped to make a Lloigor. For good this time."

Lady Twilight had gone. The choice had been made.

Rose pulled Madoc's head onto her lap and stroked his face as he closed his eyes. He was fading.

"What do you want us to do, Madoc?" John asked.

"Take me out of this place," said Madoc weakly. "Take me to the water."

Madoc was a large man, and his burns and fractures meant he was already in almost constant agony. It took all the companions to make a litter that would allow them to transport him down to one of the docks that jutted out into the Thames.

Within an hour, the torchlit processional had made its way
to the water's edge, where John, Jack, and Burton gently lifted
Madoc from the litter.

"Take me in, Caretakers," he said to John. "You, and Jack,
and—and my daughter, if she will."

"Of course, Father," Rose said, weeping. "Of course I will."

"Don't cry, little dove," said Madoc, touching her face with his
blackened hand. "I'm not going to die, after all."

"But you won't be with me anymore," Rose said, "and I feel like
I only just got you."

"I wasn't with you for the whole of your life," Madoc said as
they moved him farther out into the river, "but after this is done,
I always shall be."

She leaned forward and kissed him on the forehead. "I love
you, Father."

"And I you, little dove."

On his signal, Rose moved away, and the three men lowered
him into the water. The swirling blackness closed over his face as
he slowly became submerged.

"What now?" Jack asked the others. "I don't want him to
drown."

"Wait for it," said John, watching anxiously. "Wait. We have to
trust he knows what he's doing."

An explosion of light suddenly lit the bottom of the river and
burst upward into the air, showering the companions with water
and debris. John, Jack, and Burton were thrown off their feet and
fell backward into the water as a sleek, massive creature erupted
out of the Thames and into the sky.

Madoc had become a Dragon—the Black Dragon.

He wheeled around, wings outstretched, and landed skillfully on the dock, where he waited until the others had clambered out of the river.

Most of the companions had seen Dragons before, but this was a new experience for Franklin and the McGees. The Doctor seemed to switch back and forth between delight and terror, but the McGees were simply awestruck, looking at the Dragon with their mouths hanging open.

For John and Jack, it was still a thrill, as it had been the first time they met Samaranth—never mind the fact that he could have just as easily eaten them.

For Burton, Houdini, and Doyle, it was a bittersweet experience. They were realizing how the wheel of destiny turns—and finally understood that as with Rose, all their choices had also brought them to this place.

Rose walked across the dock to the Dragon and without a pause reached up and wrapped her arms around him. In response, he enfolded her with his wings.

"So," the Black Dragon rumbled in a voice not unlike Madoc's. "Speak. Ask of me what you will, and I shall do my best to answer."

"The riddle," Rose said. "The one given to me by Mother Night. I need to know what it means."

She repeated it in a clear, unhurried voice. There was no need to hurry now.

> To turn, from time to time
> To things both real and not,
> Give hints of world within a world,
> And creatures long forgot.

With limelight turn to these, regard
In all thy wisdom stressed;
To save both time and space above—
Forever, ere moons crest.

The Dragon made a huffing noise, and the companions realized he was laughing. "She was not telling you what you needed to learn to fix the Archipelago," said the Dragon. "She was telling you what must happen in both worlds: no more secrets."

"That's it?" said Fred. "What a lousy riddle."

"Hardly, little Child of the Earth," the Dragon said. "It is a great truth, and one any honest creature should recognize."

"Mother Night said I needed to find you and say those words," said Rose. "Why was that so important?"

"Because," the Dragon replied, "only a Dragon could give you what you needed. Once, all the doors to the Keep of Time were locked, but the Dragons created the doors, and made them work by giving a piece of themselves to each one. They gave their hearts to the times they guarded. You came here through the last door, and I am the last Dragon. And I will give you what you need, Rose . . .

". . . I'll give you my heart."

The Black Dragon reached into his chest, which had begun to glow with an ethereal light, and removed a small stone circlet. "Take this with you," he said as he unfolded his wings. "When the time comes, use it wisely. Use it well. And never forget your father, my dove."

"Madoc," John began, realizing as he said it that it sounded rather stupid to call the Black Dragon by his human name, "what will you do now?"

"What I have already done," he said as he prepared to take flight. "I'm going to go where all Dragons go until I am summoned. And when that time comes, I will give myself to the making of a ship, so that the events that have played out will play out."

In a flash of imagery, John saw the future of this great beast— he would become the very vessel that the Winter King would use to sail into the Archipelago. "But why?" he called out as the Dragon lifted itself into the air. "Why, when you can still choose and change everything?"

"Because," the Dragon replied, "every choice I've made, good or ill, has made me what I am now. And what I am is a father who has given his heart to his daughter, and who I think has finally earned hers. What more would I wish?"

And with that, he wheeled away and disappeared into the night sky.

"Well, that's going to change one thing in the future," said Fred.

Jack frowned. "What's that?"

"We're going to have to stop referring to the Black Dragon as a 'she.'"

As one, all the watches belonging to the Caretakers Emeritis began to hum, then just as quickly, fell silent.

By reflex, all of them checked the watches, and one by one expressed relief, or joy, or both.

"A new zero point," Verne murmured, waving Bert to his side so they could compare readings. "It's a new zero point at last."

Several other Caretakers were shaking hands and nodding, while voicing various platitudes of congratulation.

"It isn't over yet!" Bert barked at them. "We know when

they are now, but they still have to find a way to come home."

"Can't they just use the watches?" asked Shakespeare. "It should be simple now, shouldn't it?"

"In the past, the zero points were located behind the doors of the keep, and the tower itself connected them," said Bert. "The zero points exist, but nothing has connected them yet. And until they find a way to connect those points, the only way to return is the way Hank Morgan did."

He looked at his watch and frowned. "This isn't over."

CHAPTER TWENTY-THREE
THE REVOLUTION

IT TOOK THE better part of the night for the fire to burn itself out. When the companions returned to Craven Street, there was little left of Ernest's house except for a stone and brick skeleton and ashes.

"I'm so sorry, Father," said Edmund. "We can rebuild it, if you want."

"No," Ernest said, shaking his head. "I think I'm done here. I have you, and I have the maps. That's all that matters."

They walked the short distance to Franklin's house, arriving there just as the sun was rising. Myrret met them at the door.

"The magistrate was here looking for you," Myrret said. "He'd like to ask if you know anything about the fire down the street."

"What did you tell him?" asked Franklin.

"I said you'd be back soon, and I'd have you contact him," the fox said. "And then he told me I'm very articulate for my species."

"Oh dear," said Jack.

The companions all went to their separate corners of Franklin's house to better come to grips with the events of the night. The Doctor graciously opened another spare room for Ernest to use, with the promise that breakfast would soon be ready.

When Doyle had dressed in clean clothes, he found Houdini in the kitchen with Franklin.

"You're obviously a man of learning," the Magician was saying, "so let me ask you. His voice dropped to a whisper. "If you were to have a box about yea big, and say, for the sake of argument, it was a magic box—"

"Harry!" Doyle said sharply. "Nix, brother."

Houdini scowled at Doyle, then switched to a charming smile for Franklin. "Another time, perhaps."

A few moments later John and Jack came in. They had questions for Doctor Franklin—which he'd already anticipated.

"Here," said the Doctor, handing a cream-colored multipage letter to John. "That should answer many of your questions."

"It's a letter from Jules," John said to Jack. "This is why Franklin helped us."

"I'd have helped you anyway," said Franklin. "As much as I could have. But this letter made it easy. Verne delivered it to me himself years ago and told me who he was, and why he needed my help. I thought it was some sort of prank—but when you showed up at my door, I knew it was all real."

"So the Mystorians . . . ," John began.

"All I know is what he told me, and what's in that letter," Franklin said with a shrug. "I knew enough to anticipate certain events, and to assist you as best I could. And that's all I was asked to do. And he gave me this," he added, holding up the watch, "so that you would trust me. And it seems you did. Although mine doesn't allow me to travel in time."

"That's all right," said Jack. "Neither do ours at the moment."

"The watch would have been more help," said John, "if you'd

shown it—and the letter—to us when we got here. We trusted you when we had to, but we wasted a lot of time thinking you might be . . ."

"Echthroi?" Franklin finished, nodding. "That's the very reason I could not confirm who I was, nor whom I worked for. I knew I could trust you Caretakers, as Verne told me I could. But you came with an entourage—including an Echthros. I couldn't reveal more until events had played themselves out. Other than mentoring the boy, assisting you was all that Verne asked of me."

"So a Mystorian is sort of a single-mission Caretaker," said John, "at least in your case, Doctor. I don't know whether to be grateful to Verne or if I want to beat him within an inch of his life."

"Let's get you home first," said Franklin with a wink, "and then I'm sure you'll be able to decide."

After breakfast, the companions reconvened in the study. "There's something that needs doing," Burton announced somberly, "and I'd rather do it quickly."

The companions all nodded in understanding, especially John and Jack. To them, it was not so long ago that they had lain their friend to rest. Now Burton wanted to do the same for his.

Theo's funeral was a small, private affair—only Burton, Houdini, and Doyle, and John, Jack, Fred, and Franklin attended. The body had been wrapped in the style of Theo's culture and placed in a shallow boat on the river.

With no platitudes, and little ceremony, Burton and John set the boat aflame and pushed it out onto the water.

"In broad daylight?" Franklin whispered to Jack. "Isn't this quite risky?"

"Not really," Doyle whispered back, pointing.

There on the dock behind them, Houdini stood with his back to them, hands outstretched. His fingers made delicate tracings in the air, but the muscles on his neck and the beads of sweat soaking his shirt showed the obvious strain he was under. They could hear him whispering arcane words of magic under his breath as he worked the illusion.

"No one will see us, or the funeral barge," Doyle explained. "Burton considered the End of Time to be his friend—perhaps his only friend. And he deserves the chance to do this in peace."

Burton stood on the dock, watching the small craft as it was consumed by the flames. Finally it drifted too far to see clearly. He spun about and cleared his throat.

"All right," Burton said gruffly. "Let's get back to work."

Back at Franklin's house, they found Rose already poring over the maps in Johnson's book.

"What are you looking for?" Ernest offered helpfully. "Perhaps I could give you a hand?"

Rose looked up at him as a flash of fear and worry crossed her features. She'd basically confessed to trying to destroy the work of his entire family—that would not be easily forgiven. But there was no guile or malice in the man's face—the offer was sincere.

"Hank Morgan traveled back to our time with a map your grandfather made him," Rose replied. "I was hoping to find something similar that we might use to duplicate his efforts."

"What are you thinking, Rose?" Jack asked as he and the others came into the room.

"Mother Night told me that I had all the things I needed to

connect the threads of time," Rose replied, "and the Watchmaker told us we needed someone who was able to map time. Doctor Franklin told us that he was instructed by Verne to help Edmund become a mapmaker. I think," she finished, "that together, Edmund and I may be able to get us home."

"When we first met," Ernest said to John, "I told you that I did not have the skills of my father and grandfather. That is still true. But," he added with no small pride, "there is a member of the family McGee who does. My son Edmund can make the kind of map you need."

"I have the extra pages," Jack said as he removed a large folder from Fred's pack. "The ones Bert and the Cartographer took out of the *Geographica* for safekeeping."

He spread out the large sheets of parchment and selected one, handing it to Edmund. "Here," Jack said. "Let's try your skills out on one of these."

"All right," said Edmund. "What do you want me to map?"

"About twenty years shy of two centuries," said Jack.

"Hmm," said Edmund. "I'm going to need more ink."

As the young mapmaker worked, John moved over alongside Burton, who was compulsively checking his watch and looking out the window. "You're thinking about the boy, aren't you?" John asked.

Burton responded with a short, sharp nod.

"We'll find him, Burton. We will," said John, gripping the man's shoulder. "I swear it."

And this time, Sir Richard Burton didn't knock aside John's hand, but allowed it to remain on his shoulder, steadying him.

John wondered if that was deliberate, or if Burton, for the first time since he'd known the man, was simply weary. It didn't really matter, he supposed. Or maybe, it just shouldn't.

"What I'm concerned about," Doyle was saying, "is whether the conflict with Defoe will have any ill effect on the future. After all, he sells the portrait of Captain Johnson to, well, *us*, in around a decade or so."

"They mean me," said Burton, turning from the window. "I came here in the *Indigo Dragon*, specifically searching for Defoe to strengthen his ties to the Society. Our pact was sealed with the purchase of the portrait."

"I don't think the future will be affected," said Jack. "That Burton isn't you, Richard—he won't have had this experience and will have no reason to distrust Defoe. And for all we know, Defoe will end up trusting you *more* then because of your having met *now*."

"He didn't mention it," said Burton. "Why?"

"I don't think he would," said Jack, "just as he won't care about having seen us here. All he'll recall is that he got the best of us."

"That's not really a consolation," said Houdini.

"I'm actually more worried about what happens when we get back than I am that we'll get back at all," said Jack.

"Why is that?" asked John.

"Aven," Jack replied simply. "How are we going to tell Bert? He's already lost his wife in Deep Time—and now we're going to have to tell him that he's lost his daughter as well."

"Time enough for that later," said Burton, sitting. "No pun intended. But we have more pressing matters to attend to, do we not? First we need to make sure we can get back at all. Then we'll deal with grief and the grieving."

"Of course you wouldn't feel that was important," Jack said, frowning. "You took the news of your own daughter's loss with barely a blink."

Burton leaned back in his chair and observed Jack with a wry expression on his face. "And you have determined from that reaction that I don't care for Tiger Lily, or mourn her death?" he said evenly. "You would be wrong, little Caretaker. I will mourn her, in my own fashion, when I have time to do so. But now is not that time.

"She lived her life as I raised her to," he continued, "rich and full and honorably. She married well, and gave me an heir. I mourn that I was not there to share in more of her years, but that does not weaken the pride I feel as her father, nor does it make me love her less."

With that he spun around and strode from the room.

John clapped Jack on the back. "I can't say he's wrong, old fellow."

"You know," said Houdini, "if Theo were here, he'd have something profound to say."

Doyle looked on impassively. "It is from the dust that we came, and it is to the dust we must all return."

"Oh, shut up," said Jack.

"And what about Coal?" Rose asked. "What can we do about him?"

"We can't stay here," John stressed, "even to try to find Coal. Wherever Defoe sent him can't be helped now. And if we are to have any hope of finding him in the future, the only way to do it is to keep our eyes on our larger goal. We have to fix the Archipelago. And then we'll have a chance of finding Coal."

"In Morgan's note, he said he and Elijah were trying to create a 'chronal map,'" Rose said. "We know they did, eventually. That's how he attuned his watch to get back."

"Shouldn't we be able to do the same?" asked Fred. "The zero point he mapped to Tamerlane House is still there."

"Except," said Jack, "he didn't start from a mapped zero point, so even when he had the map, he spent two centuries trying to leap forward in time."

"Which," Burton noted, "is exactly how long it would have taken him doing it the ordinary way."

"Do you remember when we moved through time using the trump?" John asked. "They tried it again and it never worked—and it didn't really work for Hank, either."

"That may not have been Morgan's fault," said Rose. "Basically, he was trying to mix two incompatible means of travel. The trumps were meant to be used in space, and the watches in time."

"That's what worries me," said Jack. "His map worked in exactly a way it wasn't supposed to. It effectively functioned as a 'chronal trump,' moving him in time *and* space. I'm worried that we'll just be duplicating Hank's efforts, and with just as little success."

"Fruitless?" said Fred. "He *did* make it back."

"Just in time to die," said Burton. "I'd rather stay here, if that's the choice."

"No, I think it may be just the direction we need to be looking," said Jack. "Think about it—the Keep of Time functioned in the same way. Stepping through the doors moved you in time and space—and they were changeable. Basically, the keep itself intuited where and when we needed to go. If we can find a way to recreate that . . ."

"I'll settle for getting to Tamerlane House in 1945," said John. "If we can."

"We're about to find out," said Edmund. "I think I'm done."

Edmund had followed the notes in Elijah's maps, as well as the calculations that accompanied them. As well as he could determine, the map he'd made was identical to the one his great-grandfather had made for Hank Morgan.

"All we have to do now," said Burton, "is figure out how to use it without spending two centuries lost in history."

"He stepped through in space, but it didn't let him step through in time," said John. "It was the same problem he had with the projected message he left at Magdalen Tower."

"I think I understand what to do," said Rose. "I think I know the reason I needed to be here." She reached into her pocket, and just as she had before, she found the glowing ball of Ariadne's Thread.

She looked at the ball, then at the others. "Reweave the threads of history, that's what Mother Night told me," she said. "Somehow I have to use this thread to get us home."

"You're forgetting the original purpose of the thread from mythology," John said. "With it, you can always find your way back."

Experimentally, Rose unwound one end of the thread and let it dangle on the table.

"Now that's very interesting," said Edmund. "How do you get it to extend into the map that way?"

"What are you talking about?" asked Rose.

"The glowing thread," Edmund said, pointing from the ball in her hand to the parchment on the table. "It's connected directly to my drawing, see?" He grabbed the edge of the sheet and slid it back and forth. "It follows the map. How are you doing that?"

"Edmund," said Jack. "We can't see anything."

The young mapmaker never heard the comment. He'd already become too absorbed in the strange light, and something deeper it seemed to mean to him.

Dipping a quill in his ink, he started adding some new notations to the map, pausing every few seconds to observe his handiwork. He added another sketch to the center, and several symbols to the edges. Finally he put down the quill. "There," he said, breathing rapidly from the anxious effort. "Now it's done. The thread just showed me a few things I hadn't understood before."

"All right," Jack said. "Let's give it a try. Everyone, please focus on the map."

Half in fear that it might work, but more out of fear that it wouldn't, the companions gathered closely about the table and stared at the map.

The parchment trembled—once, then again. And again. And then suddenly it started to expand.

"Here!" Jack exclaimed. "Hold up the other side, John!"

Together the Caretakers held up the sheet as it continued to grow. In minutes it filled the whole width of the room, and as they watched, a picture began to form amid the symbols and equations.

"What do you think?" Jack asked. "Should one of us go through first, to test it?"

John shook his head. "It's either going to work, or it isn't," he said, his voice full of resolve. "We all go together."

"What about Edmund?" Laura Glue asked. "Don't we have to take him?"

"She's right," said John. "If this works, and we want to do it again, we're going to need him, just as the Watchmaker said."

"I agree," said Ernest. "This is your destiny, my boy. You must go."

Edmund hugged his father. "What of Elijah's maps? And all of his notes?"

"You saved them from obscurity," Ernest said to his son with honest pride. "They should stay with you."

"What of the rest of these?" said Houdini, eyeing the treasure maps. "These could be very . . . ah, useful."

"Not in our purview," John said. "We aren't treasure seekers, Harry."

"It was worth a shot," said Houdini.

"I'll take the treasure maps with me," Ernest said. "My time here in London is done, I think. The fire decided that, if for no other reason. I'm now officially retired from this whole business of maps, and I think maybe I'll spend some time on a plantation in the Caribbee Sea."

"As a gentleman farmer?" asked Jack.

"Or as a pirate," Ernest replied, "but then again, these days, who can tell the difference?"

"Doctor Franklin?" John said. "I'd like to invite you along, but I don't think I can."

"Not a problem," said Franklin, holding up his hands. "My place is here, in this time, and I'm content to leave it that way. Give my best regards to Verne—whenever he is."

"All right," John said. "Bring the animals from Paralon down. I think we're ready to go."

Good-byes were said, farewells given. And then the companions stepped through the map and into the future. It did not take long to discover if it worked. One moment they were in Franklin's study in London, and the next they were elsewhere.

They were in Rose's attic room at Tamerlane House.

"It worked!" Jack exclaimed. "Well done, Rose!"

"Wait," Burton said, holding up a hand. "We've moved in space, but we don't yet know if we moved in time."

Together, he, Houdini, and Doyle all checked their watches, then nodded in agreement. "It's all right," Burton proclaimed with uncharacteristic relief in his voice. "They all say we're back in 1945. Right when we're meant to be."

CHAPTER TWENTY-FOUR
THE THIRD ALTERNATIVE

THE COMPANIONS' SUCCESSFUL return was met with great rejoicing at Tamerlane House. Not only were they home, safe and sound, but the journey had given them the seeds of hope that time might be fixed, and the Archipelago restored. But none of the good news made relaying the bad news any easier. During the celebration, Jack took Bert aside and told him privately about Aven's last moments.

"I can still hope," Bert said somberly. "The Archipelago runs according to Kairos time, and that is not absolute. If it were here, in the Summer Country, I would be more fearful. But I'm glad you were able to speak to her, Jack. Very glad."

"You won't be able to interact with her as we did," Jack said as he pulled the reel from Paralon out of his pack, "but you'd still be able to see her, if you like."

Bert began to reach for the reel, then hesitated. He seemed to be debating the matter in his mind; then finally he decided.

"Thank you, Jack, truly," he said, curling up his fingers and folding his hands together. "Perhaps later."

The Far Traveler quickly moved on to give more instructions

to the Caretakers Emeritis, and Burton moved over to a slightly puzzled Jack. "He's putting up a brave front," he whispered. "Give him time."

Jack tilted his head and replaced the reel in his pack. "I guess I was expecting him to respond more as you did."

"Maybe," Burton said as he moved past Jack to grab a bottle of wine, "I was just putting on a brave front too."

Deftly Burton maneuvered himself alongside Bert, and then drew them both to a balcony where they could speak privately.

"So, Far Traveler," Burton began.

"So, Barbarian," Bert answered. "What did you want to speak to me about that was not for the ears of our colleagues?"

Burton looked at him oddly for a moment, then poured wine into a glass that he handed to Bert before taking a swig from the bottle. "It seems we have something in common, you and I," he said at length. The lost boy, my heir . . . he's your descendant too."

Bert nodded thoughtfully and sipped at the wine. "I've considered that. It certainly gives him a colorful heritage."

"That's an understatement. He has the potential to conquer the world, if he wished it."

"Lineage isn't everything," Bert countered. "Environment and upbringing have a lot to do with one's potential. And all this boy knew was a legacy he couldn't touch, a sheltered Aladdin's cave of fairy tales read to him by hedgehogs, and several well-meaning adults who didn't pay attention to him until someone else did. Yes, what he'll grow up to become is exactly what troubles me about him, never mind his lineage."

"Do you think it's possible?" asked Burton. "Will we be able to discover what's happened to him?"

Bert didn't reply. After a minute, Burton returned to the party.

Edmund McGee was already settling nicely into a suite of rooms Poe had offered him at the opposite end of the corridor from Basil Hallward's studio. In a matter of hours, Edmund and Laura Glue had set up drafting tables, shelving, and enough reference material that the main room had already begun to resemble the old Cartographer's room near the top of the Keep of Time.

The main differences, Jack noticed, were that this Cartographer's room had windows that opened, and a door that would never be locked.

He even noted, with some amusement and a little mild understanding, that Archimedes had all but nested in one of the alcoves, which pained Rose ever so slightly. He had been her most constant companion and teacher during those years when she was maturing from a child into a young woman, and he was her closest friend.

Still, he was also what he was—and his memories of the early days with Rose's father and uncle still resonated strongly. Rose had a passing interest in her uncle's handiwork, and she certainly had the facility for mapmaking—but it was not her passion. For young Edmund, it was. Not only did he have three generations of mapmakers behind him, but they had developed the family trade during one of the most exciting, thrilling, and unpredictable periods in human history.

If anything, Jack concluded, Edmund was better primed and prepared to become a Cartographer of imaginary lands than Merlin was.

✦ ✦ ✦

"Hank knew exactly what he was doing," said Twain. "He didn't choose Elijah McGee at random, and the skills of the family McGee are not mere coincidence."

He flipped open one of the Histories that Hank Morgan had been annotating through his jaunts in time and indicated a series of notes along one margin. "It's here, you see—in the genealogy."

"This says that Elijah McGee was descended from François Le Clerc," John said. "He was a pirate, wasn't he?"

"Among the first who were called so," Edmund Spenser said as he entered the room and the conversation. "In some quarters, he was even called the Pirate King. Quite a scoundrel—which, I suppose, is not a bad quality to possess if you're going to be a pirate. He was a contemporary of mine, and we met on two occasions before his presumed death."

"Presumed?" said Jack. "There was a question?"

Spenser nodded. "Eminently so. He supposedly perished after trying to commandeer a Spanish galleon and sail it, unassisted, through the Frontier."

John's mouth gaped. "He knew about the Archipelago?"

"Of course he did," Spenser replied. "He was *from* the Archipelago. Sinbad wasn't the only seafarer who made a practice of crossing from world to world when the occasion presented itself. He was just better at it than Le Clerc."

"Spenser never confirmed that the pirate was dead," Twain said, "but Verne's Mystorians have a working theory that he and his subsequent ships became the original source of the Flying Dutchman legends. Spenser did, however, manage to save Le Clerc's ship."

"What did you do with it?" asked John.

Spenser smiled, a broad, warm expression. "You know as well as anyone," he said impishly. "It's sitting in the south boathouse."

"The *Indigo Dragon*," Jack exclaimed. "Brilliant!"

"So you see," Twain finished as he added a new notation to the book, "that boy was not selected at random. He has a fine lineage from the Archipelago itself—all Hank did was to bring the family trade full circle."

Eventually, as the companions knew it must, talk turned to the topic of Hank's note, and the mysterious others who were able to manipulate time.

"They must have discovered some way to combine the attributes of the trumps with the mechanism of the watches," Verne said, looking askance at Bert, "and there are very few among us who could even conceive such a thing."

"Do you think the Watchmaker may have had a hand in it?" asked John. "Could Dee have coerced him, or somehow bribed him to modify them?"

"I doubt it," said Verne. "He may be above our petty little alliances with their shifting lines, but he's also a good judge of character. And he can tell a Namer from an Un-Namer."

"At least we're in the Summer Country now," said Bert. "Our experiments would not have worked if we were still in the Archipelago."

"Why not?" asked Jack.

"We have never been able to traverse time inside the Archipelago," Verne explained, "only in the Summer Country. It's the nature of Kairos time, you see. It's more pure, more fluid—almost imaginary. Events there are given meaning only because of the connection to Chronos time, here in the Summer Country. That's why residents there age slowly, or not at all, and why without the keep, time travel was impossible. There are exceptions to this, of course, but we have come to realize that this should be treated more as a rule than a guideline."

"We'll have plenty of opportunities to practice," said Rose, "but even with all of our successes, I can't help feeling sad for all that we've lost. It seems too high a price to have paid."

"Maybe not so high as you think, dear child," said Verne. He was smiling broadly. "We have a surprise for you—for all of you, in fact." He pointed to the door of the banquet hall, where a tall, lanky man was just stepping through.

"Hello, Rose," he said warmly.

Rose looked up, and her gasp of surprise turned into a squeal of glee as Charles walked toward her.

Rose's delighted reaction was echoed by John and Jack, both of whom were moved to hug their colleague several times while tears filled all their eyes.

"Well done!" John kept exclaiming as he clapped his friend on the back, as if Charles not being dead was some sort of carnival award. "Well done, my man!"

"Thank you, John, Jack," Charles said amiably. "I'm only disappointed that when you needed me, I wasn't ready to accompany you. So sorry about that."

"It's fine, it's fine," Jack exclaimed. "We managed somehow, and your stand-in comported himself very well, very well indeed."

"Stand-in?" said Charles.

"We recruited Hugo," said Jack.

Charles's face froze in a mix of amusement and horror. "You're joking! Ah, no offense, Rose."

"They are joking, and none taken," Rose said as she chucked Jack on the shoulder. "It was Fred, of course."

"Right," said Charles. "Where is the young fellow, anyway? I should quite like to see him."

"He'll be down in a bit," John assured him. "He's upstairs assembling a lamp for our new Cartographer."

It was Charles's turn to be surprised. "New Cartographer?" he sputtered. "I die and everyone starts rearranging things on me."

"You don't know the half of it," said Jack. "But there'll be time for that later. Tell us how . . ." He stopped. The initial excitement now past, they could finally take a good look at their old friend—who was no longer quite so old.

"I say," Jack murmured as he squinted at Charles. "Did you do something to your hair?"

"Got it back," Charles said jovially. "That's one of the positive things about becoming a tulpa—the body you create is exactly the one that you think of when you think of 'yourself.' It's the ideal you, so to speak—and mine happens to be around thirty."

"That's about how old you were when we first met, back in 1917," said Jack. "Remember, Bert?"

Bert nodded. "I do very well," he said, clearing his throat. "It was a good age for a Caretaker."

"The third alternative, they call it," Charles said when they'd settled back in their seats. "Everyone dies eventually. And there's also the course that almost all the Caretakers have chosen for ethical and moral reasons, which is to become portraits in the gallery and reside at Tamerlane House. But there's also the third way, becoming a tulpa, which Jules and Bert both advocated to me after that meeting at the Inn of the Flying Dragon."

"*Bert* advocated?" John said, surprised. "I didn't expect that."

"My personal feelings about it haven't changed," Bert offered, "and it remains a sore point between Jules and me. But something very significant happened that we've never had to deal with before. And that changed everything."

"What was that?" asked John.

"Stellan," said Bert. "We've always known the risks of leaving Tamerlane House, but never in our history had we lost a Caretaker in that way."

"We defeated the Shadow King only by the slimmest of margins," said Verne, "and Stellan was key to that victory. But had the journey taken just a little longer, or had they been delayed . . ."

"We'd never have reached the wall, or my father," said Rose, "and we'd have lost everything."

Bert nodded. "None of which would have been an issue if Stellan had been a tulpa," he said, not really enjoying the admission. "Charles is still vitally important to the work we're doing now, and we didn't want to risk the same thing happening to him. So we offered him the choice, and he accepted."

"Also," added Charles, "I'm getting on amazingly well with Rudyard Kipling."

"It doesn't make you immortal, you know," Jack cautioned. "As we saw with Defoe, a tulpa body can still be destroyed."

"Oh, I'm completely aware of that possibility," said Charles, "and if we see that coming, I can still have my portrait done by

Basil, and join the others in the gallery. And if that happens, then I'll have something really interesting to explore. I'm not terribly worried about it."

"After our discussion about his impending, uh, discontinuity," said Bert, "progress on Charles's portrait was halted while Jules and Rudy began to prepare him to create a tulpa."

"What did you do with the uncompleted portrait?"

"We found another use for it, which didn't require as much alteration as you'd think," said Verne.

"And I'm very glad you did," said a familiar voice, "or else I'd have missed out on too much fun."

Jack pulled out a chair next to himself and waved Ransom over. He paused to shake hands with Charles, who, Jack noted, looked less like his other-dimensional counterpart now that he was younger. Ransom sat next to Jack and winked at Rose.

"My days as a Messenger may be a lot more restricted now," he said with undisguised melancholy, "but that's better than not having any days at all."

"Doesn't it take a long while to create a tulpa, though?" asked Jack. "When did you do it?"

"It does take some considerable time, yes," said Verne, "and more so in Charles's case, because we weren't there when he actually died. If he hadn't begun the process in 1943, then there might have been no way to save him—except with a portrait."

"It's an act of visualization, as much as anything," said Charles. "The Buddhists were particularly adept. You simply create a spirit form in your mind, and then, at the time of your death, it takes on solid flesh as your, ah . . ." He scratched his head and looked at Verne. "Spirit? Soul? Aiua? Well, whatever it is that makes you 'you' moves into the new body."

"Even if I don't fully comprehend it, I'm impressed," said Jack. "Especially since you could do it so well on the first try."

Verne and Bert both reddened and pulled at their collars at the same time, in a gesture the companions had come to realize meant they were slightly embarrassed about something.

"There was a practice run, so to speak," Charles offered, glancing a bit nervously around the room as he tried not to tug at his collar, "sort of like a final exam before graduation."

"What was that?" Jack asked with a wry grin on his face. "Making a tulpa of the Queen?"

"I, ah," Charles stammered, "I made a tulpa of *you*, Jack."

"Me?" Jack exclaimed. "You practiced by making another *me*?"

"Really, you ought to take it as a compliment," said Verne. "If he didn't respect you greatly, and have a good understanding of what makes you tick, he wouldn't have been able to do it at all."

Jack was still frowning, and he looked distinctly uncomfortable. He glanced around the room. "So is he—ah, I mean, am I around here somewhere?"

"No," Verne said firmly. "As I said, it was only a dry run, to see if Charles could do it. One doesn't have to make a tulpa out of himself—traditionally, it was done to create workers, or guardians of some sort. But those would fade after the death of their maker. It was Dee, and then Blake, who realized that by making a tulpa of oneself, the consciousness, the soul, if you will—"

"Or intelligence, which I prefer," said Charles.

"Or intelligence," Verne added, "could be transferred after death to the tulpa, and thus could live on indefinitely. But a tulpa of anyone else, be it a manservant or a colleague, would simply have to be ignored to make it fade back into the ether. A tulpa can only be maintained by a deliberate act of will—and when he was certain it could be done, Charles switched his attention to his own."

John ran his hand through his thinning hair and smiled crookedly at his now more youthful friend. "I can't say I'm not slightly jealous," he said, "but you do realize that in some respects you're now more like Burton than us?"

"I'll learn to cope," said Charles.

"You don't miss your old body?" asked Jack. "The, ah, deceased one?"

"This is where I reside now," Charles said with a touch of somberness. "Here in this body, and at Tamerlane House, and wherever else I might traipse around to with Verne and Kipling. I don't miss what I was, because I'm still me. Still your Charles."

"So," said Twain to the Magician and the Detective, "did you fellows learn anything on this trip, or were you just window dressing?"

"Yes," Houdini said with a hint of gloomy self-realization. "I found out that I don't need to find everything out."

"Really?" exclaimed Twain. "I'm actually rather impressed, if that's truthful."

"Oh, it is," Houdini complained. "I'm not very happy about it, but it's true. As a magician, I should have realized it all along—some secrets are better off remaining mysteries."

In that instant, the Serendipity Box suddenly reappeared on the tabletop in front of Houdini.

"Oh good Lord," said Doyle. "Quick, someone take this thing away before he changes his mind."

✦   ✦   ✦

There was still one reunion to be had, which Charles was a little less prepared for. Fred stopped in the doorway with crackers falling out of his mouth.

"Hey ho, Fred!" Charles said, arms outstretched. "Aren't you happy to see me?"

Unexpectedly, the little mammal took a step backward, then another. "You in't Scowler Charles," Fred whispered, his whiskers trembling. "You in't. You just in't."

"Of course he is," John offered, stepping forward. "He's just been, ah, youthened, is all."

But the badger wasn't having it. As far as he was concerned, this personage might be Charles in appearance, and in voice and mannerisms, but in one way he was sorely lacking—a way that was a crucial part of identity to the Children of the Earth.

"He din't smell right," said Fred. "He din't smell like Scowler Charles. I—I mean he does in some ways. But he in't quite right."

Charles was utterly crestfallen. This was one reaction he had not anticipated in any way.

"My memories are the same," he said gently. "I remember finding Perseus's shield with your grandfather. I remember meeting you for the first time, and how we could not have rescued Hugo without you. And I remember when I chose you to be my apprentice."

"If you're back," Fred said hesitantly, "and you're the third Caretaker again, then what happens to me?"

"You've read the story of the Three Musketeers, haven't you?"

Fred nodded.

"Well then," said Charles, "this will be like the sequel, when they became Four Musketeers. Just like that."

The little mammal's whiskers twitched. "Four Musketeers? Can I be D'Artagnan?"

"I'd be D'Artagnan," said Jack, "obviously."

"You're more like Athos," said John. "Or maybe Porthos."

"I am not Porthos!" said Jack, self-consciously rubbing his stomach. "I'll be Aramis. Charles can be Porthos."

"Look at him," said John. "He's *maybe* thirty. *He* should be D'Artagnan."

"I hate to interrupt," Alexandre Dumas said, waving a turkey leg, "but Charles does make a better Athos."

"So who would be Lady de Winter?"

"I vote Byron," said Shakespeare. "Do any here dispute me?"

"I do!" pouted Byron.

"You don't get to vote," said Hawthorne. "Eat your soup."

"It doesn't matter who gets to be who," Charles said, "as long as we know we're all for one, and one for all." He knelt down and looked his old apprentice in the eye. "Are we, Fred?" he asked, holding out a hand.

Fred looked around the room at the assembled Caretakers, and then back at Charles. True, he didn't smell right—but then again, neither did badgers, most of the time. And he didn't smell any worse than the rest of them, who mostly smelled of turpentine anyway.

"All for one and one for all," said Fred.

"So everything that happened, everyone we met," said John. "The McGees. Franklin. Madoc. Is that all supposed to have been coincidence?"

"There are no coincidences, John," Bert said, his eyes bright.

"None. All things happen for a reason. You see it as coincidence, as mere happenstance, that unusual people meet under extraordinary circumstances, but those meetings are not random. Like attracts like, and those like us are drawn to one another, not just in space, but also in time."

"So for now," John replied, "the means to remedy the discontinuity is still a mystery."

"Not a mystery," said Houdini. "A secret. Mysteries are secrets that no one knows the answers to. But secrets can be found out. Someone knows a secret. And if someone knows, they can tell."

"To what end?" asked Jack. "Time in the Archipelago has continued to flow unchecked—and everything we knew and loved is already long gone. We can't get them back, Harry."

"Yes," a soft, ethereal voice answered from the landing above them. "We can."

Poe descended the stairs and took a seat next to Rose. "The Archipelago is not lost, nor are your friends and loved ones," he said placidly, holding her hands in his. "Once there was no separation—Kairos time and Chronos time were one and the same. Unveil the secret that may reunite them, and all may yet be restored."

"No more secrets," Rose said. "That's what Mother Night and my father told me. All the secrets must be revealed."

"But what secrets?" asked Bert. "The greatest secret we knew was the identity of the Cartographer, and that was discovered. What else don't we know that isn't already in the Histories?"

"There's a great deal," said Verne. "What we have to do is discover what among the mysteries of history are, in fact, secrets—including the most profound secret of all, which I think will be the key to saving the Archipelago and our future."

"What is that?" asked John.

Verne smiled and arched an eyebrow. "Rose knows. Don't you, my dear child?"

Rose nodded. "Who built the Keep of Time?"

The entire room went silent as they realized that she was right. Of all the mysteries, all the secrets, that was the one question that had eluded them all. No one had questioned it, not even the Dragons, because the keep had always been. Its origins were lost so deeply in time that no one believed it had an answer at all. But if it was indeed a secret, and not a mystery . . .

"And if, by some miracle, we do answer that question," said Jack, "what then? How will knowing help our terrible situation?"

"Because," Rose answered, "if we can find out who built it, we might be able to find out how. We can't keep jumping through time and space trying to bandage the symptoms—not when what we really need is the cure. We need to repair what was broken. To mend what was torn. And to finally weave all the threads back together the way they were meant to be."

"What are you proposing, Rose?" John asked, although he already knew what her answer would be, and he could feel the electric crackle of the hair rising on the back of his neck.

Rose stood, folded her arms, closed her eyes, and smiled. "We must seek out the Architect," she said, simply and openly, "and rebuild the Keep of Time."

EPILOGUE

EVENTUALLY THE LAST *embers from the fire at the mapmaker's house on Craven Street were extinguished, and nothing remained but ash and memory. Scavengers, the kind that walked upright, picked through the charred remains seeking something to steal, or barter with, or sell, but found that nothing of value remained. All that had been worthwhile had been carried away on the winds of time.*

From the narrow townhouse across the street, the Chronographer of Lost Times watched impassively as a blind magistrate chased away the low-born rabble, who abandoned their scanty finds as they ran.

"When Sir John appears, order cannot be far behind," a voice said from the rear doorway. The Chronographer turned.

"Good afternoon, Mr. Defoe."

"Good afternoon, Dr. Dee," Defoe replied as he entered the room and sat heavily in a chair.

"It went as you expected?" Defoe asked.

"Well enough," said Dee. "You'll be paid, as agreed. Now if you'll excuse me, I am expecting visitors."

Defoe scowled but rose to his feet; then, with a bow, he walked out the door. In his place a Shadow arose, and soon formed into something solid. Something alive.

"He suspects something. He knows you keep secrets from him," the Shadow said.

"All the more reason to have kept our distance," said Dee. "We

knew Burton would eventually defect to join the Caretakers, and the others were weak-willed to begin with. Defoe will be much the same—and only by remaining strong in our convictions will we prevail."

"The girl is learning too much," said the Shadow.

"Is she what they think?" Dee asked. "Is she the Imago?"

The Shadow shook his head. "It's possible. The Mystorians have yet to confirm it. She may not be the person she—and the Caretakers—believe her to be. Her lineage is false."

"If hers is, then isn't the boy's also?" said another voice.

"Ah, Tesla," Dee said primly. "So glad you could join us."

"I was only late because I was fetching Crowley, as you asked."

Dee turned to the Shadow, which now looked more like a cat. "You may go," he said.

"Remember our deal," Grimalkin answered, as he began to disappear. "When this is done, you will remove the Binding, once and for all."

"Of course," answered Dee. "That's the promise I made when I bound you to begin with. And so many centuries of service deserve a just reward."

Satisfied with the answer, the Cheshire cat smiled its cheshire smile and vanished.

"And what of the boy?" asked Tesla. "What's to be done with him?"

"I'm taking a page from Verne's own book," answered Dee. "I'm going to hide the boy when no one else will be able to find him."

"Where is that?" Tesla inquired. "Between the Caretakers, the Mystorians, and the Imperial Cartological Society, all of history is open to them."

"I'm going to put him where he truly belongs," Dee replied. "In the future."

"*Elegant, elegant,*" said Crowley. "*Well done, Dee. So, do you think she noticed? That the shadow she returned with isn't her own?*"

"*Unlikely,*" said Dee as he peered at a small vial. Inside, a shadow writhed about, seeking a way to escape—but the glass vessel was too securely stoppered. "*But even if she does, it's already too late. The Caretakers' secrets are an open book to us now.*"

"*So the plan moves forward?*" asked Crowley.

Dee nodded. "*Yes. The daughter of the House of Madoc,*" he said, "*will be the downfall of them all.*"

With that pronouncement, Dr. Dee removed the silver watch device from his pocket, spun the dials, and, as one, the Cabal disappeared.

Author's Note

If it's possible to both broaden and narrow the scope of an extended storyline simultaneously, then the closest I have come to doing so is in writing *The Dragon's Apprentice*. I had to mix together time travel (in several directions at once), the destruction of imaginary worlds, the introduction of new enemies (the Echthroi) and new allies (the Mystorians), and the death (so to speak) of a major character, and begin the introduction of a new pantheon of Caretakers—while at the same time telling the next more personal chapter in the story of the unlikeliest of heroes: Madoc.

Because of his real-world prominence, many readers have assumed John is the central protagonist of the Chronicles of the *Imaginarium Geographica*, but in my heart of hearts, I've always believed it to be Jack (and remember, there are more books to come, so I'm by no means done with his story arc). He was my youngest Caretaker, and so almost by necessity will undergo the most changes. Similarly, Madoc has evolved from our original villain (who never quite went away) into a conflicted character whose story is closer to the heart of the series than any of the others. He has swung through what are probably the most dramatic transformations of any of the characters, and yet, he remains somewhat of an enigma. Asking if he is good or evil may be too simple a way to pose the question, and the answer would not be a very interesting one, because it wouldn't be true—not as long as Madoc is still actively playing a role in my story. In fact, I don't really believe it would be true of almost anyone, fictional or otherwise. As long as there is an opportunity for choice, there is an opportunity to change direction.

Dag Hammarskjöld said, "In any crucial decision, every side of our character plays an important part, the base as well as the noble. Which side cheats the other when they stand united behind us in an action? When, later, Mephisto appears and smilingly declares himself the winner, he can still be defeated by the manner in which we accept the consequences of our action."

I believe this to be a Thing That Is True. And it is why I wanted to write this story.

The evolution of Rose as the possible Imago was necessary to the plot, as was the chaos in the Archipelago, and the looming menace of the Dark Caretakers. The inclusion of Franklin was great fun, as was the full-circle introduction of Edmund McGee as a possible new Cartographer, fulfilling the early promise of his mapmaking family from the book I created with my brother, *Lost Treasures of the Pirates of the Caribbean*. The deepening mystery of Tamerlane House is a thrill to write, and the story of the vanished young Prince has, in part, already been told elsewhere, in another series of books I wrote for publication in a faraway land. But all of that is plot and story. To me, the heart of this book, and perhaps, when I'm done, of the series as a whole, is character and theme.

A writing acquaintance recently asked the open question as to whether the theme of a writer's work could be summed up in a single word. I replied that it could, and wrote, simply, "Redemption."

There is always a chance to choose. And, as in Hammarskjöld's example, even when you believe you have chosen the wrong path, how you accept the consequences of that choice, and then choose anew, can be redeeming in and of itself. This is true in all the best stories, all the ones we hope are real, and want to believe in. And in this story, it was true for Madoc. Just as it would be true, I hope, for me. Just as it would also be true . . .

. . . For *you*.

James A. Owen
Silvertown, USA

THE DRAGONS
OF WINTER

PROLOGUE

PULLING HIS TRENCH coat tighter against the cold drizzle of the Northampton rain, the Zen Detective sighed and checked his watch. His appointment was late, as usual. He wondered how people who seemed to spend half their lives consulting their watches could ever be late for anything.

Their watches were not like his, which was a Swiss-made, gold-plated chronograph with a pleasant little chime that played Rachmaninoff on the hour and half hour. The watches carried by his clients were less like watches and more like magic devices that could do anything asked of them. He had witnessed the watches being spoken to, as if they operated as a sort of two-way radio. Once, he saw a watch actually project an image of a creature that was all but tangible. And then there seemed to be their most frequent use, which was enabling the bearer to disappear into thin air. All of which shouldn't have detracted from their ability to keep good time, which was why he wondered how his clients always seemed to be running late.

He was still wondering when the trio of gentlemen appeared behind him, silent as a whisper. "Hello, Aristophanes," one of them said softly. "Well met."

"Hades!" the detective exclaimed under his breath, half in shock and half in relief. "I hate when you do that. And I told you—I'd prefer to be called Steve, if you don't mind."

The three men ignored his remark and simply stood there, waiting.

It was annoying, the way they played these childish games that seemed to do little more than test his patience. Still, he could ill afford to lose their business. Work in his profession was scarce enough to come by as it was, never mind the fact that his being just a shade lighter than purple, as well as being a Homo sapiens unicorn, always complicated client relations. Even when he wore a trench coat with his collar up and kept the horn on his forehead filed down, just taking a meeting was risky.

Finally the Zen Detective broke the silence. "Well?" he said gruffly. "You wanted to hire me?"

"Yes," one of the men said. "You know of the Caretakers, correct?"

The detective nodded. "They're the ones with that book," he said. "That bloody big atlas, or whatever it is."

"Indeed," said the speaker. "You've worked for them before, I believe."

"Just the Frenchman, and only now and again," came the reply. "Why?"

"They're going to want to hire you again," the second man said. "They will want you to find something . . . special. We simply want you to take the job. And to succeed."

The Zen Detective peered at them. Easy job requests got his hackles up, as well as his radar for a scam. "Is that it? Just take someone else's job? That's all you want me to do?"

"There is one other matter we'd like you to deal with, Aristophanes," the second speaker said. He moved closer to the Zen Detective and spoke softly into the other's ear. The detective's eyes grew wide, and against his will his mouth flew open as he uttered a loud, particularly vulgar curse.

"You can't be serious!" he said in disbelief, stepping back and looking at each of the three men in turn.

As before, none of the men replied, but simply stared impassively back at him.

Each time the three men had hired the Zen Detective, he always had the unnerving impression that they were not the same three men as the time before, even though they appeared to look almost alike.

No, he thought—exactly alike.

"There are only eleven personages still walking the Earth who knew, firsthand, those who were driven from Eden," the first speaker finally said. "Only thirteen more who were alive before the Flood, and fewer than a hundred who have memories of the Inversion that occurred when the Erl-King was born in Bethlehem.

"You live among a very privileged group, Aristophanes," he continued, and the tone made the statement more a threat than a compliment. "Don't give anyone cause to lessen that number. You are too valuable to lose."

The Zen Detective looked up sharply. "Better men, and greater beasts, than you have tried. Killing me is harder than you think, and if you doubt my words, you're welcome to try."

"I didn't say we'd try to kill you," the speaker replied, "I said you were too valuable to lose. And you should know that death is always preferable to exile."

Aristophanes held the speaker's gaze for a long moment, then dropped his eyes and nodded once, then again. "Immortality," he muttered, more to himself than the others. "It's a mug's game."

"No one lives forever, Aristophanes," the shadowy figure said as he twirled the dials on his black watch and disappeared. "Not even Caretakers of the Imaginarium Geographica."

PART ONE

THE WAR OF THE CARETAKERS

CHAPTER ONE
THE MISSION

---✳---

"IT'S AMAZING HOW productive dead writers can be," John commented to Jack as he scanned the shelves in the great library at Tamerlane House. "Some of our colleagues have been more productive after their natural lives than they were beforehand."

"I would chance a guess that having died brings a lot of focus and clarity to one's goals," Jack ventured. "Not that I'm planning on testing that myself any time soon."

"Take a look at this," John said, removing a fat volume bound in bright red leather and handing it to his friend. "It's Hawthorne's book *Septimius Felton*. I never realized he'd finished it."

"Finished it, and written a sequel," a familiar voice answered. The two men turned to see their friend Charles at the door, nodding enthusiastically as he strode into the room, arms outstretched. "He's having a bit of trouble with the third one, though. Twain and I are helping him work through it."

John's self-control was such that he managed to bite his tongue before blurting out what he wanted to say, but Jack was startled enough by Charles's appearance that he actually dropped the book he was holding.

"Charles!" Jack sputtered. "Your hair . . . it's—it's—"

"Purple," said John.

"Burgundy, actually," Charles said, preening slightly. "Rose helped me color it. Isn't it striking?"

"It's purple," Jack said, still staring openmouthed as he bent to pick up the book. "Whatever possessed you, Charles? That's hardly a becoming color for an editor."

"Possibly," said Charles, "but it's also the exact shade of burgundy as Queen Victoria's throne. I have it on good authority. And besides, I'm not really just an editor anymore, am I? More of a soldier of fortune."

Jack and John traded disbelieving glances, and the latter asked, "So, ah, who told you that was the color of Victoria's throne?"

"Geoffrey Chaucer."

"Mmm," John hummed. "I see."

It was traditional, in the old-fraternal-order sort of way, for the Caretakers Emeriti to prank the newer members of their secret society. The problem was that every time John, Jack, and Charles had been present at Tamerlane House, it had been in a crisis situation, and there was no time or inclination for tomfoolery. But now that Charles was a full-time resident, John suspected that the Elder Caretakers—specifically Chaucer—were having a bit of fun.

"Rose helped me do it," Charles said again as he ran a hand through his full head of hair. "She changes hers on a weekly basis."

"I'd noticed," said John, "but she's still a teenager, and you're . . ."

"Dead," Charles said. "But still optimistic about the future."

Jack laughed, and both he and John shook Charles's hands. "Fair enough," John said. "We're always happy to see you, old fellow."

The friends had gotten accustomed to having easy access to Tamerlane House through the use of Shakespeare's Bridge in the garden at the Kilns. Despite the pain they all still felt over the loss of the Archipelago, it was a comfort to be able to simply cross over and be in the company of the other Caretakers, and thus remind themselves of the value of the work they had done—and the work they still had to do.

Jack was busying himself with preparations for the eventual establishment of a reborn Imperial Cartological Society, including Apprentice and Associate Caretaker programs. It would have to remain an underground project until the Caretakers were truly ready to make it more public, but he and John had already begun actively recruiting the next generations of Caretakers, and were deliberately making it more of a global endeavor than it had been under Verne.

"I see you've found Nathaniel's book," a voice whined from the doorway. It was Lord Byron, a disgraced Caretaker who was tolerated only reluctantly by the rest of them because of Poe's insistence that he be included. "It isn't as good as he thinks it is, you know. It was better when it was unfinished."

"Say, George," Jack said, turning to address Byron, whose real name was George Gordon. "I noticed that there's nothing new in your section of the library. Has inspiration finally failed you?"

"Hardly," Byron sniffed. "I have more inspiration in my little toe than you have in your whole body. I don't need to write to demonstrate that—my life is my art."

"You're dead, you idiot," said Sir James Barrie as he entered the room, accompanied by Charles's apprentice Caretaker, the badger Fred.

"Death is but a new adventure . . . ," Byron began before the others' laughter cut him off. "What?" he said, a blush rising in his cheeks. "What's funny about that?"

"I'm sorry, George," Jack said, giving the poet's shoulder an appreciative squeeze. "All I meant was that I've often wondered why someone of your talent never applied it to some grand epic, or an ongoing work of proportions worthy of your ability. That's all."

"Oh," said Byron, who wasn't certain whether that was actually an apology. "I simply never found the right tale for that kind of treatment."

"I thought Bert might be with you," John said, shaking Barrie's hand. "Does he know we're here?"

"I couldn't say," Barrie answered. "He's been keeping to himself lately, but I'm sure he'll be along shortly. The war council was his idea."

As the Caretakers talked, Fred maintained a respectful distance and kept his opinions to himself. Technically speaking, an apprentice Caretaker had all the standing of a full Caretaker, especially among those at Tamerlane House. But Fred was still a little uncertain about his own position, considering his predecessor was technically deceased. Charles was himself still considered a Caretaker, but a Caretaker Emeritus. He was, like Verne and Kipling, a *tulpa*—a near-immortal, youthful, new body housing an old soul. And unlike the majority of the other Caretakers, who were portraits in Tamerlane, and who could leave the frames for only one week, he could go almost anywhere—as long as it wasn't somewhere he'd been known when he was alive.

To the animals, dead was dead, and while they tolerated the portraits, none of them—especially the badgers—could quite accept the tulpas. It was something about their smell, Fred once said to Jack—there was none. Tulpas gave off no odor at all. And to an animal, who determines friend or enemy, truth or lies, based on smell—that made the whole idea completely suspect.

Still, he was sworn to serve the Caretakers, as were his father and grandfather before him, and of them all, Charles had the strongest bond to the badgers. So Fred was cheerfully stoic. Mostly.

"You could do as John is doing," Jack continued, "and base a great work on stories of the Archipelago."

"I learned my lesson about that ages ago," Byron grumbled. "They set fire to me, remember? And that was just on general principles. I'd hate to see what the others would do to me if I broke one of the cardinal rules of the Archipelago."

"Others have done it before me," said John. "Most of them, actually. And as long as the stories or characters are disguised or altered, and no secrets of the Archipelago are revealed, it isn't really a problem."

"Technically speaking," said Charles, "you aren't revealing any secrets about the Archipelago, because there's nothing left to keep any secrets about."

"Believing is seeing," Fred murmured in a low voice. "Believing is seeing, Scowler . . . Charles." He twitched his whiskers as if he were about to say something more, then turned abruptly and scurried out of the room, closing the door behind him.

"Ah, me," Charles said, sighing. "I've put my foot in it again, haven't I?"

"No argument there," said Jack.

"You'd think finding his father was really alive, and not lost

with the rest of the Archipelago, would have cheered him somewhat," said Barrie, "but he can't push past the loss of everything
else, I fear."

"It was his world," said John. "And it's gone. You can't fault the
little fellow for feeling as he does."

Charles sighed heavily. "No," he said. "No, we can't. But I wish
it were at least easier for him to accept that I'm, well, me. Myself."

"Remember, Charles," said Barrie. "All good things happen . . .

". . . in time."

There was a knock at the door. Percy Shelley opened it and
stepped into the room. He scowled at Byron, then regained his
composure and faced the other Caretakers. "Gentlemen," he said,
gesturing back down the hall. "Summon the others to the meeting
room, if you please. The war council will begin within the hour."

Charles led his companions to the inner courtyard of the house,
where Sir Richard Burton and the Valkyrie called Laura Glue
were instructing Nathaniel Hawthorne, Mark Twain, and Rose
Dyson in the ancient art of the samurai sword.

Each held a *katana* about three feet long and was in a stance of
readiness. The girls faced each other, while Burton faced both of
the other men. He barked a command, and all of them erupted in
a flurry of shouts and clashing metal.

"I never caught the knack of it," Charles said over the din. "I'd
land a good blow with one of the wooden practice swords, then
pause to apologize to my opponent and allow him to regain his
footing. It's an honorable discipline, but it really doesn't mesh well
with gentlemanly chivalry."

The girls were evenly matched, and fought to a draw—but

after handily disarming Hawthorne, Burton found himself driven to his knees by Twain, who finally relented when he realized they had an audience.

The combatants turned to face their visitors, and John was struck by how Rose seemed to have changed since his last visit. There, in battle gear, with newly colored blue hair and holding a sword, she seemed to have grown older overnight, and for a moment he felt a wistfulness for the child she had been when they first met. But then again, he reminded himself, she had never truly been a child—something for which he felt honest regret.

"Uncle John! Uncle Jack! Uncle Charles!" Rose exclaimed as she tossed away her sword and jumped across the lawn to hug and kiss the three companions. "I didn't know you were here!"

Laura Glue also went to greet the Caretakers, but only after retrieving Rose's sword. "I told you," she said, glaring at the other girl as she hugged Jack, "never drop your sword. It must be a part of you."

"Something Samuel here has learned too well," Burton said as he dusted off his trousers and rose to his feet. He glowered at Twain as they greeted the others.

"He may look older than the rest of you," Burton said to John, "but he's really full of—"

"Spirit," Twain said, winking at John. "I'm full of so much spirit it just spills out of me."

"Percy asked us to fetch you," said Charles. "It's almost time for the council."

"All right," Burton said, handing his *katana* to Hawthorne. "We'll just pick up the lesson another time. Maybe next time you can fight Laura Glue, Caretaker."

"Thank you, no," said Hawthorne. "She's better than *you* are."

John pulled Twain aside as the others gathered their weapons together. "Where is Bert?" he asked, concerned. "He's usually first to greet us, and we were expecting to have seen him well before now."

A look of concern mixed with worry crossed the older Caretaker's features as he gestured at the three of them. "Come with me," he said, turning down one of the corridors. "There's something you need to see."

As the others went to the room where the war council was to be held, Twain led John, Jack, Charles, and Rose to a large screening room. It was darkened, save for the light coming from the projector in the center of the room.

"Is that . . . ?" John asked, staring at the projection in astonishment.

"Yes," Twain answered. "That's the film you brought back from the Archipelago."

The reel had been created by Bert's daughter, Aven, and left in the ruined palace on Paralon for the Caretakers to find—but neither they nor she had expected it would be two thousand years of Archipelago time before that would happen. Two millennia, during which Aven had lain in a deathless sleep. Most of those centuries were spent in a rarely interrupted hibernation inside a bed of crystal; but before that, she had ensured that there would be a way for her friends to find out what had happened, as well as a means to try to make things right, via the film Bert was now watching.

They'd been able to speak to the projected image when they

found it, but now it was simply a recorded memory of the friend who never lost hope that they would come—and who paid the ultimate price to do so.

"It's a rare day that goes by," Twain said, his voice low, "that he hasn't watched it through at least once. More commonly, he watches it several times at a sitting. Then he goes back to his work as if he hadn't a trouble in the world."

Bert's daughter had been a reluctant queen of the Silver Throne of Paralon. She much preferred her life as a dashing buccaneer and captain of the *Indigo Dragon*, and after her marriage to King Artus, did her level best to maintain that life, even as she kept an eye to her responsibilities on Paralon. But then Artus was killed in the conflict with the Shadow King, and suddenly the entire Archipelago was looking toward Aven to lead. And lead she did, right up to the moment the Keep of Time fell—and then for two thousand years after.

The companions were at a loss as to what they could say to console the old Caretaker. Of all that they had lost in their many conflicts, John thought, it was their mentor who had paid the dearest price. And it was a loss that could not be mended.

Bert finally noticed the group at the door and quickly reached out to shut off the projector. The image of Aven vanished abruptly from the screen, and the room darkened to twilight. "Ah, I'm sorry," he said, wiping at the tears on his face. "I didn't realize you were there. Just, ah . . ."

"We know," John said gently. "It's all right, Bert."

"How far can I go?" Rose asked abruptly. She was looking at Bert as she spoke. "With Edmund's help, how far in time can I travel?"

The others looked confused, but Twain realized what she was asking, if not entirely why.

"It would be my wager," Twain said, puffing on his cigar, "that young Rose here, with assistance from our new Cartographer, could go anywhere—anywhen—she chose. Isn't that correct, Bert?"

"Yes," Bert replied, looking back at Rose. "At least, that is our hope. That's what we've been working toward, after all," he continued, "finding a way to go far enough back to rebuild the Keep of Time. That will be your mission, and the reason I've called the war council. It's time. And you're ready, I think."

"That may be the primary mission, but it doesn't have to be the only one," Rose said. "Before we can attempt to go back into Deep Time, we'll have to go forward into the future anyway, right?"

"Farther than *almost* anyone has ever been," Twain agreed, nodding as he ushered the others out of the room, "to one of the only zero points we have recorded that distantly in the future. About eight thousand centuries, wasn't it, Bert?"

The old man didn't answer, but his bottom lip quivered, and his eyes started to well with tears. "Rose," he began, "I've never asked you to—"

She stepped closer to him, taking his hands in hers, and shook her head. "You don't need to ask," she said, smiling. "Of course we're going to try—as I said, we have to go there anyway."

"You've lost me," said Charles, scratching his head. "Where are you going?"

"Weena," Rose answered. "We're going to go find Weena."

CHAPTER TWO
THE BUNGLED BURGLARY

·—✳—·

AS THE COMPANIONS made their way through the labyrinth of
rooms and hallways that comprised the upper floors of Tamerlane
House, Bert chatted happily with Jack and Charles, as if nothing
significant had just taken place. But John knew that Rose's suggestion was incredibly significant—and that she must have been
thinking about it for a very long time.

It was an open secret among the Caretakers that Bert himself was the very time traveler he had written about in *The Time
Machine*, and that the woman he met there, called Weena, bore
him their daughter, Aven. But what was not discussed so openly
was the fact that after Bert returned to visit the Summer Country
in his own time, to show his daughter the world he had come from,
he had never found a way to get back to the future. Weena had
been lost to him—and not even Poe himself had conceived of a
way to go back to the far future. But Rose and Edmund, together,
could do just that.

"Can she really do it?" John whispered to Twain, out of earshot
of the others. "Do you really believe it's possible?"

"Bert thinks she is ready," Twain answered. "And I believe our
war council will concur. Rose is, for all her unique experiences,

still a youth. And she's made her share of youthful mistakes. But she has learned from them, John. And she would not have said what she did to Bert if there were a doubt in her head that she and Edmund could do this."

As he spoke, they rounded a corner to the Cartographer's Lair that had been set up by young Edmund McGee. There were maps and diagrams scattered around the main room, which was decorated in accordance with Edmund's late-eighteenth-century upbringing, but the space was dominated by a large construct that stood in the center of the room. The Cartographer was standing amid the tangle of rods and wires, making some sort of adjustment to the mechanism, when he looked up and saw his visitors.

"It's a tesseract," he said, answering the question that was on all their minds. "Diagramming the different trips through time and space that Rose and I have been experimenting with on paper was becoming too tedious, so I thought I'd try to build a working model of it all instead."

"Impressive," said Jack. "How's it coming?"

"It's been a struggle, I'll admit," Edmund said as he stepped gingerly out of the tesseract, "but a few of the new apprentice Caretakers—especially the young woman, Madeleine—have been very helpful."

He shook hands with each of the Caretakers in turn. "I take it you've come because of the burglary?"

"Burglary?" John said, surprised. "I hadn't been told anything about a burglary. We were summoned to a council of war."

"It's all part and parcel of the same thing," Edmund said as they stepped out of his lair and back into the corridor. "A number of things at Tamerlane House have come up missing—and my great-grandfather's maps were almost among them."

He pointed at the door as he closed it behind them. The handles were tied together with string, and the locks had been pried out entirely.

"Nothing else was touched," he explained, "but the maps were scattered around on the floor. If Archimedes hadn't been rooting around in the rafters where he could hear the intruder, they might have gotten them, too."

"Hmm," said John. "That's quite unthinkable, to invade Tamerlane House! Those maps must be more important to someone than we realized."

"They are important to me," said Edmund, "and they have some historical significance, I suppose, since they were drawn by my great-grandfather. But I don't know what use they'd be to anyone else—not so as to make them worth stealing."

"I agree," said John. "If anything, I would have thought it was all your own more recent maps that were most valuable."

"That's true," Twain said. "They probably are more valuable—but only to those who can use them. And as far as we know, there are only two groups on Earth who have the ability to travel in time."

John sighed heavily and nodded in agreement. When the Keep of Time fell completely, the connection between Chronos time, which was real, day-to-day clock time, and Kairos time, which was pure, almost imaginary time, was completely severed. This had several effects on both the Archipelago and the Caretakers. In the Archipelago, time fell out of sync with the Summer Country, and it began to speed up until thousands of years had passed, destroying anything familiar that was left there. It was only because of Aven's sacrifice, and her willingness to stay behind, that the Caretakers learned that somehow, the great Dragon Samaranth had taken the rest of the Archipelago someplace beyond the world itself. Someplace where it could be safe, until the Caretakers figured out how to restore the proper flow of time.

Unfortunately, the fall of the keep had also handicapped the Caretakers, rendering their Anabasis Machines, their time-traveling watches, almost useless. The doors of the keep had created focal points, called zero points by the Caretakers, that allowed them to align and utilize their watches. But when the keep was lost, so were all the reference points—and one of their own, a Messenger named Hank Morgan, paid the ultimate price to learn the truth.

It was only with the discovery of the McGee family, and particularly young Edmund, that the Caretakers found that time could be mapped; new zero points could be created. And with the help of Rose, Edmund could reestablish the Caretakers' ability to traverse time at will. But according to Edmund, none of those maps, which he kept in a book he called the *Imaginarium Chronographica*, had been touched. Only the maps made by his great-grandfather, Elijah McGee, had been disturbed, and those only depicted a handful of places in the Summer Country.

"I guess we'll find out soon enough," Twain said as he threw open the doors to the great hall where the war council was to take place. "It's time."

In the year since the fall of the Archipelago, the last vestiges of World War II had drawn to a close—but the War of the Caretakers had barely begun. It was a passive war, fought in small skirmishes on the outskirts of history, but that fact made it no less a war, nor its effects any less potent.

It was a war of ideas, and the battlefields were the smoke-filled taverns, and libraries, and stages, where stories were whispered with an urgency that gave them the ring of truth. Stories that were believed more and more as time passed. And that belief was what allowed the darkness in the shadowed corners to creep closer and closer, crowding out the light.

For many years the Caretakers had believed their greatest enemy was the one called the Winter King, and more than once they fought and defeated aspects of him. But his rise to prominence had been fostered by a coalition of rogue Caretakers who formed the original Imperial Cartological Society, which had even darker goals than establishing the Winter King. Many members of the Society, including Richard Burton, Harry Houdini, and Arthur Conan Doyle, realized that a greater evil had permeated their group, and so they left, defecting back to the Caretakers. But that evil, which had formerly operated in secret, was now becoming bolder and bolder. And in the last year, the Caretakers were finally able to give it a name: Echthroi—the primordial Shadows. The original Darkness. And through the Lloigor, corrupted agents recruited by the Echthroi, they had taken over the Archipelago—and now threatened the Summer Country.

A war of stories was still a war—even if the only ones who knew it was being fought were a group of storytellers, gathered together in the house of Edgar Allan Poe.

The Caretakers took their customary seats around the great table. At the head sat Geoffrey Chaucer, who, as an Elder Caretaker, often presided over their meetings. The other Elders, including Edmund Spenser and Leonardo da Vinci, took their seats to his left and right, with the younger Caretakers seated at the far end. The other guests of the house who were not Caretakers, such as Edmund McGee, Laura Glue, Rose, and the clockwork owl Archimedes, took up positions along the walls where they could watch and, when invited, participate.

Rudyard Kipling, away on assignment for Jules Verne, attended the council via trump, as he usually did. Being one of the only other Caretakers who was actually a tulpa gave him exceptional freedom to travel with none of the constraints the others had, and so he was their de facto eyes and ears in the world.

Burton leaned close to John. "What happened to Charles's head?" he whispered. "He looks as if he's been dipped in a boudoir."

"He colored it burgundy," John whispered back, "because Chaucer told him that was the exact color of Queen Victoria's throne."

Burton's brow furrowed in puzzlement. "But it wasn't . . . Ah," he said, as the realization dawned and a smile spread across his face. "Geoff's having a bit of fun, I think."

"Probably," said John.

Chaucer saw the two men conversing, and sussed out what subject they were discussing from their covert glances at Charles. He gave them a quick wink and a grin before shifting his expression to a solemn one and rapping on the table to bring the meeting to order.

"As the current Caretakers have joined us," Chaucer said with a nod to John, Jack, and Fred, which thrilled the little badger immeasurably, "we may now begin this council of war." He paused and looked around the table—one seat at the opposite end was empty. "Where is the Prime Caretaker?"

"He's, ah, indisposed at the moment," Bert said suddenly. "I'm sure Jules will be here as quickly as he can manage."

"Ah," Chaucer said in understanding. "He's with his goats again, isn't he?"

"This is behavior unbecoming of a Caretaker," da Vinci sniffed. "Especially for the Prime Caretaker."

"Oh, be quiet," Charles Dickens said, scowling at da Vinci. "This has been a difficult time for all of us, and each of us needs a way to blow off some steam before our boilers explode. Give the man his goats."

"I agree," said Spenser. "After all, Samuel there has his butterfly collection, and Dumas loves to cook."

"True," said Alexandre Dumas. "And Tycho over there steals things."

"I do not!" said Tycho Brahe. "You can't prove that I do!"

"Tycho, my young moron," said Twain. "We live on an island. Everyone knows you stash the evidence of your crimes in the north boathouse. Nathaniel gathers it all up and replaces everything each Thursday."

"Oh," Brahe said, crestfallen. "Uh, thanks for that, Nathaniel."

"My pleasure," said Hawthorne. "It's easier than cleaning up after the things George Gordon, our Lord Byron, does to de-stress."

"I resent that," said Byron.

John, Jack, and Charles had long become accustomed to the fact that a meeting of the Caretakers Emeriti never went straight to the business at hand. There was always a breaking-in period when the various personalities traded brickbats with one another until things finally settled down enough to discuss the real issues.

"Who is the fellow in the west alcove?" Jack whispered to Charles as the other Caretakers continued to argue. "I don't recognize him. Is he one of Burton's people?"

Charles and John glanced up to where Jack was looking. There, some ways back in the alcove, but still near enough to comfortably observe the whole room, was a man in a sand-colored cloak. He was hooded, but his face was clearly visible, and he had taken note of the fact he was being observed.

"Well, don't look right at him!" Jack said, blushing.

"It's all right," Charles said, grinning. "He isn't one of Burton's. He's one of Verne's. That's one of the Messengers—Dr. Raven, I believe."

"A Messenger," Jack said, now glancing back up against his own will. "Interesting. I thought Jules usually had them traipsing about on errands."

"Apparently he thought this was worth sitting in on," said Charles, "although I must admit, it is a bit unusual."

"Unusual?" John said. "I should say so. This is the Caretakers' war council. Outside of Laura Glue, Edmund, Rose, Archimedes, and maybe Houdini and Conan Doyle, I wouldn't have thought anyone else would be allowed."

"You trusted Ransom and Morgan, correct?" Charles asked. "He's no different. We just know him less well."

"I don't know . . . ," Jack said doubtfully. "What do you think, John?"

Before the Caveo Principia could reply, Chaucer rapped on

the table again to try to bring the meeting to order. But John had
noticed that the whole time they were discussing the Messenger,
Dr. Raven had not been watching the other Caretakers. . . .

He'd been watching *John*.

"There has been a burglary at Tamerlane House," Chaucer said
somberly. "Verily, we have been burgled. The Cabal has brought
the war to our very doorstep."

"The Cabal!" Jack said, shocked. "Are you certain?"

"As certain as we can be," Dickens said in answer. "The
Echthroi themselves have no need of common burglary, so it can
only be their agents who have done this."

"John Dee may have been a renegade Caretaker," Burton said
gruffly, "and the other members of the ICS might have disagreed
with your beliefs about the Archipelago, but I hardly think that
means they're Lloigor."

"They may not know whose cause they serve, Richard," said
Chaucer. "You yourself know that better than any else here."

"Harrumph," Burton growled in response. "Still, how would
they have even found Tamerlane House?"

"The bridge," Jack said simply. "Shakespeare's Bridge, which
connects the house to the Kilns. We've trusted that secrecy has
been enough—but the location, and where it leads to, could be
found out, I suppose."

"Yes," Chaucer agreed, "the way is open. And we do not know
enough about our enemies' capabilities to rule out some sort of
espionage effort to find and use it."

"It would seem to me," Twain said, lighting another cigar,
"that the *what* of it is no longer in question, because it has already
taken place. The *how* of it is, and may remain, a mystery. But what

concerns me at the moment is the *why* of the thing. Why was it necessary to burgle our abode?"

"Edmund said that they tried—and failed—to steal old Elijah's maps," said John, "but if that was a failure, then what was taken?"

"A portrait," a loud voice boomed from the entry doors. "A few trinkets, a few baubles, and one of Basil's portraits. That's what was taken—and that's how we know, without doubt, that Dee's Cabal is responsible."

Jules Verne strode into the room and took his seat at the head of the table opposite Chaucer.

"How?" John exclaimed, too surprised to even offer a greeting to the Prime Caretaker. "Which portrait?"

"The only one," Verne replied, "dangerous enough to be sealed up behind a brick wall."

"Oh dear," said Jack. "You mean . . ."

"Daniel Defoe has escaped," said Chaucer, "and to where, we have no idea."

"We had opened up the wall," Chaucer explained, "in order to interrogate Defoe about the lost prince—but he was reluctant to offer any information that could be deemed as helpful, even under extreme coercion."

"What he means," said Burton, "is that we tried our level best to torture it out of him, even to the point of setting fire to the portrait. But he held his tongue. Apparently, he's made of sterner stuff than others among us."

"Rude," Byron sniffed.

"We know that whoever broke out Defoe's portrait also

wanted Elijah McGee's maps," said Chaucer, "although they failed to claim those."

"So other than Defoe, what was stolen?" asked John.

"A key, which was important but not irreplaceable," said Verne, "a statue of Jason's wife, Medea, which is irreplaceable but not important, and," he added with a slightly puzzled look on his face, "every pair of eyeglasses in Tamerlane House."

"That's a very strange laundry list for a burglar," said Jack. "Any idea why those things were taken?"

"Not particularly," Verne said, giving Bert an odd look, "but it's the escape of Defoe that we've focused on—because it's the only theft that includes a timetable."

"How do you mean?" asked John.

"Defoe's a portrait," said Verne. "He can leave the frame outside of Tamerlane House, but only for seven days."

"Yes," Bert said, nodding. "And we believe that the Cabal is planning some sort of initiative in that time, which is why I called for this council. We have spent a year reestablishing the zero points in time to allow our watches to function, but if we are truly to be able to defeat our enemies, we must resolve once and for all the question of how to rebuild the Keep of Time. And we must do it now."

"I understood that such a leap in time as that would require is not yet possible," said da Vinci.

"Rose believes that it is," Bert said, gesturing to the girl, "and I believe her. She *is* ready. It's time."

"It's time to pursue your personal agenda, you mean," said Burton. "Going to the past means going to the future first. And only an idiot couldn't guess when you want to go to, and why."

"It's not just for personal interests of my own that we're doing this," Bert shot back. "Ask Poe. He knows."

The reclusive leader of the Caretakers Emeriti nodded impassively from his post at the landing high above the room. "He is correct. In order to attempt a crossing of Deep Time into the past, to discover the identity of the Architect of the keep, a journey into the future must be made. It is the only way to balance out the chronal energies. And to go to a point that has been traveled to before only increases the odds that it will become a zero point. What Bert suggests is the only wise course of action."

"Crossing back to the present from eighteenth-century London is one thing," said Jack. "This seems like it will take more than a map and a piece of string."

"Machines have always been required to go into the future," said Verne. "That was one aspect of the Keep of Time that we realized from the start: It was recording time as much as anything else. The fact that it continued to grow, but somehow also continued to keep its connections to the past, was forever a mystery to us. As a means of travel into the past, however, it was both consistent and reliable. That ended once it fell."

"It had its own link to the future, though," said Charles. "The last door, up at the top."

"The door the stairs couldn't reach," said Bert, "but it did exist. The future was tangible, behind that door. That's how we knew traveling to it was possible."

"Anything within recorded history was reachable," said Verne, "through the means we developed here at Tamerlane House. Backward and forward within around twenty-five hundred years could be done with reasonable fidelity and accuracy. But that was when the tower still stood, and the doorway to the future still existed."

"Hah!" Burton laughed. "If we'd thought about this sooner, perhaps we could have salvaged that door. But it's a little late for that now. All the doors are gone."

"It wasn't the doors that were important," said one of the other Caretakers, who had been silent until now. "It was the *stone*."

William Shakespeare rose to his feet and continued. "If we can't yet rebuild the keep of the past, we might still be able to build a gate to the future," he said placidly. "If the council would just permit me—"

"And the time may yet come to put your plans into motion, Master Shaksberd," Chaucer said, dismissing the Bard's request with a wave, "but now is not that, uh, time." He turned to Edmund. "What does our young Cartographer say? Can you truly do this?"

Edmund swallowed hard and stood. "I believe we can, sir," he said, glancing at Rose. "It will take me most of the day to prepare the chronal map, but once that's done, we can go as soon as you give the word."

Chaucer glanced at the other Caretakers, then at Verne, who nodded, and Poe, who simply arched an eyebrow. "The word is given," Chaucer said finally. "May the light be with us all."

CHAPTER THREE
THE RINGS OF JULES VERNE

—✳—

THE NEXT ORDER of business was the security of Tamerlane House, to prevent any further intrusions while Edmund prepared the new map. Shakespeare's Bridge was the only substantial access point from the Summer Country, and Hawthorne and Laura Glue were both stationed there as guards, rotating in shifts with Byron and Washington Irving. There were others among the Caretakers who were willing to serve as guards—but who hadn't the physical prowess or inclination to really be any good at it. However, there were other means of entry, and those were not so easily guarded against. The most obvious were the trumps—the illustrated cards carried by Verne's Messengers and several of the Caretakers, which allowed them to communicate with one another, and to travel between places depicted on the cards.

"There's no way of knowing what trumps the Cabal has use of," Verne said once the Caretakers had reassembled in the meeting hall, "so we must be prepared for any eventuality."

"They couldn't come here anyway," John said pointedly, "since except for the one Kipling uses, there aren't any trumps that lead directly to the Nameless Isles or to Tamerlane."

"None they'd have had access to, anyway," Verne said, frowning. "But they might have access soon. Dee knows the process, and Defoe spent a lot of time here. So the whole place could be an entry point, if they create a new trump for it."

"How do we defend against that?" asked Charles. "If they can make a card for any spot Defoe's seen?"

"With these," said Verne. He took a small pouch from his vest pocket and emptied the contents onto the table. A scattering of silver rings spread across the surface, glittering in the light.

Charles picked up one of the small circlets and examined it. "Rings?" he said curiously. "How will these help protect Tamerlane House?"

"Hold it close to the candle flame," Verne instructed. Charles did so, and as the silver touched the flame, runes began to appear on the surface of the ring.

"Deep Magic," said Chaucer. "We had them made by the Watchmaker, after the method he used for the watches. But the runes are linked to those carved on standing stones, which Shakespeare is placing around the perimeter of the main island, and on either side of the bridge."

He pointed to the *Imaginarium Geographica*, which sat on a pedestal where it had rested, unused, since the fall of the Archipelago. "There is an incantation in the earliest pages, which will activate the stones, and the rings. And when it is spoken, no one without a ring can set foot on this island."

"How many rings are there?" asked John. "Enough for all of us?"

Verne nodded. "They were modeled after the one that Poe wears," he said, tipping his head up at the alcove above. "There are rings for everyone at Tamerlane, and all our apprentices and associates in the world beyond these doors, some of whom already have theirs. In short, there will be a ring for every agent of the Caretakers, given by my own hand. That's how we'll know who is to be trusted, and who isn't."

"It sounds complicated," Jack murmured. "How do you make sure all our allies are given rings? Can more be made if we need them? And if so, what's to stop the Cabal from having their own rings made?"

"Hell's bells, Jack," Verne snorted. "To be frank, I really can't answer most of that. I'm making this up as I go along, and just trying to do the best I can to serve the needs of whatever crisis is before us. Some of my Messengers, like the knight and his squire, have them already. Others are waiting. But in any case, I don't think it's wise to have an excess over what we actually need, and the fewer people who have access to Tamerlane House, the better."

"So this was your idea, Jules?" John asked.

"Mine, actually," a voice purred above John's right shoulder. He turned his head just in time to see the Cheshire smile appear, followed by the eyes and whiskers of his cat, Grimalkin. "Easier to say who can come and go, if those coming and going have a Binding to protect them."

"So will th' Caretakers still need th' watches, then?" Fred said glumly, looking down at his own watch. "I haven't even had mine all that long!"

"The pocket watches have long been the sole means of identifying fellow Caretakers and our agents, but in truth, they had never been intended as such," said Chaucer. "It was more in the spirit of camaraderie to approach one of our number and realize, with both joy and no small relief, that he carried a watch. He was of one's tribe."

"The rings just mark someone as an ally," Charles said to his apprentice, "but the watch still says you're a Caretaker. And you are, Fred," he added. "One of us."

"As a covert identifying marker, however," said Verne, "the method was far from infallible and had been subverted more than once." He gestured at the half-formed cat wrapped around John's shoulders. "And Grimalkin is correct," he said. "To accept a ring is to accept the Binding that comes with it. And once accepted, it cannot be taken from you, and can only be given if offered freely, and accepted on the same terms. And those are terms," he finished, "we know the Cabal will never accept. Not while they serve the Echthroi."

"Why not?" asked Jack.

"Because," said Verne, "the Binding invokes Deep Magic, which can only be used by one of noble worth, in a cause of selfless intent—and the Echthroi have only ever served themselves."

"Enough speechifying, Jules," said Bert. "Let's just get on with this, shall we?"

One by one, each of those gathered at Tamerlane House accepted a silver ring from Verne. When they had all been given out, Rose read the passage in the *Geographica* that Chaucer indicated. As she spoke the last word, a wave of energy swept over the entire island.

"Well," said Verne. "That's it and done. Unless someone has one of these rings, or is already here, they're not setting foot in the Nameless Isles."

"Amen," said Grimalkin.

+ ◆ +

After the ceremony of the rings, the Caretakers separated briefly to reflect on the events of the day and plan their next strategies. John, Jack, and Charles, however, held back, and indicated for Twain to do the same. After a few minutes, the room had cleared, and they were alone except for a few of the Elder Caretakers who were still talking at the far end.

"What can I do for you boys?" asked Twain.

"Bert has been very, ah, anxious this entire time," said Jack, "no pun intended. I've seen him under stress before, and it's always been like water off a duck's back. It never sinks in with him. So why is he so testy now? It can't just be because he wants to go find Weena."

"It isn't," Twain said, drawing them away from the others into the corridor so he could speak to the three friends in complete privacy. "Our friend is operating under a severe time constraint. And he's aware of every tick of the clock."

"What kind of constraint?" asked John. "Is he ill?"

"Nothing like that," Twain replied. "You know that he is an anomaly, that he has a temporal near-twin, correct?"

"Sure," said John. "Herb—the real H. G. Wells, or at least, the one Verne started with."

"Precisely," said Twain. "And you know that our Bert has aged a great deal more than Herb, due in large part to all his wandering around time and space."

All three companions nodded, afraid to speak of what they feared was coming.

"Bert is," Twain said softly, "the only non-tulpa time traveler, but he is still bound by the rules of Chronos time, or real time, here in the Summer Country. And the person he was, the person he may still have a connection to, is about to kick the bucket."

"Oh dear," John said, closing his eyes.

"What?" Charles said, looking at Jack. "I don't . . ."

"What I mean to be clear about, and apparently failed at," said Twain, "is to tell you that in seven days, H. G. Wells is going to die. And that means Bert may too. So he has just one week left in which to go find his ladylove."

The statement hit the three companions like a thunderclap, shaking them so badly that for a moment, none of them was able to speak.

"Like Ransom, when Charles . . . ," John said finally, swallowing hard. "Like that."

"Yes," said Twain. "That's exactly what we expect to happen."

"That's awful, of course," said Charles, "but if I can offer my own very informed opinion, I died, and I got over it. Won't Bert? I mean, after the fact, he'll still be a Caretaker. And we have ways of dealing with these things."

"Yes," Twain agreed, "except you chose to become a tulpa, whereas Bert has never strayed from the plan that when he eventually perished, he would join the rest of us here in the portrait gallery. We've tried to convince him to do otherwise, but he simply won't be swayed. His will to do what he believes is best is simply too strong."

Finally it dawned on Charles what the real urgency was. If Bert became a portrait, he might never be able to travel through time again—and certainly not into the far future or the deep past. There was simply too great a risk that he would not make it back to Tamerlane House in the allotted week. And then . . .

"What happened to Stellan could happen to him," Jack said, completing Charles's thought. "No wonder he's so stressed."

"Indeed," said Twain as he began to guide them back into the room where the other Caretakers had started to gather again. "So, best efforts, eh, boys? For Bert, if for no other reason."

"That," John said, "is more than reason enough. And all the reason we'd ever need."

The Caretakers were gathering again in the meeting hall because there had been a crossing over Shakespeare's Bridge. Two of Verne's most trusted agents had just returned, and just in time—because they would be needed to fulfill the next part in his battle plan.

"Well met," Don Quixote said, bowing deeply as he entered the meeting hall. "Greetings, Caretakers."

John and Jack both stood to take the knight's hand—which John noticed already bore one of Verne's silver rings—and Rose gave him a hug and a kiss on the cheek, which made him blush. It was a deserved warm welcome—but it was nothing compared to the response his squire Uncas got.

Every time Uncas visited Tamerlane House, with or without the old knight, there was the equivalent of a hero's reception and parade held in the library. The library of Tamerlane House had been all but taken over by two dozen foxes and hedgehogs, all Paralon-trained librarians and archivists, who were led by the new head librarian—a fox called Myrret. And to these animals, Uncas was not merely a knight's squire or an associate of the Caretakers—he was a legendary badger.

"Since I became Don Quixote's squire," Uncas had explained

to the starstruck animals, "I hadn't had as much time as I'd liked to visit back t' th' Archipelago. It was only luck that we wuz doing a secret errand for Scowler Jules that spared us bein' lost with everyone an' everything else."

"Your name was well known to all the Children of the Earth," Myrret said admiringly. "The son of the great badger Tummeler, who saved the Scholar Charles in the battle with th' Winter King . . ."

"'Saved'?" asked Charles.

"Poetic license," said Jack, "I'm sure."

". . . and the father of the Caretaker Fred," Myrret went on, "you deserved the honors given to you and monuments named for you—even if you did not perish so long ago, as we once believed."

"How many badgers can there be with the name Charles Montgolfier Hargreaves-Heald?" asked Charles.

"In point of fact," said Myrret, "there were eleven. Not counting juniors and thirds."

"All right then," said Charles. "I'm so glad I asked."

"I have another mission for you," Verne explained to Quixote and Uncas as he handed them a slender, cream-colored envelope. "Your instructions are there, as per usual. And yes," he added, with a wry look at Uncas, "you get to use the Duesenberg."

"Hot potatoes!" Uncas said, jumping onto his chair. "Let's get going!"

Several of the Caretakers accompanied the knight and his squire back to the bridge and over it, to the Kilns. Charles relished each opportunity to return to the Summer Country, given that he could only do so occasionally since he'd become a tulpa. To Jack it was simply going home. And for John, it was a chance to keep the world he lived in connected to the one he'd become responsible for. At times, long years passed between visits to the Archipelago—and it sometimes seemed as if that other world was only a dream. But now that it was gone, John thought wistfully, it seemed more real than ever. And he missed it.

"We no longer have the resources of the Archipelago to draw upon," Verne was saying, "but that does not mean we are wholly without resources—however questionable some of them may be."

"What's that supposed to mean?" asked Jack.

"That we use what resources we have," Verne said as he opened the door to the 1935 Duesenberg that sat alongside the house, "and we call in the favors that we can, from those who are able to grant them."

Uncas gleefully took the wheel as Quixote bent his lanky frame in the seat beside the badger. "We'll be back soon, Scowler Jules," Uncas said as the engine growled to life. "You c'n count on us."

"I know," Verne said, almost inaudibly. "I know we can, little fellow."

"Is it really prudent to just let them go driving around in the Duesenberg like that?" John asked as the vehicle roared away, scattering gravel as the tires spun.

"It's not really a problem," Verne replied. "Everyone in England drives like that. No one will notice one more insane driver."

"That's not what I meant," John persisted. "Quixote may be able to pass, but isn't it a little irresponsible of us to let a talking badger go driving around out in the open? In the old days, that would have gotten us in a lot of trouble."

"Ah, but it isn't the old days anymore, is it, young John?" said

Verne. "The world is turning its attention away from certain things, and the loss of the Archipelago has made this even more pronounced. No one sees . . .

". . . because no one is looking. Not anymore."

"That's terrible, Jules," said John. "Someone should look. Or at least, remember."

"That's a large part of the reason it's our practice to recruit writers as Caretakers," Verne replied, looking intensely at his protégé. "It's part of your job to write down the stories so the world doesn't forget.

"So no one ever forgets."

Verne held John's eyes a moment, then wheeled about, waving to the others. "Come on, then," he called out over his shoulder as he strode back to the bridge. "We've done what we can do for now. It's up to Uncas and Quixote to see where we'll go next."

CHAPTER FOUR
THE RUBY ARMOR OF T'AI SHAN

———✳———

FOLLOWING THE DIRECTIONS in the cream-colored envelope, Quixote and Uncas drove northward from the Kilns and Oxford, to the gray, industrial town of Northampton. It took more than two hours to make the trip, and another two once they'd gotten there to find the address they were seeking. At first they had argued a bit as to whether they were reading the map properly— but when they found the actual building, both realized that they would have been hard-pressed to find it even if they'd been there a hundred times before.

It was a low, sloping edifice, which was tucked away on an alley off a side street near a seldom-used thoroughfare, and it looked as if it had been built at least three centuries earlier, and had not been repaired since just after that.

A dimly lit speakeasy was housed on the ground floor, and none of the windows on the two floors above showed any evidence of occupancy. Quixote was about to declare the whole adventure a misfire when Uncas tugged on his sleeve and pointed at the narrow stairs leading down to an apartment below street level.

"There," the badger said softly. "I think that's where we're sup-posed t' go."

Cautiously they made their way down the steps and were debating using the half-attached door knocker when a gruff, scratchy voice within called out, "Well, come on in! No sense standing out there waiting for the plaster to peel."

The knight and the badger entered the apartment, which was one large room, divided only by the struts and braces that supported the structure above. On the far side were greasy windows, framed with ramshackle blinds that let in bands of light from the street outside.

There were filing cabinets of various sizes scattered around the room, which formed rough, concentric circles around the gravity of a massive, dark desk, at which was seated a large, heavyset man who wore a hat and a tattered trench coat. He didn't rise to greet them, but waved them over to stand in front of the desk.

"I'm Steve, the Zen Detective," the man said without offering his hand or asking his visitors to sit. "But if you knew how to find me, then you probably already knew that."

"Zen Detective?" asked Uncas. "What do you detect?"

"I help people to find themselves, among other services," the detective replied, giving no sign that he cared that the question was asked by a badger, "although most don't actually like what I find, so I've learned the hard way to ask for my fee up front, cash on the barrel."

"How do you lose yourself?" Uncas asked, patting himself on his stomach. "I'd 'a' thunk that'd be hard t' do."

"It's easier than you think," said the detective. "Mostly it happens through inattention, but sometimes it's deliberate." He snorted. "Those are always the ones who have the most urgent need, and are always just as reluctant to pay."

"Hmm," Uncas mused, looking around at the shabby office. "Do you really make a living doing this, uh, 'Zen Detecting,' um . . . Steve?"

"His name," said Quixote, "is Aristophanes."

"I prefer Steve," the detective replied, sniffing, "but yes, you speak the truth."

"That's awfully familiar to me," said Uncas. "How is it that I would know you?"

"Well," the detective replied, "I was once a noted philosopher. Perhaps you read—"

"Naw," said Uncas. "I'm not a big reader—you're thinking of my son. Say," he added, leaning closer. "Are you, uh, purple?"

"It's a birthmark," the detective replied testily.

"Over your whole body?" said Uncas.

"Don't you have any birthmarks?" Aristophanes shot back. "Or doesn't your species have such a thing?"

"Of course we do!" said Uncas. "In fact, I myself have a birthmark around a mole on my—"

"Decorum, Uncas," Quixote interrupted, waggling a finger. "Decorum."

"Heh." Aristophanes chuckled. "A badger with a mole. That's funny."

"How does a philosopher end up becoming a detective?" asked Uncas. "That seems like two very opposite perfessions."

"All philosophical inquiry," said the detective, "can be boiled down into just two questions. The first"—he counted off on his fingers—"is 'Am I Important?' And the second is 'Can I Survive?' There's nothing in philosophy that isn't somehow covered by those questions. And every case I take as a detective ends up asking them as well."

"Hmm," Uncas said, tugging on his ear and squinting. "I don't recognize it. It is from Aristotle?"

"No, it isn't from Aristotle!" the detective shot back. "It's from one of my own teachers, who was relatively unknown, but a great philosopher still."

"What was his name?" asked Quixote.

"He didn't have one," Aristophanes replied. "He preferred to be known by an unpronounceable symbol, so most of his less imaginative students just called him 'the Philosopher.' That's part of how Johnny-come-latelies like Aristotle got credit for some of the stuff he actually thought of."

"What did *you* call him?" asked Uncas.

"He started all his dialogues by making this glottal sound with his throat," said Aristophanes, "so I called him 'Larynx.'"

"A great Greek philosopher named, erm, *Larry?*" Quixote asked, confused. "That sounds very, ah, improbable."

Uncas shrugged. "Detectives named Steve could have teachers named Larry," he theorized. "It could happen."

"Not Larry, *Larynx!*" Aristophanes retorted angrily. "And it was only a nickname, anyway. Besides, it doesn't matter what he was called—the quality of the thinking is what is important to a philosopher. The rest is just advertising."

"And yet you became a detective," said Quixote. "Interesting."

Steve scowled. This wasn't going the way it was supposed to have gone. He had assumed that a lanky, out-of-sorts knight and a talking badger would be pushovers, but somehow, this unlikely duo had managed to get him talking about himself—which simply wouldn't do. Not at all.

"So," Aristophanes said gruffly, tapping the desk. "Enough talk. Time is money. Let's see your dough, and then we'll find your Zen, or whatever."

"Is this really the right feller?" Uncas asked behind his paw. "He seems a little . . . off t' me."

"He's the right fellow, all right," Quixote said as he rummaged around in his duffel. "I know I had it here somewhere . . . ," he muttered.

"Aha!" Quixote finally exclaimed as he found what he'd been searching for. "Here you go," he said, dropping a small drawstring bag on the detective's desk. "Thirty pieces of silver—your traditional price for this kind of job."

The Zen Detective made no move to retrieve the bag, but simply sat, staring at it with a passive expression on his face. At length, he inhaled deeply, then exhaled the air in a long, melancholy sigh. "Silver," he said at last, eyeing Quixote. "Verne sent you, didn't he?"

The knight nodded. "He did, yes."

"And whom is it you would like me to find?"

"It in't a whom, it's a what," said Uncas.

"We've been instructed," Quixote said with all the formality of an official request, "to ask you to locate the Ruby Opera Glasses."

Aristophanes fell backward over his chair and crashed to the floor. He rose in an instant, cursing under his breath, then more loudly as he set his chair back on its legs and took his seat.

"You don't ask for much, do you?" he said, squinting suspiciously at the knight and the badger. "Why not ask for the Cloak of the Paladin, or a shard of the true cross, or the Spear of Destiny while you're at it?"

"Actually," Uncas said, brightening, "what happened with the spear was this, see. . . ."

"Never mind that," Quixote said as he scowled at the badger. "We really do just need the Ruby Opera Glasses."

"If I *could* locate them," said the detective, "I would require an additional fee. And then there might be an additional cost to acquire them. How much is Master Verne . . ."

In response to the unfinished question, Quixote reached back into his duffel and removed a second bag of silver. Then a third. And a fourth.

Uncas let out a slow whistle of appreciation. "That's a lotta nuts," he said, looking from Quixote to the detective and back again. "What's so special about these glasses anyhoo?"

"The glasses are the only object in all of the Summer Country that can detect the presence of an Echthroi," said Aristophanes.

"Is this sufficient?" Quixote asked, indicating the bags on the desk. "I'm not authorized to pay more, but I could ask if needed."

"To locate them, yes. But it won't be nearly enough," the detective answered, "for what we're actually going to propose to the Frenchman."

"And what is that?"

"The rest of the armor," Aristophanes said simply. "It still exists. And what's more, I know where to find it."

It was a credit to Quixote's self-control that he did not react to this news, but kept his expression steady; and it was a credit to Uncas's self-control that all he did was whoop with excitement.

"Th' scowlers will be so excited to know that!" Uncas exclaimed. "Th' rest of the armor! Imagine that!"

"Do you even know what the armor is?" asked the detective.

"Not at all!" Uncas admitted. "But it sounds right stellar!"

"What do you ask of us?" said Quixote.

"Simple," Aristophanes replied as he leaned back in his chair and crossed his feet on top of his desk. "I want to be dealt back in."

The old knight looked confused. "Dealt back in? You want to play cards?"

Aristophanes groaned. "No, you idiot. Dealt back into the *game*. The Great Game. I want my seat at the table. I want to rejoin the flow of the world."

"That's for the Prime Caretaker to decide," Quixote said after a moment, "and I daren't even consult him with such a request, when we don't even know if you're capable . . ."

Aristophanes ignored the knight's comments and opened up a drawer on the left side of his desk. He reached in, removed an object, and placed it on the desktop.

"There," he said. "The Ruby Opera Glasses. That alone should convince Master Verne that I can find the rest of the armor."

The knight and the badger peered curiously at the glasses, which, other than the thick red lenses, looked like any other pair of antique opera glasses. "Tell us about this armor," Quixote said, gingerly touching the glasses. "To whom did it belong?"

"A great warrior named T'ai Shan," Aristophanes answered, "who lived many, many thousands of years ago. She was the Imago of this world, which made her the mistress of time and space, and she was respected and feared by all. Even," he added darkly, "the Echthroi."

Uncas frowned. "So this, Inag . . . Imuh . . . This person lived thousands of years ago, did she?" he said as he examined the opera glasses. "Beggin' y'r pardon, but these seem t' be a bit too muchly on th' contemporary side t' be real."

"Master, uh, mistress of time and space, remember?" said Quixote. "Perhaps she acquired them during the dispatching of her duties as Imago—whatever those entailed."

"She disappeared long ago, even before the Archipelago of Dreams was created," said the detective, "and the armor was thought to be lost. But it was found again during the Bronze Age, by those who knew of its power and sought to use it.

"The helmet, breastplate, and gauntlets are still intact," Aristophanes continued, "but the leggings were dismantled so that the ruby could be used in the creation of five other objects of power."

"Like the opera glasses," Uncas said. "I get it."

"The light dawns," said Aristophanes. "As I told you, the glasses can be used to detect the presence of the Echthroi, and also their servants, the Lloigor. The second object that was created is a brooch, which does exactly the opposite: It can hide someone from being seen by an Echthros or a Lloigor.

"The third object, which has been missing for several centuries, is a comb. That's the one I really wish I could find," he added ruefully. "Using it banishes an Echthroi Shadow from its host.

"The fourth object is almost as useful—a Ruby Dagger, which can actually cut an Echthros, even those who have bonded themselves to a mortal. Although," Aristophanes said, "the damage to the Shadow is mirrored in damage to the host. So it's a weapon of last resort, unless you really don't care about the host."

"I suppose that would depend," said Uncas, "on who th' host was."

"A pragmatic attitude," the detective philosopher replied with a surprised expression on his face. "Very wise."

Uncas shrugged. "Animal logic. What's the last object?"

"Objects, not object, actually. A pair," Aristophanes corrected. "Ruby shoes. They allow the wearer to instantly transport to anywhere they wish, simply by fixing the location in their mind, then tapping the heels together."

"What of the intact armor pieces?" asked Quixote.

"Of those, the helmet may be the hardest to find," said the Zen Detective, "which is ironic, because it enables the wearer to find their way between any two places. Someone wearing the Ruby Helm cannot get lost.

"The breastplate has been the object most sought after through the centuries, because the general perception was that it was the most powerful. He who wears the Ruby Breastplate is invulnerable in battle against any mortal foe," Aristophanes said, with a slight emphasis on "mortal."

"And against, say, the Echthroi?" asked Quixote.

The Zen Detective shook his head. "Against them, not so much. It's still very powerful, but without the comb and the brooch, no defense against an Echthros."

"And the gauntlets?" asked Uncas. "What about them?"

"Strength," Aristophanes said. "The more opposition, the stronger the wearer becomes, with," he added, "one proviso. They don't give you strength, they just allow you to draw more of the strength you already possess. So if they are used for too long in battle, you could conceivably win . . ."

"And still lose your life," Quixote finished. "Worth noting, I think."

"You really know where all these things is? Uh, are?" asked Uncas.

"I do," Aristophanes said. "They are secreted away, in the corners of the world where magic is real and still worth looking for."

"Alas, but those lands are gone now," said Quixote. "The Archipelago of Dreams—"

"There was a lot of magic in the lands of the Archipelago, that's true," the detective interrupted, nodding. "But they were not all the magic places there are."

"And you can find these places then?" asked Quixote. "We've already paid a considerable fee just to find the glasses—which you already had in your possession. So for the rest . . ."

"I'm not bartering with you here," Aristophanes said gruffly. "This is an all-or-nothing deal. If you take me with you and Verne agrees to my request, then I'll help you find the rest of the objects. If you decline to do even that much, then I swear on all the gods of Olympus that you will never see me again."

Quixote sighed heavily, and with a nod of assent from Uncas, held out his hand. "Your word?"

Aristophanes paused long enough that Quixote dropped his hand, then the detective nodded sharply. "For whatever it's worth, you have it," he said brusquely. "Give me just a moment, and then we can go."

He took the bags of silver and locked them all in a heavy safe set within one of the filing cabinets. Then he opened another and removed a large black case, which he handled very carefully.

"This should be all we'll need," he said, looking at the two companions. "Let's go find your armor."

It was perhaps the most unusual group to ever arrive at the Kilns, Warnie decided, and after the last several years, that was not an easy benchmark to clear. He had procured the 1935 Duesenberg specifically for the Caretakers to modify for Quixote and Uncas's use—mostly because of the small windows, which made it harder to see the badger. Unless, he noted ruefully, Uncas was driving, which happened more frequently than not. Quixote complained that he simply hadn't the temperament for dealing with a horse-less carriage, and so was perfectly content to let the badger drive. This was again the case as the battered old vehicle came skidding into the drive next to the cottage.

"Almost like driving one of th' old principles back home," Uncas chortled as he clambered from the driver's seat. "'Cept it smells. Steam and ecstatic lectricity is so much cleaner."

A stout man with an unusually dark complexion stepped from the seat behind the driver. "You mean static electricity," he said brusquely. "There's no such thing as 'ecstatic lectricity.'"

"That's a very skeptical outlook," Quixote said as he unfolded himself from the passenger seat and stretched out his cramped frame in the sunlight. "Especially coming from a two-thousand-year-old philosopher unicorn detective."

Before any of them could comment further, a delegation of Caretakers emerged from behind the house. Jack and John led the way, followed by Charles and Byron, Bert and Verne, and behind them, Dickens and Burton, with Twain and Hawthorne, both of whom carried samurai swords, bringing up the rear.

"You come bearing arms, Caretakers?" asked Aristophanes. "A strange way to greet your guests."

"You're a contractor, not a guest," Verne said without both-ering to make introductions. He turned to Quixote and Uncas. "What's the meaning of this?"

"We did as you requested, Master Verne," Quixote said. "The price was acceptable, and he located the Ruby Opera Glasses right away." This last was said with a wink at the detective—the old knight's effort at camaraderie. "As to the cost for acquiring them, he has a proposal he'd like to make. I think you should give him a hearing."

"Why did you bring the detective with you? For all we know, you've just brought the serpent into the heart of the garden, so to speak."

"I'm not *that* old," Aristophanes snorted.

"It is my understanding," said Quixote, "that this fellow excels in finding things that are hidden, and he already knows a great deal about the Caretakers. So we trusted him the full mile—but only because of what else he has to offer."

Verne and the others looked at the detective expectantly. "Well?" asked Verne.

"The Ruby Armor of T'ai Shan," Aristophanes replied. "I know where it is. All of it. And if you bring me into the inner circle, I'll lead you to it all."

Quixote and Uncas briefly recounted the Zen Detective's proposal, along with the description of the armor and what it could do. When they finished, John and Verne both asked if they could look at the glasses, and after a moment's reluctance, Aristophanes handed them to the two Caretakers.

"You didn't say anything about these, Jules," John murmured as he peered into the ruby lenses. "Why? Especially if they'd be so useful against the Echthroi."

"I didn't know if they could be found," Verne admitted, "so I didn't want to get anyone's hopes up. But now," he added, taking back the glasses and returning them to the detective, "it seems they may have led us to an even greater treasure—if we can afford the price."

The detective nodded. "I think you can."

"Well, possibly," John said. He turned to Aristophanes. "I'm sorry, but I know nothing of you. And I'm not that prepared to trust you. The fact that Verne could not bring you in openly, as one of his Messengers, gives me pause. And if he does not trust you fully, then I don't believe the rest of us can either. Revealing the secrets of the Caretakers is too high a price to pay for this armor, or whatever it is."

"Speaking as one who has been on both sides of this debate," said Burton, "I have to agree."

John turned to Bert and Verne. "This deal is suspect. I don't trust his motives."

"My motives?" Aristophanes exclaimed. "My motive is the one you can depend on most—self-preservation. If that is a man's true motive, then all his other causes may lay exposed to the world, naked as a babe. Because you can always determine the truth of his words, by simply asking whether he benefits from his choices."

"I hate to be the bearer of bad tidings," said Charles, "but we have a *lot* of enemies, and their number seems to be growing almost daily. How exactly is it an act of self-preservation to plant your flag on Caretaker Hill?"

"You're not a fool," the detective replied, eyeing Charles's pocket watch. "Men are judged by the quality of their enemies, and that makes you powerful indeed. And I know"—he glanced at Verne—"who it is that runs the secret machineries of the world."

"Your benefit is obvious," said John, "but ours is not."

"If this armor is that important," Jack suggested, "can't the Messengers find it?"

"They're engaged in other work," Verne replied. "And there aren't as many of them as there used to be."

"The truth of it is that you need me," said Aristophanes. "That swings the weight to my side of the scale."

"You're not as indispensable as you think," said Verne. "We have maps of all the places the armor may be hidden—finding it is just a matter of time."

"Maybe you do," the detective said quickly, "but you are unable to make good use of them—or you wouldn't really need me at all. And after the recent burglary at Poe's house, you almost didn't have *those.*"

Verne turned and raised an eyebrow at Uncas.

The badger squirmed. "Uh, was I not s'pposed t' tell him about that?" he asked apologetically.

"Well, since we already have the glasses . . . ," Verne murmured. "But on the rest of the matter, we seem to be at an impasse."

"In point of fact," Aristophanes said, raising a finger, "you paid me to locate the glasses, not give them up. I think I'll hold on to them, for now. And it's you who are at an impasse, not me.

"I've named my price, Frenchman," the detective continued, feeling his boldness grow in the opportunity of the moment. "The whole package—you hire me to find and acquire all of the Ruby Armor, and I will deliver it to you complete—including the glasses. If you decline, then I go, and the glasses go with me."

John looked at Jack, Charles, and Bert, who all nodded. "The glasses alone seem invaluable," said Jack, "and it seems he *can* deliver what he's asked to find. So I think it's worth risking."

The Caveo Principia held the detective in his regard a few moments longer, then nodded his assent to Verne.

"All or nothing, is it? Then it seems we have no choice but to trust you," Verne said heavily. "We have our agreement, detective."

"Excellent. Shake on it?" Aristophanes said, sticking out his hand and laughing as Verne recoiled. "Sorry. Just a little joke."

"Very little," said Verne.

Warnie bid his brother and friends good-bye, making certain to give Charles an especially warm handshake, before going inside to put on a pot of tea. Verne excused himself to retrieve Elijah McGee's maps from Tamerlane House—taking great care not to allow Aristophanes to see the bridge—leaving the other Caretakers to keep an eye on the Zen Detective.

"I like your hair, Caretaker," Aristophanes said to Charles. "It's very distinguished."

"Thank you," Charles said, beaming. He gave a look of *I told you so* to his friends. "It's the exact shade of Queen Victoria's throne, you know."

Aristophanes looked puzzled. "No, it isn't. Her throne was black—black velvet."

Charles looked flustered. "But—but—" he stammered. "Chaucer said—"

"Chaucer?" Aristophanes exclaimed. "*Geoffrey Chaucer?* He wouldn't know the truth if it bit him in the—"

"Hang on there, detective," Twain said, swinging his *katana* up under the other's nose. "Let's not be maligning senior staff now, hey?"

"Whatever," Aristophanes said, holding up his hands. "I think all you people are crazy." He chuckled grimly. "I must be crazy myself to want to side with you."

"You're probably right on both counts," Twain said as he twirled the sword in the air, "and don't you forget it."

The detective grunted in response as Verne crossed back over the lawn and handed Uncas a leather folder.

"Here they are," he said to the badger. "The maps of Elijah McGee. They should be everything the Zen Detective needs to find the armor, and I am entrusting them to your care, Uncas."

The badger's eyes widened, and he gulped as he accepted the parcel of maps, but he nodded in understanding and gave the Prime Caretaker a dignified salute. "You can count on me, Scowler Jules," he said. "I mean, uh, on us. Except for Aristophanes, I mean."

"By Zeus's knickers!" the detective exclaimed as he climbed into the passenger seat of the Duesenberg. "I told you—call me Steve."

"We'll keep an eye on him, too," said Quixote. "Never fear," he added as he lowered himself into the rear seat. "We'll see this through."

"We have no doubt," Jack said as the automobile roared to life. "Do we, fellows?"

But none of the men answered. John was looking at the vehicle as it sped off into the distance, and Verne . . .

. . . was looking at John. His brow creased with worry for the young Caretaker and what was to come, but only for a moment. His face broke into his customary smile, and when John turned, Verne winked at him.

After a moment, the sounds of the Duesenberg faded, and without speaking further, the Caretakers crossed back over the bridge.

PART TWO

THE CHRONIC
ARGONAUTS

CHAPTER FIVE
DAYS OF FUTURE PAST

·—✳—·

THE CHRONOGRAPHER OF Lost Times stood at the tall windows in his athenaeum and considered the small stoppered flask he held in his hand.

Inside, a wisp of smoke curled against the glass in a slow, almost deliberate motion. In the right light, it sometimes seemed to coalesce into a face, and the expression it wore was one of confusion.

The Chronographer smiled grimly. Confusion was acceptable, but fear would have been better. It would come in time, however. Everything comes in time.

"Dr. Dee," someone called out to the Chronographer from the doorway. "I trust it's as you hoped?"

"It was nearly too late," Dee snapped back before composing himself. "You took too long, and we nearly lost our opportunity."

Tesla clenched his jaw, then strode into the room to stand next to the other man. Tesla was tall and fit, and his features were handsome, although he often wore a cold, clinical expression, which ensured that no one looked at him for long, or twice. "We nearly lost Crowley in acquiring it as it was," he said, his voice

434 JAMES A. OWEN

clipped and precise. "The Caretaker's brother returned to the cottage as he was leaving, and that would have undone us all."

Dee scowled. "He wasn't supposed to be near the house at all!" he snapped. "It was too great a risk."

"It was a necessary one," Tesla replied soothingly. No point in irritating Dee for nothing. "He couldn't risk transporting from the Caretakers' fortress itself—we still don't even know if it exists in real space or not. Better to have risked exposure than to lose them both. It was difficult enough just to get across the bridge."

Dee eyed the flask. "Yes—yes, you're correct. I had just assumed that more precautions would be taken."

Tesla shrugged. "The cat was watching out for any interlopers and could have dealt with them accordingly. And Lovecraft and I were waiting here on our side should he need any intervention in Oxford. Really, it went about as well as it could go. And now," he said, pointing at the flask, "we have it."

"Indeed," said Dee. He handed the flask to the scientist and noticed a marked increase in the motion of the smoke inside. "You know what to do. Is the other one ready?"

"Quite nearly," Tesla replied as he turned on his heel and began to walk out of the room. "I'll give you a further report later today."

"And our Archimago project?" Dee added. "How goes that, Nikola?"

The scientist stopped, and paused for a moment before answering. "It goes . . . according to plan," he said, measuring his words carefully. "Complete isolation, as you'd instructed. He will have grown to adulthood without having the slightest idea of who he really is."

Dee turned to look at his colleague. "You still disapprove, I take it?"

Tesla ran his hand through his hair and looked at the floor. "Blake believes—"

"Blake is not the Chronographer!" Dee shouted. "He is an adept, but he is not irreplaceable. No one is, except for the boy. The girl whom they believe is the Imago was raised to believe she had a great destiny, and that makes her unpredictable. So the only way to control the Archimago was to make sure he believed he had no destiny at all."

Tesla looked up. "If he is what we believe, then he won't believe that for long, once we bring him back. And once he realizes what he can do . . ."

"He will already be sworn to serve our ends," said Dee. "And if for some reason he chooses not to, we'll just cast him back into the future. Irreplaceable does not mean necessary," he added, looking at the flask in the scientist's fingers. "The girl is Shadowed, remember. And if we can't use him, then perhaps we'll still be able to turn her. Either way," he finished, eyes glittering, "we win."

Tesla seemed to want to say something further, but instead pocketed the flask and walked out, shutting the door harder than necessary.

"Excellent," the Chronographer murmured to himself when he was alone once more. "All things pass, in time. And soon enough, they will. And then . . . at last . . . I will truly be the Master of the World."

Almost as if responding to his words, the long shadows in the room rose from the floor and swirled about until the entire athenaeum was cloaked in darkness.

✦ ✦ ✦

The returning Caretakers were greeted on the East Lawn of Tamerlane House by Fred, who rushed to embrace Uncas; Laura Glue, who was still brandishing her own *katana*, and upset that she hadn't been allowed to go with the others to the Kilns; and Edmund and Rose.

"I'm one of the best fighters at Tamerlane," Laura Glue pouted. "I should have been with you, even if you didn't really need me."

"There will be a much more important mission at hand for you, little Valkyrie," Verne chided gently as they walked to the house, "and against much more dangerous adversaries than old Aristophanes."

"She ought to go with Rose and Edmund, then," Byron offered, trying to lighten the mood. "Not much point to saving the world if you can't save your woman, too, eh, Bert?"

"Shut up, George," said Hawthorne.

"What?" said Byron. "I was being sincere! How can I ever participate if you try to shut me up whenever I say anything at all?"

"You can't," said Hawthorne. "And just so you know, I'm not agreeing with you here."

"Well," Byron grumbled, "I'm just saying I think Bert's reason for going is better than everyone else's."

"Mmm, thank you, George," said Bert. "But it really is more important to repair the Keep of Time. Anything else must be secondary to that goal—however much I would want it to happen."

"Whoever else goes with Rose and Edmund," said Verne, "you'll be among them. You've earned that, Bert."

"If push came to shove, I suppose *you* could always have just tried taking the machine in the basement yourself, Jules," Bert replied, not entirely with conviction. "After all, we know it worked at least *once*."

Verne started, then shifted in his chair, as if the suggestion was an uncomfortable one. "I . . . appreciate that, Bert," he said with a bit too much joviality, "but the machine wouldn't work for me. Not again, at any rate."

Bert looked at his associate, puzzled. "You've taken it out? And come safely back? I wasn't aware of that."

Verne waved off the remark. "Yes, yes. It went . . . well. But it's not important now. Our concern is how to get you to the future and back safely, so we can finally go about this business of rebuilding the Keep of Time."

"I meant to ask," Jack said to Verne, "what's this about goats in the Himalayas?"

"It's a lake in Mongolia, actually," Verne said. "Not many people know about it. I keep the herd in the ruins of an old castle there."

Jack suppressed a grin. "I, ah, never took you for a goatherd, Master Verne."

Verne drew himself up and frowned. "I don't spend all my, ah, time traipsing around in history," he huffed. "I have to have a way to vent my stresses. Everyone does, or they turn into Byron."

"Hey, now," said Byron.

"Interesting," said Charles. "What do you call your herd?"

"The Post-Jurassic Lower Mongolian Capra Hircus Horde," Verne said with such obvious pride that Rose feared he might actually pop a vest button or two. "I'm raising two of them in particular to be show goats," he went on. "Elly Mae and Coraline. Fine, fine stock. Took first and third in their classes at the Navajo County Fair last year."

"Erm, Navajo County Fair?" Charles asked.

"Arizona," Verne answered. "No one knows livestock better than the Navajo, except for perhaps the Lower Mongolians. They appreciate the exotic lineage of my goats in ways the European cultures cannot."

It was John's turn to suppress a grin. "And what lineage would that be?"

Verne's eyes narrowed and he pursed his lips, unsure if he was about to be made the fool, but he explained anyway. "My goats," he said, resuming his prideful tone, "are descended from the stock of Genghis Khan himself, and were brought into the West by Marco Polo. Some mingled with the lesser stock of the northern Europeans, but Elly Mae's line bred true, and Coraline's almost as much."

"Hmm," said Charles. "I take it that's where the third-place award came from?"

"The judge cheated," Verne replied. "He put a foot out of place when I wasn't looking."

Jack looked at John and shrugged. "Jules Verne showing goats descended from the herds of Genghis Khan in a county fair in an Indian nation in America," he said. "Now I think I *have* heard everything."

"I would have thought you would raise goats from the Archipelago," said Charles, "if you really wanted to make a showing, that is."

"Considered it," said Verne, "but for one thing, they're harder to breed, and for another, they kept insisting on driving the car themselves."

"And," Byron added, "there is no Archipelago anymore. It's all Shadow."

Hawthorne cuffed Byron across the back of his head. "You see?" he huffed. "This is why we don't take you anywhere."

More quickly than any of them had expected, including himself, Edmund finished the chronal map. It was almost three feet across, mostly to allow for the symbols that ringed its border, which were necessary to accurately pinpoint the date to which they would travel.

In celebration, the Elder Caretakers called for a dinner in honor of the mission. John and Jack exchanged silent glances of frustration with Twain, knowing that every second that passed was another one lost to Bert, but nothing could be done. To the Caretakers Emeriti, who were largely confined to Tamerlane House, ceremony was everything. In the dining hall, Alexandre Dumas and the Feast Beasts quickly put together what Dumas referred to as "a light dinner," which nevertheless consisted of enough food to have stocked the Kilns for a year.

"So," said Twain when they had all eaten their fill, "who's up for an adventure?"

Burton let out a loud belch. "What you're really asking is, 'Who gets to go?'"

The Caretakers and their associates all looked up from their plates. It was not an academic question—the group selected to go on the mission had to be carefully chosen, if for no other reason than if they ran into trouble, they would not be able to draw on the Caretakers' resources for help. Those chosen would be on their own.

"Rose and Edmund, as per usual," said Verne. "And of course, Bert will go," he added, clapping his colleague on the shoulder.

"Th' three Scowlers should go," said Fred. "For something this important, *they* should make the trip, if anyone."

Verne hesitated and looked at the other Caretakers. Until this moment, none of them had considered whether—or if—they wanted to actually make this trip. But now, faced with the possibility, they realized that all of them wanted to, badly.

"I'm sorry," Verne said before any of them could volunteer, "but of the three of you, only Charles should be allowed to go."

John and Jack were immediately crestfallen—but they also understood right away what Verne meant. They were still living Caretakers, in the Prime Time of their actual life spans—but Charles was a tulpa, like Verne, Kipling, and a few others. He could withstand stresses and injuries that they could not—but more importantly, if he were lost, it would not affect the natural timeline.

"But Scowler Verne," Fred started to protest, clutching his paws in sympathetic anguish. "Scowler John an' Scowler Jack . . ."

"No, no, it's all right," John said, chuckling softly. He bowed his head for a moment, then looked up at his friends. His eyes were shining with tears. "I suppose in a way, I was looking forward to one last, great adventure, just like we had when all this began. That's how we all met, remember? When Bert came to the club at Baker Street?"

"Impossible to forget it, old friend," Charles said, giving in to his impulses and hugging his friend. "I'm, ah, sorry you're still alive and can't come along."

"I've had my adventures," Jack said, putting his arms around both Edmund and Rose. "It's time for a younger generation to earn their teeth."

"To, uh, *what?*" asked Edmund.

"It's a rite of passage," Jack replied, "for every crewman aboard a Dragonship."

"Do you remember, Jack?" Bert asked. "Do you remember the day you earned your dragon's tooth from Aven?"

Involuntarily Jack put a hand to his chest and felt the small bump where the tooth hung around his neck underneath his shirt. "I remember," he said, smiling wistfully. "I've never taken it off."

During their first adventure together, when a younger Jack was infatuated with the older captain of the *Indigo Dragon*, he had performed many feats of bravery, and more than once had saved the ship and its crew. And so during a quieter moment, she had presented him with a dragon's tooth—the mark that he had earned his place among the crew. It was more than decorative—it was one of the original dragon's teeth sown by Jason of the *Argo*, in his quest for the Golden Fleece, and thus it had several magical properties that came in handy onboard a ship. It could be turned into a stave for fighting, or a grappling hook. But mostly it was a symbol to other sailors—a statement that his place among them had been earned, not given.

Later, after having made some terrible mistakes, Jack had tried to give it back, but Aven refused. "No," she had told him firmly, "it's not an honor you lose. You earned this. But you're learning some hard lessons—and that's part of the deal too." So he kept it. And in that moment at Tamerlane House, he was glad he had. It was one of the connections he had had with Aven that neither of his friends had been given, and for that reason, he treasured the memories it brought.

"Yes," Bert said as he looked at Jack and wiped away the tears that were welling in his eyes at the memory of his daughter. "I can see that you do."

None of the Caretakers Emeriti could go, because of the limitations of the portraits—they could survive for one week outside the bounds of Tamerlane House, and no more. This was a guideline that had been underscored by the terrible loss of John's mentor, Professor Sigurdsson.

For the same reasons that John and Jack couldn't go, a petulant Laura Glue was also denied the chance to join the others, as was Fred. Burton, however, insisted on going, and stated it flatly, as if the matter was not open to debate.

"Technically speaking," he said, "I still represent what's left of the official ICS, and I'm not really a Caretaker. So I have a right to go. Also," he added, "like our friend Charles, I'm a tulpa, so there will be less risk."

"We don't have other tulpas who can go?" Jack asked Verne. "Like Kipling? Or maybe . . ." He stopped and looked around at the gathering. "Where are Houdini and Conan Doyle, anyway, Jules?"

"Er, ah," Verne sputtered, caught off guard by the question. "Kipling is on other business, and Houdini and Conan Doyle are, ah . . ."

"Tell them," said Dickens.

"They're tending my goats," Verne admitted sheepishly. "I've taken them on as apprentice shepherds."

"Good Lord," Burton said, slapping his forehead. "I weep for this and all future generations."

◆   ◆   ◆

The discussion continued as the Caretakers left the banquet hall and repaired to the lawn outside, where Shakespeare had constructed a simple stone platform to mark the point where the company of travelers would cross into the future.

"It's cavorite," he explained to the others. "Edmund and I realized it would give him and Rose a stronger point to link to for the return trip."

"Brilliant," said Jack. "Marlowe would never have come close to anything this clever."

Shakespeare tried not to beam with pleasure at the compliment, but failed miserably. "My thanks, Jack."

Fred was quite put out at not being allowed to accompany his friends on their journey into the future, particularly since Charles was going.

"It's my job," the little badger protested. "I'm the fourth Caretaker, after you, an' I should be going along to watch your back."

"I understand," Charles said with sincere sympathy, "but it's precisely because of that that I need you to stay here at Tamerlane House. John and Jack are going to need you here—no one else is as skilled a researcher as you are, Fred. That's part of your job too."

The little badger tried not to pout, but wasn't very successful. "Th' *bird* is going, though."

"Archie is the best reconnaissance agent we have," Bert said, winking at the clockwork owl perched on Rose's shoulder. "Taking him along is a safety precaution."

"Also," Burton interjected, "there's very little danger of the Morlocks accidentally eating the bird."

"Well, all right," Fred said with obvious reluctance. "But at least take along my copy of the Little Whatsit. I won't need it here, since I'll have th' whole library at my disposal. But you never know when it might just save your lives with some tidbit or another you didn't know you needed to know until you needed to know it."

Charles took the book and scratched Fred's head. "Of course, my friend. Thank you." He stored the book in his duffel alongside the *Imaginarium Geographica* and a few of the Histories that Verne and Bert had selected.

"Humph," Byron snorted. "He scratches the badger and the animal preens, but I try to do it as a friendly gesture, and the little beast bites me."

"Badgers are excellent judges of character," said Twain.

"Oh—right," said Byron.

Charles shouldered the duffel bag and moved to stand alongside Bert, Rose, Burton, and Edmund. Archie hopped to Charles's shoulder and beamed at Fred, as Rose tucked her sword, Caliburn, under one arm.

"We have our company then," said Bert, "and all of you have my gratitude."

"Close your eyes and think of Weena," Rose whispered, taking Bert by the hand. "You're going to see her, very soon."

Edmund and Rose held the map in front of them and concentrated on it. Instantly it began to glow, then expand, and in seconds was large enough to cross through. It was dark on the other side, but the sun was setting behind Tamerlane House as well, so that meant little.

"Farewell, my friends," said Verne, "and safe return."

The Chronic Argonauts, as Archie had dubbed them, in honor of one of Bert's stories, stepped through the portal and into darkness.

CHAPTER SIX
THE ANACHRONIC MAN

—*❈*—

IT WAS DEFINITELY not the world they came from, or at least, it was obvious that it was a different time. The air smelled different, and there was a startling sort of energy that vibrated through the gloomy twilight.

As soon as they were through, the portal closed, becoming a map once more, and where there had been the images of all those they had left behind at the Nameless Isles, there was now only more of that penetrating darkness that surrounded them.

"We were right," Rose said in both delight and relief as she turned to Charles and embraced him. "We did it!"

"Well done, both of you!" Charles said, returning Rose's hug and clapping Edmund on the back. "I daresay you're getting better at these jaunts all the time."

"Quiet, all of you!" Burton snapped. He was looking at Bert, who had already walked several paces away from the others. "Something's wrong."

The other companions moved to stand with Bert, so they could have a better look at where and when they'd actually come to. Charles and Burton removed two electronic flashlights from

Charles's duffel, so they could illuminate the area and get their
bearings.

The portal had opened onto a small plaza, which was paved
with some form of concrete. It was seamless, and nearly smooth,
and it spread outward in geometric patterns from where they
stood on Shakespeare's platform all the way to the buildings that
formed yet more geometric patterns in the distance. Beyond those,
they could see the shapes of great, dark pyramids, which rose
above the rest of the city like silent guardians.

Charles whistled. "Impressive," he said, looking at Bert. "You
never mentioned the city in your book."

Bert looked back at the taller man, his brow furrowed with
worry. "That's because there *wasn't* one—not one like this, at any
rate. There was no London, no Oxford. No cities of any kind.
None of this should be here, Charles."

"I read it too," Rose said, pointing up at the sky, "and I don't
remember any mention of those, either."

Higher in the sky, above the spires of the city and obscured
by the clouds, were the faint outlines of massive structures that
arced across the sky from horizon to horizon. The companions all
gasped in shock at the immensity of what they now realized were
all-too-familiar shapes.

They were *chains*.

Unimaginably massive, each link was larger than the tallest
building before them, and there were at least seven chains that
they could see crisscrossing in the atmosphere.

"No," Bert breathed when he could find his voice again. "Those
were definitely not here."

"Who could have built such incredible chains?" said Edmund,

clearly overwhelmed with the concept. "And raised them so high into the air?"

"I'd be more concerned with why," Burton said as Charles nodded in agreement. "Chains are made to keep something out, or . . ."

"To keep something in," Charles finished.

"I think," Bert said, his voice trembling, "that we are in trouble. This is not my future," he continued, the trepidation and fear rising in his voice as he spoke. "Not the future I came to before."

Charles checked the date on his watch. "No," he said, trying to sound reassuring even as he fought his own rising panic at Bert's words. "It's the correct time. Ransom and Will calculated it from the point you left the first time, plus almost four years, so that we would arrive almost exactly after you and Aven left. This should be exactly the right place, exactly the right time."

Bert looked at Charles, then opened his own Anabasis device. "Eight hundred thousand years?"

"And a pinch more," said Charles. "It should be the year 802,704 AD, and a few months."

"Something *has* changed," Bert said, the anguish in his voice tearing at their hearts. "Something happened, and the future changed . . . and Weena is not here."

"Wouldn't the Histories of the future give us some clue?" asked Rose. "Surely there would be some sort of pattern to them that can be traced, to see if we miscalculated."

"Not over eight hundred thousand years," said Burton. "Not over that long a time. Too many things may have changed for the same lives he remembers to have been lived. He's right—she's gone. She's not here, and she never was."

Bert turned to the Barbarian and swung his fist, connecting hard with the other man's chin.

Burton staggered backward and rubbed his jaw. "I'm getting very tired of being struck by Caretakers."

"You aren't that stupid, Richard," a glowering Bert said, almost breathless with anger. "You understand better than most how this all is supposed to work. If something's gone wrong, it can still be fixed. If reality has been changed, then it can be changed *back*."

"If it's a reality that no longer exists in this time, Bert," Charles said gently, "then why do you believe it can still be put right?"

"Because," Bert said, opening his hand to show them what he kept in his inner pocket, "I still have Weena's petals."

Charles whistled, then reached out and gently stroked the fragile wisps of color in Bert's hand. "The flower she gave you before you left," he said admiringly. "You've kept them all this time?"

"I have," Bert said as he replaced the petals inside the jacket pocket, "to remember. And now I keep them to believe," he added, jabbing a finger at Burton. "She existed. She exists. And somehow, I will find my way back to her."

"Fair enough," Charles said, realizing that his largest role in this expedition might be that of peacemaker. "So let's start by finding out what's happened to the world in the last eight thousand centuries."

The companions walked slowly along the paved pathways, being cautious about their surroundings. At Rose's behest, Archie took flight to better scan the area, but on Bert's advice never flew higher than twenty or thirty feet. Something about the great chains in the atmosphere made him wary of intruding into the airspace of this world any more than absolutely necessary.

"Is this anything like the Winterland?" Burton asked Charles. "That alternate reality we, ah, accidentally caused with the Dyson incident?"

"I wasn't there," Charles said, looking a bit crestfallen. "I'm sorry. Whatever aspects of Chaz I may have don't include his memories of that time—so I have no idea if this is a similar situation or not."

Bert was paying less attention to the men conversing than he was to Rose and Edmund, who were trying to work out something that seemed troubling to them both.

"It's Ariadne's Thread," Rose explained when Bert inquired as to what was the matter. "I can't manage to connect it to Edmund's map. If it won't connect, we can't establish a zero point here, and the Caretakers will have no idea of when we really are. And," she added, "we might have a really difficult time getting *home*."

Ariadne's Thread was the magical cord given to Rose by the Morgaine—the three near-eternal goddesses also called the Fates. The thread was what allowed Rose to connect the maps of time made by Edmund to other zero points.

"It's always worked before," said Edmund, "ever since that first time, in London. There's no place in real time we *haven't* been able to connect to."

Bert smacked a fist into his other hand. "By the cat's pajamas," he exclaimed. "I knew it! This is a might-have-been, not the real reality. Otherwise, Edmund would be able to connect Rose's thread to his map. It won't connect because this is only an imaginary land. Which means," he added with a note of hopefulness

that matched the expression on his face, "we can go back and try it
again. And this time, I know we'll succeed."

Hastened by their shared desire to leave the dismal Night
Land and return as quickly as possible to Tamerlane House and
the Kilns, the companions made their way back to the plaza much
more quickly than they'd anticipated. And so it was still only twilight when they finally reached the platform.

Edmund opened his *Chronographica*, where all his maps
were stored, and retrieved the one that would take them back to
Tamerlane House in 1946. Together he and Rose concentrated on
the map, but nothing happened.

"That's odd," said Edmund.

"Worse than odd," Rose said. "Ariadne's Thread isn't connected to this one either—and it's a confirmed zero point."

They tried several other maps, but to no avail. None of them
were working, or connected by Ariadne's Thread.

"Oh dear," Bert said weakly. "I think that we are in trouble."

"The usual kind?" Charles said.

"No," Bert replied. "The special kind. With nuts and caramel
sauce. And a cherry. A great big, red, flaming cherry on top of
a huge, delicious pile of nut-and-caramel-coated, special-delivery,
once-in-a-lifetime trouble. That kind."

"It's this might-have-been business, isn't it?" Charles asked,
rattled by the realization of what was happening. "That's the
problem."

"Going from a place that exists to a place that doesn't exist is
easy," Bert lamented, nodding. "But going from a place that doesn't
exist to a place that does . . . not so much."

Rose gasped. Edmund scowled. And Burton uttered a string

of curse words that had not been spoken aloud by a human more than twice since the fall of Babylon, just as a large stone came flying through the air, striking him viciously in the face.

The companions spun about to look in the direction from which the rock had come, expecting to see some fearsome enemy, or a clutch of Morlocks. That wasn't what they saw.

To one side of the plaza, a hunched, shabby-looking man was muttering to himself and cradling a rock in his hands as if preparing for another throw.

Shouting, Burton and Charles rushed forward and grabbed the man's arms, throwing him down and pinning him to the pavement.

Burton, who was bleeding profusely from the wound along his left cheekbone, removed the second rock from the wailing man's hand, and was not gentle about it. There was a snapping sound as the man's wrist broke, which only caused him to howl all the louder.

"Stop that infernal screeching!" Burton bellowed, "or I'll really give you something to howl about!"

"Oh," Bert said. He'd suddenly gone pale, as all the blood drained out of his face.

Rose recognized the expression on her teacher's face. "What is it?" she asked as she looked from Bert to the strange man and back again. "Do you know him? Is he one of Weena's people? One of the Eloi?"

Bert shook his head. "Not one of the Eloi, no," he said, his voice trembling with emotion. "One of us."

Charles blanched as he and Burton lifted the man roughly to his feet. "What? He's a Caretaker?"

"Not a Caretaker," Bert answered. "A Messenger, and the only time traveler to become so completely lost that no trace could be found to even hint as to where he went. Jules called him the Anachronic Man—the man lost in time."

At the mention of Verne's name the man took a breath to start howling again, but a stern look from Burton silenced him, and he simply swallowed hard, then looked at Bert with wide, frightened eyes. "Far Traveler?" he said meekly. "Is that you? Have you come to rescue me at last?"

"Rescue?" Burton said in surprise. "Who is this, Bert?"

Bert sighed heavily before answering. "Rose, gentle sentients," he said with a tight grin, "I'd like you to meet Arthur Gordon Pym."

"Had to do it," Pym said once he'd calmed down and gathered his wits. Rose and Charles were using bandages from the kit Bert always carried to bind up his broken wrist as he spoke. "No telling whose side you were on," Pym went on. "Can't leave one's enemies just strolling about."

"But," said Edmund, "we aren't your enemies at all. We didn't come to rescue you, but you've just attacked your friends."

"The irony is delicious to me," said Pym.

"He's an idiot," said Burton, who was gingerly touching his own bandaged face as the others tended to the injured Messenger. "We didn't have any idea you'd be here."

"Oh," said Pym. "Did you come here for the others, then?"

That stopped everyone in their tracks.

"What others?" Charles asked carefully, fully aware that the Messenger might still be speaking stuff and nonsense. "Other Caretakers?"

Pym seemed about to answer when his eyes widened in shock as Archie circled low enough to join in the conversation.

"If he's a friend, I fear to see our enemies in this place," the mechanical bird said, "but I suppose there's no accounting for taste."

"It . . . it isn't real!" an astonished Pym stammered.

"No, he's real, all right," Burton said wryly. "Nothing imaginary could be so irritating."

"What do you think, Archie?" Edmund called to the bird circling overhead. "Are you real, or aren't you?"

"All of you sound smarter," the bird replied, sneering at Burton's feigned respect, "when you aren't trying to sound like philosophers."

"So speaketh the adding machine," said Burton. "I can barely hear you over the sound of your gears."

"That's why I keep a small oilcan in my pack," Edmund said, glancing at the dark clouds. "In foul weather, Archimedes tends to, um, squeak."

"I do not!" Archie squawked in indignation. "I emit nothing but the sounds of my proper functioning. To squeak would be uncouth."

"You squeak," Rose said, nodding and holding up her hands in resignation. "Sorry. Edmund is right."

Suddenly, without warning, Pym's right arm shot up in a curving arc, launching a large, jagged rock high into the air . . .

. . . where it struck the hovering Archimedes with a terrible, grinding crunch.

"Spies," Pym said, panting. "His spies are *everywhere*."

Edmund and Rose cried out and rushed to where the damaged

bird had fallen. Edmund reached Archie first, and he cradled the bird in his arms.

"Are you *insane?*" Charles exclaimed, shaking the hapless Pym by the shoulders. "No wonder Verne stopped looking for you! You're worse than Magwich!"

The stone had struck the bird with such force that it tore a gash in Archie's torso from just above his right leg to his neck. Only luck or the bird's quick reflexes had allowed him to tip his chin back at the last instant and avoid having his head torn off his neck.

As it was, the damage was bad enough. Gears and wires were spilling out of his chest and onto the ground, where a tearful Rose was attempting frantically to gather them up and stuff them back in.

"Oh, my Archie!" Rose cried. "You've killed him!"

"He's a clockwork, Rose," Bert explained gently. "He can be repaired back at Tamerlane. We have Roger Bacon's books, and Shakespeare has become quite adept at working with delicate machinery. We'll fix him, I promise."

Pym seemed to have already forgotten the entire incident and had gone back to muttering to himself. Charles and Burton joined the others and circled around Edmund and the damaged bird.

Edmund seemed almost numb with shock. He knew, intellectually, that his recently acquired companion was a mechanical bird—but it was a different thing to have that point clarified in such a violent manner.

"Well," said Charles, "Messenger or not, when we get back to Tamerlane House, there's going to be an—" He stopped and looked around, groaning. "Drat! Where's Pym gotten off to?"

"I couldn't say, since I didn't see him go," Burton said, his voice low but steady. "I did, however, see the new arrival, who is watching us now."

He tipped his head to the north, and the others turned to see a man calmly watching them from about twenty paces off.

The man was pale—no, more than that, Rose realized. He was an albino. His skin was almost entirely free of pigmentation. He wore something that resembled sunglasses over his eyes, and was dressed simply, in a tunic and breeches made of the same unbleached fabric.

On his forehead was a strange marker, or perhaps a tattoo: a circle, surrounded by four diamonds.

"I don't recognize the symbol," Burton murmured to Charles. "Do you?"

"Not at all," Charles concurred, "but it's been such a long time, who knows what is meaningful, and in what ways? We might have to resort to using sign language, just to be understood."

"Greetings," the strange man said in perfect, unaccented English, "and salutations. May I be of assistance?"

Bert gave a gasp and dashed forward, almost grasping at the strange man. The old Caretaker seemed to have difficulty finding the right words to say, and it also appeared to the others that this was more than an overture to a stranger—this was recognition of . . .

. . . a friend?

"Is it you?" Bert said, his voice faint in his breathlessness. "Nebogipfel?"

"He was my sire," the pale man replied. "You may call me Vanamonde."

"Nebogipfel?" Charles asked. "You know this man's father, Bert?"

"Dr. Moses Nebogipfel," Bert said, relieved to have another touch point of familiarity in that dark place. "He is a Welsh inventor, who had developed some remarkable theories about time travel."

He strode over to Vanamonde and extended his hand. After a moment's hesitation, the pale man shook it, bowing slightly.

"I knew your father well, Vanamonde," said Bert. "How is he?"

"He died many years ago," Vanamonde replied with no obvious emotion, and enough finality that Bert knew not to ask further. "Your mek," he said, gesturing at Archie. "It has been damaged. We have the means to repair it, if you like."

"That's very kind of you," Rose said, before the others could answer. "Yes. Help him, please."

A look passed between Charles and Burton that expressed the same thought—caution was necessary, but there was no reason not to agree.

"Here," Vanamonde said, turning toward the towers of the city. "Follow me, if you please."

The companions fell into step behind the mysterious man as he began to walk. In a few minutes, it was obvious that their destination was the largest, tallest, darkest tower on the skyline.

"Heh." Charles chuckled and gestured at Rose. "'Childe Rowland to the dark tower came,'" he said jovially. "She is our Childe Rowland."

"Child?" asked Edmund.

"Childe, with an *e*," said Charles. "It means an untested knight."

"Hmm," said Bert. "Are you quoting Browning?"

"Shakespeare," said Charles. "*King Lear.*"

"Oh dear," said Bert. "You couldn't have quoted from one of the happy ones, could you?"

"Hey," Charles said, shrugging. "At least it's not *Macbeth.*"

As they walked toward the dark tower, Bert was unable to contain himself and continued to pepper Vanamonde with questions, which the albino answered patiently.

"The city is called Dys," he said without taking his eyes from the path. "It has always been called Dys, since the earliest days of the master's reign."

"And how long is that?" asked Bert.

"Since the beginning of time."

"You mean since the beginning of Dys," Burton corrected.

"What," Vanamonde asked without turning around, "is the difference?"

Occasionally, the companions would pass other people, some nearby, some in the distance. All were dressed similarly to Nebogipfel's son, but only a few bore the same markings on their forehead.

Charles asked if the markings had some sort of meaning, and Vanamonde bowed his head. "They do," he said. "They signify that one is a Dragon."

The pale man did not see the others' reactions to this remark. They were intrigued, to say the least. And more than a little surprised.

"You know, Vanamonde," Burton suggested, "some might say that it takes more than a tattoo to signify that one is a Dragon. What do you think of that?"

Vanamonde's eyes flashed briefly to Burton's forehead, but he kept walking and chose not to answer.

"What of the others?" Bert pressed, intent on finding out something about what had befallen Weena's people, the Eloi. "If they are not, ah, Dragons, what is it they're called?"

At this, Vanamonde merely shrugged, as if the question was of no importance. Before Bert could ask him anything further, they reached the base of the tower.

Vanamonde pressed a panel on the wall and a door irised open, revealing a staircase. Motioning for the others to follow, Vanamonde started walking up the stairs.

After climbing for what seemed an eternity in the deep, windowless stairwell, Vanamonde led the companions to a landing where there was a door with a traditional handle and lock.

"Here," he said, opening the door and gesturing inside. "You may wait here as our guests while I see to the repairs on your mek and inform my master of your arrival. He will want to meet you. Of that I'm certain."

The companions filed into the room, which was simply furnished, but expansive, and more comfortable than anything they had seen on the outside.

Rose and Edmund gently handed Archimedes over to Vanamonde, who cradled the mechanical owl in his arms and, with no further comment, turned to leave.

"Vanamonde, wait!" Bert implored. "You said that you are a Dragon, is that right?"

Vanamonde did not speak, but answered with a single nod.

"All right," said Bert, "then tell us this. Is everyone here a

Dragon? Everyone on Earth? You never answered me when I asked you earlier."

A light of realization went on in Vanamonde's eyes. "No," he said. "Dragon is an office of high regard. Only a few are Dragons here."

"Then the rest," Bert pressed. "The other people. Are they Eloi, or Morlocks?"

Their host furrowed his brow, as if trying to comprehend the question. "Eloi and Morlocks . . . ," he said slowly. "These are not ranks, like Dragon?"

"No, you idiot," said Burton. "We aren't asking what people do, we're asking what they are. The others here—people like us."

"Ah," Vanamonde said as he stepped back onto the landing outside the door and grasped the handle. "But there are no others like you. All are like me."

"Eloi?" asked Bert. "Or Morlock?"

"No Eloi," Vanamonde said, "no Morlocks. Only us," he finished as the door closed. "Only Lloigor."

CHAPTER SEVEN
THE MESSENGER

-—✳—-

"SO," SAID BYRON. "Did it work?"

"Of course it worked, you biscuit," Twain snorted. "The minute they stepped through, they vanished, just as they have with every other trip. I'd say the mission is off to a rousing start."

Dickens moved closer to the platform and tapped the cavorite with his shoe. "I wonder, Jules . . . wouldn't they be able to return almost the instant they left? I mean, wouldn't they have the capability to do that?"

"Could, but shouldn't," Shakespeare said quickly. "That would involve reworking the markings on the maps, because the time differential would change."

"That's why it's actually safer to allow them to explore in real time," Verne said. "It keeps the maps synchronized between the two times—the time they left and the time they arrived both move forward in Chronos time, so that nothing needs to be redrawn. Otherwise, a whole new set of calculations would have to be made. Rose might be able to do it, but it's going to be far easier for them to simply reverse the procedure when they've done all that they need to do."

"So an hour here is an hour there, and vice versa," Jack said, rubbing his chin. "Exquisite."

"How long are they expected to be gone, then?" asked John.

"They need to spend at least one full day there, in order to bank a chronal reserve of time for the trip into the past," Verne explained, "which gives them plenty of time to make their way to London."

John nodded in understanding. The site formerly known as London in the future time was the region where Weena would most likely be found.

"We allotted up to one day there, and one day back," Verne continued. "If all goes well, they should be coming back on Thursday, midday."

"Will they be bringing Weena with them?"

Verne paused and looked at John and Jack. "If at all possible, I'm sure that they will," he said, not entirely convincingly. "Chronal altruism aside, that is, after all, the reason that Bert went to begin with."

"An hour here is an hour there, and vice versa," Twain murmured, echoing Jack's earlier words. "And a day there is a day here. And a week there . . ." He let the words trail off as he looked up at the other Caretakers, who all understood what he was getting at. Bert's last clock had started—and every tick that did not see his return was another tick closer to the possibility that he might not return at all.

With that sobering thought heavy on their minds, the Caretakers and their friends left the platform and went back into Tamerlane House.

"Do we need to return to your office first," Don Quixote asked the Zen Detective, "or do you have what you need to find the Ruby Armor in that box you placed in the boot of the car?"

"I may have been exaggerating just slightly," Aristophanes admitted as the Duesenberg sped away from the Kilns. Uncas was driving erratically, as usual, which hadn't unnerved the detective the first time, but was a little more troubling now that he'd agreed to an extended trip. "What I really meant is that I know how to find the people who know how to find the armor."

"That in't what you told us," Uncas said without taking his eyes off the road, "or the Scowlers."

"I find it difficult to condemn a man for the same moral failings I myself have grappled with time and again," said Quixote, "and besides, the truth of things now will be borne out upon the success of our quest later."

"That's a very pragmatic attitude," Aristophanes said admiringly. "You'd have made an excellent philosopher, Don Quixote."

"I couldn't have afforded it," Quixote said. "That's one profession that pays even less than being a questing knight. And then there are the occasional missteps—one irritated audience, one awkward philosophical comment, and then someone starts talking about hemlock, and that's about the point you wish you'd listened to your mother and just become a fisherman."

"Does he always take compliments that poorly?" Aristophanes asked the badger.

"You have no idea," said Uncas. "I am surprised, though, that no one kept better track o' this armor, if it's as important as all that."

"The pieces could not be kept in the Archipelago, and neither were they safe in the Summer Country," said the detective, "and so the only way they could be kept completely safe was to hide them in the Soft Places—the places that aren't there."

"And no one kept a ledger?" Uncas said. "Impractical."

"Whose job is it to keep track of the places that aren't there?" Aristophanes asked. "Yours?" He pointed at the badger next to him. "Or his?" he said, hooking his thumb over his shoulder at Quixote. "The Caretakers cared only about the real places of consequence—those in the Archipelago of Dreams. But the rest were just overlooked, or," he added with a touch of rancor, "exiled.

"Only someone like Elijah McGee had the skill to set down maps of the unknown places, and only his children had the presence of mind to preserve them. That the Caretakers have them now for us to use is—"

"Zen?" offered Quixote.

Aristophanes started to scowl, then lowered his head and smiled before turning to look at the knight in the backseat. "I was going to say 'luck,' but Zen will have to do. That's how we're going to find the places we need to find. With a little Zen, and a little luck. And hopefully, the world won't end before we've done it."

"Someone's world is always ending," said Quixote.

"And I care less about that," said Aristophanes, "than I care about making sure the world that does end isn't mine."

Quixote sat back and sighed. "You'd have made a terrible knight."

"I know," Aristophanes replied, turning to face the front again. "That's why I became a philosopher."

"Our first destination should be no trouble to get to," said Aristophanes. "But we'll need to arrange passage to all the rest."

"Not necessary," the badger replied. "Not when we've got old Betsy here." He patted the dashboard.

"No, you don't understand," said the detective, irritated. "I'm talking about places that are thousands of miles away, so we've got to—"

"No problem," Uncas said, "as long as you know precisely where you want to go. Pick anyplace in th' world, an ol' Betsy can take us there."

Aristophanes blinked. "How about Madagascar?"

Quixote opened up a large compartment in the dashboard, which was filled with rows and rows of photographic slides, all ordered alphabetically. "Ah!" the knight finally exclaimed. "Here it is. I had it in Mauritania's slot. Took a minute to find."

He removed the slide and inserted it into a device on the dash that resembled a radio but had an external motor and some sort of arrangement of lenses.

"It's Scowler Jules's latest innovation," Uncas said proudly. "It projects an image through a special lamp on the bumper, like . . . *so*," he said, switching on the device. Immediately a large projection of the image on the slide appeared on the wall of fog in front of them, and Uncas gunned the engine.

"It works best with brick walls," said the badger, "but fog works pretty well too."

Before the detective could vocalize his astonishment, the Duesenberg had barreled through the projection, bouncing jarringly from the country road in England and onto a nicely paved cobblestone road in a hilly area that was clear of fog. Palm trees lined the streets, and the smell of seawater was strong in the air.

"I'm impressed," said the detective.

"So," Uncas said. "Where to first?"

"I'm almost afraid to say," said Aristophanes, "but you're going to need to turn around."

As the rest of the Caretakers converged in the portrait gallery to discuss the recent events, Jules Verne quietly pulled John down the adjacent hallway and closed the door behind them. "I need to take you with me to consult some of our allies in the war," Verne said, his voice quiet until they were a safe distance away from other ears, "and I don't want anyone else to know we're going—not yet."

"Isn't that a bit chancy?" John asked, glancing around. "We ought to—"

"Poe knows," Verne said, interrupting, "and Kipling. And for now, that must be sufficient."

He chuckled to himself, then looked at John. "You'll never believe that the pun wasn't intentional, but I told Poe we're going to see the Raven. Dr. Raven, to be precise."

"The Messenger?"

Verne nodded. "The only one among them who is still wholly mobile, and therefore wholly useful," he explained, "and that in itself brings some degree of risk, because he is also the most unknown."

"How so?"

"He's the only one we didn't actively recruit," said Verne. "Bert and I were taking a breakfast meeting in Prague in the late eighteenth century, and we observed that we were being observed ourselves. We took no notice of him, but quickly made our departure so as not to attract more attention—but then he turned up again at a café in Amsterdam."

"You have refined tastes," John said. "Perhaps he was simply running in similar epicurean circles."

"Ahh, that explanation may have sufficed," offered Verne, "if our lunch in Amsterdam had not been a century later."

John stopped in his tracks, blinking in amazement. "He was a time traveler?"

Verne nodded. "All the Messengers are, of course—but he was doing it before he became a Messenger, and," he added, with just a hint of menace in his voice, "he already had an Anabasis Machine."

John removed his watch from his pocket and examined it carefully. His was identical to the one Verne himself carried: a silver case, emblazoned with a red dragon. "How is that possible? I thought only the Caretakers possessed the watches."

"The Watchmaker gives them to us to use," said Verne, "but we may not be the only ones he has made them for. I've never been able to wheedle a straight answer out of him regarding that particular question. But in any regard, Dr. Raven, as he introduced himself, has never been anything but faithful to our goals. We asked him to join us, and he has made himself available at each point where he's been needed. As far as I know, he keeps rooms in Tamerlane, but as to the rest of his life, he is still a mystery."

"He sounds more like a secret," John said as he pocketed his watch.

"Secrets and mysteries, mysteries and secrets," a voice purred from somewhere above their heads. "Answer one and win, answer the other and lose. But who can tell which one is which? And which of you shall choose?"

John glanced above his left shoulder and smiled. "Hello, Grimalkin."

The Cheshire cat began to slowly appear a piece at a time as the men made turn after turn down the seemingly endless corridors. He had once been Jacob Grimm's familiar, but he seemed to have bonded himself to John. He was, however, still a cat, and he came and went as he chose.

"So," Grimalkin said as his hindquarters appeared, "you're going to see the Raven, are you?"

"We are," said John.

"Mmmmrrrr," the cat growled. "We do not like him. He has no place."

"What do you mean?" John asked, puzzled. "Jules said he has a room here."

"Not room, *place*," the cat spat back, clearly irritated. "The Raven has no place. He is here, but not here. It's very confusing, and it vexes us."

"What the Cheshire is trying to explain," said Verne, "is that Dr. Raven is unique among the Messengers, and even among the Caretakers, in that he has no trumps."

Again John stopped and looked at the older man. "He doesn't travel by trump? So how does he get to where you need him to be?"

Verne shrugged. "We aren't really sure. He just . . . goes to wherever he is needed. We tried to press him about it once, and he vanished for six months. When he returned, he acted as if nothing had happened, so we never addressed it again."

"No place," the cat repeated as it started to vanish again. "We will be watching, Caretakers."

"Can we really trust him then, Jules?" John said as Verne indicated a rather plain green door at the end of the last hallway.

"He sounds more like someone we should be worried about than entrusting with our future."

"The best assessment we were able to make is that he is a fiction, like Herman Melville, or Hank Morgan," said Verne. "Or possibly an anomaly, like Bert himself. But he has never acted against us, and in this war, we may be less able to choose our friends than we are our enemies."

He rapped sharply on the door, which swung open immediately. The room was small, obviously an antechamber to a larger warren of living spaces, but it was utilized fully. There were desks and shelves filled with antiquities and relics of the distant past—and, John observed, some from possible futures. Toward the right side, sitting in a tall, straight-backed chair, was a slender, slightly hawkish man who immediately rose to greet them.

"You assess correctly, Caveo Principia," Dr. Raven said, noting John's interest in the items of the collection that were not antiques. "We once kept most of these items at the Cartographer's room in Solitude, but for obvious reasons, they had to be relocated."

John gave a slightly formal nod and handshake to the other, still chewing over what Verne had been telling him in the hallways. "I recognize a few things," he said, moving over to a shelf filled with record albums. "Merlin was very fond of his Marx Brothers collection."

"He also enjoyed the films of Clint Eastwood," said Dr. Raven, "although you'd never have gotten him to admit it." He spoke in a friendly and courteous manner, but his eyes never left John's face, and John had also noticed that Dr. Raven addressed him using his most formal title.

The Messenger was hooded, but enough of his face was visible that John could see the honest smile of greeting, and the well-earned wrinkles at the corners of his eyes. The other Messengers had been roughly John's contemporaries, but this Dr. Raven was somewhat older, perhaps closer to Bert in age. Regardless, John understood some of what Verne saw in the man—he seemed immediately trustworthy, which bothered John, because nothing else he knew about him was.

"So," Dr. Raven said, rubbing his hands together. "What may I do for the Caveo Principia?"

"Harrumph." Verne cleared his throat and stepped slightly in front of John. He was used to being deferred to, and Dr. Raven's seeming interest in John was off-putting. "We need you to be a chaperone, basically. No time travel will be involved, simply spatial travel—to the Soft Places."

"Ah," Dr. Raven said, as if he understood more than Verne was saying aloud. "The badger and the knight. You've sent them on another quest, I take it? Are they after another Sphinx?"

"Not quite," said Verne. "They're looking for the Ruby Armor. And Aristophanes is guiding them."

For the briefest instant, John thought he saw the Messenger's expression darken, as if this was a disturbing surprise.

"The Zen Detective," said Dr. Raven. "I see. And that's all you need? For them to be chaperoned?"

"Shadowed," Verne corrected. "No assistance, unless their lives are in imminent danger. If they succeed, we'll have won a major victory against the enemy. But if they fail, then the armor remains out of reach to our enemy as well."

"Understood." The Messenger bowed to Verne, but he kept his eyes firmly locked on John, as if they shared some sort of secret. "I serve at the will of the Caretakers. It shall be done."

"Thank you, Doctor," Verne said as he opened the door and ushered John outside. "We'll expect a report soon, then." He closed the door, and the Messenger was alone.

The room shimmered, as if it were slightly out of focus with the rest of the world; then it clarified again, and the room was just as it had been—with one exception. Dr. Raven was younger. The wrinkles at his eyes were fewer, and he stood just a bit straighter, with just a little more vigor. It was as if several years of his life had suddenly fallen away.

"Be seeing you," Dr. Raven said to no one in particular, before he removed the watch from his pocket, twirled the dials, and disappeared.

CHAPTER EIGHT
THE LAST CARETAKER

VANAMONDE'S LAST WORD hung in the air and echoed in the companions' minds so strongly that it took a few seconds for them to realize that they might actually be prisoners, and not merely guests.

Burton got to the door first. It was locked.

"Fools," he muttered, eyes downcast. "We are all fools. Especially"—he turned, pointing at Bert—"*you*."

"We were all taken in," Charles said mildly. "We can't blame Bert for trusting in a familiar face."

"We all chose to follow him," said Edmund, "and he did offer to help Archie."

"It isn't that stout a door," Burton said, flexing his muscles. "I think I can take it down." He threw his weight against the door—which didn't move. Charles joined him, but even together, they couldn't budge the door.

"This door has a Binding," Bert mused, rubbing his chin. "Rose, try using Caliburn."

As her mentor suggested, Rose swung the great sword at the door. It struck with an explosion of sparks—but made no mark at all where the sword hit.

"Deep Magic, then," said Bert. "We're in this room until Vanamonde—or his Master—say otherwise."

There was nothing the companions could do but wait for Vanamonde to return and hope for the best. But hope was in short supply, after the reversals they'd experienced in the last few hours. They paired off into different corners of the room, to commiserate, and try to rest, and prepare themselves for whatever might come next.

"All Lloigor," Charles said bleakly. "That's a bad, bad circumstance, I think."

"Not all," Burton corrected. "Pym certainly was no Lloigor—I think."

"Perhaps, but then again, he's the one who attacked you and nearly demolished poor Archie," Charles replied. "At this point, I'm feeling less threatened by the Lloigor than by Verne's own lieutenant."

"Been there, done that," said Burton.

Across the room in the far corner, Rose and Edmund were sprawled out on their coats, using their duffels for pillows and trying to rest. Sleep was unlikely, but Burton had taught them both how to meditate, so they decided it was as good a time as any to balance their minds. Mostly, though, they were just talking about the friends they'd left behind at Tamerlane—particularly Laura Glue.

There had been a curious sort of dance among the three of them, since Rose and Laura Glue first met Edmund in Revolutionary War–era London. There had been flirtations—after all, Edmund was the only available male at Tamerlane House who was not a portrait, tulpa, or small forest creature—but Rose, for the most part, kept a discreet distance whenever an opportunity arose to be alone with the young Cartographer. An innocent romance had developed between Edmund and Laura Glue, and she didn't know whether—or if—she should complicate several friendships by seeing if there was anything deeper between herself and Edmund.

In terms of education, all three were equally balanced, with expertise in different areas—but in terms of life experience, Edmund and Laura Glue were closer. Rose simply had been through too many experiences that they could not relate to for them to be true equals. So, while the interest had been there, she had never so much as flirted with Edmund.

But now, in impossible circumstances, and facing the very real possibility that they had been caught in an Echthroi trap, she wasn't thinking about anything except the handsome young man drifting in and out of a meditative trance, who lay just inches away from her.

He was, she thought as her shadow curled up and around her like a scarf, right next to her.

And Laura Glue was very, very far away.

"Do you ever regret coming back with us from London?" she asked abruptly, taking him out of his trance.

Edmund blinked as he thought about the question and wondered what kind of an answer she was asking for. Sure, there were times when he missed his father, and the life he had led as a student of Doctor Franklin's. But there had always been that deeper yearning, the inner conviction that he was destined for greater things. Of course, that could also be his pirate blood speaking to him—not that that would be such a bad thing.

"Regret, no," he said finally, taking her hand in his as he spoke. "But there are days when I do wonder if I was crazy to have followed you."

"I don't think we could have gotten back without your help," said Rose.

Edmund smiled. "Yes, you could have. Once I made the chronal trump, you just needed to step through. And the connection was yours, anyroad."

"If you hadn't come back with us then, you wouldn't be stuck here with me now."

He sat up so that he could look at her more directly, and he squeezed her hand just a bit more tightly.

"I'm happy that I did follow you, though, whatever else may come, Rose. I am. Even ending up here has already turned into an adventure. Traveling with you is just too much fun to be had."

Her eyes flashed with anger for just a moment, until she realized that he was teasing her, and she moved closer to him and lifted her chin. "I'm glad you came with us too. Whatever may come."

He smiled at her briefly, but with an expression in his eyes that said he was worried. And afraid. So she clutched his hand a little more tightly against the darkness, and they were afraid together. And that made it more bearable. A little, at least.

From the other side of the chamber Charles watched the shadows shift and move where Rose sat with the young Cartographer. Bert moved alongside him, where he could speak without being overheard by the others.

"They're a good team," the Far Traveler said softly. "She complements him, and he, her."

"I know," Charles agreed. "His abilities to make maps may actually rival Merlin's, although I'd never have confessed that to him. And combined with her understanding of time . . . Well. It's an impressive combination, even if it did result in our getting stuck here in the far future."

Suddenly the room was shaken by a loud rumbling from outside—a tremendous noise that made the tower sway to and fro as if it were caught up in an earthquake. The sound and motion brought everyone to their feet, concerned that something awful was happening.

Bert took Charles by the arm. "That was no earthquake," he said, a spark of fear in his eyes. "I've felt that before, in another tower."

"The Keep of Time," Charles said flatly. "When it grew."

"Shades," muttered Burton. "That would explain the Deep Magic that's sealed us here in the room, too."

"It isn't a Keep of Time, though," said Rose. "Otherwise I'd feel it. This is simply a tower."

"But a living one, like the keep," said Bert, "which makes me very curious who Vanamonde's Master is."

"Begging your pardon, sir," said Edmund, "but maybe it's an enemy we already know.

"I've read about the, ah, Dyson incident," he went on, casting a sidelong glance at Rose, who pursed her lips in return. "It created the Winterland because of what Hugo Dyson changed in the past, but the Caretakers were able to largely restore everything by going into the past themselves, and fixing what Dyson set into motion. So might that not be the case here as well?"

"Not quite," Charles said, shaking his head. "The Winterland was an altered present, because of changes made in the past. But here we're in the future. Things aren't as they are because of something we've done that has to be undone," he explained. "The world has become this . . . this terrible place because of something we haven't done *yet*."

"Speaking as one who was largely responsible for initiating the, ah, 'incident,'" said Burton, "I have to say that it may also have been inevitable. There were events that we caused that had already happened in the past—such as the Winterland's version of Charles, Chaz, going back in time to become the first Green Knight."

"As awful as it is to admit, what *has* happened had to happen," said Bert. "Circumstances were thrust upon us like a football thrown to a one-legged player, and we simply played through as best we could. That it turned out that the plays we made had already been scumbled in some sort of cosmic playbook was neither to our credit nor our blame. The important fact here is that we never asked for the ball."

"So what do we do?" asked Edmund.

Bert squeezed the young Cartographer's shoulder. "Rest. Try to regain some strength. And then be prepared for anything."

The shadows that enveloped the city were not static: They were living things that flowed like the tides, overlapping one another and blocking all but the faintest of twilit gloom from reaching the surface. But every so often, they would shift in such a way that a small, insignificant corner of sky was left exposed. And it was through just such an opening that the Lady sent her moonbeam to wake the sleeping Grail Child.

The light that awakened Rose wasn't terribly bright, but it was soft, and tinged with blue. It seeped underneath the doorway and through the lock—which, with a gentle clicking, disengaged, slowly swinging the door open.

Curiosity won out over caution, and Rose got up to investigate. She was careful not to disturb any of her slumbering friends— somehow she understood that they would not wake, were not meant to wake, to see this light. It was sent to awaken only her, and as it retreated down the long hallways outside the door, she felt compelled to follow it.

The light led her to a door several landings above the room where they'd been imprisoned. The door was slightly ajar, and the light was emanating from within. Slowly Rose pushed it open and entered.

In the center of the room were three chairs. The first was occupied by a corpse wearing a dress of fine red silk, embroidered with pearls. The third chair was empty. And in the middle sat a beautiful woman in a blue silk dress, who gestured for Rose to come closer.

"Hello, daughter," the woman said. "Please, come in. Sit. We have much to tell you, and only these few moments in which to do it."

"Are you Mother Night?" Rose asked as she moved closer.

"We are," the woman said, "but before that I was Lachesis, and I am the only one who may speak to you here. Clotho is no more, and Atropos is no longer permitted on this world."

"What is it?" asked Rose. "What has happened? I tried using Ariadne's Thread, but—"

"It will not work, not in this place," Lachesis confirmed. "This is now a fully Shadowed world. Its connections have been severed. But there is still a chance for you to change what has happened."

Lachesis reached out her hand and gave something to Rose. It was a small, multifaceted mirror. "Use this only when you must. Solve the riddle of the last Dragon. And you may yet claim your destiny as protector of this world, before it is too late."

Before Rose could ask any questions, Lachesis suddenly turned her head in alarm. "Oh!" she exclaimed. "Something fell."

Then she disappeared, along with the corpse of her sister and the empty chair. And Rose woke up, still sleeping next to Edmund.

She almost imagined that it had been a dream—but in her hand was the mirror.

Rose was about to rouse the others to tell them what had happened when they were all brought to their feet by a soft tapping at the door.

"Greetings," Vanamonde said as he entered the room. "I trust you all rested well."

Burton started to respond with a well-built-up reserve of expletives, but Vanamonde stopped him with an upraised hand. "All your questions will be answered in due time," he said placidly, "and so you are not concerned, the repairs on your mek have gone well, and he will be returned to you soon. But for now," he finished, standing to one side and bowing, "Lord Winter has requested your presence, if you will be so kind as to follow me."

At the mention of the name 'Lord Winter,' Charles scowled at Burton, whose face had gone red. But Bert put his hands on both of their shoulders and smiled broadly at Vanamonde. "Yes," he said, agreeing for all of them. "We shall."

Vanamonde led them to the stairway, where they climbed

farther than they had to reach their cell, and eventually got to the very top of the dark tower.

The stairs opened onto a broad terrace, so high that the wind should have been ferocious—but it was cold, and the air was calm. At the far end of the terrace, Vanamonde spoke to a man who had been looking out over Dys, who now turned to greet the companions.

"Welcome," he said. "I'm very pleased to see you all. It has been . . . a very long time."

Lord Winter was not terribly tall, but he had unmistakable presence. He was dressed entirely in black, in fashionable clothes that would not have been out of place in their own century. His hair was nearly as long as he was tall, and he wore the same dark spectacles as Vanamonde. He was flanked by three of his Dragons—long-robed attendants, who wore masks of stone that bore the markings of their office and that flared up and away from their faces as if they were the tails of comets falling to Earth. Behind them, floating in the sky, but considerably lower than the great chains high above, were several geometric shapes. Charles couldn't shake the feeling that these hexagons and cubes were somehow sentient, and there to observe the meeting.

"Well," he whispered to the others, "that isn't Mordred. That's something, at least. Although," he added nervously, "his voice does sound quite familiar."

"No," Bert said, a chill in his voice—and loudly enough to be heard by Lord Winter. "It isn't Mordred. But it is someone else we know."

"Ah," Lord Winter said as he suppressed a wry smile. "You've recognized me after all. I was afraid that after so many thousands of years, you might not. . . . But then again, it hasn't been quite so long for any of you, has it? By your reckoning, it's been barely a day since you last spoke to the man I once was."

"It can't be," Rose whispered. "Not here. Not like this."

"I'm sorry, child," said Burton, "but it is."

Edmund looked around, confused by the growing horror he read in his companions' faces. It was obvious that Lord Winter, this dark and terrible figure, was someone they knew well. He turned to the pale man. "Your Highness," Edmund began, only to be silenced by a crisp wave of the other's hand.

"Now, now, my young Cartographer," he said smoothly. "You needn't be so formal. We are, after all, old friends, are we not? So please," he said, his voice dropping to a soft tone that nevertheless rang clearly in their ears, "call me *Jack*."

PART THREE

THE MYSTORIANS

CHAPTER NINE
THROUGH THE LOOKING-GLASS

·—✳—·

THE MAN WHO knelt looking at his reflection in the lake at the ends of the Earth appeared younger than he really was. Everyone in the lands where he had been born lived very, very long lives, in the manner of the first men, and so youth lasted not merely for decades, but for centuries. By the accounting of this world, he was in fact very advanced in years, even before his exile from Alexandria.

He had been compelled, by a Binding of Deep Magic, to journey to the farthest ends of the Earth—and that compulsion had brought him here, to the mountains on the far side of the Mongolian plateau. It was not the farthest place where men dwelled, but it was the farthest place that had been named.

The man was considering whether this meant he might have to travel farther still when the Dragon landed behind him, silent as a dream. He didn't turn around but merely considered the great beast's reflection, behind and beside his own.

"Greetings, Madoc, son of Odysseus," the reflection of the Dragon said. "I have been seeking you a long while."

"I'm not Madoc any longer," he replied. "I stopped being Madoc when my brother betrayed me and drove me from Alexandria.

"The people here call this place Baikal," the young man continued, *"and they call me Mordraut. Baikal refers to the lake, apparently. It means 'deepest.'"*

The Dragon growled. *"And Mordraut?"*

The man turned and looked up at him. *"Driven,"* he said after a moment. *"They say it means driven."*

"And are you driven?" the Dragon said. *"You must have been, to journey so far."*

Mordraut's face darkened. *"The journey,"* he said softly, *"wasn't my idea."*

"Hmm," the great Dragon rumbled. *"The Binding. Of course. I apologize, Ma—Mordraut."*

The man considered the Dragon before deciding to ask a question—something not lightly done with Dragons.

"You are from the Archipelago, are you not?"

The Dragon did not answer, but merely met his gaze.

"Can you take me there?" Mordraut pressed. *"Can you take me home?"*

The Dragon shook his head. *"I'm sorry,"* he said, *"but I cannot. Not bound, as you are now. But perhaps . . . there might be a way. It is why I have come to find you."*

The man Mordraut had listened only to the first part of the Dragon's response and was already deflating when the second part registered on his consciousness. *"You came here for me?"* he asked, more earnest now. *"Why? And how can that get me back?"*

"My brethren and I guard the barrier that separates the Archipelago from this, the Summer Country," the Dragon said, *"but we only guard, we do not govern.*

"Long ago," he continued, *"it was decided that a king from this world should be chosen to rule over both. But the one chosen was*

betrayed and fell from grace. There has been none who could replace him, until now.

"There is to be a competition, judged by the bloodline of the first king, to choose who will sit on the Silver Throne of the Archipelago. If you would become my apprentice, I will prepare you to sit on that throne and rule. But you must first win, and there will be many vying for the honor. You will have to defeat them all."

Mordraut shook his head. "I'm not interested in defeating anyone," he said brusquely. *"And I'm no fighter."*

"These people here can train you to fight," said the Dragon, "and I can prepare you to rule. But I think you will find the drive to win on your own."

"Why?"

"Because," the Dragon rumbled, "if you choose not to compete, the first king of the Archipelago will be the strongest contender—your brother, Myrddyn."

There was no way to parse the complex mix of emotions that passed across the man's face as the Dragon spoke the name of the brother who had bound him, and betrayed him, and it took several moments for Mordraut to regain his self-control. When he finally did, he looked up again.

"What are you called, Dragon?"

The great beast raised an eyebrow. "You, youngling, may call me Samaranth."

Mordraut nodded and turned back to the lake.

"Yes, Samaranth," he said finally. "I shall become your apprentice."

"Good," the Dragon replied. "Then let us begin."

John and Verne's journey back to the main wings of the house took considerably less time, due in large part to a more direct route, but also, John was certain, to Tamerlane House's penchant for moving the rooms around when the Caretakers weren't looking.

As opposed to Dr. Raven's quarters, which occupied the lowest level above the basements, and which were therefore windowless, the part of the house Verne was leading John to was in the upper floors, as evidenced by the scatterings of windows and skylights that began appearing in hallways and over stairwells.

"There are eleven arboreta in Tamerlane House . . . that I know of," Verne said as they reached the end of one of the uppermost corridors, "but this one can only be unlocked with one of three keys: mine, Poe's, and the occupant's."

He spun a large key ring out of his pocket and twirled through several brilliant gold and silver keys before choosing a rather ordinary-looking iron key, which he inserted into the lock. Verne turned the key once, then again, and with a click, the door swung open into an enormous room, which was dimly lit despite the expanse of windows in the walls and the ceiling.

The air was cloyingly thick with the scent of pollen and decay. Along the walls—which, except for the one where the door was located, were all glass—were wooden tables lined with flowerpots and trays bearing an amazing array of plants. Some were flowering, punctuating the swaths of green with bursts of magenta, orange, and turquoise. Others were climbers, and had escaped the confines of the trays to spread along the walls, nearly obscuring the glass with their leafy expanses.

On the floor, loam was scattered freely over the Oriental carpets, a clear indication of the priorities of the occupant. The room was there to house the flora, and housekeeping was a distant second.

"Step where I step," said Verne, "and don't touch anything."

"All right," said John.

As John and Verne crossed the threshold, the room's occupant, a disarmingly attractive young woman, rose from between two of the planter boxes and drew a soiled arm across a forehead damp with sweat.

She raised her chin in acknowledgment of her guests, and Verne stepped forward.

"John," he said, gesturing at the young woman, "I believe you know Beatrice—Dr. Rappaccini's daughter."

She was one of the Messengers—Verne's special envoys who traveled by use of the trumps, and each of whom had a special affinity for matters of time and space. The first of them, Hank Morgan, had recently perished during the events that had separated Tamerlane House from the Archipelago. Soon after, the second Messenger, Alvin Ransom, also died when his dimensional counterpart, Charles, reached the end of his chronal lifespan—but unlike Charles, who'd been revived as an unaging tulpa, Ransom joined the other Caretakers in the portrait gallery, and could only leave Tamerlane House for seven days. The third Messenger, Arthur Pym, had been on a mission when he became lost in time. Beatrice was the fourth, and the one least known to the other Caretakers. Except to go on missions for Verne, she seldom left her own quarters, and when she did, she spoke even less frequently. They all knew of her, of course, but this was the first time Verne had ever deigned to make a formal introduction.

"I'm pleased to meet you," John said pleasantly, offering his hand. "I'm John."

"Don't touch her!" Verne shouted as he struck the younger

man's hand, pushing him away. "Forgive me," he said, more to the girl than to his fellow Caretaker. "I should have cautioned him beforehand."

"It's all right," John said as he rubbed the top of his hand. "I meant no harm."

Verne shook his head. "Nor would you have caused any," he said, his voice softer now. "When I said 'Don't touch anything,' what I really meant was, you can't touch everything. Including the lady Beatrice.

"Some stories are true," Verne added. "Hers is one of them. Her father's experiments made her a mistress of toxins—and unable to touch anyone else. Anyone living, that is. Even her voice can be deadly to others, so she seldom uses it."

"Point taken," said John, who bowed to Beatrice before Verne guided him across the room.

In the far corner stood three massive mirrors. They were each fully six feet tall, and almost four feet wide. They hung inside frames carved from a dark wood that seemed to absorb the dim light in Beatrice's arboretum. Moving closer, John could see that there were hundreds of intricate figures carved into the frames with such detail he could almost make out the expressions on their faces.

"They were patterned after a Brueghel," Verne said, noticing John's admiration of the frames, "but the mirrors are far, far older. Walk around to the other side and take a look."

John did as he was instructed and was startled to get to the back of the mirrors and see Verne's smiling face grinning at him from the other side.

"Are they transparent?" John asked. "An invisible backing of some kind?"

"Not transparent, nonexistent," said Verne. "Go ahead, try to touch them. It's safe enough from that side."

John put out his hand to touch the center mirror, and to his astonishment it went through where the mirror was supposed to be, right through the frame.

"They're literally one-way mirrors," Verne said as John came around to the front. "There are no backs to them, only a front. Poe told me about them, although I don't think even he knows who made them."

"Astonishing," said John. "Where did you get them?"

"Aristophanes found them for me," Verne answered. "He's been useful in that way. They actually belonged to one of the fellows you're going to meet."

"So what are we supposed to do with them?"

"Do?" said Verne. "Why, go through one of them, of course. "Lots of interesting things can happen when you go through a looking-glass."

"One of them?" John asked. "They don't all work in the same way?"

"Oh, they all work," said Verne, "but only one goes to the place we need it to. The other two are, shall we say, the last line of defense—here within the house proper, that is."

"Where do they go?"

"No place you want to be," said Verne, "unless you feel like you missed something in life by not being at Pompeii."

"The other two lead to the volcano?" John exclaimed. "But isn't it dormant now?"

"The top of it is." Verne chuckled. "Look at the frame, and follow what you see."

John examined the figures along the frames and noticed that they were all similar in one regard: Each had a bas-relief carving of the Minotaur at the top, and all the figures were facing right.

"Just like in the labyrinth, then," said John.

"Take the right-hand side," Verne said, nodding, "or, as our Minotaur friend would say, the right-hand right-hand right-hand side."

Chuckling at his own joke, he turned and offered a courtly bow to Beatrice, who nodded her head in return. Then, with no further commentary, Verne stepped into the glass to the right, pulling John along with him.

The sensation was not unlike moving through water—water with the consistency of molasses. It was not at all as natural as using one of the trumps. Still, it took only a few seconds to go through, and they found themselves in an alleyway facing a broad cobble-stone street. The sun was high and bright, and the air was crisp, with a cold bite to it.

"Are we in one of the Soft Places?" John asked, pulling his collar closed. "One of those in-between places that's neither here nor there?"

"You might say that, John," said Verne. "Welcome to Switzerland."

"The mirror," John exclaimed, turning about. "It's gone?"

Verne smiled wanly. "It's a one-way mirror, young John," he said. "We can't be having people just popping through to Tamerlane House now, can we?"

"I wanted to ask but didn't want to offend Beatrice," John said, biting his lip. "You said Dr. Raven is the only Messenger who remains wholly mobile. Is she ill, or has she been hurt in some way, that she can no longer travel for you?"

Verne shook his head. "It's the end progression of her father's meddling in nature, I'm afraid," he said with sincere regret. "Her toxic nature makes her the ideal guardian of the mirror, but she's no longer just exuding the essences of the plants she cares for—she's starting to become one. She's taking root. And in time, she'll have to leave Tamerlane and join others of her kind in the jungles of the South American continent, along the River Tefé."

"How can there be others of her kind?" John asked. "Are you talking about living plants? Plants that were once human?"

"Something like that," said Verne. "More like living tree-creatures . . . Guardians of the Green. As we look after the world of men, so they look after the flora."

John scowled. "They aren't like Magwich, are they? That would be . . . well, Charles wouldn't be happy, knowing there's a grove of Magwiches in the world."

Verne laughed. "Not quite, but that really should be looked into. We ought to ask Bea about your little shrub when we return. She can consult with the grove about him."

"Will I ever meet them?"

"Perhaps," said Verne, "but trust me—once you do, you'll never feel the same about pruning your roses."

Verne led John out of the alley and onto a busy street. As they walked, he explained that they were in the canton of Fribourg, which was near Lake Neuchâtel, but that their specific destination was a small, well-appointed hotel a few blocks away.

"Not that I doubt the precision of your planning," John said as he threw a backward glance at the alleyway where they had come through the looking-glass, "but if it's a one-way portal, how are you planning to get us back?"

In reply Verne flashed open his jacket. There, in the inner breast pocket, John could see one of the trumps peeking out over the top. Just enough of the card was visible for him to recognize the towers and minarets of Tamerlane House.

"You have a trump back to the Nameless Isles?" he said, more impressed than surprised. "I thought it was forbidden for anyone but Kipling to have one."

"It was," Verne replied, "by *me*. Being the Prime Caretaker does have its privileges, you know. Here," he said, pointing across the street. "We've arrived."

The hotel stood at the corner of a busy intersection—busy enough that John was nearly clipped by an automobile speeding past. He spun around and shook his fist at the rapidly receding car.

"Curse it all, Uncas!" he yelled. "Slow down!"

Suddenly he realized what he'd just shouted, and he turned crimson from the neck up as Verne roared with laughter.

"Sorry," John said. "Force of habit."

CHAPTER TEN
THE HOTEL D'AILLEURS

-·—❈—·-

THE HOTEL WAS only three stories tall, and the exterior was not especially imposing. It was a Swiss building in a Swiss town, and so it was practical, efficient, and just a little bit bland. John was about to make a comment to that effect when Verne opened the front door and ushered him inside.

To the left of the clerk's desk—which Verne bypassed with a wave of his hand—was a bar, which was to be expected, and a small kitchen from which a delicious aroma was wafting. But to the right was a great room, and suddenly John started to realize what it was about this hotel that kept Verne's attention. From Persian-rug floor to pressed-tin ceiling, the walls were covered with perhaps the greatest collection of fantastic art John had ever seen.

There were framed paintings, and etchings, and pencil drawings, and in the corners even a few sculptures—and the common theme that tied them all together was that they were based on great works of science fiction. John also noted, wryly, that a large percentage of the art was based on the work of Jules Verne.

"But of course!" Verne exclaimed when John commented on it. "It's my hotel, so why shouldn't most of the decoration be based on my own best works?"

"I see," John said as he examined a painting based on one of Verne's earliest works, *In Search of the Castaways*. "And how many of Bert's works are represented here?"

"A goodly number," Verne replied, "at least fifteen percent."

"Fifteen percent?"

"All right, ten," Verne admitted, "but it's a really excellent ten percent."

He led John past all the paintings to a doorway located under the stairs to the rooms above. The door led down to an older structure that the hotel was built on. As they passed, John could see the notches in the walls that were meant to hold lamps before the gas lines had been installed.

Verne continued down the corridor to a cramped foyer, which was lit by a small Chinese lamp on a rather rickety oak table. Opposite the lamp were double doors, which were fitted with an elaborate lock. On the center of the right-hand door was a large knocker.

John had noticed as they walked through the hallway that in the older part of the hotel there were ancient Icelandic runes carved into every bit of exposed wood, and around these doors, they were so thick that they looked like another layer of graining in the wood.

"You know," he said as he peered more closely at the runes, "with a good magnifying lens I could probably translate these in fairly short order."

"I've no doubt you could, young John," said Verne, "but I'll save you the trouble. They basically say 'Here you leave the world of the flesh and enter the realm of the spirit,' or something like that. Shall we go in?"

"Knock, or do you have the key?"

"Both," replied Verne. "Knock to let them know we're coming, and use the key to actually get in. After the recent incidents at Tamerlane House, security is ever more on my mind."

The door knocker was an ornate carving of a face, with a kerchief tied around its jaw. "A Marley knocker," Verne said as he reached for the tappet. "Charles gave it to me as a Christmas gift some years back, and I couldn't think of anything else to do with it."

He rapped with the knocker once, then again, then a third time before inserting the key into the lock below and turning the handle.

The door opened, and John's jaw dropped as he recognized the man behind it as Benjamin Franklin.

"Why, John, my fine young fellow," Franklin said, roaring with laughter. "What's wrong? You look as if you've seen a ghost!"

"That's not funny," said Verne as they stepped across the threshold. "I haven't explained everything to him yet."

"I apologize, then," Franklin said, ushering them inside. "It's good to see you again, John."

"And you, Doctor," said John. "What is this place?"

"Some of us have taken to calling it the Wonder Cabinet," Franklin answered. "It's the place where wonderful, improbable things are kept. And also," he added, "we're in Switzerland, so, you know, of course no one knows about it who isn't supposed to."

The room was expansive, but crowded with individuals who all stopped what they were doing to take note of their visitors. It was appointed to resemble a private club, much like the club on Baker Street in London—except that instead of being a club for gentlemen scholars, this one was more of an eclectic think tank populated by Caretaker candidates.

"John, my boy," said Verne, "meet the *Mystorians*."

He immediately recognized Charles Dodgson, also known as Lewis Carroll, sitting with George Macdonald on a riser over to the right. Christina Rossetti was arguing with the American writers Robert E. Howard and L. Frank Baum on another riser over to the left, while Arthur Machen and Hope Mirrlees were in the center, debating politely with Sir Isaac Newton and two other men whom John didn't recognize.

"This is Dr. Demetrius Doboobie, and Master Erasmus Holiday," Verne said in introduction, "both here by way of the novel *Kenilworth*."

"Sir Walter Scott's book?" John asked, scanning the room again. "Is he here?"

"Sorry," Dr. Doboobie said, standing, but not offering his hand. "He was a fiction—but luckily, we are not."

"Not as long as we're here, anyroad," said Holiday.

"Agatha Christie is also with us," said Verne, "but she's less able to travel, since on her last mission, her absence was noticed— a little too prominently, shall we say."

"When was that?"

"In 1926," said Franklin. "She was shadowing you, incidentally, John. But it turned out all right. I'd have done it myself, but"—he gestured at the room—"being dead, I was a bit more limited than she was."

It was only then that John realized that most of those in the room were actually well past their allotted time spans.

"Yes," Franklin said jovially. "We're dead—well, most of us

anyway. We served as Mystorians in our own times, and now we exist here, to help those who serve during yours."

Suddenly John understood. "The runes, outside, on the walls."

"Yes," said Verne. "That's what allows these spirits to exist here, alongside the living."

"It's why I also impolitely declined to shake your hand," said Franklin. "My substance has not kept pace with my influence, it seems."

"They are present, but insubstantial," Verne explained, "so they can't touch anything. They can only advise and discuss—and they do a lot of that."

"You don't have to speak as if we're not here," sniffed Carroll.

"Sorry, Doctor," said Verne. "I apologize."

"Doctor?" asked John.

"There's no real seniority or ranking among them," said Verne, "and the living Mystorians got irritated by Franklin's insistence that he be addressed as 'Doctor,' and so at some point they all started requesting it."

"Is this hotel the only place where ghosts are actually visible to, ah, the still living?" asked John.

"Not at all," Franklin said, chuckling, "but it is the only place where ghosts are visible *by design*."

"Hmm," said John, rubbing his chin. "What do Houdini and Conan Doyle think about all this?"

"I've thought now and again about bringing them here," Verne replied, "in part because they both have an affinity for the realm of the spirit, but also because they are both brilliant minds. And then," he added ruefully, "Harry says or does something so completely irresponsible that I want to throttle him, and I think better of it."

"And Sir Arthur?"

Verne shook his head. "Tell the one, tell them both," he said dismissively. "They really are decent Caretaker material, or would be, if they weren't perpetually sixteen."

"I take offense at that," said Frank Baum, who was in a corner immersed in a stack of comic books. "Sixteen was a good year to be alive."

"All our scientific research is done here," said Verne, "away from the prying eyes of the Cabal, or traitors like Defoe."

"Forgive my ignorance," said John, "but other than Doctor Franklin and Sir Isaac, I don't see any other . . ."

"Scientists?" Carroll said, rising from his seat. "You do not look deeply enough, boy. My prime specialty is mathematics, and Frank's—"

"Ahem-hem," said Baum.

"I apologize—*Doctor* Baum is a technological genius greater than even Doctor Franklin. It's part of what makes us effective as Mystorians," he concluded. "I can tell you all the secrets of time travel in a poem. And have. It's just that no one has bothered to look to poetry for the secrets of the universe."

"I'm sorry," John said, shaking his head in disbelief, "but you make it sound as if time travel were much simpler than it really is."

"In actuality," said Carroll, "*everything* is much simpler than it appears to be. Everything."

Another young man from the back of the room stood up to meet John.

"My name is Joseph," the ghost said as he started to offer his hand to the Caretaker, then, with a wry smile, thought better of it. "I admire your work very much."

"Thank you," John replied. He looked over the young ghost, trying to ascertain where he fit among the pantheon of noted men and women in the Mystorians.

When Joseph realized why he was being scrutinized, his ghostly cheeks pinked self-consciously. "No, good sir, you do not know me," he said, answering John's unspoken question. "At least, not in this form."

"Some of the Mystorians were not so much engaged in active work on our behalf, as they were in observing and reporting on the players in the Great Game at the time they were alive," Verne explained. "Young Joseph here was just such an observer—and later in his life, he was as famous as any of those he reported on. That was his shield—he was so famous that no one noticed the activities he engaged in for himself."

Again, the young ghost's face reddened. "That's very charitable of you to say, Mr. Verne, but we both know that's not the reason no one paid attention."

He looked John squarely in the eye and smiled a sad smile, which was made more beautiful by the perfect symmetry of his features. "The reason no one gave credence to me or what I was covertly doing for the Prime Caretaker was that I was hideously deformed, and no one among the members of polite society could fathom that my mind was not similarly deformed."

John considered this for a moment, then stepped back in surprise. "Joseph . . . *Merrick?*" he said hesitantly. "You're Joseph Merrick!"

The young ghost nodded gravely. "I am. You would have known me by the appellation 'The Elephant Man.'"

John looked at Joseph, then at Verne and back again. "I'm not sure I understand," he said. "Are you a tulpa? How is it that . . . ah . . ." He stumbled over his words, unsure of what to ask without offending the young man.

Joseph smiled. "How is it that I have the appearance that I do? It's simple—this is how I really am."

"But you were so terribly deformed—," John began.

"No," Joseph said firmly, cutting him off. "My *body* was terribly deformed. I was not."

"I don't understand."

"I *am* a soul," Joseph answered. "I *had* a body."

The clarity of it suddenly flashed across John's face. "Ah," he said. "I do understand, and I apologize. My friend Jack would have seen that right away."

"Here," Verne said, drawing John to the far side of the room and pulling out two chairs so they could sit. "Let me show you what the good Doctors Baum and Carroll have been doing.

"They've been working on a theory that the trumps are actually opening something called wormholes," Verne explained, gesturing at some diagrams on Carroll's table. "The smaller ones permit communication, and the larger ones actual travel. And what Carroll here has been working on—"

"Doctor Carroll, if you please," said Carroll.

Verne sighed, then went on. "Yes—what *Doctor* Carroll has been working on is the instances where the trumps were used to traverse time."

"It was actually that Clarke fellow who thought of it," said Baum. "He's got a lot of good ideas, that one."

Now it was Carroll's turn to scowl. "Yes, yes he did," he said with an irritated look at Baum, "but I've been the one developing the actual science behind the theory."

"The young theoreticians have been invaluable to our processes," said Franklin. "Especially that Asimov fellow, the Russian. He's going to outshine us all, I think."

"Easy for you to say," Newton said without really joining the conversation. "It's easy to create great works when one stands on the shoulders of giants."

"He's a little sensitive," Baum whispered. "The first time Newton met Asimov, the joker offered him an apple."

"It's young Asimov's work that has allowed the Mystorians to help us calculate probabilities on the might-have-beens to come," Verne explained. "It's one reason I have the Messengers traveling so frequently gathering information. The more we know about what has happened, the better we can predict what may happen in the future. And the wonder of it all is that it's completely based in scientific principle. He calls it 'psychohistory.'"

"No offense," John said, hesitant to speak, as he fully expected he was about to offend someone, "but there's something slightly disconcerting about knowing that such intense scientific research is being carried out in a hotel in Switzerland by a group of ghosts and children's book authors."

"I should like to point out that most of your colleagues at Tamerlane House," Franklin said sternly, poking his walking stick at Verne, "including your French tour guide there, are in fact themselves deceased. So I'd like to know just what you have against ghosts."

"I'm doubly offended," said Baum, "seeing as how I'm both a ghost and a children's book author, as is Charles."

"I'm a mathematician," sniffed Carroll. "And it's Doctor Carroll, if you please."

"Really, I meant no offense," John said, holding his hands up in either supplication or surrender. "Honestly, some of my best friends write books for children."

"And you don't?" asked Baum.

"Not really, you see," John began.

"Wait a moment," said Holiday. "Didn't you write the book about the little fellow with the furry feet? And trolls? And dwarves?"

"Well, yes," John admitted, "but—"

"What do you call that, then?"

"It's actually an initial tale that I'm broadening into a much wider invented mythology for—"

"Blah, blah, blah, blah," said Baum. "Elves and dwarves and trolls. Fairy tales. You're a children's book author, John."

Before John could argue the point further, they were interrupted by another knock at the door.

"Ah," Verne said as he rose to usher in the new arrival. "Unless I miss my guess, that'll be our secret weapon coming along now."

John stood and took a place next to Verne to greet the newcomers. The first was tall, firmly built, and had a crest of white hair that gave him the appearance of a classical philosopher. His eyes flashed briefly as he noticed John's presence, but he said nothing and merely smiled as he took his companion's coat.

The second man was smaller, more slender, and noticeably older than the other. Verne stepped forward to greet him first.

"Hello," the slight gentleman said as he entered the room and removed his hat. "I apologize for being late. I had a concern I was being followed and so some extra precautions—and delays—were necessary."

John nearly fell off his feet, astonished, confused, and delighted all at once. He was so taken off guard that he forgot to offer his hand to the bemused man, who was clearly enjoying the effect his arrival had on the younger Caretaker. John looked at Verne. "Is this some sort of illusion? How is he here?"

"Not an illusion," Verne replied, smiling broadly. "A Mystorian. One our adversaries would never have suspected, never watched, because they thought that they already were watching him. It was just a *different* him."

John recovered a small degree of his composure. "So, the last person they would suspect of becoming one of your special operatives was someone who was already a Caretaker," he said, "so to speak. Ingenious." He wiped his hand on his trousers and quickly offered it to the bemused Mystorian. "It's a pleasure to be meeting you at last."

"The pleasure is all mine, I assure you," the gentleman said, taking John's proffered hand. "My name is H. G. Wells."

CHAPTER ELEVEN
LOWER OXFORD

—◆—✳—◆—

ACCORDING TO ARISTOPHANES, the first destination they needed to travel to in their quest for the Ruby Armor was very close—practically in the neighborhood.

"Oxford?" Uncas said, surprised. "That's right under the scowlers' noses."

"Literally, in this case," said the detective. "Quite literally, in fact."

The street Aristophanes guided them to was less than two miles from the building where Jack kept his teaching rooms at the college, and it was small enough that they were able to park the Duesenberg and get out without attracting undue attention.

"Shouldn't you be wearing a hat, or a scarf, or something?" Aristophanes said to Uncas as he glanced around the street. "I know this is a university, and everyone has their nose buried in books, but some deliveryman or other passerby might take notice we're strolling along with a talking animal."

"I'll be honest," said Uncas, "it's not indifference to th' opinions of passersby that lets me walk around in th' open." He produced a small piece of parchment from his vest pocket. It was covered in runes.

"Ah," the detective said in understanding. "A glamour. That makes sense."

"All most people see is a short feller with hairy feet," said Uncas. "Maybe a beard."

"Well then," Aristophanes said as he led them to a nondescript door at the end of the alley, "you'll not be surprised at where we're going. Everyone there is using one glamour or another."

The door opened onto a stairwell, which dropped away several floors below ground level—much farther than any basement should have extended. It was lit with torches that were set at regular intervals, but nothing other than the granite walls of the stairwell was visible until they reached the bottom.

Aristophanes threw open the great green wooden doors at the bottom of the stairs, and revealed an enormous cavern that seemed to contain a city at least the size of Oxford above.

"Welcome," the detective said, "to Lower Oxford."

The three companions wove their way through the warren of buildings that seemed to have been cobbled together from every culture on the continent—none of which had been updated since the fifteenth century, and many of which seemed far, far older.

"These buildings seem to predate Oxford itself," commented Uncas.

"Little badger," Aristophanes said with a touch of irritation at the animal's small thinking, "most of these buildings predate *England*."

There were Moorish harems, and Byzantine bazaars; English banks and colleges; and Ottoman markets that could have been operating since the first millennium.

As they walked, Aristophanes explained that this was one of the Soft Places that were known only to the lost and disenfranchised—that it was all but lost to those who never looked, and only findable by those who were truly lost.

"The Caretakers would barely take note of such a place," he said brusquely, "although perhaps that Burton fellow might. And most other people would take no notice of it at all. In a way, what happens every day in Lower Oxford is exactly what happened long ago to the entire Archipelago."

He stopped. "They just stopped believing. Here," he said, gesturing down a crowded street. "This is the district we want."

All the buildings along the street bore Chinese markings, including the one where they stopped.

"This is one of the oldest libraries in existence," Aristophanes explained, pointing at the cracked, faded sign above the door. "It was here, in this spot, for two thousand years before I was born, and was collecting stories of the earliest cultures of the world when our ancestors were living in caves and hunting with obsidian spears."

"What does the sign say?" asked Uncas.

"You know it already," said the Zen Detective. "The statues in the window should give you a clue."

Inside the windows on either side of the door were paper lanterns, a stringer of plucked, headless ducks—which made Uncas shiver just a bit—and four soapstone statues. Each was of a different Chinese man, but all four bore attributes . . .

. . . of *Dragons*.

"Ah," Quixote said, looking up at the sign. "'Go ye no further, for here, there be Dragons.'"

Aristophanes nodded. "Or something to that effect. Those four statues represent the four great dragon kings of ancient China, and this shop is what remains of the library that began when they ruled under the Jade Empress."

Quixote wanted to ask something about who the Jade Empress might be, but the detective had already pushed open the door with a loud jangling of bells and entered the shop.

The shop that purported to be a library was tightly packed with shelves, which made passing down the aisles difficult for Quixote, and almost impossible for the stouter Aristophanes. Smoke from a brazier hung cloyingly in the air, and there were small birds in cages hung randomly throughout the clutter.

Toward the back, the aisles suddenly opened up to a wider working space that was ringed about with more shelving that reached to the ceiling ten feet above. To one side, atop a ladder, was a woman who could only be the librarian Aristophanes had told them about on the drive.

She was short and plump, and wore a tight silk dress, which was straining at the seams in a number of potentially inconvenient places. Her black hair was pinned up neatly with long sticks carved into the shape of dragons. And she was not in a very receptive mood.

"What it is, what it is?" the librarian called down from the ladder. "I cannot be bothering now. I am very busty."

Uncas turned to Quixote. "Does she mean something else?"

"Probably," the knight whispered, "but better not to ask. Just smile and nod."

Aristophanes removed his hat and spoke in a respectful

manner. "Song-Sseu," he said, hat in hand, "thank you for allowing us to enter your library. We have come to ask for your help."

At the mention of her name, the librarian stiffened, but did
not turn to look at them. A long moment passed, and then she
answered. "I am not who you think me to be, strange, and am to
work much, too much mind, to talk. To help."

"You are the person we're looking for, Song-Sseu, to find what
we're after," Aristophanes said. "If you cannot help us, then there
is no one else who can. We're looking for the Ruby Armor of T'ai
Shan."

She turned her head slowly and fixed the detective with a
thousand-yard stare that would have driven a lesser man, or
perhaps a more prudent one, right out the door. But as it was,
Aristophanes held his ground, and she descended the ladder.

"Wait here," the librarian said, "and don't think to be touch
anything."

She descended the ladder without actually tearing any seams,
and removed herself to a room farther back. After some rattling
around, followed by unintelligible cursing, she returned holding a
ring of keys. "How would you know that even I know, the place of
the armor?"

Aristophanes shrugged. "I didn't know. But it's apparent that
you do. That's Zen for you."

"Hmm." She folded her arms and pursed her lips. "What
would you know of Zen, Westerner?"

Aristophanes stiffened at that, but he kept his demeanor
and voice steady. "More than you would believe, Song-Sseu," he
replied. "Can you help us?"

"Help you, or help Caretakers?" she asked. "It not surprise," she added before he could react. "Who else send purple unicorn, talking rat, and crazy man to ask about T'ai Shan?"

"I'm a badger," said Uncas.

"And I'm, uh," said Quixote. "I have no defense."

"Yes, they sent us," said Aristophanes.

"You know the Archipelago, that it is gone," she said. "Something happened to it. All Shadow now. So now they Caretakers of air."

"We know," said Quixote. "That's why we need the armor—to fight the Shadows."

She looked at the three of them for a few moments—at Aristophanes for longer and more critically than the others—before she finally assented. "Yes," she said primly. "I help you. But it cost you much, I think."

"I expected it would," the detective said, rummaging around in his pockets. "Ah!" he exclaimed. "Here it is!"

It was a very old piece of parchment, covered in Arabic writing.

The librarian peered at it. "A Scheherazade story? Pfah! I have all already. All thousand and three."

"This," said Aristophanes, "is the one thousand and *fourth* tale."

Her eyes grew wide as she realized he was quite serious, and the parchment, quite authentic.

Song-Sseu snatched it out of his hand and filed the parchment in a desk drawer, which she then locked with a key. Using a second key, she opened a different drawer and took out a sheaf of paper.

"You know these not work by themselves," said Song-Sseu. "Need the Quill of Minos, or Letter-Blocks of—"

"I have an Infernal Device," Aristophanes said, giving a sideways glance at Uncas and Quixote.

"Ah," she said, as if that explained everything. "How many sheets you need?"

"Seven," said the detective. "Seven should do."

Song-Sseu's brow furrowed in puzzlement. "Seven? But there are eight pieces. . . ."

"We already got the Ruby Opera Glasses," Uncas offered, and Aristophanes's complexion turned a full shade darker, "so we don't need t' look fer them."

"You do know," she said as she counted off seven sheets and handed them to the Zen Detective, "that knowing that places exist, and be able to locate those places, are two different thing. And there be places in the world that even Caretakers know not about."

"Maybe they don't," Aristophanes said as he folded the papers and stuck them inside his coat, "but we do. We have the maps of Elijah McGee."

The expression on her face, Aristophanes thought, was worth all the grief he'd had to take just to be able to witness that moment.

"You lie," she finally said after closing her mouth and regaining her composure. "They were lost in fire, in London."

"Not all of them," Aristophanes said, "and not the important ones."

She tried to look casually uninterested, and was failing miserably. "Do you have with you?" she asked. "Could I have to look at them?"

"Maybe next time," Aristophanes said as he slowly guided Uncas and Quixote out of the shop. He bowed, then quickly closed the door before she could say anything further.

"Stupid, stupid, stupid," he muttered as they retraced their steps to the stairwell. "Never should have mentioned the maps!"

"Then, uh, why did you?" asked Uncas. "We already had what we wanted, didn't we?"

Aristophanes glowered, then nodded. "I was showing off," he said. "Wanted her to know I was in a loop she wasn't in. And now maybe I've compromised us."

"How so?" Quixote asked, looking a bit worried.

"Because," the detective said as he pushed open the great green doors, "people who are willing to sell what they know always have a price. And we just gave her something very, very valuable. And you," he growled at Uncas, "should not have told her we had the glasses, either. But what's done is done, and it's not to be helped, now.

"Come on," he finished, jumping to the stairs. "We've just sped up our timetable."

"We shouldn't discuss the details of the pieces here," Aristophanes said as they reached street level and Oxford Above, "and we sure as Hades shouldn't look at the maps anywhere in the open. Does your instant-travel-projector have a slide for someplace more private?"

"We have just th' place," said Uncas. "Hop in. We'll be there in two shakes of a fox's tail."

The three companions climbed into the Duesenberg, and Uncas pulled out the appropriate slide. Starting the motor, he wheeled the car around and, projector whirring, drove straight into—and through—a solid brick wall.

They were so intent on getting someplace more secure, where they could talk unmolested, that none of them had noticed the tall, hooded man at the end of the street, who had been observing them since they entered Lower Oxford. No one else, not even the few ragged denizens who were coming and going through the door to the stairwell, took any more notice of him. He was simply another near-invisible lost soul, minding his own business. And so no one noticed at all when he took the watch out of his pocket, twirled the dials, and vanished.

"Have you ever noticed," Uncas said conversationally, as the barmaid brought another round of drinks to their table, "that all th' so-called 'Soft Places' seem t' be centered around taverns and th' like?"

Aristophanes snorted and took a long swallow of ale.

Quixote frowned. "I'm sure I don't know what you mean," he said. "There are plenty of Soft Places with no ale whatsoever."

"Yeah?" Aristophanes replied, wiping his mouth on his sleeve. "Name *three*."

"Hmm," mused the knight. "There's, ah, Midian. And, um . . ."

"I thought so," said Uncas.

"Oh, just be quiet and drink your prune juice," said Quixote.

The Inn of the Flying Dragon was one of the Caretakers' favorite meeting places to discuss Archipelago business, and it had come as a huge relief to all of them that the loss of the Archipelago did not mean the loss of the Flying Dragon.

It was not the only Soft Place where they could drink away the night, but it was one of the few that consisted of a single edifice at a Crossroads. There were some, like Club Mephistopheles, that existed in London, for those who knew how to see them. Others, like Midian, were entire cities. Some, like Abaton, were both a city and a country, with indefinable borders.

Fortunately, according to Aristophanes, the Soft Places they would need to go to were a bit smaller in size.

"So," Quixote said, having downed his second ale, "how are we going to find the pieces, anyroad?"

"With this," Aristophanes said. He opened the box he'd taken from his office and removed a device that resembled a typewriter's larger, more complicated, slightly preindustrial brother. "It's called a Machine Cryptographique," he explained as he set up the contraption on the table. "It was invented by a printer in Marseilles in 1836, and he claimed it could write as fast as a pen."

The detective showed them how each letter had its own bar, which would rotate into place to type a letter. Uncas noticed that there were several bars that were engraved with numerals—as well as several more that bore marks he didn't recognize.

"The inventor had more than commercial uses in mind," Aristophanes was telling Quixote, "which is why he added the Hermetic markings to some of the bars. The problem was, he didn't know enough about what he was getting into, and the device became possessed by a djinn."

"By gin?" asked Uncas.

"A *djinn*," the exasperated detective said. "An imp. Something that can grant wishes, tell your fortune, and make predictions."

"That sounds like something th' Caretakers would like, all right," said Uncas.

"Actually, it was deemed too dangerous for the Caretakers," said the detective. "The power to use it came with a condition— if you died while it was in your possession, yours became the next soul that powered it. The Frenchman—Verne—acquired it in 1882 and quickly realized the danger of keeping and using it. So he sold it to someone less likely to die than even a Caretaker."

He stroked the gears and wheels of the device and grinned. "I call it Darwin, after the last supposed owner who died while he had it," Aristophanes said. "It's been very reliable. Just don't," he added, "ask it any questions about the Garden of Eden. It gets very testy when you do that."

"If you have this machine," Quixote asked, "then what did we need to acquire the parchment from Song-Sseu for?"

"The original djinn is gone," said Aristophanes, "and Darwin has no predictive powers of his own. So," he continued, as he pulled out the seven sheets of parchment, "we needed some oracular parchment to do the job instead."

"Hmm," said Uncas. "Where d'you get oracular parchment?"

"From an oracular pig."

"An oracular pig?" Uncas asked, shuddering. "D'you mean like the famous one, from the farm on Prydain?"

"The very same," said Aristophanes. "Same pig, actually."

"That's a shame," Uncas said, shaking his head. "Sacrificing an entire oracular pig just for some stupid parchment."

"Oh, I don't think they killed her," the detective said quickly. "They just used her hindquarters. A pig that valuable, you can't use all at once."

"Ewww," said Uncas.

"Well," said Quixote, "I have seen those little carts with the wheels they can attach...."

"Never mind about the pig!" Aristophanes snorted. "Let's find out where we're to go first."

The Zen Detective threaded a sheet of parchment into the machine, then slowly, deliberately, pecked out a question, which appeared in faint, reddish-gray letters.

Suddenly the machine took charge of its own operation, and more quickly than Aristophanes had typed, click-clacked out an answer one line below the question.

"There we go," Aristophanes said, whipping the parchment out of the machine and stuffing it quickly into his pocket. "We'll compare it with the maps in the morning."

"In the morning?" asked Quixote. "Why not right now?"

"Because for one, I don't think it's safe to pull out the maps in sight of others, even here," said Aristophanes. "And for another, I'm tuckered out and could use some sleep before we start off on this treasure hunt."

"Why not just take a room here?" Uncas protested as the detective boxed up his machine and rose to leave. "The rooms are very nice."

"They are," he replied in a soft, low voice, so he couldn't be overheard past their table. "It's the other clientele that I'm wary of, like the fellow in the corner—no, don't look, Uncas!—wearing the hood, who has been watching us since we got here."

Neither Uncas nor Quixote turned to look in the direction Aristophanes indicated, but simply dropped some coins on the table and followed him out the door.

The detective instructed Uncas to drive the Duesenberg back to the Summer Country, to a wooded hilltop in Wales, where he said they would camp for the night.

"This ought to be safe enough," Aristophanes said as he

removed his hat and ran his fingers through his hair. "The Welsh mind their own business, and not everyone else's."

Both Uncas and Quixote, who were taking some camping supplies out of the boot of the Duesenberg, stopped short at the sight of the hatless detective. They had both known he was a unicorn, but thus far in their acquaintanceship, he had never removed the hat.

The base of his horn spread a full five inches across his forehead, like a thick plate of cartilage, and the markings from his having filed it down were easily visible. But from the base, a wicked-looking point had begun to grow, and it was already curving upward several inches from his brow.

"I like to grow it out when I'm working," said Aristophanes. "And besides, where we're going, no one will notice anyway."

"No one noticing is pretty much why I don't wear pants," said Uncas.

"I like to sleep under the stars," Quixote complained as he and Aristophanes unfolded the seemingly endless tent. "I really don't see why we have to go to so much trouble."

The Zen Detective nodded his head to the eastern horizon. "Those clouds are why. There may be weather later, and I'd rather not spend the night in a downpour, thank you very much."

"I'd really rather have stayed at th' Flying Dragon," Uncas grumbled as he struck some flint to spark a fire.

"Not while we're being observed," said Aristophanes. "For all we know, that fellow was someone sent by Song-Sseu, to see what we're using the parchment for."

"She seemed like such a nice lady," said Uncas.

"Everyone," Aristophanes said as he handed his own knapsack to the badger, "can be bought. Get the bedrolls set out. I have to go find a peach tree to water."

"You have a peach tree in Wales?" asked Quixote.

The detective groaned. "I have to pee, you idiot."

"Hey," Uncas whispered as the detective cursed his way to the trees. "Look at this!"

It was the Ruby Opera Glasses. They were inside the knapsack.

"Manners, my squire," Quixote scolded. "You shouldn't be looking in his bag. And besides, those won't do us much good out here, anyway."

"They might," Uncas disagreed, tipping his head at the tent flap. "Anyone can be bought, remember?"

The knight shook his head. "Being a thug for hire and giving oneself entirely to the Echthroi are different things. If he has simply been bought, the glasses wouldn't show it, would they?"

"If he's a Lloigor," the badger replied, "they will."

Quixote chewed on that thought a moment. It might be worth having a quick peek at the detective—just to be sure he was, as he claimed to be, on the side of the angels.

"What are you doing?" Aristophanes exclaimed as he suddenly entered the tent. "I told you those are only good for . . ." He made the connection and scowled, then smirked. "Oh. I see. Wanted to check out your partner, did you? You were wondering if I was an Echthros?"

"Technically, you'd be a Lloigor," Uncas said as Quixote elbowed him in the arm. "Uh, I mean, well, yes. Sorta."

"Hmph," the Zen Detective grunted as he sat next to the old

knight and opened a bottle. "I suppose I can't blame you," he said as he tipped back the bottle to have a drink. "Very well, then. If it'll make you feel better, go ahead and have a look."

With a nod from Quixote, Uncas held the opera glasses up to his eyes and peered through them at the detective.

"Well?" asked Aristophanes. "Satisfied?"

Uncas nodded and handed the glasses to Quixote. "He's not one of them. Not a Lloigor."

"You just needed to ask," Aristophanes said, a genuine note of hurt in his voice. "I could have told you."

"Not to degrade our already shaky position with you," Quixote said, clearing his throat, "but couldn't you just have lied?"

"Maybe," said the detective, "but not about that. I'm a unicorn—we can't be possessed by Shadows, nor can we lose our own. It's one of our more useful features."

"Ah," exclaimed Quixote. "So that's why Verne trusts you."

"No," Aristophanes corrected. "That's why Verne uses me. He sent you two along precisely because he doesn't trust me. And, it appears, neither do you." Without waiting for a response, he got up and opened the tent flap. "I'm going to go stretch my legs. I'll be back later . . .

". . . *partners.*"

The way he said that last word left Uncas and Quixote both flustered enough that they couldn't say anything. Worse, they realized there wasn't much they *could* say. Aristophanes was right. They didn't trust him. They hadn't trusted him from the beginning.

"But Verne didn't . . . doesn't," said Uncas. "Is it really any wiser of us if we chose to, just to avoid hurting his feelings?"

"Something I have learned in my long years as a knight," said Quixote, "is that everyone rises to the level of trust they earn. Your part in that is to simply give him a chance to rise or fall as his actions dictate."

The little mammal's whiskers twitched as he looked from the knight to outside the tent and back again. At last he smacked his badger fist into the other paw. "Then I'll do it," he declared. "I'm going to trust him."

Quixote nodded approvingly as his little companion busied himself with getting their bedrolls ready to sleep for the night—but inwardly, he felt a twinge of regret. Not that the little badger was so willing to be trusting, but because, in Quixote's experience, such trust could be easily justified . . .

. . . and just as easily betrayed.

Outside, there was a flash of light, followed by a low rumble of thunder. Moments later the first drops of rain began to speckle the ground outside.

"Looks like Steve was right about the storm," Uncas said as he rolled over to sleep. "G'night, sir."

"Good night, my little friend," Quixote replied as the rain began falling harder, and a second burst of lightning illuminated the tent.

The knight could see that outside, silhouetted against the fire-light, the detective had once again donned his hat. The rain didn't seem to be bothering him, so Quixote decided that rather than press the issue, he'd just follow Uncas's example and go to sleep. The detective could do as he wished.

Quixote wondered as he blew out the light which choice Aristophanes might make, to justify or betray the trust the badger—the trust that both of them—were giving to him. And he wondered what Uncas was going to feel if they were proven wrong.

He was still wondering when, finally, he drifted off to sleep. It was still raining.

CHAPTER TWELVE

THE CABAL

—◦❋◦—

"I HOPE YOU'RE ready for another shock, young John," Verne said as he put his arm around the shoulders of the man who had entered with Wells. "This is the true leader of the Mystorians, and the one without whom the Caretakers would have been lost long ago.

"John," Verne continued in introduction, "I'd like you to meet William Blake."

Almost involuntarily, John jumped backward, ignoring the man's outstretched hand.

"*Blake?*" he exclaimed angrily. "John Dee's right-hand man? The second great betrayer of the Caretakers?"

"*My* right-hand man," said Verne, "and the one who has given us what few actual advantages we have over the Cabal."

"I understand your misgivings, John," Blake said, unruffled by the younger man's reaction, "but what I'm doing is very similar to Kipling's own covert missions among the ICS—I'm just playing a deeper game."

"It's the idea that it is a game at all that bothers me," John said testily. "Our circumstances are far more serious than that."

"It is exactly that degree of importance that makes it a game worth playing," Wells cut in. "The Little Wars, the small games of conflict, and one-upmanship, all add up into history. The timeline of the world has ever been nothing but games.

"And," he added, "as Heraclitus said, those who approach life like a child playing a game, moving and pushing pieces, possess the power of kings."

"Is that what the Mystorians are?" John asked. "Kings playing games?"

"No," Wells replied. "The Caretakers are the true kings. We're just the ones who make sure no one removes you from the board."

John sighed and turned to Verne. "I can see why he's your secret weapon. He's smarter than we are."

Verne laughed, as did Blake. Wells merely smiled and removed his coat, nodding in greeting to the other Mystorians.

"It was always my strategy to use those whom I recruited only in their own Prime Time," said Verne, "but then as events started to accelerate, I realized the value of having them available to consult with, and so in secret, we established the hotel, and this room, to better serve the cause."

"Thereby having the help of men like Doctor Franklin both in life and in death," said John. "I understand that. But why, ah, continue to work with them as ghosts, rather than create portraits, as with the Caretakers?"

"The portraits only work within the walls of Tamerlane House," said Verne. "Outside, they would only last a week. And we needed to preserve the secrecy of our operations."

John chuckled. "It almost seems like cheating," he said blithely. "To continue to draw on all these great minds, after their deaths."

"How is that any different from influencing the minds of those who read our books?" Carroll asked. "Or our overinflated autobiographies, in some cases."

"Noted," said Franklin.

"Your books are full of thoughts you've already, ah, thought," said John, "but everything you're doing here is . . ."

"New?" said Franklin. "So our influence should end, just because our earthly lives have?"

"I suppose if I really believed that," John admitted, "I wouldn't be a Caretaker."

"As I told you, our adversaries were no longer playing by the rules," Verne said, "so I started changing a few rules myself."

"How is it that they haven't suspected you before now?" John asked Blake. "Especially after the defection of Burton, Houdini, and Conan Doyle?"

"You're confusing the frosting with the cake," Blake replied, "if you think the Imperial Cartological Society had anything to do with Dee's Cabal. He founded the ICS, sure—but only as a cover for his true goals. Burton, however, really believed in what the ICS set out to do, and that made his transition back to the Caretakers much easier."

"Easier for you, maybe," said John. "He put us through a lot of grief before coming back over. He—"

John stopped, and watched, dumbfounded, as a second William Blake, and then a third, walked out of one of the back rooms and began conversing with Sir Isaac Newton.

"Blake perfected the creation of tulpas," Verne said, amused at John's shock, "and he liked himself so much, he made more."

"How many more?"

"We call them Blake's Seven," said Verne, "although in point of fact, there are now only six of you, aren't there?"

"Yes, six," Blake acknowledged as if he were tallying bags of flour instead of tulpas. "We lost the one on that ill-advised trip past the Edge of the World. From what I understand, he was turned to solid gold, or some such."

"And losing yourself doesn't, ah, bother you?" John asked. "I would think you'd be slightly more put out. If it was me, I'd be rather traumatized."

"There are no limitations on those who are serving the cause of the Echthroi," said Carroll, "so why should we have limitations on those of us who are in the service of the angels?"

"I wouldn't mind a few of the angels themselves popping in to lend a hand now and again," murmured Macdonald.

"There must be some limitations, er, ah, Doctor," said Baum, "or else what's to keep us from becoming them?"

"There are *some* limitations," said Wells. "Just enough."

"So what are the Mystorians working on?"

"The problem the Caretakers haven't yet taken the time for," said Jules. "They're trying to find Coal—the missing boy prince of Paralon who was kidnapped by Daniel Defoe."

"Where do we stand on it?" asked Verne. "Any leads?"

"A few," Wells said, "mostly by virtue of the leads Blake has given us, and with help from young Asimov's psychohistory."

"Herb is the best resource we have," Verne said, gesturing at Wells, "in part because he and I disagree about a great many things."

"How is that helpful?" John asked.

"Too often scholars limit themselves by working with what

they know they know," said Baum, "when what they really need to know is what they know they need to know but don't yet know. So we aren't bothering with looking in the places we think he might be—we're looking in all the places we would never think to look. Because otherwise, we'd have already found him."

"I'm starting to understand why you keep them sequestered in a hotel in Switzerland," John said to Verne. "He's not steering with both hands."

"It's probably true," Baum admitted cheerfully.

"All we know is that he's in the future," said Blake. "We believe that's why the Cabal broke Defoe free from Tamerlane House."

"You knew about the burglary?" John said in astonishment. "And you did nothing about it?"

"Better than that," said Verne. "He facilitated the burglary, but also prevented their success by interfering with their attempt to get the maps of Elijah McGee. And nothing else they took was of any value."

"We'll find him, Jules," Franklin said, more somber now. "If it takes an eternity yet to come, we'll find him."

"Speaking of Defoe, I need to leave," said Blake. "One of my tulpas is still helping Harry and Arthur with the goats, and three of me are expected for the meeting with the Cabal."

"Be careful," Verne said. "Call if you need us."

"I shall," said Blake. "Farewell, Caveo Principia."

"Sure," said John. "You too."

As Blake left, John turned to Wells. "So, I imagine you're aware of what our Bert is doing," he said. "Is that matter creating any anxiety for you, as it has for Bert?"

"Not if he's successful," Wells replied. "If they made the first swing of the pendulum into the future, I'm confident they'll be able to ride it back into the past."

"I meant his, uh, his other mission," said John, "and the . . . timetable, so to speak."

"Ah," Wells said, blushing slightly. "No. I never met Weena, so I never lost her. And Aven was never my child. So my path diverged dramatically from Bert's, and I have never been under the same compulsions as he to solve the riddles of time travel. I've been perfectly happy to do research for the Mystorians, and, of course, to spend my time writing more books."

He stood and offered his hand to Verne. "I'm sorry I can't stay longer," Wells said. "I needed to bring you my reports, but now I must repair. It was a pleasure, young John. A true pleasure."

"Thank you . . . Mr. Wells."

"Please—call me Herb," Wells said, with a twinkle in his eyes that very much resembled John's mentor.

"I've enjoyed your work very much, ah, Herb," John said, shaking the older man's hand. He looked askance at Verne. "Ah, does he . . . I mean . . ."

"Yes," Herb said, looking John in the eye and giving his hand another firm shake. "I know what's coming. I've known for a very long time. And I'm all right with it. I've had a very full and successful life. And I've had a number of friends who have made it rich beyond compare. So don't fret—I'm going to be fine."

Soon after, John and Verne also took their leave of the hotel so that they could return to Tamerlane House and await word from Blake.

"I'm curious," John asked as they crossed the busy street

outside the hotel. "Is searching for the lost boy really a job for the Mystorians? That fellow Aristophanes certainly seems capable enough, if not entirely trustworthy. Surely he'd be your man for this, too?"

Verne shook his head. "It's a different kind of problem," he explained. "The boy was deliberately hidden from us, by those whom we know to be our enemies. They can therefore plot and counterplot against all the moves we make, which is why having Blake among them is so necessary.

"Normally," Verne continued, "this would have been a task for the Messengers. But after losing Henry Morgan, and then with Alvin Ransom's effectiveness being lessened, all I've really had to work with is Raven—and he has had no luck in finding the lost boy. So the Mystorians really are the best option, even with a Zen Detective at our disposal.

"And besides," he added ruefully, "I *don't* trust Aristophanes. I can't risk trusting him."

"And yet you sent him to search for those talismans of incredible power."

Verne shook his head again. "Not alone," he said with a wry grin. "As you already saw yourself, I made certain one of our best agents was with him and will be keeping me apprised of everything."

John furrowed his brow. "Do you really think Quixote is up to that?"

The Frenchman paused a moment, and then laughed. "Quixote? You're joking, surely. I meant Uncas."

The younger Caretaker seemed unconvinced. "He's not exactly Tummeler."

"No," Verne replied. "But he is a badger, and his heart is mighty. He won't let us down."

They walked along in silence for a few moments as they made their way back to the alleyway where they could safely activate their trump to Tamerlane House.

"There's something more you want to ask me," Verne said without taking his eyes from the path in front of them. "So ask."

"What I'm wondering about," John mused, "is that if there are so many ways for one's essence to survive death—Basil's portraits, or becoming a tulpa, or these ghosts of yours in a hotel in Switzerland—then is there really any reason to fear death at all? Doesn't all that mean that death, far from being the end, is just another state of existence?"

Verne turned to look at the younger Caretaker with an expression of delighted admiration. "John, my boy," he said, grasping the other man's arm, "if you understand even that much, then you are already a greater Caretaker than I ever dreamed you might be. And a far better man."

Before the younger man could respond, Verne activated his trump, and in a few moments it had grown large enough for them to step back through to Tamerlane House. They were both so focused on returning to the other Caretakers to report on the work of the Mystorians that they didn't notice the Shadow that slipped through underneath their feet, and that stayed behind when the portal closed.

He arrived, as usual, in a room of near-total darkness. He was John Dee's most trusted lieutenant, and one of the most powerful and influential members of the Cabal. But William Blake had never seen the exterior of the House of John Dee. None of the Cabal had.

Blake had designed the black watches the Cabal used to transport between places and times, but Dee himself had calibrated their primary orientation. Setting the dials to midnight always returned the bearer to Dee's house, but never on the outside, always to some inner chamber. So in point of fact, Blake had no earthly idea where the house was actually located in space. If he had, then perhaps the Caretakers' War could have been resolved long before then. Verne had certainly pressed him to find it often enough. But Blake had always resisted, feeling that it would be a mistake to confront the enemy on their home ground—particularly when no one knew where that home *was*.

Dee's residence had been at times referred to as the Nightmare Abbey, and sometimes as the House on the Borderlands. But mostly, it was just referred to as the House.

From Blake's limited explorations of the interior, it appeared to be an old family manse, possibly even a castellated abbey, as one of the names suggested. From the smell, Blake knew there was a moat, or, barring that, a nearby marsh. But sometimes that changed.

Blake wondered if perhaps the House moved from place to place, much in the same way the rooms at Tamerlane House often moved of their own accord. That would make it even more difficult to attack.

The house was maintained by a veritable army of young, attractive men and women, all of whom bore the name Deathshead. There were rumors among members of the Cabal that a young squire named Diggory Deathshead had once visited and made the acquaintance of the maidens in residence—leaving behind a colony of young Deathsheads. However, in all the years Blake had been visiting, none of the staff had seemed to age. He suspected it was because they were, in fact, all dead. But there were some questions he preferred to avoid asking.

He rounded a corner to the meeting hall, which was filled with a massive oak table. At the head, perched on a chair, sat an enormous crow.

"Greetings, Loki," said Blake. "How goes the effort?"

The large bird bowed in deference to a guest of the house and made a clicking noise with its tongue. Blake knew from experience that this meant the bird was irritated about something but was trying to maintain a sense of decorum. It was Dee's familiar, and always preceded his appearance.

Blake assumed the great black bird served the same purpose as Dee's shadow once did, as a sort of conscience. But it had been a long time since Dee had actually possessed a shadow, so Blake couldn't really be sure.

His second and third tulpas entered the meeting hall from the opposite corridor and nodded a brief greeting as they took their seats. Blake himself had only just sat down as Dee and the rest of the Cabal entered the room.

The Cabal seldom met in full quorum—whether this was by chance or by design, Blake could not guess. Ever since Jules Verne had convinced Richard Burton to defect to the Caretakers, and to bring Arthur Conan Doyle and Harry Houdini with him, Dee had become more and more suspicious, and kept his activities cloaked in greater and greater secrecy. Part of the reason was because the three defectors had been the primary operatives of

Dee's Imperial Cartological Society—and were therefore the most visible of John Dee's disciples. The other part was Rudyard Kipling's infiltration of the ICS, which resulted in the destruction of the Shadow that had belonged to the Winter King, and the second Keep of Time the ICS had been constructing.

Blake had to suppress a shudder at the memory of Dee's response to that fiasco—which was that it wasn't a total loss, because they'd managed to destroy all the Dragons in the process.

All but one, as far as they knew. And a second, about which the Cabal knew nothing.

But the main reason that Dee had become more secretive, even to the point of abandoning their cover of the ICS, which allowed them to operate in semi-secrecy, was that his true goals were finally coming to the fore.

It had never been about the misguided goals of the Caretakers, or the secrets of the Archipelago, or even about the injustices done to the man who became the Winter King. For Dr. Dee, it was about knowledge, and power—both of which had been promised to him by the Echthroi. They had offered to reveal the secrets of creation to Dee, and in doing so, make him Shadows' agent of hell on Earth.

If Dee's plans succeeded, the entire world would be open to the Echthroi. That could not be allowed to happen. And that reason alone had been motivation enough for Blake to continue to help Dee and the Cabal, even to the point of doing things that were reprehensible to him.

Someone once said that it was sometimes necessary to commit small acts of evil, if those acts were in the service of a greater good. Blake knew that if he didn't believe that, on some deep level, then he wouldn't be able to bear sitting at this table, among these men, putting these plans into motion.

But he also knew, with some regret, that this was a reason he was not comfortable being among the Caretakers. Perfect knights, who saw the world in terms of black and white, good and evil, right and wrong, were very difficult to argue with. But he understood that living that way to begin with made them far stronger—and far better—men than he.

Dr. Dee, as usual, took his seat at the head of the table. The three Blakes sat to his left, and the inventor Nikola Tesla sat on his right. Next to Tesla were Aleister Crowley, the occultist, and the original discoverer of the House, William Hope Hodgson.

To the Blakes' right were the writers James Branch Cabell, H. P. Lovecraft, and, three seats farther down, G. K. Chesterton, who preferred a bit more personal space than the others—perhaps because other than Blake, Chesterton was the only member of the Cabal who had retained his own shadow.

At the far end of the table sat a very fidgety and disgruntled Daniel Defoe. He had been recruited into the ICS by Burton when he was still a Caretaker—but by then, he had already performed several services for Dee. And during the battle with the Winter King's shadow, when he overstepped his mandate and tried to seize power for himself, he was captured and imprisoned by the Caretakers.

He'd been left there, mortared up behind a wall, for several years—and as far as Dee was concerned, could have been written off completely as a minor casualty in the Caretakers' War, except for one salient fact.

The boy whom Defoe had hidden in the future was not

trackable by any means known to the Cabal—which meant that only Daniel Defoe knew when and where he could be retrieved. And so Defoe himself had to be retrieved from the Caretakers' fortress. Fortunately, Dee also had other reasons for ordering the burglary, so the effort, which nearly failed, was worthwhile.

"It took you long enough," Defoe complained. "Don't think I don't know that the only reason you broke me out of that dratted wall was because you need me to find the boy."

"No," Dee said coolly. "We broke you out because it was convenient. And it will be just as convenient to put you back, if you don't hold your tongue."

Defoe glowered, but wisely said nothing.

"What do you have to report?" Dee asked the Cabal.

"Aristophanes is not looking for the boy at all," said Crowley. "They approached him, just as we expected, but to ask him to find something else. Not the child."

Dee's eyes narrowed. "What, then?"

"The Ruby Opera Glasses."

A murmur of consternation rippled through the group. "If they sent him looking for the glasses," exclaimed Tesla, "it won't be long before he offers to seek out the rest of the armor for them, if he hasn't already."

"They do have someone looking for the boy," Chesterton said. "Or several someones, in point of fact. They call themselves the Mystorians."

A chill ran up Blake's spine, and it was a testament to his self-control that neither he nor his other tulpas reacted visibly to Chesterton's remark. Apparently, Verne's secrets were not as well kept as they believed.

"They have nothing," said Tesla. "Some fiction writers, a few students, a few women, Newton, and Lord Kelvin. Their technology will be not only out of date compared to ours, but functionally useless. We have nothing to fear from the Mystorians."

Dee turned to Blake. "Monitoring Verne's activities has been under your purview, William. Do you know anything about these 'Mystorians'?"

Blake wasn't sure whether he was being tested. "I do," he said finally, "but since none of them are actually Caretakers, I didn't see any import in addressing the matter. They are no threat to our plans. The Caretakers can enlist whomever they wish. But our devices, and our knowledge of how to use them, are greater. I think these Mystorians are merely a distraction."

"Indeed," said Dee. "Interesting that the Caretakers have chosen to recruit outside of their fortress in the Nameless Isles. And more interesting," he added, pointedly glancing at Blake, "that these allies, these Mystorians, are only now coming to our attention."

"We got all that we needed, even without the maps," said Tesla. "We won't need to go back."

"I beg to differ!" Defoe exclaimed, pounding his fist on the table for emphasis. "If they're watching too closely, I can't get back into Tamerlane House!"

"And this is a problem, how?" asked Tesla.

"You know good and well how it's a problem," Defoe shot back. "I'm limited to seven days without going back across that threshold."

"This would not be a problem if you hadn't gotten yourself crushed, Daniel," said Lovecraft. "That this problem has fallen at your feet is entirely your own fault."

"Actually, you owe the Caretakers a debt of gratitude," said Crowley. "If they hadn't created a portrait of you, you'd simply be dead now."

"Yes, well," Defoe said. "You brought me back for a reason, I assume, Nikola?"

"It's time to bring the boy back into our Prime Time, Daniel," said Tesla. "We cannot wait any longer. And," he added, swallowing hard, as if reluctant to make the admission, "so far, none of us have been able to, ah, locate the precise time in which you have him hidden."

Defoe smiled and slouched in his seat. "I'm cleverer than you give me credit for," he said, preening in his rare moment of prominence. "I didn't just hide him in the *future*—I hid him in an *imaginary* one."

"A might-have-been?" Dee said slowly. So that was the reason that despite their collective skills, they had been unable to locate the boy on their own. The idiot Defoe had basically hidden him inside a living *fiction*. If the boy had Defoe's original watch, they could still possibly track him—without Daniel Defoe—but someone would have to physically retrieve him. Even with a means to do so, which the Cabal had, it was still almost impossibly dangerous and risky to even attempt.

"If you know his physical origin point," Dee said to Tesla, "could you track the boy?"

Tesla nodded. "The number of zero points Daniel had access to are limited. If we know where the boy was left, we should be able to ascertain when."

"The boy," Dee said, eyes glittering, "is in London."

Defoe sat up with a start. "Uh, how did you . . . ?"

"There's only one means of travel back from a might-have-been to the real world," said Dee, "and it's in the subbasement of the British Museum. You left him in London because you wanted easy access to your means for returning here."

Defoe swallowed hard. "There's no need to search for him," he said, a frantic tone creeping into his voice. "I can retrieve him for you, no problem."

Blake and the others watched Dee's face as he debated what to do. Finally, and to Defoe's relief, Dee nodded at him.

"Do it, then," he said. "Bring him back. Don't show your face here again until you do."

Defoe removed the ebony watch he'd been given as a replacement for his own, twirled the dials, and disappeared.

Dee looked at his own watch. "This meeting is adjourned. You all have things to be doing. Attend to them."

Without further discussion, each of the Cabal removed their own watches and disappeared. The three Blakes went last, leaving only Tesla and the black bird in the meeting hall with Dee.

"William didn't react to the mention of the Mystorians," Tesla said. "Impressive."

"Maybe," said Dee, "but we cannot let him interfere with our endgame—not until he's finished with the new tulpas."

"Do you really think he'll finish them?" Tesla asked. "At some point, he'll realize that one of them is—"

"We'll deal with that when it happens," Dee said, rising from his seat, "but for now, we must take the next step. We must close their ears and cover their eyes."

"Then the word is given?" said Tesla.

"It is," said Dee. "Destroy these Mystorians. And then, when that has been accomplished . . .

". . . we're going to cut off the head of the Dragon and kill Jules Verne."

PART FOUR

THE WINTER WORLD

CHAPTER THIRTEEN
THE DRAGONS OF WINTER

THE CASTLE THAT *stood on the shores of Lake Baikal was as gray as the surrounding mountains, and nearly as timeless. It had been built for functionality, not vanity, and when, at long last, Mordred had been summoned to compete in the Gatherum, he had closed the castle doors with no intention of ever opening them again.*

He reflected bitterly on the memory, and the second betrayal at the tourney, and the twenty lost years that only resulted in another, final betrayal, and worse, the loss of his right hand.

This, he thought coldly, was the result of believing too strongly in the nobility of men—and in the Dragon who had promised him a reward that was now as insubstantial as a dream.

The Dragon had been waiting for him when he arrived, and stoked a fire in the long-cold hearth. It had burned down to glowing embers before Samaranth chose to speak.

"Your brother has been exiled," the Dragon said.

"Exiled?" Mordred answered, a glimmer of interest rising in his eyes. "To where?"

"Solitude."

Mordred's face fell. "You mean in the Archipelago. You've let him return. . . . But not . . ." The words trailed off as the expression on his face hardened once more into an inscrutable mask. "And his son, the Arthur?"

"He is king," Samaranth answered, "and has claimed the Silver Throne."

Mordred's shoulders slumped forward, and a bit of the craziness that had possessed him when he lost his hand seemed to have returned.

"So," he said, giggling, "my brother betrayed me, more than once, and his punishment is to return home, where we have been trying to go for centuries. And his son, who betrayed me utterly, and took this," he said, waving the still-bloody stump of an arm, "is punished by being made the High King and steward of two worlds.

"And I," he continued, his bitterness adding sanity as he spoke, "have done nothing but honor my obligations, love my family, accept unjust exile, and spend my life being schooled to become the last Dragon, and for what?"

He spun around before the Dragon could answer.

"I'll tell you," Mordred said. "It's to become educated—and I have learned my lesson, oh yes, I have. And I know, Samaranth, who has betrayed me the most."

The Dragon did not answer, but merely regarded his apprentice with an expression closer to sorrow than pity.

"I'm through as your apprentice," Mordred said. "And you can leave now."

The Dragon growled in response. "You are still the apprentice," he said sternly. "And as poor a student as you have been at times, it is a calling, not a cloak to be dropped on the floor when you grow too hot. You may refuse my teaching, but you will remain a Dragon's apprentice until the end of your days."

"Then I'll be what you made of me, Samaranth," Mordred said, turning back to the fire, "and the next time I see you, we shall see if one Dragon may kill another."

He said nothing more, and after a time, the great Dragon gave a sigh, and with a stroke of his wings, lifted silently into the night.

It was not an hour later when the Scholar appeared, quietly, unobtrusively, in the corner of the room, just out of range of the firelight.

"Greetings, young Madoc," he said, his voice quiet but firm. "Well met."

"My name," Mordred spat, not bothering to turn around, "is Mordred. And you have chosen a poor time to introduce yourself, whoever in Hades's name you are."

"Wrong twice," the Scholar said. "I have neither chosen poorly nor introduced myself."

Mordred spun about, reaching for his sword, then flushed with both anger and embarrassment when he realized he'd reached with his missing hand.

"You have been the victim of a grave injustice," the Scholar said. "I have come to right that wrong."

"I've heard that before," Mordred said, hiding his stump under his cloak as if it were naked.

"From the Elder Dragon, yes," the Scholar replied. "But his agenda is not mine. And I am not going to ask you for anything. I am merely here to serve."

"Serve?" Mordred barked. "Whom do you serve, here, in this place?"

The Scholar bowed. "A king, my lord. I serve you."

Mordred's face grew tight. "I am no king," he said brusquely. "Especially not here."

"*You are a king with no country,*" *the Scholar said,* "*but you remain a king, nevertheless.*"

Mordred hesitated—the Scholar's soothing words were doing the job they were intended to do.

"*Winter is approaching,*" *he said, turning to stoke the fire and add tinder to it.* "*A poor time to become a king.*"

"*Winter's king now,*" *the Scholar said persuasively,* "*and king of all else in time.*"

"*Do not promise that which you cannot give,*" *said Mordred.*

"*I never do,*" *said the Scholar.* "*May we sit, and speak further . . . my lord?*"

Mordred regarded the Scholar warily. His manner was not impos- ing, and his words dripped with honey. . . . But somehow, this strange, slight man who wore a monk's robe and called him lord understood what he needed to hear. And, Mordred realized, it had been a very, very long time since anyone had understood that, much less spoken the words.

"*All right,*" *he said, gesturing to the chair opposite his seat by the hearth.* "*Whom am I conversing with?*"

The Scholar took a seat and extended his hand. "*Dr. Dee,*" *he said firmly.* "*But you can call me John.*"

"Call me Jack." Hearing those terrible words, spoken by this pale man who called himself Lord Winter, was like stumbling into the Styx and feeling the cold death of the water splashing against one's soul.

Lord Winter noted the companions' shocked reaction with a wry expression, then walked across the terrace to where a long table had been set up for a feast.

The geometric shapes and the attendants marked as Dragons stayed where they were, watching silently.

The settings at the table were familiar, as were the dishes the food was served on—it was patterned after the Feast Beasts' dinner table at Tamerlane House. Except none of the foods were recognizable, and the details of the plates were not quite right.

They were made of bronze rather than silver, and the designs were imprecise, as if they were being viewed through a fuzzy lens, or had been made of wax that had softened over time. Or, thought Rose, as if they had been remade from old, imperfect memories of what the real dishes looked like.

Lord Winter took his seat at the head of the table and gestured for his guests to join him—but none of them moved. A look of irritation flashed across his features, and with a gesture, he signaled to his Dragon aides to escort each of the companions to their seats around the table. Winter watched as each of his "guests" pulled out their chairs to sit, giving each one a thorough once-over, but paying particularly close attention to Rose.

When everyone was in their place, Burton broke the tension by blurting out the first question that was on all their minds: "Your servant, Vanamonde, said that everyone on this world is Lloigor. Are you also a Lloigor, 'Jack'?"

"Right to the point, eh, Sir Richard?" Lord Winter said, unruffled by the question. "The answer is yes, I am. But the larger question is, why aren't all of you?"

"Why would we be?" asked Charles. "If you were truly Jack—"

"I am," Lord Winter replied, "just as much as you are who you are, Charles."

"You haven't answered me," Charles said, his voice reflecting the misery in his face. "Why would we be Lloigor?"

"On the rare—exceedingly rare—occasions that we encounter someone who has not chosen the path," said Winter, "their shadows are severed, and they are assigned new shadows, from those of the Echthroi who are still waiting for hosts." His eyes flickered up to the geometric shapes in the air, which vibrated slightly with the attention. "It is a condition of living in Dys."

"And if they choose not to, are they permitted to leave?" asked Burton. "I only wonder this because we were called your guests— but last night, the door was locked."

"That was for security," said Winter. "I shall order it kept unlocked in the future."

The companions exchanged uneasy glances at this suggestion that their stay might be longer than they wished—whatever their choice would have been.

"Have you ever had 'guests,'" Burton pressed, "who wanted to stay in Dys but didn't want to become Lloigor?"

"A few," Winter admitted, "like Vanamonde's father—your old colleague, Bert. Moses . . . Nebogipfel, I think it was. I'll have to check the label on his skull."

"Keeping the skulls of your enemies as trophies?" Bert asked with a barely suppressed shudder. "Isn't that a bit . . ."

"Barbaric?" Lord Winter finished for him. "Perhaps. But one man's barbarism is another man's culture. Isn't that right, Sir Richard? And besides," he added with a grin at Bert, "I learned it from *you.*"

Bert looked horrorstruck. "I've never taken a head from anyone in my life!" he exclaimed vehemently. "Nor would I keep the skull as a trophy!"

"Ah, not to quarrel," Charles put in, "but according to what John and, ah, Jack, told me, that isn't precisely true."

"How do you mean?" asked Bert.

"You did exactly those things in the country of the Winter King during the Dyson incident," Charles said, a pained expression on his face. He seemed to hate the appearance of supporting this Lord Winter's point of view on anything, least of all on a point regarding their mentor. But the truth was the truth.

"That wasn't me!" sputtered Bert. "That was—"

"A version of you, who had lived through some terrible tragedies," said Lord Winter, "and in the process, had to make some terrible choices. But make no mistake, Bert. It was you. I know. I remember."

"It weren't—I mean, it wasn't," Bert shot back. "I wasn't there."

"We all like to think that we will always make the choices that flow in line with our image of ourselves," Lord Winter said, turning to look out over the city, "but the truth is, we never know what we'll really do until we're already in the soup. And then, we do what we must, just as you did. It doesn't diminish the good choices you made to have chosen to do something you abhor," he continued, "but neither does it mean you suddenly changed character when you made those other choices. You are who you are."

Bert shook his head. "I would not have done those things— not if I had any choice," he added before Charles could correct him. "It just isn't in my character."

Their host spun about to face him. "Nothing we actually do," Lord Winter said, "is out of character."

He stood, and with a little encouragement from Lord Winter's

Dragons, the others rose as well. None of them had so much as touched a morsel of food.

"No one was hungry, I guess," Winter said. "Come—let me escort you back to your room. After all, traveling so many thousands of years must have made you all very tired."

The companions followed Winter and Vanamonde back down the stairs to the room where they'd spent the night. None of their belongings seemed to have been touched. Not their duffels, or their books, or . . .

. . . their *weapons*.

"Perhaps we may speak again later," Lord Winter said from the open doorway, "and I can tell you more about my decision to join the Echthroi and why"—he smiled broadly—"you will make the same choice, in the end."

Rose had already been considering a choice, and there, in that moment, as Lord Winter spoke those words, she made it.

Steeling herself to her task, she carefully, quietly removed the sword Caliburn from its sheath underneath her duffel, and before he could speak, she whirled around and rushed over to Lord Winter.

"You," she cried, "are *not* Jack!" and she buried the sword to the hilt in his chest.

It had absolutely no effect.

She stared at him, eyes wide and unblinking in disbelief.

"I was wondering why it was taking you so long to try that," Winter said, not even trying to conceal the pleasure in his voice. "I decided that you were either too timid to actually strike, or you were too overwrought with emotion for your dear uncle Jack to try it. But I'm glad to know that you weren't too weak to try. And I'm sorry that you had to fail so badly."

He gave her a shove, and she flew backward into the corner, hitting her head roughly against the wall.

"And," he said, taking little notice of the companions who had flown across the room to Rose's aid, "I'm sorry that I have to break your little toy."

He reached up and grabbed the hilt of Caliburn—and snapped it off. Then he simply pulled out the blade, which emerged clean and bloodless from his chest. He dropped it to the floor with a clatter.

"Impossible!" Burton breathed. "That sword should have defeated any Shadow!"

"Any mortal's shadow, eh, Sir Richard?" Winter said, winking. "But not primordial Shadow. Not Lloigor. Not Echthroi. And especially not while I wear this armor."

The fear in the companions' eyes was evident, and he chuckled, then held up his hands.

"It's all right," Lord Winter said. "I've no desire to harm you. Step closer, and observe."

To better facilitate their examination, Lord Winter stepped forward himself and raised his arms, turning slowly so they could see all the armor he wore.

"What is it?" asked Burton. "Where did you get it?"

"There was an old Chinese legend," Lord Winter began, "about a young girl named T'ai Shan. In the beginnings of time, there came upon the gods of the world a great drought—and I say gods, and not peoples, because in those days, all were considered as gods. They spoke with the beasts of the Earth, and lived long lives, and knew all the secrets that there were. But not the reasons for the drought.

"Crops died, livestock perished, and soon starvation followed. And all the great gods came together to try to find a solution, but none was forthcoming. No one knew what had caused the drought, and no one knew how to resolve it. But one child, a crippled girl named T'ai Shan, who lived as a beggar on the outskirts of the first city of the gods, knew what must be done.

"She recalled a story told by her grandfather, who was one of the elder gods, that when the gods needed aid, they prayed to the stars, and the stars came to Earth and aided them. So she rose on her crutch and hobbled away from the city, which was radiantly bright, into the darkness where she could see the stars, and she began to pray.

"One of the stars heard her prayer and descended to Earth to give her aid. He said that far to the west there grew a flower, a rose, which contained within it a single drop of dew. If she were to find that rose and return to the city, the drop of dew would become a torrent that would restore rain to the world and fill the oceans again.

"All he required of her was that when this was done, she give the rose to him. And T'ai Shan agreed.

"So the star took from himself scales of fire and gave them to the girl, instructing her that she should find a smithy to forge them into armor. And when she had done so, she would be able to traverse the great distance and retrieve the rose."

Lord Winter paused, as if he were struggling to remember— but after a few moments he regained his composure and contin- ued on, his voice strong and unwavering.

"T'ai Shan found a smith, and her armor was made. And as the gods of the Earth began to die, she went on her great journey, defeating terrible beasts and overcoming immense obstacles to succeed in her quest. And succeed she did—but when at last she returned, the star declared that he wished to keep the rose, and the dewdrop, for himself, and thus force the gods to swear homage to him, that he should rule over all the Earth.

"But T'ai Shan knew that this was wrong, and she resisted. The star tried to take the rose from her, but he had given her too much of his own fire, and in the great battle that followed, he was defeated, and fell.

"T'ai Shan succeeded in bringing the water back to the world, but she could not control it, and a deluge flooded all the Earth. Only through great sacrifice were the gods able to save parts of their world—and when the waters again receded, they found that the world had changed. It was no longer theirs—T'ai Shan had given it to their children, as it should have been all along. As her grandfather, the elder god, had told her the world was meant to be. To ensure that the gods would not try to reclaim it, she left her armor to the children, so that they might defend the world themselves. And with that, she walked into the mountains and vanished forever."

Lord Winter lowered his head, and the companions looked at one another, uncertain whether he was done—and more uncertain whether they dared to say anything.

Edmund was the one who finally broke the silence. "Begging your pardon, lord," he said respectfully, "but why did you tell us that story?"

Lord Winter laughed, a short, sharp bark, and turned to face the boy. "Innocence," he said, more to himself than to any of them. "It's a refreshing thing, after so long."

"I told you that story, my young Cartographer," he said, holding Edmund by the chin so the boy was looking him in the eye, "so that you would understand—I serve the Shadows, but fire still has its uses."

"You are not wearing the Ruby Armor of T'ai Shan," Bert said firmly. "As powerful as that armor is, an Echthros would not be able to countenance its touch. And the armor forged from a star would not shatter Caliburn. Only Deep Magic could do that. So your armor is something else."

Lord Winter started to respond in anger, but caught himself and replaced the harsh words on his tongue with a sickly sweet smile. "Very good, old friend. I'm impressed."

He released Edmund's chin. "I told you the story, boy, because somewhere in time and space, the bearer of that armor still exists. And unlike this sword, he does have the ability to injure me. So I forged armor of my own."

"Armor strong enough to break the sword of Aeneas?" asked Rose. "How?"

"As useful as the Spear of Destiny once was as a weapon, I found it to be far more useful as armor," Lord Winter replied, stroking his chest. "It heals any wound, deflects any blow against me. And together with the energies of the Echthroi, makes me all but immortal. And so I have had all the time needed to create this," he continued, spreading his arms to indicate the city that stretched into the distance, "my perfect world."

As it had before, the tower began to shake with a loud rumbling, lasting longer this time.

Bert snorted. "Hardly perfect, 'Lord Winter,'" he said. "Your dark tower seems to be coming apart."

"Not coming apart," Winter replied. "On the contrary—Camazotz is *growing*."

Charles threw a surreptitious glance at Burton, who nodded almost imperceptibly. So they were right—it was like the keep, in some ways at least.

"Growing?" said Edmund. "Why?"

"It no longer matters," Winter replied, trying—and failing—not to glance at Rose. "My plans have recently undergone a change, and soon I'll no longer need the tower."

"Why?" asked Burton.

"Because," Lord Winter said as he turned to walk away, "I've realized it is a world of perfect order, just as the Echthroi have ordained it to be. Just as it was always meant to be. Just as it will always be. And soon," he added as the door closed with an almost imperceptible hiss, "just as it will have always *been*."

Again the companions were alone, and in the silence, they let the full possibility of his words sink in.

"It's us," Charles said. "We're the somethings that changed him doing whatever it is he plans to do."

"Agreed," said Burton. "What think you, Bert?"

But the Far Traveler wasn't paying any attention to the discussion. Instead he was listening at the door. Then he reached down, grasped the latch . . .

. . . and pulled it open.

"The door!" Rose exclaimed. "It's unlocked! We can leave!"

"Of course," Edmund said, still not entirely grasping whether they were supposed to be prisoners. "He did say we are his guests."

"Guests are always free to leave the party," Bert said hastily, cutting off whatever sarcastic remark Burton was about to make to the boy, "and a good guest knows when it's time to dust the crumbs off his lap and bid the host good evening."

"If it's all the same to you," Charles said as the companions headed out the door, "I think we'll pass on saying good-bye."

"Agreed," Burton and Rose said together.

"Wait!" Edmund exclaimed, stopping in the doorway. "What about Archie? We can't just leave him behind!"

Rose started to answer, but it was Bert who turned around. "That can't be helped right now," he said, sternly but also with honest regret and sympathy. "You may not realize this yet, young Edmund, but it's a miracle enough that we're leaving this room alive."

"B-But Lord Jack . . . ," Edmund stammered.

"That is *not* Jack," Rose said firmly. "I don't know who he is, but Lord Winter is not our Jack. Listen," she added, putting a comforting arm across his shoulders, "we aren't leaving him for good. We'll come back for him. But right now, we are in the heart of the enemy's stronghold—and we aren't safe. We have to find high ground, where we can make a plan. But we'll come back. I promise."

Comforted, Edmund nodded and followed her and Bert out to the corridor where the others were waiting. Swiftly, and thanks in part to Edmund's unerring sense of direction, they retraced the path that Vanamonde had used to bring them along to their room, and in short order were again outside the tower.

Keeping close to the buildings, they made their way back to the massive entry doors, trying to avoid being seen—but very quickly they noticed that no one was looking for them. The few of

Lord Winter's Dragons they passed took no notice of them. And so their escape proceeded swiftly and without event. Their flight from the tower was done in silence, each of the companions keeping their thoughts to themselves. There would be time enough to talk and commiserate later. But as they ran, all Rose could think of was whether she would be able to keep the promise she'd made to Edmund.

And whether, if they were given the chance, she would be brave enough to.

CHAPTER FOURTEEN
THE UNFORGOTTEN

—*—

"SOMETHING'S GONE WRONG," Jack said as he and John examined the cavorite pedestal in front of Tamerlane House. "I can feel it in my spleen. Something's wrong. They should have come back before now, don't you think?"

"It's only been a couple of days," John replied as he sat on a nearby rock and started pulling at the long grass that grew in patchy clumps all over the islands. "That's the point of them staying there in real time—so that they'll have more time at the other end of the mission, in the past. And as to their other goal, well, there's no telling what's needed."

"I understand," Jack said, "but you've read the book. England isn't that big. They should have found her and returned by now. And Bert . . ."

"I know," John said irritably. They didn't speak of it much, but both men were constantly aware of the time—and how little of it Bert had left.

"At least," Jack said as he moved over to sit in the grass next to John, "when they do get back, we'll have another solid zero point connection for our *Imaginarium Chronographica*."

"That's the thing that disturbs me about our *Imaginarium*

Chronographica," John murmured. "I think our adversaries already have one, or something very much like it. And," he added, "it's better than ours."

"One of the reasons," said Verne's voice behind them, "that the Cabal's *Imaginarium Chronographica* is, well, not necessarily better . . . let us say, more complete than ours, is that not only did they have a head start in creating one, but somehow, they are adding all our zero points to their own—as we discover them."

Verne, Dickens, Twain, and Byron stepped off the porch and walked to where John and Jack were sitting. Verne lowered himself to the ground and sat with the younger men. "We do not know 'when' they have gone, but they know 'when' we have. And in that," he finished, "they have a decided advantage over us."

"But if a zero point isn't created until Rose and Edmund create it, how could they do that?" asked John.

"Bread crumbs," said Byron.

"If this is the start of a poem, I'm going to clock you," said Dickens.

"I mean, they're leaving a trail of bread crumbs," Byron said, irritated at being marginalized—again. "Rose and the Cartographer must somehow be leaving a marker that the Cabal can follow to each zero point. It's the logical explanation."

"Perhaps," Verne said, stroking his beard. "But how?"

Jack sighed. "This was all a whole lot easier when we just had to climb up some stairs and open a door in a tower someone else had already built."

"That is part of our quest," a quiet voice said. "It's part of why the travelers needed to undertake their journey—to restore what was."

The companions turned in surprise at hearing the speaker. It was Poe. Edmund Spenser was also with him.

It was surprising not that Poe had spoken, but that he had left the confines of the house. He rarely ventured outside—at most once or twice during the time that John and Jack had known him.

"That's the other thing I miss about the good old days," said Twain. "We didn't have to rely on a blasted deck of cards to go anywhere. We had the Dragonships."

"The trumps are more convenient, Samuel," said Verne, "and let us do our work more efficiently."

"But it's a device our enemies also use to go where they want to," said Dickens. "In fact, I think they've figured out some way to travel in space better than we do."

"Like the cat," Twain said, puffing thoughtfully on his cigar. "Grimalkin can appear wherever, whenever he pleases, and he does so without benefit of a trump."

"Yes," Dickens agreed, "but he is a cat, and obeys as well as the rest of his species—which is to say, not at all."

"We'll have the means ourselves soon," Verne said firmly. "Someone wearing the Ruby Shoes will be able to go anywhere they please—perhaps even into our enemy's stronghold."

"If we can acquire them," John pointed out. "Uncas and Quixote still have to find them first."

"Finding them is one thing," said Twain. "Keeping them is a horse of a different color."

"They're meant to be used by an adept, like Rose," Verne said. "Perhaps she can give them a try when they get back."

John looked at the others. "Maybe we ought to try to send someone after them with one of the devices in the basement, just in case there's been trouble," he said. "I'd certainly volunteer. Anyone else game?"

For a few long moments, none of them moved, until finally Twain reached out and squeezed the younger man's shoulder. "We are all with you, my boy. To the last man, to the last mouse. We are with you. But we cannot follow them into the future. Not until they return."

Suddenly it dawned on John why his suggestion couldn't be followed—and why it hadn't been suggested and implemented already by one of the others.

"The chronal energies," he said, crestfallen. "I'd forgotten. We can't go after them."

"Not," Verne said cautiously, "with what we now know about time travel, young John. But there are those working on . . . new ways."

"Who?" asked Jack.

"Top men," Verne answered cryptically. Which angered John, who stood up and clenched his fists.

"Your Messengers, you mean, like Dr. Raven, and the Mystorians!" John exclaimed, barely containing his frustration. "I don't care if we're meant to keep them a secret. Now is the time to play your cards, Jules!"

"The who?" said Byron.

"The thing you should know about cards, young John," Verne replied, "is never play an ace when a two will do."

"Jules learned that from the badgers," said Twain.

"How is this not the time to play all your aces, Jules?" said John. "How much larger do the stakes have to be?"

"It's not the stakes that you're misunderstanding, Caretaker,"

Edmund Spenser said, moving past the others and standing next to John, "but the size of the game."

It was an accepted tradition that due respect and deference was given to the Caretakers in accordance with their seniority. The only exceptions to this were Verne and Poe, who were accorded more because of their more prominent roles in the work of the Caretakers, and da Vinci, who was accorded less because of his arrogance among his peers. And thus Spenser or Chaucer usually presided over meetings, but less frequently got involved in the debates. So when one of them actually went out of his way to make a point, the rest of them listened. John sat back down on the rock and waited.

"All it takes for the opposition to win is to defeat us once— because the corruption that will cause can never be completely winnowed out again. And thus for us, a victory means never letting that take place. Constant, eternal vigilance—in all the times past, and all those still to come.

"So have patience, Caveo Principia," Spenser finished, holding out his hand to John. "Trust in your mentor, and the Grail Child, and the Cartographer. Trust in those you believe in. And they will find a way to come home."

John puffed his cheeks and blew out the air to calm down. "All right," he said, shaking Spenser's hand. "Let's go back into the house, shall we?" He glanced at Verne, still clearly annoyed. "All this hot air out here is giving me a headache."

As the others moved into Tamerlane House, Verne held Poe back to speak with him more privately.

"I need . . . ," Verne began. He stopped. Poe was holding a key in his outstretched hand.

"I know," the master of Tamerlane House said simply. "She is downstairs, where she has been since Quixote and the Child of the Earth retrieved her from the museum in London."

"I've prepared some memory rings," said Verne, "but if they're truly lost that far in the ancient future . . . If they indeed did just as you fear, and ended up in a might-have-been . . ."

"The Sphinx will persist, but the rings themselves may not last," Poe confirmed. "She may be the only one who can help them there, then."

It did not take Defoe long to return to the House on the Borderlands, but against Dee's express request, he returned without the boy prince.

"I have some good news and some bad news," Defoe said, slumped in his chair at the Cabal's table. He looked as if his head were splitting in two. "Which do you want to hear first?"

"I only care about why you came back without the boy," Dee replied through clenched teeth. "Tell me that before I have you drawn and quartered and fed to Loki."

Defoe glanced up at the huge black bird and gulped. "I went to find the Sphinx at the British Museum, but she's, uh, she's no longer *there.*"

"Moved?" asked Tesla.

"Stolen," said Defoe. "Burgled."

"Well, there's irony for you," said Chesterton. "Can't say we didn't deserve *that.*"

"Without the Sphinx, there's no way to return him from a might-have-been—," a now livid Dee started to say before Defoe interrupted him.

"That's just it," he insisted. "The boy *is* here, in the *House*. He's waiting in the next room. I just can't decide if that's the good news or the bad news."

On hearing the boy was there, Dee started to calm down, but now he stiffened up again. "How is that bad news?"

"*I* didn't bring him," Defoe said. "He found us entirely on his own."

The Chronographer's eyes narrowed, and he looked at Blake. "How is that possible?"

"Because," Blake said testily, "he's not just an heir to the powers that be. It seems he's also an adept."

Dee's eyes widened, and he leaned forward. "Explain."

"He has all the abilities we hoped he might have," Tesla said, glancing sideways at Blake, "and more, he is using them. He has learned how to activate his Anabasis Machine, and he has already been traveling in time."

Dr. Dee turned to look at Defoe, eyes blazing with anger. "You left him with a *functional* watch?"

"I had to!" Defoe exclaimed. "If he had been left in the past, no problem. We record where he is and retrieve him at our leisure. But in the future, especially in a might-have-been, we needed to leave a marker. And that meant giving him a watch and making sure it was activated."

He slumped back in his chair, pouting. "It isn't my fault, you know," he said to no one in particular. "How was I to know the boy would figure it out on his own?"

Blake knew from Dee's expression that he was considering whether to just dump Defoe in the ocean and be done with him.

"He more than 'figured it out' if he returned from a might-have-been all on his own," Dee murmured, more to himself than to the others, "and to have found the House so easily . . ."

He looked up at Defoe. "Bring him here. Now."

Defoe leaped out of his chair and vanished through the door. He reappeared a moment later, followed closely by a young man of perhaps nineteen who stood next to him as he took his seat.

"Greetings," said Dr. Dee. "You can call me John."

"If it's all the same to you," the young man replied, "I'll call you Dr. Dee."

Dee and the others reacted in surprise. "Daniel has told you about who we are?"

"No," the young man replied, "but I learned about you and who you are from my studies. And I know you can help me. That's why I decided to find you."

Interesting, Blake thought as he observed the young man, who was unruffled and very, very self-assured. *Dee may have actually bitten off more than he can chew.* He thought they'd taken a hostage who could be converted to an acolyte. But now, Blake realized, even if the others in the Cabal did not quite yet, they might have created a predator.

"We can help you," Dee said persuasively.

"I know I have these abilities," the young man said. "I just don't know what I have them *for.*"

"I can tell you that," said Dee. "You shall use them in the service of a great cause. There are immense forces at work in the world, and I am offering you the chance to shape what the world will become. If you work with us, there is no limit to what your destiny may be. Will you accept?"

In response, the young man simply nodded, once.

"Good," said Dee. "Daniel, will you see to it our young guest is made comfortable? We'll finish our business here, and then I'll come to personally instruct him."

Defoe again rose from his seat and motioned for the young man to follow, and without another word, they left the room.

"We should simply kill him now," Tesla said flatly. "He's more dangerous than he appears, Dee. And he's too unknown a quantity."

"He's an adept!" Dee snapped. "Like Mordred before him. Only we've gotten him before he's had a chance to lose his focus."

"His focus is precisely what worries me," said Tesla. "And if he's already learned to use the watch *on his own* . . ."

"Then he'll be at least as useful as Daniel Defoe," said Dee, "and longer-lived, to boot."

"What is his name?" Chesterton asked. "No one asked him."

"What does that matter?" Dee replied. "He's here, and he's ours. The plan proceeds apace."

"Where should we go?" Charles asked the others as they hurried down one of the paved pathways amid the dark buildings. "Back to the plaza, perhaps?"

Bert shook his head. "If that's really Jack up there, that'll be the first place he comes to look for us. We should find somewhere else where we can try to plan our next move."

"I'm all for going to find that Messenger, Pym," Burton growled, "and wringing his scrawny little neck."

"In that," Charles said, "we are absolutely agreed."

As it turned out, the companions had the opportunity to do both. When they exited through one of the city gates, they also found Arthur Pym, who seemed to have been waiting for them.

The scruffy Messenger threw himself to the ground, wailing. "Please!" he howled, tears rolling down his cheeks. "Forgive! I did not realize the birdy was a hurdy-gurdy! Only Echthroi fly here! Forgive!"

"Archie isn't a hurdy-gurdy," Edmund said sternly. "He's a *Teacher*."

"Oh for crying out loud," Charles said, rolling his eyes. "Have a little dignity, man." He pulled the still wailing Pym to his feet and offered him a handkerchief, which the Messenger promptly covered in snot.

"You can keep that," Charles said when Pym offered it back. "I've got a perfectly good sleeve here."

"Do you think the Lloigor will be looking for us?" Rose asked the others.

"Possibly," Bert said, looking around, "but we're still in the open here. We need to find someplace safe."

"Safe haven!" Pym exclaimed, tugging on Bert's arm. "That's where the others are. Safe haven."

"You mentioned 'others' before," said Burton. "Are they Lloigor too?"

Pym shook his head. "Not Lloigor. Not Messenger, either. People of the Book."

"Librarians?" asked Bert. "Or writers?"

"A little yes, a little no," said Pym.

"Which one?" asked Rose.

"Exactly," said Pym.

"All I care about," Charles interrupted, "is if this 'safe haven' is away from the city."

Pym nodded and started walking across the pavement. "Yes,"

he answered over his shoulder with a loopy, triumphant grin. "Very far." He motioned for the others to follow and picked up his pace.

"That," Charles said as they all fell into line behind Pym, "sounds pretty darn good to me—at least, better than our alternative. Lead on, Arthur."

The companions, led by the Anachronic Man, Arthur Pym, followed a paved path that led due east away from Dys. They walked in relative peace—the denizens of the city apparently didn't venture beyond its gates, or so Pym told them.

The Messenger kept up a rambling travelogue about their surroundings, none of which made an impression until they came to the canyon.

"This," Pym said, his voice echoing even though he spoke barely above a whisper, "this I wanted to show you especially, Bert."

Ringed about the high canyon walls were the great, skeletal remains of several ships, which had nonetheless survived enough of the passing centuries to be easily recognizable.

"It's all the ships," Bert said breathlessly. "All the Dragonships, come together again."

"Come together in a graveyard, you mean," Charles said scornfully, giving Burton a withering glance. "They're all dead, Bert. All of them. They would have been dead, as living ships, anyway, long before he ever brought them here."

"I . . . didn't know," Burton said, looking away, unwilling to face any of the others. "I swear to Christ—I didn't know the Dragons would be lost, when we took all their shadows."

None of them responded to Burton's apology, but Rose

stepped forward, simply taking Burton's hand and squeezing it in empathy.

"I don't see the *Blue Dragon* anywhere," said Bert. "The Elves' ship."

"Nor would I expect you to," said Charles as he climbed over a protrusion of rock for a better view. "It was left behind, there on Paralon, and perished with the island when the Echthroi took over."

"But the rest of them are here," Bert said, pointing, "including the old *Black Dragon*. Which means that at some time in the past, the Archipelago was restored."

Before any of them could comment further, Pym moved farther down the path on the canyon floor, toward an old, ramshackle gate. "There's more to see," he said, beckoning for the others to follow. "Much more."

They followed him through the gate, where they saw a massive, gleaming pyramid that rose up from the ground and dominated the horizon. It was surrounded by an immense wall that was nearly twice Burton's height. "The Last Redoubt," said Pym, trying to hurry them on. His eyes kept darting from side to side on the path, as if he were waiting for some beast to leap out and attack them.

At the pyramid's base, they saw something else familiar. "These are the rune stones!" Bert exclaimed as he examined the wall around it. "The ones we set up as wards around Tamerlane House. They've been repurposed to protect the pyramid and whatever else is behind this wall."

"The entrance is here," Pym said, showing them a looming, ornate door a little farther down the slope.

"It's of Caretaker manufacture," Bert said, excitement rising in his voice. "What's inside, Arthur?"

"Don't know." Pym shrugged. "Never been inside. Can't. Have to have a watch or a silver ring to get in at all—but you need two Caretaker's watches, just to open the entrance—and Lord Winter took my watch ages ago."

That piece of information elicited a quick glance of concern between Charles and Rose, but Bert was too excited to notice.

"Tried without using a ring," Pym said plaintively. "Tried and tried and tried. Don't like it out here a'tall. But no use. I couldn't get through."

"Maybe you can't," Charles said, "but I'm betting that *we* can."

There was a protective ornamental lock that was affixed to both sides of the door, where Pym said that the watches must be inserted to allow passage. "Otherwise," he said, "can't get through, even with a ring."

"Nice," said Burton. "Good forethought. Whoever built this place wanted to make sure that at least two Caretakers or their emissaries were present for it to work. Just one wouldn't do the trick."

"No," Pym echoed. "Wouldn't."

"Arthur was lost in time before Jules conceived of the rings," said Bert, "and so of course he wouldn't have one. But," he added, "I have mine, so he can use my watch to pass through."

He handed the device to Pym and nodded at Rose. She inserted her own watch in the indentation on the left of the door, as Edmund inserted his on the right. Then she reached out her hand and pushed the door . . .

. . . which swung soundlessly open.

"There," said Bert. "We're in."

From inside the wall, they realized the pyramid was in fact still a good distance away. There were crumbling temples and fallen archways, all overgrown with foliage, lining the gentle slopes of land that led to the pyramid's base. It was an architectural and arboreal disaster area—but somehow, it all managed to look deliberate. And the atmosphere was far less oppressive than that just on the other side of the gate.

"Well enough and good," said Bert, looking around. "There are people here." He pointed to the right of the pyramid. Against the dark sky, they could see the wispy trails of smoke rising.

"Why I brought you here," said Pym. "To meet the Unforgotten."

"Who are?" asked Charles.

Before Pym could answer, a tall creature with the beaked skull of a bird and the skin and claws of a reptile stepped out of the trees just ahead of them. He was carrying a spear and was adorned with ringlets of beads and feathers.

He stood watching the companions a moment, then tipped his head back and spoke—and it was then they realized it was a man, dressed as some kind of creature.

His words were unintelligible, but he was immediately joined by several others, all dressed as similar creatures.

The tallest of them cocked his head, as if he, too, were appraising these strange visitors; then he strode forward—to *Charles*.

"It's the glasses," Bert whispered. "They give him presence."

The strange man looked Charles over, then began to recite in a surprisingly delicate and refined voice:

He that is thy friend indeed,
He will help thee in thy need:
If thou sorrow, he will weep;
If thou wake, he cannot sleep;
Thus of every grief in heart
He with thee doth bear a part.
These are certain signs to know
Faithful friend from flattering foe.

"Dear Lord," said Bert, "That's—"

"Shakespeare!" Rose exclaimed. "He's reciting Shakespeare!"

Another of the strange people, a female this time, approached Charles and examined the silver ring he wore. As one, all the companions held up their rings, and Pym held up Charles's soiled handkerchief, grinning.

The response was unexpected, to say the least.

"You are of our tribe," the tall man said in perfect, unaccented English, his face breaking into a bright, gapped smile. He turned and raised his arms in triumph. "*They are of our tribe!*" he shouted, and the others broke out into loud cheering.

They clustered around the companions and started herding them toward the smoke. "They have a village there," Pym explained. "In this good a humor, just go along."

"How did these people survive?" Burton asked as they were jostled along by the exceedingly happy bird-skull-lizard-dressed people that Pym called the Unforgotten.

"Big world," Pym said, shrugging. "Even Echthroi couldn't take it over all at once. Some parts, didn't want to take over."

"So they just ignored those parts?"

"No," said Pym. "Usually, simply obliterated whatever they couldn't possess. This place, though, think they couldn't take over."

"Because of the wards," said Bert. "The protective rune stones."

"This isn't all that far from the city, or Dys, or Camazotz, or whatever it is that he's calling that dark tower," said Charles. "I wonder where we are."

"Thought you'd know where we are," said Pym. "From what I've learned, when the world fell to the Echthroi and Lord Winter began his rise to power, was the only place of free, truth-seeking, higher learning left on Earth."

"The Last Redoubt," Bert said, echoing the Messenger's words from earlier. "The last haven."

Pym nodded, as interested in what was inside as the others. "Didn't find this place until after I'd lost my watch," he said, "or else I'd have been in here, being Unforgotten myself.

"An ironic shame," he added with a tone of sincere regret, "that it happened to be the very place your friend Jack taught . . . you know. Before."

Charles slapped his forehead and Rose suppressed a grin, while Bert rolled his eyes at both of them.

"What?" asked Edmund. "I don't get it."

"Inside joke," Bert replied, "that's either gotten funnier or lamer depending on which side you're on."

"Cambridge," Charles muttered. "My old friend Tummeler would be absolutely appalled."

CHAPTER FIFTEEN
THE SPHINX

·—✳—·

THE COMPANIONS WERE led to an outdoor amphitheater that bore traces of Greek design, as well as designs of China, India, the Navajo, and other cultures that perhaps hadn't even existed yet in their own time.

When these "Unforgotten" removed the bird skulls and lizard cloaks they wore, the companions could see that they were simply men and women—and, Bert was thrilled to note, children—like those they had known in the past. And these people were far from being Lloigor. They were simple but happy, and, once they had established tribal affiliation, more than happy to receive guests.

There were homes fashioned from the fallen buildings that stood in the clear spaces between the wall and the pyramid, and more in the overgrowth of shrubbery and trees that pockmarked the area. There were cooking fires, and foods of the same sort that Lord Winter had offered—but this time the offer was combined with genuine hospitality, and the companions happily accepted.

"Have you noticed," Rose said, keeping her voice deliberately low, "that they almost all wear silver rings?"

"The adults do," Pym said as he bit into what appeared to be a roast hen—with six legs. "Rings are passed to the tribal elders from generation to generation. Allows the Unforgotten who wear them to pass freely into the outside. Although," he added with a shiver, "they seldom do, unless they must."

"Why are they called the Unforgotten?" Rose asked.

"Last remnants of our civilization," Pym replied, "the most important parts, some would say. Preserved that which was most important, which would otherwise not have survived so many centuries."

"Not engineering, or science," Charles said, looking around at the feather-clad children sitting nearby.

"Architecture?" Burton said, glancing at the pyramid.

"The books," said Edmund. "The stories—that's what's most important in any culture, I think."

As if that was a request, one of the group that had met them at the entrance leaped to his feet and began, in a rough American accent, to recite:

> "CAMELOT—*Camelot*," said I to myself. "I don't seem to remember hearing of it before. Name of the asylum, likely."

> It was a soft, reposeful summer landscape, as lovely as a dream, and as lonesome as Sunday. The air was full of the smell of flowers, and the buzzing of insects, and the twittering of birds . . .

"Dear Lord!" Bert exclaimed, nearly dropping his plate. "Those are the first lines of Samuel Clemens's book! Do you mean to tell me he's memorized the *whole book*?"

Pym nodded. "As his forefathers before him do, done, did. In fact, he *is* the book. So are they all."

The man shyly walked over to Bert and offered his hand, which the Far Traveler shook, slightly dazzled and definitely bewildered.

"This is A Connecticut Yankee in King Arthur's Court 417," Pym said by way of introduction, "although among friends and family, he's simply known as 'In.'"

"'In'?" asked Charles.

"If that whole title was your name, you'd want a short nickname too," said Pym.

"Good point," said Charles. "Who's this fellow?"

Pym put his arm around a slim, fair-haired man who appeared to be in his forties. "Treasure Island 519. And his brother, the fellow just there by the pylon—Oliver Twist 522."

"So everyone here is a living book?" Charles asked. "Amazing!"

"Not all the books that started in the beginning have survived to this day," said Pym. "There have been accidents, and natural deaths before books could be passed on in their entirety. The family line that had *Anna Karenina* lost the last chapter around ninety generations ago, and subsequent generations have decreed it to have improved the book immeasurably.

"Also," he continued, "*Silas Marner* didn't last into the fifteenth generation."

"Was that because of an accident, or a natural death?" asked Edmund.

"Neither," said Pym. "Just couldn't stand it anymore. Ended up marrying into and merging with *The Wizard of Oz*."

One youth stepped forward hesitantly, trying to decide whether he should introduce himself.

"Go ahead, lad," said Pym. "He'll be very pleased to meet you in particular."

"I am The Time Machine 43," the gangly, copper-headed youth said, unsure whether to offer a hand to Bert. "Are . . . are you really my creator?"

"*The Time Machine?*" Bert said incredulously. "I can't believe it!"

The young man was a bit flustered at this and took Bert's statement as a request for verification. So he gulped down his nervousness and began to recite: "The Time Traveller (for so it will be convenient to speak of him) was expounding a recondite matter . . ."

Bert rushed forward and embraced the startled young man before he could continue. "Oh my stars and garters!" he exclaimed. "You know it! You do know it!"

"Of course," Pym said, a hangdog expression on his face. "Told you he did—these people are the books, Bert. And he is one of yours, as were forty-two generations before him."

"Oh my," Bert said, unable to keep the tears from streaming down his face. "Do you know what this means, Rose, Charles?" The expression on his face was a mix of joy and pain. "It means that in a way, Weena is still here, in her future. Because I wrote her into the book, and because these people have kept it alive all these centuries, she's still here."

"I say," Charles asked, craning his neck to look at all the Unforgotten gathered around them. "Which, ah, which of these fellows or families represents *my* books?"

Pym looked at him curiously. "Sorry, Charlie, but I don't know that any families here ever really took to any poetry."

Charles frowned. "Oh. Uh, of course not," he stammered, "but I was asking more about my novels."

"Novels?" Pym asked, scratching his head. "Thought you were an editor."

"Editors can *write!*" Charles exclaimed. "I mean, I'm a novelist, besides being an editor. And a poet." He looked crestfallen. "So—no one here memorized any of *my* books?"

"Wait a moment," one of the Unforgotten said, stepping closer to Charles. "He said you were friends with the Caveo Principia and the Caveo Secundus?"

"Yes!" Charles said. "They are my friends. My good friends. Actually," he added with a nervous glance at his companions, "I was, ah, a bit of a mentor to them, in fact."

A light came on in the Unforgotten's eyes. "Aha!" he said, turning to the others. "Yes! I do know you."

Charles exhaled. "That's quite a relief."

"You are the Third!" the man said. "This is the *Third!*" he cried to the crowd. "He *did* truly exist after all!"

"Oh for heaven's sake," Charles said, totally deflated. "Shoot me. Shoot me now."

"Is the Unforgotten all that they are called?" asked Rose. "It seems a shame that such a noble group, with such a worthy calling, is simply known as 'Unforgotten.'"

"Not only name," said Pym. "Unforgotten describes their purpose, but they have another name to describe identity. Forefathers many generations ago chose another name. Felt it did honor to the path they chose. Called themselves that ever since.

"They," Pym said, "are known as the Children of the Summer King."

After a wonderful, plentiful meal, during which they were entertained by many great and classic stories, the companions were shown to a small tumbledown building where they could rest for the night and gather their wits.

"May I bring you anything else, Third?" one of the young women asked Charles, who answered with a weary smile and a deep sigh.

"No thank you," he said. "We're all fine here. And," he added, "please, call me Charles."

"As you wish, Third," she said, bowing.

"I think he's getting really annoyed with that," Edmund said with as much sincerity as he could muster.

"He ought to be looking on the bright side," said Burton. "It's been eight thousand centuries—to even be remembered as 'Third' is quite a testament to him and his place in history."

"Easy for you to say," Charles grumbled, "seeing as *Arabian Nights* is one of the books that survived."

"That's just because it was full of all sorts of lewd, lascivious, awful things that gave people something to feel ashamed about," said Bert. "You should feel proud that your books faded into obscurity in part because they had none of those things."

"Thanks," said Charles, "but that doesn't really help, you know."

"Have you noticed," said Rose, "the longer we've been here, the more composed Arthur seems to be getting?"

"His madness does seem to be fading," Burton agreed, "a bit."

"At least he's starting to use pronouns again," said Charles. "Just listening to him talk was making me itchy."

Pym, along with the Unforgotten he called Twist, after Dickens's book, had been explaining more details about this strange world, about the Unforgotten, and especially the dark city, Dys, and Lord Winter.

"The rings they wear are the rings of the Caretakers," said Pym, "as are the rune stones in the walls. But outside of that, they know little else about how and why this place came to be. They were focused on preserving the books."

"It's interesting, don't you think?" Rose said to the others. "How the Children of the Summer King are essentially the last vestiges of civilization, of all the learning of humankind . . . and yet they live almost as savages, in the most basic ways possible. But the city dwellers, living in thrall to Lord Winter and the Echthroi, who don't know anything of their own history, live in relative luxury, in that extraordinary metropolis."

"It's the same division as the Eloi and the Morlocks," said Bert. "The Eloi were simpler, purer—but the Morlocks were the ones who retained the technological knowledge that allowed their society to function."

"So what are we to make of Lord Winter, then?" asked Edmund. "Or the fact that it is Shadow that has ruled the world for all these thousands of years?"

"I'm not sure," Bert said, frowning. "I had always believed that the Echthroi represented chaos, but that apparently isn't true. In fact, it's just the opposite—the Echthroi have imposed an incredible state of order on the whole world."

"But shouldn't that have been the goal of all humanity?" asked Charles. "Isn't a world of perfect order something to have striven for?"

"You tell me, Caretaker," Burton said as he tore off a piece of chicken with his teeth. "You've spent time in both worlds now. Which place were you more comfortable? There in the city, or here with these wild folk?"

"If I had to choose," said Charles, "I'd take this place, no doubt.

Plus indoor plumbing, if there was an extra wish in the genie bottle."

"Choice," Rose said, her voice low and cool, "is the entire point of it all. Choice is the difference. The Echthroi do not allow those whom they make Lloigor to choose to be thus. They compel it. That these people managed to preserve their ability to choose seems almost . . . accidental."

"You think all this was an accident?" Pym sputtered. "Are you serious? This was no accident—nothing Verne does is accidental. It's all part of a plan, his and Poe's. Even my being here, in this horrid place—it was a plan, I'm sure of it."

"And yet you're the one who chose to do their bidding," said Burton. "You idiot."

"I am prone to occasional lapses of judgment," Pym admitted, "but those are mostly confined to time travel, and trips to the Arctic Circle."

"There's no way to know if Verne or Poe foresaw this," said Bert. "Not unless they can send a message across eight thousand centuries."

At this, Twist brightened. "But he did, great creator," the Unforgotten said. "Follow me—I can show you."

Twist led them through a warren of tunnels that wrapped around the base of the pyramid to an entrance. As with the gate, it opened for a ring bearer, and they all went inside. The narrow entry corridor opened into a large anteroom that was torch-lit, and empty save for a round, metallic table that was slightly concave. On it rested three golden rings, each about four inches in diameter.

"Oh my stars and garters!" Bert exclaimed. "These are memory rings! Jules created them, after the ones I saw here—well, in Weena's future, anyway." He picked up one of the rings and peered through it. "Sort of a 'chicken-and-the-egg-and-the-chicken' kind of setup. I told him about the rings I'd found that recorded history, and he thought it was a capital idea and tried to duplicate them. He designed them to last for as long as ten thousand years."

"Ten?" asked Burton. So for these to have existed eighty times that long . . ."

". . . is exceptional and extraordinary," said Bert. "But they're here, nonetheless. And we may as well, ah, give them a whirl, so to speak."

Delicately, he picked up the other two rings, then set one on edge on the table and gave it a spin.

As the ring whirled about, the voice of Jules Verne suddenly echoed across the anteroom:

"No way to know which of these rings may survive into the ancient future," Verne's voice was saying. ". . . last of the Caretakers in exile after the restoration of the Archipelago . . ."

"It's fading in and out," said Edmund. "I can't hear it clearly."

"They're too old," said Burton. "It's been too long."

"Shush," said Bert. "Listen!"

". . . all the lands put in their proper place, then . . . at the waterfall . . . Lloigor . . ."

The ring slowed and clattered to a stop.

"Oh dear," Charles murmured. "Perhaps the next one will be more cheerful."

It wasn't. When Bert spun the second golden ring, it emitted nothing but hissing and scratching, then a few unintelligible words, and then . . . a scream.

"That was Laura Glue," Rose said numbly as the ring slowed and stopped. "I'm sure of it."

The third ring was shorter, but infinitely more promising— at first. ". . . not forgotten you!" were the first words, followed by ". . . given you the means to return, which only you can use . . . answer to the riddle . . . the last Dragon . . . Sphinx . . ." then static. And just as the ring began to spin down, one final, chilling hint of what befell them in the past:

"Jack . . . at the waterfall . . . Lloigor . . . and there was . . . he fell."

The ring stopped. That was all.

"So," Charles said glumly, "Lord Winter really *is* our Jack."

"He is not the Caveo Secundus!" Twist exclaimed. "He is dust! He is the smoke!"

That got Burton's attention. "Smoke?" he asked, more to his companions than to Twist. "Was Jack planning to become a tulpa?"

"As far as I know," Charles said, "Jack's plan is to follow your own course of action, Bert, and join the portrait gallery at Tamerlane House. He has never spoken to me about becoming a tulpa."

"Well, unless he changed his mind, or someone made a tulpa of Jack against his will, we may never know what really happened," said Burton.

"Oh," Charles said, as all the blood drained out of his face. "Oh dear."

"What?" asked Bert.

"I, ah, I made a tulpa of Jack, just for practice, remember? But once I knew I could, I stopped concentrating on it, and it just faded away into . . ." He swallowed hard. "A whiff of smoke."

"You infernal fool!" Burton shouted. "It takes time to dissolve a tulpa! Time! And effort! And if even the smallest whisper still existed . . ."

"Then someone could steal it, and build it up again," said Bert. "As I think the Cabal did. Yes. Exactly that."

"B-But even if they did," stammered Charles, "how would he have become Lord Winter?"

"A tulpa that you make of another person has no aiua, no soul," said Burton, "because unlike one you make and claim for your-self, it would just be a shell, a copy of someone who already *has* a soul. It would be the perfect vessel for an Echthros to possess.

"Your choices destroyed the Archipelago," he added, his face an inch from the hapless Caretaker's, "and it's your choices that may have doomed this world as well."

"Wait!" Rose exclaimed. "I'd completely forgotten!" She turned to Bert. "Can we play the rings again? Please? It's important."

Bert complied, and again they listed to the rings. When they had done so, the companions all turned expectantly to Rose.

"In all the rush to get away from Dys," she said, "I forgot to tell you what happened to me while you were sleeping. I think I know now what it all meant, and what we're supposed to do."

Quickly Rose told them of the moonbeam that led her to the Morgaine, and about the message she'd been given. They might have believed it was just a dream except for Rose's conviction that it had really happened—and the fact that she actually had the multifaceted mirror Lachesis had given her.

"Technically speaking, I think my father, as the Black Dragon, was supposed to be the last Dragon," Rose said. "And we lost him when the Archipelago fell to the Echthroi, so I'm at a loss as to what riddle she meant."

"Maybe she meant the *other* last Dragon," Twist offered helpfully. "The one in the next chamber."

The companions all turned to Twist, who returned their slack-jawed amazement with a wan smile. "I was going to mention it sooner," he said helpfully, "but I don't like to interrupt."

"Like the door in the wall outside, it takes two watches to open the inner chamber," Pym explained, "and they are greatly treasured, so they almost never take them out."

Twist and several of the other Unforgotten ceremoniously unwrapped a box of folded palm fronds, which contained their greatest treasures: two of the silver Caretaker's watches.

"So that's how they get to the outside," Burton murmured. "Verne always was the good Boy Scout."

"One is Jules's," Bert confirmed, "and the other is . . . Twain's? Or maybe Dickens's."

"The watches survived all these centuries?" Edmund exclaimed. "I've never seen a watch that could last that long."

"These aren't the silver watches the McGee family worked with," said Bert. "These are covorite. They'll outlast pretty much everything!"

Twist fumbled with the placement of the watches into the two slots, and an exasperated Pym stepped forward to help. "Here," he said a bit gruffly. "You're getting them in backward."

When the two watches were properly in place, something in

the walls shifted, and a wedge of stone slid up into the ceiling. There, in a much larger room, was what Twist had called the last Dragon—but it was not really a Dragon at all. It was a Sphinx.

It was perched atop a squarish, solid-looking structure that was approximately twenty feet wide, with a semicircular arch in front that held a metallic door. The Sphinx itself was greenish-gold, and indeed resembled a Dragon—but not a full-bodied Dragon, as they were thinking they'd see.

She had wings, and the lower body, legs, and hindquarters of a Dragon—but her torso, neck, and head were those of something much more human, and her eyes were closed. Still, she had a terrible kind of beauty, and just looking at her inspired a hushed reverence.

"Here," Twist said, pointing to a plate set in the wall of the structure. "This may be the riddle you're seeking."

It was. There were several lines of text, written not in English, but in . . .

"Elvish," said Rose. "If Jules left this here for us, and made certain only ring bearers and Caretakers could enter, then he left this riddle that could only be read by someone like John. Or," she added with a wink at Bert, "his best student."

Rose brought the torch closer and translated for the others:

> *Come not between the Dragon and her wrath;*
> *But give unto her a choice;*
> *Redeem her life, that distant past,*
> *By easing others' strife;*
> *Or choose again, the folly path,*
> *In anger or in sorrow,*

And once more sleep, 'gainst her will,
Till there be no tomorrows.

Naming is waking, speak loudly and clear;
Then offer the choice, and pay what is asked;
No passage is free, all prices are dear;
The heart of the Dragon belongs to the past.

"So we're to give her a choice?" asked Charles. "That's not really a riddle, is it?"

"The riddle is in naming her," said Bert. "To wake a Sphinx, you must speak its name."

"They wouldn't have left this for us without the means to solve it," said Rose. "it's probably in a book."

"The answer to the riddle is in a book?" Charles groaned, looking at Twist. "But *which* book? There are hundreds of them here, running all over the place, and it's not as if we can simply skim through them for what we want."

"Then maybe it's something we already know," said Bert. "There are surely many stories where hidden names are the solution to the problem."

"Got it!" Charles said, snapping his fingers. He stood in front of the Sphinx, taking a heroic stance—feet spread apart, hands on his hips, chin lifted in anticipation of victory.

"Rumpelstiltskin!" he declared in triumph.

In response, the Sphinx didn't even acknowledge that he had spoken, but merely continued to sleep.

Bert slapped his hand to his forehead, and Rose blushed in sympathetic embarrassment.

"What?" asked Edmund, clearly confused. "Is it working? Was that the right name?"

"No, that wasn't the right bloody name," Burton growled. He frowned at Charles. "I can't believe you thought that was worth trying, you idiot. And you call yourself a scowler!"

"Actually, I think it's pronounced 'scholar,'" Edmund said helpfully.

"Never mind," said Charles, who was now both deflated and embarrassed. "That was the best example I could think of where a name was the answer."

"Maybe that's just the wrong address on the right road," Bert said, rubbing his chin. "John was including just such a thing in that new book he's been working on, remember?"

"That's it!" Charles exclaimed. "The lock on the door to Samaranth's cave. It opened when we spoke the word 'friend' in Elvish."

"Really?" said Burton. "That's a stupid idea."

Charles smirked. "That's what he said too. At first."

"Just try it," Rose said, clambering to her feet. "Speak the word 'name' in Elvish, Uncle Charles."

He did, but to no avail. The Sphinx remained impassive, unmoved, and the eyes stayed closed up tight. Burton argued that the original riddle was too easy to break—but noted that the door was also guarded by a large dragon—Samaranth—who had no problem roasting unwelcome visitors, so any other riddle using the same premise would, by necessity, need to be more difficult. So Charles tried both "friend" and "name" in Elvish once more—just for good measure—before trying both words again in Dwarvish, Orc, Goblin, Badger, and French.

"Why French?" asked Bert after the last failed attempt.

"Because," Charles answered, "for all we know, Verne set the terms here, and not John."

"But John is the Caretaker Principia," said Edmund.

"And Jules Verne is the Prime Caretaker," Burton said, answering the young Cartographer's unspoken question, "and thus has greater latitude to muck about with history than his understudy."

"Oh," said Edmund, looking up at the Sphinx. "Maybe when we left, that was true. But we have no idea when this was put here for us to find, or who among them was still alive to leave it."

"The boy has a point," Burton admitted, "even if it's a brutal one." He turned to Twist, who was eager to help, but helpfully staying out of the way. "What about you? Do your people have a name for the Sphinx?"

"Sure," said Twist. "We call her Isis."

Charles tried that, but the results were the same—no response. "Why do you call her that, anyway?"

"It's engraved on the wall behind her," Twist said, pointing at the near-obscured letters. "There."

"Not Isis!" Charles exclaimed, crouching for a closer look. "I—C—S! The initials of the Imperial Cartological Society! Someone in the past must have just started calling the Sphinx by these letters, and eventually that's all anyone remembered."

"There's no way any of the Caretakers, or Jack's version of the ICS, could have anticipated the Unforgotten," Bert said. "How could they? None of this should have been here. So any riddle they left, they would have expected us to be able to solve with whatever we had on hand. Unfortunately, I don't think any of the books we have will be helpful."

"There's *one!*" Rose said excitedly. "The Little Whatsit. If there's only one real book left on Earth to use for solving a riddle, that would be the one I'd want. And Fred made certain that we'd bring it with us. That had to be their plan."

Burton scoffed. "The badger's book isn't going to tell us how to escape from this place," he said, scowling at her. "We need a practical solution."

"That's as practical as it gets," Bert said. "The Little Whatsit can tell us when the Sphinx was created, and the *Imaginarium Geographica* can tell us where. And between the two, we may be able to discover her name."

"There's only one problem," said Charles. "We left all our things—including the books—back in Dys, at the dark tower."

"Then we know what we have to do," said Rose. "We've got to go back."

CHAPTER SIXTEEN
THE LAST DRAGON

PYM CHOSE TO remain with the Unforgotten, which suited the companions just fine—especially Burton, whose main contribution to the group seemed to be that he was suspicious of everyone. Not that Pym didn't invite it—more than one of them noticed he knew how to open the Sphinx's chamber in the pyramid, a place he had supposedly never been.

No one the companions passed even glanced in their direction as they made their way up into the tower, to the room where they'd left their belongings. The door was open, but the room was not entirely as they'd left it.

"It's Archimedes!" Edmund exclaimed joyfully as he dashed to the far side of the room. There, perched on a beautiful mahogany stand, was the owl—whole again. The gash across his torso had been completely repaired.

Forgetting the urgency with which they'd arrived, the companions circled around Archie in grateful relief.

The bird was silent, but his head pivoted to each of the companions, observing them with an unblinking gaze. Rose almost hugged him, and for a moment, she thought Edmund actually would.

But it was Rose, the one who had known Archimedes the longest, who realized something was wrong.

"Step back," she said, gesturing for the others to move away from the still-observant bird. "Something is amiss here."

"What's wrong?" Edmund said, unwilling to move away. He stroked the owl's back and beamed. "Tell them, Archie. Tell them you're all right."

Archie looked at him, but still didn't speak.

"Archimedes," Rose said slowly, "how long is a rope?"

The workings of the bird whirred and clicked as it answered. "There is no answer to that query. It has no absolute value."

Rose frowned. "He taught me that question, when I was younger. It's a test of numbers, but also of philosophical thinking. The answer is, 'Exactly twice the length of the distance from the center to one end.' But he answered it like . . ."

"Like a machine." Vanamonde appeared at the doorway and bowed.

"We have taken the chaos from him," a chilling and familiar voice said from the corridor behind Vanamonde. "We repaired his form and cleared all the clutter from his mind. He is now a creation of perfect order."

Lord Winter stepped inside the doorway and stood next to his servant. "How, pray tell, was he broken?"

"He was . . . ah, damaged," said Edmund. "Outside the city, when we found—"

"It was an accident," Rose said, interrupting Edmund before one of the others could. He was a smart young man, but he did not have the kind of experience the rest of them had in dealing with a Shadow-possessed person—especially one he might believe he could trust. "Thank you for fixing him."

"Of course," Lord Winter said, almost dismissively. "Such repairs are a simple thing in the city of Dys."

"What clutter are you talking about?" Edmund asked. "Archie was smarter than all of us, and he never hesitated to say so."

"Indeed, and that is exactly my point," Lord Winter said as he stepped into the room and closed the door behind him. This time, the click of the lock was definite. "His brilliance was cluttered with the detritus of free will—but we removed that. And now he functions as he was meant to—as a machine."

"We're grateful that you helped Archimedes," Bert said, "but it appears that we're expected to stay here now, whether we like it or not."

"I apologize for treating guests in such a manner," Lord Winter said with a tone of sincere regret. "I had assumed that you would be unable to cause any mischief if I allowed you to wander freely. It is obvious that I was mistaken."

"What mischief?" asked Charles. "We simply went to—"

"The Renegades," Lord Winter said. "The ones who have prevented us from completing our control of this world."

"The keepers of the faith, you mean," said Bert. "The ones who preserved your own legacy . . . *Jack.*"

Lord Winter tried to suppress a slight smile. "Not for much longer, I fear."

He spun about on his heel and opened the door. The corridor outside was filled with Winter Dragons—far more than the companions could evade or fight. "It is time to begin our negotiations," he said curtly, "regarding what place each of you shall have in Dys. I would speak with Charles first."

He walked out of the room, with Vanamonde close behind. It was clear they expected the Caretaker to follow.

"You aren't going to go?" Rose said, aghast.

"I must," Charles replied. "Following him, negotiating . . ." He dropped his head and gestured with his hands in frustration. "We may have nothing else left."

"Yes we do," Bert said. "We have hope. And that cannot be taken from us."

"How can you say that, Bert?" asked Charles. "You've even lost your wife. Here, in this time, she never even existed."

"She did exist," Bert said simply, his eyes brimming with tears. "She existed, and I loved her, and together we had a daughter whose name was Aven. And Aven lived a long, full life, and was brave and beautiful, and when it seemed as if all hope was lost for her, she found a way to keep it alive. And that act is what paved the way for your own redemption, Charles. To make right a mistake you have paid too dear a price for already. And you know, as much as the rest of us, that it's in the darkest moments that hope shines brightest.

"Here," he finished, pressing Weena's petals into the Caretaker's hand. "Let these guide your choices. As they have mine."

Charles gave Bert a long, appraising look before slipping the petals into a pocket and turning away. The door closed behind him with silent efficiency as he strode away from the room. He did not look back.

The Winter Dragons escorted Charles to an expansive room where Lord Winter was already waiting. He was looking out a window toward the Last Redoubt and did not turn when Charles entered.

"Once, you were my mentor," Winter said, never taking his

eyes from the window, "and now it seems I have become the teacher, and he who was once my teacher may now become my apprentice."

"You were made a similar offer long ago," Charles said softly, "by someone who also had no shadow. And as I recall, you declined the invitation."

At that, Jack lowered his head and smiled. "Not without a struggle, I assure you, old friend. I was young and far too innocent to understand what Mordred was offering me."

"As I recall," said Charles, "he also had a penchant for stabbing his teachers."

"Just the one," replied Winter. "Otherwise, he was an excellent student himself. He just had his own ideas of how to go about things. It never went well when his affairs were guided by someone else's intentions."

"As your intentions guide the choices of your Dragons, Jack?"

"They're Dragons in name only, you know," Winter said, indicating the masked servants who stood at posts around the great room. "It was my way of establishing a hierarchy among the Lloigor. But none are really Dragons. There have been none here for millennia who even knew what becoming a true Dragon meant, and then," he said, turning, "*you* came."

"The Echthroi are mighty," Charles said, "and obviously dominate this world, even if there are places left that still defy your rule. So what need have you of Dragons?"

Winter inhaled sharply, and the breath rattled in his throat. "Because," he answered, "only a Dragon can leave this world and travel to another."

All at once Charles understood. A real Dragon, who had

accepted his calling, as Madoc once had, could cross even the great wall that existed at the far edge of the Archipelago.

"Then the chains in the sky . . . ," he said.

"My fetters," Winter answered, "imposed by Shadow."

Charles started, surprised. "Your own masters imprisoned you here? Why?"

"Because of that," Winter said, gesturing to the pyramid in the distance. "Because I do not control the whole of this Earth, I am not permitted to leave. But with a Dragon as my apprentice, who could also take me as her apprentice, there will be no boundaries to stop me."

"I hate to tell you, old fellow," said Charles, "but I'm not . . ." He stopped, suddenly realizing what Winter had actually said: *her* apprentice. "You mean . . ."

"Rose," Winter said, nodding. "When Madoc became the Black Dragon, he entrusted her with his heart. That is how the mantle of responsibility is passed. She is now the Dragon's apprentice. And all she need do is choose it, and she will become a Dragon in more than name."

"And the reason you asked to speak with me first . . ."

"We are old friends, are we not?" said Winter. "Together we could convince her. The others need not be involved. Just you and I. Just like old times."

He turned and placed a hand on Charles's shoulder. "I know you," Winter said, his voice dropping to a whisper. "I know you chafed, as John and I received the recognition and the glory. But what I'm offering you now can be far greater than that, Charles. Greater than you are able to imagine."

"Yes," Charles replied. "But at what cost?"

"I paid the cost myself, long ago," said Winter. "All your friends died, long ago. Their work turned to dust, long ago. All you have to do now is say yes."

"If I agree to help you," Charles said slowly, "will you let the others go?"

"I'm sorry, but that just isn't possible," Winter said, an almost gentle tone in his voice. "They cannot remain as they are. But join me, help me convince Rose to take the mantle of Dragon, and I as her apprentice, and we will all be together forever, living lives of perfect order as servants of the Echthroi."

Charles couldn't contain his reaction, and he recoiled in horror. "You want us all to become Lloigor? Are you *insane?*"

"I understand," Winter said soothingly. "But you have no idea how free will has burdened you all. You may argue, but eventually you must agree."

Charles shook his head. "That isn't a reality I have the right to choose for my friends. And I refuse to choose it for myself."

"There *is* no other reality," Lord Winter hissed, irritated that the Caretaker was not ceding his point. "There has been no other reality for eight thousand centuries. There has been no opposition to my dominance of this world for a longer time than all of human history before it, many times over. Open your eyes, Charles, and see the world as it truly is."

Almost absentmindedly, Charles put his hand into his pocket and removed what he found there, cradling them gently in his hand.

Weena's petals.

"My eyes *are* open," said Charles, "and what I see is that you have nothing to give me that I do not already have. I decline your offer. I will not join you, nor will I help you convince Rose to do so. And that is *your* reality."

Lord Winter stared at Charles, trembling, then with a gesture had him escorted from the room.

"He wants us to *choose* to become Lloigor?" Bert exclaimed. "He *is* insane."

"It's greater than that," Charles said after he'd related the gist of the conversation with Lord Winter to his friends. "He wants our Dragon to make him her apprentice."

Rose went pale and touched the circlet that hung on the chain around her neck—the Dragon's heart her father had given her. "My apprentice?" she said in disbelief. "But that would mean . . ."

"Yes," Charles said. "When your father gave you his heart, he marked you as his apprentice. You were meant to become the next Dragon, Rose, if you chose to be—and if in turn you made Lord Winter your apprentice, then he could learn to become a Dragon too. And that's what he wants."

"I'm a little unclear on the power structure," said Burton. "He's practically the absolute ruler of the entire planet, and he has the soul of an Echthros. So what would he have to gain by becoming a Dragon?"

"The one ability that has only ever been invoked by one Dragon I know of," said Bert. "The choice that is all-encompassing, and for which an impossible price must be paid. But still the only thing a Dragon can do that an Echthros or Lloigor cannot."

"What?" asked Rose.

"Heaven," Bert said grimly. "He wants to become a Dragon so that he can storm the gates of heaven itself."

◆ ◆ ◆

Before any of them could remark on Bert's words, there was a tapping at the door, which opened. They all expected it to be the ever-polite Vanamonde, but it wasn't Lord Winter's chief Dragon—it was Arthur Pym.

"Oh my stars and garters!" Bert exclaimed. "Am I ever so glad to see you, Arthur!"

"Quickly, quickly!" Arthur exclaimed, eyes darting back and forth in fear. "Distracted the guards, and there's no one in the corridors! To escape, it must be now!"

Hastily the companions gathered up their belongings, including the broken sword Caliburn, and the books they'd come back to retrieve in the first place.

"That's everything," said Burton. "Let's go!"

"What about Archie?" Edmund said. "We can't just leave him here!"

"Lad," Bert said, as gently as he could manage. "That isn't the Archimedes we know. Not any longer."

The young Cartographer backed away and shook his head. "I don't believe that. They may have been able to change around some of his parts, but what made him our Archie is still in there somewhere. I know it."

Bert looked at Rose, then at Charles, who shrugged.

"I'm here now because my soul, my aiua, my . . . whatever it is that makes me *me*, didn't need my old body to go on," he said. "So I found a new one. So who am I to tell Edmund that Archie's soul isn't still there, somewhere, buried under all those cogs and wheels and wires?"

"I can carry him," Edmund said, ending the discussion. "We

won't leave him behind. Maybe Shakespeare can fix him."

"I've got him," Burton said, putting the compliant clock-work into his own bag. "We aren't leaving anyone behind. Not today."

At the gates, Pym's anxiousness eased visibly, and swiftly they made their way back through the canyon of ships and toward the entrance of the Last Redoubt.

"What is it?" Burton asked Charles, keeping his voice low so the others couldn't overhear them. "You're chewing on something, I can sense it."

Charles nodded. "It's Pym, the Messenger. Before, he wouldn't go anywhere near the doors to Dys. Was absolutely terrified just at the prospect of it. But suddenly, to rescue us . . ."

Burton tipped his head in agreement. "I see where you're going. Somehow he overcame his fear, made his way deep into a city he'd never been in before, snuck into the tower where Lord Winter lives, located us, and is now leading us to . . . safety?"

"Wherever this leads," Charles whispered, "be prepared for it to go terribly wrong."

"I hope you're wrong," Burton said, glancing ahead at where Pym was animatedly chatting with Bert and Charles.

I hope so too, Charles said silently to himself, *but I'm not.*

As they moved along the paved pathways, Rose, Bert, and Edmund were scanning through the Little Whatsit and the *Imaginarium Geographica* for clues to the riddle of the Sphinx.

"What I don't understand," Rose said, "is why Lachesis called it the last Dragon's riddle. What would the Sphinx have to do with my father?"

"Technically you're the last Dragon," said Edmund, "in waiting, as it were."

"You're letting your own notions guide you, rather than the riddle itself," said Bert. "Obviously, the Sphinx was a Dragon once. So she has to be who the Morgaine was referring to."

"I think that's what Lord Winter brought the Dragonships here to do," said Edmund. "He was trying to find a Dragon to make him its apprentice."

"And one was here, in the only place he couldn't get to," said Rose. "No wonder he wanted to get into the pyramid."

"If the Dragon's heart is what he needs," said Edmund, "why didn't he simply take it? Rose even tried to kill him and couldn't, so he obviously could have overpowered all of us anytime he chose to."

"It's a matter of free will," said Bert. "It's an office that must be conferred, then accepted—not taken by force. She had to choose it—that's why he needed Charles's help to persuade her."

"I never would have—," Charles began.

"I never doubted, Uncle Charles," Rose said, hugging him. "You'd never let me fall."

"Here," Edmund said, pointing to a map in the *Geographica*. "This looks like the Sphinx, doesn't it?"

The map was one that Bert had seen before—and he knew the drawing well. It depicted a chariot being drawn by two Dragons, one scarlet, the other the greenish-gold of the Sphinx.

"Oh my stars and garters!" Bert exclaimed. "I think I know

what her name is. Rose," he said, eyes wide, "I want you to look up the Little Whatsit's entry on Samaranth."

"You think the Sphinx is Samaranth?" asked Charles, who was listening in with one ear.

"No," Bert replied, "I think the Sphinx is Samaranth's *wife*."

The companions crossed the plazas inside the wall and entered the passageway to the chamber of the Sphinx.

"I'm guessing that Jules left something inside for us," said Charles. "Maybe something we can use to reestablish a connection to another zero point."

"They wouldn't even know what had happened," Burton said, looking up at the sleeping Sphinx, "so how could they know what we needed to come home?"

"The Sphinx knows—," Pym started to say before Burton finally lost his temper and clocked the Messenger upside his head. "We know that, you cretin! That's why we have to solve the riddle!"

Pym, in a rare moment of assertion, actually shoved Burton and spun away, pressing his back to a wall. He took a deep breath. "No," he wheezed, "not 'knows.' Nose. The Sphinx *nose*. Look at the nose."

They all looked at the Sphinx. The nose, and places along the wings, were more worn than in other spots, allowing the underlying material it was made of to show through. "It needs a little plaster," said Charles. "Why is that significant?"

"Because," Bert said as the realization suddenly dawned on him, "underneath the centuries of paint, and soot, and dust, the Sphinx's nose—in fact, the entire Sphinx—is made of cavorite. Including the structure—and the arch."

Rose suddenly beamed. "They knew a machine would never

survive all those centuries," she said brightly, "but something made entirely of cavorite *would*."

"Here," Edmund said, indicating an entry in the Little Whatsit. "There's not much about Samaranth or his wife, just that they pulled a chariot for the legendary Jason, of the Argonauts. It also says that she was punished for betraying the Archipelago," he finished, "but that's about all."

"Her name is here in the *Geographica*," Bert said, handing the atlas to Rose. "It can't hurt to try."

"It will work," Rose answered. "Somehow, I know it." She looked up at the Sphinx and laid a hand on the cool stone. "Azer," she whispered, hardly daring to breathe. "You're Azer."

For a long moment, the Sphinx did not answer. Then, slowly, she opened her eyes.

"Greetings, Moonchild," Azer said in a voice that sounded of silk and ancient gardens in a long-ago place. "What do you desire?"

Before Rose could answer, there was a terrible noise outside—the sounds of combat, and screaming, and suffering.

"Oh no," Charles exclaimed. "What's happened now?"

The companions rushed out of the chamber and into the amphitheater—which was in flames. The Unforgotten were running away from the center of the chaos: a dozen masked servants of Lord Winter, who was standing at the top of the steps, where the dark geometric shapes of the Echthroi hovered in the air above him.

He was holding one of the old Caretakers' books in his hand. One of their future histories—a book that would have turned to dust long ago, were it not for the Lloigor's eldritch magicks running through it.

"This was once a prophecy," Lord Winter said, "that warned of what might happen if the Echthroi were to finally conquer this world in full. And now I'm going to turn prophecy . . .

" . . . into *history*."

The companions' minds raced to try to figure out what could be done. There were too many Lloigor to fight, and the Unforgotten were already scattered.

"I think," Bert said, mostly to buy them more time, "that you are not completely in the thrall of the Echthroi. I think you are not wholly Lloigor."

"Really," Lord Winter said with an amused smile. "Do tell."

"All this power," Bert said, gesturing widely with his arms, "and such absolute domination for so many centuries, and somehow you never managed to overcome the Unforgotten until *we* arrived?"

"Oh, on occasion I captured and killed or converted a few," Winter said. "Those who strayed too far, or for too long, from their haven. I still have the skull of The Golden Compass 519 on my wall. But," he went on, "until you came, I didn't have *this*."

He was holding Bert's watch. A terrified Arthur Pym stepped out from behind one of the servants. He looked overcome with sorrow—but he was standing behind Winter, not the Caretakers.

Charles and Burton glowered, but Rose and Edmund held them back as Bert continued to talk.

"Speaking of Pym," he said, gesturing at the terrified Messenger, "he's been here, what? A decade? And he aided us. He's been running freely around this world of yours, and yet you never managed to stop him, either. And it's not because you couldn't—I think it's because you wouldn't."

"He betrayed us, Caretaker," Burton said coldly. "It was his choice."

"No," said Pym. "It wasn't."

Trembling, he held out his arm and pulled back his sleeve. There, tattooed on his forearm, was the mark of Lord Winter—a circle, surrounded by four diamonds.

"Not useful enough to be a Dragon, I'm afraid," said Lord Winter, "but useful enough, when the time came."

"What did he promise you?" Charles asked.

"Freedom," said Pym. "I get to go home."

"And I always keep my promises," said Winter. He lowered his glasses, and dark bolts of ebony fire leaped from his eyes and in a trice had consumed the hapless man.

"Arthur!" Bert screamed. "Oh dear me, Arthur!" He dropped to his knees, scrabbling after the drifting wisps of flame-singed cloth that were all that remained of the Anachronic Man.

"I kept him around far longer than I should have, anyway," Winter said dispassionately. "He had begun to bore me."

As one, Burton and Charles both stepped protectively in front of Rose and Edmund, who scowled and moved forward to stand shoulder to shoulder with them. Charles also kept a steadying hand on Bert, who was trembling with anger.

"Don't worry, I have no intention of destroying any of you," Winter said blithely. "You're all very interesting, and you will make excellent Lloigor."

"We'll find out how we failed, and we'll make things right," Bert said. His voice was trembling, but his face was a mask of defiance. "We'll find a way to defeat you, Lord Winter."

"Mmm, all formal now, are we, old friend?" Lord Winter said with a trace of sarcasm. "You should just call me Jack."

He shook his head. "You aren't Jack. I'm not sure who you are, but you're not him."

"I thought you wanted to become a Dragon," said Charles, "to get past your masters' chains."

"Pym told me about the Sphinx," said Winter, "and that she may, in fact, be a time travel device. And if that's true, I can use her to go back and correct my own mistakes—and I can make sure that this place," he added, gesturing at the pyramid, "will never be built, and all the books destroyed."

"What if I accept your offer?" Rose said suddenly. "What if I become a Lloigor and make you my apprentice Dragon?"

"Rose, no!" Charles cried. "Don't!"

"Hmm," said Winter. "That's an interesting proposition. I might even consider sparing your friends, just for old times' sake."

As the others cried out in protest, the Winter Dragons parted and allowed Rose to approach Lord Winter.

"Just take my hand," Winter said, "and kneel."

Instead of taking Lord Winter's outstretched hand, Rose picked a shard of flint off the ground and jabbed it into her thumb, drawing blood. She stepped to one side and spun around, too quickly for Lord Winter to respond. Rose locked her arm around Winter's neck and warned the servants to back away. Then, she reached up and swiftly marked the Lloigor's forehead with blood.

"What are you doing?" Winter screeched. "What—"

"Silence!" Rose commanded, with the full confidence and authority of her heritage. The Lord of the Night Land went instantly quiet. "I am the Grail Child Rose Dyson, daughter to Madoc the Maker, apprentice to the Black Dragon, and I thus bind thee."

Lord Winter trembled and shuddered, but stood stock-still as Rose continued to speak:

> *By right and rule*
> *For need of might*
> *I thus bind thee*
> *I thus bind thee*
>
> *By blood bound*
> *By honor given*
> *I thus bind thee*
> *I thus bind thee*
>
> *For strength and speed and heaven's power*
> *By ancient claim in this dark hour*
> *I thus bind thee*
> *I thus bind thee*

Rose released her hold on Lord Winter, who remained frozen in place. The Winter Dragons kept a discreet distance, waiting to see how this would play out—but the shapes floating overhead were vibrating madly enough to make the air buzz with their anger.

"That won't hold him long," Rose said, panting with the effort of the binding, "but it'll hold him long enough, I think. Now," she declared to her companions, "we must run for our lives, and for the sake of the world we left, and all we hold dear. Now! Run!"

Without a backward glance, the friends gathered up their belongings and ran into the pyramid.

PART FIVE

THE CORINTHIAN LEGEND

CHAPTER SEVENTEEN
THE GOBLIN MARKET

OF THE MANY *notable events that marked the Victorian age, the most significant was one witnessed by only three people.*

The creation of the Black Dragon was attended only by Mordred, the Winter King, who summoned the Dragon that was to become one with the ship; Argus, the shipbuilder, who was compelled by a Binding and an ancient promise to perform the task; and Mordred's mentor, Dr. John Dee, who watched from a nearby rooftop as Mordred and Argus went about their work.

It wasn't until the shipbuilder was done, and dismissed, and Mordred had sailed the newly christened Black Dragon out of the harbor on the Thames and into the open sea that the great red Dragon, Samaranth, spoke to the doctor.

"Ill met, Dee," the Dragon growled, not bothering to cover the rising anger in his tone. "You should not have done this."

"I," said Dr. Dee, "have done nothing—nothing except teach the student that you betrayed and abandoned."

"You have corrupted his spirit," the Dragon rumbled.

"His brother did that when he betrayed him," Dr. Dee spat back. "I have simply shaped what was already there." He turned and faced the great beast with no trace of fear. "You had your chance, Old Serpent,"

Dee said. "Now I am going to shape him into the great man he was always meant to be."

"He is not the Imago," Samaranth said. "Once, perhaps, he might have become such. But that time is past."

"The Imago, if he exists, will be made, not found, Dragon," said Dee. "We have differed on that point before."

"Regardless, he is not now worthy, even if he has the skill. And now you have given him a Dragonship—the means to cross through the Frontier."

"Yes. I have."

"To what end?"

"Order," said Dee. "To bring order to two worlds that have fallen into chaos under your stewardship."

"You are not seeking to create the Imago at all," the Dragon concluded, more to himself than to Dee. "This cannot be permitted to continue."

"There are many streaks of white in your beard, Dragon," said Dee. "You are getting old."

"Your services are no longer needed, Dee. There are others better suited to the task. I only hope," Samaranth said with a hiss of melancholy, "that it is not too late to undo what you have done."

"There are none qualified to replace me," said Dee. "Whom would you have, Old Dragon? Will Shaksberd? Or that old fool, Alighieri?"

"I have all of history to choose from," Samaranth replied, "and choosing wisely is the one thing that I must take the time to do, whomever it is that I choose."

He stopped and drew in a breath, as if intending to exhale on the Scholar—but stopped, as he realized Dee was completely unconcerned.

It was only then that the Dragon noticed Dee's shadow was moving about completely independently of its owner.

Samaranth took a step backward and hissed. "You have fallen," he said, his voice laced with sadness. "You have joined the enemy, John Dee. And that choice will result in nothing but suffering for your protégé."

"The Winter King may surprise you yet, Dragon," said Dr. Dee. "It took me decades to choose to give up my shadow in the cause of order. It took Mordred far less time to do the same."

The Dragon stretched out his wings and shook his head. "He will never sit on the Silver Throne," Samaranth said as he took flight. "The Caretakers will see to that. And he will never," he added as he vanished into the clouds, "be the Imago."

The Scholar watched until the Dragon disappeared from view, then took a small pocket watch out of his coat.

"Perhaps," he said to no one in particular. "But if not him," he finished as he twirled the dials on his device, "then certainly another of my choosing will."

The rain on the Welsh mountainside lasted only three-quarters of an hour and was sufficient to settle the dust, and little more. When Don Quixote and his squire, the badger Uncas, awoke during the morning's sunrise, the Zen Detective Aristophanes was already busying himself with breakfast. His bedroll seemed untouched. Quixote couldn't tell whether the detective had slept much, or at all, and decided it was the better part of knightly decorum not to ask.

After a surprisingly delicious meal, during which Quixote reversed yet another judgment he'd made about the gruff detective, the three companions set about determining their plan of action.

Uncas carefully opened the vellum folder Verne had entrusted to him and spread out the fourteen maps of Elijah McGee.

"There really aren't too many of them, you know," said Quixote. "We could practically go about locating the armor by trial and error."

Aristophanes scowled. "No, we really couldn't," he said. "There isn't time."

"I know this is important," said Uncas, "but until we met you, and asked about th' glasses, we didn't even know the armor existed. So why do we suddenly have a timer on finding it?"

"Anything to which attention is paid becomes a magnet for more attention," Aristophanes said primly. "I promise you, even if Song-Sseu has not already sold the knowledge that we are looking for the armor and in possession of the McGee maps, there will still be a dozen other denizens in every one of the Soft Places who will take note of our arrival. And once the first piece has been found, word will spread—and from that point, it will be a race. And those who would also seek the armor will think nothing of killing us to get even a single piece, much less the whole set."

"So, this quest becomes more dangerous the more successful we are," said Quixote. "That sounds like a Caretaker's mission, all right."

"Fair enough," said Uncas. "We'd better get cracking, then!"

Aristophanes unfolded the first sheet of parchment, on which he had asked the location of the Ruby Dagger, and read the name the machine had typed: "Castra Regis."

Uncas scanned the maps and quickly found the one that matched the name. "It's a close one," he said happily. "Staffordshire."

The detective's brow furrowed in puzzlement as he looked at

the map. "Castra Regis was the ancestral home of an infamous family called Caswell," he said, "but both it and the neighboring mansion, Mercy Farm, were destroyed when . . ."

He stopped and put a finger on the map. "Here," he said, voice rising with excitement. "This is the place, I'm sure of it."

The knight and the badger peered closely at the spot on the map. "Th' crossroads?" asked Uncas. "Why there?"

"All the interesting stuff happens at a crossroads," Aristophanes said, "and especially at this one. It's in a wood called Diana's Grove. And that's where we'll buy the dagger."

"Buy, and not find?" asked Quixote.

"Yes," the detective said, standing. "Diana's Grove is the site of one of the oldest Goblin Markets in the world. That's the place, I'm sure of it."

"A market!" Uncas said, brightening. "I love markets. That don't sound dangerous at all."

"I said 'interesting,' not safe," retorted the detective. "Just follow along with me and pay attention. And don't touch anything."

"I wasn't planning to," said the badger.

Aristophanes smirked and hooked his thumb at the knight. "I was talking to *him*."

"Rude," said Quixote.

The Goblin Market was not the Victorianesque tapestry the companions might have been expecting, but rather a ramshackle collection of carts, wagons, and makeshift pens for various horses and horselike creatures.

"This is, ah, quaint," said Quixote. "It seems a little horse-centric for a market. Or is it run by Houyhnhnms?"

The detective sighed and gave the knight a withering look. "This isn't the market, you idiot. This is where all the pack animals are stabled. I thought it would be better to leave the Duesenberg here than to drive up to a Seelie Court–run Goblin Market in a 1935 automobile. The market," he finished, only slightly less exasperated, "is over that rise, there."

Both Quixote and Uncas chuckled in understanding as they topped the small hill and the full wonder of the market came into view.

Sitting just beyond the crossroads indicated on the map, the Goblin Market was a cacophony of ornate wagons, huts, tents, and all other manner of temporary structures, which nevertheless looked as if they had always stood there. That was because, according to Aristophanes, they always had.

The explosions of color were scattered among and amid the trees, which themselves seemed to be first growth, and in a few places were built into the fabric of the market, lending their trunks and branches to the anchoring of the tents.

In the distance, the ruins of both Castra Regis and Mercy Farm stood over the small hollow like watchful sentries, but slightly more benignly than the real sentries, armored wraiths, who gave the companions a careful once-over as they crossed the road and entered the market.

At one of the tents, a man in a turban was selling the wind, in various gusts and gales. Each one came with a caution about when and where the bag could be opened safely, as well as a customer satisfaction guarantee that promised the wind would work—but allowed that no promise could be made about the destination to which it carried the purchaser.

At a small cart, another vendor, a stout, bespectacled shop-keeper, was demonstrating various clockwork animals, some of which were real, and some mythical. He winked at Uncas, intuit-ing that the badger might be an easy mark. "The windup monsters are good company for extended trips," the shopkeeper explained, "but for some real entertainment, it's hard to beat the Steam Crows." He proffered one to Uncas. "Would you like to see how it works?"

Aristophanes rather brusquely guided Uncas and Quixote away from the tempting display of toys. "Keep your eyes open and touch nothing—*nothing*," he said, waggling his finger for empha-sis. "Have you ever heard the expression 'you break it, you buy it'? Well, here, just touching something can be considered an ironclad contract. It's Seelie Court law. So don't touch anything I don't tell you to touch."

One small woman was selling hand-painted calendars, which changed the seasons as the pages were turned. Patrons were look-ing through the various works, and as they did so, the seasons in her tent changed from summer, to fall, to winter, and back again. Summer was by far the most popular, with fall a close second, so the tent was full of gentle, warm breezes that scattered crimson and gold leaves, amid the only occasional flurry of snow. No one, it seemed, was all that interested in spring.

"Here's the fellow we want, unless I miss my guess—and I seldom do," Aristophanes said, pointing down the slope to a smithy's shop. It was set against the side of the hill so it could take advantage of the slope for the bellows on the forge.

"My name is Schmendrick," the smithy said, giving the com-panions the once-over. "What can I be doin' f'r y' t'day?"

"We're looking to barter," Aristophanes said with as much authority as he could muster. "We have relics from the Summer Country to trade, and"—his voice dropped to a softer tone—"even a few from the Archipelago."

"Really?" Schmendrick exclaimed. "Those be rarer and rarer these days, ever since th' Day of Charles's Lament."

"Ooh," Uncas groaned to Quixote. "We best not tell Scowler Charles there's people callin' it that."

"He shouldn't be surprised," said Quixote. "He does berate himself over the whole destruction-of-the-keep matter rather often."

"I'm working here!" Aristophanes said to the badger and the knight. "Why don't you two go browse around in the next tent? And remember . . ."

"Don't touch anything, I know, I know," Uncas grumbled. "Come on, sir," he said to Quixote. "Let's fraternize with th' wee folk."

"Do y' have any deadly nursery rhymes?" the smithy asked. "They're really useful for takin' care of changelings, if y' know what I mean."

"No," said Aristophanes, "but I'm sure I can find something to your liking, if you have what it is we're looking for."

Schmendrick squinted up at him. "An' that is?"

"The Ruby Dagger."

The smithy's eyes widened and darted from side to side, to see if anyone was listening. "I might be able t' help you," he replied. "Come, let us discuss what you have t' offer."

As the detective and the smithy continued to speak in hushed whispers inside the shop, Uncas and Quixote browsed the wares of the tent three spaces down, in the lee of a large stone. The proprietor was a wizened old woman with a hat that resembled a tree growing from her head, on which were perched two buzzards, who seemed to be doing all the negotiating with the customers.

The goods the woman—or possibly the vultures—were selling were ornamental crystals of every color, shape, and size. Some had been set into pendants, and others, sculpted into miniature cathedrals. Some had even been set into the hilts and scabbards of weapons.

"Asking a smithy who makes weapons for a dagger that already exists isn't very Zen," Uncas said as he peered through the tiny doors of an amethyst city. "He'd be better off looking over—"

The little badger gasped, then slowly, carefully, drew a bronze-hilted ruby knife from out of the back of the display.

"Is it . . . ?" he breathed.

"I think so," said an astonished Quixote. "We should go get Steve."

"Don't worry," Uncas said smoothly. "I got this."

"Badgers?" one of the vultures squawked as Uncas examined the dagger. "We don't need no steenkin' badgers!"

"Why not?" the other vulture replied. "Iff'n his money's good."

"We can pay," said Uncas. "No fuss, no muss."

"See?" said the second vulture. "Say hello to my leetle friend."

The first vulture sighed. "All right, all right. That one ees a bad piece, anyway. Eet can only damage Shadows. No good for cutting oxen or Harpy. What you got to trade, leetle badger?"

"Hmm." Uncas thought a moment, then rummaged around in his pocket. "Y' seem t' like crystals," he said, producing a small ebony shard from his pocket. "P'rhaps you'd trade f'r this, straight across?"

Both vultures snorted in contempt, and even the old woman tsk-tsked at Uncas.

"You be crazy badger," said the first vulture, "to be thinkin' we take a sliver—"

"It's a shard, actually," Uncas corrected, "and it's from th' Nameless Isles."

That stopped both vultures cold, and the old woman's jaw dropped open. It also got the attention of several other patrons at nearby shops.

"Deal," the second vulture said, snatching up the shard before Uncas could change his mind. "A pleasure do business with you, my leetle badger friend."

With a broad smile that would light up a barn, Uncas leaped into the pathway to find the detective, who was still arguing with the smithy. "I have it!" Uncas proclaimed proudly—and loudly. "I have the Ruby Dagger!"

"Oh fewmets," Schmendrick cursed, apparently having been close to a deal for the dagger he didn't have. "C'n I interest you in a carnelian ice pick, mebbe?"

"Never mind." Aristophanes strode out of the smithy's to meet the triumphant badger. "At last!" he exclaimed as he lunged forward—and tripped over a discarded Spanish helmet at the edge of the tent.

Aristophanes went sprawling, and his hat flew off, landing at Quixote's feet.

The smithy, the old woman with the vultures on her head, and several others circled around to look at the strange purple man who was cursing under his breath as he dusted himself off.

"A unicorn!" Schmendrick whispered in astonishment. "I haven't seen th' like! Not in a hound's age!"

"Unicorn!" the haggard old woman echoed, bellowing at the top of her lungs. "Uuuuunicooorrrnnn!!!!"

"Oh dung," said Aristophanes. "Run."

"What?" said Quixote. "They—"

"Just shut up and run!" the Zen Detective shouted as he grabbed the knight by the arm and the badger by the collar and propelled all three of them down the pathway and out of the wood.

The news of the unicorn spread through the market like the Black Plague, but at lightning speed, and as the companions crested the hill and headed for the Duesenberg, they realized they were now being chased by quite a sizeable mob.

"Oh my stars an' garters," Uncas exclaimed as they ran, "but I wish Sir Richard was with us!"

"Burton?" Quixote blurted out as he glanced backward at their pursuers, who were rapidly closing the distance between them. "You think he would have fared any better?"

"Not really," Uncas replied, "but he'd give them a bigger target than us."

Under the spreading branches of a chestnut tree, the Messenger watched. The sunlight that broke through the clouds above passed through the leaves to form mottled patterns of light and shadow on Dr. Raven's face, which remained impassive, observing.

"They seem to be in a bit of a pickle, neh?" a voice said from somewhere above in the branches. "We wonder why you are not helping them to evade their pursuers."

Dr. Raven didn't look up—he didn't need to, to know who was speaking. "That wasn't my responsibility. I'm to shadow them, and nothing more."

"Lies," Grimalkin purred as an upside-down smile appeared in the air next to the Messenger's face. "All lies. You are the Caretaker's errand boy, are you not? And he is nothing but wheels within wheels, and games within games. You serve a greater purpose, we think, than to simply watch."

The doctor didn't flinch at the cat's slight insult, but turned to look at Grimalkin as the badger, the Zen Detective, and the knight disappeared over a rise in the distance. "They'll do fine without my help," he said, not caring to distinguish whether he meant the Caretakers or the hapless trio running from the irate merchants of the Goblin Market. "And as to games, methinks you would know something of those . . . *cat*," he added with emphasis. "Don't you? Or else you'd have already told Dee all about me."

"We serve our own interests, and none other," said Grimalkin, who had now begun to vanish again, starting with his half-formed head.

"Now who is lying?" Dr. Raven said, looking pointedly at the Cheshire cat's ornate collar. The runes on it glowed slightly, whether or not the rest of the cat was visible. "You serve whom you are compelled to serve, as do I."

"Well, of course," said the voice of the disembodied cat, more weakly now. It was obviously bored, and returning to wherever it spent its time in between appearances. "If we were not compelled, would we choose to serve anyone at all? Even ourselves?"

Dr. Raven wanted to ask if the cat was including him in that statement, or was still merely speaking with the royal "we" as it so often did. But by the time he opened his mouth to speak, the cat was already gone—as was, he noted with some relief, the Duesenberg. Uncas, Quixote, and the Zen Detective had evaded their pursuers and moved on to the next destination.

Looking around to ensure that no one would notice his own departure, and assuring himself that he was alone, the Messenger removed the watch from his pocket, twirled the dials, and disappeared.

If anyone had been watching, they might have noticed that there, under the shadows of the chestnut tree, the silver casing of the watch appeared darker.

In fact, it was almost black.

Shakespeare, Laura Glue, and the badger Fred closed the doors and drew curtains over the windows in the small room that was far from where the other Caretakers ventured throughout Tamerlane House.

"Have we heard anything from them?" Laura Glue asked hopefully.

"Nothing yet, it seems," Shakespeare said, dropping the last curtain. "They haven't returned. And the other Caretakers do not seem overly encouraged that they will."

"If the Scowlers are all stumped," said Fred, "then us figuring out a way t' help will be impossible."

"Nothing's impossible," Laura Glue said, folding her arms. "Nothing."

"But some things really are," Fred said sadly. "Like making crème brûlée with a kerosene torch, or teaching Byron t' fight with a *katana*."

"Everything is impossible until someone does something for the first time," said Laura Glue. "Half the time I've been here the Caretakers are usually discussing why a trump did or didn't work the way they thought it was supposed to, or how the keep really worked, or all sorts of other stuff that nobody really knows anyway. So I think if nobody really knows how anything is supposed to work, then anything is worth trying, neh?"

"Neh," said Fred, tapping her fist with his. "Our unknowledge is our only hope."

"'Our doubts are traitors, and make us lose the good we oft might win, by fearing to attempt,'" said Shakespeare.

"Ah," Fred said, nodding. "*Measure for Measure.* One of your great plays."

"Well," Shakespeare said, reddening. "Yes. But that particular line actually did come from Kit Marlowe, thrice curse his eyes. But he spake it while deep in his cups, and I wasn't going to let it go to waste."

"So," he said, wiping his hands on his trousers. "What be our plan, my children?"

"Our plan be to have their back, neh?" said Laura Glue. "Sometime soon, someone is going to have to go after them, to help them. And we're not going to let them down. We're going to find a way, even if every scholar who has ever lived and died says it's impossible. We'll find a way. And when they need us," she concluded, a determined look in her eyes, "we're going to be *ready.*"

CHAPTER EIGHTEEN
THE SORCERESS

THE COMPANIONS DASHED through the passageways to where the Sphinx sat, silently watching.

"We aren't going to have enough time!" Charles said, panicked. "That was the bravest act I've ever witnessed—but they aren't going to be able to hold him for long."

"We won't need much time," said Rose. "We just have to let Azer make her choice."

"What choice is that, Moonchild?" Azer asked impassively.

"The one in the riddle," Rose said. "Here, on the wall. It says we're to give you a choice. So we discovered your name and woke you. Can you help us?"

"Help you?" the Sphinx said. "How?"

"Can you help us go back in time?" Charles asked, getting straight to the heart of their urgency. "Are you able to travel in time?"

The Sphinx ignored him completely. "There is a price, Moonchild, for all things. Pay the price, and you shall have what you wish."

"What do you want?"

"A Dragon's heart," she said, looking at Rose, "to restore me to what I was, long ago."

"To become a Dragon again?" asked Rose.

"No," said Azer, still looking at the Grail Child. "To once again ascend, and leave this world at last."

Rose removed the circlet of stone she wore around her neck, which her father had given her when he became the Black Dragon. She looked up at the others, doubtful.

"Your destiny is greater than just being a Dragon, Rose," Bert said gently, "and you don't need that circle of stone to fulfill it. In truth, I don't think you ever did."

"Then I think . . . ," Rose began—but she was interrupted by an unearthly shrieking sound coming from the passages outside the chambers.

"Lord Winter is freed," Burton said, "and this world now belongs to the Echthroi."

"Not fully," Azer said, looking at Rose. "Not if a Dragon remains. The Shadows cannot prevail against a true Dragon. You can choose to stay, or you may give the heart to another and save the world as it is. Or you may give it to me, and return to your own world as it was. The choice is yours."

"No, it isn't," Rose said in sudden understanding. "The choice is yours."

Azer stared at Rose, who held the Sphinx's gaze, unafraid. A thousand regrets passed through the eyes of the once-Dragon, as she considered the truth of Rose's words.

"He's coming!" Charles shouted. "Hurry!"

At last the Sphinx made her decision. She closed her eyes, and below where she sat, the doors set into the arch slid open. "Give the heart to another," she said, "and go to thy journey."

The companions suddenly realized what had to happen—Azer

had agreed to give them passage, but unless a Dragon stayed behind, the world would still be lost to the Echthroi.

"The world must have its defender, it seems," Rose said sadly. "Maybe this is my destiny. You should all go. I'll stay."

"No," Burton said, laying a muscular hand on Rose's shoulder. "Not this time you're not."

Rose began to protest, but the old adventurer shushed her.

"I served the man your father once was because I believed a grave injustice had been done to him," Burton said calmly, clearly, "and somehow along the way, the cause I served became as distorted as the man, and I lost my way. But I found it again. I found myself. And I lived to see him redeemed. So this is not a request—this is what I was meant to do. This is the reason I am here. And taking his daughter's place is the best way I know to honor your father's memory."

Rose nodded in understanding. She handed the stone circlet to Burton, then stood on tiptoe and kissed him on the cheek. He blushed, and pushed them all toward the open doorway, then turned to meet the Lloigor.

"I never got to see my own daughter grown and married," Burton called over his shoulder as he strode to the antechamber. "But I can do this thing for you, Rose. For Lord Mor—for Madoc."

The Scholar Barbarian stepped into the passageway. Dark Shadows were cascading up against the pyramid, swirling so thickly he could barely make out the features of Lord Winter standing just outside.

Burton turned and called back to his friends. "Bert, don't . . . don't stop looking. . . . Find him. Find our boy."

Rose lifted her head, locking eyes with Burton, and answered for all of them. "We won't, Sir Richard. None of us will stop looking. We'll find your heir, if we have to travel to the beginning of time."

He didn't reply, but gave a curt nod, then slipped the Dragon's heart around his neck and stepped out to do battle with the Lloigor.

Rose looked up at the Sphinx. "I'm ready to make my wish," she said.

"Speak."

"Take us home," Rose said. "That's all. Just take us home."

In answer, the Sphinx closed her eyes and nodded once. "It shall be as you desire."

Rose stepped inside with the others, and the door underneath the Sphinx slid closed.

"In another life, in another reality, you were a Namer, Jack," Burton said, reaching to grasp the Lloigor's arms. As he grappled with the slender man, Burton's features, his very form, began to ripple and change. "So, name me now. Name me for what it is I have become because of you."

Lord Winter glowered, and his footing slipped. He lurched to one side, and his glasses fell from his face. Where his eyes were supposed to be were orbs of impenetrable blackness. "You are Chaos," he hissed, steadying his stance and tightening his grip. "You are disorder!"

"Damn straight I am," said Burton.

The air vibrated around him, almost as if it were responding to his will and expanding his presence; and perhaps it was doing just that. He resonated with the countenance of a Dragon, a true, living Dragon—and suddenly the Echthroi that attended Lord Winter trembled themselves—and began to withdraw.

For the first time in many millennia, Lord Winter felt a thrill of fear run through him.

"No, wait!" he called out to the ascending geometric shapes. "Stop! Grimalkin! Loki! Do not abandon me!"

"What," Burton hissed, eyes narrowing, "did you just say?"

Lord Winter's only response was to howl in despair. He was losing—had lost. And he knew it, and so did his masters.

"Name me!" Burton roared. "Name me, Jack!"

"*You are Dragon!*" the Echthroi screeched, as much from the darkness that enveloped Burton as from the throat of the Lloigor Jack. "*Dragon!*"

"Yes," Burton said, almost as a whisper. "And I have made the right choice at last."

When the doors of the Sphinx closed behind them, none of the time-lost companions knew what to expect. Certainly, that they might be transported to another time, at least. Edmund and Rose were hopeful that they would end up back at Tamerlane House, although that was longer odds than they could really expect. Bert harbored a secret hope that they might actually end up in the future they were aiming for—with Weena. And Charles simply wanted to get away from Lord Winter.

"So, uh," Charles stammered. "Is it on?"

"Not yet," said Rose, who had been examining the interior, "otherwise there'd be too much risk of someone else using it." She didn't need to say more.

"This panel," said Edmund. "The symbols on it match some of those in the *Geographica!*"

"It's how we activate the Sphinx," Rose said, running her fingers across the engravings in the stone. "I'd bet my life on it."

"Actually," said Bert, "I think we have."

"Are there any, ah, instructions?" asked Charles.

"No," she replied, "just these markings." Among them was a crescent moon, set in an indentation within the panel. She pressed it, and instantly they were surrounded by a glow of radiant light.

"Excellent, Moonchild," Bert murmured. "You are less and less the student, I see."

The light lasted only a few seconds, and then as quickly as it had risen, vanished.

"Now what?" said Charles. "Is it over?"

"Only one way to find out," Edmund said. He stepped to the doors and slipped his fingers between them. Then, with a great effort, he slid them open, and at once the companions were blinded by bright, golden sunlight.

"Well, Toto," Charles said in relief, "I don't think we're in Camazotz anymore."

They stepped out onto a low, grassy hilltop that overlooked a broad, sandy beach. The structure they emerged from was the same as it had been in the future, but there was no sign of the Sphinx.

"It doesn't smell right," said Charles, sniffing. "Not like England smells. But it smells . . . familiar."

"I agree," said Rose.

"I must confess my ignorance," Edmund said, "being that my education in these things is more limited than I'd have liked it to be, but aren't those runic columns over there?"

They were—and not ancient ones, but freshly constructed, newly painted columns. And farther back, they could see larger structures.

"Greek temples?" asked Charles. "In 1946?"

"This isn't 1946," said Bert. "I think we may have overshot our mark."

"Not really," Edmund said as he consulted his chronal maps. "We did go back approximately eight hundred thousand years . . . give or take. My chronal map might have taken us back to England in 1946, but it was designed to do that. We came through a different device that couldn't be set for a specific time, because they had no way of knowing when—or if—we'd use it. And we've moved in space as well as time, so something else had to determine why we came here now."

"But then how . . . ," Bert began before the realization struck him and his face fell. "Oh . . . oh my stars and garters."

Charles groaned and put his face in his hands. His shoulders started to shake, and for a moment the companions were concerned for him—until they realized he was laughing.

"Not determine," he said, clapping Edmund on the back. "Choose. Someone chose to bring us here. You are correct, Edmund. I don't even have to see your maps to know that."

Rose sat on a boulder, her shoulders slumping forward in misery as she realized what the others all meant. The Sphinx had done precisely as she had asked—she had taken them home. But to *her* home, her time and place—not theirs.

"Can't we simply go through it again?" the young mapmaker asked, his face eager with hope.

"Even if we could reuse the Sphinx," said Rose, "I don't know what else we'd use to barter with her for passage. We'd also be risking ending up stranded in the future again. And anyway," she added, looking around at the dunes, "she's gone."

"Look at it this way," Edmund said, "at least we're not still in that awful might-have-been future. We're much closer to home here."

"Indeed!" said Charles. "Instead of being stuck a million years from home, we may only be trapped a few thousand years from home. Luck is definitely with us."

"Have you ever noticed," Edmund said to Rose, "that these Caretakers' view of reality differs widely from pretty much everyone else's?"

"All the time," said Rose.

Edmund made a few calculations on one of his chronal maps and confirmed that they were approximately somewhere around the era of 2500 BC.

"If we're at that point in the past," Rose asked, "wouldn't the keep itself still exist? Could we use that to either go home, or maybe even go farther back to find the Architect?"

"You spent more time there than any of us, Bert," Charles said, thinking. "Would that work?"

"It doesn't have a basement, if that's what you're asking," Bert retorted. "When the Dragons created the doors, it was already standing. I don't know that there's any way to use it to go back to a point before its own making. And besides, it burned from the ground up—meaning the passages to the oldest times were lost *first*. So it may not actually be here at all anymore."

"Great," Charles groaned. "I not only botched up the future, but I've retroactively messed up the past."

"I want to go home too," said Bert, "but if we returned now, we'd simply have to come back this way again anyway. Or," he added with a bit of a catch in his voice, "someone would, at any rate."

"If we're somewhere in Greece," asked Edmund, "where would we go to find the keep if we did look?"

"In this era," Bert said, turning to look at the ocean, "it would be . . ."

His voice trailed off as his jaw dropped. The others looked out over the water and were similarly shocked by what they saw.

Far in the distance, with the bearing of thunderclouds, and the slow, steady movement of tectonic plates, giants were striding through the ocean. They were pulling islands behind them by great chains, much like the ones the companions had seen circling the Earth in the ancient future.

These were the giants of old, not the misshapen, mythological creatures. These were Titans, and they were awesome to behold.

"What are they?" Edmund asked, his voice trembling with awe.

"The Corinthian Giants, of course," a voice said as they gawped. "They are almost finished here, and will soon move on to other climes."

It was a woman, tall and regal, and speaking with the bearing and manner of a queen. She was dressed in a simple tunic, but her belt and jewelry were equal to the cost of entire cities.

She was speaking in ancient Greek, which Rose understood

easily, and Charles less so. Bert and Edmund would have been completely out of luck—but somehow they understood her.

"What are they doing?" Edmund said, motioning to the giants.

She seemed taken aback by the question, as if she expected they would already know. "They are taking the rest of the lands through the Frontier and into the Archipelago, as was agreed at the—" She stopped and examined them more closely. "You are not the Watchers. And you are not of Corinth. Who are you?"

Edmund was the most startled to be spoken to in Greek and to realize he understood it completely, being the companion with the least amount of experience with magic. "How is it that I can understand your words?" he exclaimed in openmouthed astonishment. "Or that you can understand mine?"

"A minor incantation," the woman said haughtily, "and if you do not know even that much of me, then it is a waste of my time to be conversing with you at all."

"We beg your pardon," Rose said. "We are strangers to your land, and meant no offense." As she spoke, she bowed deeply and took one knee to the sand—a gesture of deference and respect. As she did so, the woman noticed Rose's bracelets, which her grandfather had given to her. They were golden, ornate, and the mark of royalty. Not something worn by someone bowing to a stranger.

The woman took a step backward. "Why are you here?" she asked. "Has my husband sent you? I have broken no laws. My children are my own, and if I choose to hide them among the islands of the Archipelago, it is my own business. He will wander an eternity before he sees them again."

"By Zeus," Bert whispered to Edmund and Charles. "She means Jason! This is Medea!"

"And the sons she is talking about are William and Hugh," Charles whispered back.

"That's terrible!" whispered Bert, remembering the wraith that Jason became after searching for his lost sons. "If there was ever a man who needed a hand, it's him."

"But we have the *Geographica*!" Charles exclaimed. "We can take him right to the island where she abandoned their sons!"

"At what risk?" Bert said with a touch of surprise. "We could irrevocably damage the future in the process."

"Haven't you already done that?" asked Edmund. "The Archipelago has already been swept away. Can anything we do here really make it worse?"

"The Archipelago is not what I'm worried about," Bert replied, casting a glance at Medea, who was still conversing with Rose. "In this time, the Summer Country is still very much connected to the Archipelago. And everything that has happened, did happen. Every moment that we spend here risks derailing that, and possibly changing our futures."

"When the rest of the islands of the Mediterranean are taken across," Medea was saying in answer to something Rose had asked, "then the Corinthian Giants will return for Autunno—this island.

"The last remnant of old Atlantis, the Silver Throne, sits in my temple," she said, "and when Autunno is taken through the Frontier, it will be the seat of power of both worlds."

Bert and Charles looked at each other, confused. The Archipelago was not built overnight—they knew that much from the old shipbuilder, Ordo Maas. It had taken centuries. But this was the first they had ever heard about Medea becoming Queen of the Silver Throne.

"Begging your pardon," said Bert, "but you *are* Queen Medea, are you not?"

She tilted her head slightly in acknowledgment. "I am. Since the death of my father, Aeetes, I have become queen of Corinth."

"And what of your husband, Jason?"

Her face darkened. "My husband is . . . occupied elsewhere. I don't expect that he shall return soon, if at all."

"A queen should not be walking thus, unattended and alone," said Rose. This was closer to her own era, Bert knew, so the mannerisms and proper courtesy to royal blood came more easily to her.

"My chariot was damaged crossing the Frontier," Medea answered. "Only one of my Dragons chose to attend me after . . . a dispute with my husband. And her strength was insufficient to weather the storms as smoothly as with both. One of my ship-builders is down the beach," she said, pointing, "but I fear it's beyond his skill to repair.

"A shame to have to have him killed," she added. "He did build good ships."

"The chariot," Bert murmured to the others. "That's how it was done, before Ordo Maas built the Dragonships. The Dragons personally escorted Jason and Medea to the Archipelago, through the Frontier."

"I have experience at a forge," Edmund said bluntly. "I could effect the repairs your chariot requires."

Medea's eyes brightened for a moment, then dimmed in distrust. "At what cost?"

"A boon," Edmund said evenly. "I shall do you this service, and you'll owe me one in return."

She shook her head. "That's too high a price," she said haughtily, tossing her head and folding her arms. "Still . . ." She thought a moment, glancing now and again at Rose's bracelets.

"Agreed," she said finally—to Rose, not Edmund. "But if your servant is unable to fix it to my liking, then you and all your servants will stay on Autunno to serve me, until I choose to release you."

Rose bowed. "We have a bargain."

Medea turned and strode down the beach. Quickly the companions gathered their things and followed her.

"You're not offended to be called 'servants'?" Rose asked her companions, smiling.

"I've been there before," Charles replied. "I'm just happy she didn't call me 'Third.'"

The stables were well-appointed and had all the materials necessary for Edmund to reshape Medea's chariot.

"I can do this," he whispered to Rose, "but just the same, I'd give almost anything to have your father with us for the next few hours."

"You'll do fine," Rose reassured him, "and for what it's worth, so would I."

"I didn't know he'd been trained as a blacksmith," Charles remarked. "I thought he came from a line of silversmiths."

"He wasn't trained by a smithy," Rose said, grinning. "He was trained by a scientist—Doctor Franklin. That may not mean much in twentieth-century Oxford, but in ancient Greece, it makes him a Magic Man."

The young Cartographer set to work, and in short order had

restructured the chariot to be pulled by a single creature instead of two.

"You did that rather easily, and quickly," Medea said as she looked over his handiwork. "Impressive. Perhaps too impressive. I think that maybe I bargained too quickly, Master Smith."

"I said I could do it, and I have done it," he replied, wiping his brow with a cloth.

"And far more quickly than that fool Argus," she said. "If I'd left him to it, he'd have taken a week, and the wheels would still rattle."

"Your shipbuilder's name is Argus?" Edmund asked, as casually as he could manage. "As in, the man who built the *Argo* for Jason and the Argonauts?"

"Yes," she said, face darkening. "Why?"

He set the cloth aside. "That is the boon I ask. Spare his life."

"What are you doing?" Rose whispered.

"I know what she did to her sons," Edmund whispered back. "She's a really horrible person, and so I asked for the one thing I know will twist her in knots to grant me."

Rose was surprised by Edmund's request, but nonetheless nodded her agreement. "That is our request," she said to the queen. "Spare the shipbuilder Argus."

"A boon is a boon," said Medea, "but this is more. This is blood. By what right do you ask a life-boon?"

Rose glanced back at Edmund, who folded his arms defiantly. "By right of blood—blood ties of family, great-grandmother," she said softly, her voice low and cool, but with a trace of menace nonetheless. "A bond that cannot be taken, only given."

Medea did not understand what she meant by these words—and

had no way of knowing that Rose was descended from the blood-line of the Argonauts. But it was Edmund's handiwork on the chariot that gave her pause. This youth was no mere servant. He was clearly a Maker—and thus, not to be trifled with. That the young woman who bore the ornament of royalty also claimed a blood-bond told Medea she should not overplay her hand.

"Agreed," she said, and made as if to leave, but paused in the doorway of the stables.

"Interesting that this should be your request, today of all days," Medea said.

"Why is that?" asked Rose.

Medea shook her head. "Just coincidence, or perhaps . . . fate," she answered. "He was to be killed in service of another blood-debt, which is still owed. But no matter—I gave you my word. And the word of a queen of Corinth is sacrosanct.

"The regent of the Old World will be arriving soon, and I must prepare for him. The shipbuilder will be freed, as you have asked."

The queen of Corinth left the stables, and a few moments later they saw she was good to her word, as a young, rather ragged man appeared at the doorway.

He looked curiously at the strange band of travelers, then walked over to Edmund and offered his arm, in the old Greek tradition.

"I understand you are the one who is responsible for my good fortune," Argus said slowly, "and I find I have no words to . . ."

Edmund took his arm. "A boon was given for your life," he said. "Perhaps someday, you'll do the same for another."

Argus stepped back and bowed. "I will. You have my

word—although my skills are rarely called upon these days. Few adventurers are bold enough to hire a shipmaker who can bind the spirit of living creatures into a vessel."

The companions all stilled at hearing this.

"Have you ever bound a Dragon to a ship?" Bert asked. "Could you, if someone wished it done?"

Argus laughed. "I have the skill, but no one will ask me to," he said. "Not while my master is still working in the trade. His are far better than mine."

"Who is your master?"

"The greatest of all shipbuilders," Argus replied. "Ordo Maas."

A bright gleam suddenly appeared in Bert's eyes. "Does anyone else have this skill other than yourself and Ordo Maas?"

Argus folded his arms and shook his head, grinning. "None living, or otherwise. Only he and I."

"That's awfully self-assured," said Charles.

"Not at all," said Argus. "Merely the truth."

"That's the boon," Bert said suddenly, glancing at Edmund, who looked startled, but nodded his assent. "Someday, perhaps many years from now, someone will ask you to build such a ship. All we ask is that you do it."

"Done and done," Argus said in surprise. "And a bargain at twice the price." He stretched his back and turned to the doorway.

"Again, you have my gratitude," he said. "I have to go find my master—but I shall always remember. Call on me if you are ever in need. And when the time comes, I'll build your ship."

With that, he trotted off down the beach.

"What was that all about?" Charles asked. "What Dragonship did you want him to build, Bert?"

"One that in our time, he's perhaps already built," Charles's mentor replied. "A ship that only Ordo Maas could have built, but didn't. A ship that no one living knows the origin of. A ship," he added, looking pointedly at Rose, "that has been at the heart of one of the great mysteries of the Archipelago."

Charles gave a low whistle. "Do you really think so, Bert?"

"I do," Bert said, nodding. "I think we've just saved the life of the man who will build the *Black Dragon*."

Before the companions could discuss this extraordinary turn of events further, another voice called out from the darkness at the far end of the stables. It sounded inebriated.

"Was that the shipbuilder, Argus?" it called out. "I was s'pposed t' kill him today. Blood-debt, you know."

Cautiously, Edmund picked up an iron bar, as did Charles, and they motioned for the others to stay back. "Who goes there?" Charles called out.

"I'd say it's the Comedian, but the Comedian is dead," said the voice. It was coming from the far stalls, away from the entrance, where the torchlight didn't reach.

"I'd say it's th' Philosopher, but the Philosopher is terrible at Philosophizing," the voice rambled on. "So I must be th' Executioner—'cept you just freed the executionee, so I think I'm out of a job again."

As he spoke, they heard another sound—rattling chains. He was not a servant of Medea, but a prisoner.

"You sound very familiar to me," Charles said. "Something in the tenor of your voice—I've heard it somewhere before. Did you say you were a philosopher?"

"I did, but I don't mind telling you again," came the answer. "I *was* a philosopher. Of some renown, I might add, although of late"—he clanked his chains for emphasis—"I seem to have fallen into disfavor with th' queen. Again."

"Ah!" Charles said as he and Edmund lowered the iron bars. Whoever this drunkard was, he was no danger to them. "A learned man, then."

"A learned man who's just been sick all over his sandals," said the voice.

"Mmm, sorry," said Charles. "I'm Charles, by the way, and these are my friends Rose, Bert, and Edmund. Despite the circumstances, we're very pleased to make your acquaintance."

"And I you," the voice replied. "My name is Aristophanes."

CHAPTER NINETEEN
THE UNICORN

—◆—

THE FLIGHT FROM the Goblin Market was marked by both the speed Uncas was driving, and the nearly endless stream of curse words being generated by the Zen Detective. Apparently, he was fluent in over a dozen languages—at least, fluent enough to competently curse.

At Aristophanes's urging, Uncas flipped on the projector and drove them through a slide to an out-of-the-way spot where they could catch their collective breath and locate the next object. The badger chose a grassy field in Finland. Other than the Duesenberg, the only thing that broke the monotony of the fields was a small fishing shack that stood on the top of a cliff in the distance. "It's th' calmest place I knows of," Uncas said as they got out of the car. "Nothing exciting ever happens in Finland."

Aristophanes inserted the second parchment into the Machine Cryptographique and carefully typed in a question. As swiftly as before, the Infernal Device returned the answer: "Pohjola."

Uncas rummaged through the maps and stopped on the second to last. He stared at it with a bewildered expression and looked up at Quixote and Aristophanes. "I, uh, I have it. I think."

"So?" said the detective. "Will we be able to find it?"

Uncas nodded. "I'm pretty sure."

Aristophanes waited. "Well? Where is this 'Pohjola'?"

The little mammal pointed at his feet. "Right here. We're *standin'* on it."

"Give me that!" Aristophanes exclaimed, snatching the map out of the badger's paws. A moment later, though, his expression changed. "Well," he admitted, handing the map back to Uncas, "this might be easier than we thought."

Quixote was dumbfounded. "You mean he's right? That we just happened to pick a place to hide from that mob, and we ended up coming to the very place we needed to go next?" He shook his head. "That's just too incredible to believe."

"That's Zen for you," Aristophanes said, shrugging. "Let's go see if anyone's home."

The little old fisherman who answered their knock at the hut acted as if they were expected and invited them in. "Would you like some *sima*? Sweet mead?" he offered as they sat on the pelt-covered benches inside. "I have just made it, fresh. But," he added ruefully, "I have no lemon. It would be lemonless *sima*."

Quixote gave Aristophanes a look that said what they were both thinking—the old fisherman had spent way too long inhaling the salt air. But Uncas cheerfully accepted, and with shaking hands, the old man poured them all a drink.

"I assume," he said, sipping mead from his own cup, "that you've come to ask for the Sampo. Well, I have some bad news for you—I have no idea where it is."

"Is that some sort of, uh, magical object?" Uncas asked, winking at Aristophanes, who rolled his eyes and groaned inwardly. The badger had no sense of subterfuge whatsoever.

"It is," said the fisherman. "Everyone thinks I have it because of those cursed stories in the *Kalevala*. 'Ask Kullervo,' they say. 'Go seek Kullervo—he's bound to have it.' And on and on. As if I'd end up with a magic box that grants you all you desire. Not after the life I've had, I wouldn't. Every time something good started to happen, someone evil would turn my cows into bears, and my family would get eaten while they were tending to the milking. Very frustrating.

"Even this," he continued, standing up. He set down his mead and walked to the corner, where he lifted up a long, black sword. "I finally won something valuable—a magic sword—but every time I remove it from the sheath, it starts singing. Do you know how embarrassing it is to go into battle with a singing sword that won't shut up?"

"The sword of Turambar," the detective murmured, making a mental note to remember where it was. "Interesting."

"We're sorry to hear about your troubles," said Uncas. "We've actually come looking for a different magical object."

"Well, you won't have much luck here," said Kullervo glumly. "About the only other thing I've got is a brooch—but it's not worth very much. Would you like to see it?"

"Yes," Uncas said, and nodded. "We would, please."

The fisherman reached into a basket of straw hanging on a hook and, after rummaging around in the straw, removed a small, red brooch. "Here you go," he said, tossing it to Uncas. "If you're interested, I'll part with it for cheap."

"How cheap?" asked Aristophanes, suspicious. Easy was acceptable, once in a while. But this was going a bit too smoothly for his liking.

Kullervo shrugged. "I'd really like some fish."

Uncas blinked. "Aren't you a fisherman?"

He shrugged again. "Not a very good one, I'm afraid. And the fish aren't as plentiful here as they once were."

Aristophanes leaned over and looked at the object Uncas held. It was indeed the Ruby Brooch.

"We don't have time to go fishing," he whispered. "I think we should—"

"Don't sweat it," said Uncas. "I got this."

The badger stood up. "I got six bottles of pickled trout in my car," he said brightly. "Is it a trade?"

Kullervo thought it over. "Is trout like herring?"

"It's fish," said Uncas, "what's been pickled."

"Deal," said Kullervo. "The brooch is yours."

"Why in Hades's name," Aristophanes asked as they drove away in the Duesenberg, "would you have *six jars* of pickled trout in the boot of the car?"

"In case of a 'mergency," said Uncas. "Also, I really like pickled trout."

"Two for two," Quixote said from the rear seats. "So far, so good. And it's been Uncas who's done all the bartering!"

"Yes, well," said the detective. "As I said—we make a good team."

"Just remember you said that," Uncas chortled, "when you gets my bill."

As the car vanished into the distance, the cloaked man stepped out of the shadow of the fishing hut and walked around to the door, which was open. Kullervo was waiting.

"Did I do it right?" he asked, the tone of his voice an odd mix of both longing and resignation. "I did as you wanted—I took off the brooch so their machine would find me, and then I treated them like guests and gave them the brooch."

"Yes," the Messenger said. "You did fine, Kullervo." He looked inside the hut. "Would you like to do it now?"

"Weeelll," the fisherman replied. "I just came into some pickled trout. So I thought, if you wanted to join me, we could have a bite first?"

The man nodded. "Of course."

The trout was excellent, especially with some dark bread that was just stale enough to be really good, and when they had finished, the Messenger walked the fisherman to the edge of the cliff, where he used the long black sword to lop off the old man's head. He tossed the sword in after, then removed his watch and spun the dials.

As he disappeared, he imagined he could still hear the sword singing. It probably was.

The next piece the companions asked about was the helmet, and the machine and the map guided them to a much smaller place than a country or an island—a place even smaller than the Inn of the Flying Dragon.

"It's a shop in Vienna," Aristophanes said, "but what's inside the Abraxas House isn't quite as unusual as the building itself."

"How so?" asked Quixote.

"You'll see," the detective said.

It took several hours of driving around the twisty Austrian streets before they actually found the place they were searching for. "There!" Aristophanes exclaimed, pointing through the windshield. "That's it just up ahead."

The Abraxas House was located mid-block just past the intersection of Laimgrubengasse and Gumpendorferstraße. The streets were lined with small cafés and pastry shops, which fronted the ground floors of stately old Viennese hotels and apartment buildings. Thus, the Abraxas House was a bit of an anomaly—but then again, as Aristophanes explained, it was an anomaly in just about every other way as well.

The first unique characteristic was obvious—the entire building was seven stories tall, but only a dozen feet wide. It was deeper than it was wide, but not by much, because it backed up to a common square used by the buildings adjacent to it and on the street one block over. That was what made it unusual from the outside. What made it unusual on the inside was that it appeared to be infinitely large; room after room after high-ceilinged room stretched away past every corner they looked around. Minuscule on the outside, the Abraxas House was massive on the inside.

The shelves were primarily full of books, but there were various other artifacts scattered in and among them: ornate boxes, weapons, earthenware, and even armor.

"It's a Whatsit," Uncas said, awed by the sight. "It's just like th' Great Whatsit, on Paralon, 'cept there are pastry shops on either side. Brings a tear to one's eyes, it does."

Quixote saw an elderly gentleman with an apron moving boxes in another room, and gestured to him for service. The man nodded in acknowledgment and came toward them, wiping his hands on a cloth.

"Greetings," the white-mustached shopkeeper said, apparently unruffled to be waiting on a purple man, a badger in a waistcoat and jacket, and a knight with all the fashion sense of a novelist. "What can I do for you today?"

Aristophanes made a judgment call and decided that in a place of commerce, he could play it straight. "We're looking for the Ruby Helmet."

The shopkeeper tapped his fingers on his chin and pursed his lips. "I had an ebony helmet once, but that tall, pale fellow came back for it not long after he sold it to me. I traded two houses of secrets and mystery for it, and he bought it back for seven dreams. I also had Mercury's helmet—the one with the wings—but sold that one to a man called Garrett, or Garrick, or something like that."

"The one we seek," said Aristophanes, "is part of a larger set, called the Ruby Armor . . ."

"Of T'ai Shan!" the shopkeeper said, snapping his fingers. "I thought that sounded familiar."

He walked to a circular bookcase in the next room and pulled a copy of Machiavelli's *The Prince* out just far enough to release a catch hidden in the shelving. A panel slid back, revealing the Ruby Helmet, sitting on a pedestal.

"There have been inquiries over the years, of course," he said as he returned to the companions, holding the helmet, "but few willing to pay an acceptable price. Pieces this old are not easy to come by."

"How old is it?" asked Uncas.

"Nine, perhaps ten thousand years old," said the shopkeeper. "It was a little before my time, so I can't be certain."

"I thought you looked familiar," Aristophanes said cautiously. "What did you say your name was?"

"I didn't," came the reply, "but as you've asked, it's Trisheros."

The Zen Detective went pale—this apparently meant something significant to him. "Thrice Great?" he whispered.

"No," Trisheros said, shaking his head. "You're thinking of my father. He's considerably older and doesn't come into the shop much anymore. What did you say your name was?"

"His name is—," Uncas began.

"*Steve*," the detective interrupted. "It's just . . . Steve. A pleasure, I'm sure." He gestured at the helmet. "What would you like for it?"

"Hmm," the shopkeeper mused, rubbing his chin. "I don't really know that I need much of anything right now," he said apologetically. "Unless you happen to have a photograph of the *Painting That Ate Paris*."

"Uh, no," said Quixote. "I don't think we do. But pray tell, why would anyone?"

"Oh, no one wants the actual painting, to be sure," the shopkeeper said, "but the photograph can fetch a good price from collectors in the know. And it doesn't devour anything—just gives the viewer a vague sense of unease. Very avant-garde."

"Is there anything else you'd consider?" Aristophanes asked, feeling that the shopkeeper might be the bartering kind—especially considering his lineage. "We have access to a great many things."

"I assumed you were not the principal buyers," said Trisheros. "For whom are you working?"

The companions looked at one another. Finally Aristophanes chose to answer. "The Caretakers."

"Ah," the shopkeeper said, as if this answered more than one question. "Then the price is a simple one. I would like a copy of the *Imaginarium Geographica*. If you can do that for me, the helmet is yours."

"No problem!" Uncas said as Quixote grinned and Aristophanes slapped his head and groaned. "I gots twelve copies in—"

"In the back of the Duesenberg," the detective finished. "Of *course* you do."

"How many would you like?" asked Uncas.

"Er, ah . . . ," Trisheros stammered. "Just one will do, thank you."

The little mammal rushed out the door, then popped the lid of the trunk and jumped inside to get the book.

"Why would he—," the shopkeeper began.

"I've learned to stop asking," Aristophanes said as Uncas returned with a copy of the fifth edition of Mr. Tummeler's abridged, annotated *Imaginarium Geographica*. "Just smile and nod."

"It's even signed by King Artus," Uncas said proudly. "No extra charge."

"Thank you," said Trisheros.

"What was that 'Thrice Great' business about, anyway?" Uncas asked as they drove away from the Abraxas House. "You seemed t' know who he was f'r a minute there."

"Not him, actually," the detective answered pensively. "His father—Hermes Trismegistus. 'Thrice Great' is what the name means. He's one of the oldest beings alive—far older than I am—and some people think he was a god. And," he added, "he might have been."

"I've read about him," said Uncas. "In th' Little Whatsit. He's the one who communed with angels, right? Learned their language an' . . ." The little mammal stopped suddenly, whiskers twitching. "An' taught it all to . . . John Dee."

"Maybe," Aristophanes said, features darkening as he turned to look out the window. "I wouldn't know anything about that."

Trisheros knew just the place to shelve his newly acquired copy of the *Imaginarium Geographica*. There was space on a special shelf in the Rare Books Room, right next to the *Encyclopedia Mythica*, *The Journal of Ezekiel Higgins*, *The Book of All Stories*, and the copy of the Little Whatsit he had acquired some years earlier from an agent of the Caretakers who called himself a Messenger. His name had been Ransom, and he had been welcomed as both a seeker of knowledge and a customer.

Not so the one who was hovering around outside the door.

Trisheros murmured a few words ripe with ancient power, and the runes above the doorway—above every doorway—glowed with eldritch energies.

"I'm sorry," he said softly, not looking up from his work. "But this is one of the few places, anywhere, anywhen, that is barred to you. I know who and what you are. Once, I might have become as you are now myself. But I chose this, and I'm all the happier for having done so."

He paused and cocked his head, as if listening to an answer. "Nor do I wish you any harm," he said. "Quite the opposite. I wish you luck. And . . ." He paused again, listening.

Whoever it was that had been outside was gone now, and the old man sighed.

"And," he finished, more for himself than for the entity with whom he'd been speaking, "I wish you peace. But I fear that is not a card in the hand you were dealt. And I'm sorry, boy. Very sorry."

He filed the *Geographica* on the shelf with the other books and turned out the light.

"This will be most difficult," Aristophanes said when they'd arrived at their next destination. "Not many people ever come here. And those who do almost never return.

"It's called Tartarus," he explained, "although it's not the common one most people would think of."

"The Greek underworld," said Quixote. "I've read my mythology."

"Have you now?" said Aristophanes. "Your mythology won't have told you about this place—it's about as dank and foul a region as exists. The only reason I'm here is that I expect a great reward at the end. And I'd better get it."

"I'm sure Verne will take good care of you," Quixote said, peering through the gloom. "Access to the inner circle, and the like."

"Right," said the detective. "Verne. That's what I meant."

The wall ahead was foreboding and seemed impossibly high. From below, the companions could just make out the shape of heads set along the length of the uppermost stones.

"Brr," said Uncas. "Are those f'r reals?"

"Plaster," said Aristophanes. "Or so I've been told."

"There's no gate," said Quixote after a brief trot around the walls. "The road encircles it, but there's no way in."

"That's what I'm here for," said the Zen Detective. "One of

these stones along the path is a catch that releases an opening in the wall."

"How do you know which one?"

"Because in a past life, I was a philosopher of unknown things," came the reply from the now-irritated detective, "and finding unfindable things is what I do best."

Aristophanes walked slowly around the pathway, not even really examining the stones but more getting a feel for the atmosphere of the place. He had explained to Uncas that sometimes being a Zen Detective was nothing more than imagining oneself as the person or thing that was lost, and then going to the place that they would go. It was apparently a very successful technique, because in less than ten minutes, he waved them over to where he stood.

Aristophanes pointed to a roundish, nondescript stone half-buried in the path and covered with scrubby grass. "There," he said. "That's the one."

Without waiting for a consensus, he stepped firmly on the stone, and immediately a section of the wall in front of them came crumbling down in a torrent of stones and dust. In moments they were looking through a broad hole into the interior of the wall.

"Oh my," said Uncas. "I thought a door would swing open, or the stones would magically rearrange themselves into an entrance, or something like that."

"Maybe in the entrance to an alley of shops in London, it would do that," Aristophanes said as he stepped over the pile of rubble and inside the wall, "but this isn't that kind of place. Don't worry about it, though," he added. "It's charmed—the wall will be back in place within the hour."

"Then how d' we get out again?" asked Uncas.

"We make sure we're already gone when it closes," Aristophanes said gruffly. "Come on. Follow me."

Within the wall the companions found a thick, tangled wood of ancient dead trees. A black river flowed through the wood, and Aristophanes advised the others not to touch the water. Along the banks, someone had placed a variety of stuffed animals, perhaps to use as a lure for unsuspecting travelers. Up ahead, the trees gave way to a clearing, where there stood a crumbling Moravian church, ringed about with willows.

"That's what we want," Aristophanes said. "There should be a staircase inside that leads into the catacombs."

There was indeed a staircase, and the companions lit a torch to follow the steps down. Inside the catacombs, they followed a winding path, led only by the Zen Detective's innate sense of direction. Eventually they came to a large chamber lined with openings in the walls.

"Boy," said Uncas, "we could sure use some Lightening Bolts right about now."

Aristophanes looked at the badger like he was insane. "Are you insane?" he asked. "The last thing we need here is a thunderstorm."

"I didn't say 'thunderstorm,' I said we could use some Lightening Bolts," said Uncas. "You know, the kind that 'luminates stuff. We had a couple in the boot o' the Duesenberg."

The detective sighed and looked at Quixote. "Do you ever win an argument with him?"

"No," said the knight. "He's usually right."

In one of the openings they could see the skeleton of a man. It had been partially gilded—the ribs and thighs glistened with gold. In another was a glass bust of a beautiful maiden.

As they passed through the chamber, they found many more such talismans: a willow rod that Aristophanes said had been used to beat to death a forgiven penitent; a carved wooden toy that resembled a top, which he said would tell the day of one's death when spun; a collection of black paper hearts; and the skeleton of a dwarf, which he told them belonged to a son of the biblical Lilith.

In the last opening was the breastplate.

Aristophanes started to reach for it, but Quixote stopped him. "Wait," he explained, pointing to the far end of the chamber. "First we must make certain we have permission."

Another skeleton sat, watching them. It held an aeolian harp in its arms, and one hand was poised to play. As Aristophanes reached for the breastplate, the hand moved nearer to the strings.

"And if we don't?" asked the detective.

Quixote pointed up, to where a hundred more skeletal warriors sat in their own alcoves, waiting for the harp to summon them to life.

Aristophanes slowly pulled back his hand. "So what do we do?"

In response, Quixote strode over to face the skeleton and removed his hat, bowing as he did so.

"I am Don Quixote de la Mancha," he said, "and I am on a quest to retrieve the Ruby Breastplate there. I humbly seek your permission to remove it, if it be the good Lord's will that I do so, that I may succeed."

The skeleton nodded once, then lowered its hand and sat back in the alcove. Quixote walked back over to the others and removed the breastplate from the wall, handing it to an amazed Aristophanes.

"I can't believe it!" the detective exclaimed. "How in Hades's name did you know to do that?"

Quixote shrugged as they made their way back up the stairs. "It's something I learned long, long ago," he said, smiling. "You should always ask for what you want in life, because you might," he added, "just actually get it."

Standing at one of the tall windows of the house, the Chronographer of Lost Times waited, something he was very unaccustomed to doing. For the boy, the adept, it was worth it, though. His was a talent Dee had never seen, not even in Tesla or Blake. A talent that would change the nature of the game itself.

A talent that would ensure the Echthroi's victory, if it could only be channeled properly.

A voice from the door startled Dr. Dee—something else that very rarely ever happened. "You asked for me, Doctor?"

"Yes," Dee said without turning around. "What do you have to report?"

"Victory," the boy said. "I've been to all the prospective futures and see nothing but victory, complete and absolute."

Dee frowned. He was expecting a report on the Caretakers' activities, not this . . . rallying cry. "That's . . . good," he said at length, "but we need to be prepared. Our first battle is approaching quickly, and soon our agent will be bringing us everything we need for—"

"Victory," the boy interrupted. "It's all going as it's supposed to go, Dee." No "Doctor" this time.

"Fine," the Chronographer said, irritated. "Tell Tesla I'd like to see him."

The boy bowed slightly and left.

It was a full five minutes before Dee realized the boy had never actually said that it was the Cabal's victory he had seen in all the possible futures—and that realization left the Chronographer of Lost Times feeling uneasy for the rest of the night.

CHAPTER TWENTY
THE FIRST KING

-·-✳-·-

RUDYARD KIPLING RAN down the street with as much speed as he could muster. He had anticipated some kind of surreptitious attack from the Cabal, perhaps on the Kilns, or even at Tamerlane House again, after the burglary. But an attack on the Hotel d'Ailleurs in Switzerland was a long way down on that preparedness list—in part because it had been kept secret even from most of the Caretakers, and in part because William Blake would have warned them.

Unless, Kipling worried, Blake didn't know. In which case, he might have been discovered as a covert operative of the Mystorians and the Caretakers.

Either way, he reasoned as he rounded the corner opposite the hotel and saw the flames shooting up into the night sky, he had a greater priority.

Stepping back into a doorway of the building next door, he pulled out his trump and summoned Jules Verne.

"All right," Verne said when Kipling had explained the circumstances. "It's time. Use the special trump we made to bring them—"

"Way ahead of you, old chap," said Kipling. "I left it with

young Joseph Merrick in case of just such an eventuality. The first of them ought to be arriving there now. I'll hold out here as long as I can, to make sure we can save everyone."

"All right," Verne said, rolling up his sleeves. "Let us see where this goes. I'm going to rouse the Caretakers. When you've finished in Switzerland, go join Houdini and Conan Doyle and see to it that they're also ready."

"I'll take care of it, Jules," Kipling said as he closed the trump. "Believing is seeing."

"Yes," Verne said. "And hope springs eternal."

Edmund, with Charles and Rose's help, was able to remove the shackles that bound Aristophanes in the Corinthian stalls. He was dressed simply, if a bit dirty—but his skin was also fully as pale as theirs was, and he had no horn.

"If this is our Zen Detective," Charles whispered, "then we've caught him at an early stage in his life, but not"—he sniffed the foul wine spilled around the hay—"at a better one."

A splash of cold water from the troughs helped Aristophanes regain a bit of sobriety, and he thanked the companions for freeing him.

"You didn't have to do that, you know," he said. "The queen will not be pleased."

"Let's say we owed you a kindness, and leave it at that," said Edmund. "Will you flee, as the shipbuilder did?"

He shook his head. "I can't. I'm bound by a blood oath to stay, until she releases me. And my chance just went running off down the beach. I'm still grateful you freed me," he added quickly, "but it doesn't help overmuch."

"If you're bound," asked Rose, "then why were you chained?"

"Too much wine," Aristophanes admitted sheepishly. "I got, ah, shall we say, a little too personal with some of the local maidens."

"Well," Edmund said, moving protectively in front of Rose, "you seem to be doing much better now."

From outside, a tremendous noise arose—trumpets, and drums, and the cheering of crowds.

"Ah," said Aristophanes. "That'll be the beginning of the coronation. The last regent of the Old World is coming to select the ruler of the Archipelago. Three guesses whom the queen expects it to be."

"Do you know where this is happening?" asked Bert.

"Yes."

"Let's go have a look, then," the Far Traveler said, beckoning to his companions. "This could get interesting."

"Is this really what we should be doing?" Charles asked as they walked into the city and toward the noise. "Shouldn't we be finding a way to get home?"

"Someone from the Old World, they said," Bert replied. "That means someone who was a ruler before the divide of the Summer Country and the Archipelago. And that someone," he finished, "may be able to lead us to the Architect."

Aristophanes led them to a broad avenue, lined with trees, fountains, and all manner of ornate, stately buildings. Crowds of people thronged the street on both sides, leaving only a narrow path for the arrival of the regent and the queen, a path that terminated at a great amphitheater built around the Silver Throne.

"Look, there," Aristophanes said, pointing, "and see how a queen makes her appearance."

To the west, the chariot that Edmund had mended dropped out of the sky in front of the setting sun. It was being pulled by a great, vivid green-gold Dragon.

"Azer," Rose breathed.

The Dragon-drawn chariot landed on the street amid the cheers of the Corinthians and sped toward the amphitheater. Most of the crowd moved out of the way as it passed, but one old man, walking with a stick, hunched and slow with age, could not move quickly enough and was thrown to the ground when the chariot wheel struck him a glancing blow. Medea did not even notice.

Edmund and Rose ran to the old man and helped him to his feet, then walked him slowly to sit by one of the trees. Charles brought him some water from a fountain, which he accepted gratefully and drank greedily, while Bert brought him the walking staff—which, he noted with surprise, was made of lapis lazuli, gold, and . . . *cavorite*.

"Thank you, my children," the old man said, "for taking note of this tired old regent."

"Regent?" Bert said, handing him the staff. "As in . . ."

The old man gave Rose a wink and nodded. "People see what they want to see, what they look for," he said. "The rest may as well be invisible."

Bert sat next to the old man. "What is your name?"

"I have been called many things in my long life," the old regent said, leaning heavily on his staff, "but of those names, the one I most value was Friend, and the one I most regret was Enemy. And often, it was by the same man. So I know of what I speak.

"I was called the first king, and Ancient of Days, although that is a worthless title, earned only by virtue of being old, and not yet having died, and in truth applies far more to another great king than it ever did to me.

"So all these titles I have had and more, but when I look at the sunset of my life, I find I am no more and no less than I was when I faced my first sunrise. I am Gilgamesh. And that is enough."

"Long after it was first created, I spent many years in the Archipelago seeking the great Lord of the Creatures and Master Maker Utnapishtim," said Gilgamesh, "and went on many quests for the lords of the lands that have been taken there. Some called me a hero. More, I fear, than did so here, in the Summer Country.

"But," he continued, "Immortality was not to be mine. I have already lived many, many thousands of years, since before the time of the Great Deluge, and I am all that is left of that world. So now," he said, gesturing at the amphitheater, where Medea was impatiently awaiting the arrival of the grand regent of old, "I am brought to this."

Aristophanes had been watching, curious, from some distance away. But now Gilgamesh noticed him.

"Do you serve the queen?" he asked.

"When I must," said Aristophanes.

Gilgamesh rose to his feet. "Then please give her this message. We will discuss the ruler of the Archipelago, but in the old manner. Not here. Tell her to meet me in the Giant's Circle in one hour, if she wishes to retain her kingdom."

Aristophanes was taken aback, both by the content of the message and the likelihood that Medea might slay the person who delivered it. "Whom should I say it is from?"

The regent rose to his full height, which was greater than it had first appeared. "I am Gilgamesh, King of Uruk, King of Sumer, Slayer of the World-Serpent, grandson of Nimrod the Maker, Blood of the Firstborn, and the regent of the world that was."

Aristophanes blinked rapidly, then nodded and disappeared into the crowd.

Gilgamesh offered his arm to Rose, who took it. "Shall we take a walk to the beach, my dear?" he asked. "It is a beautiful night."

The companions and the old regent chatted companionably as they walked away from the city, and Bert chanced to ask him if he knew of the Keep of Time.

"The Eternal Tower?" Gilgamesh answered. "Yes—I know of it."

"Do you know who made it?" Rose asked.

To the companions' disappointment, he shook his head.

"As old as these bones are," he said, "it was there long before my time. Long before the Archipelago was formed, after the Great Deluge. Everything was closer then. Smaller. But the world has grown.

"I saw the tower in my youth, when I sought to find the Garden of the Gods and learn the secret of their immortality. Had I known then what I know now, I simply would have stayed in the First City."

"The First City?" asked Edmund. "Ever?"

Gilgamesh laughed. "If not, certainly among them," he said. "Would you like to hear about it?"

"I would," Edmund said as he quietly opened one of his books and grabbed a pencil. "Very much, please."

"What are you doing?" Charles whispered.

"Just a thought I had," Edmund whispered back. "Keep him talking and let me work."

"Some called it the Dragon Isle," said Gilgamesh, "and others, the City of Enoch."

"Atlantis?" Bert asked, barely able to draw a breath with the wonderment of all they were hearing. "Is it Atlantis?"

Gilgamesh considered this, then nodded. "Yes, I think I have heard some of the younger races calling it thus. But among those who have built it, and who lived among its gleaming towers, they had a different name.

"They called it the City of Jade. And there was no place like it anywhere else on Earth, nor shall there ever be again. It was destroyed during the Deluge—and on that day, the world was irrevocably changed. It was the end of the Earth's childhood. And those of us who remember the innocence still miss it."

Gilgamesh was still describing the wonders of the First City when they arrived at the Giant's Circle—a Ring of Power, to the companions—and found the Dragon Azer, Aristophanes, and a livid Medea already there.

"How dare you humiliate me in front of my people!" she shouted, not realizing she'd nearly run down the regent not an hour before. "What do you mean by this?"

"These circles were made for summonings and ordinations," said Gilgamesh. "And I asked you here to tell you that should he return, it is my intention to ordain your husband, Jason, as

King of the Silver Throne of the Archipelago of Dreams. And only him."

"By what right?" said Medea. "Do you know what he's done?"

"He has made many mistakes," said Gilgamesh, "but he is also the first of the great heroes, and he is whom I have chosen."

Azer growled and circled around the outside of the ring as Medea considered her response.

"Is that your last word?" she asked.

"It is," said Gilgamesh.

"Then so mote it be," Medea replied, nodding not at the regent, but at Aristophanes.

The failed philosopher sighed heavily, then drew a blade from his tunic. Before the companions realized what was happening, he had leaped forward and plunged it into Gilgamesh's heart.

"If you will not choose me," Medea said coldly, "then you will choose no one."

"And any idiot can swing a hammer and chisel at a block of granite," Aristophanes was saying as Uncas bumped the Duesenberg across a poorly maintained road, "but only an artist with vision and experience can make the stone reveal a sculpture."

"So which do you have?" asked Quixote. "Vision, or experience?"

"Both," came the reply. "But not enough vision to do me any good, and much more experience than anyone can handle.

"There," the detective said, squinting out the windshield through the foggy haze outside. "That's the place we're after."

The structure that dominated the desert landscape was called the Tower of the Two Dragons. There were six distinct levels to the tower, and each represented whichever culture was dominant in the region at the time new portions were built. Going from the uppermost tier, which was built by the Moors sometime after the first millennium, Quixote could trace the history of the tower downward, citing each culture's contribution through the ages, until he came to the lowest, oldest tier, which stumped him completely.

Laughing, Aristophanes explained that it had been built by a race of giants prior to the Bronze Age, which was why Quixote couldn't identify it. He simply had no frame of reference for something architectural that was so old.

"Actually," Quixote harrumphed, "I have extensive experience with giants, and in the days of my prime, even tilted at two or three, to their eternal regret."

"Hardly giants like these," the detective said over his shoulder as they approached the base of the tower. "They're anthropophagous."

"I make no judgments about that," said Quixote. "That's for each living being to decide on their own."

Aristophanes slapped his hand to his face. "No, you idiot," he said. "That means they eat human flesh."

Uncas gasped. "Cannibobbles!" he squeaked. "Like that awful Burton. He's done that before." The little mammal shivered involuntarily and looked nervously from side to side. "I don't want t' be runnin' into no cannibobbles."

"Not to worry, little fellow," said the detective. "The giants hereabouts have been gone for many moons. And I don't think they'll be coming back during the short time we're going to be here retrieving the Ruby Gauntlets. Besides," he added reassuringly, "almost everyone else who even tries to get in is usually killed immediately, so we don't really have to worry about being bothered."

"Swell," said Uncas. "T'anks for sharing."

"Frenchmen in particular are forbidden to come here. When such have tried in the past, they first shed their skins like snakes before dying a horrible, horrible death," said Aristophanes. "That's why Verne would never set foot in this tower."

"Hmm," said Quixote skeptically. "I rather question the truth of that. I think you're having a bit of fun with us."

"It's true enough that he sent us here, rather than come himself," said Aristophanes, "and unless either of you is French, you're safe as long as you stay close to me."

"Well then," Quixote said, moving noticeably closer to the detective, "I am glad to be a Spaniard."

"So am I," said Uncas. "Not t' be French, that is."

"So would anyone be," said Aristophanes, "except the French themselves. And they're usually just grateful not to be Italian."

The desert sands gave way to smooth, flat stones, set in geometric patterns around the base of the tower. Aristophanes cautioned his companions to make sure to step only on the rectangular stones, and avoid the diamond-shaped ones altogether.

The doorway of the tower was made of stone and wooden beams, and consisted of two high arches set one within the other, which were then framed by larger rectangular patterns of delicately carved friezes.

"There are very old rituals involved in entering a place such as this," Aristophanes said, indicating the stained wood in the arches as they passed through. "There were wards set here to keep out unwelcome visitors under pain of a terrible death. And without an invitation, the only way to avoid the wards was to slay one's parents, and then anoint the symbols carved into the entryway with the sacrificial blood."

"Well," Quixote said jovially, "at least those particular wards no longer function as they're supposed to."

"No," Aristophanes said, turning around. "The wards are still up."

"But," Uncas said, looking back at the doorway, then at their guide, "we walked right through th' door, no fuss, no muss. And I certainly never kilt my parents."

"Nor did I," said Quixote as he also looked intensely at Aristophanes. "But if the wards are still up . . ." The sentence trailed off into the stillness of the tower.

The Zen Detective met their questioning look with a steady glare of his own—but said nothing. After a long moment, he turned and disappeared up the stairs.

Quixote and the badger both swallowed hard; then, after another moment, followed.

"I think," Uncas whispered to the knight, "that I might have preferred running into th' cannibobbles."

"I recognize the dragon on the right," said Quixote, indicating the design of one of the friezes.

"As do I," Uncas said, his tone one of reverence. "As would any animal from the Archipelago. He's the Lightbringer. The great red Dragon. Th' wisest and oldest of all the creatures, an' th' protector of all the lands that are."

"Do you know the other one?" asked Quixote. "The green-gold Dragon?"

"I don't know," said Uncas. "They seem to go together, judging by the carvings in this tower, but I have no idea who that is s'pposed t' be. An' I thought I knew all th' great Dragons."

"She does look familiar to me, though," Quixote said, scratching at his beard. "Something about the way the light falls on the sculpted features . . ."

Suddenly his eyes grew wide, and he moved closer to better examine the frieze. "Does she look like the Sphinx?" he asked Uncas. "The one we brought Master Verne last year?"

"Naw," Uncas said. "That'd be too unlikely t' believe."

"If you're done interpreting the art on the walls," said the detective, "I could use a little help here. I'm stuck. Stumped. Don't know what to do next."

"But," Quixote interjected, thinking about the blood at the entryway, "haven't you had business here before?"

"Yes," Aristophanes replied, disgruntled, "but on the fifth tier. I haven't had to open anything on the third tier before. I don't know how to resolve the cipher."

"Ahem-hem," Uncas said, clearing his throat. He removed a small parcel from his pocket. "This is, I believe," he said with a slightly puffed-out chest, "the very reason you brung me. Bringed me. The reason I'm here." He opened the Little Whatsit and, humming a little badger tune, began thumbing through its pages.

Aristophanes leaned in to ask a question, and the badger scowled. "Give me some room," he said without looking up from his task. "I'm *workin'* here."

The Zen Detective held up his hands in surrender and retreated to the far end of the room.

"It's some combination of pictographs and Aramaic," Aristophanes whispered to Quixote. "It's pretty unlikely that he'll find any reference to those languages in his little handbook, don't you think? Shouldn't we consider—"

"Oh ye of little faith," Uncas murmured, still absorbed in his task. "If only you had the faith of a mustard seed, oh, the mountains you could move."

Aristophanes snorted. "Now he's going to quote scripture at us? And badly at that."

Uncas turned and looked at the detective, one eyebrow raised. "Scripture?" he said. "Naw—I'm quoting Gran'ma Badger. Moved a mountain t' plant her mustard seeds. Made th' best mustard in th' whole of the Archipelago. Can't eat potatoes without it."

He turned back to the frieze and, with no hesitation, swiftly touched five spots on the pattern. A foot above his head, a heavy stone slab slid open to reveal a hidden chamber. Inside, pulsing with an unearthly red light, were the Ruby Gauntlets.

"Don't underestimate Gran'ma Badger's mustard," Uncas said, pointing a claw at Aristophanes, "and don't be disrespectin' th' Little Whatsit."

"Unbelievable," said the detective.

"That's my squire," Quixote said proudly.

At the Ring of Power on Corinth, the companions stood in stunned silence and disbelief at the terrible act Aristophanes had just committed.

He wiped the blade on the regent's cloak, then moved back to stand behind Medea.

"Why?" Rose cried.

"I made a deal," he said simply. "Medea meant to feed me to the fishes, but she said that if I were to win your confidence and your trust, and discover what you were doing here, she would free me.

"Then he asked to come here, and she warned me what might happen—but said I could repay my blood-debt by slaying the regent. And so I have."

"I thought we could trust you," Charles said dully. "We did trust you—have trusted you, far more than you realize."

"Of course you can trust me," Aristophanes replied. "Right up until the point where you can't."

Of all the pieces of the Ruby Armor found thus far, the comb was the easiest to locate—a fact that both delighted and vexed the Zen Detective.

The sixth oracular parchment and the corresponding map pointed them to a place called Taprobane, which was a densely wooded island at the mouth of the Indus River. Aristophanes told Uncas and Quixote that he had often heard the island referred to as "Tanelorn," and that deep within the forest there was supposed to be an impossibly old city. Fortunately, they did not have to venture that deeply—the box containing the comb, a smooth black stone, and a human finger bone was buried underneath a stone marker on the edge of Taprobane's northern shore.

A marker that bore the sign of a Caretaker.

"Which one?" Aristophanes asked.

"My old friend, Cyrano de Bergerac," answered Quixote. "Interesting that he should have come here, but not recorded it in any of the Histories."

"Maybe he took the record with him," suggested Uncas, "before he got lost riding that comet."

"Before what?" Aristophanes asked as he pocketed the comb and closed the box.

"Long story," said Uncas. "Six down, one to go."

The final objects they needed to complete the Ruby Armor were the shoes. The last of the oracular parchments led them to a place that had no map, because no map was necessary. It was in London, in the secret subbasement of the Natural History Museum.

Unlike some of the other Soft Places, it could be gotten to without a slide, or a trump, or by other mystical means. But like Lower Oxford, the entrances to the secret level were all but impossible to see for most people, who weren't looking to begin with.

The lower levels of the museum were already a treasure trove of Egyptian artifacts and fossilized dinosaur bones, but the real worth of the collection was to be found farther down.

A docent called Trent, who appeared to be of Elven descent, met them at the reception desk and listened to their request for the shoes with a growing look of incredulity.

"I can't sell you the shoes," he said flatly. "The Board of Regents would simply never stand for such a thing. I'd be dismissed, and they'd be very, very vexed. As it is, they're still in a bad mood after someone managed to steal our Sphinx last year."

"That's a shame," Quixote said, reddening. "These things happen."

"I've dealt with regents before," Aristophanes muttered under his breath. "This could take a while."

Uncas, however, noticed that the docent had taken a keen

interest in Don Quixote, and decided that they might have more leverage than they thought.

"How would the board feel about a trade?" Uncas offered. "The helmet of Don Quixote de la Mancha, in exchange for the Ruby Shoes of . . . uh . . ."

"Marie Antoinette," said the docent, who seemed to be considering the offer. "She apparently couldn't get them on in time and . . ." He made a chopping motion with his hand. "Well, you know."

"My helmet?" whispered Quixote. "I've had it for centuries—it's just now broken in."

"Shush," said Uncas. "We'll get you a new one, with a phoenix feather or something."

"Deal," said Quixote.

"Deal," said Trent. "I'll get the shoes. But," he warned, "be careful with them. You don't have to be wearing them to use them—just in contact with them. We've lost three janitors, a schoolboy from Surrey, and a beagle that way."

"I have to tell you," Aristophanes said as they opened the trunk of the Duesenberg, "you've been the most unusual, helpful, and irritating clients I've ever had. And despite my initial reservations, I've actually enjoyed working with you."

"Thanks," said Uncas. "I think."

"Here," the detective said to the others. "Gather up the ends of that tarpaulin, will you?"

Together the three of them made a makeshift sack out of the tarp, which held all the ruby objects, as well as the Infernal Machine. Aristophanes lifted it out of the car and slung it over his shoulder.

"What are you doing?" asked Quixote. "Aren't we taking all this back to Tamerlane House?"

"We have one more little trip to take," said the detective. He unwrapped the Ruby Shoes and slipped them into his pockets—then took hold of Quixote's arm.

"Uncas," he said, "please take my arm."

"Okay," said the badger. "But . . ."

In a trice, the trio vanished, leaving the empty Duesenberg sitting outside the museum.

". . . whyfor?" Uncas finished, as the three companions reappeared on the grassy slope of an island that was definitely not England.

"Well," said Quixote. "At least now we know the shoes work."

"Where have you brought us to?" Uncas said, looking around in wonder. In the distance, they could see the mist-shrouded statues, great elongated heads, that stood along the paths of the island as silent sentries.

"This is the only actual island of the Archipelago that stayed on this side of the Frontier," said Aristophanes. "Welcome to Easter Island."

"Fascinating!" said Quixote. "I've always wanted to come here. Although," he added, "all the giants are long gone."

"Yes," the detective said. "They are."

"Maybe we should come back on a different day," said Uncas. "After we've taken the Ruby Armor t' Scowler Verne."

Aristophanes sighed, deeply and long. He turned to the badger and the knight, his expression a mix of regret and resolve. "Have I ever told you that you shouldn't trust me?"

Quixote and Uncas looked at each other, puzzled, then back

at the detective. "No," Quixote said slowly. "I don't think so. And we haven't felt the need to ask—not for quite a while, anyway."

A pained look crossed Aristophanes's features. "Well then," he said abruptly, "I'm sorry to tell you this—but you shouldn't have trusted me."

Uncas's face fell. "Are you going t' keep th' armor for yourself, then?"

"No," Aristophanes said as he drew the dagger from its sheath, "we're going to deliver it all to my client. My true client."

Uncas let out a strangled squeak when he saw the dagger. "We aren't taking this back to Jules Verne, are we?" he asked, whiskers drooping.

"No," said the detective. "We're going to take it all, every piece, to Dr. Dee."

PART SIX

MYSTERIOUS ISLANDS

CHAPTER TWENTY-ONE
THE HOUSE ON THE BORDERLANDS

·——✳——·

DR. DEE STOOD *at his window in London, watching as Benjamin Franklin and the magistrate exchanged pleasantries outside before continuing on their respective paths. He wondered, not for the first time, whether Franklin would be worth recruiting into the ICS—and then, as before, pushed the thought out of his head. Something about the American gave him a terrible sense of déjà vu—and that was not just a feeling, but a caution. Especially for one who travels in time.*

Since formally leaving his position with the Caretakers, he had accelerated his plans for the Imperial Cartological Society. And, as the Caretakers became more and more obsessed with imaginary geographies and protecting the past, Dee had concerned himself with the substance of the real world, and the possibilities of the future.

Working with William Blake, he had all but perfected the Anabasis Machines, incorporating spatial transportation abilities that none of the Caretakers had even begun to suspect were possible. That meant that his travel in the Summer Country was all but unrestricted, and his ability to leap back and forth in time, even more so.

It amused him to realize that it had been his younger self who last met with the Dragon Samaranth not far from this place, but a century in the future. To be older, and now standing in his own past, was something that would have clouded the minds of lesser men—but he had never been that kind of a man, not even centuries earlier, when he first proposed the founding of the ICS to Queen Elizabeth.

It had taken him many years to establish it as an organization separate and apart from that of the Caretakers—and those they rejected from their membership had made excellent candidates for his. Especially the learned barbarian, Burton. Yes, Dee thought. That one has potential. He could even be my successor—if, that is, I ever intend to step down from my position. So, Second in command, then. Burton would have to be satisfied with that—as would Dee. None of the other recruits were even close to being in Burton's league.

As if in response to Dee's unspoken thoughts, there was a knock at the door. He turned to see Daniel Defoe walk in, wearing a cunning smile.

Defoe approached his master and quickly whispered his report. Dee frowned at first, and then, slowly, began to smile as broadly as his protégé.

"At Franklin's, you say?" *he said, mentally checking the box that said his intuition was sound.* "And they carry the watches, as we do?"

"And the Imaginarium Geographica," *said Defoe.* "The real one. They are Caretakers, I've no doubt."

Dee turned and looked out the window again. He knew that the Caretakers had blundered badly in the future, and that the Archipelago was no longer connected to the Summer Country. More, he knew that the Keep of Time had fallen, and with it, their ability to use the Anabasis Machines.

He reached down and stroked the large, leather-bound book on his desk. It was only the maps he had recorded within, the maps of time, rather than space, that had preserved the ability of the ICS to travel in time—and the Caretakers had no Chronographer of their own. So if they were here, in Revolution-era London, he mused, then they must have found a way to begin to reweave the threads of time. And that could not be countenanced.

"I don't know who all the men are," Defoe was saying, "but they also have several animals with them—talking animals—and three children. Two girls, one of whom can fly, and a young boy."

"And why is this of interest to me?" asked Dee.

"The second girl," said Defoe, "has no shadow."

"Hmm," Dee said. "That is interesting."

There was another knock at the door, and Dee gestured for Defoe to leave, but not before giving him instructions. "Find out all that you can about them," he said firmly. "Do not come back until you have."

Defoe stepped out of one door as another of Dee's associates entered through the first. "Greetings, Doctor," Nikola Tesla said. "I couldn't help but overhear. You're right to wonder about the girl."

"Who is she?"

"Rose Dyson," Tesla answered. "The Grail Child."

Dee whirled on his colleague. "The Grail Child! Here? Then the Caretakers who are with her . . ."

Tesla nodded. "Two of the three Caretakers of prophecy," he said, "and several others—including Burton, and the End of Time."

The Chronographer frowned and put his hand to his chin, stroking it in thought.

"Burton . . . ," he said at last. "That . . . is an unexpected defection. We should keep a tighter rein on him. But he's not my immediate concern—it's the End of Time who could discern our true natures. Have him dealt with as quickly as possible. I'll brook no delay in this, Nikola."

"Fine," Tesla said, chagrined at the other's tone. "And the girl?"

"Defoe said she has no shadow," he said at last. "This is an opportunity, Nikola. One we should not miss. Do we have a spare we could use, back at the House? Lovecraft's, perhaps?"

Tesla shook his head. "We have assigned that one to Defoe. We do have Crowley's, though."

"Fine," Dee said, waving his hand. "They are at Doctor Franklin's—have the Lloigor fit her with the Shadow, as soon as possible. It will take time to corrupt her fully, if it can be done at all."

The other shrugged. "She lost her own shadow," he said blithely. "That is not coincidental. There is one other thing, Doctor. The boy—he is special."

"How so?"

"Here," Tesla said, holding out his ebony-colored watch. "Look for yourself."

Dee examined the display on the watch for a moment, and a look of astonishment suddenly blossomed on his face. He looked at Tesla in disbelief, then took out his own watch to verify the other's findings. They were correct.

"He has no zero points," Dee murmured, "no life-thread binding him to this time, or any other. How is this possible?"

"He's from a might-have-been," said Tesla. "A possible future. That's the only reason there are no zero points connected to him. They haven't happened yet. But that isn't the most significant thing about him."

Dee waited. "Well?"

"His aiua," Tesla said, smiling. "It's almost identical to the Grail Child's. His lineage is the same. So I thought he might be a candidate—"

Dee silenced him with a gesture. "Don't even say the word," he said sharply. "We put too much weight on Mordred as a candidate, and now he is forever out of our reach. I won't make that mistake again."

He turned back to the window. "Keep an eye on Defoe. Have the cat deal with Burton's guide, the Time Lord. And learn all you can about this child."

"And if he is what he appears to be?" asked Tesla. "Do we bring him here, or . . ." He paused. "Kill him?"

"No," said Dee. "They found him in a future, so we should hide him in the future . . . in a might-have-been. The Caretakers are far too enmeshed in the past—they will never think to look for him in a past that hasn't happened yet. Have Defoe do it—he's reliable, and expendable.

"And," Dee continued, more to himself than the other, "when the time is right . . .

". . . what is theirs will become ours. And this boy may be the key to winning it all."

The open secret that was Verne's Mystorians became much more open with the destruction of the Hotel d'Ailleurs, and the subsequent evacuation to the refuge that he had prepared for them.

It was a smaller place than the hotel, but it didn't need to be larger than it was. It was built on one of the smaller of the Nameless Isles, just to the east of Tamerlane House. The island was also ringed about with rune stones, but these were not merely protective. They were essential.

Evacuating the still-living members of the Mystorians was not a problem—but moving out those who were ghosts took much more preparation. Their new home had to be identically prepared with the markings that allowed the ghosts to manifest, and Verne's special trump had to be used to allow them to pass. Kipling activated it just in time, and nearly didn't make it through himself before the hotel roof collapsed in flames.

At Verne's behest, the Caretakers Emeriti had gathered together to hear Kipling's report. The tulpa had survived the flames but was not unscathed—his jacket was terribly scorched, and his hair and mustache were singed badly.

"And everyone is now safely here?" Verne asked when Kipling had finished.

"Almost," he replied. "Young Joseph Merrick stayed the longest, to make certain everyone else was safe. But I didn't see him come through the trump, and he has not as of yet manifested again at Haven."

Verne dropped his head and sighed. "I see."

"Is it the principal duty of the Prime Caretaker to form secret organizations?" asked an angry Alexandre Dumas. "And to keep it from his colleagues?"

"The principal duty of the Prime Caretaker," Verne said slowly, "is that of finding, and training, the Imago—the one who will become the protector of this world."

"Pfah," Leonardo da Vinci snorted. "That is a myth."

"It is not," said Verne. "Rose may be such a being, but the lost prince may be also. That's why the Cabal wanted him—and why we have sought him."

"To use him for ourselves?" asked Dumas.

"No," said Geoffrey Chaucer, in a tone that said he would brook no dissent. "To prevent the Cabal from turning him into the Archimago—the destroyer of worlds."

"In the days before the Caretakers," said Verne, "there were those of wisdom and learning who were asked by the Dragons to perform the same function. The greatest of these whom you may know of was Chiron."

"The centaur?" Jack asked. "Achilles's teacher?"

Verne nodded. "And the teacher of many, many others—most of the great heroes, in fact. He was the great-umpty-great grandsire to your friend Charys, I believe.

"He also taught those who were to become the protectors of the Archipelago, including Jason. But Medea's betrayal prevented that, and the Silver Throne sat empty for almost three thousand years. When John Dee became a renegade, his primary purpose—we thought—was to create and control a king of the Archipelago. But we now know it is much worse—he intends to create the Archimago and open our world to the Echthroi."

"How is it that a renegade Caretaker knows so much that he can cause us such great trouble over and over again?" John said, exasperated. "Not even Burton gave us as much grief as John Dee!"

"Burton never even became a full Caretaker," Twain said, answering before Verne could reply, "but Dee was. And more than that, for many years he was the most significant one."

"Oh dear," said Jack. "You mean . . ."

"Yes," Twain said. "Before my apprentice, Jules Verne, was appointed to the position, the office of Prime Caretaker was filled by Dr. Dee."

"So what do we do now?" asked John. "I hope you have some sort of plan."

"I always do," Verne said as he removed a trump from his breast pocket. "Gather close, and listen in. The endgame is about to start."

◆ ◆ ◆

There was nothing Uncas and Quixote could do except follow Aristophanes up the hill on Easter Island. He was walking toward a massive, dark house, which was too Gothic to have belonged there. With a chill, Quixote realized that their detective was not lying—he had been working for another client the whole time, and this edifice they were approaching was the House of Dr. Dee.

"You'll serve Dee, and betray th' Caretakers?" Uncas asked. "Shame, Steve. Shame, shame on you."

"I have been in the service of the Caretakers for over two thousand years," Aristophanes said, his voice gone low and menacing, "and it was not by my own will, but out of necessity—just as it was a necessity to ask for your help to find the Ruby Armor. You needed my machine, but I needed your maps."

"And th' Little Whatsit," said Uncas. "We did a lot more than read maps. We were your gosh-darn partners, Steve!"

The unicorn detective took a deep breath. "Aye," he admitted. "You were. But now that time is done."

Several men were walking from the house to meet them on a broad field. Quixote only recognized John Dee, but Uncas knew the others from his son's enthusiastic descriptions of them, as Fred was a voracious reader of fantastic fiction. Many of his favorite writers—several of whom were dead—were standing before them now.

"Scowlers Lovecraft, Tesla, Cabell, and Chesterton," said Uncas, "John Dee, and Aleister Crowley. And," he added, frowning, "Daniel Defoe."

Defoe bowed and smiled at the badger. "I've met your offspring, I believe," he said with a smirk. "He looked like he'd make good eating. So do you."

"Try if you like, but you'd better do it quick," Uncas said, looking at his watch. "Your dinner bell is about to be rung, you self-righteous—"

Defoe scowled and turned to Dee. "What did we need to bring them here for? Couldn't the unicorn just kill them and be done with it?"

"I brought them," Aristophanes said as he showed them the tarpaulin containing the Ruby Armor, "so they wouldn't go running off to tell their Caretaker friends what I was really up to. And I didn't kill them, because that's not what you paid me for."

"That can be rectified," said Defoe.

"Bring it on," said Uncas.

Lovecraft laughed and walked forward. "Brave words, little badger, when you're surrounded by the enemy."

"Tell you what," said Uncas. "If you surrender now, I'll put in a good word for you with th' Caretakers."

"Surrender?" an astonished Lovecraft asked as he stopped in front of Uncas. "Are you *insane?*"

"You're a storyteller, ain'tcha, Mr. Lovecraft?" Uncas asked. "Well, this is that part of the story where th' heroes snap their fingers and th' cavalry rides to th' rescue."

"Except," said Lovecraft, "you are on an island in the middle of the greatest ocean on Earth, and there is no one who even knows where you are, much less how to ride to your rescue. Face the facts, little animal." He bowed low to look the badger in the eye. "We hold the upper hand. And you have no cards left to play."

"Oh, I gots one," Uncas said, stepping backward as he reached into his jacket. "But it'll do th' trick, I think."

It was a trump. Jules Verne's own trump to Tamerlane House.

"You get all that, boss?" Uncas said into the card.

"Perfectly well," said the voice of Jules Verne. "Bring us through, Uncas."

"It's one of Dee's cursed *cards*!" Crowley snarled. "And it's *open*!"

Before any of the Cabal could stop him, the badger had concentrated on the card, which began to grow. In seconds it was a full-size portal between Easter Island and the Nameless Isles, where, as Uncas had said, the cavalry was waiting to cross over.

"Greetings and salutations," Nathaniel Hawthorne said as he stepped across the boundary of the card. He was carrying a sledgehammer, and he hefted it with purpose. "I'm in the mood for popcorn and cracking skulls. And I didn't bring any popcorn."

Behind him were John, Jack, and Verne, followed closely by Dickens, Twain, Irving, the badger Fred, and Laura Glue, all bearing drawn weapons.

"Keep the portal open," Verne said to Uncas. "More will be coming through in a moment. The advantage is ours."

"It's still Dee's battlefield," said John.

"You have your warriors, and I have mine," said Dee. "I see that you have brought samurai swords. Shall we settle this in the old samurai way, then?"

"What is he talking about?" asked John.

"There's an old story," Verne said, not taking his eyes off Dee and the Cabal, "about two samurai who met on a bridge. Neither one would give way to the other, and so they drew their swords—and instead of attacking, froze. Every little while, one of them would change position, and the other would change his to match."

"A battle of perceived skills, not actual combat," said Hawthorne. "I remember the tale."

Verne nodded, still watching Dee, who seemed only too content to listen in with the rest. "Each was assessing the other's abilities, and they were each so skilled that a single pose revealed a lifetime of training. So each would pose, and the other would assess, and counterpose.

"Finally, after nearly a day and a night, one of the samurai finally realized that he would be beaten, and he bowed, sheathed his *katana*, and stood aside to let the other pass."

"So was it the good samurai or the bad samurai who won?" asked John. "We're dealing with a good-versus-evil matter here, and it would be nice if you'd clarify."

"I can't remember," said Verne. "That was not the point of the story."

"Which is?"

"That assessment of your opponent can also be a weapon," said Dee, "and may decide the battle, all on its own."

"That's the stupidest thing I ever heard," Jack said as he drew a second blade. "We can take them, Jules. That's my assessment."

"Ah," said Dee, "but all the pieces are not yet on the board." He raised a finger, and a door on the house behind him opened. Three William Blakes strode out and joined the members of the Cabal. "Your move."

Verne smiled and cleared his throat. Three more William Blakes appeared in the trump portal and stepped through to join the Caretakers.

Dee frowned. "Matching bishops, then."

"Not quite," said Verne. He waved at the Cabal's William

Blakes, and they walked across the field to join the Caretakers. "Sorry," they said in unison.

"I told you not to trust him!" hissed Tesla. "I mean, them. Him. Whatever it is."

"Six Blakes will not defeat us," said Dee. "What else do you have?"

"We have the resources of every Caretaker who has ever lived, as well as every worthy member of the Imperial Cartological Society who was wise enough to leave," said Verne.

"Point," said Crowley.

"Oh, shut up," said Tesla.

"I have the Ruby Armor of T'ai Shan," said Dee. "Every weapon in the world that can defend against or be used to attack an Echthros is *mine*."

"Actually," Aristophanes said, "in point of fact, it isn't."

Before any of the Cabal could react, the Zen Detective swung the tarpaulin full of armor over his shoulder and quickly crossed over to stand beside Verne.

"Well, I'll be dipped," Uncas said, squinting up at Quixote. "I though we wasn't supposed t' trust him."

"I still don't know that you can," Aristophanes said with a sigh. "I'm not a very trustworthy guy. But I'd like to think I've learned a few things in the last couple of millennia, and one thing I try to do is not be on the wrong side of a battle. They," he finished, gesturing at Dee, "are definitely the wrong side."

"You've always served us well," Verne said, "and I for one have always had faith in you, Steve."

It wasn't possible for the detective's skin to redden, but it was obvious he was uncomfortable with the compliment. "I made a bad choice a long time ago," he said brusquely, "and I've worn the punishment on my skin ever since. That's a difficult weight to carry without some kind of remorse."

"We have a contract, detective," Dee hissed.

"You never paid me," Aristophanes shot back, "and the Caretakers made me an offer you can't match. No deal."

"If you were on our side all along," said Uncas, "then why did you let them think you were on their side a'tall? And why bring us here?"

"Because," said Verne, "we really did need Steve to find the armor, and Dee would never have let that happen if Blake hadn't convinced them that he would do it for the benefit of the Cabal. And he brought *you* here, so you could bring *us* here."

"That's pretty smart," said Uncas.

"Thanks," Verne and Steve said together.

Verne turned back to Dee. "Your move."

In response, Dee raised his hand, and suddenly the doors of his house all opened at once. The fields behind the Cabal were flooded with every manner of foul creature who had ever haunted children's nightmares: the half-men Wendigo; the skull-headed Yoricks; and a dozen other kinds of monstrous beings who had been collected from the Archipelago years earlier. Now they were led by Dee's new lieutenant, William Hope Hodgson.

"I have an army," said Dee, "and I have your people to thank for it. Burton gathered them, and Kipling led them. They may have defected to your side, but the army is still mine."

"And I," Verne said, "have *goats*. If you want to surrender gracefully now, Dee, I'm sure no man here will think the less of you for it."

Without waiting for a response, Verne opened a second trump—this one to Lake Baikal, where three of the Caretakers were waiting to step through.

Kipling, Houdini, and Conan Doyle came through the portal, then clambered for safety atop the rocky ledge as a wave of armor-clad battle goats swept past, heading straight for the enemy.

"Hello, Hodgson," called out Houdini. "I see you've finally found your proper position in life."

"Hello, you *hack*," Hodgson replied. "You still cheating people with the milk can trick?"

"I never . . . !" Houdini began.

"Save it for another time," said Conan Doyle.

"He can't be serious!" Crowley exclaimed. "*Goats?* He actually thinks we're going to be afraid of goats?"

"I don't know," Defoe said, hesitant to voice his skepticism. "Those badgers don't look like much either, but give them some stale baked goods and they can take you out at a hundred paces."

"And we hear pretty good too," Fred called out, gesturing for Defoe to cross the field. "C'mon, you dragon turd," he said defiantly. "I'll be your blueberry."

The goats lined up across the battlefield in front of the Caretakers in one long column, three rows deep.

"Help me, help me, Dr. Dee!" Crowley cried in mock terror. "Jules Verne is here, and—and—he's pointing a bunch of *goats* at me!"

Verne's response to the mockery was to raise a finger and gesture to one of the goats. A shaggy, potato-colored goat in heavy armor clanked her way over to the Prime Caretaker.

"My war leader, Elly Mae," he said to the others by way of introduction. He scratched the goat behind the ears and pointed at one of the smaller iconic statues, which stood only twenty yards off to the left.

"Elly Mae!" he commanded the war leader. "Bonk! Bonk the noggin!"

Elly Mae bleated an acknowledgment and darted off toward the statue, picking up far more speed than any of them would have expected in a goat.

She lowered her armored head and struck the statue with a tremendous bonk that threw her back on her haunches.

"Hah," said Crowley. "That's just—"

"Wait," said Verne.

With a great noise that sounded like an enormous tree splitting, a crack ran up the height of the statue, and it shattered into a dozen pieces.

"Shades," hissed Tesla.

"I'm in awe," said Jack.

"Meh," said Elly Mae, and ambled her way back to rejoin the ranks of the battle goats.

"Cavorite armor, laced with runic silver," Verne said, smiling broadly. "We've been working on it for years, and the goats know how to use it. Nothing your creatures of Shadow have can penetrate it. And now the goats are angry. You shouldn't have made them angry, Dee."

"You can still rejoin us, Kipling," Dee said, moving his attention to a different kind of attack. "What Burton once offered you is still there to be taken. Your son can still be returned to you."

For the briefest of instants, Kipling seemed to hesitate before steeling himself and shaking his head.

"Why not?" Dee exclaimed, the slightest tinge of frustration starting to creep onto his voice. "Isn't it what you want? To have your son again, living and whole?"

"My son died honorably," said Kipling, "and my time with him is cherished—but past. To try to reclaim it would be to mock those memories. And while you are right, that I do long to be reunited with him, I have learned something from these men." He looked at John and smiled. "Sometimes there are things that are more important to the world than what I want."

Across the field, Crowley slapped his head. "Idiot," he grumbled. "I told you not to even try to tempt him, Dee."

"Shut up!" Dee said, striking Crowley a blow across the face. The game was not going as he had planned.

"I gave you a chance," Dee said to Kipling. "My army is going to tear you all to pieces."

"Oh, I really don't think that's going to happen," Kipling replied. He walked to the front of the battle lines and began to recite a verse:

> From ghoulies and ghosties and long-leggedy beasties
> and all creatures which go bump in the night may the
> good Lord preserve us, amen.

"Hah!" Lovecraft barked. "What, is that supposed to be some kind of a prayer?"

"Not a prayer," Kipling said, smiling slyly. "A *Binding*."

There was a low vibration in the air as the invocation Kipling spoke triggered the Binding, which swept through the ranks of Dee's army like a plague in London. As one, all the Wendigo, Yoricks, and the rest of the creatures that had been in the thrall of the Lloigor crossed the field, where they formed ranks behind Kipling, who bowed gracefully at his opponent.

"My bishop takes your pawns, Dee," said Verne. "*All* your pawns. Your move."

"I have just one left," said Dee.

To John's right, next to Verne, Dr. Raven suddenly appeared out of nowhere. Verne was startled, and slightly puzzled, by the Messenger's appearance.

"Dr. Raven!" John exclaimed. "What are you . . . ?"

"All good things happen, Caveo Principia," Dr. Raven said to John, "in time."

Dr. Raven strode away from the Caretakers and across the field to stand next to Dr. Dee. He turned to face his friends from Tamerlane House, and as he did so, his form shimmered and changed. He youthened, and where Dr. Raven had been standing there was now a younger version, not much older than Edmund McGee.

Only this younger version wore two watches: the silver watch of Verne's Messengers and the Caretakers, and the ebony watch of the Cabal. He also wore one of the silver rings, but none of that was what struck fear into those on the Caretakers' side of the battlefield.

As he walked, the Ruby Armor of T'ai Shan vanished from the bag Aristophanes had carried it in and reappeared—on the young Dr. Raven.

He was now wearing the armor Jules Verne had told the Caretakers would give the bearer near-infinite control over time and space—and he was standing with the Lloigor Dee.

"That," said Dr. Dee, "is checkmate, my dear Verne."

CHAPTER TWENTY-TWO
THE FURIES

THE SKIES OVER the beach at Corinth suddenly grew dark. As Rose cradled the body of Gilgamesh in her arms and tried to understand what had happened, the others formed a protective triangle around them.

"That was not worthy of a queen," Bert said, "and not worthy of a Dragon."

Azer seemed to take pause at the Caretaker's admonition. "This world was meant to be ruled," the Dragon hissed, "not cultivated and given over to *children*—even one who calls himself a king."

"That decision," said a voice that echoed across the sky, "was not yours to make."

Above their heads, where the clouds were swirling together, a terrible apparition appeared.

The woman was ten feet tall, with flowing robes, and appeared at times to have three faces, or perhaps even three bodies. The lines were indistinct and flowed into one another so that it was never entirely clear if this was one woman, or three. One of them carried a hammer, and another carried a torch. But in all three faces, the eyes blazed with the flames of vengeance.

"Hecatae!" Aristophanes breathed. "The goddess of the crossroads!"

Rose was equally taken aback by the extraordinary apparition before them. The goddess was, after all, of the pantheon Rose had been raised to believe in. She gently set Gilgamesh's body aside, then knelt and bowed her head. Following her example, Bert and Charles did the same.

"The Furies," Rose said under her breath. "The first Morgaine."

"He was of the blood of the firstborn," the Hecatae said, voices ringing out in a terrible harmony. "It is forbidden to harm those of his line. Forbidden to spill their blood. Forbidden to kill."

Aristophanes cowered. "I had to do it!" he cried. "I had no choice!"

"You have not acted as a man should," said the Hecatae. "You have acted ignobly, in haste, and for the weakest of reasons, little philosopher. And henceforth, you shall be marked, so that those around you in this world will know of your crime, and of your shame."

The Hecatae pointed a finger at Aristophanes, who was looking to Medea, hoping for some kind of intervention or protection—but the sorceress ignored him. He had done what she wanted, and now she had no further use for him.

"Wait!" he called out to the goddess. "Wait! I can serve you instead! Please!"

"You wished the freedom from responsibility to your fellows," one face of the goddess said. "Now you shall stand forever apart from them, cloaked in the colors of a king, that all shall know your coward's heart."

As she spoke, Aristophanes clutched at his arms, which had

begun to turn crimson, as if he were covered in blood, then a rich shade of purple, which began to spread up his arms and over his entire body.

"You wished the attentions of the crowd," the second face of the Hecatae said, "now be among the most sought-after of creatures, desired and pursued, so that your only refuge will be in the shadows you served this day."

The philosopher screamed, as a bright red whorl appeared on his forehead. In moments it had grown into a bump, which burst with a spray of blood and skin as a horn sprouted out of his skull.

"And you, who spoke truths, and betrayed those truths with the sting of a blade, now be in the flesh what you summoned with your actions, and never know another's touch, lest they be poisoned by your own.

"All these things you now are, and forevermore shall be, until the end of time. So mote it be."

With a scream, Aristophanes fled, running across the top of the dunes. In seconds he had disappeared from sight, but the companions could still hear the echoes of his scream.

The Hecatae turned their attention to Medea.

"It is forbidden," they said again. Medea scowled. She had hoped—no, expected—that using the philosopher as the hand that killed Gilgamesh would spare her the vengeance of the Furies. Apparently that was not true.

Medea stood facing them, defiant. "It was my right, as queen," she said, all but spitting out the words in anger. "My right to rule. He should have chosen me, not my husband!"

"Jason will pay the price for his choices, as you will pay the price for yours," the goddess said. And Medea's stolid composure finally cracked, and she fell to her knees, trembling. "But it's not fair!" she cried. "Before his betrayal, I believed I was to rule with him, on the Silver Throne! And after, if not with him, then in his stead! And this old fool," she continued, gesturing at the body of Gilgamesh, "would not grant me his blessing, even though he knew I would kill him if he did not!"

"Your words have caused great pain, great misery," they said to the cowering Sorceress, "and so has your vanity. Thus, forevermore, these shall be all that you have."

"Daughter," the Hecatae said to Rose. "You are our heir. You are the Moonchild. And you have served us honorably and well. The punishment must come from your hand."

Rose gasped. "Me?" she exclaimed. "How—how could I possibly punish her?"

"It is your responsibility," the Hecatae said. "None other has the right. And we have already given you the means, in your past, which is still our time to come."

Rose nodded slowly, finally realizing what the goddess meant. She reached into her pocket and removed the multifaceted mirror, which, on impulse, she threw into the air. It began to spin and expand—and then it began to draw the queen of Corinth toward itself.

Medea screeched in protest, but the sound was drowned out by a thunderclap. Lightning flashed, blinding the companions for a few seconds, and when their vision cleared, Medea was gone.

Where she had crouched was the mirror, larger now, which reflected nothing of its surroundings, but which bore the image of the sorceress. She was weeping and pounding her fists against her transparent prison.

"So mote it be," said the Hecatae. "Forevermore you will dwell as an image in a cave of images, until such time as your children have redeemed you."

The mirror vanished from the sand. In that instant, Azer, who had witnessed all that had transpired, stroked her wings into the air and took flight.

Rose and her companions saw, for the first time, something that was rarely if ever seen in the face of a Dragon—*fear*.

"Stop," said the Hecatae, and in midair the Dragon froze, suspended above them.

"You have betrayed your calling," the Hecatae said, their voices reverberating in the air, "and a price must be paid."

"I did not choose this!" Azer hissed through gritted teeth. "I did not choose to descend! He did this, he chose—"

"The choice was yours, as it always was," asserted the Hecatae. "And the price you pay is yours also, until such a day when you choose to serve someone other than yourself once more."

As they watched, Azer transformed from a Dragon to a terrible, beautiful woman, then back to a Dragon again, before finally falling to the sand as a half-formed Dragon with the woman's head and torso. Azer had also been transformed to stone—to *cavorite*.

"This is why she brought us here, to her home on Autunno," Burt murmured to the others. "This was the day she became the Sphinx."

Rose looked up at the goddess. "What of Gilgamesh?"

"We shall bear his body to the Elysian Fields," the Hecatae said, dropping closer to gather up the old regent's body, "where he shall rest until such a time as he may be called upon to rise, as great heroes are needed to do."

"I'm sorry," Rose said. "I'm sorry we couldn't stop them from killing him."

"Daughter," the Hecatae said as they bore the body of Gilgamesh up into the clouds, "you have ever pleased us with your choices, and you please us still. Go now, and do the work you have set to do, and be not troubled. For your path is just."

With that, the Hecatae disappeared. The clouds cleared, and the moon was rising. And once more, the companions were alone.

They spent the night on the beach, if for no other reason than that the Ring of Power was familiar and gave them a measure of security. Although after what had happened with Azer, none of them was quite so sure summoning Dragons would ever be such a good idea again.

"Samaranth always did mention," Charles said, "that he wasn't a tame Dragon. The same apparently went for his wife."

"What are you doing?" Rose asked Edmund, who had been busying himself with his drawings all night.

"I've tried using the old trump to Tamerlane House," he replied, "but we're simply too far away from any other recorded zero points for it to work across space and time. It still isn't working well enough. And anyway, if we try to go back, whether by trump or by trying to find the keep, we'll be going in the wrong direction."

"Wrong direction?" Charles exclaimed. "Don't you want to go home?"

"What I want," Edmund replied, "is to put an end to all this and restore what's been broken. But it's not my choice—it's yours." This last he said not to the Caretaker, but to Rose.

"Mine?" she exclaimed, blushing slightly. "We're all making these decisions together, I thought."

"Yes," Bert said, "but it's been obvious all along who is the true factotum. Rose, you are the true fulcrum of history, and we will do as you feel best. It's your choice. Decide, and we will follow."

"Then I say yes," Rose answered. "We should keep pressing into the past. What are you thinking, Edmund?"

"While Gilgamesh told us about the First City," he explained, "I was making a drawing on one of the trump sheets in the *Geographica*. I think we can use it to go there and learn more about the Architect."

"And this one?" Rose asked, picking up a copy he had made on a sheet of bronze. "What is it for?"

"The Caretakers."

"So they can try to rescue us somehow?"

"No," said Edmund. "Not to rescue us. We can't risk anyone else interfering with the course of Chronos time. We've done too much already."

"What's happened had to happen, because it did happen," Bert said, "and it could not have happened any other way."

"So if we aren't going to ask someone at Tamerlane House to attempt a rescue," said Charles, "what is it you're thinking of, Edmund?"

"He's thinking of a legacy," said a voice behind them. "That's the only reason to craft something in metal."

It was the shipbuilder, Argus.

"I heard rumors that the queen had disappeared," he said, "along with her Dragon. And in their place, the Corinthians have found a Sphinx. They have asked me to stay and help them create a temple around it, as a tribute to the gods."

"If you want," Charles said, "there's a nice, sturdy little building about a mile that way that would be perfect for the Sphinx."

Argus nodded. "And what of Medea?" he asked.

Rose looked at her friends. "She got the immortality she was looking for."

The shipbuilder smiled and sat, leaning back against the rock to soak in the sun. "No one lives forever, my young friend."

"Maybe not forever," said Rose, "but long enough for all practical porpoises."

"Hmm?" Argus raised his head. "What do you mean?"

"It's a badger joke," Rose replied, grinning. "It means you will live long enough to do what we want to ask of you."

"Ah," Argus said, bemused.

"The Corinthians asked you to construct the temple of the Sphinx?" Edmund asked.

Argus inclined his head in answer.

"Would you do something for me?" Edmund asked. "Just a small, simple request?"

"What is it?"

Edmund handed him the drawing on the sheet of bronze. "When you're done," he said, "simply place this inside the base of the Sphinx."

Argus frowned. "When the structure is finished, it will be considered sacred," he said. "It isn't meant to be used. No one will ever go inside, not without some extreme compulsion to do so."

Now it was Edmund's turn to smile. "That's what we're counting on. Will you do it?"

Argus smiled. "I am here in the sun today because of your good will," he said. "I will do as you ask."

After breakfasting together, the companions bid Argus good-bye and began to gather their things together. All except Bert, who had rolled up his trousers and waded out into the ocean.

Rose waded out of the surf and toward Bert. The Far Traveler had been consulting his watch, with a grim expression on his face. As she approached, Bert hurriedly snapped the watch closed and adopted a halfhearted smile that failed miserably to conceal his turmoil.

"What is it, old teacher?" Rose asked him. "That's the third time this morning you've checked your watch and not been pleased with what you saw there."

Bert sighed. "I didn't realize that anyone had noticed."

"I think we've all noticed," she said, looking over to where the others were, near the rocks. "I'm just the one who lost the draw about which one of us would mention it to you."

"As Argus said," Bert remarked with tears in his eyes, "no one lives forever."

"Your time isn't up yet," said Rose. "Come and see—our young Cartographer has a plan."

"Verne sent us the only object he knew would survive eight thousand centuries," Edmund was saying to the others, "namely, the Sphinx. So at some point in the future, he is going to have to open it, and when he does, he'll find the bronze I made of the drawing and know where we're going to go—because I've tested it, just a little, and I think we can use the drawing I made as a chronal map."

"That's a tall order," said Rose. "According to Gilgamesh, it was thousands of years ago."

"We're going to have to try it," Edmund said. "I believe in you, Rose. And I think that I've drawn it accurately enough. We can see this through. We just have to believe."

She took his hand, and the others stood next to them inside the Ring of Power as Edmund concentrated on the drawing he held.

The young Cartographer's hand trembled, and he bit his lip, hoping the pain would steady his hand before the others noticed. In response, Rose squeezed his arm supportively, then added her own concentration to the drawing. But still, nothing happened.

And then, deep inside the drawing . . .

. . . a leaf fell from a tree and floated gently on a breeze in the faraway place, coming closer and closer until it brushed past Edmund's fingers before drifting out of the frame.

The trump shuddered, and then, much to the companions' relief, it began to grow and expand, until it was more than a dozen feet across, and nearly as high.

"Well done!" Charles exclaimed, applauding respectfully. "I doubt the original Cartographer could have done any better."

"Well," Bert began.

"Hush that," Charles admonished. "He did very well."

"Shall we?" Edmund said, beaming at the others.

"Absolutely," said Rose.

♦ ♦ ♦

On the broad field in front of the house on Easter Island, the two armies faced each other, waiting, each wondering what this new defection meant to the Great Game.

"I am the true heir of this armor," said Dr. Raven, "and I always have been."

"Dee's plans do not serve reality," Verne said cautiously. "They serve the Echthroi."

"This is not the only reality there is," Dr. Raven said, his voice even and clear. "There are other places and times where a man may reinvent himself, even if that reinvention is a fiction."

"Is that what he is?" John said to Verne. "Is he a fiction, like Henry Morgan?"

"No," Raven said, answering John's question. "Not like that. I am as real as you are, Caveo Principia. But sometimes, reality gets in the way of what's really important. And the only way you can learn what you need to learn is to practice being fictional for a while."

"There is no time for this, boy!" hissed Dr. Dee. "We must—"

Dr. Raven cut him off with a glare. "There is time enough for everything, Dr. Dee," he said, as if it was a command. Dee opened his mouth to respond, but Dr. Raven had already turned back to face the Caretakers.

A thought passed among several of the Caretakers, which John and Twain confirmed with a glance—that exchange with Dee was significant. Not only was Raven not cowering before Dee, as the other members of the Cabal did, but he had in fact put him firmly in his place—which seemed to be subservient to Raven.

Was it possible? John wondered in amazement. Was Raven

the true leader of the Cabal, or had Dee actually created a paladin he couldn't control?

"Even now," Raven continued, "we're creating new fictions where we all play our parts. But it's all just a continuation of an old tale, already begun."

He nodded to the members of the Cabal, who scrambled up the hillside and into the House, where they closed the doors behind them. After a moment, and a last glance at Verne, Dee followed.

Verne took a few steps toward the armor-clad Messenger, hoping that with Dee gone, the younger man might be more open to reason, but Raven held up a hand, stopping him.

"This part of the story is ended. It's time for us to go away, to lick our wounds and rewrite the fiction that is to come." He turned to John. "We will meet again, Caveo Principia, on a different battlefield."

Something clicked in John's mind, and he moved in front of Verne, who was at a complete loss for words.

"You know me, don't you?" John asked Raven. "Somehow we know each other, from before Jules introduced us."

For the first time since he had donned the armor, Raven smiled—and it was a brilliant, charismatic smile.

"We do, Caveo Principia," the young man replied. "Long ago, and also, not so long ago.

"I am the age you see now because I choose to be. It was the age when I was brought back into this story by Dr. Dee and his Cabal. It was when I had lived through another fiction, in another time, and I had leaned to make my own way in the world.

"In that fiction, I chose my own names. There were times I

was known as Jude, and others as Obscuro, the Zen Illusionist. At one point I thought I might be Saturn, but it turned out I was mistaken. At some other point in my future, I become Dr. Syntax, and then Dr. Raven, and it was as Dr. Raven that I made myself known to the Caretakers and began my work as one of the Messengers for Jules Verne. But," he continued, "before that, you and I met, and I was known by a different name."

With a thrill of fear, John suddenly realized what that name might have been, but he wasn't sure he should ask it, for fear the young man would vanish altogether.

"If you're serving the Cabal," he said carefully, "then why become Dr. Raven at all? Was it merely to spy on us?"

"Not spy, observe," said Raven. "I had been left entirely alone, and I found out, also on my own, who had created the life they thought I should lead, and why. In learning about the Cabal, I came to learn of the Caretakers—and I wanted to know you better."

"It hasn't helped you to choose more wisely," said John, "or else you just hadn't learned enough about the difference between right and wrong."

"You may be correct on the latter point," Raven ceded, "but as to the former, I haven't chosen anything yet. I'm simply assessing the rest of the pieces on the board."

As he spoke, the entire structure of the House on the Borderlands began to shimmer, as if it had been immersed in a wave of hot air. A moment later Raven himself began to shimmer and grow transparent.

"We always seem to be seeking what we already have," Raven said as he grew less and less visible, "like Jason of old, searching for his lost sons. Even when he found them, he couldn't see them. And so even with a father within their reach, they were still orphans."

He stopped and considered what he'd just been saying. "That's a terrible story," he said, frowning. "I don't much like it. The tale of Odysseus and Telemachus is a better one, I think."

"Odysseus missed his son's entire childhood," said John. "Telemachus never knew his father when he was growing up."

"Ah, but Odysseus did return to Ithaca," said Raven, "and Telemachus never, ever, believed that he had been abandoned. His father was simply delayed—and when he finally returned, Telemachus helped him to reclaim his kingdom. Yes," he said, nodding in satisfaction. "That's a much better story."

"Telemachus was Rose's uncle," Verne said cautiously, having found his voice, "and John Dee is no Odysseus."

"No, he isn't," the young man said, keeping his eyes focused on John, "but perhaps I might become a Telemachus."

Behind him, the House had begin to shudder and rise. Stones were dropping from the foundation, and strange lights were beginning to appear all around it.

"Telemachus," John said, realizing that only moments might be left, "what was your *first* name?"

"I don't remember the name I was given at birth," the newly self-christened Telemachus said, "but when I was a child, I chose my own name, as I have done before, from the books I was reading, from the stories I liked. And although I couldn't read, the animals who cared for me could, and I loved being read nursery rhymes as I fell asleep each night there in my room on Paralon."

Hearing that word, Jack sat up in shock, staring at the nearly vanished Telemachus, as did all the other Caretakers. Verne gave a quiet moan and dropped to his knees, and John barely managed to remain standing himself.

"Oh my dear Lord," John said under his breath.

"Yes," Telemachus said, his smile now showing as much sadness as goodwill, "we met in a place that was once in the future but is now long in the past, and my name . . .

". . . was *Coal*."

And in that instant, Telemachus, once called Coal, the missing boy prince of Paralon, vanished, and with him, the entire Nightmare Abbey.

The young man, John Dee, the Cabal, and the House on the Borderlands were gone.

CHAPTER TWENTY-THREE
CHOICES

—✳—

BERT AND EDMUND had no idea where they'd suddenly appeared, but Charles and Rose recognized where they were immediately—not because there were familiar landmarks with which they could orient themselves, but because there were no landmarks at all. There was literally nothing but an expanse of whiteness in every direction. There was no shadow or context to even indicate whether they were in a small white space or standing on an infinite expanse of nothingness. There was, simply, nothing. And then he appeared.

The old man was just as Charles and Rose remembered him. Thin, impossibly old, and hunched more with responsibility than with age. He was dressed simply in a white embroidered tunic, and he was holding a watch—one of the silver pocket watches that belonged to the Caretakers. And he was smiling—at *them*.

"Excellent, excellent," he said, the smile never faltering. "You are right on time. This pleases me. It pleases me very much. How are you, Rose?"

"You remembered this time," Rose said. "I'm well, thank you."

"And you?" he said, turning to Charles. "You've been youthened. I don't know that the hair suits you, though."

"Oh, ah, thanks," said Charles. "I think."

"And you," the old man said to Bert. "You have traveled often in time, I think."

Bert drew himself up to his full height and answered with as much dignity as he could muster. "I have. They call me the Far Traveler."

The old man nodded as if Bert had just recited a grocery list. "Oh, do they now? Yes, yes," he said, waving his hand and smiling—condescendingly, Bert thought—"that's very nice for you. Now, Rose," he continued, "what is it that you're trying to do, that brings you back to Platonia?"

"We're trying to discover the identity," she said, "of the Architect of the Keep of Time."

"The Architect?" the old man said. "That's what you've gone flitting about searching for? Why would you need to know that?"

"Because, ah," Charles stammered, "we broke it. That is, I did. I broke time."

"You broke time, you say?" the old man answered. "Not possible. Time is eternal. Only we ever change."

"We broke the keep," said Bert, "and now we're just trying to find a way to repair it."

"But," the old man said gently, "that was not the reason you wanted to go into the future, was it?"

Bert took a breath as if he meant to respond, then slumped inward and pursed his lips, thinking. "No," he finally said, looking not at the old man, but at his companions. "No, it really wasn't. Not the entire reason, anyway."

"I understand," the old man said, resting a hand on Bert's shoulder. "But it is the others who must go on." He checked his watch. "Your time is nearly done, Far Traveler."

"There's still a task to be done, still work—," Bert began, but he stopped and looked mournfully at Rose. "It is time, isn't it?"

"In more ways than one," Charles admonished. "You've done all you needed to do, Bert. Now it's up to us."

The old man turned to Edmund. "It was a very good drawing you made. If you had been using it in conjunction with an actual time machine, instead of just as a trump, you'd have made it through easily."

"Oh," Edmund said, crestfallen.

"Don't worry, young Cartographer," the old man said. "You get better. Much better."

He turned to Rose. "And you, Rose. All I can tell you now is to trust in yourself, and to not be afraid of your shadow."

She blinked at that. "Why would I be?"

"You shouldn't," he repeated. "It's the only way you will find it again."

The old man bowed his head and spun the dials on his watch. "Close your eyes," he instructed them, "and do not be afraid. Remember . . . ," he finished as his voice began to fade, "all good things happen . . .

". . . in *time*."

John Dee's house on Easter Island was gone—but not all the members of the Cabal had vanished with it. Standing there in the expanse of grass where the house had been was Daniel Defoe.

"No!" Defoe howled with rage. "You promised! You promised me, Dee! I want my amnesty!"

"Amnesty?" asked Jack. "What is he talking about?"

"His time is nearly up," said John. "If he doesn't go back to Tamerlane House right now, he'll vanish forever."

"This," said Jack, "does not sound like a problem to me."

The former Caretaker had no choice but to approach his former colleagues and appeal for mercy. He had been abandoned by his masters and had no way to even begin to fight against the army of creatures that he faced.

"Defoe has a watch," said Verne. "Why doesn't he use it to escape?"

"And go where?" asked Jack. "There are wards around Tamerlane House. And without one of these," he said, holding up his ring, "he's not getting in."

"Well, we can't just leave him here to die in a puff of smoke," said John. "I say we take him back to Tamerlane and then decide what's to be done with him."

"Shame, shame," Uncas said to Defoe. "You could have come with us and been a part of everything. But now you belong to no one at all."

"All I need," Defoe said, "is one of those rings, and I can hide forever in Tamerlane House. And you, little rodent, are going to give it to me!"

Suddenly Defoe pulled a wicked-looking dagger out of his boot and launched himself at Uncas.

None of the other Caretakers was close enough to rush to Uncas's defense—but someone else was.

Aristophanes threw himself against the little badger just

as Defoe thrust out the dagger. Uncas tumbled to the grass unharmed, but the former Caretaker had delivered a terrible wound to the detective—a wound that Aristophanes had returned in kind. Defoe had plunged the dagger deep into Aristophanes's stomach, but he had forgotten that the detective was not unarmed.

The Zen Detective had removed his hat—and for the first time, the Caretakers saw that his horn had not been filed down, as he claimed. It was stout and sharp and protruded from his brow very much like the thorn on a rose stem—and it was lodged deep in Defoe's shoulder.

Defoe pulled back and screamed in pain as the horn stabbing into his shoulder broke off, dissolving into poison.

"I'm sorry," Aristophanes gasped, clutching at his wound. "So, so sorry."

"It's only a flesh wound," Defoe spat. "You'll die long before I do."

"You're wrong, Daniel," Verne said sadly. "Steve has all the time in the world, and you don't."

The Prime Caretaker turned to the others. "You've noticed no one ever touches Aristophanes. That's because he was cursed, thousands of years ago. His skin is toxic enough to make a man seriously ill. But the poison in his horn is potent enough to kill any living thing. Even," he said, looking at Defoe, "those who reside in magic portraits. I'm sorry, Daniel—but you brought this on yourself."

The alarm on Defoe's watch suddenly rang, but was drowned out by his frustrated howl. He pushed away from the Caretakers and fell to the grassy field just as the last rays of the setting sun streamed across the top of Easter Island.

"May God have mercy on you," said John, "if it be right that he do so." And with one last cry of anguish, Daniel Defoe evaporated into the sunlight.

John turned and looked at where the other Caretakers were standing protectively around Aristophanes, who had gone pale from the wound, which was bleeding profusely.

"That's Defoe taken care of," said Hawthorne, "but what's to be done with the unicorn here?"

"We're taking him back to Tamerlane House," Verne said. "I owe him a payment, and I think he's more than earned it."

"But the armor is gone!" the detective exclaimed. "I didn't fulfill—"

"Earned it," Verne said again, looking at Uncas. "Armor or no, you've earned it."

"Let's go," John said, suddenly weary. "There's nothing more to battle over here now."

"No," a voice said from somewhere behind them. "Not here. And not now. But soon, Caretaker."

It was Defoe's shadow speaking—with the voice of someone else they thought was a friend.

The shadow twisted and spun on the ground, assuming first Lovecraft's silhouette, then Dee's, and Defoe's, and finally it coalesced into the shape . . .

. . . of a cat. A Cheshire cat.

"Grimalkin?" John said in disbelief. "Surely you haven't betrayed us too?"

"Not betrayed, boy," the cat answered, licking at its fur as if entirely unconcerned that it had just revealed itself as an enemy agent. "I am simply doing what I must, what the Binding compels me to do."

"The collar," said Verne. "I never realized it, but it must be the collar. Dee has had a spy with us all along."

"There are greater Shadows than I in the House of Tamerlane," Grimalkin said as he began to fade in the twilight, "and they are no less prisoners of fate, for as surely as this ring around my neck binds me, so are they also bound."

"But why reveal yourself to us now?" Blake asked, suspicious. "We would never have known."

"There are Bindings, and there are covenants," Grimalkin replied. "I was bound to serve Dee, but I did not choose it. Long ago I made a covenant, which I am only now able to fulfill by giving you a warning."

"What warning?" said John.

"The girl," said Grimalkin, as he continued to vanish. "The Grail Child. Her shadow is not her own, but an Echthros, and everywhere she has gone, or will go, the Cabal can also go. She carries with her the seed of your destruction. Do with this what you will."

"Farewell, little Caretaker," the Cheshire cat's grin said as it vanished into the rising light. "And fear not. We will meet again—and sooner than you think."

And then the cat was gone.

"All right," John said to the other Caretakers. "Let's get Aristophanes home and tended to. I'm done with all this business today."

It took some time for the Caretakers to sort out who would be responsible for dispersing or attending to what parts of the

Wendigo-Yorick-goat army, so it was late in the evening when John finally pushed open the doors of the great hall at Tamerlane House to collapse into a chair with a tall, tall ale. However, he had one more shock to experience before the day was over.

"We tried to summon you sooner," said Jack. "Someone is here to see you."

The other Caretakers, who were crowded around the table, parted, and John saw who was sitting in the chair opposite Jack.

"Hello, my boy," said Bert. "It's . . . good to see you again."

Joyfully, John rushed forward and embraced his mentor. "Bert! You're back!" he exclaimed, looking around. "Where are the others?"

"It's just him, John," said Jack. "But the others are fine, as far as we know. Bert's just been telling us about it all now."

Bert clapped John on the shoulder, then took Jack by the hand. "I wish Charles were here," he said. "Otherwise, it's just how I had hoped it would happen."

"How you hoped what would happen?" asked John.

Almost as if answering his question, Bert's watch began to ring with a strange chiming—a noise John had never heard it make before.

Bert's eyes grew wide, and he looked up at the other Caretakers, several of whom had moved closer to him. "Oh dear," he stammered. "I've forgotten. I needed one more sitting with Basil. . . ."

His eyelids fluttered, and he grew pale. Twain and Dickens moved around the table and gently helped the Far Traveler sit back down into his chair, where he immediately slumped into the cushions.

"What is it?" John whispered to Verne. "What's happening to him, Jules?"

"Not him," Verne replied quietly. "Well, not just him, I should say." He checked his own watch and nodded as if in confirmation. "That's it, then," he said to the others. "H. G. Wells has died."

The house at 13 Hanover Terrace, in Regent's Park in London, had no runes carved in its doors, nor along its hallways, or in the room where the aged author took his last breath. But even though those attending to the body could not see those who had come to pay their respects, he was not without friends.

"It was a good death," said Baum.

Franklin nodded. "Agreed."

"Do you think he'll join us?" Lewis Carroll asked. "I mean, join us as, you know, a spirit?"

"No, I think not," said Macdonald, looking around the room. "I think he did the things he needed to do, and that was enough."

"He also knows," Franklin added, "that he has a brother elsewhere to continue the work. So there's no need for him to stay the way that . . ."

He couldn't quite bring himself to finish the sentence, nor did he need to. And for a brief moment, the thirteen ghosts gathered around the bedside of H. G. Wells felt a twinge of regret, and the slightest envy.

Then, murmuring words of blessing and personal prayer, the members of the Mystorians took their leave of London.

In the portrait gallery of Tamerlane House, the Caretakers Emeriti gathered closely around the new portrait that had just been hung at a place of honor in the center of the west wall, among

the portraits of the greatest and most distinguished members of
their group.

"That really should have been my spot, you know," grumbled
da Vinci, "instead of over in the corner, next to George Gordon."

"Oh, shut up, Leo," said Irving. "Someone had to be next to him."

"I resent that," said Byron.

"Hush, all of you," said Twain. "He's waking up."

It was a slow rise back to consciousness. The light around him
came up gradually, but when his vision finally cleared, Bert could
see the gathered Caretakers all beaming up at him.

"Let me," Verne said, placing his watch into the frame just out
of Bert's field of vision. "Here," he said, extending his hand as the
frame blazed with light. "Come join us, Far Traveler."

Bert stepped out from the portrait on the wall and into the
midst of his colleagues, who burst into spontaneous applause.

"Basil finished," Bert said, a bit dazed by all the attention. "He
finished my portrait."

He wheeled around to Verne. "What if I'd changed my mind
and decided I wanted to be a tulpa instead?" he said. "I thought
there'd be more time to choose."

"Bert, my old friend, my old sparring partner," Verne said,
clapping a large hand on the smaller man's shoulder. "You chose
long ago, and we both know it. This was the path you preferred.
And so we'd had it prepared for some time."

"Humph," Bert snorted indignantly. "You could have prepared
a tulpa, too, if you'd wanted."

Twain puffed on a cigar and blew a plume of smoke into the air.
"Certainly we could have," he said, "but then if you'd chosen not to
take it, someone would have had to spend a lot of time dispersing

it. They don't just go away on their own—not right away, that is. And it wouldn't have done to have another you wandering around where just anyone's will could step in and mess with his—your—head."

"Ah," Bert said. "So you figured it out. The Cabal did steal the wisp of a shadow of—"

"We'll deal with that later," Verne said quickly, glancing at Jack.

"It also means," Bert said with a heavy sigh, "that I'm restricted to Tamerlane House. Forever."

"Forever may be just long enough," Dickens said with a wink at Twain, "and I think staying at Tamerlane House will be your preference from now on. Turn around."

"What the blazes are you talking about, Charles?" Said Bert. "I'm not—"

"Bert," John said, grasping his mentor by the shoulders. "Trust us. Just turn around."

Still complaining under his breath, the Far Traveler did as he was told—and what he saw left him without words or breath.

There, hanging next to his own portrait, was a full-size portrait of a woman. She was lithe, and simply dressed, and had the innocent beauty of one who had only known trust and love in her world.

Bert reached a trembling hand out to touch the portrait, but he stopped an inch short of it, as if it were a gossamer dream that might disappear if it were disturbed. "Jules," he whispered softly. "How . . . ? How did you . . . ?"

"Using young Asimov's psychohistory, the Mystorians had calculated a high probability of the might-have-been future you and the others traveled to," Verne replied, "and with each passing day, the percentage grew higher. So I took a risk and took your machine into your future. Into *her* future. I knew that someday you would try to return, if you found the means to do so. But my messengers found more and more future timelines were *changing*. And I didn't want to risk that this future would change, and take with it any hope of finding Weena again.

"Because you'd been there, you had already made it a zero point, so I knew I could get there. I was a little more concerned about having the same trouble you did in getting back."

Something clicked together. "Your missing year," Bert said. "The year we thought you'd been lost, right after John, Jack, and Charles became the Caretakers."

"Yes," Verne answered, nodding, "and just as I founded the Mystorians. I didn't want to risk making an anomaly out of myself—being a tulpa, I had no clue what that might do to the timestream—so I pulled back and returned a year after I'd started. But I accomplished what I went there to do."

"I explained to her why you hadn't been able to return, and I got her permission to take this." He pulled a small cube out of his pocket. "I took along one of my optical devices and took a remarkable image of her that I could bring back."

Bert reached out again but still didn't dare touch the picture. "So . . . this is a photo, then?"

"Not at all," Verne said, smiling broadly. "A portrait. One of Basil's best."

"There was a concern," said Twain, "that you wouldn't be able to bring her back, the way you had Aven. But only the one machine had ever gone that far into the future, and having used it once, you had no way of going back—until young Rose and Edmund came to us."

"But Jules could go, using my machine," Bert said. He spun

and looked at Verne, then the other Caretakers, all of whom were beaming. "You were all in on this?"

"Some of us knew," said Dickens, "but you know Jules—he likes to keep his own counsel. This is the first time we've invited a non-Caretaker to have their portrait done, and so this was hung only a few moments before yours was."

"So she's never come out of the portrait?"

Twain stepped forward and gave Bert a push. "No," he said with a grin, "we figured that'd be your job, young fellow. So," he added, "what are you waiting for? Bring her out!"

He paused. "Will it—will she still be . . . my Weena?"

For the first time, Poe spoke. "She will. She chose this, freely, and as with your own portrait, she lives because her aiua is the same. Only the form is different."

"As you are still our Bert, she'll be your Weena," said Twain. "Do it, son."

Trembling, Bert removed his watch from his pocket and placed it into the indentation at the base of the frame. The light from the portrait washed over him as tears streamed down his face.

Almost hesitantly, a hand reached out from the portrait. Bert took it, and gently pulled her forward into the room, before losing his composure and embracing her amid the cheers and claps of his colleagues.

"Hello, my sweet Weena," he said into her hair as they embraced. "Welcome home."

Somewhen, far in a future that may yet come to pass, the Barbarian who had become a Dragon prepared to tell his stories, as he had once done long ago, in another life, another time.

It had taken nearly a year of hard labor to create a new amphitheater where the stories were told, to re-create a stage and carve rows of terraced seating out of the earth and stone that formed this small, natural canyon.

Above, the Dragonships watched, silent sentries and testaments to a long-vanished past—a past from which the storyteller had come, and to which he could never return. Not without a price that was too costly to pay, and risking all the good work that had brought him here, to this place, and this time.

Sometimes, at night, he could feel the waves of time shimmering off the stones of the amphitheater, and in those moments, he felt regret—but as always it passed quickly, for he knew that being in this place was his destiny. It was his great work.

"All the best stories are written in books," he said, smiling at the children clustering around him, "as they once were, and as they will be again."

The grown-ups who came to listen sat to either side of him, as the smaller children clambered on top of them, eager, waiting to hear the story he would tell them tonight.

"It has been one thousand nights, and I have told you one thousand stories," the storyteller said, "and tonight will be the one thousand and first.

"How?" the children asked. "How does it begin, Sir Richard?"

"It begins," he said, "as all the best stories do. Once upon a time . . ."

CHAPTER TWENTY-FOUR
THE ANCIENT OF DAYS

"PRAISE THE LORD and bless Basil's sainted head," said Bert as he took a seat alongside John in the banquet hall. "He was prepared, or I ought to say, Jules was. They had a portrait waiting to be finished in the event of my eventual demise. I was rather hoping it would be later in coming—but their second surprise more than made up for it."

Weena sat alongside Bert and was being patiently cheerful as she tried to take in everything her husband was explaining to her. It would be a very long process, but in the meantime, Bert was happy—and still among the Caretakers. And to John and Jack, that was all that mattered.

Bert had told most of his story when he reappeared at Tamerlane House, and the rest after he died and then reemerged from his portrait. And while the Caretakers were happy to know that Charles, Rose, and Edmund were safe, the rest of what he'd had to say about the city of Dys, and Lord Winter, and the Last Redoubt created more questions than answers.

Almost as much attention was being paid to the newest resident of Tamerlane House: the Zen Detective, who took a seat next to

Uncas, and who, to everyone's surprise, was not only fully recovered from his wound, but was noticeably lighter skinned than when he'd arrived.

"That's not all that's changed," Aristophanes said. He reached across the table and offered Verne his hand—which the Prime Caretaker took and shook, once, then again.

"Uh, isn't he supposed to be poisonous to the touch?" asked Quixote. "No offense, Steve."

"None taken," the detective replied, "and no longer."

"That was the deal we made," said Verne, nodding at another guest who was just joining them at the table—the Messenger Beatrice.

"His horn is still quite deadly," Verne said, "but the Lady Beatrice is just as adept at removing toxins as she is at creating them."

While everyone commented on Bert's account of the future, no one was quite bold enough to address the matter of Lord Winter, which was just fine with Jack. He was less concerned about the ancient future and the possibilities that a shadow-version of himself might become a tyrant and a servant of the Echthroi, than he was about the still-missing boy prince, who Blake confirmed had been Dr. Raven all along.

"Raven—or Telemachus, I guess—is, in fact, the boy Coal," he told the Caretakers. "When I discovered it for certain, I was not in a position to leave Dee's House, and the Cabal were watching me too closely to send a message out. But there is no doubt—he is the missing prince."

"But Dr. Raven was looking for the boy too, wasn't he?" asked Jack. "How is it he kept his true identity so well hidden?"

"He's a true adept, like Rose," said Blake, "maybe even better than she is."

"But why couldn't we find him?"

"He was in a might-have-been in the future," said Verne. "That's the only place where Defoe could have hidden him where we'd have little hope of ever finding him."

"Why?" asked John. "You find things lost in time all of the, ah, time."

"In the past, yes," said Verne, "but the future is a different matter. The past already exists, and thus can be treated as archaeology. What we want is there, it just needs to be looked for patiently enough. But the future is all possibility, and must be treated as psychohistory. And even Isaac's best techniques can do little to find one lost child amid a myriad of possible futures."

"It was Crowley who figured out that the Sphinx could travel not just in time and space, but also between real time and might-have-beens," said Blake. "That's how we knew that it could be used to give a lifeline to Bert and the others when we realized they'd gotten lost in their own might-have-been."

"But shouldn't they have gone to the same time, uh, place, that Bert had?" Jack asked. "Isn't it a zero point?"

"That may be my fault," said Shakespeare. "We think, but can't be certain, that the cavorite platform is what threw them askew. I'm working on it."

"Wait a moment," John said, thinking about everything they'd discussed. "Blake, you said that Defoe couldn't go retrieve Coal because they didn't have the Sphinx—because we had it here. Why couldn't we use it to go after him ourselves once you knew how to track him?"

"Because of how the Sphinx works," Poe said from his alcove above. "The payment she has always required has been a human life—a price Defoe and the Cabal would willingly pay, which we would not."

"But a life wasn't required for Bert and Rose and the others to use in the future," said John.

"Because Rose had the only other thing Azer would accept," said Verne. "The ability for Azer to choose her own redemption, and the promise of being a full Dragon again. Despite the sum of those efforts as they stand, I still believe it was all worth the risks we've taken."

"Worth the . . . ," John began, astonishment choking his words. "But Jules, we lost the armor! To a possible enemy who can now do almost anything!"

"Yes, but you heard the boy," Verne replied. "He's still deciding what to do, and how he'll choose. For all we know, he's already on our side, and working against the Cabal from within."

John blinked a few times, then looked over at Jack, who was sitting with an inscrutable expression on his face. Wordlessly, John rose from his chair and walked to the head of the table, where he delivered a devastating right cross directly to Jules Verne's jaw.

The Prime Caretaker went sprawling across the floor as blood splattered across his shirt and coat. He rolled over, his eyes flashing with anger, preparing to lash out over the unfair blow. . . .

And then he realized that not a one of the Caretakers Emeriti had risen to his defense. John stood next to his chair, panting with anger and effort, and Jack sat where he was, with a slightly stunned look. But all the other Caretakers had remained in their seats, and only a few even dared to meet his eyes.

"Well," Verne said heavily as he pulled himself to his feet and straightened his waistcoat, "I see that your opinion of me is in the majority, young John."

"No more secrets, Jules," John said, his voice firm and steady. "The warning about the Echthroi that was given to Rose last year, when she was told to seek out the Dragon's apprentice, the whole key to the restoration of the Archipelago—it's all there in that one simple phrase. *No more secrets.* And keeping secrets seems to have been all that you've done, since even before we met.

"Even nearly losing our friends to that might-have-been," John continued. "You even planned for *that*, didn't you?"

"Now, John," Twain started to say, "how could he possibly—"

"If he didn't know," said John, "then why did he have Quixote and Uncas steal the Sphinx a *year* ago, when we were in eighteenth-century London?"

"I know he hasn't always planned for the big picture," Bert said, trying to steer the discussion into more pleasant waters, "or else he'd have made other plans for Richard Burton instead of letting him defect to the ICS."

"It's too bad you didn't think of that earlier in your career as Prime Caretaker," John said to Verne. "Burton would have made an excellent candidate for a new Mystorian."

Jack chuckled at this, as did one or two of the Caretakers Emeriti—but Verne didn't even smile, or acknowledge the comment except to keep a level gaze at John. At first John thought Verne simply misunderstood what he'd suggested—and then he realized, Verne did understand. Far too clearly.

John rose slowly from his seat. "How long?" he asked, his voice low and vibrant with restrained anger. "How long has Burton been working for you, Jules?"

At this, several of the other Caretakers gasped in dismay, and Bert simply put his head in his hands. Chaucer, Spenser, and Cervantes clucked disapprovingly, while da Vinci gave a small smile of smug satisfaction. Poe, for his part, simply continued to observe impassively from above.

"Since just after the Dyson incident," Verne said, still looking steadily at John.

"Chaos," John muttered, shaking his head. "It's all chaos, Jules."

"Entropy is life," said Poe. "Chaos is life. Perfect order is stagnation, is death. Only in disorder is there the possibility of change."

"So what do we do now?" John asked. "Of what are we still Caretakers?"

"We continue the work that we are doing," said Verne. "We monitor the events of the world and ensure that Dee and his cohorts don't manage to cause any trouble. We keep our eyes and ears open for young Telemachus, so that when the time comes, we might help him choose our side instead of theirs. We continue to develop the new mandate of the Imperial Cartological Society to seek out new apprentice Caretakers to further the spread of knowledge about the Archipelago with those who would help us protect it. And . . ."

"And," said Twain, "we wait."

"Yes," Verne said, nodding. "We wait. And see if Rose manages to do the task she has been set to do since the moment she was born."

"And how long do we wait?" asked John. The frustration he felt was evident in his voice, if not his expression, which remained steadfast and calm. "Do we wait a year? Five? Ten? Twenty? How long a time do we wait for some sign of them before we make some sort of effort to find them and help them?"

"Our part in Rose's quest is done . . . at least for now," Verne added quickly. "They will either find the Architect and the secret of the keep, or they will not. It's now entirely out of our hands."

"Well," John said, "I hope the angels are watching, and send them whatever help they need."

"I'll drink to that," Shakespeare said, lifting his glass and winking at Jack. "I was just thinking the exact same thing."

Rose opened her eyes to find she was no longer in the white space of Platonia. Instead she was standing on a gentle slope that overlooked a magnificent city.

Gilgamesh had remembered the details of the First City far better than he believed he had, and Edmund had transcribed them as an illustration on the parchment with remarkable fidelity.

There, in the near distance, was the City of Jade. It would have been impossible to mistake in any landscape, but here, in this time, it was all-dominating.

"By Jove," Charles said, hugging Edmund. "Well done, my boy. Well done!"

"Take a deep breath, breathe it in," Rose said. "That's the air of a new world, a world that is whole and unbroken. A world," she added with a note of relief, "that knows nothing of Shadows."

"It doesn't really feel any different . . . ," Edmund began to say, but then, as he spoke, he realized that wasn't quite true. It was different, in the same way that the Night Land of Dys in the ancient future was different from 1946.

Just ahead of them was a paved footpath. A boy was approaching, carrying a large, flat marble tablet. He looked like a normal child, except for two things: The expression on his face was one of someone far older than he appeared, and he bore markings on his forehead identical to those of the Winter Dragons.

Involuntarily, Edmund took a step back. "More Lloigor?" he said, swallowing hard. "Are we back in the Night Land?"

Charles shook his head. "Look around," he said, sweeping about with his hands. "There is nothing of the Echthroi here. No darkness that isn't natural, and no chains cover the sky. And the boy may appear strange, but he's not a Lloigor. I'd stake my right arm on it."

The boy stopped when he saw the companions looking at him. He scrutinized them, puzzled. "You really are unusual creatures, aren't you?" he said with unabashed curiosity. "You must be in the Book—but I can't seem to remember you. What was it you were called again?"

"I'm Rose, and this is Edmund," she said, gesturing at the others, "and this is Charles."

"I am Nix," the boy replied, frowning. "You should know me by my countenance."

Rose laughed. "By my body and blood," she said, hands on her hips. "I don't think I've ever seen such a mirthless child as you. Not in my whole long life. If she were here, Laura Glue would give you *such* a beating."

"I am not a 'child,'" said Nix, "I am the second assistant Maker of the thirty-fifth Guild of Makers, of the nineteenth Host of Angels of the City of Jade." He punctuated the statement with a huff. "And now, having conversed with you, I am thusly behind schedule, and with little regret, I must repair."

"Pardon me," Edmund said pensively. "But did you say you were an *angel?*"

"Of course I am an angel," Nix said, so irritated he spat as he spoke. "How did you get Named if you aren't even complete enough to know that?"

It was only then that Nix really noticed Charles—in particular, his height.

"Oh!" the angel said. "I beg forgiveness. I did not realize . . ." His eyes narrowed, and he looked Charles over from top to bottom, seeming to note the pale color of his skin and his burgundy hair as much as his features. "You carry no sigil," he said at length. "Are you Nephilim?"

Charles had been observing the angel's reactions and sensed the loaded nature of this question. "No," he said quickly. "Seraphim."

Nix visibly relaxed. "Ah," he said, consulting his tablet. "I apologize. There are many powers and principalities whom I do not know arriving for the summit."

"Yes, the summit," Charles said. "Can you tell us where it is? We've only just arrived and have not yet gotten our bearings."

Again Nix looked at them suspiciously, as if there were something amiss. But he couldn't quite put his finger on it, and still, they were in the company of a Seraphim. . . .

For emphasis on Charles's request, Rose reached into her bag and withdrew the hilt of Caliburn, just enough to show that she carried a weapon. Nix nearly dropped the tablet.

"I am already late," the angel said, glancing down at whatever list was scrolling across the stone tablet, "and I would be later still were I to tarry any longer with you. But I can tell you how to find someone who can. He's likely got nothing better to do."

"That should do nicely," Charles said. "Thank you. Who is he?"

"He is a minor Namer from a minor guild," Nix continued as he began to immerse himself in his tablet once more, "but as I said, he is more likely to be able to help you than I. He is the eldest of us all, save for perhaps one or two of the original masters of the upper guilds, and therefore quite useless."

"And is he an angel as well?" asked Edmund.

Nix snorted his disdain but didn't bother even turning around to answer the question. "Of course he is," the angel called back over his shoulder. "What kind of question is that for minions of a Seraphim? There are none here in the City of Jade save for the Creators and the Created, and even those who add little value to the work may still contribute. You will find him in the lower rooms of the tower just ahead."

"How will we know him?" Rose called out.

"Ask for him," Nix answered as he disappeared over the crest of the hill. "His name . . .

". . . is Samaranth."

"The rest of the household is sleeping, I take it?" John said to Jack as he entered the gallery at Tamerlane House and took a seat next to his colleague.

"Yes," Jack said, offering his friend a cup of Earl Grey. "It's been a very, very long season, but it's an old habit, I'm afraid, this working till the wee hours. I've just been working on some notes for integrating more of the Little Whatsit into the curriculum for the ICS."

"That was an inspired choice," John said, "renaming it as the International Cartological Society."

"All Warnie's idea," said Jack. "He never really approved of it being called 'Imperial.'"

The Caretaker lowered his head and sipped at his tea. "They haven't failed, you know," he said softly. "It isn't over, John."

"How?" John murmured. "How do we know they haven't failed? We've had no word at all, and it's been months!"

Jack gripped his friend's arm in reassurance. "Because," he said steadily, "we are still here. The world continues to turn. And the Echthroi have not defeated us."

"Will it all be worth it, in the end?" John asked. "All this effort, and all that we've had to endure?"

"It's worth protecting the stories," Jack said simply, "when the stories are all we have left to protect."

"I miss him," John said suddenly. "I miss Charles."

"So do I."

"Ah, well," John said, rising. "It's getting late. Thank you for the tea."

"Gentlemen," a voice said from the far end of the gallery. "Before you retire for the evening, may we show you something?"

The speaker stepped forward into the light. It was William Shakespeare. Laura Glue and the badger Fred were with him. "With your permission." He said mildly, "I think we should move this discussion outside. I may have discovered a way to help our friends."

John and Jack followed the trio outside Tamerlane House, to see what it was that Shakespeare had built.

"This hasn't exactly been authorized," Shakespeare explained, "so we've been working on it on the sly, just Laura Glue, Fred, and

I. We wanted to make certain it would function before we showed anyone, and you two gents are the first."

The group traipsed across a rickety, fragile-looking bridge that had been hastily constructed to make Shakespeare's latest creation, which he called the Zanzibar Gate, easier to reach. To build it, he had commandeered one of the smaller border islands to the west of the main island where the house stood, and had constructed it there, just past where the wooden bridge ended.

The Zanzibar Gate was shaped like a Mayan pyramid and was about twenty feet high and half again as wide, with a fifteen-foot aperture in the center. It stood at one end of the small island, looming like an old monolith that had existed for ages—giving that impression in part because of the ancient stone of which it was constructed. There were symbols carved into the settings at several points along its radius, and on the right, a pedestal lined with colored crystals that could be used to activate the gate.

"It is, I have reason to believe, truly representative of the best of both worlds," Shakespeare said, beaming. "The technology I have integrated into it will allow us to travel into the future, and then it can be used in the same way as the keep to travel into the past. The design is, if I do say so myself, flawless."

Laura Glue suppressed a giggle, remembering how difficult it had been to get him to admit that he had any kind of proficiency at all, much less claim credit for his work. And now the opposite was true—he was good at what he did. And more, he reveled in it.

"I don't believe it!" John said, marveling. "You've repurposed the stone from the actual keep! Brilliant!"

"The doors are gone, as Sir Richard had noted, as is the original bracing," Shakespeare explained, "but the bracing was merely for support, and the doors were to create focal points. The power itself is located in the stones."

"How did you get these?" Jack said in amazement as he examined the flame-scorched stones of the gate. "When we set fire to the second keep, I assumed the remains were left in Abaton. And after the Archipelago fell . . ."

"Abaton isn't in the Archipelago," said Fred. "It exists in one of the Soft Places, which abut this dimension. We had access to them the entire time—but, like you, we believed the power was in the doors. It wasn't. Only Will figured that out."

"So the trip into the deep past you've proposed is possible?" asked Jack.

"Yes, well," Shakespeare said hesitantly. "In theory. There's only one slight glitch to the gate I haven't yet been able to overcome."

"Uh-oh," John said, frowning. "Here it comes."

"It operates on the same principle as the doors within the original keep," Shakespeare said with obvious melancholy. "Through the work I had been doing with Rose and Edmund, we can basically calibrate it, and point it at the time and place we need to go. . . . But we still can't activate it, not without a power source—and the keep operated on a very . . . ah, *unique* source of power."

"How unique?" asked John.

"The Dragons," Shakespeare said. "Without a Dragon on one side or the other, there's no way to activate the portal. The stones simply won't work. And we've tried everything we can think of—but in truth, we really just need a Dragon. And unfortunately for us, there are no Dragons left."

EPILOGUE

SOMEWHERE BEYOND ELSEWHERE *and Elsewhen, the last of the Dragonships waited.*

It had carried out the duties for which it had been created, including this, the last voyage into the Archipelago of Dreams. It had been many years since its creation, and it had grown accustomed to waiting, and serving. This was its purpose, its function.

Those who had sailed the ship here to what was once a great island had not returned. So the ship waited on the long, lonely expanse of sand where it had landed, but no one came.

Then there was an explosion of darkness at the center of the island, followed by a spreading shadow that covered land and seas alike. The island was slowly consumed, but still, no one came to take the ship away, to find safer waters or another sheltering harbor. The ship vibrated with restless energy, anxious for action, but it held its place and waited. Then, finally, when the darkness had nearly devoured the island and rose up to blot out the sun itself, the Dragonship decided to act.

Gradually, almost painfully, it slid itself back into the waters from where the beach had begun to make a claim on the ship. Farther down, another of the ship's siblings had not been as fortunate—but then, that ship no longer had a living Dragon on its prow.

Somewhere within, the Dragonship felt a pang of shame and regret, then steeled itself against the distraction of the emotions to better focus on the task at hand as it turned from the island and headed for more open waters. The darkness sweeping across the horizon behind it was almost as foreboding as the darkness ahead.

The Frontier was a living storm front, and the very air reverberated with the constant sound of thunder. From ocean to the limits of the sky, lightning flashed and exploded with violent energies, and the sea itself rose up into crushing waves that battered the ship as it crossed the threshold.

The journey across the expanse of the Frontier seemed to take an eternity. In reality, it was only a thousand years. In times past, the transition was between worlds, from the Summer Country to the Archipelago of Dreams, and back again. But the Archipelago was no more, having been swallowed up by an evil from outside space and time—and what was hours or days on one side was centuries on the other. The ship was crossing the boundary between entropy and order, and it was not an easy passage.

The stresses of the transition nearly ripped the ship apart—stresses that it bore because it was built by a Maker; and because it had will. Will to endure. Will to return. Will, because something greater had reached across the vast distances and spread of years and called to the Dragon within—and it was a call it could not deny, from someone it could not abandon.

Someone to whom the Dragon had given its heart.

Someone to whom the Dragonship it had become was determined to return.

Someone who needed the help that only it could provide. And so it would not brook failure in this—it would, somehow, cross the uncrossable barrier.

And then, it was through.

The ship slid roughly onto another beach, on an island that was of both the Archipelago and the Summer Country. In the distance were the familiar towers and minarets of the place that was its home—the one place the ship had sought to find.

The last of the Dragonships had returned to Tamerlane House at last.

The Black Dragon had come home.

Author's Note

This is not the book I intended to write.

In point of fact, it isn't even the book I *wrote*—not at first. Between the initial draft of a book and the final revision there are often a lot of changes made, but I don't think I've revised anything as dramatically as I did between the first two passes of *The Dragons of Winter*.

There are challenges that are unique to writing series fiction, the biggest of which (for me) is making sure that each book is a standalone read while keeping the momentum of the overarching storylines going. It was difficult with Book Four, harder with Book Five, and darn near impossible to do with Book Six. I think the realization that the final volume was quickly approaching only added to the difficulty. I'd known for a few years now that Book Seven would be the conclusion of the story I began with *Here, There Be Dragons*, and so it was tempting to leave a lot of threads unresolved in Book Six. By now readers have become accustomed to my unusual mix of literature, history, mythology, and pop culture, and fully expect that the details (of which there are many) really matter, that story bits planted in one volume may not fully spring into bloom until a later book. But that wasn't the reason for the change.

I rewrote the book in its entirety to make certain that it fulfilled the primary goals—being a satisfying read while advancing the series storyline—while also augmenting the one thing I felt was lacking in the first go: *hope*.

I rewrote the entire book in order to point everything toward these final pages of the epilogue, to those final lines, to the *last* line. Because to me, that last line is what ties together the entire series. It is what matters most to me, in both fiction and in waking life— the knowledge that when it seems everything is on the verge of utter disaster, someone will still step forward, extend a hand, and say, "Don't sweat it. I've got this," and be believed, and in doing so restore hope where before there was none.

I love the idea of someone being capable of saving the day— that's part of what makes all heroic fiction so thrilling, I think. I've tried to instill that in my own work, and I knew that I was going to be bringing everything together in the final volume in a (hopefully) exciting and satisfying way. But while this book had all of the necessary dramatic elements, and all of the really fun things I enjoy writing, it was lacking in hope. And that, to me, is too necessary an ingredient to exclude. The first draft, as it stood, was already a good book—but I needed what I'd written to be questioned aloud. And once that was done by my editors, the path was absolutely clear to me.

The story was a huge amount of fun to write. I'd been waiting a while to use some of the new characters, like Aristophanes; the same goes for the collected Mystorians. Uncas and Quixote all but write themselves; young Telemachus opens up the backstory to include some of my other works; and the chance to include battle goats made me a hero to my children. But all of that whimsy and spectacle and drama was to get to the last pages of doom and despair, so that I could end with the epilogue that I wrote.

The conclusion is coming, but no story—not even that of John, Jack, and Charles—is ever truly over (this is a series involving lots of time travel, after all) and there is one more chapter to go for the most unlikely hero of them all, who chose redemption, and in doing so, restored hope. I can't ask any more of a character, or a book.

James A. Owen
Silvertown, USA

THE FIRST
DRAGON

PROLOGUE

STORIES HAVE EXISTED *since the beginning of the world, and human history itself consists of little more than the stories that survived. All stories are true—but some of them just never happened.*

The story of the first murder is one that is both true, and real.

There is, however, a secret part of the story about the first murder that almost no one knows, because there were only two witnesses, and one of them was bound not to speak what he knew. The other, of course, was dead. And the world where dead men speak had not yet come into existence, not really—because it was the murder itself that created it.

The first Maker was their mother, and the first Namer, their father. They were brothers, twins, although as in the way of all things, one was called the elder, and the other, the younger. It was their parents who called them such, and so they did not question it. It was only after they had grown to manhood that they were given their secret names and were told what their true purpose in the world was to be. With purpose came callings, the first of their kind in the world, and the most crucial.

One was the Imago, meant to be the protector of the world; the other, the Archimago, meant to be the bringer of destruction. One was the agent of order; the other, of chaos. Locked in a perpetual struggle, the brothers were meant to create balance in the world, but that was not what came to pass.

The elder son raised up a stone and struck the younger son a blow across the head, killing him. Thus did Cain murder Abel, in the first story that gave meaning to the power of choice in the world.

His family cast Cain out, and marked him, that the other peoples of the world would know him for what he was. Thus, he chose to become someone else and clothed himself in the stories of humanity so that he could walk among them unseen, unknown.

In the centuries that followed, the elder son wandered the world, taking a thousand names and living a thousand lives before he found his purpose again. He found it in the last life he created for himself, as a storyteller, who wrote of mystery, and murder, and solving unsolvable riddles, and the mechanics of creation itself.

In time, he tired of simply telling stories, and once more inserted himself into the affairs of two worlds. He built a house in a distant corner of the Archipelago and named it for one of his creations. There, he gathered together all those of his brotherhood who would help him to defend both the Archipelago of Dreams and the Summer Country against the darkness that was coming.

He shared many secrets with those who gathered around him, but of himself he shared very little—especially the greatest secret of them all.

Only a few personages still walking the earth knew that the first Imago and Archimago had been brothers, but what none of them knew was which one had been murdered.

One was killed; the other survived. Only he knew which he was: the agent of chaos, or the agent of order; and he had been bound not to tell. Not until the last battle between Darkness and Light, when all things would stand revealed and all allegiances declared.

On that day he would speak their secret names, and in doing so give voice to his brother from the grave, the way so many other dead men had made their voices heard there within the bounds of Tamerlane House.

On that day he would finally discover if the choice he'd made, oh so long ago, would be responsible for saving the world, or destroying it.

And on that day the elder son, also called Cain, also called Nimrod, also called Prospero, also called Poe, would discover if finally, he could lay down his burden, and rest.

PART ONE

THE RETURN OF THE
BLACK DRAGON

CHAPTER ONE
ANCIENT PROMISES

—✴—

"I MISS SAMARANTH," the young Valkyrie Laura Glue said as she descended the ladder, arms laden with ancient books and scrolls. "In fact, I miss all the Dragons. They may not have always been there when you wanted them . . ."

"But they were always there when you needed them," the Caretaker named Jack said, finishing the expression all of them had said at one time or another in recent weeks.

"That's only because," Harry Houdini said, raising his finger to emphasize his point, "none of them ever threatened to roast and *eat* any of you."

Jack's colleague John, the former Caveo Principia and current Prime Caretaker, chuckled and clapped the magician on the arm. "You did ask for it, Ehrich," he said, using Houdini's given name. "Both you and Arthur. You should have known better than to step on the Dragon's tail, even metaphorically."

"I'm sure Conan Doyle did know better," said Jack, "but he was swayed by . . . *Other* influences."

"I resent that," said Houdini.

"I meant Burton," Jack said, feigning innocence. "Perhaps your conscience heard differently."

He took the bundle of documents from Laura Glue and handed them to John, who winked at him, not necessarily out of agreement, but just to give Houdini a tweak. The former members of the Imperial Cartological Society might have rejoined the Caretakers, but some of the old divisions were still present in every conversation. "These are pre–Iron Age," John remarked as he peered more closely at the topmost parchments. "They're in surprisingly good shape."

"Everything here is," Jack agreed. "Unfortunately, we're still no closer to finding anything useful."

"We must persevere," John replied. "If there is anything that can give us a clue as to how to find our friends, it will be here."

The Repository of Tamerlane House was located in the center-most room, accessible only by the master of the house, who rarely involved himself directly in the affairs of the other Caretakers, and by the Prime Caretaker, who until very recently had been Jules Verne.

There were several libraries within the walls of Tamerlane, including one that contained all the unwritten books of the world, but the Repository was different: It held the books that were the most rare, the most sacred, to the Caretakers and all those who came before who tried to make better worlds out of the ones they had been given. The Histories, written by the Caretakers during each of their tenures, were there, as were the Prophecies, which were future histories that had been compiled primarily by Verne and his immediate protégé Bert, also known as H. G. Wells, the Caretaker who had chosen John, Jack, and their friend Charles to become Caretakers themselves.

There was also the *Telos Biblos*, the Last Book, which was both history and prophecy. It contained the names of all the Dragons, which the Caretakers' enemies had used to capture their shadows and compel them to service—which led to the destruction of all the Dragons save for the oldest one. Unfortunately, since the incident that severed the connections between the Archipelago and the Summer Country, time itself had become more and more erratic. Might-have-beens and alternate histories were taking the place of pasts and futures that previously, Verne had relied on as being set in stone. But that stone, it seemed, was fluid, changeable; and so the Last Book was no more helpful to them than the books in the last case: the *Imaginarium Geographicas* of other worlds yet to be explored.

Jack looked wistfully at the case with the other *Geographicas* and chuckled ruefully when John smiled and shook his head.

"I understand, old friend," John said, not for the first time. "I want to explore them too, but our first responsibility must be to the restoration of the lands from the *Geographica* we're already Caretakers of."

"I'm just feeling the weight of it all, John," his friend replied. "No one is going to suddenly appear with a magic solution to fix everything, are they?"

"We have only ourselves to rely on, I'm afraid," John said with a heavy sigh. "We can only hope that we will prove to be a fraction as effective at keeping the evils of the world at bay as the Dragons were."

In the centuries since the *Imaginarium Geographica* was created, it had been entrusted to many Caretakers for safekeeping—all of whom had the same reaction to the legend inscribed on the maps.

It read, *Here, there be Dragons*, and to a man, every Caretaker had at first assumed this was a warning. In time, they came to learn it was not.

Here, there be Dragons was meant to reassure the Caretakers and all those living in the lands depicted on the maps that there would always be someone watching over them; someone older, wiser, and stronger than any forces who might seek to destroy the world of the Archipelago of Dreams. Since the creation of the Archipelago, when it was separated from the world called the Summer Country, there had always been a Dragon—at least one—standing watch.

That was before the coming of the Winter King, who sought to rule the Archipelago, and the Caretakers of prophecy from the Last Book, three young scholars from Oxford, who defeated him and saved both worlds. But the price was high—before the Winter King was defeated, the Keep of Time, which connected the two worlds, was set on fire and gradually destroyed, severing the connection.

Time in the Archipelago was severed from the Caretakers' base at Tamerlane House in the Nameless Isles, as well as the rest of the world, and in the process, had begun to speed up. Thousands of years passed in the Archipelago, and it was eventually taken over completely by the Caretakers' great enemy: the eternal Shadows known as Echthroi, and their servants, the Lloigor.

The Nameless Isles were spared the same fate only because of a temporal and interdimensional bridge built by William Shakespeare that connected Tamerlane House to the Kilns, Jack's home in Oxford.

With the destruction of the keep, the Caretakers also lost the ability to travel in time—something that their adversaries, led by the renegade Caretaker Dr. John Dee, seemed to have a greater facility for. Only the Grail Child, Rose Dyson, and the new Cartographer, Edmund McGee, working together to create chronal maps that could open into any point in time, could give the Caretakers any hope of repairing the damage that had been done and restoring what once was in the Archipelago.

Somehow, the Keep of Time had to be rebuilt. And the only way to do that was to find the Architect—and no one in history seemed to know his identity, or when the keep had been built to begin with.

Rose and Edmund, along with the tulpa Caretaker Charles, his mentor Bert, the clockwork owl from Alexandria named Archimedes, and the once leader of the Imperial Cartological Society, Sir Richard Burton, were dispatched into Deep Time to try to find the Architect—and the mission was a disaster.

Burton was trapped in the far future, after narrowly defeating an Echthros-possessed alternate version of their friend Jack; Archimedes was nearly destroyed; and Rose's sword, Caliburn, was irreparably broken. Only the intervention of a mysterious, near-omnipotent old man in a white, timeless space called Platonia saved the other companions. Bert was returned to Tamerlane, just in time to die and become a portrait in Basil Hallward's gallery; and Rose, Charles, and Edmund were sent more deeply into the past, to a city that might have been Atlantis.

Since Bert's reappearance and the discovery of an engraving of the city that Edmund had left inside a Sphinx for the Caretakers to find, nearly two months had passed, with no sign of the companions, and no further word of where, or when, they were.

Shakespeare, who had a gift for constructing chronal devices, had fashioned a pyramid he called the Zanzibar Gate out of the fallen stones of the keep, in order to use it to go after the missing companions. Unfortunately, it had to be powered by the presence of a living Dragon—and there were no Dragons left. Even the great old Dragon Samaranth had vanished when the Archipelago was lost—so the Caretakers couldn't even seek him out for advice, much less ask him to go through the gate. That left everything at a standstill for weeks—and when Rose, Edmund, and Charles failed to reappear, John, Jack, Laura Glue, Houdini, and some of the others at Tamerlane House began searching for other options. But even the fabled Repository of Tamerlane House had given them nothing.

"It seems there are times when only a Dragon will do," Houdini said, slamming shut another ancient tome. "There simply isn't any substitute."

"Do you need a hand with those?" Jack asked, rising from his chair as Laura Glue again descended a ladder carrying a precariously arranged assortment of boxes.

"It's all right," Laura Glue said as she carefully balanced the stack on the table. "I got this."

"Actually," Jack said, "the proper way to say that would be 'I've got this.' The way you say it makes you sound . . ."

"Uneducated? Like a wildling, maybe?" Laura Glue replied.

Jack frowned. "I was going to say, it makes you sound less intelligent than you actually are."

Laura Glue frowned back. "'Ceptin'," she said, deliberately

using Lost Boy slang, "you knows I be intelligent as all that, and I knows I be intelligent as all that, so what be the problem, neh?"

"The problem," Jack said, now in full professor mode, "is that no one else who heard you speak that way would know how intelligent you really are."

She shrugged and smiled at the Caretaker. "Why should I care what anyone else thinks? I know, and that's enough."

"She has you there, Jack," John said, clapping him on the back. "Best just shut up now and help her move the boxes."

"Nah," Laura Glue said, waving one hand at them as she hefted another stack of boxes with her other arm. "Like I said—I got this."

"An' I gots some munchies," the badger Caretaker Fred announced as he strolled into the room, carrying a large basket filled with fruit. "It's midafternoon, and you missed lunch, so I thought I'd better bring something up."

"Thank you, Fred," Jack said as he selected a bunch of grapes and sat down. "Anticipating a need is the mark of an excellent Caretaker."

"Don't go quoting Jules, now," said John. "Especially regarding anticipating our needs."

"That's not entirely fair, is it?" Houdini asked as he examined some pears a moment before selecting a peach. "He hardly could have anticipated a crisis like this one."

"He seems to have anticipated every other kind of crisis," John grumbled, "including an entire alternate timeline set into motion by Hugo Dyson closing a door at the wrong time, which, as I recall, was partially *your* fault. So why didn't he anticipate this? Where's the backup plan for the backup plan?"

Jack stood and sidled around one of the tables to move another stack of scrolls and parchments, which he dropped onto the floor next to John's chair. "Perhaps we have gotten too accustomed to his being our deus ex machina," he said, sitting heavily in the wingback chair next to Laura Glue. "We count on his always having the answers, because before we knew how many strings he was pulling, he always seemed to have all the answers. And then, even after we found out just how many events he was manipulating, we still allowed it because it always seemed to work out. It was only after something finally went terribly wrong that you took matters into your own hands and stepped into the role yourself."

John scowled. "You are referring to the role of Prime Caretaker, I hope," he said with a hint of irritation, "and not Jules's predilection for meddling with time."

"What's the difference?" Laura Glue asked as she selected an apple from Fred's basket and bit into it. "Isn't that precisely what the job be, neh?"

"That's the problem in a nutshell," John said with a sigh. "It really is, but it *shouldn't* be."

At that moment, Nathaniel Hawthorne stuck his head around the corner. Before he could speak a word, he exploded with a violent sneeze, then another, and another.

"You would think," he said as Fred handed him a handkerchief to blow his nose, "that Basil Hallward could have painted some version of my portrait that left out my allergy to dust."

Jack chuckled. "That's not how it works," he said blithely, referring to their resident artist's technique for preserving life by painting portraits of Caretakers who were about to end their natural life spans. "As you were in life, so you remain in Tamerlane House."

"That's slender consolation sometimes, Jack," Hawthorne grumbled as he wiped his nose. "You'll understand when you eventually join us."

Jack hesitated. "I . . . haven't yet decided," he finally said. "I know I don't want to become a tulpa like Charles did when he passed, but I'm not certain that I want to be a portrait, either."

"It's not so bad—as long as you don't go on vacation for longer than seven days," Hawthorne said, referring to the one limitation of portrait-extended life: They could only live as long as they were never away from Tamerlane House for more than a week—a lesson the Caretakers learned all too well when both their mentor, Professor Sigurdsson, and their once-ally-turned-enemy Daniel Defoe perished after being gone for too long.

"Time enough to decide that later," said Jack. "Hopefully decades. Was there something you needed, Nate?"

Hawthorne hooked his thumb over his shoulder. "There's some kind of commotion down at one of the beaches. I've dispatched Jason's sons to go down there just in case it's trouble, and I'm going to go have a look myself. I just thought the, ah, Prime Caretaker . . ." He paused, looking at John. "I thought you ought to know."

John waved his hand. "You're head of security," he said. "I trust in that. Let me know what you find, though."

Hawthorne winked and disappeared.

"Mebbe I should go too," said Fred, "seein' as I'm one of th' actual Caretakers now."

"Actually, we could use your help here," said Jack. "There are some cubbyholes in and around the bookshelves that are too small for us to reach, and, not to put too fine a point on it . . ."

"I know, I know," Fred said with mock annoyance. "You need a badger to bail out your backsides—*again.*"

"I'll never begrudge the help of a badger," John said with honest appreciation, "especially considering that you're the closest thing to a Dragon we have left."

"That may not be entirely correct," said a breathless Hawthorne, who reentered the room in such a rush that he nearly skidded into a bookcase. "Come quickly, everyone! You must see what we've found on the South Beach."

Hawthorne's alert roused everyone at Tamerlane House, and so almost every Caretaker, Messenger, Mystorian, and creature arrived on the beach at the same time and saw the same impossible sight:

There, half out of the water and leaning slightly where it rested on the sand, was the *Black Dragon*.

CHAPTER TWO
THE PRODIGAL DRAGON

THE INITIAL SURPRISE that was felt by all the residents of Tamerlane House at finding the long-missing *Black Dragon* on the South Beach was quickly eclipsed by their arguing about what it meant, and more, what was to be done next.

Shakespeare, for his part, was thrilled by the arrival of the *Black Dragon*. But several of the Caretakers Emeriti, led by da Vinci, were convinced it was some sort of Echthroi trick—a Dragonship version of the Trojan Horse—and advocated burning it on the spot.

The younger Caretakers, led by John and Jack, suggested it was merely synchronicity that a Dragonship had turned up at just that point in time that a Dragon was needed, and protested that burning it would destroy their only chance of powering Shakespeare's Zanzibar Gate.

The rest were basically skirting one side or the other without taking a definitive stance, all of which meant that there was nothing but chaotic bickering right up to the point that Harry Houdini fired the cannon and silenced them all.

"Hell's bells," he said as he moved around the still-smoking cannon, which sat along one of the battlements. "I thought we kept this loaded in case of an attack from the Echthroi, but it seems it's just as useful in shutting up Caretakers."

"Now, see here," Hawthorne started.

"You're all forgetting," Houdini went on, ignoring Hawthorne, "that the Archipelago isn't on Chronos time anymore. So this ship didn't just leave a year ago to make its way here. It's been sailing for . . ." He looked at Twain. "I can't do math."

"Oh, uh," said Dumas, who was good with numbers. "About a . . . um, a thousand years, give or take."

"A thousand years," Houdini repeated, glaring at da Vinci. "So we know there's still a living Dragon at its heart. And as far as using it," he added, looking at John, "that isn't our choice. It's his. And we all know who the *Black Dragon* once was—so what he'll choose to do is anybody's guess."

"He'll do it," said John.

"You sound pretty confident of that," said Dumas.

"I am," said John, "because he's already sacrificed himself once for his daughter, and I have no doubt he'll do it again."

"Why?" asked Houdini.

"Because," said John, "I'm a father too, and it's what I would do."

"There's just one problem," said Shakespeare. "It's a Dragon*ship*, not a Dragon. I don't know if that will work to activate the portal. It may be that the only use for it is *as* a ship."

"It's all well and good," Dumas said, giving the *Black Dragon* a cursory glance, "but of what use is a Dragonship with no Archipelago to cross over to?"

"More to the point," said John, "if we can't separate the Dragon from the ship, how can we power the gate?"

"Do you really need to, though?" asked Jack. "The bridge didn't need anything but a Dragon's eyes to work."

"I was hoping to engineer the gate to operate on the same principle as the bridge," said Shakespeare, "but that's, it would seem, apples and oranges."

"I think I understand," said John. "The Dragon eyes were sufficient enough talismans to permit us to cross between worlds . . .'"

"But to traverse time, to activate the mechanism, requires a *living* Dragon," Shakespeare finished. "It's a conundrum, to be sure. That's why this new development is so thrilling—the *Black Dragon* still has within it a living, breathing Dragon . . . and that may be sufficient to activate the Zanzibar Gate."

"In other words," Jack said, grinning from ear to ear, "the Caretakers are back in the game."

"Bangarang!" said Fred.

Under Shakespeare's direction, Houdini and John piloted the *Black Dragon* off the beach and around to the small island where the Zanzibar Gate had been constructed. But proximity was not enough.

"It has to go through the gate," Shakespeare said glumly. "The Dragon has to go through first, or else it can't be activated properly." He turned to Jules Verne, who had typically taken charge of situations like the discovery of the ship—but who had instead chosen to stand back in deference to John. "Is there any way to . . . separate the Dragon from the ship? To perhaps remove the masthead?"

Verne glanced at John and Twain, then shook his head. "No method that I know of," he answered. "As far as I know, no one's ever tried. No one except Ordo Maas knew the process for making a Dragonship—and when the Archipelago was lost, we lost him as well."

"That's not entirely true," offered John. "He admitted that the *Black Dragon* wasn't one of his, remember? Someone else must know the secret, because someone had to *create* the *Black Dragon*."

Verne looked at John, eyes narrowed. "Yes," he said. "You might have something at that." He turned and tilted his head at Bert. "Someone one of us may have already met."

Bert moved quickly to Verne's side, eyes glittering. "Surely he can't still be alive?" he said, his voice trembling with excitement. "I mean, it could only be . . . He'd be the only one . . . But to still be alive, after all these centuries . . ."

"Maybe," Verne said, pulling at his beard. "It *is* possible, Bert."

"Who are we talking about?" asked Jack.

"A possibility," Verne said enigmatically. "Ordo Maas was not the only shipbuilder to construct living vessels—and the only other one we know of in history made an ancient promise that may have been fulfilled with the creation of the *Black Dragon*. And if that is so, then he may be the one who can reverse the process too."

John looked at the others, and a bit of the starch seemed to have gone out of him. "I'd forgotten," he said, slightly crestfallen. "That fellow they saved in the past. The one who owed Edmund a boon."

"And may have fulfilled it," said Verne.

Bert frowned. "We're wasting time, Jules," he said testily. "If he has actually survived since Jason's time . . ."

Verne held a finger to his lips and turned to the rest of the gathering. "I agree, time is of the essence now," he said, almost contritely. "But it is no longer my call. John? What do you say?"

The Prime Caretaker drew a sharp breath. It was the first time in the two months since their friends had been lost that Verne had actually deferred to him in front of the others, all of whom were now watching expectantly.

"First things first," he said firmly. "Let's secure the ship in the boathouse where it ought to be. Then we must attend to other matters, such as the security of Tamerlane House. And then," he added with a tight smile at Bert and Verne, "we'll make our battle plan."

Once the ship was safely ensconced in the boathouse, John, Jack, and Bert retreated to the main house to set another part of their newly minted plans in motion.

Bert had been largely absent from the activities of Tamerlane House for the last two months, for reasons both good and shoddy. The good reason was that upon finding out he had died and was now a portrait, he also discovered that Verne had rescued his love, Weena, from the far future, and made her over into a portrait as well. The love he thought lost to the mists of time was now, here, present, and in his new life. John couldn't begrudge his old mentor that.

However, Bert had also been complicit in many of Verne's plans, including keeping the truth of many things from his protégés simply because Verne had deemed it necessary. And so when John had enough of Verne's games and declared himself to be the new Prime Caretaker, Bert also bore some of that judgment. So when an opportunity emerged for Bert to actively contribute to the plan of action, he jumped on it with relish—and possibly out of hope of a small measure of forgiveness from the Caretakers whom he had come to love like his own sons.

On the walk to the house, Bert told the others everything he could remember about the strange shipbuilder he and the other time travelers had encountered in the past—and then, together, they repeated it all to the two residents of Tamerlane House whom they could depend on to carry out their plan.

"Interesting," said Don Quixote as he nibbled on a cookie. "Don't you agree, Uncas?"

His squire climbed down from the chair where he'd been perched and frowned at the knight. "Interesting?" he exclaimed, whiskers twitching. "Sounds more like a 'mergency t' me. Finish your snickerdoodle and let's get going."

"Uh, we haven't even told you what we need you to do," said Jack.

"That's never stopped us before," said Uncas.

"What is the task?" Quixote asked, swallowing the last bite of cookie and pocketing two more before dusting off his lap. "I'm not sure where to begin looking for a shipbuilder who might have died thousands of years ago."

"You may not," said Bert, "but someone else you know does. In fact, they were well acquainted at one point."

"Of whom are we speaking?"

"The Zen Detective," said John.

"He's just upstairs, with Rappaccini's daughter," said Quixote. "Why not just go ask him yourselves?"

"Because," said John, "despite his sudden turnabout in the battle with Dee and the Cabal, the detective still harbors a lot of deep-seated and unpleasant feelings about working with Caretakers. But *you* two," he said, pointing at the knight and the squire, "are not Caretakers. And he still feels a sense of obligation for betraying you."

"And you want us to play offa that, hey?" asked Uncas. "That in't th' Animal way."

"It's the way that will work," said John. "Will you do it?"

Quixote stood and saluted. "For you, Master Caretaker, I would march alone through the gates of Hades itself."

"And I'd go with him," said Uncas.

The knight and his squire made their way through the warren of hallways and corridors to the room that had been provided to the Zen Detective, but as they suspected it might be, it was empty. Since taking up residence at Tamerlane House, he could almost always be found with one of Verne's time travelers, the assistants known as Messengers. Her name was Beatrice, but everyone called her Rappaccini's daughter, after her famous father. Her room was less a living space than it was an arboretum, and nearly everything growing in it was poisonous. This might have been a cause for concern to the detective had he not also recently been poisonous himself. Beatrice corrected that unfortunate condition, and in the most unlikely pairing possible, the two fell in love.

It took several knocks at Beatrice's door before the detective opened it in a huff. "What is it?" he said, not even trying to disguise the ire in his voice. "We're busy."

Uncas drew a breath, intending to ask what they were busy doing, but Quixote kicked him in the shin and shut him up. "Hello, Aristophanes," the knight said pleasantly. "We'd like to ask a favor, if you don't mind."

Aristophanes looked back into the room at his dark, quiet companion and snorted. "Don't insult me. The Caretakers need a favor, you mean."

"We need you to find a shipbuilder," Quixote said, ignoring the deflection. "Someone of approximately your own vintage."

"*My* vintage?" Aristophanes said in honest surprise. "There's no one living who . . ." He paused, eyes widening.

"Back in the day, he built a ship you might have heard of," said Quixote. "It was called the *Argo*."

"Argus," the detective said, shaking his head. "You want me to find Argus."

"Ah!" Uncas said brightly. "You know him!"

"I was supposed to execute him," said Aristophanes. "Plans changed. Mistakes were made. And now I'm being harassed by a geriatric knight and a talking beaver."

"I'm a badger, you—you—*unicorn*," Uncas replied before he noticed the slight gleam in the detective's eyes. He was teasing.

"So," said Aristophanes, "the Caretakers have need of finding a shipbuilder, do they?"

"Yes," the knight said, nodding, "and we need you to do so right away." He reached into a knapsack at his side and drew out a small bag, which he handed to the detective. "We came prepared," he said somberly. "Thirty pieces of silver—your usual fee, I believe."

The detective's eyes widened slightly, but he didn't answer. Instead he reached out a hand and pressed the bag back toward Quixote.

"All debts were paid," he said softly, the gruffness gone from his voice. "Tell Verne that he was as good as his word, and I have rejoined the flow of the world."

"So, do you think you can find Argus?" Quixote asked.

"Consider it done," Aristophanes said brusquely, as if trying to regain his earlier gruff demeanor. "I can take you to him now if you like."

"Really?" asked Uncas in astonishment. "That's pretty amazing."

"I'm actually very good at this," the detective said as he cast a longing, heartfelt look at Beatrice, then grabbed his hat and coat. "Also, if I'm not actually charging you to find him, then there's no point in dragging things out to drive up my expenses."

Together, the three unlikely companions crossed Shakespeare's Bridge to the Kilns, where they kept the Duesenberg. It was no ordinary vehicle—it had been modified with a special spatial projector that could transport them instantly to any number of places that were depicted on an assortment of special slides. It made missions like these a great deal easier to manage.

"Is that a new hat?" Uncas asked as they clambered into the car.

"It is," Aristophanes said, trying and failing to hold back a wistful smile. "A gift from Bea. I'm no longer poison to the touch, but I'm apparently still a unicorn," he went on, fingering his fedora, "so I still need a hat if we're going to go mingle with civilized society—or whatever passes for that where we're going."

"You're the guide," said Quixote as he started up the car. "Where to, Steve?"

"Here," the detective said, holding up a slide. "Thousands of years in obscurity, and the Caretakers have a portal that leads almost right to his door. Amazing."

Aristophanes inserted the slide, and the Duesenberg roared forward just as the portal opened up on the side of a building a few hundred yards from the Kilns. The car slid to a stop atop a grassy hill, in the bright afternoon sunlight of Greece.

"Welcome to Lemnos," Uncas said, flipping off the projector. "Where to now?"

Aristophanes pointed ahead to a fork in the road, indicating that they should drive to the right. Then, consulting a small note-pad he pulled from his coat, he told Uncas they'd be looking for a seaside cottage about three miles farther along.

"This seems like a nice little hamlet," Quixote observed as they passed a number of small but tidy houses. "Hardly where you'd think an ancient shipbuilder could find peaceful refuge away from prying eyes."

"It's the standing stones," the detective said, pointing them out as the car passed between two sizable rocks that stood alongside the road. "They act as a sort of screen, keeping out the looky-loos and troublemakers. They're as good as hiding in plain sight, because someone living within the boundaries of the stones can't be found—not by the methods the Caretakers use, anyway."

"And what method do you use?" asked Quixote.

"That," Aristophanes said, pointing at the small red book he carried in his breast pocket. "With that and a stub of graphite, I can keep track of anyone I like. I just write it down."

He frowned at the look of incredulity on the old knight's face. "What?" said the detective. "Like everything has to be done with magic?"

"It's like our Little Whatsits," Uncas said, nodding in approval. "Very wise."

"Thank you, badger," said Aristophanes.

"Don't mention it," Uncas said, pointing at a small cottage. "Look—I think we've arrived."

CHAPTER THREE
THE SHIPBUILDER

—❈—

THE COTTAGE WAS a traditional whitewashed stone structure common to the Greek isles, save for the windows, which were stained glass that depicted ancient Greek myths in spectacular bursts of color. There were chimes outside the doorway that swayed gently in the breeze of their passing and announced the companions' presence to the occupant inside.

The shipbuilder's shop at the rear of the cottage was bright and airy and had tall, whitewashed walls that curved up into ceilings. At the center of the room, the proprietor was descending a staircase carrying a box of supplies. He paused when he saw the three visitors, then smiled and continued down the stairs.

"Please," he said, setting the box on the floor, then gesturing around the room with his hands. "Feel free to look around at my work. Much to see, more to buy, as long as the price is right."

All around the room were tables and low shelving laden with globes, clear glass jugs, and bottles, and in them floated miniature ships of various designs. Some appeared to be simple, traditional sailboats, but most were of a far more elaborate design, incorporating scrollworks and ornate carvings in the hulls. But what was most intriguing to the companions was that every ship bore a masthead that resembled an insect. Several had the aspect of a praying mantis, but most of the others were moths or butterflies with magnificent, delicate wings. As Uncas watched, some of the wings appeared to flutter with the gentle motion of the water in the bottles.

The shipbuilder was pleased to see them admiring his handiwork, and he smiled a lopsided grin. "For some reason," he said matter-of-factly, "I seem to be skilled in merging creatures that fly with craft that float."

"That's why we've come seeking you," Quixote ventured. "We understand you have had some experience with merging a ship and a larger creature—say, a dragon?"

"Hah!" The shipbuilder exclaimed. "You want someone to make you a Dragonship? Easier to ask for the Golden Apples of the Sun, or a sword made by Hattori Hanzo."

Aristophanes snorted. "Hattori Hanzo doesn't exist."

"True," the shipbuilder replied, "but that doesn't stop people from seeking out his swords."

Uncas slumped, dejected. "So it isn't possible to make ships larger than these toys?"

"Oh, it is possible, but I seldom have," Argus replied, sitting. "And not for a very long time. You don't want me, anyway. You'd be better off with my master, Utnapishtim. He's the true virtuoso for what you want."

"Utnapishtim?" Quixote said, puzzled. "I don't think I've heard . . ."

"Sorry, sorry," Argus said, rolling his eyes. "I forgot he took a different name when he'd crossed over for good. You might know him better by his Greek name, Deucalion. Or perhaps as . . ."

"Ordo Maas," Uncas finished for him. "All th' Children of th' Earth knows Ordo Maas."

Argus reached out and scratched Uncas on top of the head, which Quixote thought would offend his little friend, but oddly, the badger didn't seem to mind. "Yes, your kind would know of him, wouldn't they, small one?" he said gently. "Ordo Maas— that's who you want."

"'Cept we can't ask him," Uncas replied. "He's not findable. Not anymore."

Argus frowned. "How is he not findable? The last I knew, he had his own island in the Archipelago."

"That's exactly the problem," said Quixote. "The Archipelago is no more."

The shipbuilder's eyes narrowed. "You lie."

"Knights never lie," said Uncas. "What happened was this, see, there was a fire—"

"I don't want to know," Argus said flatly. "It's none of my business. Not anymore." He stood up as if to indicate that the discussion was over. "I'm sorry. You'll have to find someone else to build you your Dragonship."

"But, that's just the thing," Uncas protested. "We don't want'cha t' *build* a ship—we need ya t' unbuild one."

Argus turned and looked at the badger, who was all frizzy with earnestness, then up at Quixote. "I'm sorry—as I said, my master was the true creator of such things. I cannot help you."

Quixote looked at Aristophanes, who had been quiet throughout the entire encounter. The Zen Detective shrugged. "You hired me to find him, not to compel him to do anything for you," he said brusquely as he turned for the door. "If he doesn't want to help you, that's no business of mine."

Quixote sighed heavily and put his arm around Uncas. "Come along, my squire. Let's go explain to the Caretakers that their ship the *Black Dragon* is going to remain just that—a ship. And nothing more."

The sound of a glass jug shattering against the stone floor stopped the companions in their tracks. They turned back to see Argus kneeling amid the shards of glass and spilled water, gently trying to lift a Monarch ship out of the mess without damaging the wings.

"The *Black Dragon*," the shipbuilder said as he delicately installed the tiny ship in another jug. "You told me a ship—you didn't say which."

"Well, now you know," said Aristophanes. "And if you're willing to help, I'm sure you'll be well compensated."

Argus folded his arms and considered them carefully for a moment. Then he pursed his lips. "A boon," he said at last. "Your masters will owe me a boon, whatever I ask. That is my price."

"Are we authorized to agree to those terms?" Uncas asked Quixote, obviously worried. "Scowler John never said anything about offering *him* an open ticket."

"Well, it did work out the last time," Quixote whispered back, "except for, you know, the betrayal and all that."

"The Caretakers have always known *my* terms," the Zen Detective remarked, winking at Uncas, as the shipbuilder gathered his tools together in anticipation of an agreement. "I get my fee, plus expenses. And if the expenses mean agreeing to pay whatever the mark asks for, then that's the client's problem, not mine."

"I think I like your job," Uncas said. "Not much seems t' bother you. It's a very Animal way t' live."

"We need him," Quixote said simply. He turned to Argus. "I think your terms will be acceptable. We can go now, if you like."

"For a moment there," the Zen Detective said to the shipbuilder as the foursome clambered into the car, "I thought you weren't going to come with us."

"For a moment there," Argus said as he took the seat behind Quixote, "I wasn't."

"What changed your mind, if I might ask?" said Quixote.

Argus paused a moment, as if the question had violated some invisible boundary of etiquette, then realized that it was, in fact, an entirely appropriate question under the circumstances. "It was the ship," he answered. "The *Black Dragon*. Any of the others would have been made by Utna—by Ordo Maas. But that one's the exception—the only one he never touched."

"How did you know that?" Uncas asked as he started the car.

"Because," Argus answered over the roar of the engine, "I'm the one who built it, as payment for a promise made . . . long, long ago. I made the *Black Dragon*, at the request of Mordred, the Winter King."

It took a few hours for the excitement surrounding the *Black Dragon* to fade away, and soon things were humming away as usual at Tamerlane House, with one exception: Nathaniel Hawthorne had doubled the patrols along the islands and the guards at the bridge, just in case the appearance of the Dragonship was somehow a precursor to another attack.

"Remember," he warned them, "discovering the Architect of the keep and rescuing our friends is not our sole concern. The Echthroi have other agents, and this ship spent a thousand years crossing from a Shadowed Archipelago. I simply want to be cautious—you never know who might also be lurking about."

John knew without asking that Hawthorne was referring to Dr. Dee and his Cabal. Dee had enlisted the Zen Detective as a double agent to locate the Ruby Armor of T'ai Shan, which was said to give the wearer almost unlimited control over time and space. But not just anyone could wear the armor—it had to be an adept; someone like Rose. Someone the Histories referred to . . .

. . . as the *Imago*.

The problem was, Dee had just such a personage: a boy, a distant descendant of Rose, who had been rescued from the Archipelago and taken into the past, where he was then kidnapped by Dee's agent, the traitor Daniel Defoe.

Defoe put the boy prince, called Coal, into a might-have-been, a possible future, for safekeeping. But he made one mistake: Defoe gave the boy a watch—an Anabasis Machine, the time-traveling device all the Caretakers carried. And, being an adept, the boy figured out how to use it on his own and spent a lifetime learning how the world worked. And finally, when Dee pulled him out of the future and gave him the Ruby Armor, the boy Coal, now grown, revealed he had been hiding in plain sight as one of Verne's Messengers, calling himself Dr. Raven.

Then, in the crucial moment when the adept could have turned the tide against either the Caretakers or the Cabal, he instead gave himself a new name and disappeared. Moments later Dee, his house, and the entire Cabal also vanished. Ever since, the

Caretakers had been on guard, waiting, watching for the attack they believed was inevitable.

"Understood," John said to Hawthorne. "Keep me posted, and keep your silver sledgehammer at the ready."

As they waited for news from Uncas and Quixote, John, Jack, and a few of the Caretakers Emeriti accompanied Shakespeare back to the smaller island, to assist him with some minor adjustments he wanted to make to the Zanzibar Gate. As the poet-inventor worked, the Prime Caretaker examined the still impressive stone structure.

"You've become quite the creator, Will," John said in honest admiration. "I think you missed your calling in life. You ought to have been an architect."

"Thank you," Shakespeare said gravely, bowing to the younger Caretaker, "but I think I am responsible for too much stress and strife already, and all I've built was that cursed bridge."

"If it wasn't for that bridge, sirrah," said Twain as he stepped across the path and joined the others near the gate, "none of us might be here now."

"That somewhat resembles my point," said Shakespeare. "So much of this is my fault."

"Responsibility, you mean," said Twain.

Shakespeare shrugged. "What's the difference?"

"That answer," said Twain, "is what makes you a good Caretaker."

"No," said Jack. "That answer is what makes him a good man."

Shakespeare blushed, and bowed his head to acknowledge the compliment. "That is exceeding gracious of you to say, Jack," he said, "but my responsibilities now are less than those of others. I cannot fathom how, as the current Caretakers, you grapple with the care of the world. It is so much larger than in my time."

"I'm just happy that we aren't expected to do even more than we are," said Jack. "I have enough trouble just running the Kilns—"

"Ahem-hem," said John.

"Ah, that is, Warnie and I have enough trouble running the Kilns," added Jack.

"And Mrs., uh, Whatsit," John said helpfully.

"Her too," Jack admitted, "or rather, her mostly. My point is, I could never run a university, much less a city. And heaven forbid that I'm ever given my own country. I think I'd go mad—probably just lock myself in a tower and shut out the whole world while I stay in my room and read."

"And that's different from what you do now, how?" asked John with a smirk and a wink at Twain.

"Oh, shut up," said Jack.

At that moment, they all turned to see Dickens walking purposefully across the path toward them. "Blast it all, Samuel," he said as he drew near. "Are you going to tell them or not? Time's a-wasting."

"I was getting to it, Charles," Twain said. "Nothing is as urgent as exchanging pleasantries as gentlemen ought, before going to business."

"What business?" said John.

"The major has summoned us to the Kilns," Dickens replied, looking at Jack. "Your brother says that our agents have returned and are bringing a guest."

"The shipbuilder?" asked Jack. "I hope."

"This is Quixote and Uncas we're talking about, remember," John said as the group followed Dickens back to the small ferry-boat that Twain piloted. "For all we know, they've brought back the Four Horsemen of the Apocalypse."

"Don't," said Jack, "even *joke* about that."

The Caretakers crossed over Shakespeare's Bridge fully armed, and prepared for any contingency. Warnie, Jack's brother, was already waiting for them, as were Quixote and Uncas. The detective and the new arrival were still in the Duesenberg, but as the Caretakers approached, Aristophanes climbed out, tipped his hat at John, and moved over to join Warnie, who kept glancing at the detective's skin tone as if it were a trick of the light.

A smaller, wizened man stepped from the other side of the car and placed his hand on the hood, taking in the heat radiating from the engine. "It's warm," he said admiringly, "almost like a living thing. I should not be surprised if one day someone chose to become one with a machine such as this."

"We brung, uh, bringed . . . ah, we got the shipbuilder," Uncas said, gesturing at Argus, who nodded his head in acknowledgment. His expression was grave, but a bemused smile played at the corners of his mouth.

John sized up the shipbuilder. "I must beg your pardon, but you don't appear to be several thousand years old."

"You have it," Argus replied, "but considering you sent a purple humanoid unicorn, a talking badger, and a Spaniard who can't drive to fetch me, I'm surprised you place such an emphasis on one's appearance."

"He's smarter than the average mariner," Warnie commented to Aristophanes.

The detective nodded. "You have no idea."

"How far can we trust him?" Hawthorne asked. "After all, we have only the detective's word he is who he says he is."

"Why would I lie to you now?" Aristophanes sputtered. "I live at Tamerlane House!"

"You did betray us to Dee," said Hawthorne. "You were a double agent."

"Triple agent," said Warnie. "He betrayed Dee and joined you lot after all."

"Thanks," said Aristophanes.

"Don't mention it," said Warnie.

"But," Hawthorne argued, "we still lost the Ruby Armor."

"We would have lost it anyway," Dickens interjected, "so that really isn't Steve's fault."

"Who is Steve?" Argus asked Uncas.

"Th' detective," the badger replied. "It's his preference."

"If I had known," Argus said slowly from the relaxed position where he was leaning against the Duesenberg, "that you people would be this entertaining, I would have agreed to come far more easily."

"It's him," said a voice from the back of the group. "I only met him a couple of months ago, remember? And I know his face. This is Argus."

The Caretakers parted to allow Bert to move to the front, where he peered more closely at the shipbuilder. "Do you remember me, Argus?"

"I remember," Argus replied, "that when we last met, you and your companions saved my life. But also that you were much more accepting of who I was and what I claimed to be able to do. After all, you are the ones who sought me out, and not the other way around."

"I'm sorry, I'm sorry," Jack said, taking the role of host and rushing around the others to shake the shipbuilder's hand. "We've had some security issues around here lately and need to be careful."

"I understand," Argus replied. "Thankfully, however, tolerance and patience can be bought."

Warnie cleared his throat and looked pointedly at Jack and John, then tipped his head at Argus.

John sighed and frowned at the other Caretakers. "I suppose since we've already made one deal with the de—"

"Hey, now," said Aristophanes.

"The detective, I was going to say," John continued, scowling, "then I suppose we must take this fellow at his word that he is whom he says he is."

"Not at all," Argus replied before any of the Caretakers could comment further. He smiled down at Uncas. "Child of the Earth," he said gently, "do you have a scrap of paper I might borrow?"

"Soitenly!" Uncas exclaimed. He popped open his Little Whatsit, deftly removed a small blank sheet from the pages at the back, and handed it to the shipbuilder.

Argus made no comment but simply began folding the paper over and over, his fingers moving too swiftly to follow, until he had fashioned a small paper dragon. Then he knelt and looked at the ground around him until he finally spied what he was looking for in a patch of grass.

Carefully he reached out and picked up the small black wasp

by the body, and again, his fingers swiftly manipulated the folded paper.

When he had finished, he held out his creation. There in his outstretched hand was a miniature Dragonship, with wings and, somehow, the living body and head of the wasp.

The wings fluttered and caught air, and the tiny Wasp-Dragon took flight and disappeared into the trees.

Argus turned to the astonished Caretakers. "Any questions?"

No one moved, or spoke a word.

"Good," Argus said. "Can we go see the real Dragonship now? We're old friends, and I'd like to say hello."

CHAPTER FOUR
ARÊTE

—✳—

VERNE LED THE group to the large south boathouse, where the *Black Dragon* had been housed—or rather, imprisoned—for many years, and was once more, but without the locks, chains, and magic wards that had made it a prison.

The ship sat in the berth, rocking gently with the swells of water that rose and fell from the bay outside.

"I never had quite the same knack for it that my master had," Argus said as he examined the *Black Dragon*, perhaps rushing forward a little more eagerly than he'd wished to do in front of the Caretakers. "I could build the vessels, but he had the greater affinity for binding them with the beasts. And I just never cared as much as he about the Children of the Earth. No offense," he added, looking down at Uncas.

"None taken," said the badger. "If you ever smelled what one of us is like when we gets wet, you'd have given up on th' idea of letting us on boats altogether."

The *Black Dragon* seemed to rise up in the water at the shipbuilder's touch, almost as if in recognition. This was an encouraging sign to the Caretakers, since, as a ship, only Burton had ever really been able to handle it. But that was also before they learned who the Dragon had actually been before it became merged with the ship.

"The wing plates were my favorite innovation," Argus said as he ran his hands along the hull. "It was something I discussed with my friend Pelias back during our quest for the fleece, but I never quite worked out how to do it properly. Not until I put my hands on her."

"Him," said Fred. "The *Black Dragon* is a he."

The shipbuilder chuckled. "I suppose it could be, little Child of the Earth," he said, not taking his eyes or hands off the ship. "I never asked Mordred, and he never offered details. Although how he managed to tame such a fierce Dragon into willingly being bonded to a ship is beyond my understanding. I wasn't given much choice in the matter myself."

John raised his eyebrows in surprise and looked at the other Caretakers. "He doesn't know? He really doesn't know who the Dragon is, or rather, was?" he whispered behind his hand. "Don't you think we ought to tell him?"

"Let it be, for the nonce," said Bert. "We don't even know if he can do as he says he can. I certainly never saw any proof of it when we met—we simply took him at his word. No need to complicate matters by bringing up old grudges. And besides," he added, "if it *does* work, he'll know the way the cows ate the cabbage soon enough."

"So," Argus said, straightening himself and turning to look at the Caretakers. "What is it you ask of me?"

"You told Quixote and Uncas that you built the *Black Dragon*," said Bert. "Now we need you to, uh, undo that which you hath done."

Houdini rolled his eyes. "We need the Dragon," he said matter-of-factly, "separated from the ship. Can you do that?"

Argus shrugged. "Of course."

"It seemed a simple enough thing to do with a wasp," Houdini said, drawing up alongside the shipbuilder, "but this is a serious matter. Don't say you can do something you cannot."

Argus looked at John. "This is a Caretaker? They're more skeptical than they used to be."

"Not really," said John. "He's just very results-oriented, and skeptical by nature."

"Building the ship itself was the hard part," Argus said as he gestured for the others to give him room to work. "Binding something living to it was much easier."

"Even with Dragons?" asked Fred.

Argus chuckled. "Especially with them, little Child of the Earth. Because binding with a ship is about choosing one's arête—which means to achieve excellence, to reach one's highest potential. I simply help guide them in the process."

"Then how is it reversed?" asked John.

"It's just as easy," Argus said, turning to face the masthead. "I simply have to persuade the Dragon that its arête as a ship is done, and now its arête is to once more be a Dragon."

The shipbuilder bowed his head and placed his hands on the Dragon's chest, where it merged with the wood and iron of the ship. Murmuring ancient words of power, or perhaps, simply a prayer, he flexed his arms, and suddenly a glow began to emanate from the Dragon.

The hull began to crack and splinter apart. For the first time, the Caretakers could see some of the manner in which the living

Dragon had been merged with the structure of the ship. It was almost more of a spiritual blending than a physical one. The head, neck, and arms were only semi-attached, as if they were part of a sculpted masthead; but the wings were attached to part of the structure of the hull, and seemed to separate from it with more force.

Argus's murmuring became more fervent, and his arms and neck were dripping with sweat. The process was generating a great deal of heat, and so much light that the others had to shield their eyes.

Suddenly the light flared, and a thunderclap echoed deafeningly through the boathouse as Argus flew backward, hitting one of the pilings. Several of the Caretakers rushed to his side, concerned that he had been injured.

"Are you all right?" Jack asked as he and John reached under the shipbuilder's arms to help him to his feet. "Did you—"

"Look," Argus said, pointing. "It is done."

The two Caretakers turned to see what had already rendered the rest of their companions utterly speechless. There, where the shipbuilder had been working, standing amid the splintered remains that had been the fore of the Dragonship, was Madoc.

His beard and hair were overgrown and tangled, but there was no question it was he. Instead of emerging from the binding with the ship as the Black Dragon, as everyone had fully expected, he had emerged as the man he had been before he had accepted the calling, and risen from apprentice to full Dragon, and thence to Dragonship.

However, he was not entirely unchanged from the experience: his right hand, once severed and replaced with a hook, was now whole again. And while he was once again in the form of a man, not all the aspects of the Dragon had been shed with the ship—two great, black wings rose from his shoulder blades and stretched out behind him like sails.

No one spoke, or moved, until Madoc's eyes fluttered closed, and he started to fall. Then John, Jack, Houdini, and Hawthorne all rushed forward to catch him—but it was the Valkyrie Laura Glue and the badger Caretaker Fred who moved the fastest, and caught their friend's father before he fell.

"It's all right," Laura Glue whispered through the tears streaming down her face. "Rose wouldn't let you fall, and neither will we."

As the rest of the group at the boathouse gathered around the newly reborn Madoc, Verne, Bert, and Twain simply watched—because they were also watching the reactions of two others: Argus and Aristophanes.

The shipbuilder's response was easier to parse—it was that of near-total surprise. Short of just being told beforehand—something he might not have believed—there was no way for him to have known that the Black Dragon he had bonded with the ship, at the request of Mordred, the Winter King, was in fact Mordred himself, in his true persona of Madoc. The dragon already existed, and at the time, not even Mordred knew that the Black Dragon was a future version of himself, who went back in time to become the *Black Dragon*. So in a way, even as the act of releasing Madoc closed a great circle, it was understandable for the old Greek to be surprised.

Aristophanes's reaction was more enigmatic: He showed fear. Of the three Caretakers watching him, only Verne really knew the detective to any degree, but he was certain that Madoc and Aristophanes had never crossed paths. So why was his response a fearful one? It was, Verne decided, something worth investigating, but later. For now, there was a more important agenda to focus on.

Fred and Uncas were helpfully offering a drink of water to the weakened shipbuilder. The retransformation process he claimed would be "easy" was anything but, and the effort had taken a toll.

"Thank you," Argus said, handing the tin cup back to the badgers as John approached. "Well, Caretaker? Are you satisfied with my work?"

John nodded, smiling. "What was your price?" he asked. "Quixote was authorized to bargain in good faith."

"I told the knight I wished a boon."

"Whatever we owe you, then," John said to the shipbuilder, "has been more than earned. Name your price."

Argus responded by turning to look at the newly released Madoc, who was being borne up in blankets by the Caretakers for rest and recovery at Tamerlane House. The shipbuilder's face twitched as he watched, and his eyes went glassy, as if he were immersed in a long-buried memory. Finally he turned to John and extended his hand.

"There is no cost," he said. "Long ago, I myself promised to grant a boon, and that debt has now been paid—twice over, I think. No more need be said about it. I'd just like to return to my work."

John took his hand and shook it firmly, then again. "Fair enough," the Caretaker said, not certain whether he ought to question the old man further. "Even all, then."

"I would make one request," the shipbuilder said, "not as payment, but simply a favor, if it is one you'd be willing to grant."

John spread his arms. "You have returned to us dearest blood, and given us the only chance to find our lost friends," he said in reply. "Ask what you will."

"As I said, I'd like to continue my work—but I would like to do so here."

"Here?" John answered, surprised. "At Tamerlane House?" He stroked his chin in thought, before replying further.

"You must understand," he said slowly, "that save for the connection to Jack's house, those residing here are all but prisoners. The Archipelago . . ."

"I'm not as naive or as uninformed as your agents seemed to think," said Argus, "and the detective keeps secrets less well than he believes. I know—a little—of what's happened. But I have been a virtual prisoner myself on Lemnos for a very long time."

John frowned and fingered his lip. "A prisoner? I had understood that you were a free man."

"A private one," said Argus, "and those conditions do not always mesh." He made a broad gesture with his hand. "I saw the rune stones as we crossed the bridge—I kept myself hidden in Lemnos in a similar manner. I could even be of use to you in assisting with your security, beyond what work I can do in the boathouse."

"But," John said, puzzled, "it seems as if you're merely trading one jailhouse for another. What can you do here that you could not do on Lemnos?"

"Be myself," said Argus. "The easiest and hardest thing a man can do."

The Prime Caretaker considered this a moment, then nodded his head. "As you wish." He turned to the badgers. "Uncas, will you see to it that Master Swift arranges for a suite of rooms at the house?"

Argus placed a hand on John's arm and shook his head. "That won't be necessary," he said, gesturing with his other hand at the fractured hull of the *Black Dragon*. "I will be more than comfortable here. This is where I belong—and where I think I shall be content."

John agreed, and with another handshake to bind the deal, he and the badgers left Argus, who was already stroking the ship and whispering words of quiet power as a smile spread slowly across his face.

"Indeed," Argus said to no one in particular. "My conscience is finally clear, and I have at last come home."

The elder members of the Caretakers Emeriti crowded at the open door to look in on Laura Glue's patient. It was startling to see Madoc as he must have been in his youth, unbearded and unscarred by the world. But it was equally startling to see, there on top of the quilt, his right hand, whole and unblemished. That alone was unusual enough to them that they could nearly overlook the great, leathery wings that were folded along the headboard behind him.

"So," Twain said softly, "he is the Hook no longer, but fully a man again, our Mordred is."

"He is more Madoc than Mordred, I think," said Dickens. "He is, at last, perhaps once more the man that he set out to be."

Laura Glue sat next to the bed, facing this strange young

man whom she had met only once before, when he was older, and weathered by the events of his long life. In a way, it felt like another first meeting to her. She wiped his forehead with a damp cloth, watching as his breathing became more regular, until he finally opened his eyes.

"Hello there," she said.

"Rose?" he asked, propping himself up with the pillows. Then his vision cleared, and he realized his nurse was not his daughter. After a moment he added, "I'm, ah, Madoc."

She giggled. "I know that. We have met, you know."

He reddened. "I remember. It's just . . . more like a dream now. It's been so, so long."

"Only a year for me, since we saw you in London."

"Which was a century before I gave myself over to my other self to become the *Black Dragon*, and then over a thousand years since that," he said, more awed by the reality of it than anything else. "And now here I sit, in this body that I remember having centuries earlier, before I . . ." He paused.

"Before you became the Winter King."

Again, he blushed. "Or at least before I became Mordred, at any rate." He stopped and looked away, out the window. "I still remember those things too, girl. I still remember the choices I made. And . . . I don't regret them. I'm sorry, but it's true."

"You must have been capable of making some good choices," Jack offered from the doorway, where he, John, and Fred had crowded past the other Caretakers. "Otherwise, you'd never have become the Dragon's apprentice."

"Mmm," Madoc answered noncommittally. "There have been times I almost regretted that particular choice too," he said, "but when I was in the presence of my daughter, it all seemed to have happened for a reason. It seemed necessary."

"Everyone makes mistakes, Madoc," said Jack.

"Not everyone was the son of Odysseus and was offered the whole world as his kingdom," Madoc replied. "But I was, and I still made many mistakes."

"So was your brother," Jack suggested, "and he had more opportunities than you did to choose a direction for his life, but for my money, he didn't turn out any better than you did. Uh, I mean worse," he corrected quickly, after a poke in the ribs from John. "Uh, sorry."

Madoc shook his head and grimaced. "I don't know. Perhaps if I had chosen a better teacher . . ."

"Better than Samaranth?" asked John.

Madoc's face darkened. "No," he said. "A . . . different teacher. Samaranth, I should have heeded more. But then again," he added, looking around the room, "Myrddyn is nowhere to be seen, and I am here—again. So that should say something, I think."

"It does," said Jack. "Truly."

"We know you've made many sacrifices," John said, "but we need your help once more—as a Dragon. As the only one left."

Madoc exhaled heavily and swung his legs to the side of the bed. "All right," he said. "Tell me what . . ." He paused, finally noticing he carried considerably more bulk than before.

He flexed his wings, which filled the small bedroom. "Well, these are new."

"Yes," Laura Glue said. "And your eyes," she added, moving closer and turning his head to the light. "They're silver."

"Silver is nothing but dragon's blood," Madoc said. "It has

healing properties, and sometimes manifests itself during a transformation." He flexed his wings again, and the Caretakers could see that the leathery black was shot through with veins of silver. "I suppose I didn't expect it to leave a permanent marker."

"I like them," she said, looking at his eyes. "I liked them when they were violet, and I like them now. The wings, too. They make you look . . . imposing."

"Yes," Jack whispered behind his hand to his friends, "because he was such a shrinking violet *before* the wings."

"And I like that you are a good and compassionate person, and very forgiving, much like my daughter," Madoc said, glancing past Laura Glue to the others crowded into the room. "Is Rose here? I was hoping to see her."

Before John could respond, Fred moved closer to the bed, whiskers twitching. "That's why we done this," he said nervously. "That's why we brung, uh, brought you back, ah, sir. We need your help. Rose needs your help."

Madoc looked at the small mammal a moment, then stood up. "All right, Caretakers," he said, addressing all of them at once. "I haven't eaten in more than a thousand years, so what say you find us something to fill our bellies while you tell me why my daughter needs an old apprentice Dragon's help."

PART TWO

THE LAST FLIGHT OF THE INDIGO DRAGON

CHAPTER FIVE
THE ZANZIBAR GATE

-–✳–-

THE PART OF *the garden at the Kilns where the bridge was located was not visible to passersby, but the driveway where the Duesenberg had been parked was. Precautions had been taken to ensure that no one passing through Oxford would notice anything out of the ordinary, but then again, usually no one was looking—it was what made the Kilns a perfect entry point to Tamerlane House.*

No one, that is, except for the two men sitting in the black Bentley across the street. They were looking, and they saw a great deal. Warnie had noticed the car parked there earlier, but thought little of it—the enemies he had been warned to watch out for didn't drive automobiles.

Thus it was that no one, not even Warnie, seemed to take note when the two men emerged and crossed the road. Focused as they had been on taking Argus to see the Black Dragon, the Caretakers had simply crossed over the bridge, sealing the portal behind them without ever looking back. There were guards posted, and magic runes protecting the entry to Tamerlane House and the Nameless Isles . . . on that side of the bridge. But no one considered that if both sides were not protected equally, then both sides were equally vulnerable to their enemies. But no one was looking for enemies in Oxford.

If someone had been looking, he might have noticed the near-identical

*black coats and bowler hats the two men wore, and the round black
glasses that hid the dark orbs that occupied the places where their eyes
should have been.*

*If someone had been looking, he might have noticed the identical black
pocket watches both men carried, which chimed at the same moment.*

"It is time, Mr. Kirke," said one.

"Indeed it is, Mr. Bangs," said the other.

*In hindsight, John thought, that was the Caretakers' greatest mis-
take. They should have been more cautious. They should have taken
better care. If they had, then perhaps things would have gone differently when the two men knocked on the door at the Kilns.*

In the dining hall, Alexandre Dumas and the Feast Beasts quickly
put together what Dumas referred to as "a light dinner," which never-
theless consisted of enough food to have stocked the Kilns for a year.
Madoc kept refilling his plate and eating as the various Caretakers
took turns explaining what had been happening in the Archipelago.
He made no comment, only nodding occasionally and grunting.
Shakespeare was last to speak, and he explained how he believed the
Zanzibar Gate would work, and why it required a Dragon.

"The question is," Madoc said as he wiped his mouth with the
back of his hand and belched as a courtesy to Dumas, "am I still
in fact a Dragon? I still have the wings, but I feel more like a man
again."

"It is an office, not merely a descriptive term," said Bert. "One
is not a Dragon until a Dragon calls you to be one. And once you
have become a Dragon, a Dragon you shall remain until a Dragon
says otherwise. And," he added, "seeing as you're the only one left,
I don't anticipate that happening anytime soon."

"And if we do this, and somehow find the Architect and convince him to rebuild the keep, the Archipelago will be restored?"

"There's no way to know for certain," said Verne, "but this is the first necessary step to finding out."

"And the *Imaginarium Geographica* is of no help to you in this? Or the Histories?"

"The Histories that record the future are little more than unfulfilled prophecies," said Twain, "and the *Imaginarium Geographica* was unmatched as a travel guide, but, I'm sorry to say, sorely lacking as a time travel aid. Anyroad, Rose, Edmund, and Charles have it with them, whenever they are."

"We know the Archipelago itself *can* be restored," John said, indicating the open facsimile *Geographica* on the table in front of them, "because all the maps were still there in the original. When the Winter King . . ." He looked at Madoc and swallowed hard. "Sorry. When, um, *you* first tried to conquer the Archipelago," John continued, "and the lands were covered in Shadow, they vanished from the *Imaginarium Geographica*. But they're all still here, so there must be some way to restore them."

"Not all," Fred said quietly. Laura Glue moved closer to him and put a reassuring arm around the little mammal's shoulders. "Avalon in't there, and neither is Paralon."

"I'm sorry, Fred," said John. "I didn't forget."

"Some of the lands are missing?" Madoc asked in surprise. "I thought they weren't Shadowed."

"Not Shadowed, as you remember it," Jack said quietly. "Destroyed, by the Echthroi. The rest, according to what Aven told us before she . . ." He swallowed hard. "The rest were somehow removed, and taken elsewhere by Samaranth. Where he went, I cannot say. But it's a moot point if we can't reestablish the connection between worlds by restoring the keep."

"Well," Madoc said, standing, "either it'll work, or it won't. So let's go see what Master Shaksberd hath wrought."

Most of the company at Tamerlane House left to walk to the ferryboat Twain would pilot over to the island where the gate stood. Washington Irving and the half-clockwork men they called Jason's sons stayed behind with Dumas to guard the bridge, and the Elder Caretakers, having wished Madoc and the others good luck, stayed in the house.

Also remaining behind at Verne's insistence were the Zen Detective, Aristophanes, and his escorts, Uncas and Don Quixote. The detective protested, claiming foul play, until Twain judiciously let slip what they had originally done with Daniel Defoe after he had defied the Caretakers. After that, Aristophanes was more than content to wait things out in the comfort of the house.

As the companions walked across the expanse of sand and stone to the boathouse, Poe watched from seclusion high above. John caught sight of him out of the corner of his eye and gave a plaintive wave, which, after a moment, Poe returned before closing the drapes.

"So, this enemy, the Echthroi," Madoc said as they clambered into the ferryboat. "They are a constant threat?"

"Mostly through their agents," Bert said with a sigh. "The shadow-possessed servants called Lloigor."

The Caretakers were almost relieved when mention of the Lloigor caused Madoc to shudder. He had, after all, been one of them—the one the Echthroi once considered their greatest weapon.

"I'm sorry," said Madoc. "Sometimes, when you live long enough, you don't realize what kind of life your choices have culminated in. It is a path of a thousand steps—but the first step in the wrong direction can change it all. I let my bitterness determine my choices, and I was swayed by having followed the wrong teacher. For what it's worth, I'm sorry for my part in it all."

"You've more than made amends, Madoc," Laura Glue said, looking not at him, but to John, for reassurance. "You have already done more than we could have hoped."

"At least there haven't been any more incidents with some of the fouler creatures who used to serve the purposes of, ah, the man you were," Jack said, shuddering at the memory of their first encounter, long ago, with the creatures called Wendigo.

"Ah," Houdini said as he raised his hand to speak, then cleared his throat, "that may be in large part because most of those creatures were in the Archipelago when it was cut off, and thus our adversaries lost access to them. They were not, however, the only creatures at their disposal. Of that, you can be sure."

"How sure?" asked John.

"Sure enough," Houdini said, reddening slightly. "I cataloged most of them myself at Burton's request."

"I will surely burn for recruiting that man," Dickens lamented. "Burn, I tell you."

The sun had set fully by the time the company of Caretakers made their way to the Zanzibar Gate. The path was well lit with lanterns, which John noticed seemed to give the whole area an unearthly glow. He mentioned this to the others, and Jack shook his head.

"I don't think it's just the lanterns," he said, pointing at Shakespeare's construct. It was radiating with a pulsing light that grew stronger the closer they got.

"Is it working somehow?" John asked Shakespeare. "Did you manage to—"

"Not my workings," the Bard replied, cutting him off. "His."

He was pointing at Madoc, and suddenly the others realized Shakespeare's guess was correct—the mere presence of Madoc was powering the Zanzibar Gate.

"How does it work?" Madoc asked. "It looks as if it was made of the same kind of stone as the keep was."

"The very same, in fact," said Shakespeare, "minus the wooden structures that made the keep, ah, well . . . burnable."

Madoc's expression darkened a bit at that, but he said nothing.

Shakespeare stepped forward and indicated the series of markings engraved on the inner ring of the gate's aperture. "These runes represent numbers in Chronos time, and can be set for up to seven different decimal places," he explained, "giving the gate a possible range of a million years or more. For this trip, we only need to set six."

He showed them a display of crystals on a pedestal that had a mirror-image duplicate on the other side. "This is the mechanism that controls the settings," he said. "Each crystal corresponds to a rune carved into the gate. As you enter, the inner ring will shift and lock into place. When all seven are locked, as they are now, all that remains"—he turned to Madoc—"is for a Dragon to step through and pass from this time into that one."

"I'd like to point out that just this sort of thing was attempted once before," Houdini harrumphed, "by the Imperial Cartological Society, and as I recall, you were so put out by our efforts that you burned it to the ground."

"Your efforts were commendable," said Twain, "but your motives were suspect, my dear magician. You, or more specifically, Burton and Dr. Dee, were trying to re-create the keep in the service of, and for the purposes of, the Shadow of the Winter King. Now, however, you serve a higher purpose."

Houdini rolled his eyes and looked at Madoc.

"I understand," Madoc replied. "That sounded like so many fewmets to me, too."

"The gate should exist in both times," Shakespeare explained, "and much like the keep did, it will persist into the future, and carry you forward. The portal will close once you've all passed through, but you should be able to open it again from the other side."

He gestured at a rectangular indentation at the top of the control panel. "This is where the plate with the destination should be inset," he explained. "The exact location, as well as the specific time you arrive, are largely intuitive, much like going through the doorways of the keep. This is important," he cautioned. "If you aren't focused, if you allow your minds to wander and drift as you enter, it might override the settings and place you somewhere you didn't plan to be.

"If there is some need to go elsewhere, or, ah, elsewhen, rather," Shakespeare continued, "Edmund should be able to create a new destination plate to use. After that, simply repeat the process as I've explained it to you, lock the settings, activate the gate, step through, and then you'll be home."

Madoc stepped toward the gate, which brightened visibly at his approach. Impulsively, he reached out and put his hands on the stone.

The world seemed to shift out of focus for a moment, before coming back to clarity in a wave that spread outward from the gate. The air underneath the arch shimmered as if it was heated, and it took on a nearly reflective quality.

"It's quite an accomplishment," John said, smiling broadly. "With this gate, and Edmund's natural talents, we practically have a replacement for the keep right here at our doorstep."

At this, Shakespeare stepped back from the other Caretakers and wrung his hands in frustration. "I'm not the Architect who built the keep," he lamented. "I'm sorry, but as adept as I have proven myself to be, I simply don't have the skills to re-create something with the . . . ah, duration of the keep."

"What are you saying, Will?" John asked. "Will it work, or won't it?"

"Oh, it shall, I'm certain of that," Shakespeare replied, glancing over at Madoc, "now that we have a viable power source. But only thrice. That, and no more."

"*Thrice?*" Jack exclaimed. "Three times? That's not ideal, but it isn't terrible, either. If we don't find them the first go-round, we'll have two more tries to get it right."

The Bard shook his head and strode purposefully to the gate, where he motioned for Madoc to step away. Immediately the light from the gate dimmed.

"That's what I'm trying to explain to you," Shakespeare said, wringing his hands in frustration. "The gate will allow three trips, in toto. Once out in any direction, past or future; once back; and then . . ."

"Once out, with no return trip," Verne said heavily.

"Or two trips out, and then one home," Jack offered, trying to be helpful. "If we find our friends—"

"Ahem-hem," said Twain.

"Uh, that is, *when* we find our friends," Jack corrected, blushing slightly, "if they haven't yet found the Architect, we can pool our resources and try one more time before coming back."

"No one is going anywhere," a voice stern with authority rang out. "Not using the gate, anyroad. Not now, and maybe not ever."

Almost by reflex, the Caretakers turned to look at Verne, but he was already looking at the man who had spoken . . .

. . . *John.*

"We can't use it," he said, stepping around Will to stand in front of the gate, as if to emphasize his point. "It's a great idea, and may be the first step on the right road, but with a limited number of uses, it's simply too dangerous. I don't want to risk losing any among our number. One would be too great a loss."

"How is it any more risky than anything else we've tried?" asked Jack.

"You're forgetting one of the rules of time travel," John said, casting a rueful glance at Bert and Verne. "Every trip into the past must be balanced by one into the future. There won't be two trips out and then one home. At most, it would be one trip out and one back, because to go out again . . ." He let his voice trail off when he realized he couldn't speak the words. But Madoc could.

". . . means those travelers will not be returning," the Dragon said simply. "Ever."

"Yes," John said, this time looking at Jack. "It's too high a price to pay, when we don't know how the story will end."

"We tell stories for a living, John," Jack said testily, "and I believe we write the endings we choose."

"Not this time, Jack. I'm sorry."

Madoc and the other Caretakers simply watched as Jack struggled to contain what he really wanted to say to his longtime friend. This was not merely an argument, but evidence of a deeper division, one that had perhaps been growing longer than any of them realized.

"We've made our lives here ones of risk taking," Jack said, his fists clenched but his voice measured and even, "and I don't see why this is any different."

"It's different," John replied, "because every other decision was made by a different Prime Caretaker." His eyes flickered over to Verne, who was standing resolute, watching. "I'm not so willing to be reckless with the lives of our friends."

"And what about Rose and Edmund and Charles?" Jack replied, a bit less measured. "Who is looking out for them?"

"We will," John replied. "Somehow we'll find a way. But for now, we simply need to make certain the option we choose is the best one. And this one," he added, glancing apologetically at Will, "is not that option. Yet."

He started to say something to Jack, but his friend had already spun on his heel and was striding back to the ferryboat. A hand on John's shoulder stopped him from following after.

"No," Madoc said. "Not now. I'll talk with him later, but don't buckle. If you are indeed the Prime Caretaker now, you did exactly as you were supposed to do."

"Betray my friends?" John said bitterly.

"No," Madoc said again, looking at Verne. "Make the hard decisions—and then stand by them."

John cast one more rueful glance at his departing friend, then turned to Shakespeare. "That's my final word, then," he said, his voice firm but laced with sadness.

"No one will be using the Zanzibar Gate to go anywhere. We'll simply have to find another way."

CHAPTER SIX
THE HOT YOUNG TURKS

—◆—

"WE'RE GOING TO be using the Zanzibar Gate," Laura Glue said in a whisper as she and Fred walked along the docks at Tamerlane House. "There simply is no other way."

The Caretakers and their companions had adjourned back to the main island to discuss what options they might have for creating an alternative to Shakespeare's gate, but the young Valkyrie was having none of it.

"We've been looking through every library in the house," she muttered, as much to herself as to the badger, "including every nook and cranny of the Repository. We've considered every device that has ever been used to travel in time, including a few completely imaginary ones. I tell you, Fred, Will's gate is the best chance we have—and time is running out."

"Not that I disagree with most of that," Fred replied, "but isn't time exactly what we have the most of?"

She shook her head and pulled him to one side of the grand porch at the main entrance. "If they were simply lost in time, then yes," she whispered, "but we are also trying to outmaneuver an enemy who is better at time travel than we are. They know more than we do. And I don't think they've spent the last couple of months just waiting on us. I think they've been busy. And that means we have no time to waste."

"So what d' you want t' do?"

She looked around to make sure no one else was in earshot, then leaned in close. "Tonight, meet me at that place where we hid that thing that one time," she said as she pushed open the door. "We're going to sort it out."

"So, how are we going to sort it out?" Houdini asked John as he diplomatically maneuvered the Prime Caretaker away from the front door and toward one of the side yards.

John realized the magician was simply trying to make sure he didn't stride right into another confrontation with Jack, and he felt more relieved by the gesture than manipulated. "I don't know," he answered honestly, "but I simply can't risk trying something that leaves us worse off than we already are. Rose and Edmund together could travel into Deep Time, and now, with Madoc, we may be able to as well. But if we lose him, we're two steps behind again."

"Two steps behind Dr. Dee, you mean," said Houdini, "but I would dare to disagree. The boy prince could have chosen sides at the battle on Easter Island, and he didn't. I think that's why Dee hasn't acted yet—his trump card is still an indecisive child."

"An indecisive child with the power over time and space," John replied, "who may yet take John Dee's side."

"Maybe," a voice said from just ahead of them on one of the paths from the west end of the house, "but we have Will Shakespeare on our side. And," Kipling added as he reached to shake John's hand, "they don't."

Twain, Dickens, Verne, and Byron were just behind Hawthorne and nodded in agreement. "That's one security we have," said Verne. "They can't duplicate what Will is able to do with his constructs. As far as I know, their watches have no greater range than ours do."

"You're forgetting two things," said John. "One, they have the Chronographer of Lost Times. Dee. His *Imaginarium Chronographica* marks far more zero points than anything we know of, so they can move about in time more freely. And," he added with a grimace, "Telemachus, and the Ruby Armor, is still a wild card here. If he doesn't cooperate, couldn't Dee just kill him and take the armor to use himself?"

"No," Verne answered as they rounded the west wing and walked toward Shakespeare's shop, "or else he'd have already done so. The armor can only be used by an adept, and there are only two we know of for certain—Telemachus and Rose. And anything else Dee could try would require cavorite, and that's not so easy to come by."

"I thought the Nameless Isles were made up almost entirely of cavorite," John said, shading his eyes to look at the surrounding islands. "Couldn't someone else just sneak over the bridge, mine some of the ore, and start making their own gate from scratch?"

In answer Hawthorne grabbed a large sledgehammer from Shakespeare's tools and strode over to where a boulder of cavorite was protruding from the scrubby lawn. Grasping the handle with both hands, he swung the hammer in a high arc and smashed it down on the stone. It impacted with a loud thunderclap of metal on rock, and the hammer shattered as if it were porcelain. The stone looked as if it had never been touched.

"Been suggested, been tried," he said, slightly breathless from the effort. "Cavorite is harder to mine than adamantium, harder to mine than unobtainium. It takes almost infinite geologic patience. More than exists in a man's lifetime. So it is, in point of fact, a far easier prospect to recover cavorite that has already been used in some capacity.

"If it had not been that the Watchmaker already had shaped cavorite, in quantity," Hawthorne went on, "then Will could not have lived long enough to mine it himself."

John frowned. "That's not the best of news," he said. "What you're saying is that the pieces we have can be reassembled into new configurations, but nothing new can be shaped. Not entirely new, anyway."

"Yes," said Verne. "The gate really is the best option we have, John. Perhaps the only one."

"We'll resort to last options when I'm convinced there's nothing else to try, and that the risk is worth it," John said flatly. "Until then, I expect every man at Tamerlane to abide by my decision."

When night fell on the Nameless Isles, Fred and Laura Glue met up at the place where they hid that thing that one time, and, making certain they weren't being followed, she then led him someplace else.

There were very few areas in Tamerlane House that were not well lit at all times—but children have a way of finding all the hidden corners. "It's very simple," Laura Glue explained to Fred as he followed her through the hallways to the secret room. "All you have to do is imagine that the longbeards—the grown-ups—have hidden some presents that they bought you, then imagine where they'd hide them, and just go there."

She pointed down the dark corridor at the northeast corner of Tamerlane House. "That's how I found this place."

"By imagining someone bought you a gift and hid it?"

"Not imagining," she said, pointing at her aviator goggles. "These were supposed to be a surprise gift from Mr. Twain."

The badger was about to respond, but the Valkyrie shushed him. A light was approaching the corner from the other end of the corridor. They both held their breath until Quixote and Uncas rounded the corner.

"And that's how I found this place," Uncas was saying, gesturing with one of his prized possessions—a copper spyglass. "It was s'pposed t' be a present from Scowler Irving."

"Well met," Quixote said as Laura Glue opened up an almost invisible door into a small room. The walls were covered with drapes, and there was no furniture. Fred and Uncas set their lamps down in opposite corners, so that the shadows would cancel each other out.

"Can't be too sure," Fred said. "At least we know no one can find us here."

As one, all four of them jumped as someone rapped "Shave and a Haircut" on the door.

Laura opened it and was crestfallen to see Jack enter the room.

"Hello, Laura my Glue," Jack said gently. "You be up to something, neh?"

"Neh," she said, answering him in the slang she'd learned among the Lost Boys, so long ago. "How did you know?"

"It wasn't me," Jack said. "Somehow Poe knew you were planning something, and he asked me to check in on you. Oh, don't worry," he rushed to reassure them. "He didn't tell anyone else."

Jack looked around at the four of them. "Is this your whole band of conspirators, then?"

"Not quite," another voice said from the corridor. "For good or ill, I must be included amongst their number."

Jack moved aside so Shakespeare could enter the room. "They needed someone to program the gate, and I'm afraid at present, I'm the best qualified, like it or not. Also," he added, "I'm as anxious to help our lost friends as anyone. It was in part because of following my counsel that they've become lost."

"That wasn't your fault, Will," said Jack. "If not for you, we'd have no chance at all to restore the Archipelago."

"Are you going to go with us, Scowler Jack?" asked Fred. "It'd be a mighty comfort to have you with us."

"I wish I could, more than anything," Jack said, his eyes heavy with honest regret. "But I cannot. With John having taken the role of Prime Caretaker, I am essentially the new Caveo Principia, and there are too many responsibilities here than I can leave at present—not the least of which is trying to talk some sense into my erstwhile colleague. I want nothing more than to be of help to you, and go along—but fortunately, I'm not the only one who knows about your plan."

On cue, another face peered around the door. "What's all the racket?" Kipling asked. "I thought this was supposed to be a secret mission."

His face still bore the burns and scars from the evacuation of the Hotel d'Ailleurs two months earlier, and he moved slowly, his limbs still stiff from his injuries. He was a tulpa, and he would recover, but it would take time.

"How did *you* know?" Laura Glue exclaimed.

"I'm head of Caretaker espionage, remember?" said Kipling. "Plus, the secret missions are always the most fun."

"Fun?" said Fred.

"Yes." Kipling nodded. "I'm going with you. I'm a tulpa, and so I can actually be away from Tamerlane as long as is necessary. Plus, you'll need some kind of adult supervision."

"I beg your pardon!" said Quixote.

"Ah, that's right," Kipling said. "Sorry, Uncas."

He turned to Shakespeare. "You realize your helping us is going to really, really tick off the Prime Caretaker, right?"

"It can't be helped," Shakespeare admitted. "Not trying the gate is the wrong decision. This is our Hail Mary, to borrow one of the old Cartographer's favorite expressions. Our last play. You are going to be our emissaries into the eternities, to find a needle in an endless ocean of hay, and I cannot in good conscience send you out without having equipped you with every advantage I can."

"When you put it that way," said Kipling, "I don't know if I want to go anymore myself."

"He's kidding," Jack assured them. "I think."

"Well, that's everyone," Laura Glue began before she was interrupted by a clattering of hooves in the hallway.

"Not quite," Jack said. He opened the door and Argus filed in, followed by two goats.

"These are Verne's two best goats, Coraline and Elly Mae," Jack said, scratching the goats' heads. "They're also going with you."

"His war leader!" Laura Glue exclaimed. "And the one who bites. We be in some deep trouble, we takes them with, Jack."

"I'll explain it to Jules later," Jack said soothingly. "He might be irritated, but he'll be happy that you have some extra protection for your journey."

"If it helps you feel better," Argus said, raising his hand, "I'm not going with you. I just helped with your transportation."

Laura Glue groaned. "This was supposed to be a secret mission," she complained, "but it seems like everyone at Tamerlane House already knows about it!"

Uncas patted her consolingly on the arm. "That's how these sooper-sekrit things tend t' go, in my experience."

"Don't worry, young Valkyrie," Shakespeare said. "Argus knows how to keep a confidence. And more than that, telling him was necessary," he added, pulling back the curtain at the end of the room, "so we could do this."

Through the window they could see the flickering lights scattered across the decks of a ship—the *Indigo Dragon*. But this was not the *Indigo Dragon* that the Caretakers had used—it had been altered by Shakespeare and Argus to be used for this specific mission.

It was shortened, bore a smaller sail that could be converted into the balloon used for flight, and now had wheels. And it had been outfitted with a harness that was just the right size for two goats.

"It's essentially an all-terrain vehicle," said Argus, "even if there's no terrain at all."

"Are the goats supposed to just sit in the crow's nest when we fly?" asked Fred. "It is primarily an airship now, after all."

"No," Kipling replied. "They're here to work.

"I once had the opportunity to visit the Saint of the Northern Isles, back when I first became a Caretaker," he said as he reached into his coat pocket, "and he gave me these. I've been saving them all these years for just the right occasion to use them."

The others looked at his outstretched hand. There in the palm were a dozen kernels of corn.

"How long was he in th' fire?" Uncas whispered to Quixote.

"Hush," said Laura Glue. "What are they, Rudy?"

"Magic seed corn," he replied. "If you plant them, they grow into a crop of corn that, when eaten, ensures that you have only good dreams when you sleep, and never bad ones. I have often been plagued by night terrors, and considered planting a little garden out back. But I'm glad I saved them, because they have one other use.

"If you feed the seed corn to any creature with cloven hooves, it will be able to fly. The Christmas Saint used them on reindeer, but they'll also work . . ."

"On goats," Laura Glue finished for him. "That's brilliant!"

"Meh," said Elly Mae.

"I've already aligned the mechanisms from the Zanzibar Gate," Shakespeare explained as the other conspirators got settled aboard the *Indigo Dragon*. "I've set it to go to the same place Bert said that the others were going to, and I have faith it will work. But after that," he added, choking back a sob, "you'll be on your own."

"How can you set the device to the right time and place?" asked Laura Glue. "I thought only Rose or Edmund could do that without a trump."

"Actually, it's because of Edmund that I can," said Shakespeare. He showed them the bronze plate he planned to insert into the mechanism of the gate. "We know from what Bert told us that they are no longer in the future, but in the past," he told them, "and Edmund found a way to tell us where.

"When Jules asked me to examine the time travel possibilities of the Sphinx that Poe had in the basement," he explained, "I opened it and found this plate. I didn't know what it meant then, but I know now. And it will take you to them. This I believe."

"There's one more thing," Jack said. He handed Fred a box wrapped in oilcloth. "It's the Serendipity Box. Laura Glue has never used it, nor has Quixote, or Kipling. It's your fallback, for when you are in real trouble. But," he added, "I hope you won't need it."

It took only a few minutes for them to sail the *Indigo Dragon* to the outer island where the Zanzibar Gate stood, and only a few minutes more to prepare for the crossing through time. Shakespeare installed the bronze plate on the control device, then stood back with Jack and Argus and looked at the small company. A Valkyrie, a badger Caretaker, his father the squire, the legendary knight, and Kipling. "That's everyone, I think," Jack said.

"Not quite," said Laura Glue, looking around in the darkness. "Where's—"

"I'm already here," Madoc said as he stepped out of the trees and climbed onboard the ship. As he approached, the gate began to glow.

"I wasn't sure you'd do it," said Quixote. "You seemed very supportive of the Prime Caretaker's decision."

"I learned the art of diplomacy in Alexandria," said Madoc, "and I know when to use it. But there is a time to talk, and a time to act. And we are going," he finished, winking at Laura Glue, "to get my daughter."

"You're the best of us all," Jack said to the small company as his eyes welled with tears, "and you are the last children of the Archipelago. Be strong. Be brave. And never forget . . ."

"Believing is seeing," Fred said as the small craft lifted up into the air. "Don't worry, Scowler Jack," he added as the ship disappeared through the gate. "We got this."

CHAPTER SEVEN
THE CITY OF JADE

—✳—

IT WAS THE first city that was, and as such, it had no need of a name—but things that are made must also be named, for that is the way of the world. And so, as travelers came from the distant parts of the earth, to seek knowledge, and trade, and in some cases, redemption, they named the city, and carried those names back with them when they returned home.

To the younger races, it was called Atlantis. To the Children of the Earth, who had assisted in its construction, it was called the Dragon Isle. Some named it for the builder who first deigned to create something great in the world, and they called it the City of Enoch, but it was not his city they saw, not truly—and those who had created and named everything else the city is, was, and would yet become simply called it the City of Jade.

When the Cartographer Edmund McGee drew the city on parchment, to use as a chronal trump for himself, Rose Dyson, and the Caretaker Charles, and later, when he duplicated the drawing as a bronze engraving to leave in the Sphinx for the Caretakers to find in the future, both renderings were based on descriptions and memories provided to him by the legendary Gilgamesh. The great king had seen the city in his youth, and his

recollections of it were strong enough that Edmund could duplicate it in line with great fidelity. But as fine as the renderings were,
there was simply no comparison between viewing a simple drawing and being in the presence of a city that had been designed and
built by angels.

The place where Rose, Edmund, and Charles had appeared
was a grassy hill on the other side of the estuary that separated
the island where the city stood from the mainland. A conversation
with a passing angel called Nix had some unusual results: First,
Charles was mistaken for a Seraphim, which was not necessarily
a bad thing; and second, when they asked for further information
about the city, and the summit that was to take place there, Nix
instructed them to seek out what he referred to as a minor angel
with the unlikeliest of names.

"Samaranth?" Charles said for the umpteenth time. "That just
can't be a coincidence. It can't be."

"I agree," Rose said as they walked down the path taken by
Nix, but at a discreet distance. They had decided that following
someone who was attending to official city business would be the
most direct route into the city, but they preferred not to arouse
his suspicion any further than they already had. "He may be the
reason this is a chronal zero point. After all, the trump could
take us to the city, but something else had to influence the reason
we arrived at this specific point in time—and Samaranth's presence might be it."

"We had some help, remember?" Edmund interjected. "The
old man, in Platonia. He has involved himself in things before, to
help you out. He must have known."

"He knew something, that's for certain," Rose answered as

they approached the bridge. It was made of the same glowing green material as the city and was several hundred yards wide. At both ends and at several points across the width of the entrance were guard towers manned by watchmen who were paying scant attention to most of those crossing—almost all of whom seemed to be boylike angels like Nix.

As the companions approached, Edmund and Rose whispered back and forth about what possible ruse they could use to pass, but the guard in the nearest tower simply looked up, nodded at Charles, then went back to his other work.

"Interesting," Charles murmured as they passed. "I would have at least expected to be stopped and questioned."

The guard overheard this and leaned out of his tower, shaking his head. "You are Seraphim, are you not?" he asked.

"Er, ah, yes," Charles said hesitantly. "I am."

"Then you are Named," the guard replied, "Naming is Being, and there is no need to ask about your business."

The three companions walked past, and for a moment, it seemed to the guard as if the girl's shadow was moving independently of the person casting it. He watched a moment more, then shook it off. After all, there were no shadows in the City of Jade that the Makers did not intend to be there—not even those that moved of their own accord.

"Back there, on the hill," Rose said to the others as they crossed the bridge, "when Nix asked if you were Nephilim, and you said you were Seraphim . . . You *Named* yourself, Charles."

The Caretaker and the Cartographer both nodded in agreement. "I think you're right," said Charles. "Somehow, how I identified myself is reflected in my countenance. It's probably a good thing I didn't identify myself as an editor or an author. We'd probably have been taken prisoner and put to work in a labor camp somewhere, just out of compassion."

There were no other guards, and no gates to pass through on the other side of the bridge—simply open boulevards between massive buildings and towers, all of which were buzzing with activity. There were angels like Nix walking to and fro, all focused on whatever was on the tablets they carried. Above their heads were other beings the companions assumed were also angels, but these creatures had wings and were flying between the great towers.

Also walking the streets were humans, who were distinguishable from the angels by the fact that they were more elaborately dressed and carried the burden of aging more obviously.

Humans could grow old, it seemed. Even in Atlantis.

Another personage paused and turned to look at the companions as they passed. He was tall, taller than anyone they had yet seen in the city. He was silver-haired and wore a silver tunic that was shot through with a streak of crimson that matched the glowing red of his eyes.

In response, Rose took both Charles and Edmund by the arms and led them around a corner, out of his sight.

"What's wrong?" asked Charles. "Who was that?"

"I've met him before," Rose answered, still hurrying them along, "twice. The first time, he said he was a star named Rao, and he had been banished to a Ring of Power on an island past the Edge of the World. And the second time," she added, unable to suppress a shudder, "was when he destroyed Paralon and revealed himself to be a Lloigor in service of the Echthroi."

◆ ◆ ◆

Having avoided a possible confrontation with the future renegade star, the companions realized that there would be no way
to locate Samaranth without asking for help. They tried asking
some of the passing angels, all of whom responded politely as soon
as they noticed Charles, but waved the question away as basically
meaningless the moment Samaranth's name was mentioned.

"I thought he was the most respected creature in the Archipelago," Edmund said, "and everyone we've approached has mentioned his being among the oldest angels here. So why are they so
quick to dismiss him as irrelevant?"

"It's the way of the world," Charles lamented. "Youth never
trusts or respects the wisdom of age and experience until they are
aged and experienced themselves, and by then, it's usually too late."

"Not every culture is like that, surely," said Edmund. "I was
raised to respect my elders."

"So was I," said Rose.

"The exceptions that prove the rule," Charles said. "Let's go ask
that fellow, there."

He was indicating a tall, finely dressed man who was writing
with a stylus on parchment instead of using one of the tablets the
angels all seemed to carry.

"Why him?" asked Rose.

Charles shrugged. "It's just something about his countenance."

The man listened politely as they explained whom they were
seeking, and as opposed to the angels' deference to Charles the
Seraphim, seemed more taken by Rose.

"Yes, I can help you," he said when they'd finished. He turned
and took a few steps into the street. "There," he said, pointing at

a broad, squat building in the distance. "All the minor guilds are ensconced there, in the Library. It keeps them out of the way of all the others, who are certain they are doing more important work."

Charles caught the hint of derision in the man's voice and couldn't help himself. "What work do you believe is more important?"

The man smiled wryly. "You have the countenance of a Seraphim but the manner of a scholar. The work of a scholar is to seek after knowledge—and there is always something new to learn."

He turned to Rose, more serious now. "The summit is coming to an end soon, and changes will be coming. Find your minor angel, and then leave. The City of Jade may not be as welcoming to you tonight as it was to you today."

The man spun on his heel and began to walk away. "Good luck to you, scholars," he called back. "Hermes Trismegistus wishes you well."

The Library was easy enough to get to, but impossibly large, which required a few more inquiries. Eventually the companions were directed to what was essentially the basement, where a large door separated in the center and slid open at Rose's touch.

"Come in, if you must," said a thin tenor voice, "but please make haste. I have a full schedule of Naming today, and a thousand and one things must be recorded for the book if I'm to be allowed into the summit."

The companions entered the vast, tall room and gasped at the size of it. They knew that it was a lower level in the Library, but to all appearances it seemed nearly endless inside, and there was no ceiling, save for distant abstract geometric shapes set among a field of twinkling lights.

"Yes, yes," the voice said again, "it is small and rather cramped—the Guild keeps all its unfinished concepts here, and they take up more room than you'd think—but there's space enough for me to do my work, and that suffices."

The speaker was sitting on a dais at the center of the room, working on one of the tablets all the angels seemed to carry. That much was not a surprise. What was a surprise was that Nix had described the angel before them as being one of the oldest among all those in the city—but the face that peered sideways at them as they approached was that of a young man, barely out of school.

He blew a wayward strand of reddish hair out of his face and scowled at the visitors. "Well? Are you going to tell me what business you bring, or do I have to Un-Name you to get your attention?"

"Well," said Charles, "that sure *sounds* like Samaranth."

"Of course," the young man said primly. "I am he. I am Samaranth. Who," he added, eyes glittering, "are *you?*"

The companions stared at the angel with undisguised shock. This was not what they'd expected to see, and this small, twitchy, suspicious, childlike creature bore almost no resemblance to the great, regal Dragon they had known. No resemblance, save for . . .

"His eyes," Laura Glue said softly. "He has Samaranth's eyes."

The angel snorted. "Of course I do. Am I not Samaranth?" He stood and stepped down from the dais to approach them. He was barely as tall as Rose, and several inches shorter than Edmund. "I am the fifth assistant Namer from the nine hundred and second

Guild of Namers, of the fifty-first Host of Angels of the City of Jade."

"Nix said he was one of the oldest of them," Rose whispered to Charles, "but he doesn't appear to be any older than I am, if that."

"Not to put too fine a point on it," Charles whispered back, "but as I recall, you're fairly advanced in years yourself, even though you don't look it."

"Oh, I am one of the eldest of the Host," said Samaranth, who apparently could hear just fine. "At least, among those assigned to this world. And," he added thoughtfully, "I might actually be younger than you, ah, what did you say you are called?"

"I'm Rose," she said, "and this is Charles, and Edmund. Just how old *are* you?"

Samaranth answered without hesitation. "According to the Chronos time established by Sol when this world was set into motion, I am approximately two billion, three hundred seventy-nine million, one hundred fifty-two thousand, four hundred and ninety-seven years old, give or take."

"Give or take?" asked Edmund.

Samaranth nodded. "It's difficult to figure precisely, because of a few things that have already been Named and Placed, like the 'Mayan conundrum' and something called a 'leap year.' It makes the calculations especially difficult, because we don't even have a name for the process of, ah, figuring yet. It involves numbers, but that's as far as I've gotten."

Charles sighed in sympathy. "I can relate. Trouble with math is one reason I became a writer."

"Hmm. Math," said Samaranth. "I like that. That could work." He jotted down a note on his tablet. "Math. Yes. Very good. You could be a Namer yourself, you know. If you weren't a Seraphim, that is."

"Ah, yes, about that," Charles began before Edmund elbowed him in the ribs.

"Don't say it," the Cartographer hissed. "If you can Name yourself, who's to say you can't Un-Name yourself just as easily?"

Hearing this, Samaranth turned his full attention to them for the first time, and his expression was dark.

"That is not something to be spoken of in the City of Jade," he said softly. "Things that are made may be Named, and sometimes, may also be Renamed, when they must choose a different path. But to be . . . to be Un-Named is something entirely different."

He set aside his work and stepped closer to Charles. "You are not Seraphim, are you? You bear the countenance, but I sense you are also Other."

"He is a Caretaker," Rose said quickly. "That is the most important job there is."

Samaranth considered this as he walked back to the dais. "A Caretaker, you say? Hmm. Someone who Takes Care. Yes, I understand. That is good." He made some notations on a tablet. "I shall remember that, thank you."

A chime sounded in the air somewhere above them, and the angel's expression suddenly changed. "Oh by the Host—it is nearly time. I must prepare to finish here so I might attend the summit." He looked at the three of them as if they'd just walked in. "Have you been fed?"

"Please, Samaranth," Rose asked, "can you tell us what this summit is about? Everyone in the city seems to be involved somehow."

"Everyone *is* involved," he replied. "There is nothing more important than what will be determined here today, after debating for so many years. The younger principalities believe that almost everything that *can* be created in this world *has* been created, and in this, they are quite nearly correct. However, they also think that now there will no longer be a great need for Makers, there will also be no need for Namers either."

"Namers like yourself," Charles noted drolly. "Just saying."

"I speak to be understood, not out of vanity," said Samaranth, "and they believe they will have little need of me, even though there is still a tremendous amount of work to be done. There will always be some need for Makers—but Naming is far more valuable, because to Name something is to give it meaning. Simply being created is not enough."

"Everything has been made?" Edmund said, gesturing out the window. "Even there?"

He was looking to the west, toward the Archipelago—or at least, where the Archipelago should have been. But there was nothing except darkness there. And not the storm-cloud darkness of the Frontier, but the darkness that Rose had seen only once before, when she and her friends sailed past the waterfall at the Edge of the World and into the darkness beyond, to find her father.

Samaranth looked at him in surprise. "That is the Un-Made World," he said as if his visitors should have known already, "and it remains Un-Named, until the Word chooses a time and a place to make it and Name it. There is nothing there except darkness, and stone, and . . ."

"And the keep," said Edmund. "The Eternal Tower. Isn't that right?"

For the first time since they'd arrived, Samaranth actually looked frightened. "*Are* you Nephilim?" he asked, his voice steady, but the fear still evident in his expression. "Have you come to Un-Name me?"

"No, we aren't Nephilim, and we haven't come to Un-Name anyone," Rose quickly assured him. "Why would you ask that?"

"Because," Samaranth replied, "only a few among the Host, the eldest of us, even know the tower exists. We have traveled to it. We know how to use it. And of us all, I alone deduced how important it is to this world and the Un-Made World both. They were not always severed. And someday, they may be made whole again. This is the secret we have kept for eons. The secret worth . . . killing for. So, I must ask you again—have you come to Un-Name me?"

CHAPTER EIGHT
THE STEWARD

•—✳—•

"THEY DID WHAT?" John exclaimed, incredulous. "You helped them to do *what*?"

"Calm down, John," Jack said soothingly, "and I'll explain everything."

"Calm *down*?!?" John sputtered, almost too furious to speak. "You've just betrayed everything we believe in!"

Jack scowled. "No, I haven't," he said as calmly as he could manage. "We just believed that—"

"We?" John exclaimed. "You mean there were . . ." He stopped, thinking, then spun around, pointing an accusing finger at Shakespeare.

"I'm surprised at you, Will," John said. "They could not have done this without your help. You should have come to me."

"That's the rub of it," Shakespeare said, moving around the table to stand in solidarity with Jack. "We don't think you made the right call. The gate was the only viable option we had."

"You've betrayed your oath as a Caretaker, Jack," John said, shaking. "And you've betrayed me."

"Well, as regards the former," Jack said, his voice becoming steadier as he grew bolder about confronting his friend, "I disagree.

I swore an oath to protect a book that is lost somewhere in Deep Time, and an Archipelago that has disappeared to heaven knows where from a world that is dominated by shadows. So there really wasn't much to betray except my own best judgment, which I used. And as to the latter," he continued, "if that's really how you feel, oh Prime Caretaker, why don't you fire me?"

It was spoken in the heat of the argument, but Jack's statement nonetheless shocked the older Caretakers. Verne and Bert stepped in to try to calm tempers on both sides.

"Focus on what moves us forward, not what moves us backward, John," Verne said, laying a hand on the younger man's shoulder.

"Don't patronize me, Jules," John said, rebuffing Verne's calming words and comforting hand. "Besides, wasn't it your man Burton who taught us that time moves in two directions? They've gone back in time, and we couldn't even check in on them if we wanted to! We'll have no way of even knowing if they get into trouble!"

"We actually may have a way," said Verne. "It's something I'd been working on with Burton ages ago that I think will come in useful now."

John glared at Jack a few seconds longer, then tipped his head at Verne. "All right. Show me."

Verne ushered the Caretakers into a large, circular room in the northernmost wing of Tamerlane House. There was an immense round table in the center. It was made of some kind of stone, more ancient than marble. It was crisscrossed with various alchemical symbols, and a hexagonal shape, inset into the middle, was polished to an almost mirrorlike finish.

"This is the table that Arthur used to conduct séances," Verne said, gesturing at Conan Doyle. "What he didn't understand at the time, and what Ehrich spent a lot of time and energy trying to debunk," he added, winking at Houdini, "is that Arthur wasn't making contact with the spirit world, but with the past.

"This table," he continued as the other Caretakers took their seats around the circle, "is one of the few artifacts that survived the destruction of Atlantis. It is possible, if that is where our friends have gone, that we will be able to observe them, and possibly even send messages as well."

"Send messages?" John said, still fuming from Jack's announcement. "If there was the possibility that this would work, then they never should have risked using the gate."

"We don't know that it *will* work," said Verne. "In fact, it never even occurred to me as a possibility until last night. You see, Arthur always assumed he was communicating with a spirit in real time. What he was actually doing was communicating with the past, with someone who, from their own point of view, was still living. Burton is the one who figured it out."

"Actually," Conan Doyle admitted with a touch of embarrassment, "that's part of the reason Burton was able to so easily recruit me into the ICS. He had already been told a lot about me by his own right-hand man, who had been speaking to me for years via the table."

"Burton's right-hand man?" John said, frowning. "What does he have to do with all this? I don't understand."

"It is attuned to the craftsman who made it," said Verne. "Arthur knew him as Pheneas, a man of Arab descent who supposedly died thousands of years ago. In fact, the maker of this table was considerably older than that. He was known at points in his life as Theopolous, and earlier still as Enkidu. But Burton, who knew him best, simply called him the End of Time, and when he introduced us, I knew I had found the first, and perhaps the best, of my Messengers. As you know, he died at the hands of an Echthros in London, but he may be able to serve us still."

"What must we do, Jules?" Jack asked. "How does it work?"

"He always seemed to appear in answer to my questions," Conan Doyle replied. "He seemed never to age, but sometimes he couldn't recall earlier discussions. I think it's because I was going further and further back along his timeline. It functions in a manner similar to the trumps—intuition plays a part."

"As does belief," Houdini interjected. "You believed, and I didn't, Arthur. That's why you saw him."

"Believing is seeing," said Shakespeare. "We should give it a go."

"All right," John said, still reluctant, and more than a bit put out that he hadn't been told about the table earlier. "How do we do this?"

"Join hands," said Conan Doyle. "There are just enough of us here to make it work. Seven seems to have been the best number for making it operate. More, and there were too many competing thoughts; less, and there wasn't enough concentration to keep a clear focus."

Jack took Shakespeare's left hand and Houdini's right. Conan Doyle sat between Houdini and John, with Bert to John's left, and Verne completing the circle.

"What question should we ask?" said John.

"The simplest one, I suppose," said Conan Doyle. "Where is the *Indigo Dragon*?"

Together, the men gripped one another's hands and focused their will and thought on the question and the table.

Nothing happened.

"If Charles were here," Jack said after a few minutes had passed, "he would be asking if we needed to invoke some sort of incantation or magic spell."

"Abarakadabara," said Houdini. Still nothing.

"Is it plugged in?" asked Bert.

"Maybe it needed a Dragon, like the Zanzibar Gate did," Shakespeare began to say, and in that instant an unearthly glow began to emanate from the center of the hexagon.

"Ah," said John. "Well done, Will."

"Thanks, but I haven't the slightest idea what just happened," said Shakespeare.

"You focused your thoughts on a living Dragon," said Verne. "Life flows to life. We simply asked the wrong question."

"Quiet, all of you," John said as the light rose from the table in a column that began to alter and shift, forming a three-dimensional, almost holographic image. "Something is beginning to appear."

On the downward slope of a gigantic sand dune, the air shimmered and hummed, and suddenly the Zanzibar Gate came into view, becoming more and more solid as the seconds passed.

Almost instantly, the *Indigo Dragon* slid through and onto the sand, coming to rest with a slight lean about twenty feet down the dune.

"Meh!" said Elly Mae.

"Mah!" said Coraline.

"Is it over?" asked Fred. "That went pretty quickly."

"Just like walking through the doors of the keep," said Madoc. "That Shaksberd is quite the talented fellow. If I'd have recruited him instead of Burton—"

"Don't," Uncas said sternly, "even *joke* about that."

Quixote had already removed his helmet and breastplate. In the heat, the armor would be almost unbearable. He wiped his brow and looked to the horizon. "There," he said, pointing. "I think we've found the city."

Indeed, off in the distance the companions could see the magnificent outlines of the City of Jade, but the view was obscured by something so much more massive that at first, what it was failed to register with any of them. It was Madoc who understood it before the rest of them.

"The giants," he breathed, shading his eyes to look as high into the sky as he could manage. "The Corinthian Giants have formed a living wall between us and the city."

It was true—the great giants of legend, who had once saved the Caretakers from an aspect of Mordred called the King of Crickets, were standing shoulder to shoulder from the western edge of the desert that met the ocean, to so far to the east that they faded from view in the distance.

All along the perimeter formed by the giants' feet were encampments of people. Thousands upon thousands of tents, and caravans, and wagons, and what might have been a million people of every creed and color. Every culture of the young world seemed to be represented, and none of the encampments seemed to be temporary. Flocks of sheep and woolly cattle were corralled at spots along the line, as well as flocks of fowl, and animals of labor of every stripe: camel-like creatures with great humps, small horses covered in fur, and great catlike creatures that were large enough to be ridden by three men.

"It looks as if generations of people have lived here, waiting for something," said Quixote.

"Or being kept from something," said Kipling.

"Or waiting for something t' happen," said Uncas. "Turn around."

In the other direction, to the north of the Zanzibar Gate, was a sight equally as stunning—not because it was as overwhelming as the sight of the massive giants and enormous encampments at their feet, but because each of them intuitively knew what they were looking at.

Not half a mile behind the gate was a gigantic ship. It was perpendicular to their position, so they had no way of judging just how broad it might be, because it was so long they could barely see the ends.

Kipling let out a low whistle. "That has to be . . ."

"Several miles long, end to end," said Madoc. "I can't see how wide, though."

"I'll take a look," Laura Glue said, unfurling her Valkyrie's wings and leaping into the air.

"Laura Glue, no!" Kipling yelled, just a moment too late. She rose sharply into the air before she understood her mistake and dropped back down to the *Indigo Dragon*.

"Uh-oh," said Fred. "I think we're about to have some company."

A group of people had indeed seen Laura Glue's brief, ill-advised flight and were making their way over to the Zanzibar Gate to investigate—but not from the encampments. The procession was coming from the huge boat.

An elderly man, dressed in desert garb, with a long gray beard streaked through with white, led the procession of women, children, and, the companions were surprised to see, a large contingent of animals.

He raised a hand in greeting as he peered curiously at Laura Glue and Madoc in turn, taking particular care to look over their wings. In response, and perhaps as a bit of a challenge, Madoc flexed his shoulders and opened his wings to their full, impressive glory.

Kipling stepped forward, expecting to address the old man, but Fred and Uncas beat him to it, throwing themselves to the sand at the man's feet. "We greet you, oh Ancient of Days," they said in unison. "Now and forever, we serve thee, Ordo Maas."

The old man chuckled and helped them both to their feet. "That's all well and good," he said, a cheerful expression on his face that bespoke earnest affection for everyone in their group, "but there's no point getting sand in your clothes, now, is there?"

"Ordo Maas?" Madoc said, dumbfounded. "*You* are Ordo Maas?"

The old man nodded. "The Children of the Earth—the animals—named me thus back in the days when all of them spoke as these two fine badgers do," he said, scratching at Uncas's head, which the badger would have hated anyone else doing, but which he seemed to love in the moment. "In my old kingdom, back in the Empty Quarter, I was known as Utnapishtim. But here, among the people of this great exodus, I am simply known as Deucalion."

"Deucalion, the son of Prometheus," said Madoc, "who built a great ark and saved all the creatures of the earth from a deluge that covered the world."

"You're mostly right," Deucalion said. "My father was Prometheus, and I have built a ship. But it hasn't rained here in decades. Water is growing scarce. And my reputation is more that of a fool than a king or savior of animals."

"Just wait," said Fred. "I think things are about to change."

"Why were we brought here?" Kipling wondered aloud as they followed the shipbuilder back to his tents in the shade of the great boat. "I thought we'd end up closer to the city itself."

"Remember what Will told us," Laura Glue reminded them. "Intuition plays a part in how the gate is guided. If we were brought to this place, it's in part because this is where we needed to be."

"Perhaps the giants have something to do with it," said Madoc.

"You may be right in that," said Deucalion. "The Corinthian Giants have prevented anyone from reaching the city who did not specifically have the Mandate of Heaven. It has been thus for generations."

"'Generations' is certainly the word for it," Quixote said, straining backward to look up at the huge ship.

"This wasn't built overnight," Madoc said with real admiration in his voice. "How long have you been working on this vessel, old one?"

"From the time I was warned about the cataclysm to come, and my wife and I fled my kingdom to come here, it has been one hundred and forty years," Deucalion said as he gestured for his sons and their wives to serve water to his guests—first to the goats, then to the badgers, and then to the rest. "We began our family with the birth of my eldest son in the same year we began constructing the ship, a decade after our flight into the desert. And now we are nearly finished, just as my youngest son, Hap, is reaching manhood.

"But enough of family histories," he said, turning to Uncas. "What is it that brings you to my tent?"

"Some friends of ours have gone missing," Uncas said, "and we've come looking for them."

"How come I can never explain our goals that simply?" Kipling whispered to Quixote.

"Poetic license," the knight whispered back. "It's a privilege, not a right."

"I see," said Deucalion. "And I take it from what you said earlier about expecting to find yourselves in the city that you hope to find them there?"

"We do," said Uncas.

"You may be right, but without the Mandate of Heaven, you'll never know," Deucalion said. "Nothing living can get past the Corinthian Giants."

In one fluid, graceful motion, Kipling rose to his feet. "I think that's my cue. I'm going to go have a look around," he said jovially. "I'll see if I can't get the lay of the land, so we can make a game plan for finding our friends."

The shipbuilder started. "You want to go into the city?"

Kipling bowed. "That is where, it seems, all the action is. And I am a man of action."

"We could all try to—," Quixote began before Kipling cut him off with a gesture.

"Alone would be best," he said. "Just reconnaissance, I promise. I'll be back as soon as I can manage."

"Is that wise?" Laura Glue asked.

"I'm head of the Espionage Squad, remember?" Kipling said, feigning hurt feelings. "I'm just going to go have a look around. And besides," he added, glancing from Madoc's wings to Laura Glue's, "I'll attract a lot less attention than the rest of you will."

Deucalion sighed heavily. "Man of action you may be, but it is impossible. As I have told you, unless you have been given passage into the city by an emissary, the giants will permit no one living to cross the boundary."

"It shouldn't be a problem, then," Kipling said with a wink as he exited the tent, "since I actually died some time ago."

Deucalion looked at Fred and Uncas for an explanation, but the Caretaker merely shrugged, and the knight's squire stifled a chuckle.

"It's kind of hard to explain," said Laura Glue, "but trust me, he's alive enough to do what he must."

This time it was the shipbuilder's turn to smile. "As are we all, my child. God willing, as are we all."

PART THREE

THE SUMMIT

CHAPTER NINE
MESSAGES

·—✳—·

THE ECHTHROS WATCHED, and waited.

It was in the house because of the Binding it wore, and so, when it was called upon, it was forced to serve the master who had fashioned it. But in between those summonings, it was still a creature of will, doing as it pleased. And it pleased the Echthros to be here, watching these little things play at the machinations of the world as if they were gods. No—as if they were the only gods; as if they were all the little gods there were.

It had played a part in the choices they made, partly in service to the Binding, and partly because it found the events taking place to be interesting. Once, in service to the Binding, it had even killed someone who had spent thousands of years doing little more than helping others.

And once, very recently, it had spilled one of its master's secrets, perhaps the most important one. The Echthros claimed to have done so because of a covenant it had made oh so long ago—a covenant made almost at the same time it had been bound, when it was not yet an Echthros, but a free creature, who walked unafraid through the streets of the City of Jade.

The covenant did not compel servitude as the Binding did. Maybe that was why the Echthros chose to honor the request and offer help to the Caretakers' friends.

*Or maybe it was simply another aspect of its service to Shadow. It
didn't know. But soon, it might find out.*

Samaranth's question hung in the air for a long moment before any
of the companions chose to answer. Rose opened her mouth to speak.

"We are not here to Un-Name you," she said again, slowly and
carefully. After all, Samaranth might have seemed afraid in that
moment—but he was still an angel. There was no way to know
what that might mean in terms of the power he could wield if he
felt threatened . . .

. . . or felt the need for retribution.

"We have come a . . . very long way, to ask for your help," said
Edmund. "We have no desire to interfere with you, or your
summit, or anything to do with the city. We simply want to ask
you a question."

Samaranth already seemed calmer, something that might
have been due more to his curiosity about these strange visitors
than to their soothing words. "All right," he said, having decided
that whatever these creatures were, they were no threat. "What
do you want to ask of me?"

"The Keep of Time," Rose began. "You say that you know how
it works, and that you understand how important it is to both this
world and the one out there. What we want to ask is if you have
also discovered who built the keep."

The angel immediately shook his head. "That is the one question we have never been able to answer," he said, "although it is an
answer I have sought myself, in secret, because unless that answer
is discovered, nothing we do here will be of any value whatsoever."

"Why is that?"

"Because it is damaged," Samaranth answered, "and unless it is repaired, it will someday vanish altogether, and the connection to this world will be destroyed. And when that occurs, there will be nothing to prevent the Un-Namers from sweeping over the face of the earth."

As Kipling expected, passing the line of Corinthian Giants was spectacularly easy. His state of being as a tulpa, a living thought-form that possessed the aiua, or soul, of Rudyard Kipling, apparently made him a different enough kind of creature that the living monoliths paid him no heed whatsoever. They remained impassive, and immobile as stone. He was still human enough, however, to attract the attention of several among the refugees encamped along the living wall—and several of them, seeing how he passed successfully, attempted to do the same.

He watched with a bemused expression on his face, wondering just what method the giants would resort to for repelling the invaders—but an instant later, the smile dropped off his face.

The first two refugees had just reached the narrow isthmus between two of the giants' feet when a horrifyingly loud booming horn sounded in the sky, and one of the giants looked down. A beam of light erupted from the giant's cowled face, incinerating the refugees to ash.

Sickened, and berating himself for not being more careful, Kipling fashioned a turban out of his jacket to protect his head from the hot sun and started the long trek to the distant city.

"It stands to reason that he wouldn't know," Charles said to the others. "If he had known, surely Bert, or Verne, or *someone* back home would have discovered the identity of the Architect years ago."

"Not necessarily," said Rose. "He wasn't tame when we knew him, you know. And there were times he did deliberately conceal information so that we'd have to discover the answers ourselves."

"Also," Edmund put in, "if he is the oldest of all his kind here, then it's not very likely that anyone else in the entire city would know more than he does."

"Age does not equal knowledge," Samaranth said. He turned to Rose, scowling slightly. "Did you just call me 'tame'?"

She blushed furiously and changed the subject. "I'm sorry we bothered you, Samaranth," she said contritely. "I hope we haven't interfered too much with your work."

"You seem to know a great deal about who I am," the angel said, giving them a look of appraisal, "and I still know nothing of you. Where did you say you hailed from?"

"There is only so much we can share," Rose began in answer to Samaranth's question, "without risking terrible damage to our own future. And yours," she added quickly. "I can only ask that you trust us, and that you try to believe that our intentions are good."

The angel considered her words and pursed his lips. "I don't have to try," he said finally. "Your countenance bears out your intentions, and I can read you like a book.

"My concern now, and the concern of all those who are eldest within the City of Jade, is in continuing the Naming of all that has already been made, so that all those who reside here may continue to live here in peace. One world should be sufficient enough to share, even among the principalities."

"There are some who disagree?" asked Charles.

"This is the reason for the summit," Samaranth said as he put away his tablet and began to tidy up his workspace—which, Rose noted, was already almost unspeakably tidy. "The principalities have fashioned a proposal to appeal to the Word to make the Un-Made World, and to Name it, so that they may claim it for their own. They wish to leave this world, which they have long been neglecting, to the peoples who have spread across it."

"Hmm," said Charles. "That doesn't sound too unfair."

"It would not be, had the principalities not used this world up in the process. They have benefited from it, and prospered, and now that it seems to be dying, they wish to go elsewhere. But," he added, "unless the Un-Made World is connected once more and fully to this one, it will perish as well."

"You keep saying 'principalities,'" said Edmund. "Forgive my ignorance, but what does that mean?"

"Gods," Samaranth said simply. "This summit is a gathering of all the gods of the earth, large and small. Some are gods who began as men, and rose to the calling out of will; and some are those who fell to earth and were worshipped for the talents they carried with them, and so were declared to be gods. And if what they have proposed is not opposed . . .

". . . then both this world and the next shall fall into utter ruin, and perish."

It was a more difficult trek to the city than Kipling had anticipated. He was actually tired. That hadn't happened often in the years following his death, but, he reasoned, it was still bound to happen sooner or later. That wasn't important, though, because he had a bigger problem. Getting past the giants was one thing. Gaining entry into the City of Jade itself was another kettle of fish entirely.

There were two bridges on the northern side, and both of them were lined with watchtowers manned by guards who were giving at least a cursory glance to every personage who crossed them. Kipling wasn't certain that he wanted to try an end run, which might attract attention, so he decided to sit and observe for a while.

After an hour, something significant sparked his attention. A number of people who had crossed the bridge with virtually no attention from the guards at all had one thing in common: They all had some kind of unusual markings on their foreheads. The most common was a circle surrounded by four diamonds.

Kipling considered his options a bit more, then shrugged in resignation. "When in Rome," he said, taking a pen from his jacket. He leaned over a shallow section of the estuary some distance from the bridge to use the water as a mirror, and drew what looked like a fair approximation of the tattoos he'd observed.

Thus prepared, he walked straight toward one of the watchtowers—and, to his delight, the guard did nothing more than glance at his forehead and wave him on.

"This may be the easiest espionage job I've ever taken," Kipling murmured to himself.

"Or," a shockingly familiar voice said from too close behind him for comfort, "at least, the last one you ever take."

He whirled around to face the speaker. It was John Dee.

"Greetings and salutations, Dr. Dee," Kipling said.

"Say good night, Kipling," said Dr. Dee. And suddenly the

Caretaker was plunged into pain, and darkness, and as he fell into unconsciousness, he realized that Dee was very probably right.

"I want to ask," Laura Glue said, once they had eaten from the food provided by Deucalion's family, "why did you decide to build this giant boat out here in the desert, where there's no water at all?"

"Actually," Uncas said, correcting her, "it's a ship."

"Boat," said Laura Glue.

"Ship," Uncas insisted.

"Actually, it's an ark," Deucalion said pleasantly. "And it wasn't so much a decision as it was a responsibility."

"How so?" asked Madoc.

"Come," Deucalion said, rising to his feet and gesturing for them to follow. "I will show you."

He led them through a connecting passage into another tent, which was guarded at the entryway by two of his sons, who regarded their visitors suspiciously, even though the guide was their own father. Inside, another son, Hap, stood guard over a pedestal.

"This is where we keep those objects sacred to us," Deucalion said as his son stepped back and the companions circled around the pedestal, "so that we carry with us the reminders of the work we are to do in the world."

On the pedestal was an ornate box made of a black wood with a latch made of bronze. The shipbuilder opened the latch and pushed back the lid. Inside, they could see several items: a brooch, a small dagger, three scrolls, and a simple, cream-colored note card on what appeared to be paper of twentieth-century manufacture. Deucalion removed the note card and closed the box.

"This is the reason I have done the work I have," he said point-edly. "Were it not for this, I would never have conceived of building the great ship, nor pursued the animal husbandry in the manner that I have. Although," he added, smiling and scratching Uncas behind the ear, "I have always favored the Children of the Earth above man, and thus, the work I have done only pleases me more."

"I can't read it," Laura Glue said bluntly. She looked at Madoc. "Can you?"

He shook his head. "It is far older than I, and of a language I never learned at Alexandria."

"There are few who can read it," Deucalion said, "but you already know the content of it—it is a warning about the Great Deluge to come, and a plea to gather all the Children of the Earth into a great ship, so that they may be taken to safety in another world, and to take all the knowledge necessary should the world need to be rebuilt. It was such an expression of madness that I would never have given it credence had I not also known and trusted he who wrote it."

"Who is that?" asked Madoc.

Deucalion smiled and tapped his chest. "*Me.*"

He explained how he had been approached at his court by someone who appeared out of thin air and seemed to be able to predict the future. This strange visitor was the one who delivered the note, which had apparently been written by Deucalion him-self, to himself, in his own hand. Thus, the shipbuilder explained, the man must have been a prophet of some kind, and after con-sulting with his sons, Deucalion left his land and journeyed to the City of Jade, where they began their work in earnest.

"To be honest, were it not for him, I might not have been so welcoming of you," Deucalion said bluntly. "Even here, in this land, you are strange personages."

Madoc frowned. "Then why did you trust us?"

"Because," Deucalion answered, gesturing at the pocket watch Fred wore, "our strange visitor carried a device just like the one you wear."

Laura Glue sighed and looked at Madoc, who was rubbing his forehead and flexing his wings in agitation. "Verne," he said, sighing. "Sometimes I don't know whether to be grateful for him, or wish that someone would get fed up enough with his meddling to seal him in a tomb."

Deucalion gave her a strange look. "Verne? No, that was not his name. He called himself something more in the manner of my own people—Telemachus."

The companions all felt the same thrill of fear at hearing that name. Laura Glue looked again at Madoc, who shook his head slightly, as if to say, *Now is not the time or place.* However, as had often been the case, the humans' discretion was completely over-ridden by the badgers.

"That's the name of th' boy prince we lost and then found again," said Uncas. "He might be evil, though."

"Or not," said Fred. "The last time we saw him, he was still thinking it over."

"Well, he apparently made his choice," said Deucalion, "because he left something for you, too."

"For us?" Quixote said in surprise.

"The badgers, specifically," said Deucalion. "He and I share an affinity for talking animals, it seems."

At the shipbuilder's urging, the badgers peered into the box, and there, underneath the scrolls, were two more envelopes, one addressed to each of them.

"Great!" Uncas exclaimed. "I *love* t' get mail."

"What does yours say, Fred?" Laura Glue asked as he broke the seal and removed the note. It read:

> You are a Caretaker, and thus, also a Namer.
> Name Madoc as a Nephilim, and you may pass
> through to the city. Look for your friends in the center,
> under the great celestial dome. Good luck.

"Nephilim?" Deucalion said with a start. He looked askance at Madoc. "Are you Nephilim? I would not have thought one such as yourself would care to keep company with Children of the Earth."

"Why?" asked Madoc. "What is a Nephilim?"

"One of the Host," Hap replied, stepping closer to his father, "but one who sees Shadow as being equal to the Light, who serves the Void while still claiming to serve the Word."

"Ah," said Madoc. "I see. I will never fully lose who I once was, it seems."

Deucalion put a hand of support on Madoc's shoulder. "Naming is not Being," the old shipbuilder said, "and anything that is Named may still be Renamed. The choice as to whom you serve is always yours."

"I just want to find my daughter," said Madoc.

"Yes," Quixote said, "that is why we came, but I'm afraid we now have a clock on it."

"What do you mean?" asked Madoc.

"This," Quixote said. He was holding the note that had been

addressed to Uncas. "It's hard to make the message any more clear."

The companions crowded around the knight to read the small note, which bore only a few words:

> *The flood is coming.*
> *Leave. Now.*

CHAPTER TEN
ORDER AND CHAOS

—�֎—

KIPLING CAME TO consciousness and found he had been bound hand and foot to a very uncomfortable chair that was sitting in a very uncomfortable room. It had the appearance of a glass conservatory that aspired to be a skyscraper, and stood along a glass-and-stone corridor that appeared to be lined with similar rooms.

"It's the same room, actually," an ornately dressed man said from his seat on another of the uncomfortable chairs, which sat in the opposite corner. "We've been having some issues with duration, and every so often it gets stuck."

Kipling didn't reply, but simply focused his attention on waking fully. He remembered being struck from behind, but other than that, what had happened after he saw Dr. Dee was a total loss.

The man was sitting facing an immense glass case, slotted with narrow vertical shelves. He was sliding thin slabs of marble that had some kind of writing on them in and out of the slots.

"Proximity matters," the man explained without looking away from his task. "Some of the scripts change others, so I have to make sure that those in close proximity are compatible; otherwise some significant meanings might be lost completely."

"What are they?" asked Kipling.

"I suppose you could call them Histories," the man said, "but since some of them haven't and may never happen, that may be erroneous."

"Who are you?"

"Hermes Trismegistus," the man replied, again without turning to look at his captive companion. "I suppose you could say I am your friend's teacher."

Kipling scowled. "Who, Dee?" he snorted. "He is *not* my friend."

"He's very intelligent," Hermes replied. "Almost like a god, but without any followers."

"Only fools would follow someone like him."

Hermes looked at him like he was a child. "You'd be surprised at how effective appearing to be a god really is."

"He's evil," said Kipling. "That's all I need to know."

"Hmm," Hermes said, rubbing his chin. "I think that's one of the more recent concepts. I don't know if it has even been recorded in the book yet."

"Why are you keeping me here, Hermes?"

"Hermes Trismegistus, please. And I'm not keeping you here," he said pointedly, "*he* is."

Kipling turned and saw Dr. Dee enter the room, then kick the door closed behind him, which seemed to annoy Hermes. Dee was carrying several of the tablets, which he placed on a table next to the shelves. "Those are the last of them," he said. "That should be sufficient, at least for . . ." Dee turned and saw for the first time that his unwilling guest was awake.

"What are you doing, Dee?"

"I am a scholar, on a scholar's quest," Dee answered, "and as much as it pained me to inconvenience you, I cannot have you interfering." He paused and furrowed his brow. "How did you get here, anyroad? You were not traveling with the Grail Child and her cohorts."

Kipling ignored the question. "Why are *you* here?"

"This is the only place and time in history where I could find a codex to the language of the angels," Dee said as he walked back toward the door and swung it open. "There are runes and markings and even a manuscript written in their manner of speech, but nothing that remained after this time that could tell me how to translate them. And that was essential."

"Why do you need to understand the angelic languages?" Kipling asked. "What possible use could that be to you?"

"If I understand the language," said Dee, "then I can speak it correctly. And if I can speak it, then I can call an angel by his name. And," he added as he closed the door behind him, "if I know an angel's name, then that angel . . .

". . . can be *bound*."

The notes inside Deucalion's box were taken just as seriously as the one he had been given that had instructed him to build the ark. The companions watched somberly as he called his family together and instructed them to begin gathering the animals together in preparation for the long-anticipated flood. It was to their credit, Madoc thought, that not a one among them hesitated or questioned their patriarch in the slightest. He had raised them to believe what he told them, and they trusted him implicitly.

"You are not of this world, are you?" the old shipbuilder asked the companions as they left his tents to make their way back to the *Indigo Dragon*.

"Of this world, yes," Quixote said primly. "Of this era, ah, no. Not exactly."

Deucalion nodded. "I could tell as much. You have the smell of Kairos about you."

"Sorry," Uncas and Fred chorused. "We got a bit wet when we were watering the goats," said Fred.

The old shipbuilder smiled. "I think the smell of wet badger fur is more pleasant than the smell of a rose garden," he said.

"Y'see?" Uncas said to Madoc. "*That's* why ev'rybody loves him."

Madoc laughed. "I'm starting to understand that."

"Uh-oh," Fred said as they approached the spot where they had left the airship and the Zanzibar Gate. "You know that whole 'don't meddle with history' thing the Elder Caretakers are always nattering on about? Well, I think we've just meddled."

The airship, which resembled a boat enough still that everyone who looked at it completely ignored it as another one of Deucalion's desert follies, was still sitting in the sand where they had left it. But the Zanzibar Gate was drawing a considerably larger amount of attention.

Craftsmen from all the tribes had formed a perimeter around the gate and were constructing their own replicas of it. Even just a cursory glance among the works-in-progress showed that pyramid-like structures from all the great cultures of the world were being sculpted: the Egyptian, and the Maya, the Chinese, and even the latecomers of Mesopotamia.

"Maybe it's just a coincidence," said Quixote.

"Not likely," said Madoc. "This is the First City. No one else on earth has built anything like a pyramid before, and suddenly one just appeared out of thin air in the middle of the desert. That's too significant a happening to be ignored."

"Well, at least we finally know the answer to the question as to why there are nearly identical pyramids in every culture around the world throughout recorded history," said Fred. "They were all inspired by the work of William Shakespeare."

Observing from the circle of Caretakers seated at Conan Doyle's table in Tamerlane House, John tightened his grip on his colleagues' hands when he saw a child moving among the sculptors who were making the replica pyramids.

"There," he said, hardly daring to breathe. "That boy—isn't he . . . ?"

"Yes," Verne said, his voice barely more than a whisper. "In this time he was Enkidu, friend of Gilgamesh. But when he grows older, we will know him as the End of Time."

"Theo," Jack whispered. "It's good to see you again."

Almost as if he had heard, the boy stopped and cocked his head. He wiped the sweat from his brow and then ran back the other way, moving closer to the companions and the Zanzibar Gate.

Deucalion had moved past the others to examine the *Indigo Dragon.* He knelt next to the hull and ran his hands along it. "A fascinating vessel," he murmured, "of impeccable construction."

"Don't let's be patting ourselves on the back too hard," said Laura Glue.

"What?"

"Never mind her," said Fred, frowning at the Valkyrie. "It's a good ship, and she's taken good care of everyone who's sailed on her."

"She's been through a lot," Deucalion said, noting the scars in the wood, "but I have no doubt she'll continue to serve you well."

He turned to Madoc. "Something you ought to know," he said as the companions reharnessed the goats to the airship. "This is not, in fact, the First City."

That froze all of them where they stood.

"It *isn't?*" Quixote said, dumbfounded. "But isn't this *Atlantis?*"

Deucalion chuckled again. "Atlantis is among the oldest cities, and it is certainly the grandest, but it is not the first. My own city, in my own kingdom, predated it by several centuries. It was far humbler, but older nonetheless."

"Oh dear," said Uncas. "That in't good."

Deucalion knelt, a look of concern crossing his features. "If your friends are in the City of Jade, does it matter if it is the oldest?"

"It might," said Fred. "That will affect what it is they came here to find. If this isn't the First City, then there's little chance they will find the identity of the first architect."

"Is that all?" Deucalion said in surprise. "I can tell you that right now."

Again, all the companions stopped doing whatever they were doing and focused their full attention on the old shipbuilder.

"Seek my great-grandfather," Deucalion said to Fred. "He left this world long before I came into it, but if any man was ever the kind of architect whom you are seeking, it would be him. He built a city. . . ." He paused, glancing around in sorrow as the enormity of the imminent destruction hit him once again. "He built the *first* city," the shipbuilder continued, "and in the beginning, before the names the younger races ascribed to it, before anything in this world had a name, it was named for him. Seek him out, and perhaps you will find the answers you seek."

He rummaged around inside his robe and withdrew a bronze disk that bore the likeness of a man on it. "Here," he said, handing it to Fred. "This was made long ago, and is said to be the best likeness of him, made by someone who knew him in his youth, before the city was built. If it will be of some help to you, you are welcome to it," he said, scanning the horizon with a visible anxiety. There were no clouds, no signs of rain, but it was clear the notes to the badgers had unnerved him more than he had let on.

"One way or the other," he said with finality, "I will have no more use for it myself."

With no farewell but a head scratch for the goats, a squeeze to the neck for the badgers, and a polite but curt nod to all the companions, Deucalion strode away to his ship.

"I don't know my mythology, uh, my history as well as you do," Quixote said to Madoc. "Who are we going to look for?"

"Enoch," said Madoc. "The city Deucalion mentioned was called the City of Enoch, and if it truly was the first, then I think he's who we have to find."

"First city, second city, or fifth city, this one is about to be covered in water," said Laura Glue. "There's no more time to waste—we have to go."

"Will the gate be safe while we go into the city?" Uncas asked. "Maybe one of us should stand guard."

"It's a pyramid built of almost indestructible stone that is older than dirt," said Laura Glue. "What can possibly happen to it?"

"The mechanisms are breakable," said Madoc, "but I would trust in Shaksberd's construction. It'll be fine." He turned to Fred. "All right, little Namer," he said. "Name me."

"Okay," Fred said. He'd been thumbing his way through the Little Whatsit, looking for the proper way to Name a Dragon as a Nephilim, but incredibly, that bit of knowledge was nowhere in the book. He shrugged and tucked it away. "You're a Nephilim," Fred said bluntly. "Congratulations."

"There's something to be said for ceremony, you know," Quixote said as the goats took a running start and the ship lifted into the air.

"Sorry," said Fred. "I'll work on that."

The airship rose into the sky, and a great hue and cry rose up from the thousands of people living in the encampments. It was not unprecedented in a world where angels walked among men and animals talked and gods rose and fell with the seasons, but it was a thrilling sight nonetheless. As the *Indigo Dragon* flew closer and closer to the impenetrable line of Corinthian Giants, every human within sight was watching its progress. Every human, that is . . .

. . . save for *one*.

Enkidu was standing away from the throng, not watching the flying ship but instead staring directly at the Prime Caretaker sitting in the circle at Tamerlane House.

"This is as far as I can take you, O spirit guides," the boy said. "I have tried to be where I felt you needed me to be, so you could see the things you hoped to see, but I can go no further. I must prepare for what is to come. And so must you."

With that the images projecting from the table vanished, and the room was plunged into darkness.

"Good Lord!" John exclaimed, jumping up from the table. He was almost choking on his own words. "Wh-what was *that*, Arthur? What just happened here?"

"I'm sorry," Conan Doyle said as he and the others also rose. "I thought you understood—it's not simply remote viewing. We are almost physically with him. That's not a hard, fast rule—none of this is set in stone—but he knew we were present the whole time we were watching. And somehow, he understood it was necessary."

"And, it seems, done," said Jack. "How are we to follow them now? We don't even know if Rose, Edmund, and Charles are in the city!"

"Yes, we do," said a voice from the doorway. It was Poe, the master of Tamerlane House.

In the hierarchy of Caretakers, Poe occupied a unique position somewhere above that of Caveo Principia, and even above Jules Verne when he was the Prime Caretaker before John took over the role. According to Bert, Poe had a unique understanding of space and time, and supposedly could manipulate both when it suited him to do so—but in John's experience, he rarely involved himself in whatever the Caretakers were dealing with unless it was a serious crisis. His appearance here was both good and bad.

"The *Telos Biblos* was written in Samaranth's own hand, from the time before the Archipelago itself was created, and there are accounts in it we have never understood until now."

He held up the book, so devoid of color that the pages appeared cold, and promptly ripped it in half.

Before any of the shocked Caretakers could react, Poe continued to tear the pages loose from the binding, then threw them into the air. They swirled about him like leaves in a storm, and then they began to slow, emitting a strange, unearthly glow.

Gradually the pages flowed past Poe and over to the table, where they reassembled themselves in order, and then began to expand until they filled the entire impression inset within the table. The light emanating from them grew stronger, and as the Caretakers again took their seats, images began to form in the light, and faint sound could be heard coming from the pages.

"Look and listen," Poe said, still standing near the doorway, "and see how the world you have cared for came into being."

CHAPTER ELEVEN
THE OLDEST HISTORY

·—✳—·

"WHAT DO YOU THINK?" Rose asked the two men as Samaranth readied himself to attend the summit. "Should we go with him?"

"I don't know," said Edmund. "It's history—whatever's about to go on has already happened, and I'm loath to get involved and possibly mess something up."

"We already *did*," said Charles. "Didn't you hear him? The keep is damaged—that means it hasn't fallen just in the future, but in the past as well. If we leave things as they are and try to go back, we may find our own history has been irrevocably changed."

"You've been spending too much time talking to Uncle Ray," Rose said, "but I think you're right. That's exactly what we'd be risking. So I don't think we have anything to lose by trying to learn as much as we can while we're here."

"I agree," Samaranth said. It was still unnerving to all three of them that this youthful man-child had the eyes of the wise old Dragon that they knew.

"Whoever you are, it is obvious to me that you understand more about how the world works than most of the principalities," he said as they left the Library. "If you listen, and learn, it may help you to better . . . take care, of your own world."

"That's pretty much exactly what we had in mind," said Charles. "Lead on, Macduff."

"Samaranth," the angel corrected. "Your memory needs work."

"Sorry," said Charles.

The great and spacious building where the summit was being held was less an amphitheater than it was an enormous ballroom—and in all the significant ways, that was exactly what it was. Staircases rose from the floor below, which was several hundred feet lower than the entrance, and connected a series of platforms that extended almost to the ceiling, which was so far above them that clouds had formed inside the room. There were fountains that fed streams of mingled light and water flowing through the air from platform to platform at varying levels. Everything was glass and marble and solidified light, except for the huge circle of fire in the center, and the dais above it, which stood at the far end of the chamber. Atop it was something familiar to all three of the companions.

"The ring of flames is the Creative Fire," said Samaranth. "It is where all things are made, and thus, this is where all things are decided. The high seat above is . . ."

". . . the Silver Throne," Rose said, breathless with awe.

"Hmm," said Charles. "Your father—uh, Mordred, that is, once said he was older than the Silver Throne. I think he was indulging in a bit of puffery."

"Obviously," said Edmund. "It's all still awfully spectacular, though," he added, gesturing at the grand spectacle with a sweep of his arm.

"It is indeed," Samaranth said, leading them to one of the staircases. "It was built by—"

"Magic?" Edmund suggested.

"Yes, that is the word," said Samaranth. "Magic. Or was it Will? I always get those two confused."

As they descended the stairs, Samaranth indicated that he was uncertain where he was expected to go, since he had not in fact attended any session of the summit before. The companions were about to ask why he had been excluded when Rose recognized someone on a nearby platform.

"Excuse me, ah, Nix?" she said to the angel. "Can you help us, please?"

Nix frowned—which Rose had noted, when they met before, was his default expression—and consulted his marble tablet. "I don't know why you weren't ordered when you arrived," he complained. "You are minions of a Seraphim, and—" He stopped, having noticed Samaranth for the first time. His eyes widened slightly. "I beg your pardon. I did not realize the elder was also with you." He consulted the tablet again, then pointed down at the floor level. "There should be some space for you there, if you hurry. The adversaries have claimed most of the upper platforms, and the principalities have claimed everything else."

"Adversaries?" said Charles. "I'm not sure I like the sound of that."

"It is the final session of the summit," Samaranth explained as they moved past several other youthful but apparently elderly angels and located an out-of-the-way corner at the lowest level of the room. "Matters of such importance that all the principalities have been invited, including our enemies."

"What are they called?" Edmund asked.

"One cannot identify one's adversaries by name," Samaranth

explained. "One can identify them only by their actions, and then act accordingly in return. And if they demonstrate that they no longer serve the Word, then, and only then, may they be Named as Fallen, and cast out."

"Cast out to where?" asked Rose.

"You really don't want to know," said Samaranth.

"So," said Charles, "all those above us, uh, so to speak, are gods?"

"Many of them," Samaranth answered, "but most above are of the angelic Host. Seraphim, Cherubim, and," he said, darkening slightly, "Nephilim. There are also the elder of us who serve in lesser capacities, but all who have a hand in guiding the course of the world are numbered among the principalities. Since the moment this world was divided from the Un-Made World, the younger races also began to splinter, and they grew and developed into their own distinctive cultures," he said in a matter-of-fact way. "As they flourished, they lost their connections to the Word and began the development of their own deities, whom they called gods. We, the Host, came here to build this city to try to reconnect the peoples of the world with the Word. But," he added with a touch of sadness, "the execution of that plan has fallen somewhat short of the aspiration.

"There," he said, pointing at a delegation several levels above. "That's one of the younger groups of gods, from a place called the Fertile Crescent. They are crude in their mannerisms, but effective. And there," he said, pointing to the left of the first group. "Those call themselves Titans. In truth, they bear many similarities to the Host—but their view is limited. Except," he added, "for that one."

Toward the bottom of the delegation a red-haired man was watching the angels just as intensely as Samaranth was watching him, only occasionally turning away to speak to another god, who carried a staff of living fire.

"He is the offspring of one of the Titans," Samaranth explained. "They call him Zeus. I expect great things of him, as well as the one he is with . . . Prometheus, I think."

Samaranth continued pointing out deities around the great room, and it was all the companions could do to keep up. "Loki, there," the angel said, "and his father, Odin, and Odin's father, Bor. And there," he continued, gesturing to a broad platform speckled with fountains, "the twin goddesses, Mahu and Mut, who represent two-thirds of the land masses of this world."

"What of the angels?" Charles asked. "Where are they?"

"Scattered throughout," Samaranth replied. "The Seraphim, like, ah, yourself," he added with as close an expression of mirth as any of them had yet seen, "are primarily of the Makers' Guilds, and constitute the bulk of the Host. The Cherubim," he went on, "are primarily Namers, and are those here on the lower levels with us."

"Have all the elder angels been excluded thus far?" Charles asked. "That hardly seems fair."

"Some of the older angels among the Seraphim would have allowed me to participate sooner," said Samaranth. "Sycorax is not much younger than I, nor are Maelzel and Azazel. But Iblis," he added, pointing to a tall, regal-looking angel near the top of the room, "is older still, and refused all my entreaties to become involved. He is more accepted among the younger members of the Host—why this is, I cannot say. Perhaps it is because he is more permissive than others among the principalities."

"It seems wrong," Rose fumed, "that those with the most experience aren't allowed any say at all in what happens."

Samaranth turned to her, eyes glittering. "You misunderstand, Daughter of Eve. We are not allowed to participate in the debates, but in the end, we most certainly do have a say.

"The oldest of a kind dictates the actions of all," Samaranth continued quietly. "It's one reason we are given work of little importance—so we are given as little influence as possible over the events of the world, until a decision has to be made—and then it is up to us to choose, so that in the end the responsibility, or blame, is entirely ours."

He spun around to point out a passing angel, apparently eager to change the subject. "That one, with the golden skin, is Telavel," he said. "He is a star-god who actually serves as the liaison between the Host and the stars. Some among us have even said he serves the Word directly, although there is no way to know for sure."

"Begging your pardon, Samaranth," Edmund said, "but do you mean these people you've been naming are the *representatives* of certain stars? Sort of like delegates?"

"No," the angel replied. "They *are* the stars themselves. Here, in the City of Jade, Naming is Being—and so even the stars may walk freely among its streets. In fact, in this case it was necessary, because the responsibility of this world's star is being called into question. It has even been rumored that the eldest star, Rao, has aligned himself with the Nephilim," Samaranth added. "That would be very, very bad."

"Why is that?" asked Edmund. "Aren't the Nephilim angels too?"

"They are," Samaranth admitted, casting a worried glance around them as if he were afraid someone might hear, "but they commune with Shadow and heed the call of the Word less and less frequently.

"If the Nephilim side with the stars, then there may be a split among the Host," he explained, "and the Seraphim are generally opposed to conflict, which means all that will stand between the Word and the principalities will be the Cherubim. If that is the case, the speaker for the Cherubim will have no choice but to declare the Nephilim as Fallen, and then Name them as such."

"Gosh," Charles said, craning his neck to look around at the other Cherubim. "What sorry so-and-so has that awful calling?"

"That would be *me*," said Samaranth. "Now please, be quiet. The final discussions of the summit are about to begin."

In his time with the Imperial Cartological Society, when he was acting as a double agent for Jules Verne, Kipling learned a great many things, and this was not the first time he had been held captive by an enemy. One of the things he learned was how to tell when he had been tied up by an amateur, and while Dr. Dee might have been brilliant in many ways, he was not a man of great physical prowess: The knots were loose.

"He wants to bind an angel," Kipling said, hoping that discussion would distract Hermes Trismegistus from noticing that he was trying to loosen his bonds. It might not have been necessary, though—Hermes was fully engaged in the work he was doing, which seemed to involve a series of pipettes, tubes, and glass spheres that were hovering around his working area.

"It is ambitious, to be sure," Hermes replied without turning around, "but hardly unprecedented."

"You don't seem to be very sympathetic toward them," Kipling countered, "even though you are a guest in their city."

"I see it differently," Hermes said. "I am not a guest in their city—they are guests on *my* world. And what is a single city compared to an entire world?"

"I'm starting to see why you and Dee get along," said Kipling. His left arm was starting to come loose from the bonds. "You have similar ambitions."

"As all gods ought," said Hermes.

"Gods?" Kipling exclaimed. "John Dee is not a god, he's just an alchemist with delusions of grandeur."

"That," said Hermes, "is *exactly* how it starts."

Rose, Charles, Edmund, and the angel Samaranth watched solemnly as a door irised open high up in the room, and a regal, impossibly dressed woman floated through and took a seat on the Silver Throne. Her flowing gown draped the dais for almost a hundred feet, and even when she was seated, the long sleeves of her robe continued to float as if suspended in water.

"The Jade Empress," Samaranth said under his breath, "and the last real connection between the city and the true peoples of this world."

"How old is she?" Edmund asked.

"Unlike us of the Host," the angel replied, "she truly *is* as youthful as she appears. She was a crippled beggar, living on the outskirts of the city, when it was discovered that she was the granddaughter of one of the four great kings of the East. And so she was welcomed here, and made empress, so that men would have a say in the fate of the world."

"That sounds awfully familiar," said Charles.

"Because we've heard the story before," said Rose. "The Jade Empress is T'ai Shan."

"Ah," Samaranth said, surprised. "You know her?"

"We have mutual friends," said Rose. "Look, something's happening."

The ambient light throughout the great room began to dim, and several glowing rings of varying color and intensity began to spread throughout the space, aligning themselves over each of the largest platforms. The rings separated into two, and each set began to oscillate, revolving in different directions. A brightening of a particular set of rings indicated that those on the pedestal below had permission to speak.

Samaranth's expression remained placid as the first rings to brighten were high above, on the platform of the Nephilim.

"I am Salathiel," the angel began, "of the first order of the ninth Guild of Diplomats of the second Host of the City of Jade, and I speak for all the Watchers."

There was a murmuring throughout the assembly, as if something very unorthodox had been spoken.

Charles glanced around at the Cherubim, all of whom were commiserating and whispering to one another. Something about Salathiel had disturbed everyone at the summit.

"What did he say?" Charles whispered. "All I heard was an introduction, but everyone is acting as if he'd just spit into the soup."

"He has Named himself and the Nephilim as Watchers," said Samaranth. "That has not been done before."

"What does that mean?"

"The Watchers," Samaranth explained, "are mostly Nephilim, and some Seraphim, all of whom are of the Diplomatic Guild. They were meant to have direct contact with the peoples of the world—and there are many among the Host who believe they did their job either very poorly, or far, far too well."

A look of astonishment spread over Charles's face as his old studies came back to him and he finally understood what Samaranth was saying.

"They had offspring with the Daughters of Eve, didn't they?" he asked. "The angels had *children*."

"The giants," Samaranth said, nodding. "Even now, they stand guard outside the city, to prevent the Sons of Adam and Daughters of Eve, and all the other Children of the Earth, from entering the city, or even from reaching the seas beyond. This is the great injustice that we hope to change today. The world, both worlds, were meant to be shared, for the prosperity of all, not just the privileged few."

"We wish to appeal to the Word," Salathiel continued, "to make and Name the Un-Made World, so that we, our children, and those of the principalities of this world may cross over, and build it up as we have done before."

Two more rings began to glow, farther down on one of the Seraphim's platforms. "And when you have used up that world," the angel said, not bothering to identify himself, "do you plan to abandon it as well, and move on to another? And another? And another after that? At what point do you actually become the stewards we are meant to be?"

"There are limits to stewardship, Sycorax," the Nephilim

answered, scowling at the challenge, "and limits to responsibility."

"Only when you lay down your burden, Salathiel," the angel Sycorax replied. "It is not worthy of you. It is not worthy of the Host."

"The worlds have been severed," another of the Nephilim said, "through no fault of ours. The connection is broken, and none living know how to repair it. We should save what we can, and leave the rest to the mercy of the Word."

"There is a way," a slight voice said. "There is a way to save this world, without abandoning it."

It was one of the stars who had spoken—a slender, nervous being with golden hair that flowed upward like living flame and matched his glowing eyes.

Before he could speak again, another star, larger, older, stepped in front of him. "That is not going to happen, Sol. I will never permit it."

The star Sol stood defiantly in the face of his elder. "We must," he said, voice trembling with emotion. "We must ascend, Rao. It is the only way to save this world. Both worlds."

"I will not," Rao answered. "The planet of my own system is flawed, and I would not ascend to save that, so why would I possibly agree to save this little world by doing so? In any event," he continued, "it is not necessary. I have made a pact with the Little Things—"

"You mean the Sons of Adam and the Daughters of Eve, don't you, Rao?" Sycorax asked.

The star frowned, but continued speaking. "I have made a pact that will ensure prosperity for this world, if the empress will support the Watchers' proposal."

To confirm this was so, he raised a hand to the Jade Empress, who nodded once. Again, the room was filled with murmurings and whisperings among the assembly.

"So," Rao said, "as the eldest star, I formally endorse the Watchers' proposal, as do the majority of the principalities. I would like to call for a vote of sustainment."

"Pardon me," a voice, quiet but firm, rang out into the great hall, "but I think this is a mistake."

Every angel's voice could be heard with equal clarity at the summit, so any angel who spoke could be heard. The shock and surprise that the words evoked was not because they were spoken, but because of who spoke them.

"It is a mistake," Samaranth said, "and not according to the plan. It should be reconsidered."

CHAPTER TWELVE
THE TEARS OF HEAVEN

—*—

IT TOOK KIPLING only a few minutes more to loosen up the ropes that bound both his arms, and fortunately for him, Hermes Trismegistus was too sufficiently wrapped up in his work to pay any attention to John Dee's captive. In a few moments more, he had loosed the ropes around his feet as well and swung around, leaping to his feet and hefting the chair to use as a bludgeon in one fluid motion.

Hermes simply continued to work, completely ignoring him.

After a moment, Kipling lowered the chair, realizing that his odd companion really did care as little as he seemed to.

"If you've finished freeing yourself," Hermes said without looking up, "would you mind setting the chair out of the way so I don't trip over it? There's a good fellow."

Dumbfounded, Kipling rolled his eyes and headed for the door. "You're lucky no one was witness to this, Kipling," he muttered to himself, "or they might take away your spy card."

"Kipling?" Hermes exclaimed, dropping a tablet, which hit the floor with a loud clatter. "Did you say your name was Kipling?"

"Yes," the Caretaker replied, hesitant to confirm much of anything. "Why?"

"This," Hermes said, actually focusing on Kipling in full for the first time, "is for you." He stood and handed the Caretaker a small, cream-colored envelope. It bore his name, and nothing else.

"Oh my hell," Kipling said. He started at the envelope for a moment, then tore it open and read the note inside. He glanced up at Hermes, who was still showing a marked interest, especially compared to his earlier detachment.

"A god who wore the armor of a star gave that to me," Hermes said, wringing his hands with curiosity, "and warned me to save it for Kipling, that you would come for it someday. What does it say?"

"It says that it's the end of the world," Kipling answered, "which happens more often than you'd believe."

Before Hermes could ask anything further, Kipling spun on his heel and rushed out the door. He didn't look back.

No rings had been dispatched to cover the Cherubim, because no one had expected any of them to speak, so Samaranth spoke in the twilight glow that emanated from the walls.

"This summit has been ongoing for almost a century and a half of Chronos time," said Samaranth, "and the Un-Made World has remained so the entire time, because we have not yet earned that stewardship.

"The Watchers and their children," he continued, "seek to claim it for themselves, and that is not part of the plan given to us by the Word. It was meant to be connected to this world, to be used by all, but we have failed. This world is dying. And to abandon it would be unconscionable. It would not be"—he glanced at Charles—"Taking Care."

"It is not our failure!" Rao exclaimed. "When the Adam was given responsibility to govern this world, he divided the responsibility equally between the Imago and the Archimago. And we have all seen how that turned out.

"But," he added, "in one thing you are correct. It *is* a divided world. We seek to do the same as you advocate, and unite it again."

"By allowing this world to perish first, and for your own purposes, Rao," Samaranth said, "and not to serve the peoples of this world, who will live or die based on what we decide here today."

"There is another way," a new voice said, which silenced the entire chamber. The Jade Empress had spoken. "There is still a chance to save this world, to end the drought that has plagued it and restore it to the state it was in at the time of the Adam."

She reached into one of her sleeves and withdrew a single, perfect red rose. On it were three dewdrops that shone with a light so brilliant that it reflected through the entire room.

"No!" Rao hissed at her. "Not now!"

Once more the assembly erupted in whisperings and murmurings over what was a clear violation of protocol.

"What is this . . . ?" Samaranth murmured. He and Sycorax exchanged bewildered glances, and both looked back to the star, then again to the empress. Rose followed their glances and realized that underneath the flowing robes, T'ai Shan was wearing armor. The Ruby Armor.

"Ah," Samaranth said. "I think at last I understand." He closed his eyes and bowed his head, and a wave of energy seemed to ripple outward from him, touching every attendee of the summit, including Charles.

"Rao gave the empress his fire," he whispered to Rose and Edmund, "just as in the story Lord Winter told us in the far future. She used the star's fire to forge the armor that she needed to find the talisman—a rose—that held the power to end the great drought. I think," he added, "that the wheels are about to come off the apple cart."

"You have no jurisdiction over our children, Samaranth," one of the Nephilim said brusquely. "Not while you reside in the City of Jade. Only here, within these walls, may you dictate what will or will not happen. Out there, we—and our offspring—are free."

A hue and cry rose up from the rest of the Nephilim, led by Salathiel, followed by equal cries of outrage and fervor from the principalities.

For his part, Rao had already begun dashing up one of the stairs, focused entirely on the Jade Empress. She watched him advancing, and the look of sadness on her face was wrenching. He had nearly reached the dais when she stood . . .

. . . and dropped the rose, and the dewdrops, directly into the circle of flames below, which exploded with light. In seconds, the entire room erupted into chaos.

The Watcher Salathiel lifted a huge, curved golden trumpet and sounded a note that rang out so loudly that it seemed as if the walls would shatter.

"Og! Ogias!" he called out. "Gog and Magog! Orestes and Fafnir! All you who are the grandsons of the Fallen angel Samhazi! I summon you to my side! Aid us, my children!"

"Fallen!" Samaranth exclaimed. "They have Named themselves as Fallen! This changes it all! We have to leave, now!"

◆   ◆   ◆

As the note had promised, Naming Madoc as a Nephilim did indeed allow the *Indigo Dragon* and all its passengers to pass by the wall of giants unmolested. But the relief the companions felt was short-lived, because as they flew past the immense limbs, the giants suddenly turned and began to stride purposefully toward the city.

Decades of dust and decay that had built up on the motionless bodies of the giants suddenly scattered and fell, forming a dust cloud that filled the air for hundreds of feet, and which stretched for fifty miles.

"What did we do?" a horrified Laura Glue said as the shadows of the giants covered them, and Madoc and Quixote both moved protectively closer to her and the badgers.

"I don't think we did anything," said Madoc. "They aren't focused on us, they're focused on the city itself."

"Well, whatever is going on," Fred said, shading his face to look up at the giants, "I bet Kipling has something t' do with it."

The great building where the summit had been held was a madhouse of frantic activity. Of the empress, there was no sign; Rao and the stars were also gone, as were several of the principalities. Only the Nephilim and certain of the Seraphim remained where they stood, as if waiting for something.

"The giants are coming for them," Samaranth said numbly. "They intend to go to the Un-Made World to try to Name it before the destruction comes."

"What?" Charles said, startled. "What destruction?"

"The empress dropped the Tears of Heaven into the Creative Fire," Samaranth replied, still in shock for reasons the companions still did not fully understand. "Everything is about to change now!"

"Because of a single rose?" asked Edmund. "I don't understand."

"Everything that is made is conceptual first," Samaranth explained as he led them back up the stairs, which were crowded with other angels also trying to leave. "Then we . . . create the thing to be made. We give it form, and substance. But then, to put it out into the world, the made thing is placed in the Creative Fire, and from then it multiplies."

"So we'll have a lot of roses to deal with," said Edmund.

"You don't understand!" Samaranth said, whirling about and grabbing the young man in the first physical act the companions had seen him perform. "That flower contained three dewdrops, but not of just any water! They were the Tears of Heaven, and they will multiply a millionfold, a billionfold. More. More."

"Oh dear," said Charles.

"Yes," Samaranth said. "Within the day, the entire world will be covered with a great flood, and there is nothing any of us can do to stop it."

A brilliant light burst upward from one of the largest buildings in the center of the city, briefly illuminating everything around Kipling as he ran. Something was afoot, and he suddenly realized that he might have very little time left to accomplish his task.

He stopped and leaned against a wall, panting. It gave him a moment to both catch his breath and consider what he was being asked to do. It made sense, in some twisted way, but he still was not certain he could trust what it said. At least one person he knew of—one of Verne's Messengers—would die in the future because of what he was being asked to do now. But it also made sense. It was, in the grand scheme of things, logical. And, he was a bit ashamed to admit, it appealed to his sense of gamesmanship.

It meant that he might never leave the city—but it also meant that he might give the Caretakers the means to defeat not just Dr. Dee, but the Echthroi as well. And in the end, that was what mattered most.

Looking over the angelic script in the note for the umpteenth time, Kipling screwed up his courage and once more began to run. If he timed it properly, the Cherubim would be somewhere near that explosion of light, and in the confusion that was beginning to spread outward into the streets, it would never be missed until Dr. Dee found it.

"The Great Deluge," Charles sputtered as Samaranth led them back to his Library. "The flood. The destruction of the world. It's really happening, isn't it?" He took off his glasses and rubbed his forehead.

"Have you got a headache?" asked Edmund.

"No," said Charles. "Tulpas don't *get* headaches, but I think one would actually make me feel *better* right now."

"What are we going to do?" asked Rose. "What can anyone do?"

"There are hierarchies of the Host of Heaven," said Samaranth, "each with its own set of responsibilities. The stars are given the task of shaping and preparing the worlds that revolve around them, but have little concern for the creatures who evolve, live, and die on those worlds. The angels are given the task of creating and Naming the higher aspects of the world, to allow the creatures on it to develop and ascend themselves. But there is an office between the two that is rarely called upon, and rarely chosen, because it carries the responsibility of directly overseeing the welfare of all the living creatures on a particular world."

"Why is it rarely chosen?" Rose asked.

"Because," Samaranth answered, "as you witnessed, the stars are reluctant to take so much responsibility upon themselves. They prefer the bigger-picture things, like the formation of mountains and the rise of oceans. The concerns of the Sons of Adam and the Daughters of Eve, and the affairs of the Children of the Earth, are of little concern to them, and so they will almost always decline the choice to ascend."

"But our star, Sol, wanted to ascend," said Edmund. "Why couldn't he?"

"Because other stars would have also needed to do so," said Samaranth, "and Rao is oldest among them, so his decision binds them all. It takes the complete commitment of one's heart, and aiua, to ascend," he continued, looking now at Rose. "You know this. I can see it in your countenance."

"Then this world may truly be lost," Rose said despairingly. "If the stars will not ascend, what is left? What can be done?"

"Just because Rao has abandoned the care of this world does not mean the world is without its . . . Caretakers," Samaranth said. For the first time, his voice seemed to be breaking with an emotion that none of the angels in the city had displayed. "There are none here in the city willing to ascend—but the elder angels can still descend to the office necessary to look after this world. We can still choose," he finished, his words more of a struggle now, "to become *Dragons*."

PART FOUR

THE DELUGE

CHAPTER THIRTEEN
REUNION

IT WAS A *caravan of worlds, and it stretched across the dunes from one horizon to the other. The great creatures that carried the lands of the Archipelago and all the peoples who lived in them were perhaps distant cousins to the Feast Beasts that served meals at Tamerlane House, reimagined for a more massive duty. They resembled the off-spring of camels that had been successfully courted by horned toads the size of elephants, and in place of humps were immense glass spheres, each of which contained the past, present, and future of a land from the Archipelago of Dreams.*

The beasts were tended to by smaller creatures of the earth, who had been given the task by the leader of the caravan: the last true Caretaker of the Archipelago itself. When the Archipelago fell to Shadow, it was he who gathered up all the lands and peoples and transported them here, where they could make their way to safe haven until the world could be made right again. "Have they been given water?" *he asked.* "The heat is terrible today."

"Henry is takin' care o' that," *said his First Assistant Dragon, a badger called Tummeler.* "I've made him, ah, my assistant, if'n that's keen by you."

Samaranth looked at the badger in surprise. "The guinea pig?

Hrrrmm," he rumbled. "Is it really wise to entrust such a large task to
such a small creature?"

"You of all, uh, people ought t' know," Tummeler said, admonish-
ing, "that size is irrelevant. 'Ceptin' when it comes to stuff like actually
hauling stuff, like entire islands from th' Archipelago. Then it pays t'
be big—but we got creatures t' do that, so Henry is just perfect t' leave
in charge as a supervisor. My point being—"

"I understand, little friend," said the great Dragon. "Better than
you realize."

He looked back at the caravan and thought about the thousands
and thousands of lives, and the history, and the culture, and most
importantly, the stories that had been preserved by his actions. He
looked at the badger, who had been a hero in the old Archipelago, and
one of those a Dragon might actually call friend. And he remembered
those who had been left behind.

"I wish . . ." Tummeler began, sensing the old Dragon's thoughts.
He stopped, whiskers quivering, and looked up at Samaranth. "I wish
we had been able t' bring Miss Aven with us," he said sadly. "I wish
she didn't have t' stay behind, all alone."

"She wasn't alone," Samaranth replied, "but more importantly, she
knew it was necessary. Someone needed to tell the Caretakers what
had happened, so that events could proceed the way that they must."

"And have they?" Tummeler asked, looking back along the caravan
of beasts. "We have been out here, wandering around with th' whole of
the Archipelago on our backs, for . . ." He paused and did some figures
in his head. "I really don't know. How long have we been out here,
anyway? It feels like we been wandering for forty years."

Samaranth chuckled, but it sounded like the rasping of a rusty
engine. "That was an entirely different exile story, little Child of the

Earth," he said. "We are no longer in any place that follows Chronos time, so it is all relative. But if I were to hazard a guess, I would say . . .

". . . that we have been gone from the waters of the Archipelago of Dreams for less than a month. Maybe two."

"Really?" Tummeler said, eyes wide. "If'n you'd asked me, I'da said we been taking care of th' Archipelago forever."

Samaranth made a rumbling noise in his chest and rose to his feet. "So would I, little Tummeler," he said, suddenly feeling the weight of his own history. "So would I."

Madoc being mistaken for a Nephilim didn't create more difficulty moving through the city; in fact, it seemed to be clearing a path for the companions as the flying goats drew the airship between the towers and deep into the heart of the city.

Angels with the ability to fly headed in the opposite direction as soon as the airship drew close and Madoc's wings became visible; and those below on the streets took shelter in whatever structure was closest and seemed to be avoiding even being touched by the *Indigo Dragon*'s shadow as it passed.

"They seem to be clearing a path for us," Quixote said as he peered over the side. "That is good, no?"

"No," said Laura Glue, pointing back in the direction from which they'd come. "It isn't us they're clearing a path for."

The giants had begun stepping over the river estuary, having crossed the miles of desert between themselves and the city in a matter of minutes. They seemed to be converging on a single huge building in the center of the city—and were leaving destruction in their wake as they passed.

"We never should have let Kipling go on his own," Madoc fumed. "Now we have four missing people to find!"

"You forget," Fred said, removing his Caretaker's watch, "the Anabasis Machines may not be as useful for time travel these days, but I can still use mine to contact another Caretaker."

Swiftly the badger spun the dials in the necessary order, then waited. A few moments later it chimed. He read the message and frowned.

"He says that everything is fine, but he has t' run an errand before we can come get him," Fred told the others, "and he said we should go find Rose, Charles, and Edmund."

Uncas and Quixote exchanged puzzled glances. "What does *that* mean?" Uncas exclaimed. "'Run an errand.'"

Madoc raised an eyebrow, less concerned about the errand than his missing daughter. "He found them? He knows where they are?"

Fred shrugged. "He said we just need t' go where the biggest explosions are."

"Bangarang!" said Laura Glue.

"It figures," said Uncas, pulling on the reins to turn the airship. "Head for the smoke, girls."

Driven by no other compulsion save for the Summoning that drew them, the Corinthian Giants were destroying the City of Jade simply by walking through it. Towers were falling; entire boulevards were crushed. Everywhere angels were fleeing, not realizing that soon there would be nowhere to flee to. No shelter would be adequate to protect them from the coming flood. The elder angels realized this, as did one other.

Deucalion stood at the prow of his massive ship, watching the chaos from afar. The departure of the giants had created a frenzy among the refugees who had lived for generations in the encampments below. Thousands saw the removal of the wall of giants as an invitation to invade the city themselves. Others realized it for what it was: a shift in the world. A change of global proportions. And so they simply waited, and went about their business. Some were weeping; others sought solace in prayer. And all of them were doomed to die.

"Not this day," the old shipbuilder murmured to no one in particular as his youngest son came running up the deck.

"We've nearly secured them all, Father," Hap said, breathless. "All the animals are accounted for and in their places."

"Good," Deucalion said, still looking out toward the city. "Tell me, we still have a great deal of room herein, do we not?"

Hap nodded. "Lots. It's a very big boat, Father."

Deucalion turned and put his hands on his son's shoulders. "Do you know that boy we have broken bread with? The quiet one?"

Hap nodded again. "Enkidu. I know him."

"Find him," Deucalion said. "Find him, and tell him to run among the peoples of the encampment. Tell them something terrible is about to happen—but all those who wish it may take shelter on our ship. If they do not wish to come, or they have their own means to survive a great flood, so be it. But make sure the offer is known."

"To all the humans?" asked Hap.

"Not just the humans," his father replied. "There are other races as well—and I would not deny them if they chose to come.

"All who wish it will find shelter here," Deucalion said, turning back to the railing, "for as long as we can give it."

The elders of the angels, mostly Cherubim but also including a few Seraphim, were gathering together far from the center of the city, on the westernmost edge, where the terraces and towers looked out over the sea.

Rose, Charles, and Edmund followed Samaranth back to his Library, where he remained only long enough to retrieve a few items. It appeared to Rose that the objects he chose were more out of sentimental value than practicality—but then again, it was hard to imagine an angel being sentimental, so she assumed the things he gathered together had some sort of meaningful purpose.

"There is no stopping it now," Samaranth said, addressing those who had assembled at one of the towers. "The waters will come, and they will all but destroy this world. But they will also cleanse it and restore it to the state it was in before it was severed from the Un-Made World. But now," he continued, his face a mask of incredible sadness, "we must do what the Nephilim and the principalities had wanted all along, and separate the worlds as definitively as we can. If we can preserve as much from this world there as possible, then both may be rebuilt. And perhaps," he added, briefly glancing back at Rose, "someday both may be reconnected, and restored, as the Word intended from the beginning."

He turned to the angels. "Seven are needed for this. Seven, and the world will be divided—and protected."

There was no hesitation. Seven Seraphim—four female and three male—stepped forward and bowed their heads to Samaranth. He moved to each of them in turn, whispering words meant only for them, then embracing them. All the Seraphim appeared older than Samaranth, so it was an unusual sight to see grown men and women being comforted by a youth—but then again, Rose especially understood how appearances were not necessarily reality.

Samaranth stood back from the Seraphim and raised his hands. "I release you from your covenants," he said, voice cracking, "but not from this life. Go forth, and guard the Un-Made World, as your brethren guarded the Garden, and guard it still."

The Seraphim drew swords of flame and raised them to their lips. Then they began to expand. Swiftly the angels became giants, and as they grew they changed: They became less corporeal and more intangible, and they took on the appearance of massive thunderheads. The flaming swords became lightning; and the cries of the Seraphim as they left the life they knew became the thunder.

In moments the seven angels had become a dark wall of storms, which moved past the city and out over the water.

"The Frontier," Charles breathed.

"As good a name as any," Samaranth said. His face was red from the angst and great strain he was feeling, but his expression was once again resolute. "None will pass, save they are given the Mandate of Heaven. A vessel touched by divinity may cross, but none other. And no Fallen may cross over, unless given passage by one of us here. And that," he said with finality, "is *never* going to occur."

In the distance, more crashing and explosions could be heard, and the Corinthian Giants loomed over the eastern horizon like a counterpoint to the Frontier the angels had created. "They may survive," Samaranth said, "but their parents will not. Nor will any of the principalities who sided with the Nephilim. Fortunately, some have proven wiser than others."

He gestured at the assembly, and the companions realized he was correct—a number of the younger gods were present, and appeared to have sided with Samaranth. Odin was there, and young Zeus, and the god Prometheus, who still carried the staff of fire.

"The Nephilim have gone," said Odin, "along with the star Rao, to do battle with the Jade Empress."

"I know where her power comes from," said Samaranth. "It will be a terrible battle, which she may lose. But it will give us the time we need. . . . Just enough, I think."

"There is one Nephilim still in the city," Prometheus said, "although he seems to be allied with at least one Seraphim and some members of an unknown principality. He is not flying himself, but is traveling in a flying vessel being drawn by goats."

A huge smile spread over Rose's face. "Does that sound like a Caretaker operation to you?" she asked, beaming.

"It certainly does," said Charles. "Look!"

The *Indigo Dragon* had just rounded one of the towers, avoiding flying directly through the smoke now billowing up from the giants' path. A shrill cheer sounded from Laura Glue as she spotted her long-missing friends.

Rose had expected some sort of rescue party and was not surprised to see Uncas, Fred, Laura Glue, and Quixote—but she was completely taken aback when the airship landed and her father stepped to the ground.

"Hello, Rose," he said, simply and plainly. "I've come a very long way to find you, girl."

✦ ✦ ✦

Kipling looked up at the ornate sculpture standing at the intersection and sighed heavily. It was exactly where the note said it would be—which meant that any moment now . . .

His jaw dropped open as the Cherubim approached. He had not realized, had not understood until this moment, that he knew this angel—not in the same form, but close enough to be familiar. Close enough to recognize.

Close enough to feel regret, even as he stepped out into the street to do what he knew he must.

The Cherubim stopped, momentarily distracted by the markings that were still on Kipling's forehead.

"You are not of the Host," the angel said, confused. "Are you of one of the principalities?"

"I'm sorry," Kipling said, and without a pause, he began to recite the words on the note, beginning with the true name of the angel before him.

It took only a few minutes to complete his task, and when he was done, the Cherubim walked away, slightly dazed, to the spot three blocks away where he would be confronted by someone else, who would repeat almost the same process Kipling had performed. Just the thought of it made Kipling sick to his stomach, and he turned and vomited against a wall. Then he walked to one of the towers, away from the destruction being done by the Watchers and their children, and found a nice fountain to sit beside, and silently, he wept.

CHAPTER FOURTEEN
THE FIRST DRAGON

·—✳—·

THE REUNION WAS joyful, but brief. Rose hugged her father in astonishment as both badgers jumped gleefully on Charles, and Edmund wrapped Laura Glue in a passionate embrace, which he punctuated with a long kiss.

"I say," Quixote chuckled, "this is like witnessing the best ending to a fairy tale you never expected to finish."

"First things first," Charles said. "There's a lot happening that we need to tell you about."

"Like the flood about t' destroy the world?" asked Uncas. "We're on top of that."

"That isn't the most urgent business," said Fred. "Rose is."

"Me?" Rose asked. "What do you mean?"

"That," Madoc said, pointing to her shadow. "It isn't yours, Rose! The Echthroi have been following you everywhere!"

At the mention of Echthroi all the angels stopped, and their eyes glowed. "She is Fallen?" one of them asked, fearful. "There is a Fallen among us?"

"Not her," Fred said, moving defensively in front of Rose. "Just her shadow—which isn't hers."

Rose spun about to look and was horrified to see that her

shadow did not turn with her. Instead it seemed to thicken, rising up and growing larger and larger, until . . .

A hand reached out to the wall and grasped the shadow.

"I'm sorry," the star Sol said to Rose. "I'm afraid this will hurt." He pulled, and ripped the shadow free from her with a single motion. Rose screamed and fell backward as her father leaped forward to catch her.

As if sensing its imminent end, the shadow thrashed about frantically, but Sol simply held it, watching.

"There can be no shadows without light," he said plainly. "So as there are shadows here, so let there be light." He flared, bright and brief, and the companions had to shield their eyes. When they could again see, the shadow was gone.

A few streets away, closer to the center of the city, Dr. Dee screamed and dropped to his knees. His primary link with this time and place had suddenly been severed, and the loss was taking a sudden and vicious toll.

He focused on breathing deeply and slowly, and in a few moments, he regained much of his strength, if not his composure. If the shadow—which had been Lovecraft's—had been destroyed, then he had enemies other than Kipling wandering through the City of Jade. But Kipling was still bound hand and foot in Hermes Trismegistus's study, and Dee knew from the Histories of the Caretakers that he would perish in the cataclysm, so it had to be someone else who'd destroyed the shadow.

No matter, Dee thought. He had what he came to the city to find. This had been the last moment in history where angels could be found walking the same streets as men—and now one of them had been bound to serve Dee.

Bound to serve the Echthroi.

Smiling wryly, Dee removed the black pocket watch he wore and spun the dials. An instant later, he was gone.

Rose looked down at her feet and exhaled, relieved. Her own shadow had returned.

"I'm sorry," Sol said again, this time to Samaranth. "If I could ascend, I would. But Rao . . ."

"I understand," said Samaranth. "You have done all you can. It is time for you to leave, Sol. Watch over us. Warm us. Be a guide to us. And never forget."

"I won't," Sol said. And then he was gone.

Other Cherubim had drawn closer to the companions to watch the star destroy the shadow, but one in particular, a stern-countenanced female, was whispering angrily into Samaranth's ear. He nodded once, then again, and whispered something back to her before they both turned to face the companions.

Rose suppressed a shudder when she realized who this angel was—and that they had met before.

"Yes," Charles said quietly. "I remember too, Rose."

Before the companions traveled further back in time to arrive at the City of Jade, they had been in ancient Greece, where they met Medea, the wife of the legendary hero Jason, and her familiar, a green-gold Dragon named . . .

"Azer," Samaranth said by way of introduction. "My wife."

"I beg your pardon," Charles said, trying to regain his composure, "but I had no idea that angels could marry."

"It is the way of things," Samaranth said, "to organize into families. In fact, we were thinking about having a child together, in another billion years or so. But," he added, with a sudden immeasurable sadness, "that may not be possible—not after this."

"I will never forgive you for this," Azer said through clenched teeth. "Know that, Samaranth. Never. You said descent would never be necessary."

The sadness in Samaranth's face was almost tangible. "We have a responsibility, my wife. One we accepted long, long ago. You, I, and . . ." He craned his neck, scanning the faces of the Cherubim.

"Who are you looking for?" one of the angels asked.

"Shaitan," Samaranth replied. "Among the Host, he is the one who is most like . . ." He turned and gestured at Charles and Edmund. "As these Sons of Adam and Daughters of Eve are. A . . . friend? I had expected him to be here."

"There have been a great many things happening today," the angel replied. "If Shaitan could have come, he would."

"No matter," Samaranth said. "We are out of time."

The angels gathered around an enormous circle of water on the terrace outside the tower. It extended out past the cliffs on which the city was built, over the ocean. "The Moon Pool," Samaranth said. "In it are the tears of the mother of us all, called Idyl, who gave birth to the world when the Word was spoken. With this pool of water, we can choose, and change, and descend."

"It's like a larger version of Echo's Well, on the Lost Boys' island in the Archipelago," Charles said to the others. "Jack used it once, years ago, to make himself younger," he explained, "because in his heart, he was still enough of a boy to become so in reality. He believed himself to be young, and young he became. I think this is something similar."

"It was touched by the Word," said Samaranth, "like the Creative Fire, and it changes not our Names, but our Being. Who we are is the same, but we will be Remade, so that the world may be saved."

He stepped forward and leaned over the pool. A lock of his red hair fell over his eyes, and he pushed it back as he stared at his own reflection.

> *In rightness's name*
> *For need of might,*
> *I thus descend*
> *I thus descend*
>
> *By blood bound*
> *By honor given*
> *I thus descend*
> *I thus descend*
>
> *For strength and speed and heaven's power*
> *To serve below in this dark hour*
> *I thus descend*
> *I thus descend*

Even as he had started to speak the words, the change had begun. Eddies of light began to swirl about the small, lithe form of the angel Samaranth, changing him as they watched. Without taking his eyes off his reflection in the glistening pool, he grew tall and broad; his flesh turned red, and wings sprouted from his back even as he was growing a tail. In short order, as the echo of the last words faded, his reflection was no longer that of a young man, but of the great Dragon Samaranth.

Of all the reunited companions, Uncas was the one who had known all the Dragonships in their glory, and he thrilled at the sight of those familiar visages appearing as, one by one, Samaranth's companions invoked the change.

"There's th' Red Dragon!" he said excitedly. "And th' Blue Dragon! And Green!" He turned to Quixote. "That one was all'ays a bit temper'mental."

"Amazing, isn't it?" Edmund said to Rose. "It's the most extraordinary thing I've ever witnessed!" He looked up at Madoc. "Uh, except your transformation. That was most excellent also."

Madoc didn't respond. He was watching Rose, and the tears in her eyes mirrored his own.

"This is where their lives as Dragons began," she said softly. "And I remember where they ended—I just wish I could forget."

Fred hugged her leg in sympathy. In one of the greatest battles of the Archipelago, all the Dragon shadows had been turned to serve a new master: the Shadow of the Winter King, her father, when he was known as Mordred. The only way to release the Dragons was for her to sever the shadows' link to the earth with the sword Caliburn—but that also meant the end of the Dragons' days as guardians of the Archipelago.

"It is not your fault," Madoc whispered to her as he hesitantly reached out to take her hand. "It was mine. My choices brought about their end. Not yours."

She didn't reply, or look at him—but she didn't let go of his hand, either.

It went more quickly than any of them could have expected, this transformation of angels into Dragons. But when it was complete, the terrace and the sky above the tower were filled with them.

"Uh, Samaranth?" Fred said, hesitant to address the Dragon directly, but doing so anyway. "I want to ask—out there, in the desert, there is a huge ship. On it are all the Children of the Earth."

"The animals," Samaranth rumbled. "We had made no provisions for them. . . ." He stopped, realizing what the little badger had actually said. "They are all on a ship, you say?"

Fred nodded so enthusiastically the others thought his head might fly off. "Several of every kind," he said, "gathered together by Ordo Maas. Uh, I mean, Deucalion. Or, uh, Utnapishtim."

"Ah," the Dragon responded, with what seemed to be a smile. "The old king from the Empty Quarter. I had wondered what it was he was building out there." He gestured with one hand and summoned another Dragon, a giant creature with the aspect of a cat in his countenance.

"Kerubiel," Samaranth told the Dragon. "Go, find the ship, and make certain it crosses over safely."

"Samaranth," the god Prometheus implored, "that . . . is my son. There are things he will need, things he must be given." He gestured at the flame. "May I accompany the Dragon?"

Kerubiel did not speak, but simply nodded at Prometheus. The god climbed atop the Dragon, who launched himself into the air and winged his way at top speed toward the desert.

"Thank you," said Fred. "That's very gentlemanly of you to do."

"It will take a long time for this world to recover," Samaranth told the companions, "but when it does, it can be as it once was, as the Garden was, in the beginning."

"Yes," said Madoc. "It will be the true Summer Country."

"The Summer Country," Samaranth said, growling in satisfaction. "So mote it be, little Namer. So mote it be, little king."

Madoc stared, shocked at the title. "I am no king, Samaranth," he murmured back, "as you will discover for yourself, in time."

At this, the Dragon rose up to his full, terrifying height and began to beat his wings to rise aloft. Even Rose flinched at the looming sight of the red Dragon. "I am a Namer, little king, and I know my own. You may not be a king in fact, but you have it in your countenance to be. You have it within you. Just remember— a king who commands by force may rule, but a king who is followed because he is loved, and trusted, will rule forever."

The Dragon turned to the rest of the former Host and indicated that it was time to leave, to attend to the responsibilities they had just taken on.

"Samaranth, wait!" Charles exclaimed. "I want to ask you something. Please!"

The great Dragon lowered himself to the ground and a growl rumbled deep inside his chest. "What is it, little Son of Adam?"

Charles shuddered inwardly and realized suddenly that this might not have been the wisest thing to do. This was not the old, tempered, world-wise Samaranth he'd met as a young Caretaker-to-be. This was a newborn Dragon, who had just sacrificed his life as an angel of the Host of Heaven in order to create the Archipelago and safeguard the entire world. Still, he couldn't help himself—he had to ask.

"The book," said Charles, "the one my colleagues call the *Telos Biblos*. It contains all the names of those angels who became Dragons—except for yours."

Samaranth leaned closer, exhaling hot breath into the Caretaker's face, and his eyes narrowed.

"To ask one's true name is to try to have power over them," the Dragon hissed, "and it is not advisable that you ask anything further."

"I don't mean to offend," Charles sputtered, slightly terrified but unwilling to let the opportunity pass. "I am a scholar of heaven, and angelic doings, and I know many of the names of the angels, uh, I mean Dragons," he corrected quickly, "but I never heard of any angel named Samaranth. And I know that that is not your true name."

"How can you know that?"

"Because," Charles said, "in another place, and another time, someone who serves the Shadows does something . . . something terrible, to your kind. And you are spared, because your name is not in the book. I don't want any power over you, of any kind. I just want to know. You don't know me now, but someday you will—and you will trust me. In the name of that trust, I—I just want to know."

Samaranth reared up on his hind legs and looked at the man before him. The Caretaker was afraid, but only because the aspect of the Dragon was terrifying—not because he feared Samaranth himself. There was trust, somehow.

"I will tell you," Samaranth said, again leaning close, "and with the name, a small Binding, so that it cannot be shared with another."

Charles nodded. "Fair enough."

The Dragon whispered into the Caretaker's ear, and Charles's eyes widened in surprise. "You—you . . . ?" he stammered as the Dragon moved back and prepared to take flight. "You are *that* angel?"

"I am not the eldest of the Host, but I am the eldest among those here, on this world," said Samaranth, "and my name has not been spoken since the dawn of creation. Even then, it was only to summon me to do my first task, which was necessary to do before anything else could be created or Named.

"Since that time, I had simply been known as the Lightbringer to those of my kind, and as Samaranth to those younger races of the earth. And now, as a Dragon, it is Samaranth I shall remain . . .

". . . until the end of time itself."

With no further farewell, the Dragon beat his mighty wings and lifted into the air. In moments, he was gone.

CHAPTER FIFTEEN
THE MAKER

AS THE CARETAKERS at Tamerlane House watched the great
red Dragon soar away with the hundreds of newly born Dragons
into the darkness of the newly made Frontier, the whirling pages
of the Last Book began to darken and crumble apart. In moments,
the images they had been watching so keenly faded completely,
and once more the room went dark.

John turned to Poe, who had not moved from the doorway the
entire time they had been watching the visions of Atlantis and the
Dragons. "What happens now?" he demanded. "We need to keep
watching!"

"We cannot," Poe replied. "The book gave us a window into
the events that were witnessed by its author, and this was the end
of his record. Thus, there is no more to observe."

"The author?" asked Jack. "But I thought the Last Book was
written by—"

"The *Telos Biblos*," said Poe, "was written by Samaranth himself, in the days after the founding of the Archipelago, when one
by one, he named all those from the Host of the City of Jade who
followed him and became Dragons, but it is not the oldest history.
There is one older still, which John Dee never acquired nor stole,

because it was never given to the safekeeping of anyone else other than him who wrote it."

"An older history?" John said, confused. "But I want to know what happens next! We know that our friends are safe—or at least, they were—but how can we discover what's become of them with an older history?"

"Because," said Poe, "their journey is not yet finished, and their quest to find the Architect must lead them deeper into the past before they can come back to the future."

"Hmm. All right," John said. "Is this book in the Repository, then? I don't remember ever seeing it."

"It has never been in the Repository," Poe said as he reached inside his breast pocket, "because it has never left my person."

The other Caretakers rose from their seats to look at the curious, small book that Poe was holding. It was very, very old, compact but thick, and resembled nothing so much as it did . . .

"The Little Whatsits." Twain chortled. "It looks like those bloody annoying books of genius and wisdom the badgers refer to all the time."

"The thing is," Bert said, "the information in the Little Whatsits is almost always spot-on."

"That," said Twain, "is precisely why those books are so bloody annoying."

"It is indeed much like the Little Whatsits," Poe said, "in that inside its pages is an accounting of all the knowledge of the world that once was. A world that was smaller, and seemingly simpler, and never to be known again except in stories."

"How did you find this book, Edgar?" Houdini asked.

"I didn't find it," Poe answered, "I *wrote* it.

"Now," he said, stepping out into the hallway and beckoning the others to follow, "gather everyone together. *Everyone*. All the Caretakers, and Mystorians, and Messengers; all the helpers, and apprentices, and associates. Everyone at Tamerlane House should attend, because I'm going to do a *reading*—one I have waited to do since the beginning of the world.

"It is time," the master of the house said, "for *all* the secrets of history to be revealed."

"What, pray tell," Charles exclaimed, "did you do to the poor *Indigo Dragon?*" He walked around the airship, fondly caressing the battered hull and once-living masthead he knew so well. He and his colleagues John and Jack had shared some amazing adventures aboard this ship, and it pained him to see it made so . . .

"Short," he said, bending over to examine it more closely. "And it's got wheels. Sweet heaven, old girl—what have they done to you?"

"It was kind of necessary," said Fred. "We needed something that could go anywhere, do anything. And the *Indigo Dragon* has been the greatest Dragonship there ever was."

"Meh," said Elly Mae.

"Mahhh!" said Coraline.

"Flying goats," Charles said, shaking his head. "The more things change, the more they, well, change."

"We need to get out of here," Rose said anxiously. "The city is coming apart, and the deluge can't be far away."

"Not yet," said Madoc. "Kipling is still—"

"Right here," a weary Rudyard Kipling said as he stepped off the staircase and onto the broad plaza where the companions were. "Sorry to have kept you waiting."

Rose ran to him, giving him a hug, and Edmund greeted him with a warm double handshake—but Charles realized immediately that something was wrong.

"Rudy, old boy," he said, his face showing open concern. "What is it? What's happened?"

Kipling sighed. "I'm not coming with you."

That stopped all of them, even the goats. "Muh?" said Elly Mae.

"I've been . . . compromised," said Kipling. "I can't—shouldn't—go with you."

It was Madoc who realized what had happened. "Your shadow," he said with a twinge of old sorrow in his voice. "It's missing, Caretaker."

Laura Glue and the badgers stared at him, dumbfounded. "What," the Valkyrie said, "did you *do?*"

Kipling looked pained, but he managed to smile anyway. "I did something terrible that had to be done. At least," he added, fishing in his pocket, "I hope it did."

He withdrew a small envelope identical to the ones that Deucalion had given to Uncas and Fred. The companions rapidly exchanged anecdotes and arrived at the same conclusion.

"Telemachus has made his choice," said Fred. "He's decided to join the side of the, um, angels. So to speak."

"Maybe not," said Charles, "if he's also giving instructions that cost Caretakers their shadows."

Rose, for her part, was still pained by what Fred and her father had shared with her about the true identity of their possible adversary. She still remembered the lost little boy prince, Coal, far too vividly to easily accept that he had been one of Verne's Messengers in disguise, was a possible apprentice to John Dee, and might be the Archimago destined to hand the entire world over to the Echthroi.

"We'll find a way to help you," she said, almost pleading. It felt terrible to contemplate leaving him there after finally seeing some hope—especially with what they all knew was going to happen. "Please, come with us."

"It's too risky," Kipling said. "Ask Madoc. He knows."

Reluctantly Madoc looked at his daughter and nodded. "If he is now shadowless, then he lost it by his own choice, by his own actions, as Jack once did," he explained, "and that leaves him vulnerable, as you were. If an Echthros somehow manages to use him as a conduit, then they can follow us anywhere. John Dee already gained access to the City of Jade because of the shadow that you didn't know had come with you. If we were to find the Architect, and an Echthros was with us . . ."

Madoc didn't need to finish the statement. Every one of them knew Kipling was right. He would have to stay.

"Edmund," Kipling said, "before you go, may I have a word?"

As the two men talked, the others readied the *Indigo Dragon* for the flight out and tried their best not to feel the despair that was all too present.

"All right," Edmund said when they stepped back over to the ship. "We need to leave now." This last he said with a wink at Kipling that only Madoc saw. The Dragon furrowed his brow but said nothing as the others all hugged Kipling and said tearful good-byes.

"One last thing," Kipling asked. "Fly me up to the tallest tower still standing. The show is going to be spectacular, and I'd like to have a really good seat."

As the reunited companions took flight up and out of the doomed City of Jade, Fred and Laura Glue explained how they had traveled there using Shakespeare's Zanzibar Gate, and also, less enthusiastically, explained what its limitations were.

"*Three trips?*" Rose exclaimed. "That's all we get?"

"Two now," said Fred. "We used up one to come find you."

"Just one, actually," Uncas said, trying to be helpful, "because now we have to go home before we can go out again. And whoever goes on *that* trip . . ."

"Will basically be in the same boat—so to speak—that Charles and Edmund and I were in the last time," said Rose. "But we aren't going to do that."

"We aren't?" said Fred.

"We aren't?" Uncas and Quixote said together.

"No," Rose said, a determined smile on her face. "After what you told us about Deucalion's great-grandfather, Enoch, I'm convinced that he is the man we're seeking. If we can get to him and restore the keep, then we won't need to worry about how to manage a return trip."

"One problem," said Edmund. "According to Verne, the rules of time travel say we must take a trip into the future to balance every trip into the past. Won't we be causing some kind of temporal problem if we don't do just that?"

"Verne lies," Rose replied. "I think the rules about time travel are more fluid than he'll ever tell us, if he can help it. Besides, we came further back again getting here without a counterbalancing trip to the future."

"Because we had help, remember?" Edmund said. "The old man in Platonia—the one who sent Bert back to Tamerlane."

Rose scanned the sky as if waiting for help from above. "I wish he'd step in to help us now—or at least, let us know we're moving in the right direction."

"Couldn't Edmund simply create another chronal map?" Quixote suggested. "That way, we wouldn't be using up the power in the gate."

"I tried it, back in the city," Edmund said sheepishly. "It didn't work. Whatever damage has affected the keep in this time is also affecting my ability to make chronal maps. If I have a machine to augment it, it could work. Hopefully."

"We do have the gate," Fred said helpfully, "and it's designed to use a chronal map. That's how we got here."

"That's the second problem," said Edmund. "I can program the gate, but I have no clue where we're going, since we don't even have a vague description of the City of Enoch."

"We have this," Fred offered, holding up the bronze bas-relief of Enoch. "It's a pretty good likeness, I think. You could make a chronal map to take us through the gate directly to him."

"I really don't know," said Edmund. "I've always created maps to places and specific times. I really have no idea whether it will work if we try to use it to take us to a specific person."

"I don't think we have much of a choice," Charles said, hooking a thumb over his shoulder at the city as they flew out over the desert. "Look."

The wall of water was more massive than anything they had

ever seen before, taller even than the Corinthian Giants, the children of the renegade angels called Watchers. As they looked, it
enveloped the City of Jade and moved past with no apparent loss
of speed or power.

"Now, Edmund," Rose said, trying not to sound anxious, "I
believe in you. This will work."

"All right," Edmund said as they approached the Zanzibar
Gate. "I guess I'd better draw quickly."

"Well," Kipling said as he watched his friends through the spyglass.
"I guess that's that, then."

He folded the spyglass closed and slid down the wall behind
him, sitting on the smooth pavement. The buildings all around
him and even the ground beneath him were vibrating constantly
now, and in the distance, he could see cracks starting to form in
some of the greater towers.

It would not be long now.

Outside in the city, those who still remained could be heard
praying. Some were reciting histories; others, poetry. Each deni-
zen who knew what was approaching had chosen to meet his fate
in his own way, as Kipling had chosen to meet his.

He started to recite one of his poems, then paused before
starting another, but he stopped reciting that one too. "Curse
it all," he muttered to no one in particular, "I really should have
written some less depressing poems."

He finally settled on "En-Dor," mostly because several stanzas
were a comfort to him, even if the overall poem was not. Still, it
was a good poem, and there, in that place, at that moment, that
was as good a legacy as any, he decided. He had written a good

poem, and he had done good things, and he thought if his son had been there, he would be proud of his father.

A loud rumbling startled him out of his reverie, and the light from outside dimmed, as if a cloud had moved in front of the sun. It wasn't a cloud, Kipling knew.

He closed his eyes and continued to recite the poem as the massive wave moved into the city, toppling towers and overwhelming everything in its path.

On their approach to the gate, the companions were relieved to see that the controls and aperture began to glow as soon as Madoc was near.

"That's what we like t' see," said Fred. "Dragon power! Boom!"

It took only a few minutes for Edmund to complete the drawing of Enoch. He added one or two more flourishes, then with Fred's assistance, he set it into the spot on the gate next to the control crystals.

"Hmm," said Madoc. "That visage looks terribly familiar to me, but I can't quite place it."

"As long as it gets us to him," said Edmund. "That's all I'm concerned about."

"I just hope," said Laura Glue, "that we don't end up parking the entire Zanzibar Gate right on top of him, like they did with that house the tornado dropped on the witch in Oz."

"I'm sure they didn't mean for that to happen," said Uncas.

"I'm sure they did," said Laura Glue. "The way I heard it, it took them three tries to actually get her."

"Well, we have one try to get this right," said Edmund. "We're good to go—all the settings are locked."

Madoc stood atop the deck, stretched his wings, and took a last look around. The refugees still in the encampments were either disassembling tents, or frantically running back and forth, or praying. In the opposite direction, Deucalion's great ark was sealed up and waiting to fulfill its purpose. And ahead of them, the future and the past were both waiting to be created.

"All right," he said finally. "Take us through, Fred."

The companions aboard the *Indigo Dragon* had no idea what to expect when they passed through the gate. There was no transition period, no time to adjust to a new environment. It was almost instantaneous, and very similar to walking through one of the doors at the keep.

What the *Indigo Dragon* moved into was a fairy forest.

It was night, and the skies were dark, but everything around them glowed with pulsing, vibrant, living lights that illuminated the airship and its occupants with greens and blues and other colors they would not have believed were possible on earth.

There was a ring of tall, mostly branchless trees that towered above a smaller grove of thicker, leafier varieties. The shrubbery was so thick that the ground was almost impossible to see, and everything seemed to glow of its own accord. Lights, like fireflies but not, floated lazily among the foliage, giving off more than enough light for the companions to see by.

"Oh," Laura Glue said as she reached for Edmund's hand. "Oh, it is so beautiful."

Uncas lifted his nose and sniffed. "It all smells like mint," he declared. "I like it."

"I thought we were coming to find a master builder. An architect," said Edmund. "Instead, we find this . . ."

"Garden," a voice said from the far side of the trees. "I know it must pale in comparison to the original, but I never had the pleasure of seeing that one in person, so I've simply done the best that I can."

They stepped off the airship and walked around the trees to better see who had spoken. There, sitting on a stool, was a man who very strongly resembled the drawing Edmund had done. He glanced briefly at the companions, then resumed his work, which was creating a city in the sky.

He was drawing with light, in the air.

A bright point of energy was emanating from his right index finger, and everywhere he touched, the light remained. There were squat, square buildings, but also majestic, soaring towers; and every inch of the miniature city glowed with the light from his touch.

"This is my next project," he said, turning around and sliding off the stool. "I thought I'd add a few things while I waited for you."

"You . . . have been waiting for us?" Rose exclaimed. "Are you . . ."

"My name is Enoch, the Maker," he said simply, "and I have been waiting for you to arrive for a very long time."

CHAPTER SIXTEEN
THE ARCHONS

AFTER THE INITIAL astonishment at Enoch's statement passed, Rose regained enough of her composure to ask him how it was he knew to expect them.

"I was told," he said, folding his arms behind him and looking at them as if he'd actually said something useful.

"If he pulls a cream-colored envelope out of his pocket," said Laura Glue, "I think I might throw up."

"I was thinking the same thing," said Fred.

"We've come a long way to find you," Edmund said, trying to change the subject, but Enoch wasn't listening. He had stepped closer to examine Laura Glue's wings.

"These are constructs, are they not?" he asked. "Used for flight, but not a part of you."

"Yes," the Valkyrie answered. "They were made for me."

"But yours are your own," he said, turning to Madoc. "Intriguing."

Rose was about to ask another question when something she caught out of the corner of her eye distracted her. It was a column of swirling clouds, like an inverted tornado, far off in the distance. "It looks like the Frontier that separated the Archipelago from the Summer Country," she said, pointing at the clouds.

Enoch looked at her in surprise. "Interesting," he said. "Few people can actually see the Barrier, and most of those see angels carrying flaming swords, the way the Adam claimed to. How unusual that you can see it for what it really is."

"Is that . . . ?" Charles asked, swallowing hard. "Is that the Garden of Eden?"

Enoch smiled wryly and shrugged. "It may be. The Barrier has been there since long before my time. Not many still live who remember the time of the Adam and the Eve, but one does. It may be possible for you to meet him. We shall see."

Edmund rubbed his chin, thinking. "You keep mentioning 'the Adam,'" he said to Enoch.

The Maker looked at Edmund, not understanding, then he realized what the young man was asking.

"It was his calling, not his name," Enoch explained. "No one living knows what his true name was—and I doubt that after what occurred with his sons, he ever shared his true name with anyone else, ever again."

"What does 'the Adam' mean?" asked Rose.

"As I said, it was his calling," said Enoch. He lowered his head, struggling to find the right words. "In the language of the Host, it means . . . purpose? Yes, that's it. To me, the Adam meant to have purpose in the world."

"That makes sense," Quixote said, nodding. "Given that he was the first man."

"But he wasn't," Enoch said quickly. "There were men and women here for thousands of years before he came, as there are many peoples here who have cultures and history far beyond my own. He was simply the first man with purpose. Regardless, it was his calling that mattered then, not his name. Names can be changed."

"My father has changed his name several times in his life," said Rose, taking Madoc by the arm.

"That would mean," said Enoch, "that either you are a great Namer, or you have not yet been completely made, and thus cannot be Named—not completely."

"We have come here seeking a Maker," said Rose. "And possibly a Namer as well."

Enoch nodded. "I know. He told us to expect you—or at least, to expect someone—who would be seeking him."

Charles stepped forward, eyes flashing with anticipation. "Someone else told you to expect us? But aren't *you* the Architect?"

Enoch blinked. "Is that a name?" He shook his head. "He never spoke that word. But he told us he had chosen to Name himself, and he was called Telemachus."

Rose's mouth dropped open in astonishment, and she turned to the others. It hadn't occurred to any of them that Telemachus, who had been manipulating events in time to keep them moving forward, might actually be the very being they were seeking.

"What did he say, exactly?" she asked.

Enoch shrugged. "He simply said he was the one who could help you, and that you would come seeking him."

"This guy," Uncas said to Quixote behind his paw, "is like the Zen master of not being helpful."

"He was here? You met him?" Edmund asked.

Enoch nodded. "He visited us here, long ago, in the days of my youth, and learned many things from us. And in turn, we also learned many things from him, such as the art of making these."

He held out his hand and from it dropped a silver pocket watch, with an engraving of a Dragon on the case.

"Azer," said Rose. "Samaranth's wife. I never realized that was who was on Bert's watch—most of the Caretakers have one like Verne's. . . ."

"With the red Dragon?" Enoch asked. "I liked those less. There's something pure and geometrically pleasing about a simpler design. The original one he brought to me was broken, but it was simple to repair, and I think I improved upon the workings in the process."

Edmund suddenly brightened. "We have something similar in one of our bags," he said, grinning, "that was damaged beyond our ability to repair. But it may not be beyond yours. Would you mind having a look at him?"

"Him?" Enoch said in surprise.

In response Edmund simply walked back over to the *Indigo Dragon* and returned carrying the clockwork owl, Archimedes. He had been damaged on their trip into the future, where they battled the man who called himself Lord Winter. The agents of Winter had repaired the bird, but in doing so had taken away . . . something. He was now completely an automaton, with none of the fire of life he had possessed before.

Madoc sighed heavily when he saw the clockwork bird. "Ah, Archimedes," he said. "Perhaps my oldest friend, and one of my great teachers." He looked at Enoch. "Can you?" he asked. "Can you help him?"

The Maker gently took the bird from Edmund and examined him closely. "It's possible," he said finally. "Physically, he is unharmed. But his aiua has been smothered, almost extinguished. I think you can call it back, though."

"Call it back?" said Rose. "What do you mean?"

"Just that," said Enoch. "His aiua is bound to yours, even after death. To restore him to life, all you need to do is call him, and he will respond."

"It's that simple?" asked Edmund.

"It's that hard," said Enoch. "The call must be with the full desire of your heart. Your aiua must draw his back. There is no other way."

"All right," said Edmund. "I'll give it a try."

"Not your aiua," Enoch said, pointing past Edmund to Madoc. "His."

Madoc stared at the Maker in surprise. "Why must it be me?"

"Your aiua is most intertwined with his," said Enoch, "so it must be yours that calls him."

Madoc took the damaged bird from the young man and cradled him in his arms. "That's all I have to do? Just believe him well?"

"Believing is seeing, Madoc," said Fred.

"No," said Enoch. "Believing is *being*. So believe."

The Dragon Madoc held the clockwork bird as gently as he could and closed his eyes. Instantly the choices and decisions of a lifetime flashed through his mind, filling him with regret, sadness, and then . . .

. . . happiness. And contentment. And a feeling of rightness about his place in the world. And as he focused on these thoughts, he realized how much a part of who he was could be attributed to the teachings of this cranky, crotchety, wise, and beloved old bird. And that was when he felt it happen—a change, like a blessing made tangible.

"What," Archimedes said, "did you do to yourself, Madoc? You have wings!"

Madoc opened his eyes. "I wanted to be more like one of my best teachers," he said, unable to suppress a grin.

"That's what it would take," Archie replied. "It certainly wasn't going to be through your penmanship."

The companions gathered around the newly himself bird, laughing and cheering in celebration. Enoch, however, simply stood apart from them, arms extended, with his eyes closed and head tipped back.

"What are you doing?" Fred asked him, curious.

"Communing with my father," said Enoch.

"Uh, you mean you're praying?"

"Hmm," Enoch said. "Yes, I think that might be the right word. It is how we Archons communicate."

"Archons?" asked Charles. "You mean as in rulers?"

"That word will do," said Enoch. "Look—they are there, above."

For the first time, the companions actually took their eyes off the entrancing scenery and looked to the sky—and they realized what it was that was creating such an ethereal glow over the landscape.

The Archons were immense personages, less giants than men and women seen through a lens of majesty. Five beings, floating high in the air, were sitting cross-legged in the center of impossible geometries of light. They were drawing in the air as Enoch had been, but where he was simply making shapes and figures, they were weaving tapestries that moved and flowed with life. It was creation itself painted in the air above them.

"Astonishing," Charles murmured. "And you can commune with them?"

Enoch looked surprised. "Of course," he said. "I am one of them. I simply wore this body to make it easier to commune with *you*."

As if on cue, the Archons turned their heads, noticing for the first time that they were being observed. The light around them brightened—and when it faded again, five men and women had joined Enoch.

"These are the other Makers," Enoch said by way of introduction, "at least, all of us save for one. This is Abraxas and Eidolon, and Sophia and Lilith, and this"—he gestured to the last man—"is Seth. My father."

"Seth," said Charles. "You are—you are a son of the Adam, then?"

The Archon nodded. "One of them, at least." He gestured at Rose. "Is that my father's box?" Seth asked. He was pointing at the Serendipity Box in Rose's bag.

"I believe it is," she answered, handing it to him. "Would you like to have it back?"

"I would," he answered, "if you have no further use for it."

"A shame," Laura Glue said. "I never actually got to use it."

"You should," said Seth, proffering the box to the Valkyrie. "The one mistake people always make with the box is waiting until the need is both mortal and immediate before deciding to open it—and ofttimes, that's the moment when they realize it's already too late."

Laura Glue grinned and flipped open the lid. Inside was a space far larger than the box could have contained—an endlessly vast void.

"Ah," Seth said, nodding in approval. "A larger gift. Those are always interesting."

"Is that good or bad?" asked Fred.

"Neither," Seth replied. "It's merely interesting."

The young Valkyrie reached into the box to her shoulder. "I can just feel it," she said, screwing up her face with effort. "It's . . . just . . . out . . . of . . . my . . . Aha! Got it!"

Triumphantly she pulled out a tall, narrow hourglass. It appeared to have been made from bone, and had a valve in the center, where the glass was narrowest between the globes. The upper sphere was empty, but the lower was half-filled with a very fine alabaster-colored sand that seemed to glow in the waning light.

"Hmm," she said, frowning. "It's just an hourglass."

"Not just any hourglass," Seth said, reaching out to examine the device, "and not filled with any ordinary sand. These particles of dust were gathered on the shores of the ocean that reaches to heaven, and can forestall death itself for a full hour. If it's carried on a vessel, all who travel aboard it will be immune from the call of death until the last of the sand runs out."

"Holy cats!" Fred exclaimed. "That's like the best thing ever!"

"Except for lemon curd," said Uncas. "But yes, all things considered, it's pretty keen."

Laura Glue handed back the box, and Seth held it to his ear. "Hmm," he said. "It sounds as if there is one gift left to it." He handed it back to Rose. "You'd better keep it, just in case. Father would be happy to know it's been so thoroughly put to use over the centuries."

"You've given us great gifts," Madoc said as the Archons and companions seated themselves in a circle around the clearing. He looked up at Archie soaring happily around the treetops, and at the Valkyrie's hourglass and the Serendipity Box. "We have very little to offer you in return."

"I have a broken sword," Rose answered wryly. "It was a great weapon, once."

At Enoch's urging, she removed the shattered pieces of Caliburn from her bag and handed them to the Archon.

"It is great still," Enoch said. "It is Named—and it still has great power. It needs only to be repaired. Would you like one of us to do so? It is easily arranged."

"No need," Madoc said, rising to his feet. "Just show me to a forge, and I can take care of it myself."

He didn't notice the looks of approval that were traded among the Archons' faces, but Rose did.

One of the Archons, whom Enoch had introduced as Abraxas, led Madoc to a forge that was as fully modern as any he'd ever used. He had repaired the sword once before, at the beach of the Great Wall at the End of the World, but that time, he had the use of only one arm. This time, with both hands strong and capable, the muscle memory soon returned, and he was hammering away at the sword from underneath a cascade of sparks and steam.

The night passed, and then a full day, before Madoc rejoined the others. "It seems I am always repairing this sword," he said with a gruffness that wasn't entirely convincing. "Here," he said as he handed it to Rose. "Try not to break it this time."

Again, a gesture made by Madoc was met with approving glances among the Archons, but this time they didn't escape his notice. "What?" he said with a note of real irritation in his voice.

"There are only ever seven Makers in the world," Seth answered, "and many years ago, one of our number, the first, the best, was taken from us. We have waited many centuries for another to take his place. And if you wish it, Madoc the Maker, you may join us."

He stared at the Archons in disbelief, not even entirely certain what he was being asked. But after a long moment, he shook his head. "I'm sorry," he said. "I'd like to pretend that it's at least a temptation, but it isn't.

"We have come a long way together, to try to make right some terrible wrongs, and I cannot step off that path, and away from my daughter. Not yet. Maybe not ever."

Instead of disappointment, this announcement brought still more looks of approval from the Archons. "Then tell us," Enoch said. "What can I do to help you? Why did you come here, seeking me out?"

"We came looking for the Architect of a great tower," Rose answered, "and we were told that you were the man who built the first city. If you could do that, then surely you might also know how to build—"

"The Keep of Time?" asked Enoch.

"You know it?" Rose asked.

"I do," he said, rising to his feet. "Come. Walk with me, and I'll show you."

The companions and the Archons followed Enoch as he took a small trail to the top of a nearby hill, where there was a clear view of the horizon, unimpeded by the great trees and mountains that ringed the valley.

"There," he said, pointing to the setting sun. "Watch, as it turns to twilight. Then you'll be able to see it clearly, even from here."

There were a few thin, high clouds, which followed the curve of the horizon, and the sky was denser, here in the distant past. Not thick, or cloying, but simply . . . *richer*. The fading light flowed through the sky in wave after wave of ambers and purples, and then, when it finally started to ebb, they saw it.

A pencil-thin line that stretched from sea to sky, lit brilliantly by the last rays of the sun.

"There is your keep," said Enoch. "It still stands, as it has always stood—and it was built long before my time. If it is the Architect of that tower you seek, you will not find him here."

PART FIVE

THE FALL OF THE
HOUSE OF TAMERLANE

CHAPTER SEVENTEEN
AT THE END OF ALL THINGS

— ✳ —

THE DESERT CROSSING *was terrible; the mountain crossing was worse. The great beasts that carried the Archipelago on their backs faltered often, and the great Dragon worried they would not last much longer—and then they were over, and the path eased.*

While they crossed the long, narrow bridge that would take them to the Lonely Isle, there to wait again until called upon by those whom the old Dragon had entrusted to make things right, he told stories to his small friend, to better pass the time.

He had not been close to any of the Children of the Earth, not really, not as an angel, and not as a Dragon. But in times of need, the badger had always been there, with loyalty, and bravery, and heart. And the Dragon realized that in this one small example, he could demonstrate why an entire Archipelago was worth the effort to save. If there were five among all the peoples and creatures who were like the badger Tummeler, it would be worth it.

"There had been Makers, and there had been many, many Namers," the great Dragon explained, *"but there is only ever one Imago, and one Archimago, walking the earth together at the same time. The Archimago had vanished into the mists of history—but the Imago, the first in thousands of years, was reshaping the world.*

"*There was a great battle between the first giants, who were the children of the angels called Nephilim and one of the Sisters of Eve called Lilith, and the Dragons. It culminated in a struggle between their greatest, Ogias, and the greatest of us, a she-Dragon called Sycorax, who finally subdued him with the help of the Imago, T'ai Shan.*

"*She was the youngest of a family of gods, who was judged to be weak and cast out of their house. What her name had been before no one knows, but she took her new name from that of an angel who saw her for what she was, and gave her introduction to the star Rao, who would give her his fire, and taught her to use it.*

"*But the angel Shaitan disappeared before the rest of his order descended to become the Dragons of this world; Rao betrayed his kind and was deemed Fallen; and T'ai Shan, after saving the world and returning it to the people she had loved and cared for, gave her armor and her power over to them for their use, and then left the world behind.*

"*First she crossed an uncrossable desert. Then she scaled an unclimbable mountain. And finally she reached an impassable sea, so she labored for the rest of her days to build a bridge of bone, so that others who followed behind her would find the path to heaven easier to walk.*"

"*A desert, a mountain, and a bridge of bone over the sea,*" said Tummeler. "*That sounds exactly like the path we've been walking.*"

"Yes," the Dragon said. "Exactly like that."

"That's impossible!" Charles declared. "The island the keep is built on is a long journey away, deep in the Archipelago. There's no way we'd be able to see it from here!"

"And yet, there it stands," said Madoc. "That *is* the true keep."

"Distance is less of an obstacle in this time," said Enoch, "and it is not so long since meaning was divided from duration, and time itself took two paths. The longer they remain split, the further what is meaningful grows apart from all else."

"If he in't a scowler," said Uncas, "he ought t' be. He sure talks like one."

"True that," said Fred.

"Have you ever seen it up close?" Rose asked. "Is it damaged?"

"It is," Enoch said, taken aback by the question, "although my father has told me stories passed down from the days of the Adam, when it was said the tower was whole, and unbroken. But no one living has ever seen it thus. I'm sorry I cannot help you find your Architect."

"What do we do now?" Edmund asked.

"The Zanzibar Gate has one more trip left in it," said Rose. "If we go home, we will be back at square one, or worse. But if we try to go out one more time, we may find what we need. I think it's worth trying."

"So those are our choices, then," said Charles. "Either we go home, or we take one more shot in the dark—literally—to try to discover the Architect."

"This *is* why we came," said Rose. "All the sacrifices, everything we've been through . . . It's all for nothing if we fail. And either we go home, or we take one more chance. I say we take it."

"Agreed," said Edmund.

"All right," said Charles.

"Ditto," said the badgers.

"In for a penny, night on the town," said Laura Glue. "I'm up for it."

Madoc turned to the Archons. "Is there anything you might

tell us to help? We simply need to find out who first built the keep—and no matter how far back in time we go, we can't seem to locate him."

"Traveling in time is a difficult proposition," said Seth. "It flows in two directions, you know."

"This in't our first time at the Sweet Corn Festival, you know," said Uncas. "We've done this before."

"My point," Seth said, grinning at the badger, "is that time and history are two separate things. They have been since the time of the Adam. Before that, they were one, and mixed together freely. After that, they moved in divergent ways."

"What happened that changed everything?" asked Madoc.

"The moment when the Imago was slain by the Archimago," said Enoch. "That is the moment when history truly began."

The companions all went still. "What Imago?" Madoc asked slowly, putting a hand protectively in front of Rose. "And what Archimago?"

"The first Maker, and the first Namer," Seth said. "My elder brothers. That was the moment when time was divided. If meaning is what you seek, search out that moment above all others, and perhaps you will find what you need."

"That's part of the difficulty," said Edmund. "The way the Zanzibar Gate—the pyramid structure we came through—works is by programming a date or period into it, which we can refine with an illumination of whom or what we're seeking. But we don't know anything about the Architect, and if time is separate from history, that's even worse—because history is what gives us the markers by which we set the dates."

"It seems to me," Enoch said, "now that you have explained

how your mechanism works, that the answer to your question is very simple."

"Simple?" Uncas all but hollered at him. "We've had the best scowlers and the best minds of all of history tryin' t' figure out how t' make this work for years now. How can it be simple?"

"Decorum, my squire," Quixote admonished him. "Always decorum, even at the end of all things."

"Exactly," said Enoch.

Suddenly the diverse pieces of the puzzle came together in Rose's head, as she realized what the Maker was trying to tell them.

"The beginning," she said, excitement rising in her face. "All this time we've been trying to figure out exactly *when* the Architect built the keep, and everyone we've met has told us the answer!"

Edmund frowned, still unsure of where she was leading them. "Except all anyone was ever told is that it was built long before their time," he said. "That it has always existed. Even the Caretakers have said as much—that it was there because it had always been there since . . ." His eyes went wide with the realization.

". . . since the beginning," he finished. "Can it be?" he asked Rose. "Can it really be that simple?"

"Nothing is *ever* simple," Fred said, looking at his father, "but sometimes, things are easier than we make them out to be."

"I'm afraid they've lost me completely," Quixote said, looking down at Uncas. "Are you following any of this?"

"I am," Laura Glue said brightly. "We've always worried about how to go back further and further, to find the right place in time when the keep was built, when what we should have been doing was trying to go back *before* it was built!"

Madoc threw his head back and laughed. "That's brilliant," he said, wiping tears from his eyes. "I am overcome."

Edmund jumped to his feet and pounded a fist into his hand. "It's too perfect not to try," he said, almost breathless with anticipation. "All we have to do is turn all the settings to zero and go through the gate. It should allow us to return, right here, at the moment of the keep's creation."

"I agree," said Rose. "We've been so worried about who built the keep that we've forgotten that it's just as important *when* it was built. And if we go to *when*, we'll finally find out *who* the Architect is!"

"*That's* what you've all been debating?" Archie said as he glided down and landed on Edmund's shoulder. "I could have told you that much." He looked at Madoc and made a clucking noise. "Did you learn nothing from my philosophy lectures?"

"This is all very exciting for you, isn't it?" Enoch said to the badgers.

"You have no idea," said Fred.

The companions bid the Archons farewell and prepared the *Indigo Dragon* for one final trip through the gate.

"Here," Enoch said as they climbed aboard. "The visitor, Telemachus, said that when you realized where you needed to go, I should give you this." He reached out and put the silver watch into Madoc's hand. "He told me that you had no watch of your own, and so this is yours."

"You don't want to keep it?"

Enoch smiled. "I'm a Maker, remember?" he said, stepping away from the airship. "I'll make more."

"All right," Edmund said, rubbing his hands together. "There is nothing guiding us but the settings on the gate, and I've set them all for zero. Everyone cross your fingers."

Fred engaged the internal motor of the airship and urged the goats forward at the same time. Within moments they were going toward the gate, which glowed as Madoc came near, and in a moment more, they were through.

At Tamerlane House, the word quickly spread that Poe had some grand revelations to share, and no one wanted to miss out, so the great hall was quickly filled with all the residents and visitors it could hold. Caretakers Emeriti took most of the seats around the table, while the Mystorians filled in the standing room next to the walls. For his part, the detective Aristophanes brought in a couch from one of the other rooms for himself and the Messenger Beatrice, and, surprisingly, a chair for the shipbuilder Argus. Only the half-clockwork men called Jason's sons, known as Hugh the Iron and William the Pig, remained outside to guard Shakespeare's Bridge. Hawthorne and Irving went out one last time just to check on them before the meeting commenced, but otherwise, everyone at Tamerlane House was present.

A bright chime suddenly rang out from all the Caretakers' watches: once, twice, and then a third time. As one, they all stopped to look at the time, to see why the watches had made such an unusual sound, and that was when they all realized what had happened.

The watches were resetting themselves.

"What is this?" asked John. "What is happening here, Jules? Bert? They've never done *that* before."

"There is a new zero point," Bert said in amazement. "The Anabasis Machines have reset themselves to it. All of them. At once."

"That's not just any zero point," Verne said, peering at his watch. "They're resetting because it's *the* zero point. The prime zero. The moment in history when everything was connected, and the Keep of Time was built."

"Does that mean they've succeeded?" asked John. "Can this really be over?"

"I don't know," said Verne. "We should ask Poe about it immediately, though. This may preclude whatever he was planning to share."

"Not just yet," John said, holding up both his hands. "We're still waiting on a few fellows to arrive, and I think everyone should be here."

"I think they're coming now," Twain said, lifting a curtain to glance out the window, "and at top speed, apparently."

Hawthorne and Irving blew through the front doors with a bang, rounded the corner, and skidded into the room. Both their faces were ashen.

"Jack, you must come, quickly," Hawthorne said, ignoring all decorum in favor of urgency. "You, and everyone! Something's happened at the bridge."

"What?" Jack implored as the Caretakers all rose to rush outside with their colleagues. "What's happened, Nathaniel?"

"It's Warnie," Irving answered. "Dr. Dee has your brother, Jack. And he's going to kill him unless we give him access to Tamerlane House and the Nameless Isles."

It was dusk in the place and time where the *Indigo Dragon* emerged from the Zanzibar Gate. As they passed through, the glow that signaled it was functioning properly waned and died.

"Well, that's that," said Fred. "I really hope this works, or we may as well start building houses."

"I don't think it worked," Edmund said, unable to hide the trace of bitterness in his voice. "Look."

In the distance, dark against the fading light in the sky, was the swirl of clouds that made up the Barrier around the Garden of Eden. "We're still in the same place."

"But not in the same time," said Madoc. "The trees are different, as far as I can see. And those stones were not here."

In the center of the clearing, similar to the one where they'd met the Archons, was a small ring of stones, with a stone table in the center.

"It's like a small Ring of Power," Charles said, barely daring to breathe, "except for the table in the center. That's different."

Uncas and Fred both sniffed the air, as did the goats. "That's blood," Fred said with a shudder. "Fresh blood. Recent blood."

The companions all held their breath when they realized Fred was right—and that the dark stains covering the stone table still glistened in the waning light of day.

"Seth was right," Rose said, choking as she spoke. "We can't go back further in time than this moment, no matter how much older the keep is."

"A paradox," a young man said as he stepped around from behind one of the stones. "The keep is what binds the two worlds together, even though they are growing further and further apart."

Uncas, Fred, Quixote, and Laura Glue recognized him immediately. They had seen him in a battle on Easter Island only a few months earlier.

The others didn't know his face, but the Ruby Armor he wore was instantly recognizable.

"To restore what has been broken, you must travel beyond the point where the worlds have been split," he continued, "but to do so is impossible without the presence of the keep. It is, as I said, a paradox."

"If we can't go beyond this point in time," Edmund said slowly, not certain of the wisdom of speaking to this mysterious man, "then how are we possibly going to restore time? We've had two last chances to find the Architect, and now we're out of options."

The young man turned to Rose. "What do you think? Is your quest hopeless? Is it over?"

"There's got to be a way," Rose said, her voice low. "There is always a way. Always."

"Ah," said the young man. "*That's* what I was waiting for."

"Waiting for to do what?" asked Fred.

"Help you," the young man replied. "One last time."

In a trice, the young man in the Ruby Armor was replaced by someone Rose had seen twice before: a very ancient man, wearing a flowing robe. He nodded at them as if this were an entirely anticipated turn of events, then looked at Rose, smiling. "Hello, my dear," he said. "I have been waiting for you for a very long time, but I knew you'd show up again . . . eventually."

Without hesitation, Rose simply asked him the first question that came to mind. "Are you him?" she said. "Are you the Architect?"

"No," the old man said firmly. "I am *not* the Architect."

"Who are you, then?" asked Rose.

"You know, Moonchild," he replied gently. "You have always known."

"Coal," she said, her voice soft. "You're Coal."

He nodded. "I was. Am. Although I think I prefer the name I chose for myself. It suits me best, when I need a name, that is. You may call me Telemachus."

CHAPTER EIGHTEEN
THE ARCHITECT

THE CARETAKERS OF Tamerlane House gathered en masse at their side of Shakespeare's Bridge. There, just on the other side, they could see Dr. Dee and two tall men in black, who wore dark glasses and bowler hats. In between them was Jack's brother, Warnie.

"These are my colleagues, Mr. Kirke and Mr. Bangs," said Dr. Dee. "They have been trained to do many things, but what they most excel at is following my orders—and I have told them that unless you do exactly as I ask, they are to tear Major Lewis into pieces."

"Sorry, Jack," Warnie said. His military reserve and strength of character gave him the appearance of fortitude, but Jack could tell he was properly scared.

"You know me well enough, Jules," Dee said. "I'm not bluffing. And if need be, my colleagues can also kill Caretakers—no matter what form they've taken."

"What is it you want?" Verne asked, casting a quick glance at John to see if he would object. John nodded his head faintly, giving Verne the go-ahead to keep speaking. If Dee wasn't aware there was a new Prime Caretaker at Tamerlane, then John certainly wasn't going to correct him.

"There are guards set in these stones, and in the bridge," said Dee. "Runic wards. I want you to cancel them."

"I see," Verne said, stalling for time. "We use silver rings to bypass the—"

"I don't want a ring, Jules!" Dee all but shouted. "I want you to drop all the protection you have built up around these islands! Now!"

To punctuate his request, Mr. Kirke twisted Warnie's arm backward and up, dislocating his shoulder. Jack's brother let out a yelp of pain, then gritted his teeth and bore it.

"What if we decline?" asked Verne, trying not to look at Major Lewis. "What if we simply say no?"

"Mr. Kirke and Mr. Bangs are very, very strong," said Dr. Dee, "and we have silver sledgehammers that can shatter even cavorite."

"And?"

"And," said Dee, "as far as I know, this bridge is the only thing keeping Tamerlane House tethered to the Summer Country. If we smash it—and we will—then you suddenly get hurled into the heart of the Echthroi's domain. Forever. And then," he added, "we'll still kill Jack's brother."

"All right!" John shouted, realizing Verne was more likely to sacrifice Warnie than give up any tactical advantage. "We'll do as you ask."

Dr. Dee's eyes glittered as he looked from John to Verne and back again, processing this apparent breach of Caretaker protocol. "Good," he said, gesturing for Mr. Kirke to ease up on Jack's brother. "I see you are going to be reasonable men. Lower the wards."

"And then what?" John demanded.

"Then," said Dee, "I'm going to go *home*."

◆ ◆ ◆

"You were taken from us, you know that," said Rose. "We've tried everything we could to find you!"

"I believe you," said Telemachus.

"So you've chosen?" asked Fred. "You decided to help the Caretakers after all?"

"I wasn't sure, not completely," he answered, "until I put on the Ruby Armor—and realized that I had more in common with T'ai Shan than I did with John Dee, or the Echthroi.

"T'ai Shan was born into a family of gods, but she was crippled, and so was cast out. She had to make her way in the world as a beggar, or perish. She survived in part because she was an adept—like you and I, Rose—but she thrived because she saw it as her purpose to serve others.

"She was given the power of a star, who then betrayed her. But she fought him and won. The giants, who were the children of angels, were subdued by her and made to serve the cause of the Dragons. She was betrayed, terribly and often, by those closest to her—and still, her purpose was to serve. And then, somehow, I was brought to this world through improbable circumstance, and given this miraculous armor, and with it, a choice. Do I serve the Echthroi, or do I serve the Light?"

"Is this one of those remoracle questions?" asked Uncas. "Because if it in't, I'm really afraid of what his answer is."

Telemachus smiled at this. "Don't worry, little fellow," he said. "With great power comes great responsibility, and an even greater awareness. I've made my choice, and I'm going to do what I can to help you set things right."

"That is exactly why I came to the end of time," said Charles.

He looked at Edmund. "Or is it the beginning? I keep losing track."

Edmund shrugged. "Where he's from, I don't think it matters."

"Wise boy," said Telemachus. "In Platonia there is no Chronos time, only Kairos time."

"Seth, the Namer, told us something similar about Eden," said Rose. "He told us time was different there, because it had only just been separated, and so both kinds of time still mixed freely, but I didn't really understand him. What did he mean?"

"Chronos time is merely about the progression of moments," said Telemachus, "but Kairos time is about the meaning held within those moments—and the meaning of a single moment can last an eternity."

"The killing," Charles murmured. "When Chronos—Cain— slew Kairos—Abel—it split the two kinds of time, because that murder was the first act of true meaning in the world."

"Yes," Telemachus said, glancing down at the stone table. "This is the moment when it all began, and so this is the moment when the keep must be built."

"But the doors," said Madoc. "I've been inside them, and time goes back much further than this. Eden, even the time of the Adam, is not the beginning."

"You're right, and wrong," said Telemachus. "The keep, once restored, will persist in time in both directions, forward and back. But history, and true meaning, began here, with this murder. The keep is what connected the Archipelago with the Summer Country, and Chronos time with Kairos time. It was not necessary before, because nothing was divided."

"So what happens now?"

"Now," Telemachus said, "the Architect must build the keep, restore what was broken, and redeem the murder that split the world in two."

Nathaniel Hawthorne and William Shakespeare were in charge of the security of the bridge. It took only a few minutes to completely disable all the runes and lower all the wards.

"All right, Dee," John said. "Now what?"

"Watch and learn," Dee said, smiling. He was not looking at any of the Caretakers, but was instead looking past them. All of them willing to take their eyes off Dee turned to see what he was looking at.

There, on the largest of the easternmost islands of the Nameless Isles, the Nightmare Abbey, the dark, gabled house of John Dee, suddenly shimmered into view, solidified, and settled with a whisper into place.

"The Cabal," Jack said. "John, he's brought the entire Cabal to the Nameless Isles! The enemy is here at our doorstep!"

"Closer than that, I think," the Cheshire cat Grimalkin said as he appeared in the air over John's shoulder. The Prime Caretaker jumped away, but the cat merely smiled at him and scratched at himself with a wicked-looking claw. "We're in your house, eating your food, drinking your wine, and criticizing the decor."

"Grimalkin!" John exclaimed. "You aren't welcome here anymore!"

"Welcome or not, I'm still here, boy," the cat said, "although it seems not even my master needed me, really. I would have thought it would take more than 'Your shoelace is untied' to get all of you to take your eyes off Dr. Dee."

The Caretakers whirled around, but to their relief, Dee was still there, along with Warnie and his henchmen.

"We've done as you asked, Dee," said John. "Honor your part of the bargain."

Dee looked at the cat. "Well, Grimalkin?"

The Cheshire cat licked a vanishing paw. "He tells the truth. The wards are down."

Dee nodded, and Mr. Kirke struck Warnie a vicious blow to the head. Without making a sound, Jack's brother fell to the ground, unconscious.

"I will kill you for that, Dee," said Jack. "You know this. Believe it."

"I kept my word," Dee said as he crossed the bridge. "He hasn't been harmed. Much."

The Caretakers drew their swords and readied their weapons. "There are three of you and a multitude of us," Twain said, leveling his *katana* at the former Caretaker. "We have you vastly outnumbered."

"Appearances, Samuel, can be deceiving," Dee countered. "You have numbers on your side, but this time I brought an ally whose loyalty cannot be questioned."

With a gesture, he signaled to the cat, who suddenly became completely visible—and who began to grow much, much larger. In seconds, Grimalkin was the size of a good-sized truck.

"Now we can talk reasonably, like civilized men," Dee said as he and his minions strode casually toward the house under the watchful gaze of the giant cat.

"I know you are bound," John said to Grimalkin. "I know that's why you serve him."

"Yes," Grimalkin said, with no trace of shame or embarrassment. "For a very, very long time now."

Twain shook his head in disgust. "I can't believe we've had a Lloigor here all this time."

"Not Lloigor," the cat insisted. "Echthros. A Lloigor is one who has given up or sold his shadow. But an Echthros is simply an Echthros."

"Echthroi are Fallen angels," said Twain. "Are you saying you're an angel?"

"Was," said the cat.

"A Binding is not the whole of your being, Grimalkin," said John. "People have resisted Bindings before! And you resisted enough to warn us about Rose!"

"What?" Dee said, startled. He turned to the cat, scowling. "You caused me to move my timetable considerably," he growled, "and there will be a price to pay, on that count you can be certain."

"Enough chatter, Dee," said Verne. "What is it you want?"

"There has always been one Imago and one Archimago on the earth," said Dee. "You chose your candidate for Imago, and I chose mine—and now it seems both have been lost."

"Ours is lost," said Jack. "Yours abandoned you out of common sense."

"Maybe," said Dee. "But I believe that yours may yet succeed in restoring the keep and the Archipelago. And when that happens, I would like to be present. That's why I have brought my house to the Nameless Isles—so that I can be here when the Imago and Archimago are together again in one place."

"You're out of your mind," John said. "There's no such person as the Archimago."

"It is one of the great secrets," said Dee. "One of the reveals the Prime Caretaker alone knows."

Several of the Caretakers automatically turned to look at John, and the Chronographer of Lost Times slowly realized that something significant had changed in the Caretaker hierarchy. He smiled wickedly.

"I see," Dee said, turning to look at Verne. "You haven't told him, have you? He doesn't know!"

"There are a lot of things I'm still learning, Dee," John said, "not the least of which is whom I should trust, and when."

"I was the Prime Caretaker before Jules was," said Dee, "until the Caretakers and I had a critical difference of opinion.

"The most significant reason it is the job of the Prime Caretaker to seek out and train the Imago," Dee continued with a flourish, "is because the Archimago resides here, with you, at Tamerlane House. He has been hiding in plain sight among the Caretakers ever since the first Imago was killed."

The Caretakers, all except for Verne, froze in shock.

"That's impossible," said John. "We would have known."

Dee shook his head. "It's not impossible. He's watching, and listening to all of us, right now," he said, looking up at one of the balconies.

As one, the Caretakers turned to look, some already realizing, and all of them already fearing what they would see.

There, watching in the shadows from between the parted curtains at his window, was Edgar Allan Poe.

"Rebuilding the keep," said Rose, "is exactly what we've been trying to accomplish. We just have no clue who the Architect is."

"You don't need clues," Telemachus replied, "because the answer you've sought has been staring you in the face all along.

"I was a good student," he went on, turning to Madoc, "and I knew well the history of the Archipelago. And I know," he continued, "that in your former life as Mordred, the Winter King, you once went to considerable lengths to try to destroy the original *Imaginarium Geographica*, am I right?"

Madoc reddened. "You are."

Telemachus shrugged. "So why couldn't you?"

"It had to be destroyed by the one who created it," Madoc replied, "and none other. No one else could even do so much as singe the pages, unless he permitted it."

"It is one of the first principles of Deep Magic," Telemachus said gravely. "The *Imaginarium Geographica* could not be destroyed save by he who had created it . . .

". . . and neither could the *Keep of Time*."

The understanding struck Laura Glue and Fred first, and they stared at the others in shock and amazement. Charles suddenly looked as if he had swallowed an oyster that was too large to choke down, and Rose simply gripped her father's hand more tightly. Of all of them, only Edmund beamed with delight at having an answer to the unanswerable question.

"Do I really need to clarify it for you?" asked Telemachus. He pointed at Charles. "You may have created the circumstances that led to its destruction, but you didn't destroy the keep." He continued, swinging his arm around to point at Madoc, "*You* did.

"You, Madoc. *You* are the Architect of the Keep of Time."

CHAPTER NINETEEN
THE KEYSTONE

"NOW, GRIMALKIN," said Dee.

Without another word, the Chronographer of Lost Times, the cat, and the two strange men called Mr. Kirke and Mr. Bangs vanished.

Before any of the Caretakers could react, two tremendous explosions rocked Tamerlane House and threw them all to the ground.

"What in Hades's name?" Verne exclaimed.

They clambered to their feet in time to see a small boat pulling up to the docks below. It was motorized but silent, so they had not heard it approach, and had in any regard been completely distracted by Dee.

In the boat were William Hope Hodgson, Aleister Crowley, and Nikola Tesla, who was wearing a device that resembled two massive engines strapped to his back. The engines were pointed forward, and Tesla smiled and pressed a contact. Immediately another explosion rocked the island, and one of the minarets crumpled in on itself.

"Sonic energy," said Shakespeare. "I'd bet my life on it."

"Oh, that is just not bloody fair," said Dumas. "Tesla always has all the best toys."

"Split up!" Verne called out. "Our weapons won't be very effective against Tesla for long!"

The Caretakers scattered around the island as Tesla advanced, still firing at the house. As he fled to the north side of the island, John glanced up at the window where Poe had been watching. It was empty.

Madoc stared dumbfounded at the old man, too stunned to speak, but Rose found her words more easily.

"It makes sense," she said, still unsure of what this revelation meant, "but how could no one have known? No one in history?"

"Because," Telemachus said, "the only ones who were present are here now. We're witnessing it as it's happening. And history will move forward from this point, and no other."

"I know the structure well enough," Madoc said slowly, "but it's made of cavorite. Where am I meant to get the blocks to build it?"

"You brought them with you," Telemachus answered, pointing at the Zanzibar Gate. "They are precisely what you need, in the right size and shape. All you have to do is assemble them."

"That's not going to make a very big tower," Uncas observed.

"Many great things start small," said Telemachus, "and any seed planted properly can grow and flower into what it is meant to become."

Rose looked at her father. "What do you think?"

Madoc shrugged. "I think we have nothing to lose if we try," he said. "Let's get started, and see what happens."

✦   ✦   ✦

"Tell me again what we're doing down here?" Shakespeare whispered. "I like to dabble in espionage, but I'm not very good at it."

He, Houdini, and Conan Doyle had taken a page from their adversaries' playbook—while Tesla, Crowley, and Hodgson were distracted by the other Caretakers, they had stolen the boat from the dock and launched their own assault on the Cabal's own headquarters.

"Haven't you studied warfare?" Houdini whispered to Shakespeare. "The single biggest advantage of being completely surrounded is that it gives you the opportunity to attack the enemy in any direction you choose."

"All right, fair point," Shakespeare whispered back. "So how do we go about breaking in?"

"This," Houdini said, "is the moment when I prove my worth to the Caretakers at large. Give me three minutes." He stopped, reconsidering. "No, make that two," he added as he scrambled up the embankment toward the house.

"Cocksure, isn't he?" Shakespeare whispered to Conan Doyle.

"Not really," Conan Doyle replied. "If he said two, that means he can do it in under one. Some of us got our reputations because we wrote good books or had clever publicists. He got his reputation through sheer hard work."

As if to underscore his colleague's sentiments, the double doors under the eaves of the house swung open on silent hinges and Houdini leaned out, winking at the others.

"See?" said Conan Doyle. "That's why he's my best friend. Never a dull moment."

The three men entered the house, prepared for a fight—but they met almost no resistance, not even the perfunctory kind, done for show. The house was practically empty—not even the servants were moving about.

Passing one gallery, Houdini noticed a former friend, and he paused. "Gilbert?" he said. "What are you doing?"

"Having a drink, for these are trying times," Chesterton said, not moving from the chair where he was sipping some sort of drink out of a small crystal glass. "Also, I wish to defect. I'm more of a strategist, not a fighter."

"Really," said Houdini. "What strategy are you advocating now?"

"Joining the winning side," Chesterton replied, "obviously."

"I can't argue with that," Conan Doyle said as he ran past with a blunderbuss. "I'll secure the south side, Ehrich."

As it turned out, without Dee driving them, not many of the Cabal were willing to put up a fight. Some, like Chesterton, who still possessed his own shadow, offered to join the Caretakers. Others, like Lovecraft, refused to even come out of their rooms. Even Tesla was finally cornered and subdued, overcome by sheer numbers. There were many Caretakers, and few members of the Cabal. From start to finish, it seemed to be a fool's errand. It was as if the entire effort to move the House on the Borderlands to the Nameless Isles was . . .

"A distraction," said Twain. "It was all just a distraction."

"I agree. I don't think the Cabal was prepared for this, at all," said John. "Other than Tesla, with his contraptions, and maybe Crowley, none of the rest of them seemed prepared for an assault. I think Dee brought them here without telling them anything about it at all."

"You don't think they might have been trying to storm Tamerlane

House?" Bert asked. "There's a lot here that I know Dee would love to get his hands on again."

"This simply doesn't make any sense, Bert," John said to his old mentor. "They're just too outmatched. What can Dee possibly hope to achieve by literally bringing the fight to our doorstep?"

"I agree," said Twain. "There's some larger plan in the works here. Otherwise, he blows a few ventilation holes in Tamerlane, we eliminate a few of his Deathshead servants and knock Lovecraft and Crowley around for a bit . . . and everything remains as it is. No, there is something he can only get access to here, and we must discover what that is."

"The house is as secure as we're going to get it," Hawthorne said, grimacing as he joined the others near what remained of Shakespeare's shop. Tesla had gotten to it before he was subdued by Hugh the Iron and William the Pig, who were the only residents of Tamerlane House large enough to literally rip the engines off his back. "Any sign of Dee yet?"

"There aren't that many places to hide in the Nameless Isles," said John, "and we've already re-secured the access to Shakespeare's Bridge, so really, where can they go?"

"Did you notice?" Twain asked. "Dee has no shadow."

"I have some experience being shadowless," said Jack. "What I'm wondering about is that threat he made to smash the bridge."

"Be glad he didn't," said Twain. "I'm all but certain that would have thrown us straightaway into the realm of the Echthroi."

"That's my point," said Jack. "We'd be at the mercy of his masters. So why not do it? And if Rose and the others do manage to restore the keep, then the Echthroi would be driven out of the Archipelago. So isn't that a huge loss for him?"

"He has his own versions of our watches," said Twain. "He would have seen the same resetting of the prime zero point that we did."

"That's why he's here!" Jack cried. "He knows that it's about to happen. So where *is* he?"

"I'm just wondering," said Shakespeare, "but has anyone thought to check the boathouse?"

Quickly the Caretakers took a head count of themselves and their allies and realized that one of them was missing.

"Argus," Jack said, his heart sinking. "The shipbuilder is missing. And I think I know what Dee is going to try to do."

Waving for the others to follow, Jack grabbed up Hawthorne's sledgehammer and bolted out the door. John, Irving, Dumas, Verne, and Jason's son Hugh followed him, taking whatever weapons they could grab along the way.

Inside the south boathouse the Caretakers found Dr. Dee and the missing Argus—but minutes too late. The shipbuilder had already completed the work Dee had forced him to do.

Where there had once been a gaping, splintered hole in the prow of the *Black Dragon*, there was now the massive, regally maned head of a cat that aspired to be a lion. It was Grimalkin, the Cheshire cat of Tamerlane House, an angel become Echthros, and it was now part of a living ship. That gave it will, and power—and it was still in the thrall of John Dee.

Argus was half sitting, half standing on the dock alongside the ship. Even from a distance the Caretakers could tell he had been beaten, and badly. His shirt was torn, and bruises were visible on his shoulder and chest. Worse, there was a bandage over his left eye that was oozing with blood.

"Dee," Jack muttered. "I've had about enough of him."

Yelling and brandishing their weapons, the Caretakers charged into the boathouse, but Dee was prepared for them. He pressed a contact on the wall, and a sudden explosion threw all of them to the ground.

Splinters of wood flew everywhere, and the billowing smoke obscured their view of the ship—but when it started to clear, they saw there was a gaping hole in the wall of the boathouse. The ship was gone, and Dee and Argus were gone with it.

"I think this must have been part of his plan all along," said John. "We lost the only Dragon we had when Madoc left, and with him, any possibility of crossing the Frontier into the Archipelago. But if Dee has a living ship, bonded with a creature that was once an angel . . ." His words trailed off into a stunned silence.

"It can cross over," Jack said, "and I say we let it. Remember what is happening in the Archipelago? Or what used to be the Archipelago, anyway. It's all Echthroi. All Shadow. I say let them go and good riddance."

Once the extra material that Shakespeare had added was stripped off the Zanzibar Gate, the stone was easy enough for Madoc to pull apart. As he began to construct the base of the keep, Rose used Caliburn to cut branches into planks to use as support beams, while the rest of their friends busied themselves mixing mud to use for mortar.

"So," Fred observed as he dropped more straw into the pit where Quixote, Laura Glue, and Edmund were stomping it into the mud with their feet, "if the stones that Will used to make the Zanzibar Gate came from the original keep, but now we're back here helping t' build the original keep, then where did the original stones come from the first time? Isn't that one of those . . . conundrum things Scowler Jules is always going on about?"

"A pair of ducks," Uncas said as he dumped his own armload of straw in, taking great care not to get wet. "That's what Mr. Telemachus said it was called."

"A paradox, you mean," said Edmund, "and no, I don't think so. Rose and I have learned that time only *seems* to move in two directions—but it really just moves forward, along with the events you perceive. So this is still the original keep, because we're building it for the first time. It's never been built before."

"But it'll still be there when we get back to our own time, because it's been rebuilt, right?"

"Yes."

"So," Fred repeated, "if the keep never fell in our timeline, then where did Will get the stone to make the Zanzibar Gate?"

Edmund frowned, and bit his lip. "Uh, hmm," he said. "I see your point. I'll tell you what. If it works, we'll never bring it up again. And if it doesn't, we'll have plenty of time to debate it. Agreed?"

"Gotcha," said Fred. "You don't know the answer either, do you?"

"Not the faintest clue," said Edmund.

"Oh dear Lord in heaven," Shakespeare said, grabbing Hawthorne by the arm. "Look, Nathaniel!"

The small island where the Zanzibar Gate had been built was

empty. The rickety bridge was still there, as was the path that had led to the gate. But the gate itself had vanished. It was simply *gone*.

Hawthorne waved over several of the other Caretakers and pointed to the now empty island, and they quickly realized that something terrible had happened.

"It's supposed to continue to exist here, in the same way that the keep had duration, wasn't it, Will?" Dumas asked. "So how can a stationary object like that have simply disappeared?"

"I really cannot say," a bewildered Shakespeare answered. "The only way it could have disappeared is if it had been completely disassembled, but I don't know why anyone would even consider doing that, especially if it was their only means of coming home!"

"That's it, then," Verne said to himself quietly. "It's time to go."

As the other Caretakers debated what to do with the Cabal, and wondered what had happened to the Zanzibar Gate, none of them had noticed Verne slip away into the house—none, that is, except for one. Verne made his way to the lower stairs that led down to the basement and closed the door firmly behind him.

"What in heaven's name is he doing?" Bert murmured to himself. "There's no way out of that basement, and there's nothing down there except for"—he slapped himself on the forehead—"time-travel devices."

Bert dashed for the stairs and threw open the door. "Curse you, Jules," he muttered under his breath. "What are you up to now?"

Bert got his answer when he reached the bottom of the stairs. Verne was sitting in the time machine Bert had used himself so long ago to travel into the far future.

"Are you mad?" Bert exclaimed, rushing over to stop his col-league. "I can't believe you're just running away from this! You've never avoided a fight, Jules! And besides, this is not the way! You've used this machine before, so you can't use it again!"

"Oh, but I can," Verne said as he flipped the switches to line them up with the dials on his watch. "There's just a price to pay for doing so, and my bill is long, long overdue."

"It's suicide!" Bert cried, backing away as the wheel behind the plush chair on the device began to spin.

"No," said Verne, "it's the endgame, at least for me. And that means it is redemption."

"What do you mean?"

"The watches have all been reset," Verne replied, "but the keep has not yet reappeared, nor has the Archipelago been restored. Something is amiss. I think I know what is lacking—and none of our friends should have to sacrifice themselves. Not after all they have been through."

Bert stared at him, puzzled, and then he realized—somehow, this had been in Verne's plans all along.

"Yes, old friend," Verne said, nodding as tears began to well in his eyes. "I always knew. They have found the true zero point, and at long last, I get to be the hero of the story instead of . . . well, whatever I've been. Tell John . . ." He paused. The lights were spin-ning faster and faster now, and the edges of the machine were beginning to blur. "Tell him I said I'm very proud of him. It may not mean much now. But someday . . ." He flipped the last switch, adjusted the last dial. "That's it, then," he said with finality. "Time to go."

"Jules!" Bert cried, shielding his eyes from the light.

"Be seeing you," said Verne. And then, in a trice, he and the time machine were gone.

"All right," Madoc said, dusting off his hands. "I think we have it."

There, constructed around the stone circle and the stone table, were the first two levels of the Keep of Time. There had been just enough stones in the Zanzibar Gate for a structure that was tall enough to permit a doorway to be included, as well as the first floor of interlocking stairs, and a landing and framework for the first door up above.

"I'm afraid I don't know enough about how it functions," Madoc admitted. "Is there something we have to do to turn it on?"

"One last thing," Telemachus replied. "One last stone. That, and that alone, is what makes the tower a living thing."

Madoc looked around, puzzled. "We've used all the stones from the gate," he said, "and I don't see any more cavorite around."

The old man shook his head. "Not cavorite. The keystone of the keep must be a living heart, willingly given. Only then can the tower come to life, and grow. Only then will time be restored."

"Oh fewmets," said Fred. "I knew there was going to be a catch in all this."

"If I must," said Madoc, before any of the others could speak. "It seems, dear Rose, that I am always sacrificing something for you. My younger self would never have believed it possible to love another person as I do you. But it's true."

"It's also the reason this is not your sacrifice to make, Madoc," said Telemachus. "You have already given her your heart, and she gave it to another."

"Curses," said Charles. "I knew Burton would find some way to give me a headache. Well," he added resignedly, "I suppose it falls to me."

Telemachus shook his head. "Your Prime Time has passed, and you now exist in Spare Time. You cannot give your heart to this, Caretaker."

Fred stepped forward, whiskers twitching nervously. "I c'n do this," he said, trying his best to control the quavering in his voice. "I'll give my heart, t' rebuild th' keep."

For the first time, the companions saw Telemachus's features soften. He knelt and put his hand on the little badger's shoulder. "Your heart is big enough to contain a thousand towers," he said gently, "but it was not meant for this, little Child of the Earth."

Rose swallowed hard and gripped Edmund's hand tighter. She knew that he was about to volunteer, but Telemachus held up a hand. "Nor you, my young Cartographer. You have a great destiny ahead of you, and this is not it."

"Then who?" Quixote said, swallowing hard.

In just that moment, a blinding flash appeared on the hill just behind them, and an object appeared, throwing off sparks and belching smoke.

"I have always wanted to ride to the rescue," said a figure emerging from the smoke, "but I always entertained a vision of being able to enjoy having done so, afterward."

"Hah!" said Charles. "That may be literally the most timely entrance I have witnessed in my life—either of them."

"Well met, Caretaker," Jules Verne said as he extended his hand to Charles. "It seems as if I've arrived in the nick."

CHAPTER TWENTY
RESTORATION

"JULES!" ROSE EXCLAIMED, throwing herself at him with a giant hug. "How did you find us?"

"You made this a zero point when you came here, Rose," Verne said, smiling broadly. "All I had to do was set the dials and throw a switch. It seems as if everything that needed fixing has been fixed . . .

". . . almost."

Charles shook his head sorrowfully. "You came here for nothing, Jules," he said. "People like you and I don't fit the billing."

Verne's eyes narrowed. "What do you mean?"

Charles walked Verne around the nearly completed keep. "It needs a keystone—a living heart, to make the keep a living tower," he explained. "Tulpas exist in what this old fellow calls 'Spare Time,' and as such we aren't suitable candidates to—"

He stopped when he recognized the carefully neutral expression on Verne's face—and grew visibly angry when he realized what it meant. "You sorry son of a—"

"What?" Rose exclaimed, glancing anxiously from one Caretaker to the other. "Uncle Charles, what is it?"

"He's not a tulpa," Charles said, still glaring at Verne. "He never *was*."

"It's too high a price, Telemachus," Madoc said. "I won't allow another to sacrifice himself just for the sake of this keep."

"Telemachus?" Verne said, eyes widening in surprise. "Well, lad, you've, ah, aged a bit, since I saw you last."

"The sacrifice has already been made," Telemachus said softly, answering Madoc but looking at Verne. "All that remains is for you to make use of the gift that has been offered to you."

The companions turned as one to look at Verne, and gasped at what they saw. His hands were already the distinctive silver-gray of cavorite; tendrils of stone were already forming on his neck and were slowly moving upward.

"It's the price that must be paid for reusing a time-travel device," said Verne. "The universe can be fooled only so many times before she claims you, and pulls you to her bosom, and makes you one with eternity."

"You must decide quickly," said Telemachus, "before the process is completed. His heart will be cavorite soon, but it must be taken while it is still beating."

"Take his heart?" Fred gasped. "Out of his chest?"

"You must do it, Madoc," Telemachus said, with a trace of both sternness and finality in his voice. "You are the Architect, and so the placement of the keystone is for you to do."

Madoc nodded and turned to his daughter. "It's a fortunate thing that I repaired your blade," he said, reaching for her bag, "because it seems I'm going to need to use it."

Holding Caliburn in front of him with his right hand, Madoc strode to Verne and placed his left hand on the Caretaker's shoulder. "I cannot say whether I consider you an adversary or an ally," Madoc said, "but I do understand the value of this sacrifice. And I honor you."

"Believe it or not," Verne said with tears in his eyes, "that is all I needed to hear."

Madoc put his hand over the Caretaker's eyes and with a few swift strokes of the sword removed Verne's still-beating heart.

"Put it there," Telemachus instructed, "where the two stairways meet."

Madoc did as he was told, then covered the heart with one of the standing stones they had found when they arrived. "Blood for blood," he said to the keep. "May it be worth the price we have paid this day."

Madoc stepped out of the keep to where Quixote, Fred, and Uncas were covering Verne's body. "We'll bury him here," he said. "If something goes wrong, we shouldn't be carrying around his body."

Reluctantly, and with great sorrow, the companions agreed. Verne had been such a presence in all of their lives that it was almost too much to bear that his own had ended so abruptly.

"Look," Telemachus said as they were finishing the burial. "See what your efforts have wrought."

Laura Glue was the first to see it and could barely contain her expression of delight, even though the sadness she felt at Verne's death was still visible on her face.

The tower had grown by several feet as they worked. And now, as they watched, it grew taller still.

"It's done, Father," Rose said, her voice barely audible. "You have come full circle at last, and restored what was broken."

✦ ✦ ✦

"The keep has been restored," said Madoc, "but the question still remains—how do we get back?"

"It's the Keep of Time, and there's only one door," Telemachus said simply. "That means when you go through it, you'll be going into the future."

"In the old keep, only the uppermost door went into the future," said Charles, "and this one has a doorway, not an actual door. How do we know it will go to the future?"

"That's just it," said Edmund. "From here, there isn't anything *but* future. It's *all* future. So we simply have to focus on the point in the future we want to arrive at, and we should go directly then." He stopped and swallowed hard. "I hope."

"You're entirely right, young Cartographer," said the old man. "It's just as if you were standing at the South Pole—the only direction you could go would be north."

"When you walk through the doorway," Telemachus explained, "it will give significance to the moment, but also duration. You will have begun the process that links the beginning of all things to the future. Here, in this place, it will begin to grow, and it will anchor Chronos time and Kairos time once more—and by connecting this moment to your own future, you will ensure that the connection between the Archipelago and the Summer Country will be restored."

"So theoretically speaking," said Rose, "after accounting for the actual days we've been gone, we should end up right about the time we left, right?"

Telemachus consulted his watch and his face paled. "Oh dear," he said softly. "I didn't realize . . ."

"What is it?" Madoc demanded. "What kind of game are you trying to play now?"

Telemachus held up a hand in supplication and shook his head. "You misunderstand. It's the avoidance of game playing that has become my purpose, and many years ago . . ." He paused, looking at Edmund. "Many years ago, in my own timeline, I made a promise not to manipulate events if it was in my power to do so. I have helped, encouraged, and prodded at times, but I have never deliberately tried to shape a particular outcome, nor will I do so now."

"Are you saying that going through the doorway won't take us home?" asked Rose.

"Not at all," Telemachus answered mysteriously. "I'm absolutely certain that it will. But it will not be the end of your challenges. There is still one trial to come, and you may have to pay your way through it with dearest blood."

She looked at him curiously. "You say that *we* have to pay, but you are coming with us . . . aren't you?"

He shook his head. "I cannot come with you, I'm afraid," he said. "This is the only place in time where the two of us can exist together, at least in the Summer Country—and that's where you're going. There can only ever be one Imago and one Archimago on earth at the same time—and until now, I have been the Imago. But when you step through the doorway, that burden will shift over to you, and someday you will be the Imago, Rose."

"Not to argue," said Edmund, "but isn't she the Imago already? Or at least, since she's the best candidate, won't that simply just make her the Imago by default?"

Telemachus's response was unexpected. His eyes welled up with tears, and silently, he began to weep.

"Here, Mr. Telemachus," Fred said, offering him a hand-kerchief. "Take a minute, why don'tcha."

When he had regained his composure, he took Rose by the hands. "No," he said, answering Edmund's question. "It is not as simple as being Named. It is not even as simple as taking the responsibility by choice. It is something that must be hard fought for, and hard earned. And there will be times when you want to cast it off, but you won't. Because you know it is your purpose to one day be the Imago, and purpose is invincible.

"One day you will have done enough, and learned enough. It grieves me that there is still so much living that you must do before that day. But it will be worth it, my dear Rose. . . ." This last he said as he transformed once more from the ancient sage into the young man wearing the Ruby Armor. "It will be worth it. Because the Imago protects life. And as long as there is life . . .

". . . it is such a wonderful world we live in, after all.

"And Rose," he added as they waved farewell, "if things go well for all of you, you may see me again, after."

Madoc had deliberately made certain the entrance of the keep was wide enough to accommodate the *Indigo Dragon*, but he had neglected to do the same for the door inside. They were debating whether to leave the airship behind when Fred suddenly noticed that the inside of the tower had expanded. Suddenly there was more than enough room to maneuver the ship inside and through the doorway.

The little badger stroked the stones on the outside of the keep. "Thanks, Scowler Jules," he said with earnest humility. "We appreciate it a lot."

"All right," Rose said to the others. "Let's see if we can go home one more time."

Together, the companions climbed into the airship, and Fred guided it through the doorway.

The *Indigo Dragon* entered the doorway of the keep, which disappeared as they passed through. On the other side, it was night, and the airship slid quietly onto the East Lawn of Tamerlane House.

"We did it," Laura Glue said, squeezing Edmund's hand, then reaching out to hug Quixote and the badgers. "We found them, and brought them home."

Growing happier by the moment, the companions leaped out of the airship and raced for the front door of the house. Throwing it open and dashing inside, they were greeted by the very familiar face of a dear friend who was taking his tea by the hearth.

"Rose! Edmund! Charles!" Jack exclaimed as he leaped from his chair, scattering tea and cakes all across the room. "Uncas! Laura Glue! Fred!" He stopped, eyes wide. "And Madoc! You are all returned, finally! At last! At last!"

The Caretaker rushed to embrace the companions, and could not hold back his tears. He wept freely, in both joy and relief, as did all the newly returned companions, including Madoc.

"I can't believe it!" Jack exclaimed. "Somehow, I knew deep down you'd return, but it's been so long. So long!" He embraced Rose again, then shook Edmund's hand. Fred and Uncas, however, both held back. Something was wrong.

Laura Glue caught the same whiff of uncertainty. "You look . . . younger than I remember," she said, not bothering to conceal her suspicion. "How do we know you aren't an Echthros?"

Jack chuckled, but Charles knew him well enough to note the fleeting expression of pain that danced across his features, as well as to realize what Laura Glue and the badgers only suspected, and the others had no clue of at all.

"I'm not the enemy," Jack said blithely, "but yes, things have changed. After all, you have been gone a very long time."

"How long?" asked Charles. "And what, specifically, has changed about you, Jack?"

"Nothing about him is different than you remember," another Caretaker said as he stepped into the room. "He's just been youthened."

It was James Barrie—one of the portrait-bound Caretakers who resided in the gallery at Tamerlane House. He spoke directly to the young Valkyrie and grasped her shoulders with an affectionate firmness. "I don't yet know how long it has been for you, Laura-my-Glue, but for us, here, it has been almost twenty years since you went on your little rescue mission into the Zanzibar Gate. And it has been almost three years now since Jack came to join us in the gallery."

As one, all the companions gasped and looked in astonishment at Jack. "You're a *portrait?*" Rose said breathlessly. "That means you're . . ."

"Dead," Jack said matter-of-factly as he stepped to her and kissed her on the forehead. "I waited for you to return for the rest of my life, and then some. And it was worth the wait—because at long last, you have come back, dear, dear Rose."

As Barrie went to alert the other Caretakers, Jack and the companions settled in around the table in the dining hall so that he could begin to tell them about what had happened in the years since they'd left.

"I married, and adopted a son," Jack told them, "as unlikely as either seemed to be in the years when you knew me. I lost her soon after, but it was still a thrilling, heartbreaking, wonderful part of my life."

"That reminds me," he added, turning to Charles. "I've also had to continue taking care of the Magwich plant, which has progressed in size from shrub to tree. Karmically speaking," he continued, "you now owe me several lifetimes' worth of favors."

"I thought Warnie was helping take care of him, at the Kilns?"

"He did, for a time," said Jack. "The problem was that Magwich would never shut up, and he was starting to attract attention, so we had to relocate him here."

"Here?" Charles said, unable to keep himself from cringing. "You brought that Maggot to Tamerlane House?"

"Not Tamerlane specifically," said John. "We planted him on one of the outer islands, where Jason's sons go to play their war games. He gets to talk to someone, and they completely ignore him. It's an entirely amicable arrangement."

"What happened here?" Charles asked as the other Caretakers began to arrive. "The house looks as if it went through some major renovations that were either poorly planned or badly executed."

"There was a battle," Dickens explained as he took a seat next to Charles, "between the Caretakers and Dee and his minions, and Tamerlane House paid the greatest price, I'm afraid."

"Several of the towers and minarets had been toppled, and almost the whole of the north wing was destroyed," said Hawthorne.

"We did add to our collective real estate, however," Twain said as he entered the room and kissed Rose on the top of her head. "The House on the Borderlands is now our neighbor."

"What?" Charles and Fred exclaimed at once.

"Yes," Bert said as he joined them at the table, eyes filled with tears. "The Cabal, or most of them, anyway, have established a truce with the Caretakers."

"Where's John?" Rose asked. "Is he . . . ?"

"Oh, he's still among the living," said Jack, "and still the Prime Caretaker. He just has a great deal of business to tend to at Oxford these days. We've sent for him, and he should be here at any—"

"Where are they?" John exclaimed as he burst through the door. "Are they really . . . ?"

"Hello, Uncle John," Rose said, jumping to her feet. "You've gotten older!"

"I have," he said, hugging her closely, "while you have stayed exactly the same, just as I'd hoped."

PART SIX

BEYOND THE WALL

CHAPTER TWENTY-ONE
TABULA RASA GEOGRAPHICA

THE GREAT BRIDGE *of bone reached across almost the entire width of the ocean, but stopped just short of the Lonely Isle.*

Poets and painters had dreamed about the island, which stood at the farthest reaches of existence, and which was the last haven for travelers before they reached the shores of eternity. And in truth, dreaming was the simplest way to reach it, and the only way most ever would.

For the great Dragon Samaranth, it meant using the last relic of the life he had lived before this one, when he was a Maker in a wondrous green city at the edge of an ocean far, far away.

It was a chest made of amethyst, and it was meant to contain worlds. Slowly, carefully, he placed all the lands of the Archipelago of Dreams into it, and then released the great beasts to return to the deserts and mountains where he had gathered them.

To his smallest, last friend, he offered a choice, and was not surprised by the badger's answer, but was surprised by his own gratitude at receiving it.

Together, they made their way through the storm-tossed sea to the island where the last inn stood, where they would be greeted by the last of the angels from the City of Jade, and where they would wait, for as long as they were able.

At their knock, an old woman opened the door. Her expression was one of joy, then of sorrow at seeing her old friend. "To cross the threshold requires a price," she said. "Will you pay it willingly?"

"I shall," the great Dragon rumbled, "for myself, and my friend, Tummeler."

"Then enter and be welcomed, Samaranth, and Master Tummeler," she said. They stepped across, and she handed them an hourglass made of bone. "You have until the last sand runs out," she admonished. "To the last grain, and no more."

Samaranth nodded. "I understand. Thank you, Sycorax."

She closed the door behind them and went to set their places for tea. If she had paused a moment more, she would have seen the black ship not far behind. Soon there would be more company. Very soon.

The companions and the Caretakers spent the entire night telling and retelling stories, to catch up the companions on twenty years of missed history, as well as to tell the Caretakers about the unknown history of the keep itself—and about the sacrifice that had made restoration possible.

They bowed their heads, and there was a long, respectful moment of silence for the man who had been one of the greatest Caretakers of them all.

"To Scowler Jules," Fred said, raising his glass.

"To Scowler Jules," the Caretakers chorused.

"And what of Poe?" Charles asked. "What happened to him?"

John's expression darkened, and he glanced at both Bert and Twain before he answered. "We haven't seen him again," he said, choosing his words carefully, "and I'm not certain that's a bad thing."

"I still don't understand," Rose said, "why we lost twenty years in passing through the doorway."

"I think I know," Shakespeare offered. "My gate was made from the keep, but it was not the keep. Not the same. It still relied on technology and mechanical programming more than simple intuition, and thus could be more precisely programmed. Whereas the doorway in the keep could not."

"Wasn't that the original reason the Dragons added doors to the keep?" Edmund asked. "To better focus the chronal energies?"

"I think so," said John. "At least, that's my understanding of how it worked for traveling in time."

"That may also be the difference between the time-travel devices and mechanisms and your own uses of chronal maps and trumps," Shakespeare said. "Those latter draw very strongly on will and intuition, and rely less on mathematics and science, and so I think they are subject to fewer laws."

"Limitations," Twain said, puffing on his cigar. "When you use science, you by definition put things in boxes. You create limits. And thus it follows you would be bound by those limits. But doing what these young'uns do," he added, gesturing at Rose and Edmund, "that is, literally and in every other sense of the word, *art*. And art has no limitation."

"So did it work?" Rose asked. "Has the keep been restored? Is the Archipelago back?"

"The keep, yes," said Twain. "The Archipelago, no."

"When it was being taken over by the Echthroi," John explained, "we know from the message Aven left on Paralon that Samaranth somehow . . . removed all the lands and peoples of the Archipelago and took them somewhere safe. The problem is, we have no idea where."

"Have you tried summoning him, from one of the Rings?" asked Madoc. "I'm not so good at it myself, but then again, I never had permission."

"We have all tried it," said John. "Every man and woman among the Caretakers, and a few associates and apprentices besides."

"He was waiting," a new voice said, "for the Imago to return, so that she would be the one to restore the Archipelago."

It was the Watchmaker, the ancient being who resided on the island to the northwest of Tamerlane House. But the companions who had just returned from the deep past now knew him by a different name.

"Enoch," Rose said as she and her companions moved forward to embrace him. The Caretakers were fairly stunned—the Watchmaker had never left his cave, as far as they knew. Ever.

"He had a name?" John said to Bert. "I never knew that."

"The Summoning was not going to be sufficient," Enoch said, ignoring the curious stares from the Caretakers, "not until the keep itself was restored. And now that has been done, you're going to have to go find the lands of the Archipelago and bring them back."

"Back from where, Enoch?" Rose asked. "Where did Samaranth take them?"

"Beyond the End of the World," the Maker said, "past the Great Wall, and to the shores of heaven itself."

"Is that even possible?" Madoc asked. "Mind you, I speak from experience at having tried."

Enoch nodded. "You are a Dragon, and those such as you are

permitted to pass, as are those with you. But," he added cautiously, "your adversary has the services of one of the Host, who is bound to serve him, and he is already speeding his way toward his destination. If he reaches Samaranth first, then the Archipelago may still be lost."

"We have not seen him in twenty years," John explained. "Not since he forced Argus to bond Grimalkin to the hull of the *Black Dragon.*"

"The cat?" Charles exclaimed. "What was he expecting to come out of that?"

"Not just a cat," John said heavily. "Grimalkin is a Fallen angel, who is bound to serve John Dee. And he can go everywhere a Dragon can go—including past the End of the World. Worse, they have a twenty-year head start."

"Perhaps not," said Enoch. "Time operated differently past the wall. What seemed to us to be years can be a far shorter time to someone on the other side."

"Great," said Fred. "That's just what we need—more time-travel issues."

"You misunderstand," said Enoch. "The moment you came through the door of the keep, you realigned Chronos time and Kairos time. It is now the same on both sides of the Frontier, and that includes the flow of time past the wall. So while years were passing here, your adversary has been in flight only a short time."

"Which means we can still catch them!" John said, rising to his feet. "What are we waiting for? Let's go!"

"Please, tell me that we are not actually this insane," Jack pleaded. "I know we have had our differences, John, but—"

"What he means to say is we have really missed you, Charles," John said, giving Jack an exasperated look. "You were a tempering agent between us, and you were sorely missed. Especially since he died. There's been no end to the arguments after that."

"What I'm trying to say is that you aren't as young as you used to be, and this is a task for others to do."

"I understand your reservations, Jack, but this is not a negotiation," John said. "I'm going to go."

"I'm sorry, John," Twain said, his voice filled with honest regret, "but you cannot go. You are the Prime Caretaker in fact as well as name, and your choices guide the path of this group. You must remain here."

John glowered at the others for a moment, then sat down, sighing heavily. "I suppose you're going to want to go with them," he said to Jack.

"It's been a long time," Jack said. "I haven't left Tamerlane House much, and, not to put too fine a point on it, I am now younger than you."

"Hah," John said. "That's just because Basil painted you younger."

"Look at it this way," Jack said, winking at Rose as he got up from the table, "someday you'll die too, and then you can go save the world with us."

"Oh, shut up," John huffed. "Go do what must be done. And then," he added, "hurry back."

It didn't take long for everyone at Tamerlane House to realize that save for the loss of Kipling, the current crew of the *Indigo Dragon* was the perfect team to undertake difficult tasks. "The Young

Magicians," Jack said as he climbed aboard. "You are the future of both worlds, you know."

"I'll be content enough just to save one if I can," said Edmund. "Let's go."

After the *Indigo Dragon* left the Nameless Isles, there was one place Rose required that they go first, before she would even contemplate pursuing the trail of Samaranth and the missing Archipelago.

"Of course," Madoc murmured. "Of course that's where we should go." Jack, Charles, Edmund, and the others all nodded in agreement. Rose blushed when she realized that she had simply given voice to an assumption they all had made before they started.

They had to see the tower first. They had to make certain the Keep of Time had indeed been restored.

"It isn't difficult to find," said Jack. "It's just about all that is left of the Archipelago."

He was right. They came upon it in a matter of hours. It was both comforting and heartbreaking to see the stark gray outline of the tower in the distance—but just seeing it was enough.

"I recall it taking far longer to get to the last time," said Charles. "Is the airship just faster, or did the Archipelago shrink?"

"Probably both," said Jack. "I think the Archipelago grew in accordance with how many lands were added, or discovered, or invented, or even imagined. And," he said, surveying the bleak, open ocean, "with no lands to fill it up, it simply got . . . smaller."

It took considerably less time for them to arrive at the only other island that couldn't be removed by Samaranth, because it was the very island that marked the edge of the original Archipelago.

"Terminus," Madoc said as he leaned heavily against the railing. "I never expected to see it again."

"Father, are you all right?" Rose asked.

"I am . . . remembering," Madoc answered slowly. "The last time I went over the side of this waterfall, it wasn't in a ship."

"Wait!" Charles exclaimed. "What about the different gates, below," he said as the ship flew down the face of the waterfall. "Aren't there dangers abounding here?"

"I don't think we'll find any," said Jack. "It's been twenty years since you restored the keep, so we've had a little time to look around. As far as we could tell, when the Echthroi occupied the whole of the region, they completely absorbed or destroyed all the gates. It's all free passage to the end now."

"That's sort of a good-news, bad-news scenario," said Charles. "It's the first thing that the Echthroi have ever done that I was actually happy to hear about."

It was dark by the time the ship reached the bottom of the waterfall and began sailing over open ocean again.

"When we came this way before, there were thousands of lights above," Rose said wonderingly, "and the Professor said they were Dragons. I wonder where they've gone?"

"I thought you had, ah, released all the Dragons with the sword," said Edmund, "and that there weren't any left."

"Those were all who descended from angel to Dragon at Samaranth's urging, when the City of Jade fell," said Madoc, "but they were not all the Dragons there are, nor were they the first Dragons of creation."

"Where have they gone?" asked Rose. "What's happened to all of them?"

Madoc shrugged. "I can't say for certain. Samaranth taught me that this plane borders heaven itself, and so that may be where they have returned to. Why, I have no idea."

"It was the Echthroi," said Fred. "The entire Archipelago was lost to shadow. I don't think any Dragon would stick around to watch over a world that we screwed up that badly."

"Maybe when we put everything right," said Rose, "the Dragons will return again." She looked up into the darkness and sighed. "Maybe."

"It shouldn't be too long now," Madoc said as he and Rose consulted the *Imaginarium Geographica*. "We're almost there, at the End of the World."

"There was a time not long ago," said Uncas, "that we believed Terminus and th' waterfalls was the End of the World, but then we found out it went beyond that. And now, we're finding out that the boundary is even farther away. I'm starting to think there's no end to anything!"

"There was also a time," Jack said wryly, "when you would have taken my shadow for the chance to have that book, Madoc. And done many other terrible things besides."

"Jack!" Rose exclaimed. "I can't believe you said that!"

"It's all right," Madoc said, shushing her. "It's better that I know these things, if he feels they are worth saying."

"This will be difficult to hear," Jack said. "You are not the man now that you were then."

Madoc considered Jack's words, then slowly nodded his head. "True," he said at last, "I am not. I have been several men since that time, and a Dragon besides. But I think I am better than I was. I hope I am. And if that is true, I should be able to bear an accounting of my own darker choices."

"Fair enough," Jack said, turning to the others. "During our first great conflict with, ah, the Winter King, we discovered something that chilled us all to the core. We were focused on safeguarding the *Imaginarium Geographica* and by extension the Archipelago, but Mordred knew how connected this world was to our own. And he knew that as devoted as we had become to seeing through what we had promised Bert and Professor Sigurdsson we would do, we might abandon our responsibilities as Caretakers if something we cared for more was threatened."

"Something?" Rose asked, looking at her father.

"Someone," Madoc replied, meeting his daughter's gaze.

"Several someones, actually," said Jack. "Mordred had dispatched several Shadow-Born to the Summer Country, to seek out and . . . murder our loved ones. Charles's wife. My mother, and best friend. And John's young wife, Edith, as well as his eldest child, then newly born."

Uncas glared at Madoc with barely contained fury. "That in't right," he said, his voice low and trembling. "Goin' after younglings . . . That in't right."

Strangely enough, it was the badger's anger that affected Madoc most of all. Everyone else—every human—he faced squarely, fully accepting that his past sins were choices for which he would continue to pay. But he struggled to meet the badger's eyes.

"Charles never knew," Jack continued, "and I was still young and brash enough not to understand the gravity of the situation. But John knew, and understood. And he realized that if we abandoned our duties here to try to race back to save our loved ones, then both worlds might be lost. So the decision was made to soldier on and try to find a way to defeat the Winter King. It was the only way we could save them."

He paused, and put a hand to his forehead. "I . . . I found out later, through James Barrie, and some of Verne's Mystorians, that the Shadow-Born came closer than we realized to killing our families. In fact, two of them were right outside Edith's door—close enough to hear her singing lullabies to young John, the baby, in his crib.

"It was in that moment that Charles and Tummeler figured out how to use Perseus's shield to close Pandora's Box and reseal all the Shadow-Born within it. At once, all the—the Shadow-Born vanished, including the assassins that had been dispatched to the Summer Country."

"I never heard that story," Uncas said, eyes shining with pride. "Your grandfather was a credit to badgers everywhere," he said, clapping Fred on the back. "A credit, I tell you."

"The reason I wanted to share that story," Jack continued as he leaned against the railing, "is so that you understand that all our choices are cumulative—and we must always keep the bigger picture in mind. Sometimes . . . sometimes the stakes that are more personal can distract us from the goals that are more necessary to achieve. And that's—that's when you must be resolute. . . ."

The Caretaker's voice trailed off as he rubbed his temple. "I—I think I need to sit down."

Before any of the companions could assist him, Jack's eyes rolled back in his head and he pitched forward, already unconscious.

CHAPTER TWENTY-TWO
THE LONELY ISLE

- ❋ -

"IT'S HAPPENED SEVERAL times," Jack admitted as Laura Glue dabbed at his forehead with a damp cloth. "Mostly just headaches, but they've been increasing in frequency and intensity over the last few years. And in the last several months, I've started having blackouts."

"And no one at Tamerlane House noticed?" asked Rose.

Jack shook his head and propped himself up to a sitting position. "I'm good at hiding the headaches," he admitted. "That's what a lifetime of British reserve will do for you. And only Dumas ever saw me black out, but I managed to explain it away. I didn't want any of them thinking something was amiss."

"You're already dead," Charles said bluntly. "You're technically a portrait, Jack, and I'm a thought-form given flesh. People like us don't *get* headaches or have blackouts. It simply doesn't happen."

"If he's stable for the moment," said Edmund, "we can discuss it later. I think we've arrived."

The wall at the End of the World stood above a shallow beach, which was barely wide enough to pull a boat onto, but the wall itself rose so high that not even the keen-eyed Archie could fly high enough to see the top of it.

"Is it even possible to get over or through?" Jack asked. "Can it be done, Madoc?"

"I could not have done it then," said Madoc. "That is indisputable, because heaven knows I tried. I walked the length of the wall in both directions until my strength gave out, and the only way to restore it was to return here, to the center. The compulsion was unbearable, but crossing was impossible. And thus is hell on earth attained. But now, yes—it may be possible."

"Because you're a Dragon?" asked Fred.

"A Dragon *can* cross," said Madoc. "A true Dragon, at any rate. I have been one in the past, and the Zanzibar Gate proved that I carry with me some of the aspect of a Dragon still. But this is different."

"How is it different?" asked Charles. "It's just a wall, isn't it?"

"On this side, yes," said Madoc. "But behind it is the true Unknown Region. It is the source of the Dragons, and all the magic that is in the Archipelago. It is the true beginning of the world, and whatever lands we may find might very well be within sight of the shores of heaven itself."

"So how do we get over it?" asked Charles.

"We don't go over," said Madoc. "We go *through*."

Two great doors, hundreds of feet high, with sculpted angels on either side, suddenly materialized out of the mist and gloom as if they had been there all along—which, the companions realized, they probably had been.

"It's like with the Zanzibar Gate," said Laura Glue. "Your presence alone activates whatever is needed."

"Such is the power of a Dragon," Madoc murmured. "If only I had known then . . ."

He took the reins to the goats from Fred and urged them onward with a gentle shake, and quickly, they crossed the wall into the Unknown Region.

"It's an old children's poem, I think," Madoc said as they surveyed the landscape past the Great Wall. "Something about an impossible desert, or something like that . . ."

"I can tell," Archie said, dropping from his perch atop the airship's balloon, "that you have sorely neglected your studies while I've been away."

"Is that what you call it?" Madoc replied with a grin. "'Away'?"

The clockwork bird ignored him and instead began to recite a poem. To his delight, Laura Glue joined in, chanting the verses along with him.

> *Cross the uncrossable desert, tally-yee, tally-yay.*
> *Climb the unclimbable mountain, tally-yee, tally-yay.*
> *Swim the impassable sea, tally-yee, tally-yay.*
> *Find the house that angels made,*
> *On the isle of bone.*
> *Pay the price that angels paid,*
> *On the isle, alone.*
> *Choose the Name that shows your face,*
> *Drink your tea and take your place.*
> *At Hades's gate or heaven's shore.*
> *There to live, forevermore.*
> *Tally-yee, tally-yay.*

"There, Caretakers," Madoc said, winking at Rose. "Find that bit of wisdom in your little *Geographica*."

"It isn't *in* the *Imaginarium Geographica*," said Fred. "That's what the Little Whatsits are for. Page two hundred ninety-six." He looked up at Archimedes. "I see what you mean about his education."

Madoc laughed. "Point taken, little fellow."

"So what does it all mean?" asked Charles.

"It's our map," said Jack. "All the wisdom in the world can be found in fairy tales and nursery rhymes. And, it seems," he added, scratching Fred behind his neck, "in the Little Whatsits."

"I see the end of the desert already," Laura Glue said, shading her eyes, "and beyond that, the mountain."

"Surely Samaranth passed this way years and years ago," said Charles.

"Perhaps," Rose said. "But remember what Enoch told us—time has been flowing differently here. It changes with one's own perception."

"And," said Madoc, "we aren't carrying the history of an entire world on our shoulders. It's going to go much more quickly for us."

As Madoc predicted, the passage over the mountain and then across the sea went quickly; in a short while, the airship passed over the last of the bridge, where it was tossed about by the storm clouds that circled the island.

"The Lonely Isle," said Fred. "The last haven in all the world."

"There's an inn on top," Charles shouted over the wind. "Aim for that, and let's see if we can't land without crashing."

They needn't have worried—once they were close to the inn,

the storm stopped. It was around the island, but in the center, it was calm. Outside the inn were some scrubby trees where they could tie up the goats and leave the airship.

"We're either just in time, or barely too late," Jack said. He pointed to the other side of the island, where a familiar black ship, also converted to an airship, had been moored.

"The *Black Dragon*, or, ah, *Black Cat*, or whatever it is now," Charles sputtered. "They're already here!"

Quickly the companions rushed up to the door, which swung open at their approach. A tall, stern-looking woman with a frazzle of graying hair spread out behind her stood there, appraising the newcomers.

"Do you know where you are?" she asked. "This is no place for visitors. There is a price to pay to sup at this inn."

"What price is that?" Madoc asked.

"One life, for one hour here," she said. "One of you must give themselves to death, or none may enter."

"All of us are coming in," Laura Glue said as she rummaged through her bag. "I've got a pass."

She pulled out the bone hourglass that the Serendipity Box had given her, turned it over, and twisted the valve. Slowly the grains began to slide through the neck of the glass.

"This is acceptable," the woman said, "as long as you understand that all of your party must abide by the glass. If any still remain on this island when the sand runs out, then all are forfeit, and if you cross the threshold again, you will die the final death, and not return."

"I understand," said Laura Glue.

The woman could barely suppress her expression of surprise

and delight. "Then you are welcome here on Youkali," she said, "but there is one more caveat—whatever you are Named, you must cross this threshold as you really are. None can be here in this place except as they truly are, and not as they appear."

"We know who we are," Rose said. "And we're not afraid to pass."

The woman stood aside, and one by one, the companions entered. Rose and Edmund simply walked across the threshold, unchanged, as did Uncas and Fred.

"We animals in't very complicated," Uncas explained as they passed.

Charles also passed unchanged. "I do feel a bit more like a writer than an editor," he said, "but I don't know if that's a good thing or a bad thing."

Quixote, however, youthened considerably as he entered the inn. "To be young in one's heart is the greatest achievement," he said.

"Good work," said Uncas.

Jack's change was much more dramatic, as was Madoc's.

On entering, Jack became a boy again, as he had once been on the island of the Lost Boys. And Madoc lost his wings, and much of his age, becoming a fresh-faced youth not much older than Jack.

"Ah," said Charles. "So now we see the truth of things. And our Madoc truly is Madoc again."

"Come," the woman said as she ushered them into the next room. "You may join our other guests for tea."

In the main room, the companions were astonished to see the tea party taking place. Sitting around an elaborately set table were five guests: a very young man with red hair that kept spilling into his eyes; a very young woman who was demurely nibbling at a cookie; an older, bearded man who wore an expression of such sadness that it was almost palpable; a very aged man, who was so old that his skin resembled the most fragile parchment, and whose eyes radiated hatred; and a badger, who immediately leaped up to greet the newcomers.

The reunion of Tummeler with his son and grandson, and with his old partner Charles, was so filled with joy and happiness that even the old woman started to tear up. The three badgers and the Caretaker whooped and hollered and hugged one another until it seemed they would burst.

"To see that, something so wonderful, I would pay almost any price," the young man said.

"Samaranth?" Rose exclaimed. "Is that you?"

"It is," the young angel replied, nodding, "but you've come just moments too late. I've already lost the Archipelago to Dr. Dee."

The companions all suddenly realized that there were hourglasses of bone identical to Laura Glue's in front of each of the guests, but only one, in front of the old man with the terrible visage, was still trickling sand through the glass.

As if in confirmation of Samaranth's words, he reached out and grasped a crystal box, which was glowing a soft purple, and pulled it across the table closer to him.

"The Archipelago," said the man they now realized was Dee, "is *mine*."

"How did you cross the threshold?" Charles exclaimed. "You would have to sacrifice a life to—"

"That's exactly what I did," Dee said, gesturing at a sorry-looking shadow in the far corner. "What do you think I brought Crowley for?"

"My time ran out, all too quickly," Samaranth said, "and as Sycorax can confirm, I cannot take the Amethyst Box with me without destroying the entire Archipelago."

"But the time limits," Jack began.

"The box is protected," the woman Sycorax said, "but it must be taken elsewhere, away from this house, before it can be opened."

"We can take it!" Rose exclaimed, reaching for the box.

"No!" Dee shouted. "I have already claimed it! By the rules of Deep Magic, it is mine!"

"Is that true?" Rose asked Samaranth as her face fell. "Is it his?"

"Yes," said Samaranth. "It is. But the box can only be opened with a Master Key, and the Master Key may only be turned by an angel, or," he said, pointedly not looking at Madoc, "by a *Dragon*."

"Hah!" said Uncas. "You really blew it then, Dee. We got the only Dragon left, an' he'll *never* help you."

Dr. Dee ignored the badger, instead focusing his attention on Rose.

"I was there, in the City of Jade, before the deluge," Dee said, his voice soft, and his eyes glittering. "I went there for two purposes. The first was to find a Master Key—one of the keys the angels used to unlock anything in creation—and the second, to find, and bind, an angel."

He stood and picked up the box. "Time to go," he said, smiling at Samaranth, and then at Rose. "Be seeing you."

Madoc, Charles, and Edmund all started to move for Dee at once, but a shout stopped them in their tracks.

"No!" Sycorax said sternly. "This is the last of the Free Houses, and no violence may be committed here."

"In other words," said Charles, "'take it outside.'"

"Just so," said Sycorax. "He still has sand in the glass and may do as he wishes."

Rose looked at the other three glasses on the table. "But you can't, can you?" she asked, already knowing the answer. "I think I understand. All of you here—you're already . . ."

"Yes," Samaranth said, nodding. "We are already on our way to the final death, where we will cross over into the next stage of being."

"I waited," the girl said, speaking for the first time, "so that I could meet you, the daughter of my heart."

"Who are you?" Rose asked.

"The one who built the bridge, but could not finish it," the girl replied. "Perhaps someday, you will finish it for me. I hope you will."

"I just didn't want to be alone," the bearded man said. "I have been here a very, very long time."

"I can tell," Jack said, looking more closely at the man. "Someone hurt you, didn't they? Hurt you badly."

"I don't think he meant to," the man said. "He was my brother. I think he was just sad, and I think it was my fault. I've waited here, in case he comes, so I can tell him I'm sorry."

Jack didn't respond, but instead reached out and gave the man a hug, which, after a moment, he returned.

"Oh . . . oh no," Uncas wailed, looking at Tummeler and suddenly understanding the meaning of the empty hourglass in front of Samaranth. "Does that mean . . . ?"

The old badger nodded. "It's all right, young one. I did good, helping Mr. Samaranth. And I got t' see you, and Fred, and Scowler Charles. That's a lot. In fact, that's everything."

"Not everything," Dee said as he stepped out the door, "as everyone in your precious Archipelago is about to discover."

Before anyone could stop him, Tummeler let out a loud howl and threw himself at Dee.

Samaranth jumped to his feet. "Tummeler, don't! Don't cross the threshold!" But it was too late.

The little badger fell to the ground, just outside the door. His eyes rolled back in his head, and his breathing stopped.

As the companions all cried out and moved to attend to Tummeler, Dee walked across the front of the island to where the black ship waited. Outside the inn, he returned to his usual appearance, but his face was still a mask of hatred.

At his approach, Mr. Kirke and Mr. Bangs stood and lifted the shipbuilder Argus roughly by the arms.

"Now," Dee said to the shipbuilder, "do as you did with the *Black Dragon*, and release the Cherubim from the vessel. And then we will unlock the Archipelago and reshape two worlds in the image of order. In the image . . .

". . . of the *Echthroi.*"

By the time the companions who had arrived on the *Indigo Dragon* approached Dr. Dee to reclaim the Amethyst Box, Argus was nearly finished with his task.

When the shipbuilder bonded him to the hull of the *Black Dragon*, Grimalkin had still resembled a Cheshire cat. But when the process reversed, Grimalkin emerged, shaken but whole, as a very different sort of creature.

In the same way that releasing Madoc had reverted him to a more human state, the way he had been before he became a Dragon and then allowed himself to be bonded to the ship, releasing Grimalkin reverted him to being what he had been before he was bound by Dee to serve the Echthroi.

Standing atop the rocks before them, drinking in the energies of the storm swirling above, was a Cherubim—one of the oldest angels from the City of Jade. And he was not happy.

The Caretakers and the companions who had been in the city and witnessed the transformation of angels suddenly realized that the aspect of children, of youth, that angels like Samaranth wore so easily was simply so they could more easily commune with mortals. Here, now, Grimalkin had shed that aspect of himself completely.

Around his neck was the collar he had worn as a cat—but everything else had changed. He stood nearly twelve feet tall, and had four feathered wings that stretched out behind him like a wall of steel feathers. He had great claws and wore armor that was stretched tight over muscles that rippled with the power of heaven itself. But most significantly, he now had four faces: the face of an ox, the face of an eagle, the face of a lion, and the face of a man, which bore some of the aspects of the Cheshire cat that so many around Tamerlane House had seen so often.

"Fear me, little thing," the angel rumbled, looking at Dee. "You have summoned your own doom."

"I'm not afraid of any Dragon who ever was," Dee said menacingly, "or of any *angel*. And I am prepared for you . . . *Shaitan*."

Shaitan, far from being cowed as Dee expected, merely smiled and spread his arms. "I am not a Dragon, as you can plainly see," he said, his voice a soft purr that nevertheless carried echoes of thunder in it. "I never descended, and so I am *still* an angel, still Cherubim, exactly as you intended for me to be."

"And still able," Dee said, "to do everything that a Dragon could do here, in this place. That is why I have released you now. To do my bidding one last time."

"Stop!" Rose shouted as she drew Caliburn from its scabbard. "Stop, Dee! You know what I can do with this."

"Little Imago," Dee sneered. "It is far, far too late."

He turned back to the angel, arms spread. In one hand, he held what looked like a green crystal. It was glowing, just like the buildings in the City of Jade. "Shaitan! The time is *now!*" Dee proclaimed, his face a mask of triumph. "Take the Master Key, so we may release the Archipelago and deliver both worlds to the eternal rule of order—so we may deliver them both to the Echthroi."

"Excuse me," Edmund said, raising a finger, "but I don't think that's going to happen."

Everyone turned in surprise to look at Edmund McGee. He seldom took point in a battle, and none of them could understand why he would challenge Dee in such a manner.

The young Cartographer was holding up a trump. It depicted the towers of the City of Jade, along with a familiar face.

"Hello there," Kipling said. "I was beginning to wonder if you'd get around to saving that world before this one meets its doom. I can see the water from here."

"Save the commentary," said Edmund. "Do it!"

"Grimalkin, called Shaitan, called the Cheshire cat," Kipling said, "I release you from your Binding. Thrice I bound you; thrice I release you. I release you. I release you. I release you."

There was a clap of thunder, and a rending of the sky as the angel's collar flew apart and shattered into fragments of light.

"Impossible!" Dee cried. "He was bound to me! To the Echthroi! He is all but Echthros himself!"

"Bound by *you?*" Kipling asked through the trump. "That's what *he* thought too. But a creature who is bound to one cannot be bound to another. And I got to him *first.*"

Dee looked dazed. "B-but all these years, he has served *us!*" he said, confused. "He has been a spy in the House of Tamerlane! He has killed agents of the Caretakers!"

Kipling's expression darkened at this, but he merely nodded. "All at my direction, I'm afraid. When I bound him, that was the one thing I ordered him to do—to serve John Dee, and follow his orders as if he were bound to him, until the day when I released him. Which," he added, smiling more broadly now, "I just *did.*"

CHAPTER TWENTY-THREE
THE LAST BATTLE

—※—

THE ANGEL SHAITAN looked down at John Dee, who suddenly seemed a lot smaller. "Little thing," Shaitan said, "you have caused my countenance to be darkened. You denied me the opportunity to serve the Word by becoming a protector of this world. And there is a price to be paid."

"Not me!" Dee shrieked, pointing at the trump in Edmund's hand. "I never bound you! Kipling! He's the one!"

"Intention counts," the angel replied, "and I can see past his countenance into his heart, just as," he said, moving closer, "I can see into *yours*."

Dee shrieked as the great angel moved down to embrace him with wings and arms and eyes of fire. "I'm sorry!" the Chronographer of Lost Times cried out as he burst into flame. "Forgive me! Please forgive—!"

The angel began to glow, brighter and brighter, and suddenly Dee burst into a thousand shards of shadow, all scattering in an effort to escape the purifying light—but it was impossible. For an instant, the island glowed like a star, and the shadows evaporated in Shaitan's light.

When the companions could see again, the great and terrible

creature that had been the angel had been replaced by a young man, dressed simply in a tunic, who had curly black hair and a look of horrible sadness.

"It's over, isn't it?" he said, to no one in particular.

"No," Samaranth said from the doorway of the inn. "It is just beginning, my friend Shaitan."

The young angel's expression changed from one of sadness to joy, and he ran to his friend. When Sycorax explained the price of entry, he didn't even hesitate.

"Quickly," Edmund said to Kipling. "The flood hasn't hit the city yet. I can still pull you through!"

But to the surprise of all the companions, the Caretaker refused.

"I'm done, I think," he said. "This was my last mission, my last hurrah for the Caretakers. It's time for the—what did you call them, Jack? The Young Magicians? It's time for you to take over now."

"But why?" Rose exclaimed, suddenly understanding where Kipling was, and what kind of price he paid and was paying still to give them this opportunity. "You can still save yourself!"

Kipling smiled. "I think I already have, dear girl," he said, stepping back, away from his own trump. Charles saw it first. "Your shadow!" he exclaimed with relief. "It's come back! Good show, old fellow."

"That's why I'd like to stay," Kipling said. "I lost my shadow by doing a terrible thing for the best of reasons, and then I earned it back by giving you a chance to save the world."

"Also, you got to stick it to John Dee," said Laura Glue.

"Yes." Kipling chuckled. "That too."

"Regardless," he went on, "I've lived two good and worthy lives now, and I get to finish this one watching the destruction of Atlantis. And when that's done," he said, wiping a tear from his eye, "I'll get to see my boy again. Can't say fairer than that."

He turned away from the trump. "I can hear it now," he said. "Time to go."

"Thank you!" Rose shouted over the increasing noise of the approaching flood. "Thank you, Caretaker!"

Kipling winked at her and turned away as the card faded and went black.

"Oh no," Laura Glue exclaimed. "My hourglass! It's almost run out. We have to go!"

"I'd love to," Quixote said, "but our transportation seems to have disappeared."

The companions' hearts sank as they realized what must have happened—while the angel was dealing with Dee, his henchmen Mr. Kirke and Mr. Bangs had taken the *Indigo Dragon*.

"It's worse than that," said Rose. "I think they took the Amethyst Box as well."

"We still have the Master Key, though," said Charles. "And we have Madoc. We just don't have any way to get back."

"The *Black Dragon*?" Laura Glue asked. "It might work!"

They rushed over to the ship, but all they found was an unconscious Argus, and a massive, gaping hole where the masthead of the angel had been.

"It's no use," Madoc said. "We'll never be able to repair it enough to fly. Not so quickly."

"We should have left a guard," Jack moaned. "What happened to Archie?"

"They must have done something to him," said Madoc. "He would have alerted us otherwise."

"Still," said Jack. "We should have taken more precautions."

"We're at the end of all things, Jack!" Charles sputtered. "Heaven itself is a stone's throw out the back door! Why would we *possibly* have worried about someone stealing the *Indigo Dragon*? Where would they possibly go with her?"

"Back to the Archipelago, for one place," said Laura Glue.

"You are *not* helping things," said Charles.

The Valkyrie turned to make a sarcastic comment to Fred, and for the first time they realized that the two badgers and Quixote were still close to the inn, sitting with Tummeler. Even during Dee's confrontation with the angel, they hadn't left him.

Suddenly Tummeler inhaled a massive breath, and then began to speak. "I am a commander, first class, in the Royal Animal Rescue Society," he said, exhaling as hard as he could, "...retired."

"He's still alive!" Charles shouted, half in astonishment and half from joy. "Come quickly! We have to help him! Tummeler is still alive!"

"How?" Jack asked, looking at Samaranth, who shook his head in response. "I don't think there's anything we can do, Don Quixote," the Caretaker said softly.

"A portrait?" Uncas said. "At Tamerlane?"

"There are no portraits of...well, any animals in Basil's studio," Jack said, casting a sorrowful, apologetic glance at Tummeler's son and grandson. "Uncas, Fred...I'm so sorry."

"A tulpa!" Fred exclaimed, clutching at Charles's coat. "Y' did it once before, with someone else, t' make th' tulpa of Jack!"

"And look how that turned out in the future," Charles answered bitterly. "He became Lord Winter and turned the whole world over to the Echthroi. No," he said, shaking his head, "I'm partly to blame for what's happened here, because I did that foolish, foolish thing—and I cannot countenance doing it again, for anyone."

"It only went badly because Jack was still alive," said Rose. "Can't you make one for Tummeler, for his aiua to enter?"

Charles shook his head. "There simply isn't enough time. It would take a miracle to save him now."

Uncas leaped to his feet. "Brilliant, Scowler Charles! That's it exactly!" The little badger dashed away to where Rose had dropped her bag when she drew her sword, and returned bearing a box.

It was the Serendipity Box. And he presented it not to Charles . . .

. . . but to Don Quixote.

Uncas trembled as he proffered the box to the wizened old knight, who knelt to receive it.

"I know I'm just a squire," Uncas said, voice quavering with emotion, "an' squires is supposed t' help their knight, not ask for boons. But . . ." The little badger risked a glance at the barely breathing Tummeler. "He's my pop. Will you . . . Will you please make a wish, and open th' box?"

"Of course I shall," said Don Quixote. And with no hesitation, he opened the box—but all that was within was what looked like an oversize playing card.

"A trump," said Jack. "It's a *trump*! And look," he said, gesturing at the illustration on the card. "It's the waterfall, at Terminus. We can escape before the sand in the hourglass runs out!"

No one else was listening. Instead they were watching in sorrow and disbelief as the Serendipity Box fell to pieces in Uncas's paws. There was nothing else inside, and now the box itself was crumbling to dust before their eyes.

"There *has* t' be something else!" Uncas cried inconsolably. "There's no time t' take him back for help!"

"No," a very weak voice answered. "But there is time for you to go catch the *Indigo Dragon* and save our world. The box knew. It gave you what you needed most. And that wasn't t' save me."

Tummeler lifted his head, trembling. His strength, his life, were nearly gone. Charles clung to him more tightly as tears streamed down his face.

"I did what I was asked," the old badger said, "and Samaranth and I saved the Archipelago. . . ."

"Balderdash," Charles said. "We know it was really you who did all the work."

"But it will all be lost," Tummeler continued, "if you don't go, now, and do what y' have t' do."

Uncas knelt next to his father. "But you . . ."

Tummeler shushed him. "I got what I wanted, my boy," he said, looking at his son and grandson, and up at Charles. "I got t' be a hero, at last."

"You were always a hero, Tummeler," said Charles, but his old friend didn't hear him. Tummeler was dead.

"We will mourn him after," Madoc said, "but he was right— the hourglass is nearly empty, and we have to leave now."

Quickly Rose and Edmund focused on the trump, and it began

to expand. In minutes they could clearly see the rocky outline of Terminus above the great waterfall, and soon it was large enough for all the companions to step through.

Fred and Uncas were still reluctant to leave Tummeler, but Samaranth assured them that he would not leave his friend alone. "Where he went, I'll soon follow," the angel said. "He is not alone."

"That's all I needed to hear," Fred said, wiping the tears from his face. "Let's go."

With one last farewell to the two angels, the reunited friends standing in the doorway at the inn on the shores of heaven, the companions stepped through the trump just as the last grain of sand circled the neck of the hourglass and fell.

"All right, what now?" Rose asked.

"Now," a voice said from above, "we are going to change history."

The companions all spun about as the *Indigo Dragon* rose up behind them. Mr. Kirke was at the wheel and held the reins.

"Curse it all!" Charles spat. "With the airship, they have the high ground!"

"Not all of it!" Laura Glue exclaimed as she spread her wings and leaped into the air. No one was surprised by the Valkyrie taking to the air—but all of them were surprised when Madoc beat his wings and rose into the air next to her.

"That won't help you," Kirke shouted over the din of the waterfall. "I still have the advantage."

"That's what you think," said Fred. He stuck his paws in his mouth and whistled shrilly, twice, then again. "Coraline! Elly Mae!" he shouted. "To the moon!"

Instantly both goats shot straight up into the air, pulling the airship with them.

"Good girls!" Fred shouted. "Left rudder! Right rudder!"

At the commands, the goats spun about and flew in opposite directions, flipping the airship upside down and releasing their harnesses at the same time.

"Oh hell," said Mr. Kirke.

The airship crashed to the ground and exploded into shards of wood and metal, which sent the companions flying for cover and threw Kirke and Bangs into the rocks at the edge of the island.

Instantly Dee's henchmen were on their feet and rushing at the companions, who were still regaining their composure after the crash of the *Indigo Dragon*.

Kirke ran first to Rose and grabbed Caliburn out of the scabbard. He circled the others warily, holding the sword menacingly in front of him.

"You're outnumbered," Madoc warned him, "and if you try to use that sword, it will break on you. I promise you that."

"Not if I'm worthy," said Kirke as Bangs circled around in the other direction. "And a part of me must be, or I wouldn't be holding it now."

"Who are you?" Rose asked, eyes narrowing.

"My friend, Mr. Bangs, was a tulpa," Kirke said. "The first Dee ever created, from a shadow of a whisper of the last words spoken by the first Imago, who was murdered by his elder brother."

"Abel," Jack whispered. "Dee made a tulpa out of Abel."

"Indeed," Kirke said. "But he was imperfect. I, however, am not. And I intend to claim my due, and inherit the earth."

"You're a tulpa too, aren't you?" asked Rose. "So who are you, really?"

"You should know," Kirke said, looking at Charles. "As should you," he added, looking now at Jack. "Having any headaches lately?"

"Oh dear Lord in heaven," Charles exclaimed, growing pale. "Why do I have to be in the middle of every awful thing that happens in the Archipelago?"

"Who is it?" Jack asked.

Kirke took off his glasses, and suddenly they all recognized him.

"You, Jack," he said, smiling. "I'm *you*."

Before the companions could react, Kirke leaped out at Rose, but it was only a feint—one he had been taught by Laura Glue and Hawthorne. Madoc immediately leaped to protect her, and Kirke cut a vicious stroke across one of his wings, dropping the Dragon to the ground in agony.

"I know everything you know, Jack," Kirke said, still smiling, "and I know all your moves before you make them."

Suddenly Bangs jumped forward and struck Laura Glue a terrible blow on the head, and she fell unconscious. Edmund let out a cry and swung a fist at Bangs, who countered it easily and then pinned the young Cartographer to the ground.

"One by one, you are losing allies, Jack," Kirke said menacingly, "and with every second that passes, I grow stronger while you grow weaker. You've lost," he continued, his voice triumphant. "You've lost everything now. All that remains is for you to kneel at my feet and acknowledge the truth of things—that this world belongs now and forever to the Echthroi."

"That," Jack said, suddenly calmer, "is the first mistake I've seen you make, 'Mr. Kirke.'"

"Mistake?" Kirke said, momentarily confused. "What mistake?"

"You're not Echthroi," said Jack. "Not if you can wield Caliburn. And that means you are more like me than you think. And you may know how to beat all my friends, but I," he said, feeling more confident with every passing second, "know how to defeat *you*."

Kirke's face drew into a rictus mask of anger. "Just try it, Caretaker," he hissed. "I am going to rule this world."

At this Jack stepped forward, and to the others' astonishment, he was smiling. "That," he said, rolling up his sleeves, "is *never* going to happen."

Kirke frowned, and his eyes narrowed. "You have nothing left, no allies who can defeat me. It . . . is . . . *over*."

"Over?" Jack snorted. "It's never over until you win—and for you to do that, all we have to do is stop. Defeating you might just be impossible—but as long as we continue to fight, you can't win. You'll *never* win. And if it takes an eternity, I swear by all that's holy on earth and in heaven, I will never stop. Never. Never. Never."

"Jack, this is the moment!" Charles exclaimed. "The one written about in the Histories! The fate of the past, present, and future of the world is at stake! If he defeats you, you'll die—and he will become Lord Winter in the future! This is the moment when the Echthroi take over! You can't just—"

His friend cut him off with a calmly upraised hand. "It's all right, old fellow," Jack said as he moved to engage Kirke.

"I got this."

✦   ✦   ✦

"We are the same," Kirke said, stepping back but still brandishing the sword. "We share the same aiua, you and I—and I am growing stronger. Soon I will have it all, and you will be dead."

"The headaches!" Rose exclaimed as she tended to the injured Madoc. "That's why Jack has been getting sick! There have been two of him this whole time! One, the living, breathing Jack in Prime Time, who then became the portrait at Tamerlane, and the other, the tulpa that Charles made and Dr. Dee corrupted!"

"Exactly so," said Kirke. "But I wasn't corrupted, I'm who Jack really is. Your father saw that in me the first time we met, all those years ago."

"You're a part of me, yes," Jack said. "A part, but not all."

"This is reality, Jack!" Kirke exclaimed. "You cannot defeat me, because I am your opposite number. I am the player on the other side, and we are as evenly matched as any two men in history—except I am stronger."

"No," Jack said as a sudden realization flooded through him. "You *aren't*."

He put down his arms and simply looked at Kirke.

"We can never stop fighting against our own nature," Jack said softly, "but we can accept it as a part of who we are, and embrace it. Look around you," he continued. "Your masters have abandoned you. It is your allies who have been defeated, not mine. And the Archipelago is about to be restored to the world, in service of the Word."

"Nnnnnaaaaghhhhh!!!!" Kirke screamed. "I won't permit it! You cannot do this, Jack! I . . ." He stopped, then dropped to his knees, and the cries of defiance turned to plaintive whimpers.

"I don't want to go!" he exclaimed, almost pleading. "I want to live! I deserve to live!"

"Yes, you do," Jack said, kneeling in front of the tulpa. "And you shall, as a part of me. The part I could not deny when I was young, and cannot deny now."

"Mr. Bangs!" Kirke cried, more weakly now. "Help me!"

But the other tulpa had already stopped fighting and was simply standing apart from the others, watching.

"Don't worry," Jack said as he reached out to embrace the tulpa. "I know who you are, and I accept you, and you are not alone."

The Caretaker wrapped his arms around his shadow-self and pulled him close. The tulpa resisted a moment more, and then gave up his resistance. Kirke started to fade, turning back into the smoke from which he was made, and in seconds, he was gone.

Jack stood up and brushed off his trousers, then walked to the edge of the waterfall and simply stood there, looking out into the abyss.

"That's all well and good," Fred said as he, Uncas, and Charles helped their injured friends, "but what's to be done with Bangs there? I don't think any of us is equipped t' hug *him* into smoke."

Rose picked up Caliburn and strode over to Bangs, but he offered no resistance. Instead he dropped to his knees and bowed his head.

"Please," he said, his voice raspy from sorrow and centuries of pain, "release me."

"I don't want to kill you," Rose began, but he cut her short.

"Already dead," he said, "oh so long ago. The man I was is sitting with the angels at the end of all things, but cannot go on until you release the aiua from this body that was created. And only an Imago or an Archimago can release their own."

Rose closed her eyes in sudden understanding and nodded her head.

"Thank you," the tulpa said. She nodded again, and the sword Caliburn rose, and then fell, and the tulpa dissolved into smoke.

"Now," a voice whispered into her ear from across the eternities, "you are truly the Imago."

CHAPTER TWENTY-FOUR
THE REIGN OF THE SUMMER KING

IT TOOK SOME time for the companions to recover from their ordeal past the wall at the End of the World, and the events on Terminus, but eventually they all healed, and soon preparations were made for the restoration of the Archipelago of Dreams.

The Caretakers Emeriti insisted on a ceremony, with a lot of pomp and circumstance, and speeches, and of course, a massive feast. But when all the ceremony was done, in the end all that was left to do was for the last Dragon, Madoc, to open the Amethyst Box with the Master Key.

It was as simple as it seemed. He inserted the key, and the lid of the box exploded with light, and color, and sound, and life. The torrent from the box filled the sky overhead in an ever-expanding curtain of strange and wonderful geometries.

"Does that look familiar to you?" Edmund asked.

"Yes," said Rose. "It's the tapestry the Archons were weaving in the sky, with light and color and all those impossible gestures they made."

"This is better," Charles said to them both. "You get to design everything about the Archipelago that the angels intended to create when they were planning it in the City of Jade—only there's no impending flood to hurry things along."

Edmund and the badgers were put in charge of island placement, using Tummeler's editions of the *Imaginarium Geographica* as a guide.

"I have to say, this is the most unusual cartographical job I've ever undertaken," said Edmund. "I've used many maps to find lost islands, but this is the first time I've ever used an atlas to tell me where the island should be returned to."

"That's kind of how things work around here," said Fred.

"Here!" Uncas exclaimed excitedly. "I found what we was lookin' for, Rose!"

He turned the atlas around and pointed at a map of a very large, very green, and very undistinguished island.

"This would work just dandy," Uncas continued. "It has mountains, but not too many, beaches and harbors, nice trees, and a huge, honking cave that we can use t' build a new Great Whatsit."

"If it's so undistinguished, then why did Tummeler include it in the facsimile *Geographicas*?" asked Charles.

Uncas shrugged. "We had to fill out a printing signature," he said matter-of-factly, "and it was either a map of this boring ol' place, or another muffin recipe. And we had four in there already."

Charles slapped his forehead. "I should have known," he said, rolling his eyes.

"It looks perfect, Uncas," Edmund said. "Absolutely perfect."

"What is it you're doing, Rose?" Charles asked.

"I'm going to summon the Corinthian Giants," she answered. "We're going to use this island to create a place that we should have never lost, and give it a name that makes certain we always remember.

"We're going to build New Paralon."

The new Cartographer of Lost Places declined to keep the rooms he had been given in Tamerlane House in favor of something that felt more fitting for his calling. Once he had moved all his maps, charts, and equipment to his new workplace, Rose and Madoc took the *Indigo Dragon, newly restored by the shipbuilder Argus*, out to go visit him and give it their blessing.

"It seemed like the place I should be," said Edmund. "Once the Caretakers explained to me fully who the Cartographer of Lost Places really was, and how significant he was to everything that happened in the Archipelago, I thought that there would be no better place for me to work than here, in his old quarters."

Rose looked around the room and realized that it was smaller than the space he had used at Tamerlane, but somehow, this was more fitting. The second-to-the-last room at the top of the Keep of Time had housed a Cartographer for a very, very long time—and it seemed fitting that it did so again.

"But," said Rose, "without the lock on the door."

"Never with a lock," Madoc said, shaking his head. "Never again."

"We're building a small cottage on one of the other islands," Edmund said. "This room is the only one that's in the present, and I need to have someplace to retreat to from time to time."

"'We'?" asked Madoc.

Edmund blushed and smiled. "I've asked Laura Glue to marry me," he said, slightly embarrassed, "and she said yes."

"That's wonderful!" Rose said, rushing over to hug the young Cartographer. "The first wedding in the New Archipelago."

"Thanks," said Edmund, "but it's the same Archipelago, isn't it? We just brought everything back."

"No," Madoc said firmly. "It's not the same. It's better—because wiser people are making better choices about it this time around, and," he added, putting his arm around Rose, "I hope that this time, I will be one of them."

Back in her quarters at Tamerlane House, Rose flopped down on her bed, exhausted, and realized there was a parcel sitting on one of her desks. Wearily, she got back up and turned on a light. What she saw made her gasp.

It was the Ruby Armor of T'ai Shan.

There was also a note, addressed to her, but unsigned—although she knew without any doubt whom it was from. She carried the parcel back over to her bed and opened up the note, which was written on the now familiar cream-colored paper. It read:

> *My dear Rose,*
> *This armor belongs to you now. I have no further use for it, but you may still do some good in the world. I hope that I have as well, though I cannot be sure. I tried to help when I could, and I hope it was enough. I know that there are still many questions, and I'm afraid you'll have to answer them on your own. That*

*is part of the path of the Imago. But I know you, Rose,
and I believe in you. And if anyone ever questions
you, if they question your motives, or your choices, you
can point to me as an example. I had every reason to
fall into shadow, but when I had the opportunity to
choose, I chose the light. Not because of some noble
cause, or for any great purpose, but because, when I
was a child, and I was afraid, the Caretakers did not
leave me behind.*

*Small gestures can change the world. Never
forget that, my dear Rose. And never forget me.*

Tears began to well up in Rose's eyes again as she read and
reread the note, and then her breath caught when she realized
that there was someone in the room with her, sitting quietly in
the shadows.

"Telemachus?" she said. "Is that you?"

Her silent visitor stood up, and she realized it wasn't the boy
prince—it was Poe.

He walked to the door, beckoning for her to follow.

The corridors and hallways were empty—all the Caretakers
were keeping themselves busy with the restoration project, and
so they were spending as little time as possible cooped up inside
Tamerlane House. So Rose simply followed Poe as they walked
silently to the uppermost minaret of the house.

Poe walked to the balcony and pushed open the doors, letting
in the sea air. Then, with no preamble, he began to speak.

"The Archimago came first into the new world," Poe began,
"because that was the way of things. Without darkness to penetrate,

light would have no meaning. And so he came to make his way, and find his purpose. The Imago followed after, but the light was too much for the Archimago to bear. He was merely a Namer, whereas his younger sibling, the Imago, was a Maker.

"He didn't realize that there could be as much meaning in Naming as in Making, and in his jealousy, he . . ." Poe stopped, his voice trailing off into silence.

"From the moment I raised my hand and struck him," Poe said, still not turning from the balcony, "and he fell to the ground . . . there was sorrow. And regret. I—I need you to know that.

"He was meant to be the Imago. The protector of the world, and I took that from him. I didn't understand what I had done, until it was too late."

He dropped a small ring to the floor, and it dissolved in smoke and ash. "A Binding," he said, "of my own devising. I could not bear to speak of it, and so I made certain I never could—not until he was truly freed, and the damage I caused was undone. It was the best I could do to live here, in Kairos time, and try to restore that which I had destroyed, and to help those who cared for the Archipelago to try to find another Imago to take his place."

At that he turned to look at her. "I am grateful that we have. I am grateful to you, Rose Dyson."

"I—I don't know what to say," she answered truthfully. "I'm not even certain what I should call you."

"I have gone by many names, and lived many lives, over these thousands of years," said Poe, "and the one that suited me best was the one given to me by my father—Cain. But the one that I think I shall return to is the one my mother called me—Chronos. I think it suits me better now, don't you think?"

"Yes," said Rose. "I do."

He didn't say anything after that, but merely turned to look out over the sea, so after a few moments, Rose turned and left, closing the door behind her.

As the restoration of the Archipelago continued apace, a meeting was called among the Caretakers to address something being asked by the reemerging peoples of the lands: Who would rule?

"I think 'govern' is a better word," Madoc said as he and the Prime Caretaker made their way to the great hall. "Ruling is an anachronism, I think."

"That's just modesty talking," said John.

"Not modesty," said Madoc. "Caution. It was my ambition to rule the Archipelago that created most of the problems to begin with, remember?"

"And it was your eventual wisdom that resolved them," John said. "You mustn't forget that, either."

"I wasted my youth." Madoc sighed. "I could have done so much better, for so many around me."

"You were a good boy, who never had the opportunity to become a good man," said John.

Madoc shook his head. "I had opportunities—I just allowed the bitterness to dominate my choices. That, and deciding to listen to John Dee instead of . . ." He sighed again heavily. "I've made a lot of mistakes in my life—and it has been a very long life."

Madoc and John had decided that the best approach would be the most direct one, and so at John's urging, the son of Odysseus stood to address the Caretakers.

"We are going to dissolve the Frontier," he said simply. "Before today is ended, the Archipelago of Dreams and the Summer Country will once more be one world."

At hearing this, da Vinci choked on his wine, spraying it across his hapless colleagues at the end of the table. "Are you mad?" he said, barely containing his anger. "If you do that, then anyone can simply cross over! It's madness!"

"Anyone who has a guide," Madoc said, gesturing at the stack of *Imaginarium Geographicas* piled on the floor next to Fred. "A guide, and the purity of heart to see the invisible world that our magic has restored."

Twain nodded in agreement. "Most humans wouldn't be able to find the Archipelago if we strapped them to a Dragonship and dropped them onto Tamerlane House," he said as he lit another cigar, "but there are some who would be able to find a way here if they were blind, deaf, and dumb. They would still feel the magic, and heed its call. And for those people, it should be as open as possible."

Da Vinci scowled. "This has all gone exactly as you wanted, Mordred," he said, deliberately using the name that had at one time struck fear into the hearts of all the Caretakers. "You wanted to rule the Archipelago, and you shall. You wanted to open the Archipelago to the world, and you will. And after all our efforts trying to defeat you over the years, and all the lives that were lost in the pursuit of that goal, you have won everything after all. Well. Done."

"I am no longer Mordred," Madoc said, his words measured and cool, "and I am dictating terms to no one. I have the support of the Prime Caretaker"—he gestured to John—"the Caveo Principia," he continued, gesturing at Jack, "the other Caretakers of this era"—he nodded at Charles and Fred—"and the Imago herself. This is the best plan we can try, and it will be worth our efforts."

"It also supports what I established with the International Cartological Society, back in the Summer Country," said Jack. "We already have dozens of apprentices, and hundreds of associate Caretakers, and we hope that number will soon grow."

"Grow?" da Vinci said, incredulous. "At this rate, anyone in the world who wants to will be able to find their way into the Archipelago of Dreams!"

"Yes," Madoc said, smiling. "If we do our jobs right, that's exactly what will happen."

It was dusk when John, Jack, Charles, and Madoc made their way to Terminus for a private discussion they had wanted to have for a very long time.

"You realize," Madoc said as they stepped off the new boat Shakespeare had built to be pulled by the flying goats, "the last time all four of us were together was here, on this island."

"So many graves here," Madoc said. In addition to Captain Nemo and Artus, they had also added markers for Kipling, Tummeler, and Samaranth. "It's a good place to think about the future. A good place to remember the good choices, and the bad ones."

"It's easy to see the good and bad in others," said Jack. "It's much harder to see it in ourselves."

"Is it?" asked Madoc.

"You knew about me," Jack said. "When we first met, all those years ago, when I was still a child, you knew. You saw the shadow-side I didn't even know I possessed."

"I was a different man then—" Madoc began, before Jack cut him off.

"You keep saying that," the Caretaker told him, "but that's not actually true. You are the same man, Madoc—you've just been Named differently. Sometimes of your own volition. Sometimes by others. But still the same man.

"When I was young, and brash, and full of good trouble," Jack went on, "you saw the potential in me to have a darker side. That was very difficult to accept. But when I finally did, I was able to do things others could not. I was able to restore a Shadowed Archipelago not because of my purity, but because I had faced my own shadows—and accepted them. That's all I did when I faced my shadow-self here on Terminus. And if it hadn't been for the lessons you taught me all those years ago, I never would have been able to do it."

"We wanted to bring you here," Charles said, "to tell you about the new History I've just begun. It's a history that starts here, today, with the four of us—just the way the last one ended."

"That one was a prophecy, though," said Madoc. "It was all about the things that happened—the things I caused to happen—that only the three of you were able to stop."

"This one is going to be a self-fulfilling prophecy, then," said John. "It's going to project all the things we want to have happen, and will make happen, because we choose for them to happen."

"Yes?" Madoc said. "And what are you going to call this work of fiction-made-real?"

"Rose suggested the name. We're going to call it *The Reign of the Summer King*," John said as the three men put their hands atop one another in front of him. "May you live forever, Madoc. Forever."

EPILOGUE

THE OLD MAN *was dying. He had, however, lived a very long and happy life, and he had accomplished many things. He had a loving family and colleagues who respected him, and he wasn't in pain. All those things were important to him.*

Two years earlier, when his wife passed away, he had returned here to his Oxford, to live at Merton College. It was a balm for him, to live in familiar surroundings.

It was, in truth, his second-favorite place in the entire world. He blinked his eyes in the soft light—someone, several someones, had entered his room.

"Who's there?" he called out. "Who is it?"

"Uncle Hugo let us know it was time," said Rose, "and we've all come to be here with you."

"Rose! Charles!" he exclaimed, rising up on his elbows. "And Jack! You shouldn't have left Tamerlane House! What if . . ."

Jack simply smiled and helped him lie back down. "Now, John—you know I've left Tamerlane a hundred times in the last ten years. Just as long as I'm not away more than a week. You know that."

"I know," John said, breathing heavily. There was a rasp in his lungs. He was not long for this world. "So has Basil painted my portrait, then?" he asked. "Please tell me he thickened up my hair and tightened up my belly."

"No portrait, Uncle John," said Rose. "You would never be content being so tied to Tamerlane House."

A look of alarm crossed the old man's features. "But I haven't prepared a tulpa! And there isn't time, unless someone else has already . . ." He looked at Charles, who raised his hands in protest.

"Not I," Charles said. "I learned my lesson the last time, remember?"

"Then what?" asked John. "What's to become of me?"

"Something you earned, Scowler John," Fred said, stepping out from behind Charles. "Something special."

"The lands of the Archipelago are restored and flourishing once more," Rose said as she removed a small pendant from around her neck, "but the restoration is not yet complete. One thing remains to be done. The Archipelago of Dreams must have a protector."

She held up the pendant. John could see it was made of clear crystal, with some kind of fluid inside that caught the light and made it dance.

"Water from Echo's Well, which is the same water from the Moon Pool of the City of Jade," Rose said, smiling even as tears began to streak her cheeks. "Just look into the water, and speak the words."

A momentary thrill crossed John's features, only to dim a moment later. "It's . . . a great, great honor," he said, "but to suddenly vanish from the Summer Country . . ."

"Your family knows," said Fred. "Your son is an apprentice Caretaker, after all. It's all been arranged."

"Well then, it's all fine and good," said John, "but I was hoping . . . I mean to say that I wished that Edith . . ."

Jack leaned forward and put a gentle hand on his friend's shoulder.

"Edmund made a chronal trump, and he and Hugo are with her now, two years behind us. She will meet you on New Paralon."

"Two hearts are as one, Uncle John," said Rose. "Of course we wouldn't give this to you, without offering it to her as well."

A great breath escaped John's lips, as if that was the only thing that had held him to life. "Then yes, please. Yes. I accept, gladly, happily, joyfully, yes."

"Just look at your reflection in the water," Rose repeated, leaning close, "speak the words . . .

". . . and ascend."

When the huge, violet-colored Dragon arrived at New Paralon, his mate was already waiting. She flexed her own great wings and lifted up to meet him as he plummeted faster and faster toward her, and to the reunion he had hoped for since her death. They had been apart for two years, but now they would never be apart again. Without speaking a word to any of those assembled on the newly built docks, the two Dragons soared up into the clouds and disappeared.

Occasionally someone would report a sighting—never of one, always of both—and the peoples of the Archipelago knew that they were close, and if they were needed, would be even closer. These were not tame Dragons, but they were Dragons nonetheless, and they knew their purpose—to protect those who needed protecting, and offer guidance when it was needed. Everything else was flying. Together.

No one was on Terminus, at the waterfall at the Edge of the World, to see it happen, but in the moment the Dragons returned to the Archipelago, a star appeared in the darkness beyond. Then another. And another. And another. And soon the sky was so full *of stars that no one would ever imagine that it had ever been a place of darkness at all, or a place where anyone in need might cry out and not be reassured with the response that was carried in a whisper across the sky. . . .*

. . . Here, there be Dragons.

Author's Note

One of the drawbacks of blazing a new trail, which writing a book always is (especially if it's part of a series), is that you can't really tell how successful your choices are going to be looking forward. You have to blaze the trail first, so that you can look back and take an accounting of how well your choices worked.

A great many things changed between the time I wrote my original series outline and the publication of *Here, There Be Dragons*. When plans went forward to do *The Search for the Red Dragon*, the outlines changed even more; and when I jumped full-bore into writing the third, fourth, and fifth books, there were not only points where I veered a long way off from what the original plan was, but also points where I wondered if the whole thing hadn't just gone completely off the rails. But that's the nature of the beast: Fiction, especially in an extended form, is more than just a narrative. It's the recording of the lives of the characters within it—and sooner or later, everyone's lives become complex and complicated. That's what makes things interesting.

I had always had the general endgame in mind—but the exact nature of the players involved changed over the course of the series. Some bad guys became worse; characters who started out as rogues transformed into friends; and the character who changed the most revealed himself to be far, far greater than I ever imagined—and in the process, gave me a big part of the ending that pulled all the threads together into a tapestry. The idea that something can be destroyed only by the one who created it was set up with the first book, and the nearly indestructible *Imaginarium Geographica*. It was a perfect circle to close to realize that I had set things up for that to apply to the Keep of Time as well.

The original outlines are really interesting to look over (to me, anyway), and might be worth doing an essay about sometime. I had envisioned three main books under the series title Here, There Be Dragons, and a second set of smaller books, to be called the Chronicles of the *Imaginarium Geographica*, which would tell the history of the Cartographer—the notes for which were used almost in their entirety in *The Indigo King*. The three primary books were to involve the three main conflicts with the Winter King and were going to be very much more straightforward adventure stories than these books turned out to be. But once I realized that merging the Cartographer's story into the main narrative made everything more fun to write, that meant that Madoc was going to play a more complex role in the stories as well. After that, the series took on a life of its own.

Someone said the best way to make a story interesting is to have a good character do something bad, or have a bad character do something good. I think that's the sort of thing that makes the best stories resonate with readers long after the cover of the book is closed: because we all have those elements within us. We all have the potential to make mistakes—and the potential to learn from them, and to try to choose better.

I am not ashamed to admit that in writing this book, I wept more than once. The characters I spent eight years writing were changing, so it was a very emotional book to finish. Most of the book had to be written to line up with everything that had gone before; but I wrote the epilogue, with only a few changed details, over five years ago.

There were times in writing these books where I felt like I was losing my way, but in the end, I think I pulled it all together and made it read as if I knew where I was going all along. And maybe, just maybe . . . I *did*.

James A. Owen
Silvertown, USA

ACKNOWLEDGMENTS

I knew from very early on in the series how everything would end, but there was a lot of work that had to be done to get there: stories that had to be told, adventures that had to be shared, and finally, grateful thanks that had to be offered to the remarkable people without whom these books could not have been written.

The Dragon's Apprentice was the first book that veered completely away from my original outlines, playing as it did off of the mythology of the Caretakers and the possibility of a huge change to one of the major characters. It was easy to write and illustrate, which lulled me into a false sense of security about *The Dragons of Winter*. I looked forward to all of the homages I wanted to do in that book, and I loved writing it—but it became the book that required the most substantial revision. The first draft now exists in an alternate dimension, where what is now the epilogue was once the prologue. *The First Dragon* brought everything home, in more than one sense of the word. It was a thrill to write, with a quarter of it done in one mad thirty-eight-hour rush, and it required almost no revision at all. The last part, the epilogue, was largely written several years earlier. All stories do, at last, come home.

Navah Wolfe had the greatest impact on these books, mostly through a single suggestion about *The Dragons of Winter* that changed many, many things about what I was planning to do with Madoc, and all for the better. My primary editor, David Gale; managing editor, Dorothy Gribbin; and freelance copy-editor, Valerie Shea; all helped me shape the words in these books into their ideal form, and I am absolutely grateful for their wisdom and guidance. The support of Justin Chanda, Carolyn Reidy, and Jon Anderson has been a big part of why I have been so happy in my relationship with Simon & Schuster. And the art direction by Laurent Linn and Lizzy Bromley has always been world class.

My representation has always looked out for me, most notably Craig Emanuel at Loeb & Loeb, and Julie Kane-Ritsch and Ellen Goldsmith-Vein at the Gotham Group, without whom this series would not have even begun.

My team at Coppervale and at home—especially my brother Jeremy, and Cindy, Sophie, and Nathaniel—kept me on track and functional, and celebrated with me as each book was completed. I cherish the memories of book festival daddy-daughter trips I took with Sophie, and I never would have imagined that Cindy and Nathaniel's goats would end up playing such a large part in my stories. I love them all dearly—the people, not so much the goats.

As I wrote these books, new family members stepped into my life and made everything easier: dear Victoria Morris, for whom no task seems impossible, and who is always there when I need her; my beloved first reader, Kristin Leigh Luna, who made writing *The First Dragon* and completing the series a delight; and my awesome design department, Heidi Berthiaume, whose patience is as great as her abilities are vast. Tracy and Lisa Mangum did more to clear my path than anyone; Daanon DeCock, Brett Rapier, and Shawn Palmer circled the wagons whenever I called;

and my mentor, Larry Austin, helped me to keep remembering who I am.

I literally could not have created these books without all of you. And I'm grateful.

WELCOME TO PERN,

A PLANET OF SOARING ADVENTURE, WHERE DEATH CAN FALL FROM THE SKY.

Journey to the world of Pern in Anne McCaffrey's bestselling Harper Hall trilogy. Menolly of Half-Circle Hold has longed to learn the ancient secrets of the Harpers while Piemur, an apprentice Harper, secretly becomes a dragonrider. Together they will change Pern forever.

ANNE McCAFFREY's tales of Pern, with all their colorful dragons and fantastic characters, have won her millions of fans around the world. The winner of the Hugo and Nebula Awards, she is one of the best-loved writers in all of fantasy literature.

ANNE McCAFFREY
DRAGONSONG
A HARPER HALL OF PERN NOVEL

ANNE McCAFFREY
DRAGONSINGER
A HARPER HALL OF PERN NOVEL

ANNE McCAFFREY
DRAGONDRUM
A HARPER HALL OF PERN NOVEL

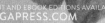
PRINT AND EBOOK EDITIONS AVAILABLE
SAGAPRESS.COM

DON'T ENVY THE DEAD.

RICK YANCEY
NEW YORK TIMES BESTSELLING AUTHOR

THE MONSTRUMOLOGIST

RICK YANCEY
NEW YORK TIMES BESTSELLING AUTHOR

THE CURSE OF THE WENDIGO
THE MONSTRUMOLOGIST

RICK YANCEY
NEW YORK TIMES BESTSELLING AUTHOR

THE ISLE OF BLOOD
THE MONSTRUMOLOGIST

RICK YANCEY
NEW YORK TIMES BESTSELLING AUTHOR

THE FINAL DESCENT
THE MONSTRUMOLOGIST

"With a roaring sense of adventure and
enough viscera to gag the hardiest of
gore hounds . . . Might just be the best
horror novel of the year."

—*Booklist*, starred review on
The Monstrumologist

PRINT AND EBOOK EDITIONS AVAILABLE
SAGAPRESS.COM

IT'S THE EPIC BATTLE OF BRAINS AGAINST MANES. WHICH SIDE ARE YOU ON?

Z

ZOMBIES
vs.
UNICORNS

"Who is the victor in this epic smackdown? Readers, of course!"
—*Kirkus Reviews*

PRINT AND EBOOK EDITIONS AVAILABLE
SAGAPRESS.COM